# RESPLENDENT

DESTINY'S CHILDREN: BOOK 4

# RESPLENDENT

DESTINY'S CHILDREN: BOOK 4

## STEPHEN BAXTER

GOLLANCZ

LONDON

The right of Stephen Baxter to be identified as the author
of this work has been asserted by him in accordance
with the Copyright, Designs and Patents Act 1988.

First published in Great Britain in 2006
by Gollancz
An imprint of the Orion Publishing Group
Orion House, 5 Upper St Martin's Lane,
London WC2H 9EA

A CIP catalogue record for this book
is available from the British Library.

ISBN-10: 0 57507 895 2 (cased)
ISBN-13: 9 780 57507 895 6 (cased)
ISBN-10: 0 57507 896 0 (trade paperback)
ISBN-13: 9 780 57507 896 3 (trade paperback)

1 3 5 7 9 10 8 6 4 2

Typeset at The Spartan Press Ltd,
Lymington, Hants

Printed and bound at Mackays of Chatham plc,
Chatham, Kent

The Orion Publishing Group's policy is to use papers that
are natural, renewable and recyclable products and made
from wood grown in sustainable forests. The logging and
manufacturing processes are expected to conform to the
environmental regulations of the country of origin.

www.orionbooks.co.uk

# ACKNOWLEDGEMENT OF PREVIOUS PUBLICATIONS

One
'Cadre Siblings', first published in *Interzone* 153, 2000.
'Conurbation 2473', first published in *Live without a Net*, ed. Lou Anders, Tor Books, August 2003.
'Reality Dust', first published by PS Publishing, 2000.
'All in a Blaze', first published in *Stars: Stories Based on the Songs of Janis Ian*, ed. Mike Resnick and Janis Ian, Daw Books, 2003.

Two
'Silver Ghost', first published in *Asimov's*, September 2000.
'The Cold Sink', first published in *Asimov's*, August 2001.
'On the Orion Line', first published in *Asimov's*, October 2000.
'Ghost Wars', first published in *Asimov's*, January 2006.
'The Ghost Pit', first published in *Asimov's*, July 2001.

Three
'Lakes of Light', first published in *Constellations*, ed. Peter Crowther, Tekno Books, 2005.
'Breeding Ground', first published in *Asimov's*, February 2003.
'The Dreaming Mould', first published in *Interzone* 179, 2002.
'The Great Game', first published in *Asimov's*, March 2003.

Four
'The Chop Line', first published in *Asimov's*, December 2003.
'In the Un-Black', first published in *Redshift*, ed. Al Sarrantonio, Penguin Putnam, 2001.
'Riding the Rock', first published by PS Publishing, November 2002.

Five
'Mayflower II', first published by PS Publishing, August 2004.

'Between Worlds', first published in *Between Worlds*, ed. Robert Silver-
berg, SF Book Club, September 2004.

Six
'The Siege of Earth', previously unpublished.

All material revised for this volume.

For my grandfathers,
Private Frederick William Richmond,
20th Battalion the King's Regiment (the Liverpool Pals), 1914–1917,
and Company Sergeant-Major William Henry Baxter,
King's Own Shropshire Light Infantry, 1903–1919.

# CONTENTS

*My name is Luru Parz.*

*I was born in the year AD 5279, as humans once counted time. Now I have lived so long that such dates have no meaning. We have lost the years, lost them in orders of magnitude.*

*Nevertheless, I am still here.*

*I was born on Earth. But Earth was not human then.*

*It belonged to our conquerors, the Qax.*

# ONE

## RESURGENCE

# CADRE SIBLINGS

## AD 5301

Before she was called into Gemo Cana's office for her awkward new assignment, Luru Parz had never thought of her work as destructive.

Cana stood before the window, a portal whose natural light betrayed her high status in the Extirpation Directorate. Red-gold sunset light glimmered from the data slates fixed to the walls of the office. Beyond the pharaoh's round shoulders Luru could see the glistening blown-silicate domes of the Conurbation's residential areas, laced by the blue-green of canals.

And on the misty horizon a Qax ship, a Spline, cruised above occupied Earth, swivelling like a vast eyeball. Where it passed there rose a churning wave of soil and grass and splintered trees.

'*Never*,' Cana murmured. 'You *never* thought of it that way, as destructive. Really? But we are destroying data here, Luru. That is what "Extirpation" means. Obliteration. Eradication. A rooting out. Have you never thought about that?'

Luru, impatient to get back to work, didn't know how to reply. If this was some new method of assessment it was obscure, Cana's strategy non-obvious. In fact she resented having to endure this obscure philosophising from Cana, who most people regarded as a musty relic cluttering up the smooth running of the Directorate. Among Luru's friends and pushy rivals, even to report to a pharaoh was seen as a career impediment. 'I'm not sure what you're getting at.'

'Then consider the library you are working on, beneath Solled Laik City. It is said that the library contains an ancestral tree for every man, woman and child on the planet, right up to the moment of the Occupation. You or I could trace our personal history back thousands

5

of years. Think of that. And your job is to destroy it. Doesn't that make you feel at least' – Cana's small hands opened, expressive – 'ambiguous, morally?'

Cana was short, stocky, her scalp covered by silver-white fuzz. Luru, her own head shaven, knew nobody else with *hair*, a side-effect of AntiSenescence treatment, of course. Cana had once told Luru she was so old she remembered a time before the Occupation itself, two centuries back. To Luru, aged twenty-two, it was a chilling idea.

She thought over what Cana had said. 'I don't even know where *"Solled Laik City"* is – or was. What does it matter? Data is just data. Work is just work.'

Cana barked laughter. 'With a moral void like that you'll go far, Luru Parz. But not everybody is as – flexible – in their outlook as you. Not everybody is a fan of the Extirpation. Outside the Conurbation you will encounter hostility. *You* see a satisfying intellectual exercise in the cleansing; they see only destruction. They call us jasofts, you know. I remember an older term. Quislings.'

Luru was baffled. Why was she talking about *outside*? Outside was a place for ragamuffins and bandits. *'Who* calls us jasofts?'

Cana smiled. 'Poor little Luru, such a sheltered life. You don't even remember the Rebellion, do you? The Friends of Wigner—'

'The Rebellion was defeated five years before I was born. What has it to do with me?'

'I have a new assignment for you,' Cana said briskly. 'Do you know Symat Suvan?'

Luru frowned. 'We were cadre siblings, a couple of dissolutions ago.' And, briefly, lovers.

Cana eyed her; Luru sensed she knew everything about her relationship. 'Suvan left the Conurbation a year ago.'

'He became a ragamuffin?' Luru wasn't particularly shocked; Symat, for all his charm, had always been petulant, difficult, incompliant.

'I want you to go and talk to him, about his research into superheavy elements . . . No, not that. None of *that* matters. I want you to talk to him about minimising pain, and death, for himself and others. He has got himself in the way, you see.'

Luru said stiffly, 'I don't think this assignment is appropriate for me. My relationship with Symat is in the past.'

Cana smiled. 'A past you'd rather forget, a little Extirpation of your own? But because of that past he might listen to you. Don't worry; this will not damage your glittering career. And I know that bonds between cadre siblings are not strong. They are not intended to be. But you might persuade this boy to save his life.

'I know you judge me harshly, Luru, me and the other pharaohs. Just remember that our goal is always to minimise distress. That is the reason I work in this place. It is my job, and yours, to mediate the regime of the Qax. Humanity's relations with its conquerors deteriorated after the Friends' Rebellion. Without *us* things would be much worse still. Which is why,' she said slowly, 'I regret asking this of you – especially you, Luru.'

'I don't understand.'

Cana sighed. 'Of course you don't. Child, Jasoft Parz, the exemplar after whom our traitorous class is named, was your grandfather.'

Luru sat in the flitter's small cabin, nervous, irritated, as the land peeled away beneath her.

From the air the spread of buildings, bubbles blown from scraped-bare bedrock, was glistening, almost organic. She could see the starbreaker-cut canals, arteries that imported desalinated water and food from the huge offshore algae farms and exported waste to the sink of the ocean. Down one canal bodies drifted in an orderly procession, glinting in plastic wrap; they were the night's dead, expended carcases returning to the sea.

Conurbation 5204 had been constructed when Luru was ten years old. She remembered the day well; the construction had taken just minutes, a spectacular sight for a little girl. There was talk now that the Extirpation Directorate might soon be moved to a new location in the continental interior, in which case Conurbation 5204 would be razed flat in even less time, leaving no trace. That was how the Qax did things: deliberate, fast, brutal, clean, allowing not the slightest space for human sentiment.

It was a relatively short flitter hop to Symat Suvan's research facility – short, but nevertheless longer than any journey Luru had taken before. And she was going to have to spend more time *outside* than she ever had before.

She didn't want to do this at all.

Luru's brief career, at the Extirpation Directorate in Conurbation 5204, had been pleasingly successful. She was working on a tailored data-cleanse package. The cleanser was to be sent into huge

7

genealogical libraries recently discovered in a hardened shelter under the site known as Solled Laik City, evidently a pre-Occupation human city. The cleanser was a combination of intelligent interpretive agents, targeted virus packages and focused electromagnetic-pulse bursts, capable of eradication of the ancient data banks at the physical, logical and philosophical levels. The cleanser itself was of conventional design; the project's challenge was in the scale, complexity and encryption of the millennia-old data to be deleted.

The work was stretching, competitive, deeply satisfying to Luru, and a major progression along her career path within the Extirpation Directorate. In fact she had been promoted to cadre leader for this new project, at twenty-two her first taste of real responsibility. And she resented being dragged away from her work like this, flung halfway across the continent, all for the benefit of a misfit like Symat Suvan.

She tried to distract herself with her notes on superheavy elements, Symat's apparent obsession.

There was a natural limit to the size of the nucleus of an atom, it seemed. A nucleus was a cluster of protons whose positive electrical charges tended to drive them apart. The protons were held together by a comforting swarm of neutrons – neutral particles. Larger nuclei needed many neutrons to hold them together; lead-208, for example, contained eighty-two protons and a hundred and twenty-six neutrons.

The gluing abilities of the neutrons were limited. It was once believed that no nucleus could exist with more than a hundred or so protons. But some theorists had predicted that there could be much larger nuclear configurations, with certain special geometries – and these were eventually discovered. The lightest of the superheavy nuclei had a hundred and fourteen protons and a hundred and eighty-four neutrons; the most common appeared to be an isotope called marsdenium-440, with a hundred and eighty-four protons and a crowd of two hundred and fifty-six neutrons. But there were much heavier nuclei still, with many hundreds of protons and neutrons. These strange nuclei were deformed, squashed into ellipsoids or even hollowed out . . .

She put down her data slate. She found it hard to concentrate on such useless abstractions as this corner of physics – and she didn't understand how this could have absorbed Symat so much. She did wonder absently why 'marsdenium' had that particular name: perhaps

'Marsden' or 'Marsdeni' was the name of its discoverer. Such historical details were long lost, of course.

As the flitter neared the top of its suborbital hop the curving Earth opened up around her, a rust-red land that glimmered with glassy scars – said to be the marks of humanity's last war against the Qax, but perhaps they were merely the sites of deleted Conurbations. A Spline craft toiled far beneath her, a great blister of flesh and metal ploughing open a swathe of land, making its own patient, devastating contribution to the Extirpation.

Her flitter drifted to the ground, a few hundred metres from Symat Suvan's exotic matter plant. She emerged, blinking, beneath a tall sky. Far from the rounded chambers of the Conurbation, she felt small, frail, exposed.

This was a place called *Mell Born*. It had been spared the starbreaker ploughs so far, but even so nothing remained of the land's pre-Occupation human usage save a faint rectangular gridwork of foundations and rubble. The place was dominated by a single structure, a giant blue-glowing torus: a facility built and abandoned by the Qax. Now it was occupied by a handful of ragamuffins who called themselves scientists – there were no scientists in the Conurbations. The humans had even built themselves a shanty town, an odd encrustation around the huge Qax facility.

Symat Suvan was here to meet her. He was tall, gaunt, looming, agitated, his eyes hollow; his bare scalp was tanned a pale pink by the unfiltered sun. 'Lethe,' he snapped. '*You*.'

She was dismayed by his hostility. 'Symat, I'm here to help you.'

He eyed her mockingly. 'You're here to destroy me. I always knew *you* would finish up like this. You actually *liked* running the mazes the Qax built for us – the tests, the meaningless career paths, the competitions between the cadres. Even the Extirpation is just another pleasing intellectual puzzle to you, isn't it, in a lifetime of puzzles? Oh, the Qax are smart rulers; they are exploiting your talents very effectively. But you don't have any idea what your work *means*, do you? . . . Come with me.' He grabbed her hand, and pulled her towards the curved electric blue wall of the facility.

She shivered at the remembered warmth of his touch. But he was no longer her cadre brother; he had become a ragamuffin, one of the dwindling tribes of humans who refused to remain in the Qax

Conurbations, and his face was a mask of set planes and pursed lips, and his determined anger was intimidating.

To get to the Qax facility they had to walk through the shanty community. It was a pit of rough, improvised dwellings, some little more than heaps of sheeting and rubble. But it was a functioning town, she realised slowly, with a food dispensing plant and a clinic and a water supply, even what looked like a rudimentary sewage system. She saw a small, dishevelled chapel, devoted to some no-doubt illegal religion, whose gods would one day free humanity from the rule of the Qax. All of this was laid over a mighty grid of rubble. There were still fragments of the old buildings, bits of wall and pipe poking like bones from the general wash of debris, some scarred by fire. Where vegetation had broken through the concrete, the remnant walls had become low hummocks coated with thick green blankets.

There was a stink of smoke and sour humanity, and the air was full of dust which clung to her skin and clothes. It was hard to believe that any cadre sibling of hers would choose to live here. Yet here he was.

Symat was talking rapidly about superheavy elements. 'It used to be thought that marsdenium and its more exotic sisters could only exist as technological artefacts, manufactured in giant facilities like this Qax factory. But now we know that such elements can be born out of the great pressures of a supernova, the explosive death of a giant star.'

She tried to focus. 'An exploding star? Then why are you looking for heavy elements here on Earth?'

He smiled. 'Because the Earth coalesced from a cloud of primordial gas and dust, a cloud whose collapse was triggered by the shock wave from a nearby supernova. You see? The primordial supernova laced the young Earth with superheavy matter. So the heavy elements have deep significance, for Earth and all that live on it or in it.'

On a heap of shattered stones a small child was sitting on the lap of an older girl, playing with a bit of melted glass. The girl was the infant's cadre sister, Luru supposed. They both had hair, thick dark thatches of it. The little one looked up, coughing, as they passed.

'This isn't a healthy place,' Luru observed.

'What did you expect? But I keep forgetting. You expect nothing; you know nothing. Luru, people die young in places like this. How else do you think I became so senior here so quickly? And yet they still come. *I* came.'

'Perhaps you were seduced by the closeness of the cadres here.'

A healthy dissolution might restore the social balance here, she thought.

He stared at her. 'There are no cadres here. The cadres, dissolved every couple of years, are another Qax social invention, imposed on humans after the Rebellion for the purposes of control. Didn't you even know that? Luru, these are *families*.'

He had to explain what that meant. And that the girl who nursed the child was not the little one's cadre sibling, but her mother.

They reached a door that had been crudely cut in the wall of the Qax facility. They passed through into an immense curving chamber where vast engines crouched. Hovering light globes cast long, complex shadows, and human technicians talked softly, dwarfed to insignificance. There was a smell of burned lubricant, of ozone.

Luru was overwhelmed.

Symat said, 'This place was thrown up by the Qax after the Rebellion. It was one of hundreds around the planet. We think it was a factory for making exotic matter – that is, matter with a negative energy density. They abandoned the place; we don't know why. Since it was built with human wealth and labour I suppose it means nothing to them. We refurbished the machinery, rebuilt much of it. Now we use it to make our own superheavy nuclei, by bombarding lumps of plutonium with high-energy calcium ions.'

That puzzled her. He'd said his goal was the *detection* of superheavy elements in Earth's crust. So why was he manufacturing them?

'Why were the Qax making exotic matter?'

'None of us knows for sure,' he said. 'There is a rumour that the Qax were trying to build a tunnel *to the future*. It's even said that the Qax Governor itself is an immigrant from the future, where humanity is triumphant. And *that* is why the Qax work so hard to control us. Because they are frightened of us.'

'That's just a legend.'

'Is it? Perhaps with time all history becomes legend.'

'This is nonsense, Symat!'

'How do you *know*, Luru?'

'There are witnesses to the past. The pharaohs.'

'Like Gemo Cana?' Symat laughed. 'Luru, there are no survivors from before the Occupation. The Qax withdrew AntiSenescence treatment for two centuries after the Occupation. *All the old pharaohs died*, before the Qax began to provide their own longevity treatments. These

11

modern undead, like Gemo Cana, have been bought by the Qax, bought by the promise of long life.' He leaned towards her. 'As they are buying you, Luru Parz.'

They emerged from the clean blue calm of the facility, back into the grimy mire of the town.

Disturbed, disoriented, she said evenly, 'Symat, the starbreaker beams are coming here. Once the Qax tolerated activities like this, indigenous cultural and scientific endeavours. Not any more, not since the Friends of Wigner betrayed the Qax's cultural generosity towards indigenous ambitions.' The Friends had used a cultural site to mask seditious activities. 'If you don't move out you will be killed.'

He clambered on a low wall and spread his arms, his long robe flapping in the thin dusty breeze. 'Ah. *Indigenous*. I love that word.'

'Symat, come home. There's nothing here. The data cleansers were sent through this place long ago.'

'Nothing? Look around you, Luru. Look at the scale of these old foundations. Once there was a host of immense buildings here, taller than the sky. And this roadway, where now we mine the old sewers for water, must have swarmed with traffic. Millions of people must have lived and worked here. It was a great city. *And it was human*, Luru. The data might have gone; we might never even know the true name of this place. But as long as these ruins are here we can imagine how it must once have been. If these last traces are destroyed the past can *never* be retrieved. And that's what the Qax intend.

'The Extirpation isn't always a matter of clinical data deletion, you know. Sometimes the jasofts come here with their robots, and they simply burn and smash: books, paintings, artefacts. Perhaps if you saw that, you would understand. The Qax want to sever our roots – to obliterate our identity.'

She felt angry, threatened; she tried to strike back at him. 'And is that what you're seeking here? An *identity* from unravelling this piece of obscure physics?'

'Oh, there is much more here than physics.' He said softly, 'Have you ever heard of *Michael Poole*? He was one of the first explorers of Sol system – long before the Occupation. And he found life, everywhere he looked.'

'Life?'

'Luru, that primordial supernova did more than spray superheavy atoms through the crust of the young Earth. There were complex structures in there, exotic chemistries. *Life*. Some of us believe they may be survivors of a planet of the primordial supernova – or perhaps they were born in the cauldron of the supernova itself, their substance fizzing out of that torrent of energy. Perhaps they breed that way, seeds flung from supernova to supernova, bugs projected by the mighty sneezes of stars!

'There is much we don't understand: their biochemistry, the deeper ecology that supports them, their lifecycle – even what they look like. And yet we know there is a forest down there, Luru, a chthonic forest locked into the substance of the ground, inhabited by creatures as old as the Earth itself. You see, even in these unimaginably difficult times, we are finding new life – just like Michael Poole.'

Wonder flooded her, unwelcome. Bombarded by strangeness, she felt as if some internal barrier were breaking down, as if Symat's bizarre superheavy creatures were swimming through her mind.

He peered into her eyes, seeking understanding. 'Now do you see why I'm prepared to fight for this place? Humans aren't meant to be drones, for the Qax or anybody else. *This* is what we live for. Exploration, and beauty, and truth.'

She returned to Conurbation 5204, without Symat. She filed a report for Gemo Cana. Her duty fulfilled, she tried to get back to work, to immerse herself once more. As always, there was much to do.

But the work was oddly unsatisfying.

She was distracted by doubt. Could it really be true, as Symat had said, that her career trajectory, with its pleasing succession of tasks and promotions, was just a Qax social construct, a series of meaning-less challenges meant to keep bright, proactive people like herself contented and contained and usefully occupied – useful for the Qax, that is?

Meanwhile it was a busy time in the Conurbation. The cramped corridors were crowded with people, all of them spindly tall, bald, pale – just as Luru was herself – all save the pharaohs, of course; they, having been born into richer times, were more disparate, tall and short, thin and squat, bald and hairy. The cadres were undergoing their biennial dissolution, and everybody was on the move, seeking new quarters, new friends, eager for the recreation festival to follow, the days of storytelling and sport and sex.

Luru had always enjoyed the friendly chaos of the dissolutions, the challenge of forming new relationships. But this time she found it difficult to focus her attention on her new cadre siblings.

At the age of twenty-two Luru was already done with childbirth. She had donated to a birthing tank; it was a routine service performed by all healthy women before they left their late teens, and she had thought nothing of it. Now, thinking of the families of Mell Born, she looked at the swarms of youngsters scrambling to their new cadres, excited, all their bare scalps shining like bubbles on a river, and wondered if any of these noisy children could be *hers*.

Gemo Cana said, 'I read your report. You're right to question why Suvan needs to manufacture his strange elements. He's obviously planning something, some kind of rebellious gesture.' She looked up from her data slate, as if seeing Luru for the first time. 'Ah. But you aren't interested in Symat Suvan and his grubbing in the dirt, are you?'

'I don't know what you're talking about.'

Cana put down the slate. 'It got to you. The outside. I can see it in you. I knew it would, of course. The only question is what difference it's going to make. Whether you will still be useful.' She nodded. 'You have questions, Luru Parz. Ask them.'

Luru felt cold. 'Symat Suvan told me that the Qax's ultimate intention—'

'Is to cauterise the past. I suppose he talked about our identity being dissolved, and so forth? Well, he's right.' Cana sounded tired. 'Of course he is. Think about what *you've* done. What did you *think* was the purpose of it all? The Extirpation is an erasing of mankind's past. A bonfire of identity. *That* is the truth.'

'But—'

'There are further plans, you know,' Cana said, ignoring her. 'For example: the Spline starbreakers penetrate only the first few tens of metres of the ground, to obliterate shelters, archives and other traces. But the Qax intend to perform a deeper ploughing-up. They have a nanotech replicator dust, which – Well. You see, with such tools, even the fossils will be destroyed, even the geology of the Earth itself: never to be retrieved, the wisdom they contain never to be deciphered.

'Another example. The Qax intend to force mass migrations of people, a mixing, a vast melting pot.' She touched her chest. 'Then even *this* will be lost, you see, in a few generations – the differences between us, the history embedded in our bodies, our genes, our blood types. All mixed up, the data lost for ever. There is a simpler proposal to replace our human names with some form of catalogue numbers. So even the bits of history lodged in our names will be lost. It will only take two or three generations before we forget . . .'

Luru was shocked at the thought of such cultural vandalism.

Cana evidently read her expression. 'So at last we've dug far enough into Luru Parz to find a conscience. At last we've found something that shocks you. And you're wondering why any human being would cooperate with such monstrosity. I'll tell you why. The alternative is worse. The alternative is *the destruction of the species* – an option the Qax have considered, believe me. That is why we are here, we who collaborate. That is what we must work ceaselessly to avoid.'

She stood, restless, and picked a slate off the wall. 'Look at this. It is data on the deletion of data: a recursive register of destruction. And when all the primary information is gone, of course, we will have to delete this too. We must even forget that we forgot. And then forget that in turn. It will go on, Luru, a hierarchy of deletion and destruction, until – on one last data slate in an anonymous office like this – there will remain a single datum, the final trace of the huge historic exercise. If it falls to me I will erase that last record, gladly. And then there will be no trace left at all – *except in my heart*. And,' she added softly, 'yours.'

Luru, half understanding, was filled with fear and longing.

Cana eyed her. 'I think you're ready. You face a choice, Luru Parz.' She reached into her desk and produced a translucent tablet the size of a thumbnail. 'This comes from the Qax themselves. They are able to manipulate biochemical structures at the molecular level – did you know that? It was their, um, competitive edge when they first moved off their home planet. And this is the fruit of their study of mankind. Do you know what it is?'

Luru knew. The tablet was the removal of death.

Cana set the tablet on the desk. 'Take it.'

Luru said, 'So it is true. You have been bought with life.'

Cana sat, her face crumpling into sadness; for an instant Luru had the impression of very great age indeed. 'Suddenly you have grown a moral sense. Suddenly you believe you can judge me. Do you imagine I *want* this? Should I have followed the others to Callisto, and hidden there?'

Luru frowned. 'Where? Jupiter's moon?'

Cana regained the control she had momentarily lost. 'You judge, but you still don't understand, do you? There is a purpose to what we do, Luru. *With endless life comes endless remembering.*

'We cannot save the Earth from the Qax, Luru. They will complete this project, this Extirpation, whatever we do, we jasofts. And so we must work with them, accept their ambiguous gift of life; we must continue to implement the Qax's project, knowing what it means. For then – when everything else is gone, when even the fossils have been dug out of the ground – *we will still remember*. We are the true resistance, you see, not noisy fools like Symat Suvan, we who are closest of all to the conquerors.'

Luru tried to comprehend all of this, the layers of ambiguity, the compromise, the faintest flicker of hope. 'Why me?'

'You are the best and brightest. The Qax are pleased with your progress, and wish to recruit you.' She smiled thinly. 'And, for exactly the same reasons, I need you. So much moral complexity, wrapped up in a single tiny tablet!'

Luru stood. 'You told me you remembered how it was, before the Qax. But Symat said all the old pharaohs died during the Occupation. That nobody remembers.'

Cana's face was expressionless. 'If Suvan said that, it must be true.'

Luru hesitated. Then she closed her hand around the tablet and put it in a pocket of her tunic, her decision still unmade.

When she returned to Mell Born she found it immersed in shadow, for a Spline ship loomed above the ruins. The Spline rolled ponderously, weapon emplacements glinting. There was a sense of huge energies gathering.

Her flitter skimmed beneath the Spline's belly, seeking a place to land.

The crude shanty town was being broken up. She could see a line of Directorate staff – no, of *jasofts* – moving through the ramshackle dwellings, driving a line of people before them, men, women and children. Beetle-like transports followed the line of the displaced, bearing a few hastily grabbed belongings. The jasofts were dressed in skinsuits, their faces hidden behind translucent masks; the raw surface of Earth was not a place where inhabitants of the great Conurbations walked unprotected.

A small group lingered near the electric blue walls of the Qax facility, robes flapping, their stubborn defiance apparent in their stance. One of them was Symat, of course. She ran to him.

'I didn't think you would return.' He waved at the toiling, fleeing people. 'Are you proud of what is being done to us?'

She said, 'You are manufacturing superheavy elements, here in this facility. What is the real reason? Have you lied to me, Symat?'

'Only a little,' he said gently. 'We do understand something of the creatures of the rocky forest that has flourished beneath our feet.'

'Yes?'

'We know what they eat. We have tried to provide them with food, to get their attention—'

Without warning a thread of ruby-red light snaked down from the hide of the Spline. Where the starbreaker touched, buildings disintegrated, panels and beams flying high into the air. From the heart of the old Qax facility came a scream of tortured air, a soft concussion, a powerful, blood-red glow. The ground shuddered beneath their feet.

'It has begun.' She grabbed Symat and tried to pull him towards her flitter. 'Symat, please. You were my cadre sibling; I don't want to see you die. *This* isn't worth a life.'

A blankness came into his eyes, and he pulled away from her. 'Ah. Not *your* life, a pharaoh's life, perhaps.'

'I am not yet a pharaoh—'

He wasn't listening. 'You see what a dreadful, clever gift this is? A long life makes you malleable. But my pitiful life – a few decades at best – what is the use of such a life save to make a single, defiant gesture?' He stepped away from her deliberately. He closed his eyes, and raised his arms into the air, robe flapping. 'As for you – you must make your choice, Luru Parz.'

And from beneath Symat's feet a bolt of dazzling light punched upwards, scattering debris and rock, and lancing into the heart of the Spline. There was a stink of meat, of corruption.

A shock wave billowed over her, peppering her with hot dust. Luru fell back in the rubble, stunned. Symat was gone, gone in an instant.

And the roof of flesh above her seemed to tip. The Spline sank with heavy gentleness towards the ground.

And she was going to be crushed beneath its monstrous belly. She turned and ran to her ship.

The flitter, saving itself, squirted towards the narrowing gap of daylight beneath that descending lid of flesh. Luru, bloody, bruised, filthy, cowered in her seat as immense pocks and warts fled above her head. A dark, steaming fluid gushed from the Spline's tremendous wound; it splashed over the ground, a lake of blood brought from another star.

Suddenly she burst into daylight. From the air she could see how the raking starbreaker beam had left a gouge in the earth like an immense fingernail scratching a tabletop. But the gouge was terminated by the dying Spline, a deflating ball, already grounded.

The flitter, in utter silence, tipped back and lifted her up towards the edge of space.

The sky deepened to violet, and her racing heart slowed.

She tried to work out what had happened. There must have been a cache of the strange, ancient supernova creatures, she decided, drawn there by Symat's superheavy-element bait. Perhaps the eruption had been purely a matter of physics, a response to the sudden release of pressure when the upper levels of the crust were stripped away. Or perhaps that great blow against the Spline had been deliberate, a conscious lashing out, a manifestation of the rage of those ancient creatures at this disturbing of their aeons-long slumber.

And now, all around the sky, she could see more Spline entering the atmosphere: four, five, six of them, great misty moons descending to Earth. A fine dust pulsed from them in thin, silvery clouds, almost beautiful. The dust spread through the air, settling quickly. Where the glittering rain touched, the land began to soften, the valleys to subside, the hills to erode. It was shockingly fast.

This was the wrath of the Qax. The overlords had learned not to hesitate in the face of human defiance. And this nanotechnological drenching would leave the planet a featureless beach of silicate dust.

She took the translucent tablet from a pocket of her skinsuit. The scrap of Qax technology gleamed, warm. She thought of the wizened, anguished face of Gemo Cana, of Symat's vibrant, passionate sacrifice. *You must make your choice, Luru Parz.*

I am too young, she thought. I have nothing to remember. Nothing but what was done today.

As the mountains of Earth crumbled, she swallowed the tablet.

\*

*We endured another century of the Qax.*

*When their reign ended it happened quickly, the result of an event far from Earth, the actions of a single human, a man called Bolder.*

*For all our conspiring, I think we never really believed the Qax would leave.*

*And we certainly never imagined we would miss them when they were gone.*

# CONURBATION 2473

## AD 5407

Rala knew there was something wrong.

For days, all around Conurbation 2473 there had been muttered rumours. A cell of counter-Extirpationists had been found hoarding illegal data. Or a group of cultists were planning an uprising, like the failed Rebellion decades ago. Rala just wanted to get on with her work. But everybody got a little agitated.

It all came to a head one morning.

The room lights came on as usual to wake them up, But when their supervising jasoft didn't come to collect them for work, Rala quickly got uneasy.

Rala shared her tiny room with Ingre, a cadre sibling. The room was just a bubble blown in nano-engineered rock by Qax technology. There was nothing inside but a couple of bunk beds, a space to store clothes, waste systems, water spigots, a food hole.

Ingre was a little younger than Rala, thin, anxious. She went to the door – which had snapped open at the allotted time, as it always did – and peered up and down the corridor. 'Luru Parz is never late.'

'We'll just wait,' Rala said firmly. 'We're safe here.'

But now there was a tread, steadily approaching along the corridor. It was too heavy for Luru Parz, their controlling jasoft, who was a slight woman. Some instinct prompted Rala to take Ingre's hand and hold it tight.

A man stood in the doorway. His skin seemed oddly reddened, as if burned. He wore a skinsuit of what looked like gold foil. And there was a thick thatch of black hair on his head. Nobody in the Conurbation, workers or jasofts alike, wore hair.

He wasn't Luru Parz. He wasn't from the Conurbation at all.

The man stepped into the room and glanced around. 'All these cells are the same. I can't believe you drones live like this.' His accent was strange. Rala thought his gaze lingered on her body, and she looked away. She had never heard the word 'drone' before. He pointed at the panel in the wall. 'Your food hole.'

'Yes—'

He smashed the transparent panel with a gloved fist. Ingre and Rala cowered back. Bits of plastic flew everywhere, and a silvery dust trickled to the floor. To Rala this was literally an unthinkable crime.

Ingre said, 'The jasofts will punish you for that.'

'You know what this was? Qax shit. Replicator technology.'

'But now it's broken.'

'Yes, now it's broken.' He pointed to his chest. 'And you must come to us for your food.'

'Food is power,' Rala said.

He looked at her more closely. 'You are a fast learner. Report to the roof in one hour. You will be processed there.' He turned and walked out. Where he had passed Rala thought she could smell burning, like hot metal.

Rala and Ingre sat on their bunk for almost the whole hour, barely speaking. Nobody came to fix the smashed hole. Before they left, Rala scooped up a little of the silver dust and put it in a pocket of her robe.

From the roof the Conurbation domes were a complex of vast, glistening blisters. Rala had been up here only a handful of times in her life. She tried not to flinch from the open sky.

Today this dome roof was full of people. The Conurbation inhabitants, with their shaven heads and long robes, had been gathered into queues that snaked everywhere. Each queue led to a table, behind which sat an exotic-looking individual in a gold skinsuit.

Ingre whispered, 'Which line shall we join?'

Rala glanced around. 'That one. Look who's behind the table.' It was the man who had come to their cell.

'He frightened me.'

'But at least we know him. Come on.'

They queued in silence. Rala felt calmer. Living in a Conurbation, you did a lot of queuing; this felt normal.

Around the Conurbation the land was a plain that shone silver-grey, like a geometric abstraction. Canals snaked away to the horizon, full of

21

glistening blue water. Human bodies drifted down the canals, away from the Conurbation to the sea. That wasn't unusual, just routine waste management. But there did seem to be many bodies today.

At last Rala reached the front of the queue.

The stranger probably wasn't much older than she was, she realised, no more than thirty. 'It's you,' he said. 'The drone who understands the nature of power.'

She bristled. 'I am not a drone.'

'You are what I say you are.' He had a data slate before him, obviously purloined from a Conurbation workstation. He worked it slowly, as if unfamiliar with the technology. 'Tell me your name.'

'Rala.'

'Rala, my name is Pash. From now on you report to me.'

She didn't understand. 'Are you a jasoft?' The jasofts were human servants of the Qax who, it was said, were granted freedom from death in return for their service.

He said, 'The jasofts are gone.'

'The Qax—'

'Are gone too.' He glanced upwards. 'At night you can see their mighty Spline ships, peeling out of orbit. Where they are going, I don't know. But we will go after them one day.'

Could it be true – could the centuries-old Occupation be over, could Luru Parz and the other jasofts really have melted away, could the framework of her whole world have vanished? Rala felt like a lost child, separated from her cadre. She tried not to let this show in her face.

'What was your sin?' It turned out he was asking what job she did.

She had spent her working life in vocabulary deletion. The goal had been to replace the old human tongues with a fully artificial language. It would have taken a few more generations, but at last a great cornerstone of the Extirpation, the Qax's methodical elimination of the human past, would have been completed. It was intellectually fascinating.

He nodded. 'Your complicity with the great crime committed against humanity—'

'I committed no crime,' she snapped.

'You could have refused your assignments.'

'I would have been punished.'

'Punished? Many will *die* before we are free.'

22

The word shocked her. It was hard to believe this was happening. 'Are you going to punish me now?'

'No,' he said, tiredly. 'Listen to me, Rala. It's obvious you are smart, you have a high degree of literacy. We were the crew of a starship. A trading vessel, called *Port Sol*. While you toiled in this bubble-town, I hid up there.' He glanced at the sky.

'You are bandits.'

He laughed. 'No. But we are not bureaucrats either. We need people like you to help run this place.'

'Why should I work for you?'

'You know why.'

'Because food is power.'

'Very good.'

The traders tried to rule their new empire by lists. They kept lists of 'drones', and of their 'sins', and tables of things that needed to be done to keep the Conurbation functioning, like food distribution and waste removal.

For Rala it wasn't so bad. It was just work. But compared to the sophisticated linguistic analysis she had been asked to perform under the Occupation, this simple clerical stuff was dull, routine.

Once she suggested a better way to devise a task allocation. She was punished, by the docking of her food ration. That was how it went. If you cooperated you were fed. If not, not.

Her food was the same pale yellow tablets she had grown up with, the tablets produced by the food holes, though less of them. They came from a sector at the heart of the Conurbation where the food holes had been left intact – the only such place, in fact. It was guarded around the clock.

After the first month or so, the battles started in the sky. You would see glowing lights on the horizon, or sometimes flashing shapes in the night, threads and bursts of light. All utterly silent. All these ships and weapons were human. The oppression of the Qax had been lifted, only for humans to fall on each other.

Actually there was a lot of information to be had from the traders' lists, if you knew how to read them. Rala saw how few the traders really were. She sensed their insecurity, despite the gaudy weapons they wielded: *so few of us, so many of them.* And now there were challenges from the sky. The traders' rule was fragile.

But though people muttered about the good old days under the Qax, nobody did anything about it. It wouldn't even occur to most drones to raise a fist. Besides there was no place else to go, nothing else to eat. Beyond the city there was only the endless nano-chewed dirt on which nothing grew.

There was never enough to eat, though.

In a corner of her cell, away from prying eyes, Rala examined the silvery Qax replicator dust. This stuff had made food before; why wouldn't it now? But the dust just lay in its bowl, offering nothing.

Of course the food hadn't come from *nothing*. A slurry of seawater and waste had been fed to the dust through pipes in the wall. Somehow the silver dust had turned that muck into food. But in the pipes now there was only a sticky, greenish sludge that stank like urine. She scraped a little of this paste over the dust, but still, treacherously, it sat inert. She hid it all away again.

She had been aware of Pash's interest in her from the first moment they had met.

She built on that tentative relationship. She talked to him about her work, and drew him out with questions about his background. He told her unlikely tales of worlds beyond the Moon, where humans had once built cities that orbited through rings of ice. Perhaps she was developing an instinct for survival; Pash's interest was something she could exploit.

Eventually he began to invite her to his room. The room, once owned by a jasoft, was set beneath the Conurbation's outer wall. It had a view of the sky, where silent battles flared.

'I don't know what you want here,' she said to him one evening. 'You traders. Why do you want a Conurbation? You aren't very good at running it.'

'There are worse than us out there.'

'It isn't *wealth* you want, is it?' She had struggled to understand that trader word, long expunged from her language; for better or worse the Qax had for centuries imposed a crude communism on mankind. 'There's no wealth to be had here.'

'No. There are only people.'

'Yes. And where there are people, there is power to be wielded. And that's what you want, isn't it?'

He fell silent, and she wondered if she had pushed him too far. She sighed. 'Tell me about *Sat-urn* again—'

The door slammed open. Somebody was standing there, silhouetted by bright light.

Instinctively Rala stepped forward, spreading her arms to hide Pash. A light shone in her face.

The intruder said, 'I represent the Interim Coalition of Governance. The illegal seizure of this Conurbation by the bandits of the GUTship *Port Sol* is over.'

'We are both drones.' She rattled off details of her identity and work assignment.

'You must stay in your cell. In the morning you will be summoned for new details. If you encounter the *Port Sol* crew—'

'I will report them.'

There was shouting in the corridor; the Coalition trooper, distracted, hurried away.

Pash murmured, 'Lethe. *Look.*'

Beyond the window, in the reddening sky, a Spline ship was hovering, a great meaty ball pocked with weapons emplacements. But this was no Qax vessel; a green tetrahedral sigil, a human symbol, had been crudely carved in its flank.

'Things have changed,' Rala said dryly.

Pash asked, 'Why did you shelter me?'

'Because I have had enough of rulers,' she snapped. 'We must be ready. You will have to shave your head. Perhaps one of my robes will fit you.'


The Coalition had its own, different theory about how to run a Conurbation.

They were all evicted from the city. The people stood in sullen ranks – mostly Conurbation drones, but with at least one trader, Pash, camouflaged among the rest. They had been given tools, simple hoes and spades. The walls of the Conurbation loomed above them all, scorched by fire.

The sun was hot, the air dry, and insects buzzed. These were city folk; they didn't like being out here. There were even children; the new rulers of the Conurbation had closed down the schools, which even the traders had kept running.

A woman stood on a platform before them. She wore a green uniform, clean but shabby, and she had the green sigil tattooed on her forehead – the symbol, as Rala had now learned, of free humanity. At her side were soldiers, not in uniform, though they all wore green armbands, and had the sigil marked on their faces.

'My name is Cilo Mora,' said the woman. 'The Green Army has restored order to the Earth, overthrowing the bandit traders. But *the Qax may return* – or if not them, another foe. We must always be prepared. You are the advance troops of a moral revolution. The work you will begin today will fortify your will and clarify your vision. But remember – now you are all free!'

One man near the front raised his hoe dubiously. 'Free to scrape at the dirt?'

One of the green-armbands clubbed him to the ground.

Nobody else moved. Cilo Mora smiled, as if the unpleasantness had never happened. The man in the dirt lay where he had fallen, unattended.

Fields were marked out using rubble from fallen Conurbation domes. Seeds were supplied, from precious stores preserved off-world. All around the city people toiled in the dirt, but there were machines too, hastily adapted and improvised.

For many, it went hard. There hadn't been farmers on Earth for centuries, and the people of the Conurbation had all been office workers. Some fell ill, some died. But as the survivors' hands hardened, so did their spirit, it seemed to Rala.

The crops began to grow. But the vegetables were sparse and thin. Rala thought she understood why – the poisoning of the soil was a legacy of the Qax – but nobody seemed to have any idea what to do about it.

The staple food continued to be the pale yellow ration tablets from the food holes. But just as under the old regime there was never enough to eat.

In the rest times they would gather, swapping bits of information.

Pash said, 'The Coalition's Green Army really does seem to be putting down the warlords.' He seemed fascinated by developments, apparently forgetting he was one of those 'warlords' himself. 'Of course having a Spline ship is a big help. But those clowns who follow Cilo around aren't Army but another agency called the Green Guard. Amateurs, with a mission to cement the revolution.'

Rala whispered, 'What this "revolution" comes down to is scratching at the dirt for food.'

'We can't use Qax technology any more,' Ingre said. 'It would be counter-progressive.' Ingre was always mouthing phrases like this. She seemed to welcome the latest ideology. Rala wondered if she had been through too many shocks to be able to resist.

'It's not going to work,' Rala said softly. 'The Extirpation was pretty thorough. The Qax planted replicators in the soil, to make it lifeless.' Their ultimate goal had been to wipe off the native ecology, to make the Earth uninhabited save for humans and the blue-green algae of the oceans, which would become great tanks of nutrient to feed their living Spline ships. 'No amount of scraping with hoes is going to make the dirt green in a hurry.'

'We have to support the Coalition,' said Ingre. 'It's the way forward for mankind.'

Pash wasn't listening to either of them. He said, 'You'd never get in the Army, but those Green Guards are the gang to join. Most of them are pretty dumb; you can see that. A smart operator could rise pretty fast.'

They spoke like this only in brief snatches. There was always a collaborator about, always a spy ready to sell a story to the Guards for a bit of food.

The cuts began.

It was as if the Coalition believed that starvation would motivate the new shock troops of its uninterrupted revolution. Or perhaps they simply weren't managing the food stocks competently. Soon the first signs of malnutrition appeared, swollen bellies among the children.

Rala had always kept her handful of replicator dust, from her old cell in the Conurbation. Now she found a hidden corner by the Conurbation walls, where she dug out the earth and sprinkled in a little of her dust. Still nothing happened.

One day Pash caught her doing experiments like this. By now he had fulfilled his ambition to become a Green Guard. The former trader had donned the green armband of his enemies with shameless ease.

She said, 'Will you turn me in?'

'Why should I?'

'Because I'm trying to use Qax technology. This action is doctrinally invalid.'

He shrugged. 'You saved my life.'

'Anyhow,' she said, 'it's not working.'

He frowned and poked at the dirt. 'Do you know anything about this

27

kind of technology? We used a human version in the *Port Sol*'s life support – cruder than this, of course. Nanotech manipulates matter at the molecular or atomic levels.'

'It turns waste into food.'

'Yes. But people seem to think it's a magic dust, that you just throw at a heap of garbage to turn it into diamonds and steak.'

'*Diamonds? Steak?*'

'Never mind. There is nothing magic about this stuff. Nanotech is like biology. To "grow", a nanotech product needs nutrients, and energy. On *Sol* we used a nutrient bath. This Qax stuff is more robust, and can draw what it needs from the environment, if it gets a chance.'

She thought about that. 'You mean I have to feed it, like a plant.'

'There is a lot of chemical energy stored in the environment. You can tap it slowly but efficiently, like plants or bacteria, or burn it rapidly but inefficiently, like a fire. This Qax technology is smart stuff; it releases energy more swiftly than biological cells but more efficiently than a fire. In principle a nano-sown field ought to do better than a biologically planted crop . . .'

She failed to understand many of the words he was using. Though she pressed him to explain further, to help her, he was too busy.

Meanwhile Ingre, Rala's cadre sibling, became a problem.

Despite her ideological earnestness she was weak and ineffectual, and hated the work in the fields. A drone supervisor, a collaborator, one of her own people, punished Ingre more efficiently than any Guard would have done. And when that didn't work in motivating Ingre to work better, she cut off Ingre's food ration.

After that Ingre just lay on her bunk. At first she complained, or railed, or cried. But she grew weaker, and lay silent. Rala tried to share her own food. But there wasn't enough; she was going hungry herself.

Rala grew desperate. She realised that the Guards, in their brutal incompetence, were actually going to allow Ingre to die, as they had many others. She could think of only one way of getting more food.

She wasn't sexually inexperienced; even the Qax hadn't been able to extirpate *that*. Pash was easy to seduce.

The sex wasn't unpleasant, and Pash did nothing to hurt her. The oddest thing was the spacegoer's exoskeleton he wore, even during sex; it was a web of silvery thread that lay over his skin. But she felt no affection for him, or – she suspected – he for her. Unspoken, they both knew that it was his power over her that excited him, not her body.

Still, she waited for several nights before she asked him for the extra food she needed to keep Ingre alive.

Meanwhile, in the Conurbation, things got worse. Despite the maintenance rotas the stairwells and corridors became filthy. The air circulation broke down. The inner cells became uninhabitable, and crowding increased. Then there was the violence. Rumours spread of food thefts, even a rape. Rala learned to hide her food when she walked the darker corridors, scuttling past walls marked with bright green tetrahedral sigils, the most common graffito.

The Conurbation was dying, Rala realised with slow amazement. It was as if the sky itself was falling. People spoke even more longingly of the Qax Occupation, and the security it had brought.

One day Pash came to her, excited. 'Listen. There's trouble. Factional infighting among the Green Guards.'

She closed her eyes. 'You're leaving, aren't you?'

'There's a battle at a Conurbation a couple of days from here. There are great opportunities out there, kid.'

Rala felt sick; the world briefly swam. They had never discussed the child growing inside her, but Pash knew it existed, of course. It was a mistake; it hadn't even occurred to her that the contraceptive chemistry which had circulated with the Conurbation's water supply might have failed.

She hated herself for begging. 'Don't leave.'

He kissed her forehead. 'I'll come back.'

Of course he never did.

The brief factional war was won by a group of Green Guards called the Million Heroes. They wore a different kind of armband, had a different ranking system, and so forth. But day to day, under their third set of bosses since the Qax, little changed for the drones of Conurbation 2473; one set of rulers, it was turning out, was much the same as another.

By now most of the Conurbation's systems had ceased functioning, and its inner core was dark and uninhabitable. Everybody worked in the fields, and some were even putting up crude shelters closer to where they worked, scavenging rock from the Conurbation's walls.

Still Rala went hungry, and she increasingly worried about the child, and how she would cope with the work later in her pregnancy.

She remembered how Pash had said, or hinted, that the nano dust

29

was like a plant. So she dug it up again and planted it away from the shade of the wall, in the sunlight.

Still, for days, nothing happened. But then she started to noticed pale yellow specks, embedded in the dirt. If you washed a handful of soil you could pick out particles of food. They tasted just as if they had come from a food hole. She improvised a sieve from a bit of cloth, to make the extraction more efficient.

That was when Ingre, for whose life Rala had prostituted herself, turned her in to the new authority.

Ingre, standing with one of the Million Heroes over the nano patch, seemed on the point of tears. 'I had to do it,' she said.

'It's all right,' said Rala tiredly.

'At least I can put an end to this irregularity.' The Hero raised his weapon at the nano patch. He was perhaps seventeen years old.

Rala forced herself to stand before the weapon's ugly snout. 'Don't destroy it.'

'It's anti-doctrinal.'

'We can't eat doctrine.'

'That's not the *point*,' snapped the Hero.

Rala spread her hands. 'Look around you. The Qax did a good job of making our world uninhabitable. They even levelled mountains. But *this* bit of Qax technology is reversing the process. Look at it this way. Perhaps we can use their own weapons against the Qax. Or is that against your doctrine?'

'I don't know. I'd have to ask my political officer.' The Hero let the weapon drop. 'I'm not changing my decision. I'm just postponing its implementation.'

Rala nodded sagely.

After that, as the weeks passed, she saw that the patch she had cultivated was spreading, a stain of a richer dark seeping through the ground. Her replicators were now turning soil and sunlight not just into food but into copies of themselves, and so spreading further, slowly, doggedly. The food she got from the ground became handfuls a day, almost enough to stave off the hunger that nagged at her constantly.

Ingre said to her, 'You have a child. I knew they wouldn't hurt you because of that.'

'It's OK, Ingre.'

'Although betraying you was doctrinally the correct thing to do.'

30

'I said it's OK.'

'The children are the future.'

Yes, thought Rala. But what future? We are insane, she thought, an insane species. As soon as the Qax get out of the way we start to rip each other apart. We rule each other with armbands, bits of rag. And now the Million Heroes are prepared to starve us all – they might still do it – for the sake of an abstract doctrine. Maybe we really were better off under the Qax.

But Ingre seemed eager for forgiveness. She worked in the dirt beside her cadre sibling, gazing earnestly at her.

So Rala forced a smile. 'Yes,' she said, and patted her belly. 'Yes, the children are the future. Now here, help me with this sieve.'

Under their fingers, the alien nano seeds spread through the dirt of Earth.

*During the churning of the post-Qax era, we undying, our actions during the Occupation misunderstood, were forced to flee.*

*The Interim Coalition of Governance consolidated its power, as such agencies do, and proved itself to be rather less than interim.*

*But from the ranks of the Coalition's stultifying bureaucracy emerged one man whose strange genius would shape human history for twenty thousand years.*

# REALITY DUST

## AD 5408

An explosion of light: the moment of her birth.

She cried out.

A sense of self flooded through her body. She had arms, legs; her limbs were flailing. She was *falling*, and glaring light wheeled about her.

. . . But she remembered another place: a black sky, a world – no, a *moon* – a face before her, smiling gently. *This won't hurt. Close your eyes.*

A name. *Callisto.*

But the memories were dissipating. 'No!'

She landed hard, face down, and was suffused by sudden pain. Her face was pressed into dust, rough, gritty particles, each as big as a moon to her staring eyes.

The flitter rose from liberated Earth like a stone thrown from a blue bowl. The little cylindrical craft tumbled slowly as it climbed, sparkling, and Hama Druz marvelled at the beauty of the mist-laden, subtly curved landscape swimming around him, drenched as it was in clear bright sunlight.

The scars of the Occupation were still visible. Away from the great Conurbations, much of the land glistened silver-grey where star-breaker beams and Qax nanoreplicators had chewed up the surface of the Earth, life and rocks and all, turning it into a featureless silicate dust.

'But already,' he pointed out eagerly, 'life's green is returning. Look, Nomi, there, and there . . .'

His companion, Nomi Ferrer, grunted sceptically. 'But that greenery has nothing to do with edicts from your Interim Coalition of

32

Governance, or all your philosophies. That's the worms, Hama, turning Qax dust back into soil. Just the worms, that's all.'

Hama would not be put off. Nomi, once a ragamuffin, was an officer in the Green Army, the most significant military force yet assembled in the wake of the departing Qax. She was forty years old, her body a solid slab of muscle, with burn marks disfiguring one cheek. And, in Hama's judgement, she was much too sunk in cynicism.

He slapped her on the shoulder. 'Quite right. And that's how *we* must be, Nomi: like humble worms, content to toil in the darkness, to turn a few scraps of our land back the way they should be. That should be enough for any life.'

Nomi just snorted.

Already the two-seat flitter was beginning its descent, towards a Conurbation. Still known by its Qax registration of 11729, the Conurbation was a broad, glistening sprawl of bubble-dwellings blown from the bedrock, and linked by the green-blue of umbilical canals. Hama saw that many of the dome-shaped buildings had been scarred by fire, some even cracked open. But the blue-green tetrahedral sigil of free Earth had been daubed on every surface.

A shadow passed over the Conurbation's glistening rooftops. Hama shielded his eyes and squinted upwards. A fleshy cloud briefly eclipsed the sun. It was a Spline ship: a living starship kilometres across, its hardened epidermis pocked with monitor and weapon emplacements. He suppressed a shudder. For generations the Spline had been the symbol of Qax dominance. But now the Qax had gone, and this abandoned Spline was in the hands of human engineers, who sought to comprehend its strange biological workings.

On the outskirts of the Conurbation there was a broad pit scooped out of the ground, its crudely scraped walls denoting its origin as post-Occupation: human, not Qax. In this pit rested a number of silvery, insectile forms, and as the flitter fell further through the sunlit air, Hama could see people moving around the gleaming shapes, talking, working. The pit was a shipyard, operated by and for humans, who were slowly rediscovering yet another lost art; for no human engineer had built a spacecraft on Earth for three hundred years.

Hama pressed his face to the window – like a child, he knew, reinforcing Nomi's preconception of him – but to Lethe with self-consciousness. 'One of those ships is going to take us to Callisto. Imagine it, Nomi – a moon of Jupiter!'

But Nomi scowled. 'Just remember *why* we're going there: to hunt out jasofts – criminals and collaborators. It will be a grim business, Hama, no matter how pretty the scenery.'

The flitter slid easily through the final phases of its descent, and the domes of the Conurbation loomed around them.

There was a voice, talking fast, almost babbling.

'There is no time. There is no space. We live in a universe of static shapes. Do you see? Imagine a grain of dust that represents all the particles in *our* universe, frozen in time. Imagine a stupendous number of such dust grains, representing all the possible shapes the particles can take. This is reality dust, a dust of the Nows. And each grain is an instant, in a possible history of the universe.' A snapping of fingers. 'There. There. There. Each moment, each juggling of the particles, a new grain. The reality dust contains all the arrangements of matter there could ever be. Reality dust is an image of eternity . . .'

She lay there, face pressed into the dirt, wishing none of this was happening.

Hands grabbed her, by shoulder and hip. She was dragged, flipped over on her back. The sky above was dazzling bright.

A face loomed, silhouetted. She saw a hairless scalp, no eyebrows or lashes. The face itself was rounded, smoothed over, as if unformed. But she had a strong impression of great age.

'This won't hurt,' she whispered, terrified. 'Close your eyes.'

The face loomed closer. 'Nothing here is real.' The voice was harsh, without inflection. A man? 'Not even the dust.'

'Reality dust,' she murmured.

'Yes. Yes! It is reality dust. If you live, remember that.'

The face receded, turning away.

She tried to sit up. She pressed her hands into the loose dust, crushing low, crumbling structures, like the tunnels of worms. She glimpsed a flat horizon, a black, oily sea, forest-covered hills. She was on a beach of silvery, dusty sand. The sky was a glowing dome. The air was full of mist; she couldn't see far in any direction, as if she were trapped in a glowing bubble.

Her companion was mid-sized, his body shapeless and sexless. He was dressed in a coverall of a nondescript colour. He cast no shadow in the bright diffuse light.

She glanced down at herself. She was wearing a similar coverall. She fingered its smooth fabric, baffled.

The man was walking slowly, limping, as though exhausted. Walking away, leaving her alone.

'Please,' she said.

Without stopping, he called back, 'If you stay there you'll die.'

'What's your name?'

'Pharaoh. That is all the name I have left, at any rate.'

She thought hard. Those sharp birth memories had fled, but still . . . '*Callisto*, My name is Callisto.'

Pharaoh laughed. 'Of course it is.'

Without warning, pain swamped her right hand. She snatched it to her chest. The skin felt as if it had been drenched in acid.

The sea had risen, she saw, and the black, lapping fluid had covered her hand. Where the fluid had touched, the flesh was flaking away, turning to chaotic dust, exposing sketchy bones that crumbled and fell in thin slivers.

She screamed. She had only been here a moment, and already such a terrible thing had happened.

Pharaoh limped back to her. 'Think beyond the pain.'

'I can't—'

'*Think*. There is no pain.'

And, as he said it, she realised it was true. Her hand was *gone*, her arm terminating in a smooth, rounded stump. But it didn't hurt. How could that be?

'What do you feel?'

'Diminished,' she said.

'Good,' he said. 'You're learning. There is no pain here. Only forgetting.'

The black, sticky fluid was lapping near her legs. She scrambled away. But when she tried to use her missing right hand she stumbled, falling flat.

Pharaoh locked his hand under her arm and hauled her to her feet. The brief exertion seemed to exhaust him; his face smoothed further, as if blurring. 'Go,' he said.

'Where?'

'Away from the sea.' And he pushed her, feebly, away from the ocean.

She looked that way doubtfully. The beach sloped upward sharply; it would be a difficult climb. Above the beach there was what looked like a forest, tall shapes like trees, a carpet of something like grass. She saw people moving in the darkness between the trees. But the forest was dense, a place of colourless, flat shadows, made grey by the mist.

She looked back. Pharaoh was standing where she had left him, a pale, smoothed-over figure just a few paces from the lapping, encroaching sea, already dimmed by the thick white mist.

She called, 'Aren't you coming?'

'Go.'

'I'm afraid.'

'Asgard. Help her.'

Callisto turned.

There was a woman, not far away, crawling over the beach. She seemed to be plucking stray grass blades from the dust, cramming them into her mouth. Her face was a mask of wrinkles, complex, textured – a stark contrast to Pharaoh's smoothed-over countenance. Querulous, the woman snapped, 'Why should I?'

'Because I once helped you.'

The woman got to her feet, growling.

Callisto quailed from her. But Asgard took her good hand and began to haul her up the beach.

Callisto looked back once more. The oil-black sea lapped thickly over a flat, empty beach. Pharaoh had gone.

As they made their way to Hama's assigned office, Nomi drew closer to Hama's side, keeping her weapons obvious.

The narrow corridors of Conurbation 11729 were grievously damaged by fire and weaponry – scars inflicted not by Qax, but by humans. In some places there was even a smell of burning.

And the corridors were crowded: not just with former inhabitants of the Qax-built city, but with others Hama couldn't help but think of as *outsiders*.

There were ragamuffins – like Nomi herself – the product of generations who had waited out the Occupation in the ruins of ancient human cities, and other corners of wilderness Earth. And there were returned refugees, the descendants of people who had fled to the outer moons and even beyond Sol system to escape the Qax's powerful, if inefficient, grasp. Some of these returned space travellers were exotic indeed, with skin darkened by the light of other stars, and frames made spindly or squat by other gravities – even eyes replaced by Eyes, mechanical supplements. And most of them had *hair*: hair sprouting wildly from their heads and even their faces, in colours of varying degrees of outrage. They made the Conurbation's Occupation-era inhabitants, with their drab robes and shaven heads, look like characterless drones.

The various factions eyed each other with suspicion, even hostility; Hama saw no signs of unity among liberated mankind.

Hama's office turned out to be a spacious room, the walls lined with data slates. It even had a natural-light window, overlooking a swathe of the Conurbation and the lands beyond. This prestigious room had once, of course, been assigned to a jasoft – a human collaborator administering Earth on behalf of the Qax – and Hama felt a deep reluctance to enter it.

For Hama, up to now, the liberation had been painless, a time of opportunity and freedom, like a wonderful game. But that, he knew, was about to change. Hama Druz, twenty-five years old, had been assigned to the Commission for Historical Truth, the tribunal appointed to investigate and try collaboration crimes. His job was to hunt out jasofts.

Some of these collaborators were said to be *pharaohs*, kept alive by Qax technology, perhaps for centuries . . . Some, it was said, were even survivors of the pre-Occupation period, when human science had advanced enough to beat back death. If the jasofts were hated, the pharaohs had been despised most of all; for the longer they had lived, the more loyalty they owed to the Qax, and the more effectively they administered the Qax regime. And that regime had become especially brutal after a flawed human rebellion more than a century earlier.

Hama, accompanied by Nomi, would spend a few days here, acquainting himself with the issues around the collaborators. But to complete his assignment he would have to travel far beyond the Earth: to Jupiter's moon, Callisto, in fact. There – according to records kept during the Occupation by the jasofts themselves – a number of pharaohs had fled to a science station maintained by one of their number, a man named Reth Cana.

For the next few days Hama worked through the data slates assembled for him, and received visitors, petitions, claimants. He quickly learned that there were many issues here beyond the crimes of the collaborator class.

The Conurbation itself faced endless problems day to day. The

Conurbations had been deliberately designed by the Qax as temporary cities. It was all part of the grand strategy of the latter Occupation; the Qax's human subjects were not allowed ties of family, of home, of loyalty to anybody or anything – except perhaps the Occupation itself. A Conurbation wasn't a home; sooner or later you would be moved on.

The practical result was that the hastily constructed Conurbation was quickly running down. Hama read gloomily through report after report of silting-up canals and failing heating or lighting and crumbling dwelling places. People were sickening of diseases long thought vanished from the planet – even hunger had returned.

And then there were the wars.

The aftermath of the Qax's withdrawal – the overnight removal of the government of Earth after three centuries – had been extremely turbulent. In less than a month humans had begun fighting humans once more. It had taken a chaotic half-year before the Coalition had coalesced, and even now, around the planet, brushfire battles still raged against warlords armed with Qax weaponry.

It had been the jasofts, of course, who had been the focus of the worst conflicts. In many places jasofts, including pharaohs, had been summarily executed. Elsewhere the jasofts had gone into hiding, or fled off-world, or had even fought back. The Coalition had quelled the bloodshed by promising that the collaborators would be brought to justice before its new Commission for Historical Truth.

But Hama – alone in his office, poring over his data slates – knew that justice was easier promised than delivered. How were short-lived humans – dismissively called *mayflies* by the pharaohs – to try crimes that might date back centuries? There were no witnesses save the pharaohs themselves; no formal records save those maintained under the Occupation; no testimony save a handful of legends preserved through the endless dissolutions of the Conurbations; not even any physical evidence since the Qax's great Extirpation had wiped the Earth clean of its past.

What made it even more difficult, Hama was slowly discovering, was that the jasofts were *useful*.

It was a matter of compromise, of practical politics. The jasofts knew how the world worked, on the mundane level of keeping people alive, for they had administered the planet for centuries. So some jasofts – offered amnesties for cooperating – were discreetly running parts of

Earth's new, slowly coalescing administration under the Coalition, just as they had under the Qax.

And meanwhile, children were going hungry.

Hama had, subtly, protested against his new assignment. He felt his strength lay in philosophy, in abstraction. He longed to rejoin the debates going on in great constitutional conventions all over the planet, as the human race, newly liberated from the Qax, sought a new way to govern itself.

But his appeal against reassignment had been turned down. There was simply too much to do *now*, too great a mess to clear up, and too few able and trustworthy people available to do it.

As he witnessed the clamour of the crowds around the failing food dispensers, Hama felt a deep determination that things should be fixed, that such a situation as this should not recur. And yet, to his shame, he looked forward to escaping from all this complexity to the cool open spaces of the Jovian system.

It was while he was in this uncertain mood that the pharaoh sought him out.

Asgard led her to the fringe of the forest. There, ignoring Callisto, she hunkered down and began to pull at strands of grass, ripping them from the ground and pushing them into her mouth.

Callisto watched doubtfully. 'What should I do?'

Asgard shrugged. 'Eat.'

Reluctantly Callisto got to her knees. Favouring her truncated arm, it was difficult to keep her balance. With her left hand she pulled a few blades of the grass stuff from the dust. She crammed the grass into her mouth and chewed. It was moist, tasteless, slippery. She found that the grass blades weren't connected to roots. Rather they seemed to blend back into the dust, to the tube-like structures there.

People moved through the shadows of the forest, digging at the roots with their bare hands, pushing fragments of food into their faces.

'My name,' she said, 'is Callisto.'

Asgard grunted. 'Your dream-name.'

'I remembered it.'

'No, you *dreamed*.'

'What is this place?'

'It isn't a place.'

'What's it called?'

'It has no name.' Asgard held up a blade of grass. 'What colour is this?'

'Green,' Callisto said immediately. But that wasn't true. It wasn't green. What colour, then? She realised she couldn't say.

Asgard laughed, and shoved the blade in her mouth.

Callisto looked down the beach. 'What happened to Pharaoh?'

Asgard shrugged. 'He might be dead by now. Washed away by the sea.'

'Why doesn't he come up here, where it's safe?'

'Because he's weak. Weak and mad.'

'He saved me from the sea.'

'He helps all the newborns.'

'Why?'

'How should I know? But it's futile. The ocean rises and falls. Every time it comes a little closer, higher up the beach. Soon it will lap right up here, to the forest itself.'

'We'll have to go into the forest.'

'Try that and Night will kill you.'

Night? Callisto looked into the forest's darkness, and shuddered.

Asgard eyed Callisto with curiosity, no sympathy. 'You really are a newborn, aren't you?' She dug her hand into the dust, shook it until a few grains were left on her palm. 'You know what the first thing Pharaoh said to *me* was? "Nothing is real."'

'Yes—'

'"Not even the dust. *Because every grain is a whole world.*"' She looked up at Callisto, calculating.

Callisto gazed at the sparkling grains, wondering, baffled, frightened. Too much strangeness.

I want to go home, she thought desperately. But where, and what, is home?

Two women walked into Hama's office: one short, squat, her face a hard mask, and the other apparently younger, taller, willowy. They both wore bland, rather scuffed Occupation-era robes – as he did – and their heads were shaven bare.

The older woman met his gaze steadily. 'My name is Gemo Cana. This is my daughter. She is called Sarfi.'

Hama eyed them with brief curiosity. The daughter, Sarfi, averted her eyes. She looked very young, and her face was thin, her skin sallow.

This was a routine appointment. Gemo Cana was, supposedly, a representative of a citizens' group concerned about details of the testimony being heard by the preliminary hearings of the Truth Commission. The archaic words of family – *daughter, mother* – were still strange to Hama, but they were becoming increasingly more common, as the era of the Qax cadres faded from memory.

He welcomed them with his standard opening remarks. 'My name is Hama Druz. I am an adviser to the Interim Coalition and specifically to the Commission for Historical Truth. I will listen to whatever you wish to tell me and will help you any way I can; but you must understand that my role here is not formal, and—'

'You're tired,' Gemo Cana said.

'What?'

She stepped forward and studied him, her gaze direct, disconcerting. 'It's harder than you thought, isn't it? Running an office, a city – a world. Especially as you must work by persuasion, consent.' She walked around the room, ran a finger over the data slates fixed on the walls, and paused before the window, gazing out at the glistening rooftops of the Conurbation, the muddy blue-green of the canals. Hama could see the Spline ship rolling in the sky, a wrinkled moon. She said, 'It was difficult enough in the era of the Qax, whose authority, backed by Spline gunships, was unquestionable.'

'And,' asked Hama, 'how exactly do you know that?'

'This used to be one of my offices.'

Hama reached immediately for his desktop.

'Please.' The girl, Sarfi, reached out towards him, then seemed to think better of it. 'Don't call your guards. Hear us out.'

He stood. 'You're a jasoft. Aren't you, Gemo Cana?'

'Oh, worse than that,' Gemo murmured. 'I'm a *pharaoh* . . . You know, I have missed this view. The Qax knew what they were doing when they gave us jasofts the sunlight.'

She was the first pharaoh Hama had encountered face to face. Before her easy authority, her sense of dusty age, Hama felt young, foolish, his precious philosophies half-formed. And he found himself staring at the girl; he hadn't even known pharaohs could have children.

Deliberately he looked away, seeking a way to regain control of the situation. 'You've been in hiding.'

Gemo inclined her head. 'I spent a long time working in offices like this one, Hama Druz. Longer than you can imagine. I always knew the day would come when the Qax would leave us exposed, us pharaohs.'

'So you prepared.'

'Wouldn't you? I was doing my duty. I didn't want to die for it.'

'Your duty to Qax occupiers?'

'No,' she said, a note of weariness in her voice. 'You seem more intelligent than the rest; I had hoped you might understand that much. It was a duty to mankind, of course. It always was.'

He tapped a data slate on his desk. '*Gemo Cana*. I should have recognised the name. You are one of the most hunted jasofts. Your testimony before the Commission—'

She snapped, 'I'm not here to surrender, Hama Druz, but to ask for your help.'

'I don't understand.'

'I know about your mission to Callisto. To the enclave there. Reth has been running a science station since before the Occupation. Now *you* are going out there to close him down.'

He said grimly, 'These last few years have not been a time for science.'

She nodded. 'So you believe science is a luxury, a plaything for easier times. But science is a thread in the tapestry of our humanity – a thread Reth has maintained. Do you even know what he is doing out there?'

'Something to do with life forms in the ice—'

'Oh, much more than that. Reth has been exploring the nature of reality – *seeking a way to abolish time itself.*' She smiled coolly. 'I don't expect you to understand. But it has been a fitting goal, in an era when the Qax have sought to obliterate human history – to abolish the passage of time from human consciousness . . .'

He frowned. *Abolishing time*? Such notions were strange to him, meaningless. He said, 'We have evidence that the science performed on Callisto was only a cover – that many pharaohs fled there during the chaotic period following the Qax withdrawal.'

'Only a handful. There only ever was a handful of us, you know. And now that some have achieved a more fundamental escape, into death, there are fewer than ever.'

'What do you *want*?'

'I want you to take us there.'

'To Callisto?'

'We will remain in your custody, you and your guards. You may restrain us as you like. We will not try anything – *heroic*. All we want is sanctuary. They will kill us, you see.'

'The Commission is not a mob.'

She ignored that. 'I am not concerned for myself, but for my daughter. Sarfi has nothing to do with this; she is no jasoft.'

'Then she will not be harmed.'

Gemo just laughed.

'You are evading justice, Gemo Cana.'

She leaned forward, resting her hands on the desk nonchalantly; this really had once been her office, he realised. *'There is no justice here,'* she hissed. 'How can there be? I am asking you to spare my daughter's life. Later, I will gladly return to face whatever inquisition you choose to set up.'

'Why would this Reth help you?'

'His name is Reth Cana,' she said. 'He is my brother. Do you understand? Not my cadre sibling. My *brother*.'

Gemo Cana; Reth Cana; Sarfi Cana. In the Qax world, families had been a thing for ragamuffins and refugees, and human names had become arbitrary labels; the coincidence of names had meant nothing to Hama. But to these ancient survivors, a shared name was a badge of kinship. He glanced at Gemo and Sarfi, uneasy in the presence of these close primitive ties, of mother and brother and daughter.

Abruptly the door opened. Nomi Ferrer walked in, reading from a data slate. 'Hama, your ship is ready to go. But I think we have to—' She looked up, and took in the scene at a glance. In an instant she was at Gemo's side, with a laser pistol pressed against the pharaoh's throat. 'Gemo Cana,' she hissed. 'How did you get in here?'

Sarfi stepped towards Nomi, hands fluttering like birds.

Hama held up his hand. 'Nomi, wait.'

Nomi was angered. 'Wait for what? Standing orders, Hama. This is a Category One jasoft who hasn't presented herself to the Commission. I should already have killed her.'

Gemo smiled thinly. 'It isn't so easy, is it, Hama Druz? You can theorise all you want about justice and retribution. But here, in this office, you must confront the reality of a mother and her child.'

Sarfi said to Hama, 'If your guard kills my mother, she kills me too.'

'No,' said Hama. 'We aren't barbarians. You have nothing to fear—'

Sarfi reached out and swept her arm down at the desk – no, Hama saw, startled; her arm passed *through* the desk, briefly breaking up into a cloud of pixels, boxes of glowing colour.

'You're a Virtual,' he whispered.

'Yes. And do you want to know where *I* live?' She stepped up to her mother and pushed her hand into Gemo's skull.

Gemo observed his lack of comprehension. 'You don't know much about us, do you, even though you presume to judge us? Hama, pharaohs rarely breed true.'

'Your daughter was mortal?'

'The Qax's gift was ambiguous. We watched our children grow old and die. *That* was our reward for serving the Qax; perhaps your Commission will accept *that* historical truth. And when she died—'

'When she died, you downloaded her into your *head*?'

'Nowhere else was safe,' Gemo said. 'And I was glad to, um, make room for her. I have lived a long time; there were memories I was happy to shed.'

Nomi said harshly, 'But she isn't your daughter. She's a copy.'

Gemo closed her eyes. 'But she's all I have left.'

Hama felt moved, and repelled, by this act of obsessive love.

Sarfi looked away, as if ashamed.

There was a low concussion. The floor shuddered. Hama could hear running footsteps, cries.

Nomi Ferrer understood immediately. 'Lethe. That was an explosion.'

The light dropped, as if some immense shadow were passing over the sky. Hama ran to the window.

All around the Conurbation, ships were lifting, hauled into the sky by silent technology, an eerie rising. But they entered a sky that was already crowded, darkened by the rolling, meaty bulk of a Spline craft, from whose flanks fire spat.

Hama cringed from the brute physical reality of the erupting conflict. And he knew who to blame. 'It's the jasofts,' he said. 'The ones taken to orbit to help with the salvaging of the Spline. They took it over. And now they've come here, to rescue their colleagues.'

Gemo Cana smiled, squinting up at the sky. 'Sadly, stupidity is not the sole prerogative of mayflies. This counter-coup cannot succeed. And then, when this Spline no longer darkens the sky, your vengeance will not be moderated by show trials and bleats about justice and truth. You must save us, Hama Druz. Now!'

Sarfi pressed her hands to her face.

Hama stared at Gemo. *'You knew.* You knew this was about to happen. You timed your visit to force me to act.'

'It's all very complicated, Hama Druz,' Gemo said softly, manipulating. 'Don't you think so? Get us out of here – all of us – and sort it out later.'

Nomi pulled back the pharaoh's head. 'You know what I think? I think you're a monster, pharaoh. I think you killed your daughter, long ago, and stuck her in your head. An insurance against a day like today.'

Gemo, her face twisted by Nomi's strong fingers, forced a smile. 'Even if that were true, what difference would it make?' And she gazed at Hama, waiting for his decision.

Obeying Nomi's stern voice commands, the ship rose sharply. Hama felt no sense of acceleration as shadows slipped over his lap.

This small craft was little more than a translucent hemisphere. In fact it would serve as a lifedome, part of a greater structure waiting in Earth orbit to propel him across Sol system. The three of them, plus Sarfi, were jammed into a cabin made for two. The Virtual girl was forced to share the space already occupied by Hama and Gemo. Where her projection intersected their bodies it dimmed and broke up, and she averted her face; Hama was embarrassed by this brutal indignity.

The ship emerged from its pit and rushed directly beneath the looming belly of the attacking Spline; Hama had a brief, ugly glimpse of fleeing, crumpled flesh, oozing scars metres long, glistening weapon emplacements like stab wounds.

The ship reached clear sky. The air was crowded. Ships of all sizes cruised above Conurbation 11729, seeking to engage the rogue Spline. Hama saw, with a sinking heart, that one of the ancient, half-salvaged ships had already crashed back to Earth. It had made a broad crater, a wound in the ground circled by burning blown-silicate buildings. Already people had died today, irreplaceable lives lost for ever.

The ship soared upward. Earth quickly folded over into a glowing blue abstraction, pointlessly beautiful, hiding the gruesome scenes on its surface; the air thinned, the sky dimming through violet, to black. The ship began to seek out the orbiting angular structure that would carry it to the outer planets.

Hama began to relax, for the first time since Gemo had revealed herself. Despite everything that had happened he was relieved to leave behind the complications of the Conurbation; perhaps in the thin light of Jupiter the dilemmas he would have to face would be simpler.

Gemo Cana said carefully, 'Hama Druz, tell me something. Now that we all know who and what we are—'

'Yes?'

'In your searching, has your inquisition turned up a pharaoh called Luru Parz?'

'She's on the list but I don't believe she's been found,' Hama said. 'Why? Did you know her?'

'In a way. You could say I created her, in fact. She was always the best of us, I thought, the best and brightest, once she had clarified her conscience. I thought of her as a daughter.'

The Virtual copy of her real daughter, Sarfi, turned away, expressionless.

Nomi cursed.

A vast winged shape sailed over the blue hide of Earth, silent, like a predator.

Hama's heart sank at the sight of this new, unexpected intruder. What now?

Nomi said softly, 'Those wings must be hundreds of kilometres across.'

'Ah,' said Gemo. 'Just like the old stories. The ship *is* like a sycamore seed . . . But none of you remembers *sycamore trees*, do you? Perhaps you need us, and our memories, after all.'

Nomi said, anger erupting, 'People are dying down there because of your kind, Gemo—'

Hama placed a hand on Nomi's arm. 'Tell us, pharaoh. Is it Qax?'

'Not Qax,' she said. '*Xeelee.*' It was the first time Hama had heard the name. 'That is a Xeelee nightfighter,' said Gemo. 'The question is – what does it want here?'

There was a soft warning chime.

The ship shot away from Earth. The planet dwindled, becoming a sparking blue bauble over which a black-winged insect crawled.

Callisto joined the community of foragers.

Dwelling where the forest met the beach, the people ate the grass, and sometimes leaves from the lower branches, even loose flaps of bark. The people were wary, solitary. She didn't learn their names – if they had any – nor gained a clear impression of their faces, their sexes.

She wasn't even sure how many of them there were here. Not many, she thought.

Callisto found herself eating incessantly. With every mouthful she took she felt herself grow, subtly, in some invisible direction – the opposite to the diminution she had suffered when she lost her hand to the burning power of the sea. There was nothing to drink – no fluid save the oily black ink of the ocean, and she wasn't tempted to try that. But it didn't seem to matter.

Callisto was not without curiosity. She explored, fitfully.

The beach curved away, in either direction. Perhaps this was an island, poking out of the looming black ocean. There was no bedrock, not as far as she could dig. Only the drifting, uniform dust.

Tiring of Asgard's cold company, she plucked up her courage and walked away from the beach, towards the forest.

There were structures in the dust: crude tubes and trails, like the markings of worms or crabs. The grass *emerged*, somehow, coalescing from looser dust formations. The grass grew sparsely on the open beach, but at the fringe of the forest it gathered in dense clumps.

Deeper inside the forest's gathering darkness the grass grew longer yet, plaiting itself into ropy vine-like plants. And deeper still she saw things like trees looming tall, plaited in turn out of the vines. Thus the trees weren't really 'trees' but tangles of ropy vines. And everything was connected to everything else.

She pushed deeper into the forest. Away from the lapping of the sea and the wordless rustle of the foraging people at the forest fringe, it grew dark, quiet. Grass ropes wrapped around her legs, tugging, yielding with reluctance as she passed. This was a drab, still, lifeless place, she thought. In a forest like this there ought to be texture: movement, noise, scent. So, anyhow, her flawed memories dimly protested.

She came to a particularly immense tree. It was a tangle of grassy ropes, melding above her head into a more substantial whole that rose above the surrounding vegetative mass and into the light of the sky. But a low mist lay heavily, obscuring her view of the tree's upper branches.

She felt curiosity spark. What could she see if she climbed above the mist?

She placed her hand on the knotted-up lower trunk, then one foot, and then the other. The stuff of the tree was hard and cold.

At first the climbing was easy, the components of the 'trunk' loosely

47

separated. She found a way to lodge her bad arm in gaps in the trunk so she could release her left hand briefly, and grab for a new handhold before she fell back. But as she climbed higher the ropy sub-trunks grew ever more tangled.

High above her the trunk soared upwards, daunting, disappearing into the mist. When she looked down, she saw how the 'roots' of this great structure dispersed over the forest floor, branching into narrower trees and vine-thin creepers and at last clumps of grass, melting into the underlying dust. She felt unexpectedly exhilarated by this small adventure—

There was a snarl, of greed and anger. It came from just above her head. She quailed, slipped. She finished up dangling by her one hand.

She looked up.

It was human. Or, it might once have been human. It must have been four, five times her size. It was naked, and it clung to the tree above her, upside down, so that a broad face leered, predator's eyes fixed on her. Its limbs were cylinders of muscle, its chest and bulging belly massive, weighty. And it was male: an erection poked crudely between its legs. She hadn't been able to see it for the mist, until she had almost climbed into it.

It thrust its mouth at her, hissing. She could smell blood on its breath.

She screamed and lost her grip.

She fell, sliding down the trunk. She scrabbled for purchase with her feet and her one good hand. She slammed repeatedly against the trunk, and when she hit the ground the wind was knocked out of her.

Above her, the beast receded, still staring into her eyes.

Ignoring the aches of battered body and torn feet, she blundered away, running until she reached the openness of the beach. For an unmeasured time she lay there, drawing comfort from the graininess of the dust.

The craft was called a GUTship.

As finally assembled, it looked something like a parasol of iron and ice. The canopy of the parasol was the surface ferry, now serving as a habitable lifedome, and the 'handle' was the GUTdrive unit itself, embedded in a block of asteroid ice which served as reaction mass. The shaft of the parasol, separating the lifedome from the drive unit, was a kilometre-long spine of metal bristling with antennae and sensors.

In a hundred subtle ways the ship showed its age. Every surface in the lifedome was scuffed and polished from use, the soft coverings of chairs and bunks were extensively patched, and many of the major systems bore the scars of rebuilding. The design was centuries old. The ship itself had been built long before the Occupation, and lovingly maintained by a colony of refugees who had seen out the Qax era huddled in the asteroid belt.

*GUT*, it seemed, was an acronym for Grand Unified Theory. Once, Gemo whispered, unified-theory energy had fuelled the expansion of the universe. In the heart of each GUT engine asteroid ice was compressed to conditions resembling the initial singularity – the Big Bang. There, the fundamental forces governing the structure of matter merged into a single unified superforce. When the matter was allowed to expand again, the phase energy of the decomposing superforce, released like heat from condensing steam, was used to expel asteroid matter as a vapour rocket.

Remarkable, exotic, strange. This might be a primitive ship compared to a mighty Spline vessel, but Hama had never dreamed that mere humans had once mastered such technologies.

But when they were underway, with the lifedome opaqued over and all the strangeness shut out, none of that mattered. To Hama it was like being back in the Conurbations, in the enclosed, claustrophobic days before the Occupation was lifted. A deep part of his mind seemed to believe that what lay beyond these walls – occupied Earth, or endless universe – did not matter, so long as *he* was safe and warm. He felt comfortable in his mobile prison, and was guilty to feel that way.

All that changed when they reached Callisto.

The sun was shrunk to the tiniest of discs by Jupiter's remoteness, five times as far as Earth from the central light. When Hama held up his hand it cast sharp, straight shadows, the shadows of infinity, and he felt no warmth.

And through this rectilinear, reduced light, Callisto swam.

They entered a wide, slow orbit around the ice moon. The satellite was like a dark, misty twin of Earth's Moon. Its surface was crowded with craters – even more so than the Moon's, for there were none of the giant lava-flood seas that smoothed over much lunar terrain. The largest craters were complex structures, plains of pale ice surrounded by multiple arcs of folded and cracked land, like ripples frozen into shattered ice and rock. Some of these features were the size of continents, large enough to stretch around this lonely moon's curved horizon, evidently the results of immense, terrifying impacts.

But these great geological sculptures were oddly smoothed out, the cracks and ripples reduced to shallow ridges. Unlike Earth's rocky Moon, Callisto was made of rock and water ice. Over billions of years the ice had suffered viscous relaxation; it flowed and slumped. The most ancient craters had simply subsided, like geological sighs, leaving these spectacular palimpsests.

'The largest impact structure is called Valhalla,' Gemo was saying. 'Once there were human settlements all along the northern faces of the circular ridges. All dark now, of course – save where Reth has made his base.'

Nomi grunted, uninterested in tourism. 'Then that's where we land.'

Hama gazed out. 'Remarkable,' he said. 'I never imagined—'

Gemo said caustically, 'You are a drone of the Occupation. You never imagined a universe beyond the walls of your Conurbation, you never even saw the sunlight, you have never lived. You have no *memory*. And yet you presume to judge. Do you even know why Callisto is so-called? It is an ancient myth. Callisto was a nymph, beloved of Zeus and hated by jealous Hera, who metamorphosed her into a bear . . .' She seemed to sense Hama's bafflement. 'Ah, but you don't even remember the *Gree-chs*, do you?'

Nomi confronted her. *'You* administered the Extirpation, pharaoh. Your arrogance over the memories you took from us is—'

'Ill-mannered,' Hama said smoothly, and he touched Nomi's shoulder, seeking to calm the situation. 'A lack of grace that invalidates her assumption of superiority over us. Don't concern yourself, Nomi. She condemns herself and her kind every time she speaks.'

Gemo glared at him, full of contempt.

But now Jupiter rose.

The four of them crowded to see. They bobbed in the air like balloons, thrust into weightlessness now the drive was shut down.

The largest of planets was a dish of muddy light, of cloudy bands, pink and purple and brown. Where the bands met, Hama could see fine lines of turbulence, swoops and swirls like a lunatic water-colour. But a single vast storm disfigured those smooth bands, twisting and stirring them right across the southern hemisphere of the planet, as if the whole of Jupiter were being sucked into some central maw.

As perhaps it was. There was a legend that, a century before, human rebels called the Friends of Wigner had climaxed their revolt by escaping *back through time*, across thousands of years, and had hurled a black hole into the heart of Jupiter. The knot of compressed spacetime was already distorting Jupiter's immense, dreamy structure, and perhaps in time would destroy the great world altogether. It was a fantastic story, probably no more than a tale spun for comfort during the darkest hours of Occupation. Still, it was clear that *something* was wrong with Jupiter. Nobody knew the truth – except perhaps the pharaohs, and they would say nothing.

Hama saw how Sarfi, entranced, tried to rest her hand against the lifedome's smooth transparency. But her hand sank into the surface, crumbling, and she snatched it away quickly. Such incidents seemed to cause Sarfi deep distress – as if she had been programmed with deep taboos about violating the physical laws governing 'real' humans. Perhaps it even hurt her when such breaches occurred.

Gemo Cana did not appear to notice her daughter's pain.

The lifedome neatly detached itself from the ship's drive section and swept smoothly down from orbit. Hama watched the moon's folded-over, crater-starred landscape flatten out, the great circular ramparts of Valhalla marching over the close horizon.

The lifedome settled to the ice with the gentlest of crunches. A walkway extended from a darkened building block and nuzzled hesitantly against the ship. A hatch sighed open.

Hama stood in the hatchway. The walkway was a transparent, shimmering tube before him, concealing little of the silver-black morphology of the collapsed landscape beyond. The main feature was the big Valhalla ridge, of course. Seen this close it was merely a rise in the land, a scarp that marched to either horizon: it would have been impossible to tell from the ground that this was in fact part of a circular rampart surrounding a continent-sized impact scar, and Hama felt insignificant, dwarfed.

He forced himself to take the first step along the walkway.

To walk through Callisto's crystal stillness was enchanting; he floated between footsteps in great bounds. The gravity here was about an eighth of Earth's, comparable to the Moon's.

Gemo mocked his pleasure. 'You are like *Armm-stron* and *All-dinn* on the Moon.'

Nomi growled, 'More *Gree-chs*, pharaoh?'

Reth Cana was waiting to meet them at the end of the walkway. He was short, squat, with a scalp of crisp white hair, and he wore a practical-looking coverall of some papery fabric. He was scowling at them, his face a round wrinkled mask. Beyond him, Hama glimpsed extensive chambers, dug into the ice, dimly lit by a handful of floating globe lamps – extensive, but deserted.

Hama's gaze was drawn back to Reth. *He looks like Gemo.*

Gemo stepped forward now, and she and Reth faced each other, brother and sister separated for centuries. They were like copies of each other, subtly morphed. Stiffly, they embraced. Sarfi hung back, watching, hands folded before her.

Hama felt excluded, almost envious of this piece of complex human-ity. How must it be to be bound to another person by such strong ties – for life?

Reth stepped away from his sister and inspected Sarfi. Without warning he swept his clenched fist through the girl's belly. He made a trail of disrupted pixels, like a fleshy comet. Sarfi crumpled over, crying out. The sudden brutality shocked Hama.

Reth laughed. 'A Virtual? I didn't suspect you were so sentimental, Gemo.'

Gemo stepped forward, her mouth working. 'But I remember your cruelty.'

Now Reth faced Hama. 'And this is the one sent by Earth's new junta of children.'

Hama shrank before Reth's arrogance and authority. His accent was exotic – antique, perhaps; there was a rustle of history about this man. Hama tried to keep his voice steady. 'I have a specific assignment here, sir—'

Reth snorted. 'My work, a project of centuries, deals with the essence of reality itself. It is an achievement of which you have *no* under-standing. If you had a glimmer of sensitivity you would leave now. Just as, if you and your mayfly friends had any true notion of duty, you would abandon your petty attempts at governing and leave it to us.'

Nomi growled, 'You think we got rid of the Qax just to hand over our lives to the likes of you?'

Reth glared at her. 'And can you really believe that *we* would have administered the withdrawal of the Qax with more death and destruction than *you* have inflicted?'

Hama stood straight. 'I'm not here to discuss hypotheticals with you, Reth Cana. We are pragmatic. If your work is in the interest of the species—'

Reth laughed out loud; Hama saw how his teeth were discoloured, greenish. *'The interest of the species.'* He stalked about the echoing cavern, posturing. 'Gemo, I give you the future. If this young man has his way, science will be no more than a weapon! . . . And if I refuse to cooperate with his *pragmatism?'*

Nomi said smoothly, 'Those who follow us will be a lot tougher. Believe it, jasoft.'

Gemo listened, stony-faced. 'They mean it, Reth.'

'Tomorrow,' Reth said to Hama. 'Twelve hours from now. I will demonstrate my work, my results. But I will not justify it to the likes of you; make of it what you will.' And he swept away into shadows beyond the fitful glow of the hovering globe lamps.

Nomi said quietly to Hama, 'Reth is a man who has spent too long alone.'

'We can deal with him,' Hama said, with more confidence than he felt.

'Perhaps. But *why* is he alone? Hama, we know that at least a dozen pharaohs came to this settlement before the Occupation was ended, and probably more during the collapse. Where are *they?'*

Hama frowned. 'Find out.'

Nomi nodded briskly.


The oily sea lapped even closer now. The beach was reduced to a thin strip, trapped between forest and sea.

Callisto walked far along the beach. There was nothing different, just the same dense forest, the oily sea. Here and there the sea had already covered the beach, encroaching into the forest, and she had to push into the vegetation to make further progress. Everywhere she found the tangle of roots and vine-like growths. Where the rising liquid had touched, the grasses and vines and trees crumbled and died, leaving bare, scattered dust.

The beach curved around on itself.

So she was on an island. At least she had learned that much. Eventually, she supposed, that dark sea would rise so high it would cover everything. And they would all die.

There was no night. When she was tired, she rested on the beach, eyes closed.

There was no time here – not in the way she seemed to remember, on some deep level of herself: no days, no nights, no change. There was only the beach, the forest, that black oily sea, lapping ever closer, all of it under a shadowless grey-white sky.

She looked inward, seeking herself. She found only fragments of memory: an ice moon, a black sky – a face, a girl's perhaps, delicate, troubled, but the face broke up into blocks of light. She didn't like to think about the face. It made her feel lonely. Guilty.

She asked Asgard about time.

Asgard, gnawing absently on a handful of bark chips, ran a casual finger through the reality dust, from grain to grain. 'There,' she said. 'Time passing. From one moment to the next. For we, you see, are above time.'

'I don't understand.'

'Of course you don't. A row of dust grains is a shard of story. A blade of grass is a narrative. Where the grass knits itself into vines and trees, that story deepens. And if *I* eat a grass blade I absorb its tiny story, and it becomes mine. So Pharaoh said. And I don't know who told *him*. Do you see?'

'No,' said Callisto frankly.

Asgard just looked at her, apathetic, contemptuous.

There was a thin cry, from the ocean. Callisto, shading her eyes, looked that way.

It had been a newborn, thrust arbitrarily into the air, just as Callisto had been. But this newborn had fallen, not to the comparative safety of the dust, but direct into the sea. She – or he – made barely a ripple on that placid black surface. Callisto saw a hand raised briefly above the sluggish meniscus, the flesh already dissolving, white bones curling. And then it was gone, the newborn lost.

Callisto felt a deep horror. It might have happened to her.

Now, as she looked along the beach, she saw dark masses – a mound of flesh, the grisly articulation of fingers – fragments of the suddenly dead, washed up on this desolate beach. This had happened before, she realised. Over and over.

She said, 'We can't stay here.'

'No,' Asgard agreed reluctantly. 'No, we can't.'

*

Hama, with Reth and Gemo, rode a platform of metal deep into the rocky heart of Callisto.

The walls of the pressurised shaft, sliding slowly upwards, were lined with slick transparent sheets, barring them from the ice. Hama reached out with a fingertip. The wall surface was cold and slippery, lubricated by a thin sheet of condensation from the chill air. There were no signs of structure, of strata in the ice; here and there small bores had been dug away from the shaft, perhaps as samples.

Callisto was a ball of dirty water ice. Save for surface impacts, nothing had happened to this moon since it accreted from the greater cloud that had formed the Jupiter system. The inner moons – Io, Europa, Ganymede – were heated, to one degree or another, by tidal pumping from Jupiter. So Europa, under a crust of ice, had a liquid ocean; and Io was driven by that perennial squeezing to spectacular volcanism. But Callisto had been born too far from her huge parent for any of that gravitational succour. Here, the only heat was a relic of primordial radioactivity; here there had been no geology, no volcanism, no hidden ocean.

Nevertheless, it seemed, Reth Cana had found life here. And, as the platform descended, Reth's cold excitement seemed to mount.

Nomi Ferrer was pursuing her own researches, in the settlement and out on the surface. But she had insisted that Hama be escorted by a squat, heavily armed drone robot. Both Reth and Gemo ignored this silent companion, as if it were somehow impolite of Hama to have brought it along.

Nor did either of them mention Sarfi, who hadn't accompanied them. To Hama it did not seem human to disregard one's daughter, Virtual or otherwise. But then, what was 'human' about a near-immortal traitor to the race? What was human about Reth, this man who had buried himself alone in the ice of Callisto, obsessively pursuing his obscure project, for decade after decade?

Even though the platform was small and cramped, Hama felt cold and alone; he suppressed a shiver.

The platform slowed, creaking, to a halt. He faced a chamber dug into the ice.

Reth said, 'You are a kilometre beneath the surface. Go ahead. Take a look.'

Hama saw that the seal between the lip of the circular platform and the roughly cut ice was not perfect. He felt a renewed dread at his reliance on ancient, patched-up technology. But, suppressing hesitation, he stepped off the platform and into the ice chamber. With a whirr of aged bearings, the drone robot followed him.

Hama stood in a rough cube perhaps twice his height. It had been cut out of the ice, its walls lined by some clear glassy substance; it was illuminated by two hovering light globes. On the floor there was a knot of instrumentation, none of it familiar to Hama, along with a heap of data slates, some emergency equipment, and scattered packets of food and water. This was a working place, impersonal.

Reth stepped past him briskly. 'Never mind the gadgetry; you wouldn't understand it anyhow. *Look*.' And he snapped his fingers, summoning one of the floating globes. It came to hover at Hama's shoulder.

Hama leaned close to inspect the cut-away ice of the wall. He could see texture: the ice was a pale, dirty grey, polluted by what looked like fine dust grains – and, here and there, it was stained by colour, crimson and purple and brown.

Reth had become animated. 'I'd let you touch it,' he breathed. 'But the sheeting is there to protect *it* from *us* – not the other way around. The biota in there is much more ancient, unevolved, fragile than we are; the bugs on your breath might wipe it out in an instant. The prebiotic chemicals were probably delivered here by comet impacts during Callisto's formation. There is carbon and hydrogen and nitrogen and oxygen. The biochemistry is a matter of carbon-carbon chains and water – *like* Earth's, but not precisely so. Nothing *exactly* like our DNA structures . . .'

'Spell it out,' Gemo said casually, prowling around the gadgetry. 'Remember, Reth, the education of these young is woefully inadequate.'

'This is life,' Hama said. 'Native to Callisto.'

'Life – yes,' Reth said. 'The highest forms are about equivalent to Earth's bacteria. But – native? I believe the life forms here have a common ancestor with Earth life, buried deep in time – and that they are related to the more extravagant biota of Europa's buried ocean, and probably most of the living things found elsewhere in Sol system. Do you know the notion of panspermia? Life, you see, may have originated in one place, perhaps even outside the system, and then was spread through the worlds by the spraying of meteorite-impact debris. And everywhere it landed, life embarked on a different evolutionary path.'

'But here,' Hama said slowly, fumbling to grasp these unfamiliar concepts, 'it was unable to rise higher than the level of a bacterium?'

'There is no room,' said Reth. 'There is liquid water here: just traces of it, soaked into the pores between the grains of rock and ice, kept from freezing by the radiogenic heat. But energy flows thin, and replication is very slow – spanning thousands of years.' He shrugged. 'Nevertheless there is a complete ecosystem. Do you understand? My Callisto bacteria are rather like the cryptoendoliths found in some inhospitable parts of Earth. In Antarctica, for instance, you can crack open a rock and see layers of green life, leaching nutrients from the stone itself, sheltering from the wind and the desolating cold: communities of algae, cyanobacteria, fungi, yeasts—'

'Not any more,' Gemo murmured, running a finger over control panels. 'Reth, the Extirpation was *very* thorough, an effective extinction event; I doubt if any of your cryptoendoliths can still survive.'

'Ah,' said Reth. 'A shame.'

Hama straightened up, frowning. He had come far from the cramped caverns of the Conurbations; he was confronting life from another world, half a billion kilometres from Earth. He ought to feel wonder. But these pale shadows evoked only a kind of pity. Perhaps this thin, cold, purposeless existence was a suitable object for the obsessive study of a lonely, half-mad immortal.

Reth's eyes were on him, hard.

Hama said carefully, 'We know that before the Occupation, Sol system was extensively explored, by *Michael Poole* and those who followed him. The records of those times are lost – or hidden,' he said with a glance at the impassive Gemo. 'But we do know that everywhere humans went, they found life. Life is commonplace. And in most places we reached, life has attained a much higher peak than *this*. Why not just catalogue these scrapings and abandon the station?'

Reth threw up his arms theatrically. 'I am wasting my time. Gemo, how can this mayfly mind possibly grasp the subtleties here?'

She said dryly, 'I think it would serve you to try to explain, brother.' She was studying a gadget that looked like a handgun mounted on a floating platform. 'This, for example.'

When Hama approached this device, his weapon-laden drone whirred warningly. 'What is it?'

Reth stalked forward. 'It is an experimental mechanism based on laser light, which . . . It is a device for exploring the energy levels of an extended quantum structure.' He began to talk rapidly, lacing his language with phrases like 'spectral lines' and 'electrostatic potential wells', none of which Hama understood.

At length Gemo interpreted for Hama.

'Imagine a very simple physical system – a hydrogen atom, for instance. I can raise its energy by bombarding it with laser light. But the atom is a quantum system; it can only assume energy levels at a series of specific steps. There are simple mathematical rules to describe the steps. This is called a "potential well".'

As he endured this lecture, irritation slowly built in Hama; it was clear there was much knowledge to be reclaimed from these patronising, arrogant pharaohs.

'The potential well of a hydrogen atom is simple,' said Reth rapidly. 'The simplest quantum system of all. It follows an inverse-square rule. But I have found the potential wells of much more complex structures.'

'Ah,' said Gemo. 'Structures embedded in the Callisto bacteria.'

'Yes.' Reth's eyes gleamed. He snatched a data slate from a pile at his feet. Lines of numbers chattered over the slate, meaning little to Hama, a series of graphs that sloped sharply before dwindling to flatness: a portrait of the mysterious 'potential wells', perhaps.

Gemo seemed to understand immediately. 'Let me.' She took the slate, tapped its surface and quickly reconfigured the display. 'Now, look, Hama: the energies of the photons that are absorbed by the well are proportional to this series of numbers.'

1. 2. 3. 5. 7. 11. 13 . . .

'Prime numbers,' Hama said.

'Exactly,' snapped Reth. 'Do you see?'

Gemo put down the slate and walked to the ice wall; she ran her hand over the translucent cover, as if longing to touch the mystery that was embedded there. 'So inside each of these bacteria,' she said, 'there is a quantum potential well that encodes prime numbers.'

'And much more,' said Reth. 'The primes were just the key, the first hint of a continent of structure I have barely begun to explore.' He paced back and forth, restless, animated. 'Life is never content simply to subsist, to cling on. Life seeks room to spread. That is another commonplace, young man. But here, on Callisto, there was no room: not in the physical world; the energy and nutrients were simply too sparse for that. And so—'

'Yes?'

'And so they grew *sideways*,' he said. 'And they reached orthogonal realms we never imagined existed.'

Hama stared at the thin purple scrapings and chattering primes, here at the bottom of a pit with these two immortals, and feared he had descended into madness.

. . . 41. 43. 47. 53. 59 . . .

In a suit no more substantial than a thin layer of cloth, Nomi Ferrer walked over Callisto's raw surface, seeking evidence of crimes.

The sun was low on the horizon, evoking highlights from the curved ice plain all around her. From here, Jupiter was forever invisible, but Nomi saw two small discs, inner moons, following their endless dance of gravitational clockwork.

Gemo Cana had told her mayfly companions how the Jovian system had once been. She told them of Io's mineral mines, nestling in the shadow of the huge volcano Babbar Patera. She told them of Ganymede: larger than Mercury, heavily cratered and geologically rich – the most stable and heavily populated of all the Jovian moons. And Europa's icy crust had sheltered an ocean hosting life, an ecosystem much more complex and rewarding than anybody had dreamed. 'They were *worlds*. Human worlds, in the end. All gone now, shut down by the Qax. But *I* remember . . .'

Away from the sun's glare, lesser stars glittered, surrounding Nomi with immensity. But it was a crowded sky, despite that immensity. Crowded and dangerous. For – she had been warned by the Coalition – the Xeelee craft that had glowered over Earth was now coming *here*, hotly pursued by a Spline ship retrieved from the hands of jasoft rebels and manned by Green Army officers. What would happen when that miniature armada got here, Nomi couldn't imagine.

Nomi knew about the Xeelee from barracks-room scuttlebutt. She had tried to educate a sceptical Hama. The Xeelee were a danger mankind encountered long before anybody had heard of the Qax; in the Occupation years they had become legends of a deep-buried, partly extirpated past – and perhaps they were monsters of the human future. The Xeelee were said to be godlike entities so aloof that humans might never understand their goals. Some scraps of Xeelee technology, like starbreaker beams, had fallen into the hands of 'lesser' species, like the Qax, and transformed their fortunes. The Xeelee seemed to care little for this – but, on occasion, they intervened. To devastating effect.

Some believed that by such interventions the Xeelee were maintaining their monopoly on power, controlling an empire which, perhaps, held sway across the Galaxy. Others said that, like the vengeful gods of humanity's childhood, the Xeelee were protecting the 'junior races' from themselves.

Either way, Nomi thought, it's insulting. Claustrophobic. She felt an unexpected stab of resentment. We only just got rid of the Qax, she thought. And now, this.

Gemo Cana had argued that in such a dangerous universe, humanity needed the pharaohs. 'Everything humans know about the Xeelee today, every bit of intelligence we have, was preserved by the pharaohs. I refuse to plead with you for my life. But I am concerned that you should understand. We pharaohs were not dynastic tyrants. We fought, in our way, to survive the Qax Occupation, and the Extirpation. For we are the wisdom and continuity of the race. Destroy us and you complete the work of the Qax for them, finish the Extirpation. Destroy us and you destroy your own past – which we preserved for you, at great cost to ourselves.'

Perhaps, Nomi thought. But in the end it was the bravery and ingenuity of one human – *a mayfly* – that had brought down the Qax, not the supine compromising of the jasofts and pharaohs.

She looked up towards the sun, towards invisible Earth. I just want a sky clear of alien ships, she thought. And to achieve that, perhaps we will have to sacrifice much.

Reth Cana began to describe where the Callisto bugs had 'gone', seeking room to grow.

'There is no time,' he whispered. 'There is no space. This is the resolution of an ancient debate – do we live in a universe of perpetual change, or a universe where neither time nor motion exist? Now we understand. Now we know we live in a universe of static shapes. Nothing exists but the particles that make up the universe – that make up *us*. Do you see? And we can *measure* nothing but the separation between those particles.

'Imagine a universe consisting of a single elementary particle, an electron perhaps. Then there could be no space. For space is only the separation between particles. Time is only the measurement of changes in that separation. So there could be no time.

'Imagine now a universe consisting of *two* particles . . .'

Gemo nodded. 'Now you can have separation, and time.'

Reth bent and, with one finger, scattered a line of dark dust grains across the floor. 'Let each dust grain represent a distance – a configuration of my miniature two-particle cosmos. Each grain is labelled with a single number: the separation between the two particles.' He stabbed his finger into the line, picking out grains. '*Here* the particles are a metre apart; *here* a micron; *here* a light year. There is one special grain, of course: the one that represents zero separation, the particles overlaid. This diagram of dust shows all that is important about the underlying universe – the separation between its two components. And every possible configuration is shown at once, from this god-like perspective.'

He let his finger wander back and forth along the line, tracing out a twisting path in the grains. 'And here is a history: the two particles close and separate, close and separate. If they were conscious, the particles would think they were embedded in time, that they are coming near and far. But *we* can see that their universe is no more than dust grains, the lined-up configurations jostling against each other. It feels like time, inside. But from outside, it is just – sequence, a scattering of instants, of reality dust.'

Gemo said, 'Yes. "It is utterly beyond our power to measure the changes of things by time. Quite the contrary, time is an abstraction at which we arrive by means of the changes of things."' She eyed Hama. 'An ancient philosopher. *Mach*, or *Mar-que* . . .'

'If the universe has three particles,' said Reth, 'you need *three* numbers. Three relative distances – the separation of the particles, one from the other – determine the cosmos's shape. And so the dust grains, mapping possible configurations, would fill up three-dimensional space – though there is still that unique grain, representing the special instant where all the particles are joined. And with four particles—'

'There would be six separation distances,' Hama said. 'And you would need a six-dimensional space to map the possible configurations.'

Reth glared at him, eyes hard. 'You are beginning to understand. Now. Imagine a space of stupendously many dimensions.' He held up a dust grain. 'Each grain represents one configuration of all the particles in *our* universe, frozen in time. This is reality dust, a dust of the Nows. And the dust fills *configuration space*, the realm of instants. Some of the dust grains may represent slices of our own history.' He snapped his fingers, once, twice, three times. 'There. There. There. Each moment, each juggling of the particles, a new grain, a new coordinate on the map. There is one unique grain that represents the coalescing of all the universe's particles into a single point. There are many more grains representing chaos – darkness – a random, structureless shuffling of the atoms.

'Configuration space contains all the arrangements of matter there could ever be. It is an image of eternity.' He waved a fingertip through the air. 'But if I trace out a path from point to point—'

'You are tracing out a history,' said Hama. 'A sequence of configurations, the universe evolving from point to point.'

'Yes. But *we* know that time is an illusion. In configuration space, all the moments that comprise our history exist simultaneously. *And all the other configurations that are logically possible also exist*, whether they lie along the track of that history or not.'

Hama frowned. 'And the Callisto bugs—'

Reth smiled. 'I believe that, constrained in this space and time, the Callisto lifeforms have started to explore the wider realms of configuration space. Seeking a place to play. Life will find a way.'

Nomi toiled up the gentle slope of the ridge that loomed above the settlement. This was one of the great ring walls of the Valhalla system, curving away from this place for thousands of kilometres, rising nearly a kilometre above the surrounding plains.

The land around her was silver and black, a midnight sculpture of ridges and craters. There were no mountains here, none at all; any created by primordial geology or the impacts since Callisto's birth had long since subsided, slumping into formlessness. There was a thin smearing of black dust over the dirty white of the underlying ice; the dust was loose and fine-grained, and she disturbed it as she passed, leaving bright footprints.

'. . . Do you understand what you're looking at?'

The sudden voice startled her; she looked up.

It was Sarfi. She was dressed, as Nomi was, in a translucent protective suit, another nod to the laws of consistency that seemed to bind her Virtual existence. But she left no footprints, nor even cast a shadow.

Sarfi kicked at the black dust, not disturbing a single grain. 'The ice sublimes – did you know that? It shrivels away, a metre every ten million years – but it leaves the dust behind. That's why the human settlements were established on the north side of the Valhalla ridges. There it is just a shade colder, and some of the sublimed ice condenses out. So there is a layer of purer ice, right at the surface. The humans lived off ten-million-year frost . . . You're surprised I know so much. Nomi Ferrer, I was dead before you were born. Now I'm a ghost imprisoned in my mother's head. But I'm *conscious*. And I am still curious.'

Nothing in Nomi's life had prepared her for this conversation. 'Do you love your mother, Sarfi?'

Sarfi glared at her. 'She preserved me. She gave up part of herself for me. It was a great sacrifice.'

Nomi thought, You resent her. You resent this cloying, possessive love. And all this resentment bubbles inside you, seeking release. 'There was nothing else she could have done for you.'

'But I died anyway. I'm not *me*. I'm a download. I don't exist for me, but for *her*. I'm a walking, talking construct of her guilt.' She stalked away, climbing the slumped ice ridge.

Gemo started to argue detail with her brother. How was it possible for isolated bacteria-like creatures to form any kind of sophisticated sensorium? – but Reth believed there were slow pathways of chemical and electrical communication, etched into the ice and rock, tracks for great slow thoughts that pulsed through the substance of Callisto. Very well, but what of quantum mechanics? The universe was *not* made up of neat little particles, but was a mesh of quantum probability waves. – Ah, but Reth imagined quantum probability lying like a mist over his reality dust, constrained by two things: the geometry of configuration space, as acoustic echoes are determined by the geometry of a room; and something called a 'static universal wave function', a mist of probability that governed the likelihood of a given Now sharing configuration space with a given other . . .

Hama closed his eyes, his mind whirling. Blocky pixels flickered across his vision, *within* his closed eyes.

Startled, he looked up. Sarfi was kneeling before him; she had brushed her Virtual fingertips through his skull, his eyes. He hadn't even known she had come here.

'I know it's hard to accept,' she said. 'My mother spent a long time making me understand. You just have to open your mind.'

'I am no fool,' he said sharply. 'I can imagine a map of all the logical possibilities of a universe. But it would be just that – a map, a theoretical construct, a thing of data and logic. It would not be a *place*. The universe doesn't *feel* like that, I *feel* time passing. I don't experience disconnected instants, Reth's dusty reality.'

'Of course not,' said Reth. 'But you must understand that everything we know of the past is a record embedded in the present – the fossils and geology of Earth, so cruelly obliterated by the Qax, even the traces of chemicals and electricity in your own brain that comprise your memory, maintaining your illusion of past times. Sarfi herself is an illustration of the point. Gemo, may I—?'

Gemo nodded, unsmiling. Hama noted he hadn't asked Sarfi's permission for whatever he was about to do.

Reth tapped a data slate. Sarfi froze, becoming a static, inanimate sculpture of light. Then, after perhaps ten seconds, she melted, began to move once more.

She saw Hama staring at her. 'What's wrong?'

Reth, ignoring her, said, 'The child contains a record of her own shallow past, embedded in her programmes and data stores. She is unaware of intervals of time when she is frozen, or deactivated. If I could start and stop *you*, Hama Druz, you would wake protesting that your memories contained no gaps. But your memories themselves would have been frozen. I could even chop up your life and rearrange its instants in any way I chose; at each instant *you* would have an intact set of memories, a record of a past, and you would believe yourself to have lived through a continuous, consistent reality.

'And thus the maximal-reality dust grains contain *embedded within themselves* a record of the eras which "preceded" them. Each grain contains brains, like yours and mine, with "memories" embedded in them, frozen like sculptures. And history emerges in configuration space because those rich grains are then drawn, by a least-energy matching principle, to the grains which "precede" and "follow" them . . . You see?'

Sarfi looked to Gemo. 'Mother? What does he mean?'

Gemo watched her clinically. 'Sarfi has been reset many times, of course,' she said absently. 'I had no wish to see her grow old, accreted with worthless memory. It was rather like the Extirpation, actually. The Qax sought to reset humanity, to abolish the memory of the race. In the ultimate realisation, we would have become a race of children, waking every day to a fresh world, every day a new creation. It was cruel, of course, but theoretically intriguing. Don't you think?'

Sarfi was trembling.

Now Reth began telling Gemo, rapidly and with enthusiasm, of his plans to explore his continent of configurations. 'No human mind could apprehend that multi-dimensional domain unaided, of course. But it can be modelled, with metaphors – rivers, seas, mountains. It is possible to *explore* it . . .'

Hama said, 'But, if your meta-universe is static, timeless, how could it be experienced? For experience depends on duration.'

Reth shook his head impatiently. He tapped his data slate and beckoned to Sarfi. 'Here, child.'

Hesitantly, she stepped forward. Now she trailed a worm-like tube of light, as if her image had been captured at each moment in some invisible emulsion. She emerged, blinking, from the tube, and looked back at it, bewildered.

'Stop these games,' Hama said tightly.

'You see?' Reth said. 'Here is an evolution of Sarfi's structure, but mapped in space, not time. But it makes no difference to Sarfi. Her memory at each frozen instant contains a record of her walking across the floor towards me – doesn't it, dear? And thus, in static configuration space, sentient creatures could have experiences, afforded them by the evolution of information structures across space.'

Hama turned to Sarfi. 'Are you all right?'

She snapped back, 'What do you think?'

'I think Reth may be insane,' he said.

She stiffened, pulling back. 'Don't ask me. I'm not even a mayfly, remember?'

'It is comforting to know that configuration space exists, Hama,' Gemo said. 'Nothing matters, you see: not even death, not even the Extirpation. For we persist, each moment exists for ever, in a greater universe . . .'

It was a philosophy of decadence, Hama thought angrily. A philosophy of morbid contemplation, a consolation for ageless pharaohs as they sought to justify the way they administered the suffering of their fellow creatures. No wonder it appealed to them so much.

Gemo and Reth talked on, more and more rapidly, entering realms of speculation he couldn't begin to follow.

Callisto told Asgard what she was intending to do. She wanted to climb that tall, braided tree. But she would have to take on Night to do it.

She walked along the narrowing beach, seeking scraps of people, of newborns and others, washed up by the pitiless black sea. She picked up what looked like a human foot. It was oddly dry, cold, the flesh and even the bones crumbling at her touch.

She collected as many of these hideous shards as she could hold, and toiled back along the barren dust.

Then she worked her way through the forest back to the great tree, where she had encountered the creature called Night. She paused every few paces and pushed a section of corpse into the ground. She covered each fragment with ripped-up grass and bits of bark.

'You're crazy,' Asgard said, trailing her, arms full of dried, crumbling flesh and bone.

'I know,' Callisto said. 'I'm going anyway.'

Asgard would not come far enough to reach the tree itself. So Callisto completed her journey alone.

Once more she reached the base of Night's tree. Once more, her heart thumping hard, she began to climb.

The creature, Night, seemed to have expected her. He moved from branch to branch, far above, a massive blur, and he clambered with ferocious purpose down the trunk.

When she was sure he had seen her she scrambled hurriedly back to the ground.

He followed her – but not all the way to the ground. He clung to his trunk, his broad face broken by that immense, bloody mouth, hissing at her.

She glowered back, and took a tentative step towards the tree. 'Come get me,' she muttered. 'What are you waiting for?' She took a piece of corpse (a *hand* – briefly her stomach turned), and she hurled it up at him.

He ducked aside, startled. But as the severed hand came by he caught it neatly in his scoop of a mouth, crunched once and swallowed it whole. He looked down at her with new interest.

And he took one tentative step towards the ground.

'That's it,' she crooned. 'Come on. Come eat the flesh. Come eat *me*, if that's what you want—'

Without warning he leapt from the trunk, immense hands splayed.

She screamed and staggered back. He crashed to the ground perhaps an arm's length from her. One massive fist slammed into her ankle, sending a stab of pain that made her cry out. If he'd landed on top of her he would surely have crushed her.

The beast, winded, was already clambering to his feet.

She got up and ran, ignoring the pain of her ankle. Night followed her, his lumbering four-legged pursuit slow but relentless. As she ran she kicked open her buried caches of body parts. He snapped them up and gobbled them down, barely slowing. The morsels seemed pathetically inadequate in the face of Night's giant reality.

She burst out onto the open beach, still running for her life. She reached the lip of the sea, skidding to a halt before the lapping black liquid. Her plan had been to reach the sea, to lure Night into it.

But when she turned, she saw that Night had hesitated on the fringe of the forest, blinking in the light. Perhaps he was aware that she had deliberately drawn him here. He seemed to dismiss her calculations. He stepped forward deliberately, his immense feet sinking into the soft dust. There was no need for him to rush.

Callisto was already exhausted, and, trapped before the sea, there was nowhere for her to run.

Now he was out in the open she saw how far from the human form he had become, with his body a distorted slab of muscle, a mouth that had widened until it stretched around his head. And yet scraps of clothing clung to him, the remnants of a coverall of the same unidentifiable colour as her own. Once this creature, too, had been a newborn here, landing screaming on this desolate beach.

He walked up to her. He towered over her, and she wondered how many unfortunates he had devoured to reach such proportions.

Beyond his looming shoulder, she could see Asgard, pacing back and forth along the beach.

'Great plan,' Asgard called. 'Now what?'

'I—'

Night raised himself up on his hind legs, huge hands pawing at the air over her head. He roared wordlessly, and bloody breath gushed over her.

Close your eyes, Callisto thought. This won't hurt.

'No,' Asgard said. She took a step towards the looming beast, began to run. 'No, no, *no!*' With a final yell she hurled herself at his back.

He looked around, startled, and swiped at Asgard with one giant paw. She was flung away like a scrap of bark, to land in a heap on the dust. But Night, off-balance, was stumbling backward, back toward the sea.

When his foot sank into the oily ocean, he looked down, as if surprised. Even as he lifted his leg from the fluid the flesh was drying, crumbling, the muscles and bone sloughing away in layers of purple and white. He roared his defiance, and cuffed at the sea – then gazed in horror at one immense hand left shredded by contact with the entropic ooze.

He began to fall, slowly, ponderously. Without a splash, the fluid opened up to accept his immense bulk. He was immediately submerged, the shallow fluid flowing eagerly over him. In one last burst of defiance he broke the surface, mouth open, his flesh dissolving. His face was restored, briefly, to the human, his eyes a startling blue. He cried out, his voice thin: *'Reth Cana! You betrayed me!'*

The name sent a shiver of recognition through Callisto.

Then he fell back, and was gone.

She hurried to Asgard. Her chest was crushed, Callisto saw immediately, and her limbs were splayed at impossible angles. Her face was growing smooth, featureless, like a child's, beautiful in its innocence. Her gaze slid over Callisto.

Callisto cradled Asgard's head. 'This won't hurt,' she murmured. 'Close your eyes.'

Asgard sighed, and was still.

'Let me tell you the truth about pharaohs,' Nomi said bitterly.

Hama listened in silence. They stood on the Valhalla ridge, overlooking the old, dark settlement; the brightest point on the silver-black surface of Callisto was their own lifedome.

Nomi said, 'This was just after the Qax left. I got this from a couple of our people who survived, who were *there*. They found a nest of the pharaohs, in one of the biggest Conurbations – one of the first to be constructed, one of the oldest. The pharaohs retreated into a pit, under the surface dwellings. They fought hard; we didn't know why. They had to be torched out. A lot of good people, good *mayflies*, died that day. When our people had dealt with the pharaohs, shut down the mines and drone robots and booby-traps . . . after all that, they went into the pit. It was dark. But it was warm, the air was moist, and there was movement everywhere. Small movements. And, so they say, there was a smell. Of *milk*.'

Nomi was silent for a long moment; Hama waited.

'Hama, I can't have children. I grew up knowing that. So maybe I ought to find some pity for the pharaohs. They don't breed true – like

Gemo and Sarfi. Oh, sometimes their children *are* born with Qax immortality. But—'

'Yes?'

'But they don't all grow. They stop developing, at the age of two years or one year or six months or a month; some of them even stop growing before they are ready to be born, and have to be plucked from their mothers' wombs.

'And that was what our soldiers found in the pit, Hama. Racked up like specimens in a lab, hundreds of them. Must have been accumulating for centuries. Plugged into machines, mewling and crying.'

'Lethe.' Maybe Gemo is right, Hama thought; maybe the pharaohs really have paid a price we can't begin to understand.

'The pit was torched . . .'

Hama thought he saw a shadow pass across the sky, the scattered stars. 'Why are you telling me this, Nomi?'

'To show you that pharaohs have experiences we can't share. And they do things we would find incomprehensible. To figure them out you have to think like a pharaoh.'

'You've found something, haven't you?'

Nomi pointed. 'There's a line of shallow graves over there. Not hard to find, in the end.'

'Ah.'

'The killings seemed to be uniform, the same method every time. A laser to the head. The bodies seemed peaceful,' Nomi mused. 'Almost as if they welcomed it.'

He had killed them. Reth had killed the other pharaohs who came here, one by one. But why? And why would an immortal welcome death? Only if – Hama's mind raced – only if she were promised a better place to go, a safer place—

Everything happened at once.

A shadow, unmistakable now, spread out over the stars: a hole in the sky, black as night, winged, purposeful. And, low towards the horizon, there was a flare of light.

'Lethe,' said Nomi softly. 'That was the GUTship. It's *gone* – just like that.'

'Then we aren't going home.' Hama felt numb; he seemed beyond shock.

'. . . Help me. Oh, help me . . .'

A form coalesced before them, a cloud of blocky pixels. Hama made out a sketch of limbs, a face, an open, pleading mouth. It was Sarfi, and she wasn't in a protective suit. Her face was twisted in pain; she must be breaking all her consistency overrides to have projected herself to the surface like this.

Hama held out his gloved hands, driven by an impulse to hold her; but that, of course, was impossible.

'Please,' she whispered, her voice a thin, badly realised scratch. 'It is Reth. He plans to kill Gemo.'

Nomi set off down the ridge slope in a bouncing low-G run.

Hama said to Sarfi, 'Don't worry. We'll help your mother.'

Now he saw anger in that blurred, sketchy face. 'To Lethe with her! Save *me* . . .' The pixels dispersed into a meaningless cloud, and winked out.

Callisto returned to the great tree.

The trunk soared upwards, a pillar of rigid logic and history and consistency. She slapped its hide, its solidity giving her renewed confidence. And now there was no Night, no lurking monster, waiting up there to oppose her.

Ignoring the aches of her healing flesh and torn muscles, she began to climb.

As she rose above the trunk's lower tangle and encountered the merged and melded upper length, the search for crevices became more difficult, just as it had before. But she was immersed in the rhythm of the climb, and however high she rose there seemed to be pocks and ledges moulded into the smooth surface of the trunk, sufficient to support her progress.

Soon she had far surpassed the heights she had reached that first time she had tried. The mist was thick here, and when she looked down the ground was already lost: the great trunk rose from blank emptiness, as if rooted in nothingness.

But she thought she could see shadows, moving along the trunk's perspective-dwindled immensity: the others from the beach, some of them at least, were following her on her unlikely adventure.

And still she climbed.

The trunk began to split into great arcing branches that pushed through the thick mist. She paused, breathing deeply. Some of the branches were thin, spindly limbs that dwindled away from the main trunk. But others were much more substantial, highways that seemed anchored to the invisible sky.

She picked the most solid-looking of these upper branches, and continued her climb. Impeded by her damaged arm, her progress was slow but steady. It was actually more difficult to make her way along this tipped-over branch than it had been to climb the vertical trunk. But she was able to find handholds, and places where she could she wrap her limbs around the branch.

The mist thickened further until she could see nothing around her but this branch: no sky or ground, not even the rest of this great tree, as if nothing existed but herself and the climb, as if she had been toiling for ever along this branch that came from the mist and finished in the mist.

And then, without warning, she broke through the fog.

In a pit dug into the heart of Callisto, illuminated by a single hovering globe lamp, Gemo Cana lay on a flat, hard pallet, unmoving. Her brother stood hunched over her, working at her face with gleaming equipment. 'This won't hurt. Close your eyes . . .'

'Stop this!' Sarfi ran forward. She pushed her hands into Gemo's face, crying out as the pain of consistency violation pulsed through her.

Gemo turned, blindly. Hama saw that a silvery mask had been laid over her face, hugging the flesh. 'Sarfi . . . ?'

Nomi stepped forward, laser pistol poised. 'Stop this obscenity.'

Reth wore a mask of his own, a smaller cap that covered half his face; the exposed eye peered at them, hard, suspicious, calculating. 'Don't try to stop us. You'll kill her if you try. *Let us go*, Hama Druz.'

Nomi raised her pistol at his head.

But Hama touched the soldier's arm. 'Not yet.'

On her pallet, Gemo Cana turned her head blindly. She whispered, 'There's so much you don't understand.'

Hama snapped, 'You'd better make us understand, Reth Cana, before I let Nomi here off the leash.'

Reth paced back and forth. 'Yes – technically, this is a kind of death. But not a single one of the pharaohs who passed through here did it against his or her will.'

Hama frowned. ' "Technically"? "Passed through"?'

Reth stroked the metal clinging to Gemo's face; his sister turned her head in response. 'The core technology is an interface to the brain via

71

the optic nerve. In this way I can connect the quantum structures which encode human consciousness to the structures stored in the Callisto bacteria – or, rather, the structures which serve as, um, a gateway to configuration space . . .'

Hama started to see it. 'You're attempting to download human minds into your configuration space.'

Reth smiled. 'It was not enough, you see, to study configuration space at second-hand, through quantum structures embedded in these silent bacteria. The next step had to be direct apprehension by the human sensorium.'

'The next step in what?'

'In our evolution, perhaps,' Reth murmured. 'With the help of the Qax, we have banished death. Now we can break down the walls of this shadow theatre we call reality.' He eyed Hama. 'This dismal pit is not a grave, but a gateway. And I am the gatekeeper.'

Hama said tightly, 'You destroy minds for the promise of afterlife – a promise concocted of theory and a scraping of cryptoendolith bacteria.'

'Not a theory,' Gemo whispered. 'I have *seen* it.'

Nomi grunted, 'We don't have time for this.'

But Hama asked, despite himself: 'What was it like?'

It was, Gemo said, a vast, spreading landscape, under a towering sky; she had glimpsed a beach, a rising, oily sea, an immense mountain shrouded in mist . . .

Reth stalked back and forth, arms spread wide. 'We remain human, Hama Druz. *I* cannot apprehend a multi-dimensional continuum. So I sought a metaphor. A human interface. A beach of reality dust. A sea of entropy, chaos. The structures folded into the living things, the shape of the landscape, represent consistency – what we time-bound creatures apprehend as causality.'

'And the rising sea?'

'The cosmos-spanning threat of the Xeelee,' he said, smiling thinly. 'And the grander rise of entropy, across the universe, which will bring about the obliteration of all possibility.

'Configuration space is real, Hama Druz. This isn't a new idea; *Pleh-toh* saw that, thousands of years ago . . . Ah, but you know nothing of *Pleh-toh*, do you? The higher manifold always existed, you see, long before the coming of mankind, of life itself. All that has changed is that through the patient, blind growth of the Callisto bacteria, I have found a way to reach it. And there we can truly live for ever—'

The ice floor shuddered, causing them to stagger.

Reth peered up the length of the shaft, smiling grimly. 'Ah. Our visitors make their presence known. Callisto is a small, hard, static world; it rings like a bell even at the fall of a footstep. And the footsteps of the Xeelee are heavy indeed.'

Sarfi pushed forward again, hands twisting, agonised by her inability to touch and be touched. She said to Gemo, 'Why do you have to *die*?'

Gemo's voice was slow, sleepy; Hama wondered what sedative agents Reth had fed her. 'You won't feel anything, Sarfi. It will be as if you never existed at all, as if all this pain never occurred. Won't that be better?'

The ground shuddered again, waves of energy from some remote Xeelee-induced explosion pulsing through Callisto's patient ice, and the walls groaned, stressed.

Hama tried to imagine the black sea, the sharp-grained dust of the beach. Hama had once visited the ocean – Earth's ocean – to oversee the reclamation of an abandoned Qax sea farm. He remembered the stink of ozone, the taste of salt in the damp air. He had hated it.

Reth seemed to sense his thoughts. 'Ah, but I forgot. You are creatures of the Conurbations, of the Extirpation. Of round-walled caverns and a landscape of grey dust. But this is how the Earth used to be, you see, before the Qax unleashed their nanotech plague. No wonder you find the idea strange. But not us.' He slipped his hand into his sister's. 'For us, you see, it will be like coming home.'

On the table, Gemo was convulsing, her mouth open, laced with drool.

Sarfi screamed, a thin wail that echoed from the high walls of the shaft. Once more she reached out to Gemo; once more her fluttering fingers passed through Gemo's face, sparkling.

'Gemo Cana is a collaborator,' Nomi said. 'Hama, you're letting her escape justice.'

Yes, Hama thought, surprised. Nomi, in her blunt way, had once more hit on the essence of the situation here. The pharaohs were the refugees now, and Reth's configuration space – if it existed at all – might prove their ultimate bolt-hole. Gemo Cana was escaping, leaving behind the consequences of her work, for good or ill. But did that justify killing her?

Sarfi was crying. 'Mother, please. I'll die.'

The pharaoh turned her head. 'Hush,' said Gemo. 'You can't die. You were never alive. Don't you see that?' Her back arched. '*Oh . . .*'

Sarfi straightened and looked at her hands. The illusion of solidity was breaking down, Hama saw; pixels swarmed like fat, cubic insects, grudgingly cooperating to maintain the girl's form. Sarfi looked up at Hama, and her voice was a flat, emotionless husk, devoid of intonation and character. '*Help me.*'

Again Hama reached out to her; again he dropped his hands, the most basic of human instincts invalidated. 'I'm sorry.'

'*It hurts.*' Her face swarmed with pixels that erupted from the crumbling surface of her skin and fled her body, as if evaporating; she was becoming tenuous, unstable.

Hama forced himself to meet her gaze. 'It's all right,' he murmured. 'It will be over soon . . .' On and on, meaningless endearments; but she gazed into his eyes, as if seeking refuge there.

For a last instant her face congealed, clearly, from the dispersing cloud. '*Oh!*' She reached out to him with a hand that was no more than a mass of diffuse light. And then, with a silent implosion, her face crumbled, eyes closing.

Gemo shuddered once, and was still.

Hama could feel his heart pulse within him. His humanity was warm in this place of cold and death. Nomi placed her strong hand on his shoulder, and he relished its fierce solidity.

Hama faced Reth. 'You are monsters.'

Reth smiled easily. 'Gemo is beyond your mayfly reproach. And as for the Virtual child – you may learn, Hama Druz, if you pass beyond your current limitations, that the first thing to be eroded by time is sentiment.'

Hama flared. 'I will never be like you, pharaoh. Sarfi was no toy.'

'But you still don't see it,' Reth said evenly. '*She is alive* – but our time-bound language can't describe it – she persists, somewhere out there, beyond the walls of our petty realisation.'

Again the moon shuddered, and primordial ice groaned.

Reth murmured, 'Callisto was not designed to take such hammer blows. The situation is reduced, you see. *Now* there is only me.'

'And me.' Nomi raised the laser pistol.

'Is this what you want?' Reth asked of Hama. 'To cut down centuries of endeavour with a bolt of light?'

Hama shook his head. 'You really believe you can reach your configuration space – that you can survive there?'

'But I have proof,' Reth said. 'You saw it.'

'All I saw was a woman dying on a slab.'

Reth glowered at him. 'Hama Druz, make your decision.'

Nomi aimed the pistol. 'Hama?'

'Let him go,' Hama said bitterly. 'He has only contempt for our mayfly justice anyhow. His death would mean nothing, even to him.'

Reth grinned and stepped back. 'You may be a mayfly, but you have the beginnings of wisdom, Hama Druz.'

'Yes,' Hama said quietly. 'Yes, I believe I do. Perhaps there *is* something there, some new realm of logic to be explored. But you, Reth, are blinded by your arrogance and your obsessions. Surely this new reality is nothing like the Earth of your childhood. And it will have little sympathy for your ambitions. Perhaps whatever survives the download will have no resemblance to *you*. Perhaps you won't even remember who you were. What then?'

Reth's mask sparkled; he raised his hand to his face. He made for the pallet, to lie beside the cooling body of his sister. But he stumbled and fell before he got there.

Hama and Nomi watched, neither moving to help him.

Reth, on his hands and knees, turned his masked face to Hama. 'You can come with me, Hama Druz. To a better place, a higher place.'

'You go alone, pharaoh.'

Reth forced a laugh. He cried out, his back arching. Then he fell forward, and was still.

Nomi raked the body with laser fire. 'Good riddance,' she growled. '*Now* can we get out of here?'


There was a mountain.

It rose high above the night-dark sea, proudly challenging the featureless, glowing sky. Rivers flowed from that single great peak, she saw: black and massive, striping its huge conical flanks, merging into great tumbling cascades that poured into the ocean.

The mountain was the centre of the world, thrusting from the sea.

She was high above an island, a small scrap of land that defied the dissolving drenching of the featureless sea. Islands were few, small, scattered, threatened everywhere by the black, crowding ocean.

But, not far away, there was another island, she saw, pushing above the sea of mist. It was a heaping of dust on which trees grew thickly, their branches tangled. In fact the branches reached across the neck of sea that separated this island from her own. She thought she could see a way to reach that island, scrambling from tree to tree, following a great highway of branches. The other island rose higher than her own above the encroaching sea. There, she thought, she – and whoever followed her – would be safe from lapping dissolution. For now, anyhow.

But what did that mean? What would Pharaoh have said of this – that the new island was an unlikely heap of reality dust, further from looming entropic destruction?

She shook her head. The deeper meaning of her journey scarcely mattered – and nor did its connection to any other place. If this world were a symbol, so be it: this was where she lived, and this was where she would, with determination and perseverance, survive.

She looked one last time at the towering mountain. Damaged arm or not, she itched to climb it, to challenge its negentropic heights. But in the future, perhaps. Not now.

Carefully, clinging to her branch with arms and legs and her one good hand, she made her way along the branch to the low-probability island. One by one, the people of the beach followed her.

In the mist, far below, she glimpsed slow, ponderous movement: huge beasts, perhaps giant depraved cousins of Night. But, though they bellowed up at her, they could not reach her.

Once more Hama and Nomi stood on the silver-black surface of Callisto, under a sky littered with stars. Just as before, the low, slumped ridges of Valhalla marched to the silent horizon.

But this was no longer a world of antiquity and stillness. The shudders were coming every few minutes now. In places the ice crust was collapsing, ancient features subsiding, here and there sending up sprays of dust and ice splinters that sparkled briefly before falling back, all in utter silence.

Hama thought back to a time before this assignment, to the convocations he had joined, the earnest talk of political futures and ethical settlements. He had been a foolish boy, he thought, his ideas half-formed. Now, when he looked into his heart, he saw crystal-hard determination. In an implacably hostile universe humanity must survive, whatever the cost.

'No more pharaohs,' Hama murmured. 'No more immortality. That way lies selfishness and arrogance and compromise and introversion and surrender. A brief life burns brightly – that is the way.'

Nomi growled, 'Even now you're theorising, Hama? Let's count the ways we might die, standing right here. The Xeelee starbreaker might cream us. One of these miniature quakes might erupt right under us. Or maybe we'll last long enough to suffocate in our own farts, stuck inside these damn suits. What do you think? I don't know why you let that arrogant pharaoh kill himself.'

Hama murmured, 'You see death as an escape?'

'If it's easy, if it's under your control – yes.'

'Reth did escape,' Hama said. 'But I don't think it was into death.'

'You *believed* all that stuff about theoretical worlds?'

'Yes,' Hama said. 'Yes, in the end I think I did believe it.'

'Why?'

'Because of *them*.' He gestured at the sky. 'The Xeelee. If our second-hand wisdom has any validity at all, we know that the Xeelee react to *what they fear*. And almost as soon as Reth constructed his interface to his world of logic and data, as soon as the pharaohs began to pass into it, they came here.'

'You think the Xeelee fear us?'

'Not us. The bugs in the ice: Reth's cryptoendoliths, dreaming their billion-year dreams . . . The Xeelee seem intent on keeping those dreams from escaping. And that's why I think Reth hit on a truth, you see. Because the Xeelee see it too.'

Now, over one horizon, there was a glowing crimson cloud, like dawn approaching – but there could be no dawn on this all-but-airless world.

'Starbreaker light,' murmured Nomi. 'The glow must be vapour, ice splinters, dust, thrown up from the trench they are digging.'

Hama felt a fierce anger burn – anger, and a new certainty. 'Once again aliens have walked into our system, for their own purposes, and we can do nothing to stop them. This mustn't happen again, Nomi. You know, perhaps the Qax were right to attempt the Extirpation. If we are to survive in this dangerous universe we must remake ourselves, without sentiment, without nostalgia, without pity. Let this be an end – and a beginning, a new Day Zero. History is irrelevant. Only the future is important.' He longed to be gone from this place, to bring his hard new ideas to the great debates that were shaping the future of humankind.

'You're starting to frighten me, my friend,' Nomi said gently. 'But not as much as *that*.'

Now the Xeelee nightfighter itself came climbing above the shattered fog of the horizon. Somehow in his ardour Hama had forgotten this mortal peril. The nightfighter was like an immense, black-winged bird. Hama could see crimson Starbreaker light stab down again and again into the passive, defenceless ice of Callisto. The shuddering of the ground was constant now, as that mass of shattered ice and steam rolled relentlessly towards them.

Nomi grabbed him; holding each other, they struggled to stay on their feet as ice particles battered their faceplates. A tide of destruction spanned Callisto from horizon to horizon. There was, of course, no escape.

And then the world turned silver, and the stars swam.

Hama cried out, clinging to Nomi, and they fell. They hit the ice hard, despite the low gravity.

Nomi, combat-hardened, was on her feet immediately. An oddly pink light caught her squat outline. But Hama, winded, bewildered, found himself gazing up at the stars.

*Different* stars? No. Just – moved. The Xeelee ship was gone, vanished.

He struggled to his feet.

The wave of vapour and ice was subsiding, as quickly as it had been created; there was no air here to prevent the parabolic fall of the crystals back to the shattered land, little gravity to prevent the escape of the vapour into Jovian space. The land's shuddering ceased, though he could feel deep slow echoes of huge convulsions washing through the rigid ground.

*But the stars had moved.*

He turned, taking in the changed sky. Surely the shrunken sun was a little further up the dome of sky. And a pink slice of Jupiter now showed above the smoothly curved horizon, where none had shown before on this tide-locked moon.

Nomi touched his arm, and pointed deep into the ice. '*Look.*'

It was like some immense fish, embedded in the ground, its spread-eagled black wings clearly visible through layers of dusty ice. A red glow shone fitfully at its heart; as Hama watched it sputtered, died, and the buried ship grew dark.

Nomi said, 'At first I thought the Xeelee must have lit up some exotic super-drive and got out of here. But I was wrong. That thing must be half a kilometre down. How did it *get* there?'

'I don't think it did,' Hama said. He turned away and peered at Jupiter. '*I think Callisto moved*, Nomi.'

'What?'

'It didn't have to be far. Just a couple of kilometres. Just enough to swallow up the Xeelee craft.'

Nomi was staring at him. 'That's insane. Hama, what can move a moon?'

Why, a child could, Hama thought in awe. A child playing on a beach – if every grain on that beach is a slice in time. I see a line sketched in the dust, a history, smooth and complete. I pick out a grain with Callisto positioned just *here*. And I replace it with a grain in which Callisto is positioned just a little further over *there*. As easy, as wilful, as that.

No wonder the Xeelee are afraid.

A new shuddering began, deep and powerful.

'Lethe,' said Nomi. 'What now?'

Hama shouted, 'Not the Xeelee this time. Callisto spent four billion years settling into its slow waltz around Jupiter. Now I think it's going to have to learn those lessons over again.'

'Tides,' Nomi growled.

'It might be enough to melt the surface. Perhaps those cryptoendoliths will be wiped out after all, and the route to configuration space blocked. I wonder if the Xeelee *planned* it that way all along.'

He saw a grin spread across Nomi's face. 'We aren't done yet.' She pointed.

Hama turned. A new moon was rising over Callisto's tight horizon. It was a moon of flesh and metal, and it bore a sigil, a blue-green tetrahedron, burned into its hide.

'The Spline ship, by Lethe,' Nomi said. She punched Hama's arm. '*Our* Spline. So the story goes on for us, my friend.'

Hama glared down into the ice, at the Xeelee craft buried there. Yes, the story goes on, he thought. But we have introduced a virus into the software of the universe. And I wonder what eyes will be here to see, when that ship is finally freed from this tortured ice.

An orifice opened up in the Spline's immense hide. A flitter squirted out and soared over Callisto's ice, seeking a place to land.

Exhausted, disoriented, Callisto and her followers stumbled down the last length of trunk and collapsed to the ground.

She dug her good hand into the loose grains of reality dust. She felt a surge of pride, of achievement. This island, an island of a new possibility, was her island now.

Hers, perhaps, but not empty, she realised slowly. There was a newborn here: lost, bewildered, suddenly arrived. She saw his face smoothing over, working with anguish and doubt, as he *forgot*.

But when his gaze lit on her, he became animated.

He tried to stand, to walk towards her. He stumbled, weak and drained, and fell on his face.

Dredging up the last of her own strength, she went to him. She dug her hand under him and turned him on his back – as, once, Pharaoh had done for her.

He opened his mouth. Spittle looped between his lips, and his voice was a harsh rasp. 'Gemo!' he gasped.

'My name is Callisto.'

'I am your brother! I made you! Help me! Love me!'

Something tugged at her: recognition – and resentment.

She held his head to her chest. 'This won't hurt,' she said. 'Close your eyes.' And she held him, until the last of his unwelcome memories had leaked away, and, forgetting who he was, he lay still.

*The Coalition, hardened by Hama Druz's doctrines of constancy and racial destiny, proved persistent, and determined. Cleansing themselves of the past, they continued to try to eradicate the undying, for we collaborators embodied the past. We had to flee, to hide.*

*But our taint of immortality went deeper than those who persecuted us could know. I, already an elder, found a new role.*

# ALL IN A BLAZE

## AD 5478

On some level Faya Parz had always known the truth about herself. In the background of her life there had been bits of family gossip. And then as she grew older, and her friends began to grey, even though she had had to give up her Dancing, she stayed supple – as if she was charmed, time sliding by her, barely touching her.

But these were subtle things. She had never articulated it to herself, never framed the thought. On some deeper level she hadn't wanted to know.

She had to meet Luru Parz before she faced it.

It all came to a head on the day of the Halo Dance.

The amphitheatre was a bowl gouged out of the icy surface of Port Sol. Of course the amphitheatre was crowded, as it was every four years for this famous event; there was a sea of upturned faces all around Faya. She gazed up at the platforms hovering high above, just under the envelope of the dome itself, where her sister and the other Dancers were preparing for their performance. And beyond it all the sun, seen from here at the edge of Sol system, was just a brighter pinprick in a tapestry of stars, its sharpness softened a little by the immense dome that spanned the theatre.

'. . . Excuse me.'

Faya glanced down. A small woman faced her, stocky, broad-faced, dressed in a nondescript coverall. Faya couldn't tell her age, but there was something solid about her, something heavy, despite the micro-gravity of Port Sol. And she looked oddly familiar.

The woman smiled at her.

Faya was staring. 'I'm sorry.'

'The seat next to you—'

'It's free.'

With slow care, the woman climbed the couple of steps up to Faya's row and sat down on the carved and insulated ice. 'You're Faya Parz, aren't you? I've seen your Virtuals. You were one of the best Dancers of all.'

'Thank you.'

'You wish you were up there now.'

Faya was used to fans, but this woman was a little unsettling. 'I'm past forty. In the Dance, when you've had your day, you must make way.'

'But you are ageing well.'

It was an odd remark from a stranger. 'My sister's up there.'

'Lieta, yes. Ten years younger. But you could still challenge her.'

Faya turned to study the woman. 'I don't want to be rude, but—'

'But I seem to know a lot about you, don't I? I don't mean to put you at a disadvantage. My name is Luru Parz.'

Faya did a double-take. 'I thought I knew all the Parz on Port Sol.'

'We're relatives even so. I'm – a great-aunt, dear. Think of me that way.'

'Do you live here?'

'No, no. Just a transient, as we all are. Everything passes, you know; everything changes.' She waved her hand, indicating the amphitheatre. Her gestures were small, economical in their use of time and space. 'Take this place. Do you know its history?'

Faya shrugged. 'I never thought about it. Is it natural, a crater?'

Luru shook her head. 'No. A starship was born here, right where we're sitting, its fuel dug out of the ice. It was the greatest of them all, called *Great Northern*.'

'You know a lot of history,' said Faya, a little edgy. The Coalition, focusing on mankind's future, frowned on any obsession with lost heroic days.

Luru would only shrug. 'Some of us have long memories.'

A crackling, ripping sound washed down over the audience, and a pale blue mist erupted over the domed sky. And now the first haloes formed, glowing arcs and rings around the brighter stars and especially around the sun itself, light scattered by air full of tiny ice prisms. There were more gasps from the crowd.

'What a beautiful effect,' said Luru.

'But it's just water,' Faya said.

So it was. The dome's upper layers of air were allowed to become extremely cold, far below freezing. At such temperatures you could just throw water into the air and it would spontaneously freeze. A water droplet froze quickly from the outside in – but ice was less dense than water, and when the central region froze it would expand and shatter the outer shell. So the air was suddenly filled with tiny bombs.

On this ice moon, cold was art's raw material.

The main event began. One by one the Dancers leapt from their platforms. They were allowed no aids; they followed simple low-gravity parabolas that arched between one floating platform and the next. But the art was in the selection of that parabola among the shifting, shivering ice haloes – which were, of course, invisible to the Dancers – and in the way you spun, turned, starfished and swam against that background.

As one Dancer after another passed over the dome, ripples of applause broke out around the amphitheatre. Glowing numerals and Virtual bar graphs littered the air in the central arena; the voting had already begun. But the sheer beauty of the Dance silenced many of the spectators, as the tiny human figures, naked and lithe, spun defiantly against the stars.

Here, at last, was Lieta herself, ready for the few seconds of flight for which she had rehearsed for four years. Faya remembered how it used to feel, the nervousness as her body tried to soar – and then the exhilaration when she succeeded, one more time.

Lieta's launch was good, Faya saw, her track well chosen. But her movements were stiff, lacking the liquid grace of her competitors. Lieta, her little sister, was already thirty years old, and one of the oldest in the field; and suddenly it showed.

At the centre of the arena a display of Lieta's marks coalesced. A perfect score would have showed as bright green, but Lieta's bars were flecked with yellow. A Virtual of Lieta's upper body and head appeared; she was smiling bravely in reaction to the scores.

'There is grey in her hair,' murmured Luru. 'Look at the lines around her eyes, her mouth. *You* have aged better than your ten-years-younger sister. You have aged less, in fact. There is no grey in *your* hair.'

Faya wasn't sure how to respond. She looked away, disturbed.

'Tell me why you gave up the Dance. Your performances weren't declining, were they? You felt you could have kept going *for ever*. Isn't that true? But something worried you.'

Faya turned on her in irritation. 'Look, I don't know what you want—'

'It's a shock when you see them grow old around you. I remember it happening to me, the first time – long ago, of course.' She grinned coldly.

'You're frightening me.' Faya said it loud enough to make people stare.

Luru stood. 'I'm like you, Faya Parz. The same blood. *You know what I'm talking about*. When you need to see me, you'll be able to find me.'

Faya waited in her seat until the Dance was over, and the audience had filed away. She didn't even try to find Lieta, as they'd arranged. Instead she made her own way up into the dome.

She stood on the lip of the highest platform. The amphitheatre was a pit, far below, but she had no fear of heights. The star-filled sky beyond the dome was huge, inhuman. And, through the subtle glimmer of the dome walls, she could see the tightly curving horizon of this little world of ice.

She closed her eyes, visualising the pattern of haloes, just as it had been when Lieta had launched herself into space. And then she jumped.

Though she had no audience, she had the automated systems assess her. She found the bars glowing an unbroken green. She had recorded a perfect mark. If she had taken part in the competition, against these kids half her age, she would have won.

She had known what Luru was had been talking about. Of course she had. Where others aged, even her own sister, she stayed young. It was as simple as that. The trouble was, it was starting to show.

And it was illegal.

Home was a palace of metal and ice she shared with her extended family. This place, one of the most select on Port Sol, had been purchased with the riches Faya had made from her Dancing.

Her mother was here. Spina Parz was over sixty; her grey, straying hair was tied back in a stern bun.

And, waiting for Faya, here was a Commissary, a representative of the Commission for Historical Truth. Originally an agency for ferreting out Qax collaborators, the Commission had evolved seamlessly into the police force of the Coalition, government of Sol system. This Commissary wore his head shaved, and a simple ground-length robe.

Everybody was frightened of Commissaries. It was only a couple of generations since Coalition ships had come to take Port Sol into the new government's deadly embrace, by force. But somehow Faya wasn't surprised to see him; evidently today was the day everything unravelled for her.

The Commissary stood up and faced her. 'My name is Ank Sool.'

'I'm not ageing, am I?'

He seemed taken aback by her bluntness. 'I can cure you. Don't be afraid.'

Her mother Spina said wistfully, 'I knew you were special even when you were very small, Faya. You were an immortal baby, born among mortals. I could tell when I held you in my arms. And you were beautiful. My heart sang because you were beautiful and you would live for ever. You were *wonderful*.'

'Why didn't you *tell* me?'

Spina looked tired. 'Because I wanted you to figure it out for yourself. On the other hand I never thought it would take you until you were *forty*.' She smiled. 'You never were the brightest crystal in the snowflake, were you, dear?'

Faya's anger melted. She hugged her mother. 'The great family secret . . .'

'I saw the truth, working its way through you. You always had trouble with relationships with men. They kept growing too *old* for you, didn't they? When you're young even a subtle distancing is enough to spoil a relationship. And—'

'And I haven't had children.'

'You kept putting it off. Your body knew, love. And now your head knows too.'

Sool said earnestly, 'You must understand the situation.'

'I understand I'm in trouble. Immortality is illegal.'

He shook his head. 'You are the *victim* of a crime – a crime committed centuries ago.'

It was all the fault of the Qax, as so many things were. During their Occupation of Earth the Qax had rewarded those who had collaborated with them with an anti-ageing treatment. The Qax, masters of nanotechnological transformations, had rewired human genomes.

'After the fall of the Qax the surviving collaborators and their children were given the gift of mortality.' The Commissary said this without irony.

'But you evidently didn't get us all,' Faya said.

Sool said, 'The genome cleansing was not perfect. After centuries of Occupation we didn't have the technology. In every generation there are throwbacks.'

'*Throwbacks*. Immortals, born to mortal humans.'

'Yes.'

Faya felt numb. It was as if he was talking about somebody else. 'My sister—'

Her mother said, 'Lieta is as mortal as I am, as your poor father was. It's only you, Faya.'

'We can cure you,' Sool said, smiling. 'It will be quite painless.'

'But I could stay young,' Faya said rapidly. She turned to Sool. 'Once I was famous for my Dancing. They even knew my name on Earth.' She waved a hand. 'Look around! I made a fortune. I was the best. Grown men of twenty-five – your age, yes? – would follow me down the street. You can't know what that was like; you never saw their eyes.' She stood straight. 'I could have it all again. I could have it for ever, couldn't I? If I came out about what I am.'

Sool said stiffly, 'The Coalition frowns on celebrity. The species, not the individual, should be at the centre of our thoughts.'

Her mother was shaking her head. 'Anyhow, Faya, it can't be like that. You're still young; you haven't thought it through. Once I hoped you would be able to – hide. To survive. But it would be impossible. Mortals won't accept you.'

'Your mother is right,' Sool said. 'You would spend your life tinting your hair, masking your face. Abandoning your home every few years. *Otherwise they will kill you*. No matter how beautifully you Danced.' He said this with a flat certainty, and she realised that he was speaking from experience.

'I need time,' she said abruptly, and forced a smile. 'Ironic, isn't it? Just as I've been given all the time anybody could ask for.'

Spina sighed. 'Time for what?'

'To talk to Luru Parz.' And she left before they could react.

'I am nearly two hundred years old,' said Luru Parz. 'I was born in the era of the Occupation. I grew up knowing nothing else. And I took the gift of immortality from the Qax. I have already lived to see the liberation of mankind.'

They were in a two-person flitter. Faya had briskly piloted them into a slow orbit around Port Sol; beneath them the landscape stretched to its close-crowding horizon. Here, in this cramped cabin, they were safely alone.

Port Sol was a Kuiper object: like a huge comet nucleus, circling the sun beyond the orbit of Pluto. The little ice moon was gouged by hundreds of artificial craters. Faya could see the remnants of domes, pylons and arches, spectacular microgravity architecture. But the pylons and graceful domes were collapsed, with bits of glass and metal jutting like snapped bones. Everything was smashed up. Much of this architecture was a relic of pre-Occupation days. The Qax had never come here; during the Occupation the moon had been a refuge. It had been humans, the forces of the young Coalition, who had done all this damage in their ideological enthusiasm. Now, even after decades of reoccupation and restoration, most of the old buildings were closed, darkened, and thin frost coated their surfaces.

Luru said, 'Do you know what I see, when I look down at this landscape? I see layers of history. The great engineer Michael Poole himself founded this place. He built a great system of wormholes, rapid-transit pathways from the worlds of the inner system. And having united Sol system, here, at the system's outermost terminus, Poole's disciples used great mountains of ice to fuel interstellar vessels. It was the start of mankind's First Expansion. But then humans acquired a hyperdrive.' She smiled wistfully. 'Economic logic. The hyper-ships could fly right out of the crowded heart of Sol system, straight to the stars. Nobody needed Poole's huge wormhole tunnels, or his mighty ice mine. And then the Qax came, and then the Coalition.'

'But now Port Sol has revived.'

'Yes. Because now we are building a new generation of starships, great living ships thirsty for Port Sol's water. Layers of history.'

'Luru, why should *I* be tainted in this way? Why my family?'

'It's common on Port Sol,' Luru said. 'Relatively. Even during the Occupation, and again under the Coalition's persecution, the undying fled to the outer system – to the gas giants' moons, to here, a forgotten backwater. Yes, this was a hideout for undying.'

'I know. That's why the Coalition were so brutal.'

'Yes. Many undying escaped the Coalition invasion, and fled further.

A flock of generation starships rose from the ice of Port Sol, even as the Coalition ships approached, commanded by undying; nobody knows what became of them. But while they were here, you see, the undying perturbed the gene pool, with their own taint of longevity. It's not a surprise that throwbacks like you, as the Commission calls you, should arise here.'

'Luru Parz, I don't know what to do. Will I have to hide?'

'Yes. But you mustn't be ashamed. There is an evolutionary logic to our longevity.' Luru clutched a fist over her heart. 'Listen to me. Before we were human, when we were animals, we died after the end of our fertile years, like animals. But then, as we evolved, we changed. We lived on, long after fertility ended. Do you know why? So that grand-mothers could help their daughters raise the next generation. And *that* is how we overcame the other animals, and came to own the Earth – through longevity. Immortality is good for the species, even if the species doesn't know it. You must hide, Faya. But you must not be ashamed of what you are.'

'I don't want to hide.'

'You don't have a choice. The Coalition are planning a new future for mankind, an expansion to the stars that will sweep on, for ever. There will be no place for the old. But of course that's just the latest rationalisation. People have always burned witches.'

Faya didn't know what a witch was.

And then a Virtual of Faya's mother's face congealed in the air before her, the bearer of bad news about Lieta.

Faya and Spina held each other, sitting side by side. For now they were done with weeping, and they had readmitted Ank Sool, the Com-missary.

'I don't understand,' Faya said. It was the brevity that was impossible to bear – a handful of Dances, a flash of beauty and joy, and then dust. And why should her sister die so suddenly *now*, why was her life cut short, just as the prospect of eternity opened up for Faya? 'Why Lieta? Why *now*?'

Sool said, 'Blame the Qax. The pharaohs never bred true. Many of their offspring died young, or their development stopped at an unsuit-able age, so that immortality remained in the gift of the occupiers. The Qax were always in control, you see.'

Faya said carefully, 'Commissary, I think I will always suspect, in a corner of my heart, *that you allowed this death to happen*, in order to bring me under control.'

His eyes were blank. 'The Commission for Historical Truth has no need of such devices.'

Spina grasped her daughter's hands. 'Take the mortality treatment, dear. It's painless. Get it over, and you will be safe.'

'You could have sent me to the Commission as a child. I could have been cured *then*. I need never have even *known*.'

Sool said dryly, 'So you would blame your mother rather than the Qax. How – human.'

Spina's face crumpled. 'Oh, love, how could I take such a gift away from you – even to protect you?'

'It's your decision,' said Sool.

'It always had to be,' said her mother.

Again she swept into orbit with Luru Parz, seeking privacy.

This is how it will be for me from now on, she thought: hiding from people. I will be one of a handful of immortal companions, like crabbed, folded-over Luru here, standing like unchanging rocks in a landscape of evanescent flowers.

That or mortality.

'I can't stand the thought of seeing them all growing old and dying around me. *For ever*.'

Luru nodded. 'I know. But you aren't thinking big enough, child. On a long enough timescale, everything is as transient as one of your Halo Dances. Why, perhaps we will even live to see the stars themselves sputter to life, fade and die.' She smiled. 'Stars are like people. Even stars come and go, you see. They die all in a blaze, or fade like the last light of the sun – but you've never seen a sunset, have you? The glory is always brief – but it is worth having, even so. And *you* will remember the glory, and make it live on. It's your purpose, Faya.'

'My burden,' she said bleakly.

'We have great projects, long ambitions, beyond the imagination of these others. Come with me.'

Tentatively Faya reached out her hand, Luru took it. Her flesh was cold.

'I will have to say farewell—'

'Not farewell. *Goodbye*. Get used to it.'

Before they left she visited the amphitheatre, one last time. And –

though she knew she could never let anybody watch her, ever again –
she Danced and Danced, as the waiting stars blazed.

*Even as the Coalition hardened its grip on mankind, and continued its hideous
cleansing of Sol system, it launched a new thrust to the stars.*

*The Third Expansion of mankind was the most vigorous yet and, driven by
the new ideology of Hama Druz, the most purposeful.*

*I and those like me tried to stay out of the way of the engines of history.*

*As the Expansion unfolded humanity once more encountered alien kinds, and
re-engaged in wider Galactic history. It was only a little more than eighty years
after the liberation from the Qax that a first contact of devastating significance
was made.*

# TWO

## THE WAR WITH THE GHOSTS

# SILVER GHOST

AD 5499

**M**inda didn't even see the volcanic plume before it swallowed up her flitter.

Suddenly the fragile little craft was turning end over end, alarms wailing and flashing, all its sensors disabled. But to Minda, feeling nothing thanks to her cabin's inertial suspension, it was just a light show, a Virtual game, nothing to do with *her*.

Just seconds after entering the ash plume, the flitter rammed itself upside down into an unfeasibly hard ground. Crumpling metal screamed. Then the inertial suspension failed. Minda tumbled out of her seat, and her head slammed into the cabin roof.

Immersed in sudden silence, sprawled on the inverted ceiling, she found herself staring out of a window. Gushing vapour obscured the landscape. That was *air*, she thought woozily. The frozen air of this world, of Snowball, blasted to vapour by the flitter's residual heat.

All she could think of was what her cadre leader would have to say. *You fouled up*, Bryn would tell her. *You don't deserve to survive. And the species will be stronger for your deletion.*

I'm fifteen years old. I'm strong. I'm not dead yet. I'll show her.

She passed out.

Maybe she awoke, briefly. She thought she heard a voice.

'. . . You are a homeotherm. That is, your body tries to maintain a constant temperature. It is a common heat management strategy. You have an inner hot core, which appears to comprise your digestive organs and your nervous system, and an outer cooler shell, of skin and fat and muscle and limbs. The outer shell serves as a buffer between the outside world and the core. Understanding this basic mechanism should help you survive . . .'

Through the window, between gusts of billowing mist, she glimpsed something moving: a smooth curve sliding easily past the wreck, a distorted image of a crumpled metallic mass. It couldn't be real, of course. Nothing moved on this cold world.

When she woke up properly, it was going to *hurt*. She closed her eyes.

When she couldn't stay unconscious any longer, she was relieved to find she could move.

She climbed gingerly out of the crumpled ceiling panel. She probed at her limbs and back. She seemed to have suffered nothing worse than bruises, stiffness and pulled muscles.

But she was already feeling cold. And she had a deepening headache that seemed to go beyond the clatter she had suffered during the landing.

Her cabin had been reduced to a ball, barely large enough for her to stand up. The only light was a dim red emergency glow. She quickly determined she had no comms, not so much as a radio beacon to reveal her position – and there was only a trickle of power. Most of the craft's systems seemed to be down – everything important, anyhow. There was no heat, no air renewal; maybe she was lucky the gathering cold had woken her before the growing foulness of the air put her to sleep permanently.

But she was stuck here. She sat on the floor, tucking her knees to her chest.

It all seemed a very heavy punishment for what was, after all, a pretty minor breach of discipline.

OK, Minda shouldn't have taken a flitter for a sightseeing jaunt around the glimmering curve of the new world. OK, she shouldn't have gone solo, and should have lodged and stuck to a flight plan. OK, she shouldn't have flown so low over the ruined city.

But the fact was that after grousing her way through the three long years of the migration flight from Earth – *three years*, a fifth of her whole life – she'd fallen in love with this strange, lonely, frozen planet as soon as it had come swimming toward her through sunless space. She had sat glued before Virtual representations of her new home, tracing ocean beds with their frozen lids of ice, continents coated by sparkling frost – and the faint, all-but-erased hints of cities and roads, the mark of the vanished former inhabitants of this unlucky place. The rest of her cadre were more interested in Virtual visions of the future, when new artificial suns would be thrown into orbit around this desolate pebble. But it was Snowball itself that entranced Minda – Snowball as it *was*, here and now, a world deep-frozen for a million years.

As the Spline fleet had lumbered into orbit – as she had endured the ceremonies marking the claiming of this planet on behalf of the human species and the Coalition – she had itched to walk on shining lands embedded in a stillness she had never known in Earth's crowded Conurbations.

Which was why, just a week after the first human landing on Snowball, she had gotten herself into such a mess.

Well, she couldn't stay here. Reluctantly she got to her feet.

With a yank on a pull-tag, her seat cushion opened up into a survival suit. It was thick and quilted, with an independent air supply and a sewn-in grid of heating elements and lightweight power cells. She sealed herself in. Clean air washed over her face, and the suit's limited medical facilities probed at her torn muscles.

She had to trigger explosive bolts to get the hatch open. The last of the flitter's air gushed out into a landscape of silver and black, and crystals of frost fell in neat parabolas to an icebound ground. Though she was cocooned in her suit, she felt a deeper chill descend on her.

And as the vapour froze out, again she glimpsed strange sudden movement – a surface like a bubble, or a distorting mirror – an image *of herself*, a silvery figure standing framed in a doorway, ruddy light silhouetting her. The image shrank away.

It had been like seeing a ghost. This world of death might be full of ghosts. I should be scared, she thought. But I'm walking away from a volcanic eruption and a flitter crash. One thing at a time, Minda. Clumsily she clambered through the crash-distorted hatchway.

She found herself standing in a drift of loose, feathery snow that came up to her knees. Beneath the snow was a harder surface: perhaps water ice, even bare rock. Where her suit touched the snow, vapour billowed around her.

To her left that volcano loomed above the horizon, belching foul black fast-moving plumes that obscured the stars. And to her right, in a shallow valley, she made out structures – low, broken walls, perhaps a gridwork of streets. Everything was crystal clear: no mist to spoil the view on this world, where every molecule of atmosphere lay as frost on the ground. The sky was black and without a sun – yet it was far more crowded than the sky of Earth, for here, at the edge of the great interstellar void known as the Local Bubble, the hot young stars of Scorpio were close and dazzling.

The landscape was wonderful, what she had borrowed the flitter to come see. And yet it was lethal: every wisp of gas around her feet was a monument to more lost heat. Her fingers and toes were already numb, painful when she flexed them.

She walked around the crash site. The flitter had dug itself a trench. And as it crashed the flitter had let itself implode, giving up its structural integrity to protect the life bubble at its heart – to protect *her*. The craft had finished up as a rough, crumpled sphere. Now it had nothing left to give her.

Her suit would expire after no more than a few hours. She had no way to tell Bryn where she was – they probably hadn't even missed her yet. And she and her flitter made no more than a metallic pinprick in the hide of a world as large as Earth.

She was, she thought wonderingly, going to die here. She spoke it out loud, trying to make it real. 'I'm going to die.' But she was Minda. How could *she* die? Would history go on after her? Would mankind sweep on, outward from the Earth, an irresistible colonising wave that would crest far beyond this lonely outpost, with her name no more than a minor footnote, the first human to die on the new world? 'I haven't *done* anything yet. I haven't even had *sex* properly—'

A vast, silvered epidermis ballooned before her, and a voice spoke neutrally in her ear.

'Nor, as it happens, have I.'

It was the silver ghost.

She screamed and fell back in the snow.


A bauble, silvered, perhaps two metres across, hovered a metre above the ground, like a huge droplet of mercury. It was so perfectly reflective that it was as if she couldn't see *it* at all: only a fish-eye reflection of the flitter wreck and her own sprawled self, as if a piece of the world had been cut out and folded over.

And this silvery, ghostly, not-really-there creature was *talking* to her.

'Native life forms are emerging from dormancy,' said a flat, machine-generated voice in her earpieces. 'Your heat is feeding them. To them you are a brief, unlikely summer. How fascinating.'

Clumsy in her thick protective suit, bombarded by shocks and strangeness, she twisted her head to see.

The snow was melting all around her, gushing up in thin clouds of vapour that quickly refroze and fell back, so that she was lying in the centre of a spreading crater dug out of the soft snow. And in that crater there was movement. Colours spread over the ice, all around her: green and purple and even red, patches of it like lichen, widening as she watched. A clutch of what looked like worms wriggled in fractured ice. She even saw a tiny flower push out of a mound of frozen air, widening a crimson mouth.

Struck with revulsion, she stumbled to her feet. With her heat gone the life forms dwindled back. The colours leached out of the lichen-like patches, and that single flower closed, as if regretfully.

'A strange scene,' said the silver ghost. 'But it is a common tactic. The living things here must endure centuries in stillness and silence, waiting a chance benison of heat – from volcanic activity, perhaps even a cometary impact. And in those rare, precious moments, they live and die, propagate and breed. Perhaps they even dream of better times in the past.'

Though she had endured orientation exercises run by the Commission for Historical Truth, Minda had never encountered an alien before. She bunched her fists. 'Are you a Qax?'

'. . . No,' it replied, after some hesitation. 'Not a Qax.'

'Then what?'

Again that hesitation. 'Our kinds have never met before. You have no name for me. What are *you*?'

'I'm a human being,' she said defiantly. She pushed out her chest; her suit was emblazoned with a green tetrahedron. 'And this is *our* planet. You'll see, when we get it sorted out. These things, these flowers and worms, cannot compete with us.'

The ghost hovered, impassive. 'Compete?'

She swivelled her head to confront the hovering ghost. 'All life forms compete. It is the way of things.' But it was as if her skull was full of a sloshing liquid; she felt herself stumbling forward.

'Try to stay upright,' the ghost said, its voice free of inflection. 'Your insulation is imperfect. To reduce heat loss, you must minimise your surface contact with the ice.'

'I don't need your advice,' she growled. But her breath was misting, and there were tiny frost patterns in the corners of her faceplate. The cold was sharp in her nose and mouth and eyes.

The ghost said, 'Your body is a bag of liquid water. I surmise you come from a world of high ambient temperatures. I, however, come from a world of cold.'

'Where?'

The hovering globe's hide was featureless, but nevertheless she had the impression that it was spinning. 'Towards the centre of the Galaxy.' Something untranslatable. A distance? 'And yours?'

She knew how to find the sun from here. Minda had travelled across a hundred and fifty light years, at the edge of the great colonising bubble called the Third Expansion, towards the brilliant young stars of Scorpio and the Southern Cross. Now those dazzling beacons were easily identifiable in the sky over her head, jewels thrown against the paler wash of the Galaxy centre. To find home, all she had to do was look the other way, back the way the great fleet of Spline ships had come. The sun, Earth and all the familiar planets were therefore somewhere beneath her feet, hidden by the bulk of this frozen rock.

She was never going to see Earth again, she thought suddenly, desolately; and because this ice-block world happened to be turned this way rather than that, she would never even see the dim, unremarkable patch of sky where Earth lay.

Without thinking, she found herself looking that way. She snapped her head up. 'I mustn't tell you.'

'Ah. Competition?'

Was the ghost somehow mocking her? She said sharply, 'If we have never met before, how come I understand you?'

'Your vessel carries a translator box. The box understands both our languages. It is of Squeem design.'

Minda hadn't even known her flitter was equipped with a translator box. 'It's a *human* design,' she said.

'No,' the ghost said gently. 'Squeem. We have never met before, but evidently the Squeem have met us both. Ironic. It is a strange example of inadvertent cooperation between three species: Squeem, your kind, mine.'

The Squeem were the first extra-solar species humanity had encountered. They were also the first to have occupied Sol system; the Qax, soon after, had been the second. Minda had grown up understanding that the universe was full of alien species hostile to humanity. She glanced around. Were there more silver ghosts out there, criss-crossing the silent plains, their perfect reflectiveness making them invisible to her untrained eye? She tried not to betray her fear.

She asked cautiously, 'Are you alone?'

'We have a large colony here.' Again that odd hesitation. 'But I, too, am stranded in this place. I came to investigate the city.'

'And you were caught by the volcano?'

'Yes. What is worse, my investigation did not advance the goals of the colony.' She sensed it was studying her. 'You are shivering. Do you understand why? Your body knows it is losing heat faster than it is being replaced. The shivering reflex exercises many muscles, increasing heat production by burning fuel. It is a short-term tactic, but—'

'You know a lot about human bodies.'

'No,' it said. 'I know a lot about heat. I am equipped to survive in this heat-sink landscape for extended periods. You, however, are not.'

It was as if cadre-leader Bryn was lecturing her on the endless struggle that was the only future for mankind. *We cannot be weak. The Qax found us weak. They enslaved us and almost wiped our minds clean. If we are unfit for this new world, we must make ourselves fit. Whatever it takes. For only the fittest survive.* If she let herself die before this enigmatic silver ghost, she would be conceding the new world to an alien race.

Impulsively, she began to stalk into the shallow valley, towards the antique city. Maybe there was something there she could use to signal, or survive.

The silver ghost followed her. It swam over the ground with a smooth, unnatural ease; it was a motion neither biological nor mechanical that she found disturbing.

She pushed through snowed-out air. The cold seemed to be settling in her lungs, and when she spoke her voice quavered from shivering.

'Why are you here? What do you *want* on Snowball?'

'We are' – a hesitant pause – 'researchers. This world is like a laboratory to us. This is a rare place, you see, because near-collisions between stars, of the kind that hurled this world into the dark, are rare. We are conducting experiments in low-temperature physics.'

'You're talking about absolute zero. Everybody knows you can't reach absolute zero.'

'Perhaps not. But the journey is interesting. The universe was hot when it was born,' the ghost said gently. 'Very hot. Since then it has expanded and cooled, slowly. But it still retains a little of that primal warmth. In the future, it will grow much colder yet. We want to know what will happen then. For example, it seems that at very low temperatures quantum wave functions – which determine the position of atoms – spread out to many times their normal size. Matter condenses into a new jelly-like form, in which all the atoms are in an identical quantum state, as if lased . . .'

Minda didn't want to admit she understood none of this.

The ghost said, 'You see, we seek to study matter and energy in configurations which might, perhaps, never before have occurred in all the universe's history.'

She clambered over low, shattered walls, favouring hands and feet which ached with the cold. 'That's a strange thought.'

'Yes. How does matter *know* what to do, if it has never done it before? By probing such questions we explore the boundaries of reality.'

She stopped, breathing hard, and gazed up at the hovering ghost. 'Is that *all* you do, this physics stuff? Do you have a family?'

'That is . . . complicated. More yes than no. Do you?'

'We have cadres. I met my parents before I left home. They were there at my Naming, too, but I don't remember that. Do you have music?'

'More yes than no. We have other arts. Tell me why *you* are here.'

She frowned. 'We have a right to be here.' She waved an arm over the sky. 'Some day humans are going to reach every star in the sky, and live there.'

'Why?'

'Because if we don't, somebody else will.'

'Is that all *you* do?' the ghost asked. 'Fly to the stars and build cities and compete?'

'No. We have music and poetry and other stuff.' Defensively, she plodded on through deepening snow. 'Soon we'll change this world. We're going to terraform it.' She had to explain what that meant. 'It will be a heroic project. It will require hard work, ingenuity and perseverance. Also we have brought creatures with us that are used to the cold. We found them on an ice moon a long way from our sun, a place called Port Sol. They have liquid helium for blood. Now we farm them. They can live here, even before the terraforming.'

'How remarkable. But there are already creatures living here.'

'We'll put them in cases,' said Minda. 'Or zoos.'

'We, my kind, can live here, on this cold world, without making it warm.'

'Then you'll have to leave,' she snapped.

She reached the outskirts of the city.

It was a gridwork of foundations and low walls, all of it half-buried under a blanket of rock-hard water ice and frozen air. The buildings and roads seemed to follow a pattern of interlocking hexagons, quite unlike the cramped, organic, circle-based design of modern Conurbations on Earth, or the rectangular layout of many older, pre-Qax human settlements.

As she walked along what might once have been a street, the pain in her hands and feet seemed to be metamorphosing to an ominous numbness.

The ghost seemed to notice this. 'You continue to lose heat,' it said. 'Shivering is no longer enough to warm you. Now your body is drawing heat back from your extremities to your core. Your limbs are stiffening—'

'Shut up,' she hissed.

She found a waist-high fragment of wall protruding from the layers of ice. She brushed at it with her glove; loose snow fell away, revealing a surface of what looked like simple brick. But it crumbled at her touch, perhaps frost-shattered.

She walked on into what might once have been a room, a space bounded by six broken walls. Though there were many rooms close by here – clustered like a honeycomb, closer than would have been comfortable for people – it was hard to believe the inhabitants of this place had been so different from humans.

She wondered what it had been like here, *before*.

Once, Snowball had been Earth-like. There had been continents, oceans of water, and life – based on an organic chemistry of carbon, oxygen and water, like Earth life, and it had worked to create an atmosphere of oxygen and nitrogen, not so dissimilar to Earth's. And there had been people here: people who had built cities, and breathed air, and perhaps gazed at the stars.

But the long afternoon of this world had been disturbed.

Its sun had suffered a chance close encounter with another star. It was an unlucky, unlikely event, Minda knew; away from the Galaxy's centre the stars were thinly scattered. As the interloper fell through the orderly heart of this world's home system, there must have been immense tides, ocean waves that ground cities to dust, and earthquakes, a flexing of the rocky crust itself.

And then, at the intruder's closest approach, Snowball was slingshot out of the heart of its system.

The home sun had receded steadily. Ice spread from polar caps across the land and the oceans, until much of the planet was clad in a thick layer of hardening water ice. At last the very air began to rain out of the sky, liquid oxygen and nitrogen running down the frozen river valleys to pool atop the vast ice sheets, forming a softer snow metres thick.

She wondered what had become of the people. Had they retreated underground into caves? Had they fled their planet altogether – perhaps even migrated to new worlds surrounding the wrecking star?

'This world itself is not without inner heat,' the ghost said softly. 'The deep heart of a planet this size would scarcely notice the loss of its sun.'

'The volcano,' Minda said dully.

'Yes. That is one manifestation. And vents of hot material on the spreading seabed have even kept the lower levels of the ocean unfrozen. We believe there may still be active life forms there feeding on the planet's geothermal heat. But they must have learned to survive without oxygen . . .'

'Do you have that on your world? Deep heat, water under the ice?'

'Yes. But my world is small and cold; long ago it lost much of its inner heat.'

'The world I come from is bigger than this frozen ruin,' she said, spreading her arms wide. 'It has lots of heat. And it is a double world. It has a Moon. I bet even the Moon is bigger than *your* world.'

'Perhaps it is,' the ghost said. 'It must be a wonderful place.'

'Yes, it is. Better than your world. Better than *this*.'

'Yes.'

She was very tired. She didn't seem to be hungry, or thirsty. She wondered how long it was since she had eaten. She stared at the frozen air around her, trying to remember why she had come here. An idea sparked, fitfully.

She got to her knees. She could feel the diamond grid of the suit's heating elements press into the flesh of her legs. She swept aside the loose snow, but beneath there was only a floor of hard water ice.

'There's nothing here,' she said dully.

'Of course not,' the ghost said gently. 'The tides washed it all away.'

She began to pull together armfuls of loose snow. Much of it melted and evaporated, but slowly she made a mound of it in the centre of the room.

'What are you doing?'

'Maybe I can breathe this stuff.' She knew little about the flitter's systems. Maybe there was some hopper into which she could cram this frozen air.

But the ghost was talking to her again, its voice gentle but persistent, unwelcome. 'Your body is continuing to manage the crisis. Carbohydrates which would normally feed your brain are now being burnt to generate more heat. Your brain, starved, is slowing down; your coordination is poor. Your judgement is unreliable.'

'I don't care,' she growled, scraping at the frozen air.

'Your plan is not likely to succeed. Your biology requires oxygen. But the bulk of this snow is nitrogen. And there are trace compounds which may be toxic to you. Does your craft contain filtering systems which—'

Minda drove her suited arm through the pile of air, scattering it in a cloud of vapour. 'Shut up. Shut *up*.'

She walked back to the flitter. By now it felt as if she was floating, like a ghost herself.

The silver ghost told her about the world it came from. It was like Snowball, and yet it was not.

The ghosts' world was once Earth-like, if smaller than Earth: blue skies, a yellow sun. But even as the ghosts climbed to awareness their sun evaporated, killed by a companion pulsar. It was a slower process than the doom of Snowball, but no less lethal. The oceans froze and life huddled inward; there was frantic evolutionary pressure to find ways to keep warm.

Then the atmosphere started snowing.

The ghosts had gathered their fellow creatures around them and formed themselves into compact, silvered spheres, each body barely begrudging an erg to the cold outside. Finally clouds of mirrored life forms rolled upwards. The treacherous sky was locked out – but every stray wisp of the planet's internal heat was trapped.

Minda wondered if this was true, or just some kind of creation myth. But the murmuring words were comforting.

'My home Conurbation is near a ruined city. A bit like this one. The ruin is an old pre-Occupation city. It was called *Pah-reess*. Did you know that?'

'No. It must be a wonderful place.'

She found she had reached the flitter. She was so cold she wasn't even shivering any more. It was almost comfortable.

She couldn't lie on the ground. But she found a way to use bits of debris from the flitter, stuck in the ice, to prop herself up without having to lean on anything. After a time it seemed easier to leave her eyes closed.

'Your body is losing its ability to reheat itself. You must find an external source of heat. You will soon drift into unconsciousness . . .'

'I'm in my eighth cadre,' Minda whispered. 'You have to move cadres every two years, you know. But I was *chosen* for my new cadre. I had to pass tests. My best friend is called Janu. She couldn't come with me. She's still on Earth . . .' She smiled, thinking of Janu.

She felt herself tilting. She forced open her eyes, frost crackling on her eyelashes. She saw that the pretty, silvered landscape was tipping up around her. She was falling over. It didn't seem to matter any more; at least she could let her sore muscles relax.

Somewhere a voice called her: 'Always protect your core heat. It is the most important thing you possess. Remember . . .'

There was something wrong with the silver ghost, she saw, through sparkling frost crystals.

The ghost had come apart. Its silvery hide had unpeeled and removed itself like a semi-sentient overcoat. The hide fell gracelessly to the frozen ground and slithered towards her.

She shrank back, repelled.

What was left of the ghost was a mass of what looked like organs and digestive tracts, crimson and purple, pulsing and writhing, already shrivelling back, darkening. And they revealed something at the centre: almost like a human body, she thought, slick with pale pink fluid, and curled over like a foetus. But it, too, was rapidly freezing.

All around the subsiding sub-organisms, the frozen air of Snowball briefly evaporated, evoking billowing mist. And the dormant creatures of the Snowball enjoyed explosive growth: not just lichen-like scrapings and isolated flowers now, but a kind of miniature forest, trees pushing out of the ice and frosted air, straining for a black sky. Minda saw roots tangle as they dug into crevices in the ice, seeking the warmth of deeper levels, perhaps even liquid water.

But in no more than a few seconds it was over. The heat the ghost had hoarded for an unknown lifetime was lost to the uncaring stars, and the small native forest was freezing in place for another millennium of dormancy. Then the air frosted out once more.

At last Minda fell.

But there was something beneath her now, a smooth, dark sheet that would keep her from the ice. She collapsed onto it helplessly. A thick, stiff blanket stretched over her, shutting out the starry sky.

She wasn't warm, but she wasn't getting any colder. She smiled and closed her eyes.

When she opened her eyes again, the stars framed a Spline ship, rolling overhead, and the concerned face of her cadre leader, Bryn.

The Spline rose high, and the site of Minda's crash dwindled to a pinpoint, a detail lost between the tracery of the abandoned city and the volcano's huge bulk.

'It was the motion of the vegetation that our sensors spotted,' Bryn said. Her face was sombre, her voice tired after the long search. 'That was what drew us to you. Not your heat, or even your ghost's. That was masked by the volcano.'

'Perhaps the ghost meant that to happen,' Minda said.

'Perhaps.' Bryn glanced at the ghost's hide, spread on a wall. 'Your ghost was astonishing. But its morphology is a logical outcome of an evolutionary drive. As the sky turned cold, living things learned to cooperate, in ever greater assemblages, sharing heat and resources. The thing you called a silver ghost was really a community of symbiotic creatures: an autarky, a miniature biosphere in its own right, all but independent of the universe outside. Even the skin that saved you was independently alive . . . This is a new species for us. Evidently we have reached a point where two growing spheres of colonisation, human and ghost, have met. Our future encounters will be interesting.'

As the planet folded on itself, Minda saw the colony of the ghosts rising over the chill horizon. It was a forest of globes and half-globes anchored by cables; gleaming necklaces swooped between the globes. The colony, a sculpture of silver droplets glistening on a black velvet landscape, was quite remarkably beautiful.

But now a dazzling point of light rose above the horizon, banishing the stars. It was a new sun for Snowball made by humans, the first of many fusion satellites hastily prepared and launched. The ghost city cast dazzling reflections, and the silver globes seemed to shrivel back.

Bryn said, watching her, 'Do you understand what has happened here? If the ghosts' evolution was not competitive as ours was, they must be weaker than us.'

'But the ghost gave me its skin. It gave its life to save me.'

Bryn said sternly, 'It is dead. You are alive. Therefore you are the stronger.'

'Yes,' Minda whispered. 'I am the stronger.'

Bryn eyed her with suspicion.

Where the artificial sun passed, the air melted, pooling and vaporising in great gushes.

*After that first contact, two powerful interstellar cultures cautiously engaged. One man, called Jack Raoul, played a key role in developing a constructive relationship.*

*To understand the creatures humans came to know as 'Silver Ghosts' – so Raoul used to lecture those who were sceptical about the mission that consumed his life – you had to understand where they came from.*

*After the Ghosts watched their life heat leak away to the sky, they became motivated by a desire to understand the fine-tuning of the universe. As if they wanted to fix the design flaws that had betrayed them.*

*So they meddled with the laws of physics. This made them interesting to deal with. Interesting and scary.*

*Relationships deepened. The 'Raoul Accords' were established to maintain the peace, and give humans some say in the Ghosts' outrageous tinkering with the universe.*

*But times changed. The Coalition tightened its grip on human affairs.*

*Three centuries after Minda, there was rising friction between Ghost and human empires. And Jack Raoul found himself out of favour.*

# THE COLD SINK

## AD 5802

I called on Jack Raoul at the time appointed, acting in my capacity as a representative of the Supreme Court of the Third Expansion. Raoul submitted himself to my custody without complaint or protest.

'I must record that the indignity of the armed escort, as ordered by the court, only added to the cruelty of the procedure I was mandated to perform.'

It was as if somebody had called his name.

He was alone in his Virtual apartment – drinking whisky, looking out at a fake view of the New Bronx, missing his ex-wife – alone in a home become a gaol, in fact. Now he looked to the door.

Maybe they'd come to get him already. He felt his remote heart beat, and his mood of gloomy nostalgia gave way to hard fear. *Don't let 'em see they've won, Jack.*

With a growl, he commanded the door to open.

And there, instead of the surgeons and Commission goons he had expected, was a Silver Ghost: a spinning, shimmering bauble as tall as Raoul, crowding the dowdy apartment-block corridor. It was intimidating close to in this domestic environment, like some huge piece of machinery. In its mirrored epidermis he could see his own gaunt Virtual face. An electromagnetic signature was quickly overlaid for him – Ghosts looked alike only in normal human vision – but he would have recognised his visitor anyhow.

'You,' he said.

'Hello, Jack Raoul.' It was the Ghost known to humans as the

107

Ambassador to the Heat Sink. Raoul had dealt with this one many times before, over decades.

'What are you doing here? How did you get past the Commission security? . . . Ambassador, I'm afraid I'm not much use to you any more.'

'Jack Raoul, I am here for you.'

Raoul grimaced. What in Lethe did that mean? 'Look, I don't know how closely you've been following human politics. This isn't a good day for me.'

'As in former times, you hide your emotions behind weak jokes.'

'They're the best jokes I've got,' he said defensively.

'The truth is well known. Today you must face the sentence of your conspecifics.'

'So you're here for the spectacle?'

The Ghost said, 'I am here to present another option, Jack Raoul.'

Raoul studied the Ghost's bland, shimmering surface. There was no hope for him, of course. But he felt oddly touched. 'You'd better come in.'

The Ambassador sailed easily into the apartment, making the walls crumble to pixels where its limbs brushed against them. 'How is the whisky today?'

Raoul sipped it, savouring its peaty smoke. 'You know, I'm more than two hundred years old. But I figure that I could live another two hundred and not get this stuff right.' Still, maybe this would be his lasting legacy, he thought sourly: the best Virtual whisky in all the Third Expansion, savoured and remembered long after the Raoul Accords had been forgotten – which time might not be so far into the future.

'You are missing Eve,' said the Ambassador.

The Ghost's perception had always surprised him. 'Yeah,' he admitted. 'In a way this place is all I have left of her. But even here she is just an absence.'

'You must leave her now,' said the Ghost. 'Come with me.'

The abruptness of that startled him. 'Leave? How? Where are we going?'

'Jack Raoul, do you trust me?'

Escape was impossible, of course; Coalition security was tight, the Commission omnipresent. But this lunatic Ghost must have come a long way for this stunt, whatever it was. Maybe it was only respectful to go along for the ride.

Anyhow, what did he have to lose? One last adventure, Jack: why not?

He put the whisky glass down on a low table, savouring the weight of the heavy crystal, the gentle clink of its base on the table. 'Yes,' he said, looking into his heart. 'Yes, I guess I do trust you.' He stood straight. 'I'm ready.'

Again he had the sensation that somebody was calling his name.

The room crumbled into blocky pixels that washed away like spindrift, and suddenly he was suspended in light.

'It is important to understand that Raoul's fully human brain was maintained by normal physiological functions. Think of him as a human being, then, flensed and de-boned, sustained within a shell of alien artifice.

'The operation was more like a dismantling than a medical procedure. It was rapid.

'Immediately after the beheading I lifted the head and observed Raoul's eyes.

'The lids worked in irregularly rhythmic contractions for about five or six seconds. Then the spasmodic movements ceased. The face relaxed, the lids half-closed on the eyeballs, leaving only the white of the conjunctiva visible. (It will be recalled that Raoul's "eyes" were quasi-organic Ghost artefacts.)

'I called in a sharp voice: "Jack Raoul!" I saw the eyelids lift up, without any spasmodic contractions.

'Raoul's eyes fixed themselves on mine.'

Raoul looked down at himself. His body gleamed, a silver statue.

He peered around, trying to get oriented. He made out a tangle of silvery rope, a complex, multi-layered webbing that appeared to stretch around him in all directions. Everywhere he looked, Ghosts slid along the cables like droplets of mercury. And beyond and through it all, a deep glimmering light shone, a universal glow made pearl grey by the depth of the tangle.

He sure wasn't on 51 Pegasi I-C any more.

Jack Raoul had spent his working life at the uneasy political interface between Ghost and human. In those vanishing days of more-or-less friendly rivalry, governed by more-or-less equable accords, it had been Raoul's responsibility to ensure that humans knew what the Ghosts were doing, on their vast, remote experimental sites, just as Ghost observers were allowed to inspect human establishments. Mutual security through inspection and verification, an old principle.

But Raoul had soon learned that asking for evidence wasn't enough. Somebody had to go out there and *see* for himself – and on Ghost terms. That meant a sacrifice, though, that nobody was prepared to accept.

Nobody but Raoul himself.

So his brain and spinal cord were rolled up and moved into a cleaned-out chest cavity. His circulatory system was wrapped into a complex mass around the brain pan. The Ghosts built a new metabolic system, far more efficient than the old and capable of working off direct radiative input. New eyes, capable of working in spectral regions well beyond the human range, were bolted into his skull. He was given Ghost 'muscles' – a tiny antigravity drive and compact actuator motors. At last he was wrapped in something that looked like sheets of mercury.

Thus he was made a Ghost.

Jack Raoul couldn't live with people any more, outside of Virtual environments. Not that he wanted to. But he could fly in space. He could eat sunlight and survive the vacuum for days at a time, sustaining his antique human core in warmth and darkness. It was odd that he was actually more at home here in a Ghost ship than anywhere in the human Expansion.

'. . . Jack Raoul.' The Sink Ambassador swum before him, spinning languidly. 'How do you feel?'

Raoul flexed his metal fingers. 'How do you think I feel?'

'You are as evasive as ever.'

'Am I on a ship, Ambassador?' If so it was bigger than any Ghost cruiser he had ever seen.

'In a manner of speaking. For now, we must ascend.'

'Ascend?'

'Towards the light. Please.' The Ghost rose, slow waves crossing its surface.

Effortlessly Raoul followed.

Soon they were passing into the tangle of silvery ropes. When he looked back, there was nothing to mark the place he had emerged from – not even a hollow in the tangle.

At home or not, he knew he shouldn't be here.

'Ambassador, I was under house arrest. How did you get me out of there?'

'Have you improved your understanding of quantum physics since we last met?'

Inwardly, Raoul groaned.

The Ambassador began, somewhat earnestly, to describe how the Ghosts had learned to break up electrons: to divide indivisible particles.

'The principle is simple,' said the Ghost. 'An electron's quantum wave function describes the probability of finding it at any particular location. In its lowest energy state, the wave function is spherical. But in its next highest energy state the wave function has a dumb-bell shape. Now, if that dumb-bell could be stretched and pinched, could it be divided? . . .'

The Ambassador described how a vat of liquid helium was bathed in laser light of a precise frequency, exciting electron wave functions into their dumb-bell configurations. Then, as the pressure within the helium was increased, the electron dumb-bells split and pairs of half-bubbles drifted apart.

To Raoul it sounded like a typical Ghost experiment: extremes of low temperature, the fringe areas of physical law.

'Jack Raoul, you must understand that the quantum wave function is no mathematical abstraction, but a physical entity. *We have split and trapped a wave function itself* – perhaps the first time in the history of the universe this has occurred,' the Ghost said immodestly.

Raoul suppressed a sigh. 'You guys never do anything simply, do you? So you split an electron's wave function. So what?'

'The half-electrons, coming from the same source, are forever entangled. Put another way, if the bubbles are separated and the wave function collapsed, an electron can leap from one bubble to another . . .'

Raoul fought his way through that fog of words. 'Oh,' he said. 'Teleportation. You're talking about a new kind of teleportation. Right? And that's what you used to get me out of my cell.'

'Yes. Time was short, Jack Raoul. Your conspecifics were closing in.'

So they were, and so they had been for decades.

Still they rose through the crowded tangle. That all-consuming light seemed, if anything, to be growing brighter. He could sense deep vibrations passing through the ship's structure, the booming low-frequency calls of Silver Ghosts. Here and there he saw denser concentrations – nurseries, perhaps, or control centres, or simply areas where Ghosts lived and played – little more than patches of silvery shadow, like birds' nests in the branches of some vast tree. It was characteristic Ghost architecture, vibrant, complex, beautiful, alive – and totally inhuman.

It had always seemed to Jack Raoul that humans and Ghosts were different enough that everybody could get along. Their goals were utterly unlike humanity's, after all. That had been the motivation behind the patchwork of treaties eventually known as the Raoul Accords. But times changed.

When Raoul was a boy, the human colonisation programme was still piecemeal, driven by individual initiative. The leading edge of the Third Expansion had been too remote from the centre, Earth, to be tightly controlled. Players like Jack Raoul had freedom of movement. But gradually the Coalition – especially its executive arm the Commission for Historical Truth – had infiltrated all mankind's power centres. The ideologues of the Coalition had provided the species with a unity of purpose, belief, even language. The Third Expansion became purposeful, a powerful engine of conquest.

But from Jack Raoul's point of view, it was all downside. The pro-human ideology grew ferocious. Soon even longevity, like Raoul's, was seen as a crime against the interests of the species. As the short generations had ticked by, and as the worlds of humanity filled up with fifteen-year-old soldiers, Raoul had come to feel like a monument left standing from an earlier, misunderstood era.

And it got worse.

Raoul had been summoned back to Earth, to appear before the Commission for Historical Truth. It was part of the great cleansing that had been pursued ever since the days after the fall of the Qax Occupation of Earth, when collaborators had been hunted down and judged. After a curt hearing, Raoul's life's work had been retrospectively labelled as counter to the evolutionary interests of mankind.

His advisers had urged him to appeal. Everything he had done had been under the specific direction of legally constituted governments and inter-governmental bodies of the time. But he wasn't about to justify himself to a bunch of children. He knew the true value of his legacy. After all, it had cost him his own humanity.

And so sentence had been passed.

'How did you and I get to be the bad guys, Ambassador?'

The Ambassador's perfect hide cast glimmering highlights from the tangle sliding past them. 'We are old, Jack Raoul. Old and out of our time.'

'That we are, my friend.'

'Nevertheless, Jack Raoul, you have been a valuable interface between our species. Many sentient beings were saved from unhappiness and premature termination by your actions. This "punishment" is absurd and disproportionate. It is probably not even legal in your own terms.'

'You're storing up trouble,' Raoul said. 'Like it or not, I was tried by humanity's highest court. If you intervene it will surely go badly for you; the Coalition is not noted for its forgiveness. As for me, maybe it's my duty to sit tight and take my punishment. I will be the greater martyr for it.'

'See what we offer you, Jack Raoul, before you turn it down for the sake of martyrdom.'

At last, Raoul saw, their steady rise was slowing, the tangle of silver cables thinning out, as if they were reaching the top of a vast metallic tree. But there was still no sign of black, star-studded sky above; rather he made out swathes of light, glowing brightly, bright as the sun. Maybe the ship was actually sailing through the outer layers of a sun; it wouldn't be the first time the Ghosts had pulled such a stunt.

But the light, so his smart eyes quickly told him, was too complex for that. It was as if the sky was crowded with stars, every place he looked.

And suddenly he understood. Olbers' paradox . . .

'Sink Ambassador. This teleportation technique of yours. It can carry you from one side of the universe to the other. Yes?'

'Further than that.'

'And the light that bathes us—'

'It is starlight, Jack Raoul. Nothing but starlight.'

Again he had the sense that someone called him. He ascended into the light, seeking the voice.

'After several seconds the eyelids closed again, slowly and evenly, and the eyes took on the same appearance as before.

'I called out again.

'Once more, without any spasm, the lids lifted. Undeniably living eyes fixed themselves on mine with perhaps even more penetration than the first time. Then there was a further closing of the eyelids, but now less complete.'

He looked down at the Ghost ship, a mass of entwined silvery cables with knots of life embedded everywhere, all of it glowing in the endless starlight. He could still make out the Sink Ambassador, a mercury droplet clinging to the tangle.

But the structure was shrinking, closing on itself. The sky was a sphere of light, glowing white, and he felt he was being drawn away from the tangle, up into the light.

'Olbers' paradox,' he whispered.

'Yes,' said the Ghost. 'A key moment in the evolution of human thought, a philosophical fossil preserved by exiles through the Qax Extirpation . . . If the universe were infinite and static, every line of sight would meet the surface of a star, and the whole sky would be as bright as the surface of a sun. Even occluding dust clouds would soon become as hot as the stars themselves. That was evidently not so, observed those thinkers of old Earth. Therefore their universe could not be infinite or static.'

'But here—'

'But here, things are different. This appears to be a pocket universe, Jack Raoul. We believe it is a bubble of spacetime pinched off by a singularity. The heart of a black hole, perhaps.'

'Infinite and static.'

'Yes.'

'It doesn't make sense,' Raoul said. 'If the whole sky is as hot as the surface of the sun – Ambassador, how do you keep cool?'

The Ghost rolled, shimmering. 'There is another pocket universe at the centre of the colony. Our heat is dumped there.'

Raoul gaped. 'You have a whole universe for a heat dump? And is that how the stars keep shining?'

'We think so. Otherwise, immersed in this heat bath, simple thermo-dynamics would soon cause the stars to evaporate. We have only recently arrived here, Jack Raoul; there is much we have yet to explore. But it is clear to us that this cosmos is heavily engineered.'

'Engineered? Who by?'

'The Xeelee,' the Ghost said.

'Ah.' The Xeelee: aloof from the petty squabbles of lesser kinds, even of sprawling, brawling humanity. The Xeelee, as remote as clouds.

'It is not certain,' said the Ghost. 'But there are certain signatures we have come to recognise . . . Such universe-modelling does appear to be a characteristic Xeelee strategy.'

Raoul laughed, wondering. 'At last you've found yourselves an inverted sky, Ambassador. A Cold Sink.' Considering their evolutionary history, shaped by cosmic betrayal and cold, this place was like a Ghost wish-fulfilment fantasy.

'Yes. Jack Raoul, *we believe we were led here*, by the Xeelee. Perhaps they have prepared a bolt-hole of their own, in case their epochal war with the photino birds is ultimately lost.'

'You see this place as a bolt-hole? What are you hiding from?'

'You,' said the Ambassador.

That took him aback.

'Jack Raoul, your Expansion is already expanding exponentially. We are in your way.'

Raoul had heard this said. The Ghosts' home range lay between mankind and the rich fields of the Galaxy's Core, and the Expansion was pressing.

But he protested, 'It's a big Galaxy. It's not even as if we are fighting over the same kinds of territory, or resource. Ghosts are adapted to the cold and dark, humans to deep gravity wells. There is room for all of us.'

'That is true,' said the Ambassador. 'But irrelevant. Your Expansion is fuelled by ideology as much as resource acquisition – and it is not an ideology that preaches of sharing. In such a situation there can be no diplomacy.

'There is already war. A series of flashpoints, all along the Expansion's growing border. Naturally we will use our every resource in our fight for survival, just as we did when our sun died. There will be epic battles. But the logic is against us. Our most optimistic projection is three thousand years.'

'Until what?'

'Until the Silver Ghosts are extinct.'

Raoul said grimly, 'I spent my life fighting against such outcomes, Ambassador. As did you. Are you telling me now it was all futile?'

'From the beginning. But there is no failure, Jack Raoul. Here we have found a sanctuary. Though the Xeelee do not intervene in the squabbles of lesser types like us, they appear to embrace diversity. *They gave us this place.* Perhaps they have prepared a haven for

115

your kind, against the inevitable day when humanity too must decline.'

But Raoul found it increasingly hard to concentrate; his attention was drawn away from the Ghost and his words, away from the tangle, up to that infinite light.

The Ghost spun on its invisible axis, this way and that. 'Jack Raoul, I urge you to consider. If we are safe here, so are you. We can provide any Virtual environment you desire.' The Ghost seemed to hesitate. 'We can give you Eve.'

Ah, Eve . . .

*You can 't stay.* It was as if he could hear her voice, see her pushing her fingers through her greyed hair. *You held on to me for too long. And now, this. You never could let go Jack. But now you have to. You see that, don't you?*

He felt himself rise further. The tangle shrank beneath him, becoming lost in the light.

*It's time to go, Jack.*

'The Sink Ambassador is a friend,' he told Eve.

'Jack Raoul?'

*Sure he's a friend. That's why he's showing you what you want to see. You don't want to die a failure. But it isn't real. You know that, don't you?*

Perhaps the Sink Ambassador somehow heard this inner voice. 'Jack Raoul, it can be as real as you desire. We have only a single moment to give you. But we can make that moment last an eternity.'

'Thank you, my friend. But this isn't my place.'

'Jack Raoul, please . . .'

The tangle faded into the light. Raoul had time for a last, brief stab of regret.

Then, artificial eyes raised, he ascended into the white glow that was calling him.

'I attempted a third call, but there was no further movement. The eyes finally took on the glazed look of the dead.

'The whole sequence of post-excision events lasted twenty-five to thirty seconds. More precise timings are of course available in the record.

'Death occurred due to separation of the brain and spinal cord, after transection of the surrounding tissues and excision of the brain from the chest cavity, which probably caused acute and possibly severe pain. Consciousness was lost due to a rapid fall of intracranial perfusion of blood. Throughout the procedure nervous connections were maintained with sensory organs, notably the "eyes", "ears" and "nose".

'As noted, Jack Raoul did not resist.

'It may be that because of Raoul's unique physical condition, this "beheading" was the only available mode of execution. However I believe that my precise observations during my administration of this case demonstrate that *Raoul was aware* of what was happening to him even after excision, thus casting doubt on the humanity of the procedure.

'I will concede that I saw a certain peace, at the last, in Jack Raoul's dying eyes. It may be that somehow he found consolation, which may in turn give comfort to those who passed sentence on this complex man.

'Death occurred at the time and place noted.

'Signed: HAMA TINIF, Attending Physician.'

*The Sink Ambassador was right. War was inevitable. The logic of the Third Expansion would have it no other way.*

*At first human forces made spectacular advances. The Ghosts, capable of manipulating physical law, were on paper formidable adversaries. But we were better at making war.*

*In the centuries of conflict that followed, the Coalition completed its control. Humanity's ideology and economics were reoriented. Our entire civilisation became a machine to serve the Expansion and the war, and in turn became dependent on those two projects.*

*But then, as we approached the Ghosts' home ranges, the Expansion stalled.*

# ON THE ORION LINE

AD 6454

The *Brief Life Burns Brightly* broke out of the fleet. We were chasing down a Ghost cruiser, and we were closing.

The lifedome of the *Brightly* was transparent, so it was as if Captain Teid in her big chair, and her officers and their equipment clusters – and a few low-grade tars like me standing by – were just floating in space. The light was subtle, coming from a nearby cluster of hot young stars, and from the rivers of sparking lights that made up the fleet formation we had just left, and beyond *that* from the sparking of novae. This was the Orion Line – six thousand light years from Earth and a thousand lights long, a front that spread right along the inner edge of the Orion Spiral Arm – and the stellar explosions marked battles which must have concluded years ago.

And, not a handful of klicks away, the Ghost cruiser slid across space, running for home. The cruiser was a rough egg-shape of silvered rope. Hundreds of Ghosts clung to the rope. You could see them slithering this way and that, not affected at all by the emptiness around them.

The Ghosts' destination was a small, old yellow star. Pael, our tame Academician, had identified it as a fortress star from some kind of strangeness in its light. But up close you don't need to be an Academician to spot a fortress. From the *Brightly* I could see with my unaided eyes that the star had a pale blue cage around it – an open lattice with struts half a million kilometres long – thrown there by the Ghosts, for their own purposes.

I had a lot of time to watch all this. I was just a tar. I was fifteen years old.

My duties at that moment were non-specific. I was supposed to stand

118

by, and render assistance any way that was required, most likely with basic medical attention should we go into combat. Right now the only one of us tars actually working was Halle, who was chasing down a pool of vomit sicked up by Pael, the Academician, the only non-Navy personnel on the bridge.

The action on the *Brightly* wasn't like you see in Virtual shows. The atmosphere was calm, quiet, competent. All you could hear was the murmur of voices, from the crew and the equipment, and the hiss of recycling air. No drama: it was like an operating theatre.

There was a soft warning chime.

The Captain raised an arm and called over Academician Pael, First Officer Till, and Jeru, the Commissary assigned to the ship. They huddled close, conferring – apparently arguing. I saw the way flickering nova light reflected from Jeru's shaven head.

I felt my heart beat harder.

Everybody knew what the chime meant: that we were approaching the fortress cordon. Either we would break off, or we would chase the Ghost cruiser inside its invisible fortress. And everybody knew that no Navy ship that had ever penetrated a Ghost fortress cordon, ten light-minutes from the central star, and come back out again.

One way or the other, it would all be resolved soon.

Captain Teid cut short the debate. She leaned forward and addressed the crew. Her voice, cast through the ship, was friendly, like a cadre leader whispering in your ear. 'You can all see we can't catch that swarm of Ghosts this side of the cordon. And you all know the hazard of crossing a cordon. But if we're ever going to break this blockade of theirs we have to find a way to bust open those forts. So we're going in anyhow. Stand by your stations.'

There was a half-hearted cheer.

I caught Halle's eye. She grinned at me. She pointed at the Captain, closed her fist and made a pumping movement. I admired her sentiment but she wasn't being too accurate, anatomically speaking, so I raised my middle finger and jiggled it back and forth.

It took a slap on the back of the head from Jeru, the Commissary, to put a stop to that. 'Little morons,' she growled.

'Sorry, sir—'

I got another slap for the apology. Jeru was a tall, stocky woman, dressed in the bland monastic robes said to date from the time of the founding of the Commission for Historical Truth a thousand years ago.

But rumour was she'd seen plenty of combat action of her own before joining the Commission, and such was her physical strength and speed of reflex I could well believe it.

As we neared the cordon the Academician, Pael, started a gloomy countdown. The slow geometry of Ghost cruiser and tinsel-wrapped fortress star swivelled across the crowded sky. Everybody went quiet.

The darkest time is always just before the action starts. Even if you can see and hear what is going on, all you do is think. What was going to happen to us when we crossed that intangible border? Would a fleet of Ghost ships materialise all around us? Would some mysterious weapon simply blast us out of the sky?

I caught the eye of First Officer Till. He was a veteran of twenty years; his scalp had been burned away in some ancient close-run combat, long before I was born, and he wore a crown of scar tissue with pride. 'Let's do it, tar,' he growled.

All the fear went away. I was overwhelmed by a feeling of togetherness, of us all being in this crap together. I had no thought of dying. Just: let's get through this. 'Yes, *sir*!'

Pael finished his countdown.

All the lights went out. Detonating stars wheeled.

And the ship exploded.


I was thrown into darkness. Air howled. Emergency bulkheads scythed past me, and I could hear people scream.

I slammed into the curving hull, nose pressed against the stars.

I bounced off and drifted. The inertial suspension was out, then. I thought I could smell blood – probably my own.

I could see the Ghost ship, a tangle of rope and silver baubles, glinting with highlights from the fortress star. We were still closing. We were going to collide in minutes, no more.

But I could also see shards of shattered lifedome, a sputtering drive unit. The shards were bits of the *Brightly*. It had gone, all gone, in a fraction of a second.

'Let's do it,' I murmured.

Maybe I was out of it for a while.

Somebody grabbed my ankle and tugged me down. There was a competent slap on my cheek, enough to make me focus.

'Case. Can you hear me?'

It was First Officer Till. Even in the swimming starlight that burned-off scalp was unmistakable.

I glanced around. There were four of us here: Till, Commissary Jeru, Academician Pael, me. We were huddled up against what looked like the stump of the First Officer's console. I realised that the gale of venting air had stopped. I was back inside a hull with integrity, then—

'Case!'

'I-yes, sir.'

'Report.'

I touched my lip; my hand came away bloody. At a time like that it's your duty to report your injuries, honestly and fully. Nobody needs a hero who turns out not to be able to function. 'I think I'm all right. I may have concussion.'

'Good enough. Strap down.' Till handed me a length of rope.

I saw that the others had tied themselves to struts. I did the same.

Till, with practised ease, swam away into the air, I guessed looking for other survivors.

Academician Pael was trying to curl into a ball. He couldn't even speak. The tears just rolled out of his eyes. I stared at the way big globules welled up and drifted away into the air, glimmering. The action had been over in seconds. That was war in space for you, journeys that can last years, combat that's over in heartbeats, and your story is done. All a bit sudden for an earthworm, I guess.

Nearby, I saw, trapped under one of the emergency bulkheads, there was a pair of legs – just that. The rest of the body must have been chopped away, gone drifting off with the rest of the debris from *Brightly*. But I recognised those legs, from a garish pink stripe on the sole of the right boot. That had been Halle. She was the only girl I had ever screwed – and more than likely, given the situation, the only girl I ever would get to screw. I couldn't figure out how I felt about that.

Jeru was watching Pael, and me. 'Tar – do you think we should all be frightened for ourselves, like the Academician?' Her accent was strong, unidentifiable.

'No, sir.'

'No.' Jeru studied Pael with contempt. 'We are in an escape yacht, Academician. A bit of the lifedome, carved out by the emergency bulkheads when the *Brightly* was attacked.' She sniffed. 'We have air, and it isn't foul yet. But we're still closing on that Ghost cruiser.'

I'd managed to forget where we were going, and how little time we had. Fear pricked.

Jeru winked at me. 'Maybe we can do a little damage to the Ghosts before we die, tar. What do you think?'

I grinned. 'Yes, sir.'

Pael lifted his head and stared at me with salt water eyes. 'Lethe. You people are monsters.' His accent was gentle, a lilt. 'Even a child such as this. You embrace death—'

Jeru grabbed Pael's jaw in a massive hand, and pinched the joints until he squealed. 'Captain Teid grabbed you, Academician; she threw you here, to safety, before the bulkhead came down. I saw it. If she hadn't taken the time to do that, she would have made it herself. Was *she* a monster? Did *she* embrace death?' And she pushed Pael's face away.

For some reason I hadn't thought about the rest of the crew until that moment. I guess I have a limited imagination. Now, I felt adrift. The Captain – dead? I said, 'Excuse me, Commissary. How many other yachts got out?'

'None,' she said steadily, making sure I had no illusions. 'Just this one. They died doing their duty, tar. Like the Captain.'

Of course she was right, and I felt a little better. Whatever his character, Pael was too valuable not to save. As for me, I had survived through sheer blind chance, through being in the right place when the walls came down: if the Captain had been close, her duty would have been to pull me out of the way and take my place. It isn't a question of human values but of economics: a lot more is invested in the training and experience of a Captain Teid – or a Pael – than in me.

First Officer Till came bustling back with a heap of equipment. 'Put these on.' He handed out pressure suits. They were what we called slime suits in training: lightweight skinsuits, running off a backpack of gen-enged algae. 'Move it,' said Till. 'Impact with the Ghost cruiser in four minutes. We don't have any power; there's nothing we can do but ride it out.'

I crammed my legs into my suit.

Jeru complied, stripping off her robe to reveal a hard, scarred body. But she was frowning. 'Why not heavier armour?'

For answer, Till picked out a gravity-wave handgun from the gear he had retrieved. Without pausing he held it to Pael's head and pushed the fire button.

Pael twitched.

Till said, 'See? Nothing is working. Nothing but bio systems, it seems. They have been spared, presumably deliberately – that is a characteristic Ghost tactic. They disable your weapons but leave you alive.' He threw the gun aside.

Pael closed his eyes, breathing hard.

Till said to me, 'Test your comms.'

I closed up my hood and faceplate and began intoning, 'One, two, three . . .' I could hear nothing.

Till began tapping at our backpacks, resetting the systems. His hood started to glow with transient, pale blue symbols. And then, scratchily, his voice started to come through. '. . . Five, six, seven – can you hear me, tar?'

'Yes, sir.'

The symbols were bioluminescent There were receptors on all our suits – photoreceptors, simple eyes – which could 'read' the messages scrawled on our companions' suits. It was a backup system meant for use in Ghost-ridden environments where anything higher-tech would be a liability. But obviously it would only work as long as we were in line of sight.

'That will make life harder,' Jeru said. Oddly, mediated by software, she was easier to understand.

Till shrugged. 'You take it as it comes.' Briskly, he began to hand out more gear. 'These are basic field kits. There's some medical stuff: a suture kit, scalpel blades, blood-giving sets. You wear these syrettes around your neck, Academician. They contain painkillers, various gen-enged med-viruses . . . No, you wear it *outside* your suit, Pael, so you can reach it. You'll find valve inlets here, on your sleeve, and here, on the leg.' Now came weapons. 'We should carry handguns, just in case they start working, but be ready with these. ' He handed out combat knives.

Pael shrank back.

'Take the knife, Academician. You can shave off that ugly beard, if nothing else.'

I laughed out loud, and was rewarded with a wink from Till.

I took a knife. It was a heavy chunk of steel, solid and reassuring. I tucked it in my belt. I was starting to feel a whole lot better.

'Two minutes to impact,' Jeru said. I didn't have a working chronometer; she must have been counting the seconds.

'Seal up.' Till began to check the integrity of Pael's suit; Jeru and I helped each other. Face seal, glove seal, boot seal, pressure check. Water check, oh-two flow, cee-oh-two scrub . . .

When we were sealed I risked poking my head above Till's chair.

The Ghost ship filled space, occluding the stars and the warring fleets. The craft was kilometres across, big enough to have dwarfed the poor, doomed *Brief Life Burns Brightly*. It was a tangle of silvery rope studded with bulky equipment pods. And Silver Ghosts were everywhere. I could see how the yacht's emergency lights were returning crimson highlights from the featureless hides of Ghosts, so they looked like blood droplets sprayed across that shining perfection.

The four of us huddled together. We had been granted a little bit of peace while the yacht drifted across space, an interval between the destruction of the *Brightly* and this inevitable collision with the Ghost cruiser. Now the interval was over.

'Ten seconds,' Till called. 'Brace.'

Suddenly silver ropes thick as tree trunks were all around us, looming out of the sky, and we were thrown into chaos again.

I heard a grind of twisted metal, a scream of air. The hull popped open like an eggshell. The last of our air fled in a gush of ice crystals, and the only sound I could hear was my own breathing.

The crumpling hull soaked up some of our momentum. But then the base of the yacht hit, and it hit hard. The chair was wrenched out of my grasp, and I was hurled upwards. There was a sudden pain in my left arm. I couldn't help but cry out.

I reached the limit of my tether and rebounded. The jolt sent further waves of pain through my arm. From up there, I could see the others were clustered around the base of the First Officer's chair, which had collapsed.

The grinding, the shuddering stopped. The impact was over.

We had stuck like a dart in the outer layers of the Ghost ship. Shining threads arced all around us, as if a huge net had scooped us up.

Jeru grabbed me and pulled me down. She jarred my bad arm, and I winced. But she ignored me, and went back to working on Till. He was under the fallen chair.

Pael started to take a syrette of dope from the sachet around his neck.

Jeru knocked his hand away. 'You always use the casualty's,' she hissed. 'Never your own.'

Pael looked hurt, rebuffed. 'Why?'

I could answer that. 'Because the chances are you'll need your own in a minute.'

Jeru stabbed a syrette into Till's arm.

Pael was staring at me through his faceplate with wide, frightened eyes. 'You've broken your arm.'

Looking closely at the arm for the first time, I saw that it was bent back at an impossible angle. I couldn't believe it, even through the pain. I'd never bust so much as a finger, all the way through training.

Now Till jerked, a kind of miniature convulsion, and a big bubble of spit and blood blew out of his lips. Then the bubble popped, and his limbs went loose.

Jeru sat back, breathing hard. She said, 'OK. OK. How did he put it? – You take it as it comes.' She looked around, at me, Pael. I could see she was trembling, which scared me.

I said, 'The First Officer—'

Jeru looked at me, and for a second her expression softened. 'Is dead.'

Pael just stared, eyes empty.

I asked, 'Sir – how?'

'A broken neck. Till broke his neck, tar.'

Another death, just like that: for a heartbeat that was too much for me.

Jeru said briskly, 'Now we move. We have to find an LUP. A lying-up point, Academician. A place to hole up. Do your duty, tar. Help the worm.'

I snapped back. 'Yes, sir.' I grabbed Pael's unresisting arm.

Led by Jeru, we began to move, the three of us, away from the crumpled wreck of our yacht, deep into the alien tangle of a Silver Ghost cruiser.

We found our LUP.

It was just a hollow in a somewhat denser tangle of silvery ropes, but it afforded us some cover, and it seemed to be away from the main concentration of Ghosts. We were still open to the vacuum – as the whole cruiser seemed to be – and I realised then that I wouldn't be getting out of this suit for a while.

As soon as we picked the LUP, Jeru made us take up positions in an all-round defence, covering a 360-degree arc.

Then we did nothing, absolutely nothing, for ten minutes.

This was SOP, standard operating procedure, and I was impressed a Commissary knew about it. You've just come out of all the chaos of the destruction of the *Brightly* and the crash of the yacht, a frenzy of activity. Now you have to give your body a chance to adjust to the new environment, to the sounds and smells and sights.

Only here, there was nothing to smell but my own sweat and piss, nothing to hear but my ragged breathing. And my arm was hurting like hell.

To occupy my mind I concentrated on getting my night vision work-ing. Your eyes take a while to adjust to the darkness – forty-five minutes before they are fully effective – but you are already seeing better after five. I could see stars through the chinks in the wiry metallic brush around me, the flares of distant novae, and the reassur-ing lights of our fleet. But a Ghost ship is a dark place, a mess of shadows and smeared-out reflections. It was going to be easy to get spooked here.

When the ten minutes were done, Academician Pael started bleating, but Jeru ignored him and came straight over to me. She got hold of my busted arm and started to feel the bone. 'So,' she said briskly. 'What's your name, tar?'

'Case, sir.'

'What do you think of your new quarters?'

'Where do I eat?'

She grinned. 'Turn off your comms,' she said.

I complied.

Without warning she pulled my arm, hard. I was glad she couldn't hear how I howled. She pulled a canister out of her belt and squirted gunk over my arm; it was semi-sentient and snuggled into place, setting as a hard cast around my injury. When I was healed the cast would fall away of its own accord.

She motioned me to turn on my comms again, and held up a syrette.

'I don't need that.'

'Don't be brave, tar. It will help your bones knit.'

'Sir, there's a rumour that stuff makes you impotent.' I felt stupid even as I said it.

Jeru laughed out loud, and just grabbed my arm. 'Anyhow it's the First Officer's, and he doesn't need it any more, does he?'

I couldn't argue with that; I accepted the injection. The pain started ebbing almost immediately.

Jeru pulled a tactical beacon out of her belt kit. It was a thumb-sized orange cylinder. 'I'm going to try to signal the fleet. I'll work my way out of this tangle; even if the beacon is working we might be shielded in here.' Pael started to protest, but she shut him up. I sensed I had been thrown into the middle of an ongoing conflict between them. 'Case, you're on stag. And show this worm what's in his kit. I'll come back the same way I go. All right?'

'Yes.' More SOP.

She slid away through silvery threads.

I lodged myself in the tangle and started to go through the stuff in the kits Till had fetched for us. There was water, rehydration salts and compressed food, all to be delivered to spigots inside our sealed hoods. We had power packs the size of my thumb nail, but they were as dead as the rest of the kit. There was a lot of low-tech gear meant to prolong survival in a variety of situations, such as a magnetic compass, a heliograph, a thumb saw, a magnifying glass, pitons and spindles of rope, even fishing line.

I had to show Pael how his suit functioned as a lavatory. The trick is just to let go; a slime suit recycles most of what you give it, and compresses the rest. That's not to say it's comfortable. I've never yet worn a suit that was good at absorbing odours. I bet no suit designer spent more than an hour in one of her own creations.

As for me, I felt fine.

The wreck, the hammer-blow deaths one after the other – none of it was far beneath the surface of my mind. But that's where it stayed, for now; as long as I had the next task to focus on, and the next after that, I could keep moving forward. The time to let it all hit you is after the show.

I guess Pael had never been trained like that. He was a thin, spindly man, his eyes sunk in black shadow, and his ridiculous red beard was crammed up inside his faceplate. Now that the great crises were over, his energy seemed to have drained away, and his functioning was slowing to a crawl. He looked almost comical as he pawed at his useless bits of kit.

After a time he said, 'Case, is it?'

'Yes, sir.'

'Are you from Earth, child?'

'No, I—'

He ignored me. 'The Academies are based on Earth. Did you know that? But they do admit a few off-worlders.'

I glimpsed a lifetime of outsider resentment. But I couldn't care less. Also I wasn't a child. I asked cautiously, 'Where are you from, sir?'

He sighed. '51 Pegasi. I-B.'

I'd never heard of it. 'What kind of place is that? Is it near Earth?'

'Is everything measured relative to Earth? . . . Not very far. My home world was one of the first extra-solar planets to be discovered – or at least, the primary is. I grew up on a moon. The primary is a hot Jupiter.'

I knew what *that* meant: a giant planet huddled close to its parent star.

He looked up at me. 'Where you grew up, could you see the sky?'

'No—'

'I could. And the sky was fall of sails. That close to the sun, solar sails work efficiently, you see. I used to watch them at night, schooners with sails hundreds of kilometres wide, tacking this way and that in the light. I loved to watch them. But on Earth you can't even see the sky – not from the Academy bunkers anyhow.'

'Then why did you go there?'

'I didn't have a choice.' He laughed, hollowly. 'I was doomed by being smart. That is why your precious Commissary despises me so much, you see. I have been taught to think – and we can't have that, can we? . . .'

I turned away from him and shut up. Jeru wasn't 'my' Commissary, and this sure wasn't my argument. Besides, Pael gave me the creeps. I've always been wary of people who know too much stuff. With a weapon, all you want to know is how it works, what kind of energy or ammunition it needs, and what to do when it goes wrong. People who know all the technical background and the statistics are usually covering up their own failings; it is experience of use that counts.

But this was no loudmouth weapons tech. This was an Academician: one of humanity's elite scientists. I felt I had no point of contact with him at all. I looked out through the tangle, trying to see the fleet's sliding, glimmering lanes of light.

There was motion in the tangle. I turned that way, motioning Pael to keep still and silent, and got hold of my knife in my good hand.

Jeru came bustling back, exactly the way she had left. She nodded approvingly at my alertness. 'Not a peep out of the beacon.'

Pael said, 'You realise our time here is limited.'

I asked, 'You mean the suits?'

'He means the star,' Jeru said heavily. 'Case, fortress stars seem to be unstable. When the Ghosts throw up their cordon equipment, the stars don't last long before going pop.'

Pael shrugged. 'We have hours, a few days at most.'

Jeru said, 'Well, we're going to have to get out, beyond the fortress cordon, so we can signal the fleet. That or find a way to collapse the cordon altogether.'

Pael laughed hollowly. 'And how do you propose we do that?'

Jeru glared. 'Isn't it your role to tell me, Academician?'

Pael leaned back and closed his eyes. 'Not for the first time, you're being ridiculous.'

Jeru growled. She turned to me. 'You. What do *you* know about the Ghosts?'

I said, 'They come from someplace cold. That's why they are wrapped up in silvery shells. You can't bring a Ghost down with laser fire because of those shells. They're perfectly reflective.'

Pael said, 'Not perfectly. They are based on a Planck-zero effect . . . About one part in a billion of incident energy is absorbed.'

I hesitated. 'They say the Ghosts experiment on people.'

Pael sneered. 'Lies put about by Jeru's Commission for Historical Truth. To demonise an opponent is a tactic as old as mankind.'

Jeru wasn't perturbed. 'Then why don't you put young Case right? How *do* the Ghosts go about their business?'

Pael said, 'The Silver Ghosts tinker with the laws of physics. The Ghosts are motivated by a desire to understand the fine-tuning of the universe, which they believe betrayed them. *Why are we here?* You see, young tar, there is only a narrow range of the constants of physics within which life of *any* sort is possible. We think the Ghosts are studying this question by pushing at the boundaries – by tinkering with the laws which sustain and contain us all.'

I looked to Jeru; she shrugged. She said, 'So how do they do this, Academician?'

Pael tried to explain. It was all to do with quagma.

Quagma is the state of matter which emerged from the Big Bang. Matter, when raised to sufficiently high temperatures, melts into a magma of quarks – a quagma. And at such temperatures the four fundamental forces of physics unify into a single superforce. When quagma is allowed to cool and expand its binding superforce decomposes into four sub-forces.

To my surprise, I understood some of this. The principle of the GUTdrive, which powers intrasystem ships like *Brief Life Burns Brightly*, is related.

Anyhow, by controlling the superforce decomposition, you can select the ratios between those sub-forces. And those ratios govern the fundamental constants of physics.

Something like that.

Pael said, 'That marvellous reflective coating of theirs is an example. Each Ghost is surrounded by a thin layer of space in which a fundamental number called the Planck constant is significantly lower than elsewhere. Thus, quantum effects are collapsed . . . Because the energy carried by a photon, a particle of light, is proportional to the Planck constant, an incoming photon must shed most of its energy when it hits the shell – hence the reflectivity.'

'All right,' Jeru said. 'So what are they doing here?'

Pael sighed. 'The fortress star seems to be surrounded by an open shell of quagma and exotic matter. We surmise that the Ghosts have blown a bubble around each star, a spacetime volume in which the laws of physics are – tweaked.'

'And that's why our equipment failed.'

'Presumably,' said Pael, with cold sarcasm.

Jeru said, 'An enemy who can deploy the laws of physics as a weapon is formidable. But in the long run, we will out-compete the Ghosts.'

Pael said bleakly, 'Ah, the evolutionary destiny of mankind. How dismal. But we lived in peace with the Ghosts, under the Raoul Accords, for centuries. We are so different, with disparate motivations – why should there be a conflict, any more than between two species of birds in the same garden?'

I'd never seen birds, or a garden, so that passed me by.

Jeru glared. 'Let's return to practicalities. *How* do their fortresses work?' When Pael didn't reply, she snapped, 'Academician, you've been *inside* a fortress cordon for an hour already and you haven't made a single fresh observation?'

Acidly, Pael demanded, 'What would you have me do?'

Jeru nodded at me. 'What have *you* seen, tar?'

'Our instruments and weapons don't work,' I said promptly. 'The *Brightly* exploded. I broke my arm.'

Jeru said, 'Till snapped his neck also.' She flexed her hand within her glove. 'What would make our bones more brittle? Anything else?'

Pael admitted, 'I do feel somewhat warm.'

Jeru asked, 'Could these body changes be relevant?'

'I don't see how.'

'Then figure it out.'

'I have no equipment.'

Jeru dumped spare gear – weapons, beacons – in his lap. 'You have your eyes, your hands and your mind. Improvise.' She turned to me. 'As for you, tar, let's do a little infil. We still need to find a way off this scow.'

I glanced doubtfully at Pael. 'There's nobody to stand on stag.'

'I know, tar. But there are only three of us.' She grasped Pael's shoulder, hard. 'Keep your eyes open, Academician. We'll come back the same way we left. So you'll know it's us. Do you understand?'

Pael shrugged her away, focusing on the gadgets on his lap.

I looked at him doubtfully. It seemed to me a whole platoon of Ghosts could have come down on him without his even noticing. But Jeru was right; there was nothing more we could do.

She studied me, fingered my arm. 'You up to this?'

I could use the arm. 'I'm fine, sir.'

'You are lucky. A good war comes along once in a lifetime. And this is your war, tar.'

That sounded like parade-ground pep talk, and I responded in kind. 'Can I have your rations, sir? You won't be needing them soon.' I mimed digging a grave.

She grinned back fiercely. 'Yeah. When your turn comes, slit your suit and let the farts out before I take it off your stiffening corpse.'

Pael's voice was trembling. 'You really are monsters.'

I shared a mocking glance with Jeru. But we shut up, for fear of upsetting the earthworm further.

I grasped my fighting knife, and we slid away into the dark.

What we were hoping to find was some equivalent of a bridge. Even if we succeeded, I couldn't imagine what we'd do next. Anyhow, we had to try.

We slid through the tangle. Ghost cable is tough, even to a knife blade. But it is reasonably flexible; you can just push it aside if you get stuck, although we tried to avoid doing that for fear of leaving a sign of our passing.

We used standard patrolling SOP, adapted for the circumstance. We would move for ten or fifteen minutes, clambering through the tangle, and then take a break for five minutes. I'd sip water – I was getting hot – and maybe nibble on a glucose tab, check on my arm, and pull the suit around me to get comfortable again. It's the way to do it. If you just push yourself on and on you run down your reserves and end up in no fit state to achieve the goal anyhow.

And all the while I was trying to keep up my all-around awareness, protecting my dark adaptation, making appreciations. How far away is Jeru? What if an attack comes from in front, behind, above, below, left or right? Where can I find cover?

I began to build up an impression of the Ghost cruiser. It was a rough egg shape a couple of kilometres long, and basically a mass of the anonymous silvery cable. There were chambers and platforms and instruments stuck as if at random into the tangle, like food fragments in an old man's beard. I guess it makes for a flexible, easily modified configuration. Where the tangle was a little less thick, I glimpsed a more substantial core, a cylinder running along the axis of the craft. Perhaps it was the drive unit. I wondered if it was functioning; perhaps, unlike the *Brightly*'s gear, Ghost equipment was designed to adapt to the changed conditions inside the fortress cordon.

There were Ghosts all over the craft.

They drifted over and through the tangle, following pathways invisible to us. Or they would cluster in little knots on the tangle. We couldn't tell what they were doing or saying. To human eyes a Silver Ghost is just a silvery sphere, visible only by reflection, and without specialist equipment it is impossible even to tell one from another.

We kept out of sight. But I was sure the Ghosts must have spotted us, or were at least tracking our movements. After all we'd crash-landed in their ship. But they made no overt moves toward us.

We reached the outer 'hull', or at least the place the cabling ran out, and dug back into the tangle a little way to stay out of sight.

At last I got an unimpeded view of the stars. Still those nova firecrackers went off all over the sky; still those young stars glared like lanterns. It seemed to me the fortress's central, enclosed star looked a little brighter, hotter than it had been. I made a mental note to report that to the Academician.

But the most striking sight was the human fleet.

Over a volume light-months wide, countless craft slid silently across the sky. They were organised in a complex network of corridors filling three-dimensional space: rivers of light gushed this way and that, their different colours denoting different classes and sizes of vessel. And, here and there, denser knots of colour and light sparked, irregular flares in the orderly flows. They were places where human ships were engaging the enemy, places where people were fighting and dying.

The Third Expansion had reached all the way to the inner edge of our spiral arm of the Galaxy. Now the first colony ships were attempting to make their way across the void to the next arm, the Sagittarius. *Our* arm, the Orion Arm, is really just a shingle, a short arc. But the Sagittarius Arm is one of the Galaxy's dominant features. For example it contains a huge region of star-birth, one of the largest in the Galaxy, immense clouds of gas and dust capable of producing millions of stars each. It was a prize indeed.

But that is where the Silver Ghosts live.

When it appeared that our inexorable expansion was threatening not just their own mysterious projects but their home systems, the Ghosts began, for the first time, to resist us systematically.

They had formed a blockade, called by Navy strategists the Orion Line: a thick sheet of fortress stars, right across the inner edge of the Orion Arm, places the Navy and the colony ships couldn't follow. It was a devastatingly effective ploy.

Our fleet in action was a magnificent sight. But it was a big, empty sky, and the nearest sun was that eerie dwarf enclosed in its spooky blue net, a long way away, and there was movement in three dimensions, above me, below me, all around me . . .

I found the fingers of my good hand had locked themselves around a sliver of the tangle.

Jeru grabbed my wrist and shook my arm until I was able to let go. She kept hold of my arm, her eyes on mine. *I have you. You won't fall.* Then she pulled me back into a dense knot of the tangle, shutting out the sky.

She huddled close to me, so the bio lights of our suits wouldn't show far. Her eyes were pale blue, like windows. 'You aren't used to being outside, are you, tar?'

'I'm sorry, Commissar. I've been trained—'

'You're still human. We all have weak points. The trick is to know them and allow for them. Where are you from?'

I managed a grin. 'Mercury. Caloris Planitia.' Mercury is a ball of iron at the bottom of the sun's gravity well. It is an iron mine, and an exotic matter factory, with a sun like a lid hanging over it. Most of the surface is given over to solar power collectors. It is a place of tunnels and warrens, where as a kid you compete with the rats.

'And that's why you joined up? To get away?'

'I was drafted.'

'Come on,' she scoffed. 'On a rat-hole like Mercury there are places to hide. Are you a romantic, tar? You wanted to see the stars?'

'No,' I said bluntly. 'Life is more useful here.'

She studied me. 'A brief life should burn brightly – eh, tar?'

'Yes, sir.'

'I came from Deneb,' she said. 'Do you know it?'

'No.'

'Sixteen hundred light years from Earth – a system settled some four centuries after the start of the Third Expansion. By the time the first ships reached Deneb, the mechanics of exploitation were efficient. From preliminary exploration to working shipyards and daughter colonies in less than a century. Deneb's resources – its planets and asteroids and comets, even the star itself – have been mined out to fund fresh colonising waves, the greater Expansion and, of course, to support the war with the Ghosts. And that's how the system works.'

She swept her hand over the sky. 'Think of it, tar. *The Third Expansion*: between here and Sol, across six thousand light years, there is nothing but mankind and human planets, the fruit of a thousand years of world-building. And all of it linked by economics. Older systems like Deneb, their resources spent – even Sol system itself – are supported by a flow of goods and materials inward from the growing periphery of the Expansion. There are trade lanes spanning thousands of light years, lanes that never leave human territory, plied by vast schooners kilometres wide. But now the Ghosts are in our way. And *that's* why we're fighting!'

'Yes, sir.'

She eyed me. 'You ready to go on?'

'Yes.'

We began to make our way forward again, just under the tangle, still following patrol SOP.

I was glad to be moving again. I've never been comfortable talking personally – and for sure not with a Commissary. But I suppose even Commissaries need to chat.

Jeru spotted a file of the Ghosts moving in a crocodile, like so many schoolchildren, towards the head of the ship. It was the most purposeful activity we'd seen so far, so we followed them.

After a couple of hundred metres the Ghosts began to duck down into the tangle, out of our sight. We followed them in.

Maybe fifty metres deep, we came to a large enclosed chamber, a smooth bean-shaped pod that would have been big enough to enclose our yacht. The surface appeared to be semi-transparent, perhaps designed to let in sunlight. I could see shadowy shapes moving within. Ghosts were clustered around the pod's hull, brushing its surface.

Jeru beckoned, and we worked our way through the tangle towards the far end of the pod, where the density of the Ghosts seemed to be lowest.

We slithered to the surface of the pod. There were sucker pads on our palms and toes to help us grip. We began crawling along the length of the pod, ducking flat when we saw Ghosts loom into view. It was like climbing over a glass ceiling.

The pod was pressurised. At one end of the pod a big ball of mud hung in the air, brown and viscous. It seemed to be heated from within; it was slowly boiling, with big sticky bubbles of vapour crowding its surface, and I saw how it was laced with purple and red smears. There is no convection in zero gravity, of course. Maybe the Ghosts were using pumps to drive the flow of vapour.

Tubes led off from the mud ball to the hull of the pod. Ghosts clustered there, sucking up the purple gunk from the mud.

We figured it out in bioluminescent 'whispers'. The Ghosts were *feeding*. Their home world is too small to have retained much internal warmth, but, deep beneath their frozen oceans or in the dark of their rocks, a little primordial geotherm heat must leak out still, driving fountains of minerals dragged up from the depths. And, as at the bottom of Earth's oceans, on those minerals and the slow leak of heat, life forms feed. And the Ghosts feed on *them*.

So this mud ball was a field kitchen. I peered down at purplish slime, a gourmet meal for Ghosts, and I didn't envy them.

There was nothing for us here. Jeru beckoned me again, and we slithered further forward.

The next section of the pod was . . . strange.

It was a chamber full of sparkling, silvery saucer-shapes, like smaller, flattened-out Ghosts, perhaps. They fizzed through the air or crawled over each other or jammed themselves together into great wadded balls that would hold for a few seconds and then collapse, their component parts squirming off for some new adventure elsewhere. I could see there were feeding tubes on the walls, and one or two Ghosts drifted among the saucer things, like an adult in a yard of squabbling children . . .

There was a subtle shadow before me. I looked up, and found myself staring at my own reflection – an angled head, an open mouth, a sprawled body – folded over, fish-eye style, just centimetres from my nose.

The bulging mirror was the belly of a Ghost. It bobbed massively before me.

I pushed myself away from the hull, slowly. I grabbed hold of the nearest tangle branch with my good hand. I knew I couldn't reach for my knife, which was tucked into my belt at my back. And I couldn't see Jeru anywhere. It might be that the Ghosts had taken her already. Either way I couldn't call her, or even look for her, for fear of giving her away.

The Ghost had a heavy-looking belt wrapped around its equator. I had to assume that those complex knots of equipment were weapons. Aside from its belt, the Ghost was quite featureless: it might have been stationary, or spinning at a hundred revolutions a minute. I stared at its hide, trying to understand that there was a layer in there like a separate universe, where the laws of physics had been tweaked. But all I could see was my own scared face looking back at me.

And then Jeru fell on the Ghost from above, limbs splayed, knives glinting in both hands. I could see she was yelling – mouth open, eyes wide – but she fell in utter silence, her comms disabled.

Flexing her body like a whip, she rammed both knives into the Ghost's hide. If I took that belt to be its equator, she hit somewhere near its north pole.

The Ghost pulsated, complex ripples chasing across its surface. Jeru did a handstand and reached up with her legs to the tangle above, and anchored herself there. The Ghost spun, trying to throw Jeru off. But she held her grip on the tangle, and kept the knives thrust in its hide, and all the Ghost succeeded in doing was opening up twin gashes, right across its upper section. Steam pulsed out, and I glimpsed redness within.

Meanwhile I just hung there, frozen.

You're trained to mount the proper reaction to an enemy assault. But it all vaporises when you're faced with a tonne of spinning, pulsing monster, and you're armed with nothing but a knife. You just want to make yourself as small as possible; maybe it will all go away. But in the end you know it won't, that something has to be done.

So I pulled out my own knife and launched myself at that north pole area.

I started to make cross-cuts between Jeru's gashes. I quickly learned that Ghost skin is tough, like thick rubber, but you can cut it if you have the anchorage. Soon I had loosened flaps and lids of skin, and I started pulling them away, exposing a deep redness within. Steam gushed out, sparkling to ice.

Jeru let go of her perch and joined me. We clung with our fingers to the gashes we'd made, and we cut and slashed and dug; though the Ghost spun crazily, it couldn't shake us loose. Soon we were hauling out great warm mounds of meat – rope-like entrails, pulsing slabs like a human's liver or heart. At first ice crystals spurted all around us, but as the Ghost lost the heat it had hoarded all its life, that thin wind died, and frost began to gather on the cut and torn flesh.

At last Jeru pushed my shoulder, and we both drifted away from the ragged Ghost. It was still spinning, off-centre, but I could see that the spin was nothing but dead momentum; the Ghost had lost its heat, and its life.

I said breathlessly, 'I never heard of anyone in hand-to-hand with a Ghost before.'

'Neither did I. Lethe,' she said, inspecting her hand. 'I think I cracked a finger.'

It wasn't funny. But Jeru stared at me, and I stared back, and then we both started to laugh, and our slime suits pulsed with pink and blue icons.

'He stood his ground,' I said.

'Yes. Maybe he thought we were threatening the nursery.'

'The place with the silver saucers?'

She looked at me quizzically. 'Ghosts are symbiotes, tar. That looked to me like a nursery for Ghost hides. Independent entities.'

I had never thought of Ghosts having young. And I had not thought of the Ghost we had killed as a parent protecting its young. I'm not a deep thinker now, and wasn't then; but it was not a comfortable notion.

Jeru started to move. 'Come on, tar. Back to work.' She anchored her legs in the tangle and began to grab at the still-rotating Ghost carcase, trying to slow its spin.

I anchored likewise and began to help her. The Ghost was massive, the size of a major piece of machinery, and it had built up respectable momentum; at first I couldn't grab hold of the skin flaps that spun past my hand.

As we laboured I became aware I was getting uncomfortably hot. The light that seeped into the tangle from that caged sun seemed to be getting stronger by the minute. But as we worked those uneasy thoughts soon dissipated.

At last we got the Ghost under control. Briskly Jeru stripped it of its kit belt, and we began to cram the baggy corpse as deep as we could into the surrounding tangle. It was a grisly job. As the Ghost crumpled further, more of its innards, stiffening now, came pushing out of the holes we'd given it in its hide, and I had to keep from gagging as the foul stuff came pushing out into my face.

At last it was done – as best we could manage it, anyhow.

Jeru's faceplate was smeared with black and red. She was sweating hard, her face pink. But she was grinning, and she had a trophy, the Ghost belt around her shoulders. We began to make our way back, following the same SOP as before.

When we got back to our lying-up point, we found Academician Pael was in trouble.

Pael had curled up in a ball, his hands over his face. We pulled him open. His eyes were closed, his face blotched pink, and his faceplate dripped with condensation.

He was surrounded by gadgets stuck in the tangle – including parts from what looked like a broken-open starbreaker handgun; I recognised prisms and mirrors and diffraction gratings. Well, unless he woke up, he wouldn't be able to tell us what he had been doing here.

Jeru glanced around. The glow of the fortress's central star had gotten a *lot* stronger. Our lying-up point was now bathed in light – and heat – with the surrounding tangle offering very little shelter. 'Any ideas, tar?'

I felt the exhilaration of our infil drain away. 'No, sir.'

Jeru's face, bathed in sweat, showed tension. I noticed she was favouring her left hand. She seemed to come to a decision. 'All right. We need to improve our situation here.' She dumped the Ghost equipment belt and took a deep draught of water from her hood spigot. 'Tar, you're on stag. Try to keep Pael in the shade of your body. And if he wakes up, *ask him what he's found out.*'

'Yes, sir.'

'Good. I'll be back.'

And then she was gone, melting into the complex shadows of the tangle as if she'd been born to these conditions.

I found a place where I could keep up 360-degree vision, and offer a little of my shadow to Pael – not that I imagined it helped much.

I had nothing to do but wait.

As the Ghost ship followed its own mysterious course, the light dapples filtering through the tangle shifted and evolved. Clinging to the tangle, I thought I could feel vibration: a slow, deep harmonisation that pulsed through the ship's giant structure. I wondered if I was hearing the deep voices of Ghosts, calling to each other from one end of their mighty ship to another. It all served to remind me that everything in my environment, *everything*, was alien, and I was very far from home.

During a drama like the contact with the Ghost, you don't realise what's happening to you because your body blanks it out; on some level you know you just don't have time to deal with it. Now that I had stopped moving, the aches and pains of the last few hours started crowding in on me. I was still sore in my head and back and, of course, my busted arm. I could feel deep bruises, maybe cuts, on my gloved hands where I had hauled at my knife, and I felt as if I had wrenched my good shoulder. One of my toes was throbbing ominously: I wondered if I had cracked another bone, here in this weird environment in which my skeleton had become as brittle as an old man's. I was chafed at my groin and armpits and knees and ankles and elbows, my skin rubbed raw. I was used to suits; normally I'm tougher than that, and again I felt unreasonably fragile.

The shafts of sunlight on my back were working on me too; it felt as if I was lying underneath the elements of an oven. I had a headache, a deep sick feeling in the pit of my stomach, a ringing in my ears, and a persistent ring of blackness around my eyes. Maybe I was just exhausted, dehydrated; maybe it was more than that.

I counted my heartbeat, my breaths; I tried to figure out how long a second was. 'A thousand and one. A thousand and two . . .' Tracking time is a fundamental human trait; time provides a basic orientation, and keeps you mentally sharp and in touch with reality. But I kept losing count.

And all my efforts failed to stop darker thoughts creeping into my head. I started to think back over my operation with Jeru, and the regrets began. OK, I'd stood my ground when confronted by the Ghost and not betrayed Jeru's position. But when she launched her attack I'd hesitated, for those crucial few seconds. Maybe if I'd been tougher the Commissary wouldn't find herself hauling through the tangle, alone, with a busted finger distracting her with pain signals.

Our training is comprehensive. You're taught to expect this kind of hindsight torture, in the quiet moments, and to discount it – or, better yet, learn from it. But, effectively alone in that metallic alien forest, I wasn't finding my training was offering much perspective.

And, worse, I started to think ahead. Always a mistake.

I couldn't believe that the Academician and his reluctant gadgetry were going to achieve anything significant. And for all the excitement of our infil, we hadn't found anything resembling a bridge or any vulnerable point we could attack, and all we'd come back with was a bit of field kit we didn't even understand.

For the first time I began to consider seriously the possibility that I wasn't going to live through this – that I was going to die when my suit gave up or the sun went pop, whichever came first, in no more than a few hours.

It was my duty to die. *A brief life burns brightly*. That's what you're taught. Longevity makes you conservative, fearful, selfish. Humans made that mistake before, and we finished up a subject race. Live fast and furiously, for *you* aren't important – all that matters is what you can do for the species.

But I didn't want to die.

If I never returned to Mercury again I wouldn't shed a tear. But I had a life now, in the Navy. And then there were my buddies: the people I'd trained and served with, people like Halle – even Jeru. Having found fellowship for the first time in my life, I didn't want to lose it so quickly, and fall into the darkness alone – especially if it was to be for *nothing*.

But maybe I wasn't going to get a choice.

After an unmeasured time, Jeru returned. She was hauling a silvery blanket. It was Ghost hide. She started to shake it out.

I dropped down to help her. 'You went back to the one we killed—'

'—and skinned him,' she said, breathless. 'I just scraped off the meaty crap with a knife. The Planck-zero layer peels away easily. And look . . .' She made a quick incision in the glimmering sheet with her knife. Then she put the two edges together again, ran her finger along the seam, and showed me the result. I couldn't even see where the cut had been. 'Self-sealing, self-healing,' she said. 'Remember that, tar.'

'Yes, sir.'

We started to rig the punctured, splayed-out hide as a rough canopy over our LUP, blocking as much of the sunlight as possible from Pael. A few slivers of frozen flesh still clung to the hide, but mostly it was like working with a fine, light metallic foil.

In the shade, Pael started to stir. His moans were translated to stark bioluminescent icons.

'Help him,' Jeru snapped. 'Make him drink.' And while I did that she dug into the med kit on her belt and started to spray cast material around the fingers of her left hand.

'It's the speed of light,' Pael said. He was huddled in a corner of our LUP, his legs tucked against his chest. His voice must have been feeble; the bioluminescent sigils on his suit were fragmentary and came with possible variants extrapolated by the translator software.

'Tell us,' Jeru said, relatively gently.

'The Ghosts have found a way to *change* lightspeed in this fortress. In fact to increase it.' He began talking again about quagma and physics constants and the rolled-up dimensions of spacetime, but Jeru waved that away irritably.

'How do you *know* this?'

Pael began tinkering with his prisms and gratings. 'I took your advice, Commissary.' He beckoned to me. 'Come see, child.'

I saw that a shaft of red light, split out and deflected by his prism, shone through a diffraction grating and cast an angular pattern of dots and lines on a scrap of smooth plastic.

'You see?' His eyes searched my face.

'I don't get it. I'm sorry, sir.'

'The wavelength of the light has changed. It has been increased. Red light should have a wavelength, oh, a fifth shorter than that indicated by this pattern.'

I was struggling to understand. I held up my hand. 'Shouldn't the green of this glove turn yellow, or blue? . . .'

Pael sighed. 'No. Because the colour you see depends, not on the wavelength of a photon, but on its energy. Conservation of energy still applies, even where the Ghosts are tinkering. So each photon carries as much energy as before – and evokes the same "colour" in your eye. Since a photon's energy is proportional to its frequency, that means frequencies are left unchanged. But since lightspeed is equal to frequency multiplied by wavelength, an increase in wavelength implies—'

'An increase in lightspeed,' said Jeru.

'Yes.'

I didn't follow much of that. I turned and looked up at the light that leaked around our Ghost-hide canopy. 'So we see the same colours. The light of that star gets here a little faster. What difference does it make?'

Pael shook his head. 'Child, a fundamental constant like lightspeed is embedded in the deep structure of our universe. Lightspeed is part of the ratio known as the fine structure constant.' He started babbling about the charge on the electron.

Jeru cut him off. 'Case, the fine structure constant is a measure of the strength of an electric or magnetic force.'

I could follow that much. 'And if you increase lightspeed—'

'You *reduce* the strength of the force.' Pael raised himself. 'Consider this. Human bodies are held together by molecular binding energy – electromagnetic forces. But here, electrons are more loosely bound to atoms; the atoms in a molecule are more loosely bound to each other.' He rapped on the cast on my arm. 'And so your bones are more brittle, your skin more easy to pierce or chafe. Do you see? You too are embedded in spacetime, my young friend. You too are affected by the Ghosts' tinkering. And because lightspeed in this infernal pocket continues to increase – as far as I can tell from these poor experiments – you are becoming more fragile every second.'

It was a strange, eerie thought, that something so basic in the universe could be manipulated. I put my arms around my chest and shuddered.

'Other effects,' Pael went on bleakly. 'The density of matter is dropping. Perhaps our bodies' very structure will eventually begin to crumble. And dissociation temperatures are reduced.'

Jeru snapped, 'What does that mean?'

'Melting and boiling points are reduced. No wonder we are over-heating. It is intriguing that bio systems have proven rather more robust than electromechanical ones. But if we don't get out of here soon, our blood will start to boil . . .'

'Enough,' Jeru said. 'What of the star?'

'A star is a mass of gas with a tendency to collapse under its own gravity. But heat, supplied by fusion reactions in the core, creates gas and radiation pressures which push outwards, counteracting gravity.'

'And if the fine structure constant changes?'

'Then the balance is lost. Commissary, as gravity begins to win its ancient battle, the fortress star has become more luminous – it is burning faster. That explains the observations we made from outside the cordon. But this cannot last.'

'The novae,' I said.

'Yes. The explosions, layers of the star blasted into space, are a symptom of destabilised stars seeking a new balance. The rate at which *our* star is approaching that catastrophic moment fits with the lightspeed drift I have observed.' He smiled and closed his eyes. 'A single cause predicating so many effects. It is all rather pleasing, in an aesthetic way.'

Jeru said, 'At least we know how the ship was destroyed. Every control system is mediated by finely tuned electromagnetic effects. Everything must have gone crazy at once . . .'

The *Brief Life Burns Brightly* had been a classic GUTship, of a design that hasn't changed in its essentials for thousands of years. The life-dome, a tough translucent bubble, contained the crew of twenty. The dome was connected by a spine a klick long to a GUTdrive engine pod. When we crossed the cordon boundary – when all the bridge lights failed – the control systems went down, and all the pod's super-force energy must have tried to escape at once. The spine of the ship had thrust itself up into the lifedome, like a nail rammed into a skull.

Pael said dreamily, 'If lightspeed were a tad faster, throughout the universe, then hydrogen could not fuse to helium. There would only be hydrogen: no fusion to power stars, no chemistry. Conversely if light-speed were a little lower, hydrogen would fuse too easily, and there would be *no* hydrogen, nothing to make stars – or water. You see how critical it all is? No doubt the Ghosts' science of fine-tuning is advancing considerably here on the Orion Line, even as it serves its trivial defensive purpose . . .'

Jeru glared at him, her contempt obvious. 'We must take this piece of intelligence back to the Commission. It might be the key to breaking the Orion Line, at last. We are at the pivot of history, gentlemen.'

I knew she was right. The primary duty of the Commission for Historical Truth is to gather and deploy intelligence about the enemy. And so *my* primary duty, and Pael's, was now to help Jeru get this piece of data back to her organisation.

But Pael was mocking her. 'Not for ourselves, but for the species. Is that the line, Commissary? You are so grandiose. And yet you blunder around in comical ignorance. Even your quixotic quest aboard this cruiser was futile. There probably is no bridge on this ship. The Ghosts' entire morphology, their evolutionary design, is based on the notion of cooperation, of symbiosis; why should a Ghost ship have a metaphoric *head*? And as for the trophy you have returned with' – he held up the belt of Ghost artefacts – 'there are no weapons here. These are sensors, tools. There is nothing here capable of producing a significant energy discharge. This is less threatening than a bow and arrow.' He let go of the belt; it drifted away. 'The Ghost wasn't trying to kill you. It was blocking you. Which is a classic Ghost tactic.'

Jeru's face was stony. 'It was in our way. That is sufficient reason for destroying it.'

Pael shook his head. 'Minds like yours will destroy *us*, Commissary.'

Jeru stared at him with suspicion. Then she said, *'You have a way.* Don't you, Academician? A way to get us out of here.'

He tried to face her down, but her will was stronger, and he averted his eyes.

Jeru said heavily, 'Regardless of the fact that three lives are at stake – does duty mean nothing to you, Academician? You are an intelligent man. Can you not see that this is a war of human destiny?'

Pael laughed. 'Destiny – or economics?' He said to me, 'You see, child, as long as the explorers and the mining fleets and the colony ships are pushing outwards, as long as the Third Expansion is growing, our economy works. But the system is utterly dependent on continued conquest. From virgin stars the riches can continue to flow inwards, into the older mined-out systems, feeding a vast horde of humanity who have become more populous than the stars themselves. But as soon as that growth falters . . .'

Jeru was silent.

I understood some of this. This was a war of colonisation, of world-building. For a thousand years we had been spreading steadily from star to star, using the resources of one system to explore, terraform and populate the worlds of the next. With too deep a break in that chain of exploitation, the enterprise broke down.

And the Ghosts had been able to hold up human expansion for fifty years.

Pael said, 'We are already choking. *There have already been wars*, young Case: human fighting human, as the inner systems starve. Not mentioned in Coalition propaganda, of course. If the Ghosts can keep us bottled up, all they have to do is wait for us to destroy ourselves, and free them to continue their own rather more worthy projects.'

Jeru floated down before him. 'Academician, listen to me. Growing up at Deneb, I *saw* the great schooners in the sky, bringing the interstellar riches that kept my people alive. I *saw* the logic of history – that we must maintain the Expansion, *because there is no choice*. And that is why I joined the armed forces, and later the Commission for Historical Truth. Not for ideology, not for misty notions of destiny, but for economics. We must labour every day to maintain the unity and purpose of mankind. We must continue to expand. For if we falter we die; as simple as that.'

Pael raised an eyebrow. 'Perhaps I have underestimated you. But, Commissary, sincere or not, your creed of mankind's evolutionary destiny condemns our own kind to become a swarm of children, granted a few moments of loving and breeding and dying, before being cast into futile war.'

Jeru snapped, 'It is a creed that has bound us together for a thousand years. It is a creed that unites uncounted trillions of human beings across thousands of light years. Are you strong enough to defy such a creed now? Come, Academician. None of us *chooses* to be born in the middle of a war. We must all do our best for each other, for other human beings; what else is there?'

I looked from one to the other. I thought we should be doing less yapping and more fighting. I touched Pael's shoulder; he flinched away. 'Academician – is Jeru right? Is there a way we can live through this?'

Pael shuddered. Jeru hovered over him.

'Yes,' Pael said at last. 'Yes, there is a way.'

The idea turned out to be simple.

And the plan Jeru and I devised to implement it was even simpler. It was based on a single assumption: Ghosts aren't aggressive. It was ugly, I'll admit that, and I could see why it would distress a squeamish earthworm like Pael. But sometimes there are no good choices.

Jeru and I took a few minutes to rest up, check over our suits and our various injuries, and to make ourselves comfortable. Then, following patrol SOP once more, we made our way back to the pod of immature hides.

We came out of the tangle and drifted down to that translucent hull. We tried to keep away from concentrations of Ghosts, but we made no real effort to conceal ourselves. There was little point, after all; the Ghosts would know all about us, and what we intended, soon enough.

We hammered pitons into the pliable hull, and fixed rope to anchor ourselves. Then we took our knives and started to saw our way through the hull.

As soon as we started, the Ghosts began to gather around us, like vast antibodies. They just hovered there, eerie faceless baubles drifting as if in vacuum breezes. But as I stared up at a dozen distorted reflections of my own skinny face, I felt an unreasonable loathing rise up in me. Maybe you could think of them as a family banding together to protect their young. I didn't care; a lifetime's carefully designed hatred isn't thrown off so easily. I went at my work with a will.

Jeru got through the pod hull first. The air gushed out in a fast-condensing fountain. The baby hides fluttered, their distress obvious. And the Ghosts began to cluster around Jeru, like huge light globes.

Jeru glanced at me. 'Keep working, tar.'

'Yes, sir.'

In another couple of minutes I was through. The air pressure was already dropping, and it dwindled to nothing when we cut a big door-sized flap in that roof. Anchoring ourselves with the ropes, we rolled that lid back, opening the roof wide. A few last wisps of vapour came curling around our heads, ice fragments sparkling.

The hide babies convulsed. Immature, they could not survive the sudden vacuum, intended as their ultimate environment. But the way they died made it easy for us. The silvery hides came flapping up out of

146

the hole in the roof, one by one. We just grabbed each one – like grabbing hold of a billowing sheet – and we speared it with a knife, and threaded it on a length of rope. All we had to do was sit there and wait for them to come. There were hundreds of them, and we were kept busy.

I hadn't expected the adult Ghosts to sit through that, non-aggressive or not; and I was proved right. Soon they were clustering all around me, vast silvery bellies looming. A Ghost is massive and solid, and it packs a lot of inertia; if one hits you in the back you know about it. Soon they were nudging me hard enough to knock me flat against the roof, over and over. Once I was wrenched so hard against my tethering rope it felt as if I had cracked another bone or two in my foot.

And, meanwhile, I was starting to feel a lot worse: dizzy, nauseous, overheated. It was getting harder to get back upright each time after being knocked down. I was growing weaker fast; I imagined the tiny molecules of my body falling apart in this Ghost-polluted space.

For the first time I began to believe we were going to fail.

But then, quite suddenly, the Ghosts backed off. When they were clear of me, I saw they were clustering around Jeru.

She was standing on the hull, her feet tangled up in rope, and she had knives in both hands. She was slashing crazily at the Ghosts, and at the baby hides which came flapping past her, making no attempt to capture them now, simply cutting and destroying whatever she could reach. I could see that one arm was hanging awkwardly – maybe it was dislocated, or even broken – but she kept on slicing regardless. And the Ghosts were clustering around her, huge silver spheres crushing her frail, battling human form.

She was sacrificing herself to save me – just as Captain Teid, in the last moments of the *Brightly*, had given herself to save Pael. And *my* duty was to complete the job. So I stabbed and threaded, over and over, as the flimsy hides came tumbling out of that hole, slowly dying.

At last no more hides came.

I looked up, blinking to get the salt sweat out of my eyes. A few hides were still tumbling around the interior of the pod, but they were inert and out of my reach. Others had evaded us and gotten stuck in the tangle of the ship's structure, too far and too scattered to make them worth pursuing further. What I had would have to suffice. I started to make my way out of there, back through the tangle, to the location of our wrecked yacht, where I hoped Pael would be waiting.

I looked back once. I couldn't help it. The Ghosts were still clustered over the ripped pod roof. Somewhere in there, whatever was left of Jeru was still fighting. I had an impulse, almost overpowering, to go back to her. No human being should die alone. But I knew I had to get out of there, to complete the mission, to make her sacrifice worthwhile.

So I got.

Pael and I finished the job at the outer hull of the Ghost cruiser.

Stripping the hides turned out to be as easy as Jeru had described. Fitting together the Planck-zero sheets was simple too – you just line them up and seal them with a thumb. I got on with that, sewing the hides together into a sail, while Pael worked on a rigging of lengths of rope, all fixed to a deck panel from the wreck of the yacht. He was fast and efficient: Pael, after all, came from a world where everybody goes solar-sailing on their vacations.

We worked steadily, for hours.

I ignored the varying aches and chafes, the increasing pain in my head and chest and stomach, the throbbing of a broken arm that hadn't healed, the agony of cracked bones in my foot. And we didn't talk about anything but the task in hand. Pael didn't ask what had become of Jeru, not once; it was as if he had anticipated the Commissary's fate.

We were undisturbed by the Ghosts through all of this.

I tried not to think about whatever emotions churned within those silvered carapaces, what despairing debates might chatter on invisible wavelengths. I was, after all, trying to complete a mission. And I had been exhausted even before I got back to Pael. I just kept going, ignoring my fatigue, focusing on the task.

I was surprised to find it was done.

We had made a sail hundreds of metres across, stitched together from the invisibly thin immature Ghost hide. It was roughly circular, and it was connected by a dozen lengths of fine rope to struts on the panel we had wrenched out of the wreck of the yacht. The sail lay across space, languid ripples crossing its glimmering surface.

Pael showed me how to work the thing. 'Pull this rope, or this one . . .' The great patchwork sail twitched in response to his commands. 'I've set it so you shouldn't have to try anything fancy, like tacking. The boat will just sail out, hopefully, to the cordon perimeter. If you need to lose the sail, just cut the ropes.'

I was taking in all this automatically. It made sense for both of us to know how to operate our little yacht. But then I started to pick up the subtext of what he was saying. *You*, not *us*.

He shoved me onto the deck panel, and pushed it away from the Ghost ship. His strength was surprising. He was left behind. It was over before I understood what he was doing.

I watched him recede. He clung wistfully to a bit of tangle.

The sail above me slowly billowed, filling up with the light of the brightening sun. Pael had designed his improvised craft well; the rigging lines were all taut, and I could see no rips or creases in the silvery fabric.

'Where I grew up, the sky was full of sails . . .' My suit could read Pael's, as clear as day.

'Why did you stay behind, Academician?'

'You will go further and faster without my mass to haul. And besides – our lives are short enough; we should preserve the young. Don't you think?'

I had no idea what he was talking about. Pael was much more valuable than I was; I was the one who should have been left behind. He had shamed himself.

Complex glyphs crisscrossed his suit. 'Keep out of the direct sunlight. It is growing more intense, of course. That will help you . . .' And then he ducked out of sight, back into the tangle.

I never saw him again.

The Ghost ship soon receded, closing over into its vast egg shape, the detail of the tangle becoming lost to my blurred vision. I clung to my bit of decking and sought shade.

Twelve hours later, I reached an invisible radius where the tactical beacon in my pocket started to howl with a whine that filled my headset. My suit's auxiliary systems cut in and I found myself breathing fresh air.

A little after that, a set of lights ducked out of the streaming lanes of the fleet, and plunged towards me, growing brighter. At last it resolved into a golden bullet shape adorned with a blue-green tetrahedron, the sigil of free humanity. It was a supply ship called *The Dominance of Primates*.

And a little after *that*, as a Ghost fleet fled their fortress, the star exploded.

As soon as I had completed my formal report to the ship's Commissary

– and I was able to check out of the *Dominance*'s sick bay – I asked to see the Captain.

I walked up to the bridge. My story had got around, and the various med patches I sported added to my heroic mythos. So I had to run the gauntlet of the crew – 'You're supposed to be dead, I impounded your back pay and slept with your mother already' – and was greeted by what seems to be the universal gesture of recognition of one tar to another, the clenched fist pumping up and down around an imaginary penis. But anything more respectful just wouldn't feel normal.

The Captain turned out to be a grizzled veteran type with a vast laser burn scar on one cheek. She reminded me of First Officer Till.

I told her I wanted to return to active duty as soon as my health allowed.

She looked me up and down. 'Are you sure, tar? You have a lot of options. Young as you are, you've already made your contribution to the Expansion. You can go home.'

'Sir, and do what?'

She shrugged. 'Farm. Mine. Raise babies. Whatever earthworms do. Or you can join the Commission for Historical Truth.'

'Me, a Commissary?'

'You've been there, tar. You've been in amongst the Ghosts, and come out again – with a bit of intelligence more important than anything the Commission has come up with in fifty years. Are you *sure* you want to face action again?'

I thought it over.

I remembered how Jeru and Pael had argued about economics. It had been an unwelcome perspective, for me. I was in a war that had nothing to do with me, trapped by what Jeru had called the logic of history. But then, I bet that's been true of most of humanity through our long and bloody story. All you can do is live your life, and grasp your moment in the light – and stand by your comrades.

A farmer – me? And I could never be smart enough for the Commission. No, I had no doubts.

'A brief life burns brightly, sir.'

Lethe, the Captain looked like she had a lump in her throat. 'Do I take that as a yes, tar?'

I stood straight, ignoring the twinges of my injuries. 'Yes, *sir*!'

\*

*The Orion Line was broken. Humanity spilled into Ghost space, slaughtering and colonising.*

*But the war would last centuries more. Such is the nature of conflict on interstellar scales.*

*In time the Ghosts learned to fight back, with new weapons, new tactics.*

*Even a new breed of Ghost.*

# GHOST WARS

## AD 7004

### I

The needleship *Spear of Orion* dropped out of hyperspace. Its tetrahedral Free Earth sigils shone brightly, its weapons ports were open, and its crew were ready to do their duty.

Pilot Officer Hex glanced around the sky, assessing the situation.

She was deep in the Sagittarius Spiral Arm, a place where stars crowded, hot and young. One star was close enough to show a disc, the sun of this system. And there was the green planet she had been sent here to defend. Labelled 147B by the mission planners, this was a terraformed world, a human settlement thrust deep into Silver Ghost territory. But the planet's face was scarred by fire, immense ships clustered to evacuate the population – and needleships like her own popped into existence everywhere, Aleph Force swimming out of hyperspace like a shoal of fish. This was a battlefield.

All this in a heartbeat. Then the Silver Ghosts attacked.

'Palette at theta ten degrees, phi fifty!' That was gunner Borno's voice, coming from the port blister, one of three dotted around the slim waist of the *Spear*.

Hex, in her own cramped pilot's blister at the very tip of the needle-ship, glanced to her left and immediately found the enemy. Needleship crews were warriors in three-dimensional battlefields; translating positional data from one set of spherical coordinates to another was drummed into you before you were five years old.

Borno had found a Ghost intrasystem cruiser, the new kind – a 'palette,' as the analysts were calling them. It was a flat sheet with its Ghost crew sitting in pits in the top surface like blobs of mercury. The ship looked a little like a painter's palette, hence the nickname. But palettes were fast, manoeuvrable and deadly, much more effective in

152

battle than the classic tangled-rope Ghost ships of the past. And just seconds after she came down from hyperspace this palette was screaming down on Hex, energy weapons firing.

Hex felt her senses come alive, her heartbeat slow to a resolute thump. One of her instructors once said she had been born to end Ghost lives on battlefields. At moments like this, that was how it felt. Hex was twenty years old.

She hauled on her joystick. The needleship swung like a compass needle and hurled itself directly at the Ghost palette. As weapons on both ships fired, the space between them filled with light.

'About time, pilot,' Borno said. 'My fingers were getting itchy.'

'All right, all right,' Hex snapped back. Gunner Borno, of all the needleship crew she had ever met, had the deepest, most visceral hatred of the Ghosts and all their works. 'Just take that thing down before we collide.'

But no lethal blow was struck, and as the distance between the ships closed, uneasiness knotted in Hex's stomach.

She thumbed a control to give her a magnified view of the palette's upper surface. She heard her crew murmur in surprise. These Ghosts weren't the usual silver spheres. They had sharp edges; they were cubes, pyramids, dodecahedrons – even a tetrahedron, as if mocking the ancient symbol of Earth. And they showed no inclination to run away. These were a new breed of Ghost, she realised.

The *Spear* shuddered. For an instant the Virtual displays clustered around her fritzed, before her systems rebooted and recovered.

'Jul, what was that? Did we take a hit?'

Jul was the ship's engineer, young, bright, capable – and a good pilot before her lower body was cut away by a lucky strike from a dying Ghost. 'Pilot, we ran through g-waves.'

'Gravity waves? From a starbreaker?'

'No,' called navigator Hella, the last of the *Spear*'s four crew. 'Too long-wavelength for that. And too powerful. Pilot, this space is full of g-waves. That's how the Ghosts are hitting the planet.'

'Where are they coming from?'

'The scouts can't find a source.'

'New weapons, new ships, new tactics,' Borno said darkly.

'And new Ghosts,' said Hella.

'You know what's behind this,' Jul said uneasily.

Hex said warningly, 'Engineer—'

'The Black Ghost. It has to be.'

Unlike any of its kind before, the barracks-room scuttlebutt went, the Black Ghost was an enemy commander that fought like a human – better than a human. The Commissaries claimed this was all just rumour generated by stressed-out crews, but Hex herself had heard that the stories had originated with Ghosts themselves, captives under interrogation. And whether the Black Ghost existed or not, you couldn't deny that *something* was making the Ghosts fight better than they ever had.

And meanwhile that palette still hadn't broken off.

'Thirty seconds to close,' Hella said. 'We won't survive an impact, pilot.'

'Neither will they,' Borno said grimly.

'Fifteen seconds.'

'Hold the line!' Hex ordered.

'Those dimples,' said engineer Jul hastily. 'Where the Ghosts are sitting. There has to be some interface to the palette's systems. They must be weak spots. Gunner, if you could plant a shell there . . .'

Hex imagined Borno's grin.

'Seven seconds! Six!'

A single shell sailed out through the curtain of fire. It was a knot of unified-field energy, like a bit of the universe from a second after the Big Bang itself.

The shell hit a dimple so squarely it probably didn't even touch the sides. The resident Ghost, a squat cube, was vaporised instantly. Then light erupted from every dimple and weapons port on the palette. The Ghost crew scrambled away, but Hex saw silver skin wrinkle and pop, before the palette vanished in a flash of primordial light.

The needleship slammed through a dissipating cloud of debris, and the blisters turned black to save the crew's eyes.

The *Spear* sat in space, its hull charred, still cooling as it dumped the energy it had soaked up. Sparks drifted through the sky: more needleships, a detachment of Aleph Force forming up.

For the first time since they'd dropped out of hyperspace Hex was able to catch her breath, and to take a decent look at the world she had been sent to defend.

Even from here she could see it was suffering. Immense storm systems swathed its poles and catastrophic volcanism turned its nightside bright.

Sparks climbed steadily up from the planet's surface, refugee transports to meet the Navy ships – Spline, living starships, kilometre-wide spheres of flesh and metal.

Hella murmured, 'That's what a g-wave weapon will do to you, if it's sufficiently powerful.'

Borno asked, 'How? By ripping up the surface?'

'Probably by disrupting the planet's orbital dynamics. You could knock over a world's spin axis, maybe jolt it into a higher eccentricity orbit. If the core rotation collapsed its magnetic field would implode. You'd have turmoil in the magma currents, earthquakes and volcanism . . .'

The destruction of a world as an act of war. The people being driven from their homes today were not soldiers. They had come here as colonists, to build a new world. But the very creation of this settlement had been an act of war, Hex knew, for this settlement had been planted deep inside what had been Ghost space until five centuries ago.

The Ghost Wars had already lasted centuries. War with an alien species was not like a human conflict. It was ecological, the Commissaries taught, like two varieties of weed competing for the same bit of soil. It could be terminated by nothing short of total victory – and the price of defeat would be extinction, for one side or another.

And now the Ghosts had a weapon capable of wreaking such damage on a planetary scale, and, worse, were prepared to use it. These were not the Ghosts Hex had spent a lifetime learning to fight. But in that case, she thought harshly, I'll just have to learn to fight them all over again.

Borno said, 'I don't like just sitting out here.'

'Take it easy,' Hex said. She downloaded visual feed from the command loops. Ghost ships were being drawn away from the battle around the planet itself, and were heading out to this concentration.

Aleph Force was Strike Arm's elite, one of the most formidable rapid-response fighting units in the Navy. From their base on the Orion Line they were hurled through hyperspace into the most desperate situations – like this one. Aleph Force always made a difference: that was what their commanders told them to remember. Even the Ghosts had learned that. And that was why Ghosts were peeling off from their main objective to engage them.

'Gunner, we're giving that evacuation operation a chance just by sitting here. And as soon as we've lured in enough Ghosts we'll take them on. I have a feeling you'll be slitting hides before the day is done.'

'That might be sooner than you think,' called engineer Jul, uneasily. 'Take a look at this.' She sent another visual feed around the loop.

Sparks slid around the sky, like droplets of water condensing out of humid air.

Hex had never seen anything like it. 'What are they?'

'Ghosts,' Borno said. 'Swarming like flies.'

'They're all around us,' Hella breathed. 'There must be thousands.'

'Make that millions,' Jul said. 'They're surrounding the other ships as well.'

Hex called up a magnified visual. As she had glimpsed on the palette, the Ghosts were cubes, pyramids, spinning tetrahedrons, even a few spiny forms like mines.

Jul said, 'I thought all Ghosts were spheres.'

Ghosts were hardened to space, and their primary driver was the conservation of their body heat. For a given mass a silvered sphere, the shape with the minimum surface area, was the optimal way to achieve that.

'But they weren't always like that,' said Borno. He had studied Ghosts all his life, the better to destroy them. 'Ghosts evolved. Maybe these are primitive forms, before they settled for the optimum.'

'Primitive?' Hex asked. 'Then what are they doing here?'

'Don't ask me.' His voice was tight. His loathing of Ghosts was no affectation; it was so deep it was almost phobic.

'They're closing,' Jul called.

The *Spear*'s weapons began to spit fire into the converging cloud. Hex saw that one Ghost, two, was caught, flaring and dying in an instant. But it was like firing a laser into a rainstorm.

Hex snapped, 'Gunner, you're just wasting energy.'

'The systems can't lock,' Borno said. 'Too many targets, too small, too fast-moving.'

'Another new tactic,' Jul murmured. 'And a smart one.'

Navigator Hella called, 'Hex, you'd better take a look at this.'

In a new visual, Hex was shown a dense mass of Ghost hide. It was a sheet, a ragged segment of a sphere that grew even as she watched, with more Ghosts clustering around its spreading edges.

'It's the Ghosts,' Hella said. 'Some of those shapes, for instance the cubes, are space-filling. They're forming themselves into a shell around us. A solid shell.'

Jul said, wondering, 'They are acting in a coordinated way, millions of them, right across the battlefield.'

'Like humans,' Hella said. 'They are fighting like humans, unified under a single command.'

The name hung unspoken between them: this was the work of the Black Ghost.

'We're losing the comms nets,' Jul said, tense. 'They're isolating us.'

Hex glanced around the sky. The other needleships of Aleph Force were being enclosed by their own shells of Ghost hide; they hung in space like bizarre silvered fruit. She thought frantically. 'If we try to ram that wall—'

'They'll just fall back and track us,' Hella said.

'What if we go to hyperdrive?'

Engineer Jul snapped, 'Are you crazy? With all this turbulence in the gravity field, surrounded by a wall of reflective Ghost hide, you may as well just detonate the engines.'

Hella said, 'It's that or be destroyed anyhow.'

Borno said, 'At least we will take down a lot of them with us. Millions, maybe.'

They fell silent for a heartbeat. Then Hella called, 'Pilot? It's your decision.'

Hex knew this was a war of economics. A great deal had been invested in her crew's raising and training, and in the ship itself. But that investment had been made to be spent. The four of them and the ship, in exchange for millions of these strange swarming new Ghosts: it was a fair price.

'It is our duty,' she said. She brought up a bright, colour-coded display and began to work through the self-destruct procedure.

She heard Hella sigh.

Borno said grimly, 'It's been good to serve with you all.'

Jul said, 'Not for long enough.'

Hex heard the tension in their voices. She had been trained for this, as for every other conceivable battlefield scenario. She knew that none of them really believed this was the end, not deep in their guts. If suicide was the only option, you did it quickly, before you had time to understand what you were doing. 'I'll set it to five seconds. Good luck, everybody.' She reached out her gloved hand to finalise the sequence.

'Wait.' It was a new voice, smooth, toneless, coming from her command net.

In a visual before her was a Silver Ghost. It was one of the classic sort, a perfect sphere. The image was about the size of her head, a ball of silver turning slowly in the middle of her blister.

'You hacked into our command net,' Hex said.

'It wasn't difficult,' the Ghost said. Its voice, translated by the *Spear*'s systems from some downloaded feed, was bland, without inflection. But did she detect a trace of sarcasm?

Jul spoke, her voice tremulous with fear. 'Hex? What's going on? Just get it over—'

'Wait,' Hex snapped.

The Ghost said, 'I will let you live, in return for a service.'

Hex could hardly believe she was hearing this. She heard the voice of her training officers in her head; in a situation like this, faced with a new stratagem by the Ghosts, it was her job to extract as much intelligence as possible. 'Why us?'

'Because Aleph Force are the supreme killers in a species of killers, and you are the best of Aleph Force. Quite an accolade.'

'And what's this "service"? You want us to kill somebody, is that it?' A military leader, Hex speculated, a senior Commissary, maybe a minister of the Coalition's grand councils back on Earth – Ghosts had never resorted to assassination that she knew of, but then this was a day when nothing about the Ghosts seemed predictable. 'Who?'

Even on this day of shocks, the answer was stunning. 'We want you to assassinate the Black Ghost.'

## II

Scarcely believing what she was doing, Hex set up a conference call involving herself, her crew, her commander at the base of Aleph Force back on the Orion Line – and a Silver Ghost.

Commodore Teel, a disembodied Virtual head floating in Hex's blister, glared at her. In his forties, Teel's face was hard, his eyes flat, and his scalp was a mass of scar tissue. 'None of you should even be alive. Pilot Officer Hex, charges aren't out of the question.'

Hex swallowed her shame. 'I know that, sir. It was a judgement call to abort the self-destruct.'

'Show me where you are.'

Navigator Hella hastily downloaded positional data to the Commodore. The *Spear of Orion* had been smuggled through some kind of hyperspace jump out of its cage of Ghosts and brought to a position at the rim of the system, where only icy comets swam in the dark. They were far from the fighting which still raged in the inner system.

Teel stared at the Ghost's Virtual, which spun silently, complacently. 'How did this creature bring you out here?'

Jul answered, 'We're not sure, sir. We didn't monitor any communication between it and any other Ghost. The Ghost, um, *broke* us out.'

'I think we're dealing with factions among the Ghosts, sir,' Hex said. 'Maybe there's an opportunity here. That's why I thought it best to pass it up the chain of command.'

'And this Ghost wants you to kill one of its own.'

'This Ghost has a name,' the Ghost said. 'Or at least a title.'

'I've heard of this,' Borno sneered. 'Ghosts like titles. They are all ambassadors.'

'I am no ambassador,' the Ghost said. 'This is not an age for ambassadors. I am an Integumentary.' The *Spear*'s systems displayed various alternative translations for 'Integumentary': prophylaxis, quarantine. 'I am part of an agency that insulates humans from Ghosts, like the hide that shields my essence from the vacuum of space.'

'Charming,' Teel said. 'But, fancy title or not, you are my mortal enemy. If you want us to do something for you, then you must give us something in return.'

The Ghost spun, its flawless hide barely showing its rotation. 'I expected nothing less. The one thing you wasteful bipeds relish even more than killing is trade. Bargaining, mutual deception—'

Teel snapped, 'If you expected it you have something to offer.'

'Very well,' said the Ghost. 'If you succeed we will decommission the new weapon system.'

'What new weapon?'

'Directional gravity waves on a large scale.'

The weapon that had churned up a planet. Hex held her breath.

'Download some data,' Teel said. 'Prove you can do this. Then we'll talk.'

Hex watched, astonished, as the *Spear*'s systems began to accept data from the Ghost.

Every human knew the story of the Silver Ghosts, and their war with humanity.

For fifteen hundred years the Third Expansion of mankind had been spreading across the face of the Galaxy. First contact between humans and the alien kind they labelled 'Silver Ghosts' had come only a few centuries after the start of the Expansion. The Ghosts were silvered spheres, up to two metres across. Their hide was perfectly reflective – hence the human label 'Silver Ghosts'; in starlight they were all but invisible.

The key to the Ghosts was their past. The world of the Silver Ghosts was once Earthlike: blue skies, a yellow sun. But as the Ghosts climbed to awareness their sun evaporated, its substance torched away by a companion star. As their world froze the Ghosts rebuilt themselves. They became symbiotic creatures, each one a huddled cooperative collective. That spherical shape and silvered hide minimised heat loss.

The death of the Ghosts' sun was a betrayal by the universe itself, as they saw it. But that betrayal shaped them for ever. Their science was devoted to fixing the universe's design flaws: they learned to tinker with the very laws of physics.

When humans found the Ghosts, at first two powerful interstellar cultures cautiously engaged. But the Ghosts' home range lay between mankind and the rich star fields of the Galaxy's Core. The Ghosts were in humanity's way. War was inevitable.

After early quick victories, for centuries the Ghosts stalled the human advance at the Orion Line, an immense static front along the outer edge of the Sagittarius Arm. The Ghosts, capable of changing the laws of physics in pursuit of weapons technology, were a formidable foe; but humans were the more warlike.

A weapon that could use g-waves to devastate worlds was a characteristic Ghost weapon, exotic and powerful. And it worked, the Integumentary said, by tapping into the large-scale properties of the universe itself.

'Perhaps you understand that the universe has more dimensions than the macroscopic, the three spatial and one of time. Most of the extra dimensions are extremely small.' A technical sidebar translated this for Hex as 'Planck scale'. 'But one extra dimension is rather larger, perhaps as much as a millimetre. You must think of the universe, then, as a blanket of spacetime, stretching thirteen billion years deep into the past and some twelve billion light years across—'

'And a millimetre thick,' said Hella.

'There are believed to be many such universes, stacked up' – the translator boxes hesitated, searching for a simile – 'like leaves in a book. Also our own universe may be folded back on itself, creased in the thin dimension.'

Engineer Jul said, 'So what? We know about the extra dimensions. We use them when we hyperdrive.'

'But,' said the Ghost, 'your applications are not currently on the scale of ours.'

'Tell us about g-waves,' Teel commanded.

The Ghost said that all forms of energy were contained within the 'blanket' of the universe – all save one. Gravity waves could propagate in the extra dimensions, reaching out to the other universes believed to be stacked out there. The Ghosts had learned to focus the gravitational energy raining into their own universe from another.

'The energy source in the other universe is necessarily large,' the Integumentary said. 'Alternatively it may be a remote part of our own universe, an energy-rich slice of spacetime – the instants after the initial singularity for instance, folded back. We aren't sure. You understand that this weapon offers us a virtually unlimited source of power. It's just a question of tapping it. Beyond weaponry, many large-scale projects become feasible.'

Hella said, 'I wonder what "large-scale" might mean for a species of universe-botherers like the Silver Ghosts.'

Teel said, 'Even when we were friendly with them the Ghosts scared us, I think.'

Hex had had enough of awe. 'Let's talk about the target. This weapon system is in the control of the Black Ghost . . .'

Recently the Ghosts had suddenly been scoring victories against the human forces. Their tactics had undergone a revolution that must reflect a change in their command structure, perhaps their very society.

'Humans work in hierarchies,' Teel said. 'Chains of command. All large-scale military organisations in the past have done so. We tend to think it's the only way to operate, but in fact it's a very human way to work.'

'An evolutionary legacy of your past,' the Integumentary said. 'When you were squabbling apes in some dismal forest, in thrall to the strongest male—'

'Shut up,' Teel said without emotion. 'Ghosts, however, have always worked differently. Their organisation is more fluid, bottom-up, with distributed decision-making. The whole of their society is self-organising.'

'Like a Coalescence,' Borno said with disgust.

'Like a hive, yes.'

'The Ghosts are this way,' said the Integumentary, 'because of *our* evolutionary past. As you would understand if you knew anything about the species you are endeavouring to wipe out.'

'Maybe,' Teel said, 'but you stayed that way because it's efficient. Even in some military applications: if you're waging a guerrilla war on an occupied world, for instance, a network of cells can be very effective. But in large-scale set-piece battles, which we always try to draw the Ghosts into, you need a command structure.'

'And now they have one,' Hex said.

'Which makes them harder to beat. But it also makes them more vulnerable, because suddenly assassination is an effective weapon.'

Hex, intrigued, asked, 'Why would any Ghost commit this treason? If the Black Ghost exists – if it lies behind these new effective tactics—'

The Integumentary said, 'The Black Ghost's is the greater treason, because of where its project will inevitably lead.'

Teel prompted, 'Which is?'

'To an arms race. Humans will steal or reinvent the gravity wave technology for themselves. Then we will conspire together, humans and Ghosts, to wreck the Galaxy between us. Or, worse—'

'Ah,' said Teel. 'The Black Ghost will unleash such power that there won't be anything left for the victors to take.'

'It's possible,' Borno said. 'Ghosts are single-minded. They choose a plan and stick to it, whatever the cost.'

In the training academies there was a joke about Ghosts that had the right of way to cross a road. But the transport drivers ignored the stop signs. So the first Ghost crossed, exerting its rights, and was creamed in the process. So did the second, the third, the fourth, each sticking to what it believed was right regardless of the cost. Then the fifth invented a teleport, changing physical law to make the road obsolete altogether . . .

Teel said, 'So you want the Black Ghost eliminated before it destroys everything. Even though this may be your best chance of winning the war and of avoiding the subjugation or even extinction that would follow.'

'Sooner extinction than universal destruction,' the Integumentary said.

'How noble.'

Hex said, 'And you, Integumentary, are prepared to make the most profound moral judgements on behalf of your whole species – and their entire future?'

Borno said, 'Who cares about Ghost ethics? They won't need ethics when they're all dead.'

'You're deranged, gunner, but you're right,' said Teel. 'We don't need to consider Ghost consciences. Our job is to consider what use to make of this strange opportunity. Certainly we need to find out more about these new Ghost variants you've come up against. I'll pass this up the line to—'

'You decide now,' the Ghost snapped.

Borno said, 'If you think a commodore is going to take orders from a ball of fat like you—'

'Can it, gunner,' Hex snapped.

'You decide now,' the Ghost said again. 'You allow this crew, in this ship, to follow my instructions, or I disconnect the link.'

Hella said, 'I guess the Integumentary has its own pressures. Imagine trying to run a covert operation like this from our side.'

'We'll follow your orders, whatever you say, Commodore,' Hex said.

'I know you will,' Teel said dismissively. 'But I've no way of assessing your chances of success – let alone survival.'

'Our survival is irrelevant, sir,' Jul said.

'I know that's what you're taught, engineer. Perhaps there are a few desk-bound Commissaries back on Earth who actually believe that. But out here we who do the fighting are still human. The mission has a greater chance of success if you're willing to take it on.'

'I'm willing,' Borno said immediately.

'I've seen your file, gunner. What about those of you who *aren't* psychopathically hostile to the Ghosts and all their works?'

Hella was uncertain. 'We're flight crew. We aren't infantry, or covert operatives. We may not be right for the job.'

'We're Aleph Force,' Hex said firmly. 'In Aleph Force you do whatever it takes.'

'Anyhow I don't think there's a choice,' Jul said. 'Us or nobody.'

Hella asked, 'So what do you think, pilot?'

Hex looked into her soul. A journey into the very heart of Ghost territory – a mission that might turn the course of the war – how could she refuse? 'I'm in.'

Jul, Hella and Borno quickly concurred.

'I'm proud of you,' the Commodore said.

The Ghost spun. 'Humans!'

Hex snapped, 'All right, Ghost, let's get on with it. Where are we going?'

More data chattered into the *Spear*'s banks.

## III

The *Spear of Orion* swept through space. The needleship moved from point to point through hyperdrive jumps, each too brief for a human eye to follow, so that the stars seemed to slide through the sky like lamp posts beside a road. For the crew the journey was a routine marvel.

But Hex and her crew had come far from the outermost boundary of human space, farther than any human had travelled from Earth save for a handful of explorers. And every star they could see must host a Ghost emplacement: if humanity was turning the Galaxy green, then this rich chunk of it still gleamed Ghost-silver. But the *Spear* remained undisturbed.

'It's eerie,' engineer Jul said. 'Ghosts should be swarming all over us.'

Hex said, 'The Integumentary promised to make us invisible to the Ghosts' sensors, and it's keeping its word.'

Jul, a practical engineer, snorted. 'I'd feel a lot more reassured if I knew *how*.'

Borno said, 'What do you expect? Ghosts don't give you anything.' His pent-up rage, here in Ghost territory, was tangible.

They sailed on in tense silence.

Borno had been born between the stars. His ancestors, who called themselves 'Engineers', had fled Earth at the time of an alien occupation. With no place to land the refugees had ganged together their spacecraft and found ways to live between the stars, through trading, piloting, even a little mercenary soldiering.

When the Third Expansion came, Borno's Engineers had been one of a number of peripheral cultures recontacted by the Coalition, the new authority on Earth. But the Engineers had also forged tentative links with the Silver Ghosts, who were undergoing their own expansion out of the heart of the Galaxy. For a time the Engineers had profited from trade between two interstellar empires. They even welcomed small Ghost colonies on their amorphous islands of relic spacecraft and harnessed asteroids.

But then Navy ships came spinning down to impose Coalition authority on the Engineers' raft culture. There had been a strange period when autonomous Ghost enclaves had been granted room to live under the new regime: Silver Ghosts, living under Coalition authority. But the Ghosts had been taxed, marginalised and discriminated against until their position was untenable. Their maltreatment had led to a rescue mission from Ghost worlds – and that had led to one of the first military engagements of the long Ghost Wars, fought out over the Engineers' fragile raft colony. Among the Engineers, many had died, and the rest had been dispersed to colonies deeper within Coalition space.

All this was centuries ago. But Borno's people had never forgotten who they were and where they had come from; they still called themselves 'Engineers'. And in their minds it had been Ghost aggression that had resulted in the deaths of so many and the loss of an ancient homeland.

Hex reflected that it would do no good to try to explain to Borno that it had been Coalition policy that had precipitated that defining crisis in the first place. And besides, Borno's wrath was useful for the Coalition's purposes. In a war that spanned the stars, he was not unique.

'Heads up,' Hella said. 'I have a visual. Theta eighty-six, phi five.'

Their destination was dead ahead.


Hex saw a double star: a misty sphere that glowed a dull coal red while a pinpoint of electric blue trawled across its face.

The *Spear*'s crew had had to find their way here by dead reckoning. This system didn't show up in the Navy's data banks. After fifteen centuries of the Third Expansion, the Commission for Historical Truth believed it had mapped every single one of the Galaxy's hundreds of billions of stars, human-controlled or not – but it hadn't mapped this one.

Anomaly or not, somewhere in this unmapped system, the Integumentary had promised, the crew of the *Spear* would find the Black Ghost.

Gunner Borno said hastily, 'We're crawling with Ghosts.'

Hex checked her displays. All around her were Ghosts: their ships, their emplacements, their sensor stations and weapons platforms. The whole system was like a vast fortress, defended to a depth of half a light year from that central double sun, with more monitoring stations and fast-response units even further out.

'None of them are reacting,' Jul said, sounding disbelieving. 'Not one unit.'

Hex said, 'Then forget them. What are we looking at?'

Jul said, 'I've seen systems like this before. That blue thing is a neutron star, right?'

'Yes,' Hella said, 'Actually a pulsar . . .'

Once this had been a partnership of two immense stars – until the larger, too massive, had detonated in a supernova explosion, for a few days outshining the whole Galaxy. Its ruin had collapsed to form a neutron star, a sun-sized mass compressed down to the size of a city block. As it spun on its axis a ferocious magnetic field threw out beams of charged particles to flash in the eyes of radio telescopes: it was a pulsar.

As for the supernova's companion, the tremendous detonation stripped away most of its outer layers. Its fusing core, exposed, had not been massive enough to maintain the central fire. The remnant star had subsided to misty dimness.

Hella said, 'But the system is actually still evolving. That pulsar is dragging material out of the parent.' She displayed a false-colour image that showed a broad disc, material the pulsar's gravity had dug out of the larger star's flesh and thrown into orbit.

'So that star blew its companion up,' Borno said, 'and now it's taking it apart bit by bit. What a dismal place this is.'

'And yet,' Hella said, 'this system has planets. Two, three, four – more off in the dark, they surely don't matter. It's the innermost that has the most Earthlike signature: air, liquid water, oxygen, carbon compounds. Smaller than Earth, though.'

Across human space people always spoke of Earthlike worlds, though few of them had ever seen Earth; the mother planet remained the reference for all her scattered children.

The original binary could have hosted Earths, if they were far enough from the brilliance of the central stars. No biosphere could have survived the supernova detonation, but once the system became stable again, any surviving worlds could have been reborn. Comets or out-gassing could create a new atmosphere, a new ocean. And life could begin again, perhaps crawling out of the deepest rocks, or brought here by the comets – or even delivered by conscious intent; this was a Galaxy crowded with life. How strange, Hex thought, a planet that might have hosted not one but two generations of life. She wondered if its new inhabitants had any idea of what went before – if those doomed by the supernova had managed to leave a trace of their passing, before being put to the fire.

'But that pulsar is still chipping away at the red star,' Jul said. 'The sun is failing.'

'And if there are Ghosts here they are suffering.' Borno snarled. 'Good.'

Hella called, 'There isn't much off-world, but I can see one large habitat orbiting the innermost planet.'

'Then that's our destination.' Hex set up an approach trajectory. She felt the needleship's intrasystem engines thrumming around her, powerful and secure, and the dim red sun swept towards them.

Borno said, 'Pilot, your trajectory will take us right through the thick of the Ghosts.'

'Gunner, they either see us or they don't. We may as well walk in the front door.'

Borno said tensely, 'Trusting a Ghost with our lives?'

'That's always been the deal.'

'You mean,' Jul said, 'the whole mission's always been half-assed.'

'Stay focused,' Hex murmured.

'Closest approach,' Hella called now.

The star ballooned out of the dark. Its dim photosphere bellied beneath Hex's blister, churning dully, disfigured by huge spots. A pinpoint of electric blue rose over the crimson horizon of the parent, casting long shadows through the columns of glowing starstuff that its gravity hauled up from the body of the parent star.

'Sunrise on a star,' Borno said. 'Now there's something you don't see every day.'

'But we've got more anomalies,' Jul reported. 'The parent's composition is all wrong. Too much hydrogen, not enough metals. Younger stars incorporate the debris of earlier generations, fusion products, heavy elements like metal, carbon. It's as if this star is *too old* – only by a million years or so, but still—'

'I'll tell you something stranger,' Hella said. 'This star system may not be in the Coalition catalogues, but it's a near-identical twin of a system that is.' She brought up an image of another system, another red star with a bright blue companion pulsar; Hex saw from the accompanying data that the system's orbital dynamics were virtually identical. Hella said, 'This other star is in Ghost space too. Only a few tens of light years away.'

Hex let all this wash through her. You weren't wise to block information flows, especially when you were flying into the unknown like this. But she couldn't see an immediate relevance in these stellar mysteries.

She was relieved when the twin stars fell away, the needleship climbed back out of the parent star's gravity well, and the target planet came looming out of the dark.

Unlike the rest of her crew Hex had been brought up on a planet, only a few light years from Earth itself. But even to her eyes this little world looked strange. Huddled close for warmth, it kept one face to the parent star. The subsolar point on the daylight hemisphere, where the sun would be perpetually overhead, must be the warmest place on the planet. Hex made out climatic bands of increasing dimness sprawling around that central point, so that the face of the planet was like a target, bathed crimson red. And on the dark side, illuminated only by starlight, she glimpsed the blue tint of ice.

As the needleship swung closer, she made out more detail on the sunward side: dark patches that might have been seas, broad crimson plains, and here and there a bubbling grey that was the characteristic of habitation, cities. But sparks crawled over the terminator, the boundary between day and night, and where they landed fire splashed.

Jul murmured, 'What are we getting into here? It looks like a war between the day and night sides.'

Hella said, 'That big orbital habitat is by far the highest technology on or around the planet. The materials, the trace radiation – it looks like it's the only example of modern Ghost technology here.'

'If the Black Ghost is anywhere,' Hex said, 'that's where it will be. Fix the course, navigator—'

The *Spear* shuddered and spun crazily, that faint sun and its huddled world whirling like spectres. Hex's blister lit up with alarm flags, flaring bright red.

She barked out commands and wrestled with her joystick. 'Report!'

'It was g-waves,' Jul called back. 'Just like the beams they used back on 147B.'

'Were we targeted? They aren't supposed to be able to see us.'

Hella said, 'The whole system is crisscrossed by the beams. We just ran into one.'

'A defensive measure?'

'I don't know. Maybe. Or something to do with the stellar system itself—'

Borno said, 'We have company. Theta thirty, phi one hundred. They are coming out of that habitat.'

A swarm of palette-ships came swooping down on the *Spear*. Maybe it had been too much to expect the Integumentary's shielding to survive the g-wave buffeting.

Grimly Hex fought with the still-spinning ship. 'Open up the weapons ports.'

'Half of them are off-line,' Jul called back. 'And our sensors are blitzed too. Right now we're de-fanged, pilot. Give me two minutes and—'

The first shot sizzled through space only a couple of kilometres from the *Spear*'s nose.

'We don't have two minutes,' Hex snapped. 'Options. Come on, guys!'

'Fight!' Borno called.

'Run,' said Jul.

'Abort to the planet's surface,' advised Hella.

At last Hex got the spin under control. But the face of the planet was a mottled crimson shield before her. More alarms lit up as the needle-ship sensed the first touch of this world's thin atmosphere. 'Looks like we don't have much choice.' She hauled on her controls, turned the needleship so its nose pointed down into the atmosphere – and she lit up the intrasystem drive to hurl the ship into the cover of air. A ball of light engulfed the *Spear*, atmospheric gases ionised and driven to white heat. In the blisters the inertial control held, more or less; Hex and her crew felt only the mildest of judders as they fell into the air of an unknown world.

All this in utter silence.

'We're kind of lighting up the sky here, pilot,' Borno called.

Hex said, 'It will get us down quicker. The ground proximity sensors will pull us out before—'

'Sensors are off-line,' Jul reminded her hastily.

'Oops,' said Hex. She hauled on her joystick.

'Land below us,' Hella called. 'Now over ocean—'

Hex's blister filled up with crash foam, embedding her like a wrapped-up doll, so tight she couldn't move a finger. She felt nothing as the *Spear of Orion* cut a tunnel through an ocean a half-kilometre deep, and then, before the waters had even closed, gouged a crater fifty kilometres across in the soft rocks of the ocean floor.

Her crash foam shattered, broke up and fell away.

She was floating. She was surrounded by misty grey-green air, illuminated by dim slanting light – no, not air, she realised as she tried to move her limbs. This medium was water. Thankfully her skinsuit was holding.

She looked around. Flecks of her crash foam fell away. Of the needleship, her crew, there was no sign in this murky soup. The *Spear of Orion* had been her first command, and now it was gone in seconds.

And here she was, immersed in an unknown sea. Hex's world was largely untamed. Her people, like humans everywhere, were drawn to the sea, but you never went swimming, for the ocean was full of monsters. She didn't even know how deep she was – or which way was up. For a moment panic bubbled, and she thrashed, wasting energy, until she forced herself to be still.

She ordered her skinsuit to use the planet's gravity field to find the local vertical. Then, when it was oriented, she made the suit climb. She glimpsed the ocean's scummy meniscus an instant before she broke through into the air, to her huge relief.

She rose into a crimson sky, where a misshapen sun hung low. Beneath her the ocean looked black, oily, and huge, languid low g-waves crossed its surface. But she could see, deep down beneath the waters, a pale pink glow that must be the crater they had made.

Another skinsuit broke the surface, popping up like a balloon. Then a third, and a fourth. Hex made them sound off and report on their status. Everybody was unscathed, physically anyhow. They bobbed over the surface of the ocean, four drifting people in bright green suits.

'The *Spear* has had it,' Jul said. She downloaded to Hex a last data squirt from the dying ship.

'We're stranded,' Hella said gloomily.

'We still have weapons in our suits,' Borno said.

Hex said, 'If we can find anybody to shoot at.'

Jul pointed down at the ocean. 'Pilot – what's *that*?'

Something moved, just under the surface. Larger than a human, amorphous, dimly glimpsed, it seemed to be moving purposefully.

Hex could hear her mother's voice: *There are monsters in the sea*. 'My turn to be phobic,' she murmured.

Hella said, 'What? . . . Look. It's breaking the surface.'

Hex glimpsed sleek flesh humping above the water. Then something like a limb protruded. Hex flinched; it was as if the limb had reached for her.

'I can't make out its shape,' Borno said.

'Maybe it has no fixed shape,' Hella said. 'I've read some creatures of the seas are like that.'

'But it's a toolmaker,' Jul said calmly. She pointed. 'It's wearing a kind of belt.'

All this seemed utterly horrific to Hex. That limb, muscular, equipped with suckers and fine manipulators, continued to writhe in the air.

'You know,' Hella said, 'I think it's *beckoning*.'

'To us?'

'Of course to us. I think it wants us to follow it – to the land, probably.'

'What land?' Jul asked.

Hella sighed. 'Some navigator you would make. Over there.'

There was a dark shading on the horizon.

Hex's sharp pilot's eyes picked out sparks descending from the sky. 'We're out of time.'

'They're tracking the wreckage of the ship,' Jul said.

'We stand and fight,' Borno snarled.

'Not here,' Hex snapped. 'Not now. Borno, we can't win.'

'We should follow the swimming thing,' Hella said. 'It might help us.'

'You think so?' Jul asked.

'It's clearly smart. And it's trying to help us right now. Why not?'

Hex looked down with huge reluctance at the blank surface of the water, the uncharted depths beneath. 'We don't have a choice,' she told her crew, and herself.

She flipped in the air and plunged head-first back into the water. Her suit's systems whirred as it sought neutral buoyancy, and made her legs kick. Her tell-tales showed her that her crew followed her in: one, two, three.

They all struggled through the water in pursuit of the 'swimming thing'.

## IV

Hex woke. She was reasonably comfortable, even warm. But when she looked up, she peered out through a translucent bubble-wall at the roof of a cave.

She stretched, sat up.

By the light of a suit lamp, the others were already eating. They sat around suit backpacks that glowed green, giving off light and warmth. Breakfast was a slab of sticky, green, manufactured by a backpack from the organic produce of this world's ocean, washed down by a visor-full of water.

On staggering into this sea-shore cave Hex had inflated her own suit to form this bubble-tent. If you looked carefully you could see the suit's seams, even one stretched-out glove. Inside, the crew had stripped off their suits, pooled their backpacks, and slept, lying on one stretched-out suit while blanketed by another. They had needed time for some essential maintenance, of themselves as much as their suits.

In the mouth of the cave, beyond their shelter, a fire burned fitfully, hampered by poor convection in the low gravity. Oddly the flickering glow of the fire seemed more human than the pale green of the suit lights, but it had been built by an utterly alien being.

It was odd for Hex to have her crew together like this. She had spent most of the last year with them, but for most of their time together they were sealed up in their blisters. Now here they were, stripped down to their heated undergarments, all crammed in. Borno, the only man, was bulky, big-boned, hard-muscled. She imagined him spending hours honing his body so he could take down Ghosts hand on hand if he had to. Hella was smaller, thin, morose and anxious, but possibly the smartest of the three. Jul looked a little overweight; maybe she had been skimping physical exercise. Of course the fact that the lower half of her body was a clunky prosthetic didn't help.

And then there was Hex – the youngest, she uncomfortably reminded herself.

Borno groused, 'We're interstellar warriors and we're reduced to this. Stuck in a cave like animals. You can't even tell if it's morning or night.'

'It's always day here, dummy,' Hella said. She sounded tired, drained; she chewed on her food tablets without enthusiasm.

'Lethe, you know what I mean. It's morning *somewhere* . . .'

Restless, Hex made her way to the wall of her suit-tent. They were in the northern hemisphere, but the cave was oriented south, so she could see the twin suns, a glum red blur with that spark of bright blue crawling over its face. It was strange to think that the double star never moved from its station in the sky, as if nailed there. The ground was worn, a thin soil lying over the melted bedrock that was all that had survived a supernova torching. The air was less than a fifth Earth's pressure: too thin for them to breathe, but enough to transport sufficient heat around the planet to keep all the water, and indeed the air itself, from freezing out on the dark side.

And on this small world, in this thin air, there was life.

Hex made out gaunt silhouettes standing on a low ridge. They looked like antennae, with dishes turned up to the sun. They were plants, something like trees – but they were colony organisms, with the leaves independent creatures, roosting on the branches like birds. The pool of shadow behind that ridge hadn't been touched by sunlight for a million years.

'We've got company,' Hella murmured.

A puddle of slime, glistening in the low sunlight, flowed in over the cave floor. It gathered itself up into a rough pillar and let fall a belt stocked with tools of stone and metal. Unstable and oozing, it seemed to warm itself by the fire, and pseudopods extended to hurl a little more fuel onto the flames. Then it collapsed again and came slithering over the floor of the cave towards the humans' shelter. It dumped organic produce by the translucent wall: what looked like seaweed, and even a fish, a triumph of convergent evolution.

This was the crew's only ally on this strange world.

His name for himself had translated as *Swimmer-with-Somethings*, the 'somethings' being an aquatic creature they hadn't been able to identify. Close to, he looked disturbingly like a flayed human, immersed in a kind of gummy soup within which smaller creatures swam. The 'he', of course, was for the crew's convenience, though there might have been genders among the myriad creatures that made up this composite animal.

The motile puddle pushed a membrane above its oily meniscus, and Hex heard soft gurgling sounds.

Hella studied her suit's translator box. 'He says—'

'Let me guess,' said Hex. '"More food." Tell him thanks.' She meant it. The humans couldn't eat the native life, but the biochemistry was carbon-based, and their suits' backpacks were able to use this raw material to manufacture edible food and to extract water.

Hella murmured into her unit, and the membrane pulsed in response. They had been surprised how easy it had been to find a translation. Swimmer's speech pattern was similar to some variants of the Ghost languages which humans had been studying for centuries, an odd fact which Hex had filed away as one of the many puzzles to be resolved about this place.

Engineer Jul was fascinated by the creature's biological organisation. 'Look at that thing. He's obviously a colonial organism. Every so often all the components go swimming.' She pointed. 'Those little blobs look like algal cooperatives. Powered by capillary action, probably. But these "algae" are jet black – probably something to do with the photosynthetic chemicals used in the local ecology. I'm not sure what those little swimming shrimp-like creatures are for . . .'

Swimmer had a skeleton of something like cartilage, and 'muscles', pink and sinewy, adhered to it. But the cartilage itself was independently mobile. And now a 'muscle' detached itself from its anchor, swam to the surface of the slimy pool into which Swimmer had deliquesced, and opened a mouth to breathe the air.

Borno's face contorted. 'How gross.'

'More gross than a Ghost?' Hex asked.

He turned to her, his eyes stony. 'Well, now, that's the question, isn't it? We know the Ghosts are some kind of colony creature too. And we know that this wriggling, dissolving thing speaks a kind of basic Ghost language. I think it's time we asked him what is going on here – and what he has to do with the Ghosts.'

'He may not know,' Jul warned. 'He is technological, but primitive. And we may turn him against us.'

Borno snapped, 'So what?'

'I think Borno's right,' Hella said. 'We're not getting anywhere sitting in here. We have to take a few risks.'

'If he knows who's shooting at him from the nightside,' Borno said, 'it would be a start.'

Hex considered. She had been trained by the Commissaries in alien psychology – or at least, how to manipulate it. 'We humans are very self-centred,' she said. 'Everything revolves around us. But for Swimmer, we're peripheral. He doesn't care what we want, even where we came from. He's helping us stay alive for his own reasons – and that's our angle. Hella, try asking him why he's helping us.'

Hella murmured into her translator unit.

He was helping them, Swimmer replied, because they were the enemies of his enemies.

Swimmer didn't know that the ecology that had spawned him was the second to have arisen on this battered world.

His sun was dark and cold to human senses, but to the creatures that evolved in its ruddy light it was a warm steady hearth. 'In fact,' Hella said, smiling, 'Swimmer doesn't believe that life on a planet like Earth is possible. A dazzling sun, a daily cycle of light and dark, seasons, ice ages – how could any ecology evolve in such a chaotic environment?'

Life here, though, had taken a different route to Earth. The continued cooling of the sun had exerted a selective pressure to huddle, to share, to keep warm. Here large animals were rare, cooperative organisms the norm.

Hex had never seen another of Swimmer's kind, but it seemed he joined with others in the depths of the sea. There the bits that made up the people danced in their own eager matings. And if you came out of the great merging with a slightly different set of subcomponents, so what? Hex suspected that 'identity' meant something rather different to these people than to her own.

When intelligence evolved among Swimmer's predecessors, their biology shaped everything they did. Unlike humans their politics was a matter of cooperation rather than competition, though there could be disagreements, even wars. They crawled out onto land – surely the low gravity helped them with that conquest – where there were raw materials to be shaped, power sources like fire impossible under water. Their different origins shaped their technology. They discovered a genius for moulding themselves and their coevals; these people were capable of advanced biochemistry, though their physical technology was no more than Iron Age.

They had even managed to achieve spaceflight. A handful of Swimmer's people cloaked themselves in a new kind of hide, a tough, silvered skin capable of retaining inner heat while resisting the harsh radiations of space. In time ice moons and comet nuclei had become home to a new variant of Swimmer's kind, who rarely visited the home planet.

But all the while the pulsar continued its slow, lethal work of slicing away the substance of the sun.

As this story unfolded, the *Spear* crew exchanged glances of recognition.

It had become increasingly clear that a crisis was approaching. A decision emerged from the interconnected councils of the people. The interplanetary wayfarers were summoned home. The most technologically advanced of their kind, perhaps they could find a way to save the world.

The space-hardened wayfarers returned. By now the ice cap on the nightside, hard and cold, was not so different a habitat from the ice moons they had made their home. But they found they resented being begged for help by those they regarded as a primitive, weaker form. They saw ways to use this fat rocky world for their own purposes – and all the better if the murky atmosphere and muddy oceans were frozen or stripped off.

Bringing the spaceborne home was a catastrophic mistake. They had diverged too much from Swimmer's kind. There were two species now, too far apart, competing for the same space. Conflict was inevitable.

The nightsiders were outnumbered by the daysiders, but were far more technologically advanced. For centuries they had been launching missile after missile over the terminator, from the dark to the light. At first the daysiders had fought back; epic invasions of the night had been launched. But as its cities and farms were devastated, the thin material base of the dayside crumbled. By now only scattered survivors, like Swimmer, remained. They mounted guerrilla actions against night-side patrols. But they knew the war was lost, and their future with it.

And recently, as if they had not suffered enough, a new peril had arisen, when a new light crossed the sky.

'The habitat of the Black Ghost,' Borno said grimly.

Suddenly the simple ships of the nightsiders had been equipped with faster drives and still deadlier weapons. Swimmer, with a resigned acceptance, had come to believe that his people's time was up – until, in the form of the humans, he had stumbled on his own miracle from the sky.

Hex was distracted by a shadow crossing the cave mouth.

Hella was growing excited. 'Pilot, I think I've figured it out—'

'Shut up,' Hex hissed. The shadow crossed again. Now she was sure: it was a palette-ship, and four, five, six Ghosts, angular rhomboids, rode it menacingly. Hastily she shut down their packs, and made her crew lie flat. Even Swimmer lay still in his puddle of slime.

The palette paused briefly at the cave mouth, but anything within was hidden by the fire. With a careless burst of an energy weapon the Ghosts smashed Swimmer's hearth, scattering its fuel. Then the palette moved on.

The crew stood up cautiously.

Borno said, 'So they're looking for us. We have to get out of here.'

Hella grabbed his arm. 'Not before you listen to me. I've worked it out. This world is—'

'The home world of the Ghosts,' Borno said, dismissively. 'And this is their origin, from a million years back or so, somehow brought forward in time. Isn't that obvious?'

Not to Hex. Her jaw dropped; she deliberately closed it.

Jul was figuring it out too. 'Yes, yes. Swimmer speaks a variant of one of their languages. Ghosts are cooperative organisms, just like Swimmer. Even their hides were once independent creatures—'

'Every Ghost is a whole ecology in a sack,' Borno murmured, repeating training-ground lore.

Hella said, still excited, 'We even found a copy of this system thirty light years away! *That* must be the present-day copy – this one is dredged up from the past . . .'

Jul said, 'The "primitive" Ghosts must come from this world. The Black Ghost recruited them here.'

'Maybe that's why this was done,' Borno said darkly. 'The Black Ghost has tapped its own deep past for raw material for the war with humans. When Ghosts told us about their origin they never mentioned this devastating civil war, did they? Funny, that.'

Hella turned to Hex. 'Pilot? You've been very quiet. What are you thinking?'

Hex looked at her, abstracted. 'About time travel.' Humans had achieved time travel, of course. Every faster-than-light ship was a time machine, and it was said that in the old days the legendary hero Michael Poole once travelled through time in a wormhole. 'We've sent a few people, a ship or two, through a few centuries. But the Ghosts have brought a star system, *a whole system*, up through a million years.'

That sobered them.

Jul said, 'The Integumentary did say that their new extra-dimension technology was opening up vast energy sources for them.'

'Yes. But I never dreamed it would be capable of something like this.'

'And,' Borno said coldly, 'it's in the hands of the Black Ghost.'

'So we have to stop it,' Hex said. The others nodded, determined.

'All right,' Hella said. 'But how? We're still stuck in this cave.'

'We have to get off the planet,' Hex said. 'And as far as I know the only launch capabilities are the nightsiders'.' She considered Swimmer. She wondered if he knew he had been projected into the farthest future of his own kind. 'Hella, do you think your new friend could help us get across the terminator?'

V

Under the guidance of Swimmer-with-Somethings, they journeyed north. They would cross into night somewhere near the planet's spin pole.

The journey took them days – Earth days. They travelled out of sight of the ur-Ghosts, as they took to calling them, these cousins of Swimmer hardened for space but not yet of the optimal spherical form they would reach later. They clambered through tunnels, along the shadowed floors of deep ravines, and swam under the sea, their suits' inertial control packs labouring to keep up with Swimmer's economical motions. When they stopped, while the humans tended their blisters, Swimmer huddled in a gelatinous mass in any sunlight he could find, or, if they were in the ocean, he discorporated with exuberant relief. It was a mystery to Hex how the little shrimps and algae and amphibians that made up his body knew when to come back, and how to reintegrate.

As they forged steadily north the sun slid down the sky, and the shadows stretched long and deep. In the dimming sky Hex glimpsed stars, and the single bright pinpoint, steadily tracking, that was the Black Ghost's habitat.

At last they came to a place where the sun sat on the horizon, glowing like hot coal. It looked as if it was about to set, but of course it never would. Life was sparse at this high latitude. An analogue of grass spread across the ground, though its native photosynthetic chemicals made it black, not green. But nothing grew in the long shadows, on this world where every shade was permanent.

Swimmer left them here. Unable to tolerate freezing temperatures, he could go no further. 'Fight well for me,' he said to them through Hella's translator box. Then he squirmed away, like rainwater disappearing down a drain.

Hex looked north into the darkness. She saw motion: palette-ships, patrolling this boundary between day and night.

Borno pointed. 'There are structures over that way.'

'Let's get on with it,' Hella said tautly.

Following Borno's lead, they walked into the night. Hex could sense Jul's fear, Hella's tension, and Borno's grim, bloody determination.

The sun disappeared altogether. They passed a few last trees, so tall that their leaves blazed in sunlight while frost gathered on their roots. 'Interesting bit of biomechanics,' Jul said nervously. 'They must have evolved to exploit the temperature differences between their crowns and their roots. And I guess these last trees must be as tall as this stock can grow, otherwise—'

'Shut *up*,' Borno hissed.

They came to a wall. It was just a heap of what looked like sandbags, glowing silvery in the dim light. They crouched behind this and cautiously peered at the structures that lay beyond.

Hex saw a kind of city, spun out of silver and ice, resting on a black velvet landscape. Necklaces swooped between cool globes, frosted, icicles dangling. Sparks of light drifted between silvered domes: Ghosts, or ur-Ghosts. The place had an organic look, as if it had been grown here rather than planned. But there was nothing of Swimmer's vibrant, swarming physicality to be seen in this chill place.

This was a typical Ghost colony. Ghosts stayed away from the heat of stars, but they had remained planet-dwellers; they tapped a world's geothermal heat for their energy, just as they evidently had on this, their own freezing world. And their colonies always had this tangled, unplanned look.

There were anomalies, though. On a slim spire that towered over the reef-city, a light pulsed steadily, brilliant electric blue. And at the very centre of the township a squat cylinder brooded. Hex's suit sensors told her this was merely the upper level of a complex dug deep into the ground, where thousands of Ghosts swarmed. This fortress, very unlike Ghost architecture, was the work of the Black Ghost, obvious even here, just inside the boundary of night.

Borno tapped Hex on the shoulder and pointed.

A handful of ur-Ghosts swarmed around a palette-ship on the ground. The Ghosts' forms were variants of parallelepipeds, like slanted boxes. They were really quite beautiful, Hex thought, their facets flashing like mirrors in the starlight as they worked.

Borno whispered, 'Four of them, four of us. We can take them out. And then we can grab that palette-ship and get to orbit.'

Jul hissed, 'We only just crossed the terminator. Maybe we should go further before—'

'What's the point? We came here to find a way off the planet. There's our opportunity.' He raised his hand, holding a knife.

Hex said, 'Borno is right. The longer we hang around the more chance we have of getting caught. Let's do this. There's a blind side over there, to their right. Borno, if you take Jul and head that way, Hella and I can—'

Hella cried, 'Look out!'

The wall behind Hex's back suddenly gave way, and she was tipped onto the cold ground. When she looked up she saw that the 'sandbags' were suspended in the thin air, heavy, rippling sacks swarming over her head. There must have been fifty of them, more.

This 'wall' had a been a reef of ur-Ghosts, huddled together. She should have known, she thought; she had seen their space-filling antics in combat. What a stupid mistake.

The ur-Ghosts descended.

Borno screamed, 'Weapons!' Snarling, his blade in his hand, he was trying to get to his feet.

Hex raised her arms. Her suit weapons powered up.

*'Don't fire.'*

The ur-Ghosts went limp, quivered, and fell. It was like having sacks of water dropped on you from a height. Hex's suit turned rigid to protect her. Then the crew of the *Spear* fought their way out from the heap, shoving the floppy sacks away with a whir of exoskeletal multipliers.

Beyond this chaotic scene a Ghost hovered, bobbing gently with a delicacy that belied its mass. It was one of the modern kind, a smooth, seamless sphere. Borno raised his blade, but Hex grabbed his arm.

'You are the Ghost we met. The Integumentary. You've dogged us all the way.'

'Yes. From one blunder to another. I am here to ensure the success of the mission. I hoped I wouldn't have to reveal myself; I hoped in vain. I never believed you would be so stupid as to hide behind a stack of warriors.'

Jul looked around at the limp ur-Ghosts that lay like immense raindrops on the ground. 'Why do they cluster like this? *You* don't.'

'Perhaps it's a relic of their past,' Hella said. 'Swimmer congregated with his kind. These strange forms long to do the same.'

'Now they know you are here,' the Ghost said. 'The Black Ghost and his hierarchy. They know *I* am here. You have little time. I suggest you hurry to the transporter you chose.'

They clambered past the heaps of fallen Ghosts and ran.

The four ur-Ghosts who had been tending the palette-ship had fallen like the others. When Borno reached the first of the ur-Ghosts he raised his knife, preparing to cut into its hide.

'It is dead,' the Integumentary said quickly. 'I had to kill it. I had to kill them all.' It hovered over the fallen ur-Ghosts, its movements agitated.

Borno, his knife still raised, laughed. 'You killed your own kind, dozens of them, to aid an enemy that is determined to eradicate your species. You really are screwed up, Ghost.'

'I serve a cause beyond your comprehension.'

'Oh, really? Comprehend this.' Borno plunged his knife into Ghost hide. A watery fluid, laced with red blood, spilled out onto the cold ground.

'I told you it is dead,' said the Integumentary.

'I know,' Borno said. With an effort he ripped back the ur-Ghost's skin, exposing glistening muscles, organs. 'Pilot, we can ride this ship up to orbit, but do you think the Black Ghost will let us just sail in? We'll wrap ourselves up in this stuff. Camouflage. Come on, help me.'

Jul said, 'That's repulsive.'

Borno shrugged and carried on cutting.

Such an unsophisticated ploy would never work, Hex thought. But maybe they could use a little psychology, let the Black Ghost think it had won a victory. She stepped forward, chose an ur-Ghost of her own, and took her knife from its sleeve on her leg. 'Let's get it over.'

The Integumentary spun, agitated. 'You humans are beyond understanding.'

'Which is why you hired us to do your dirty work,' Borno snapped, contemptuous.

As she worked Hella said, 'Integumentary – what is *that*?' She pointed at the tower that rose from the Ghost city, with its electric-blue light pulsing at its tip.

The Ghost said, 'You understand where you are, what world this is. In these times, my ancestors understood full well that it was the pulsar that was destroying their sun. So they venerated it. They made it a god. They called it—'

Hex's translator unit stumbled, and offered her a range of options. Hex selected *Destroyer*.

Hella said, 'Fascinating. Humans have always worshipped gods who they believed created the world. You worship the one that destroyed it.'

'It is a higher power, if a destructive one. It is rational to try to placate it. All intelligent creatures are shaped by the circumstances of our origins.'

Borno sneered. 'It's terrible for you to be brought here, isn't it, Ghost? To confront the darkest time of your species. You'd prefer to believe it never happened. And now humans are learning all about it.'

The Ghost spun and receded. 'You haven't much time.'

Borno had already got the skin off his ur-Ghost. An independent entity in its own right, it was flapping feebly on the cold ground, and the ur-Ghost's innards were creatures that flopped and crawled. Borno kicked apart the mess with a booted foot.

## VI

The cup-shaped indentations in the surface of the palette-ship were just shallow pits. Hex had to sit cross-legged.

Borno set up an ur-Ghost hide over her, like a crude silvered tent. Hex was sealed in the dark. The hide, freshly killed, was *still warm*, and she felt blood drip on her back. But she shut her suit lamp down, set her visor to show her the exterior of the ship, and tried to forget where she was.

The palette-ship turned out to be simple to operate. After all, analysts in military labs had been taking apart Ghost technology for generations. All Hex had to do was slap her gloved palms flat against the palette's hull, and her suit found a way to hack into its systems. Experimentally she raised her arm. The palette lifted, tipped and wobbled, a flying carpet on which they were all precariously sitting. But then the inertial control cut in properly, interfacing with their suits' inertial packs, and she felt more secure.

'Some ride this is going to be,' Borno said.

'Yes, and then what?' Jul snapped.

'We'll deal with that when it comes,' Hex said. 'Have your suit weapons ready at all times.'

'I think we'd better get on with it, pilot,' Hella murmured.

Hex, through her visor's systems, glanced around. She was a hundred metres above the ground, and the Ghost city was laid out beneath her, a chaotic tangle of silver cables. She could still see the bloody smears that were all that was left of the ur-Ghosts they had skinned. And silvery sparks were converging.

Hex called, 'Everybody locked in? Three, two, one—' She raised her arm again, and the palette shot skywards.

From space the extent of the ur-Ghosts' betrayal of their cousins was clear. Their chrome-dipped cities clustered over every scrap of land, with only the ghostly blue-white of the ice cap left untouched. No wonder this terrible fratricidal episode was expunged from the Ghosts' racial memory.

'Pilot,' Hella whispered. 'The habitat. Theta ninety, phi twenty.'

Hex looked ahead. Riding high above the icy nightside clouds a structure was rising. At first glance it looked like typical Ghost architecture, a mesh of silver thread. But Hex made out a darker knot at the centre of the tangle.

So this was the bastion of the Black Ghost. It was no more than a kilometre away.

'End game,' Borno said softly.

'Let's move in.' Hex raised her arms, and the platform slid forward.

Suddenly palette-ships came rushing out of the tangle like a flock of startled birds.

Jul cried out, 'Lethe!'

Hella said tightly, 'They're going around us, pilot. Hold your line. Hold your line!'

Hex ground her teeth, and kept her hands steady as a rock. The fleet swarmed around her and banked as one, swooping down over the limb of the planet.

'You've got to admire their coordination,' Hella said. 'I've never seen Ghost ships move like that.'

'That's the influence of the Black Ghost,' said Borno.

'They're heading for the dayside,' Jul murmured. 'Swimmer and his people are going to get another pasting.'

Hex said firmly, 'Then let's see if we can put a stop to it.'

They covered the remaining distance quickly.

The palette slid into the habitat, among threads and ducts; it was like flying into the branches of a silvered tree. Though individual ur-Ghosts slid around the inner structure, nothing opposed them.

Soon the clutter of threads cleared away, and the big central bastion was revealed. It was a sphere, black as night, kilometres across. In the jungle-like tangle of Ghost architecture it didn't fit; it was alien within the alien.

'That wall is a perfect absorber of radiation,' Jul called. 'A black body.'

'You see what this is,' Borno brayed. 'The Black Ghost built its central bastion in its own image. What arrogance!'

Hella murmured, 'Haven't human rulers always done this?'

Hex said, 'I'm hoping we can use its arrogance against it.' She inched forward cautiously. Still they weren't challenged. The hull of the bastion was a smoothly curving blankness before her, reflecting not a photon of starlight. She sensed the Black Ghost in there somewhere, watching, drawing out the moment as she was. 'Come on, you bastard,' she muttered. 'You know I'm out here. Let's see what you got.'

The black wall quivered. Then it split along a seam, revealing a pale silvery glow. When the wound stopped dilating it was a vertical slit hundreds of metres long, more than wide enough for the palette to pass.

'I can't see inside,' Jul said.

'Our suit sensors don't work,' Hella said, sounding alarmed.

'But the invitation's clear,' Hex said tightly. She brushed her hands forward.

The walls of the bastion slid past her; the fortress's hull looked no more than paper-thin. Twenty metres inside the hull she brought the palette to a stop. Her visor showed her nothing but empty space, a sphere kilometres wide filled with a cold silver-grey glow.

Then the ur-Ghost hide around her began to crumple and blister, and a harsher light broke through, shining directly on her. She threw up her hands to protect her vision. She heard the others cry out. The hide, scorched, crumbled and fell away.

Cautiously she lowered her arms. Now she could see what the sensors hadn't been allowed to show her. This space wasn't empty at all. It was filled with Silver Ghosts, spheres like droplets of molten metal, and ur-Ghosts of every shape and size, faceted and spiny, ranked around her in a hexagonal array that filled space as far as she could see. They were motionless, positioned with utter accuracy, objects of geometry rather than life. And, scattered through the ranks of silent Ghosts, lanterns pulsed, blue-white: models of the pulsar that was destroying the world, they were marks of adherence to the Ghosts' Destroyer god.

This was nothing like the way humans had seen Ghosts behave before, over centuries of contact and warfare. The command of the Black Ghost, here at the heart of its empire, was total.

Hex's palette-ship hung like a bit of flotsam before this symmetrical horde. With their skin covers burned away, her crew sat cross-legged in their little hollows, cowering. 'Everybody OK?'

'What do you think?' Jul said.

Borno was staring at the arrayed Ghosts greedily. 'Lethe,' he said. 'There must be thousands of them.'

'Actually more than a million.' The voice, delivered through their translator boxes, was flat, impersonal, artificial.

Hex looked into the geometric centre of the sphere, for she knew that was where *it* would be; its sense of its own importance would admit nothing less. And there she saw a black fist, a sphere twice, three times the size of those clustered around it. The ranks of Ghosts parted in shining curtains, and that central dark mass slid forward.

Hex heard the harsh breathing of her crew. 'Take it easy,' she murmured. 'We've come this far—'

'I've *let* you come this far,' said the Black Ghost. 'Did you think your absurd concealment would fool me?'

'Actually no,' Hex said. 'I thought you would be so arrogant you would let us in anyhow. You're very predictable.'

The Black Ghost rolled before them, its coating black as the inside of her own skull. Hex was guessing at the psychology of an alien being exceptional even among its own kind. Well, the Black Ghost showed some characteristics of humanity, and no human, especially the arrogant sort, liked to be mocked.

Almost experimentally, Hex raised her arm and held it out straight, pointing at the Black Ghost. An energy weapon was built into the sleeve of her suit. She fired; her suit reported the energy drain. But there was no sign of the discharge.

Her crew quickly tried the other weapons at their disposal. Nothing worked. With an angry cry Borno even hurled his knife. It crumbled to dust before it left his hand.

The Black Ghost said, 'And you call me predictable?'

'We're here to kill you, you bag of shit,' Borno said.

'To kill me, yes. Humans walk in death. Each Ghost is a complete ecological unit. When we went into space we brought the life of our world with us. Whereas you killed off your ecology, killed the world that produced you, all of it except yourselves, and the pests and parasites too wily to be eradicated. You even call us *Ghosts*, named after imaginary creatures you associate with death. How appropriate.'

'And what about you?' Hella asked. 'How many humans have you slaughtered – how many of your own kind have you put to the flame?'

'Ah, but I am different. I relish death, as you do. Can you see my black hull? These others are silvered to save their heat. I relish the obscenity of waste – as you do. I am like you. Or I am like our Destroyer god of old.'

'Your own kind despise you,' Borno said.

'That may be. That is why I brought back these others . . .' Hex's translator box interpolated, *the ur-Ghosts*. 'These, forged in the cold desperation of our race's most difficult age, don't deny what they are. It is strange. Once the ur-Ghosts were called back from space, to help save a dying world. Now I have called them again, back from the deeper darkness of the past, to help me save my kind from humans.'

'It's crazy,' Hella whispered.

'So you have us,' Hex said. 'What now?'

'You will serve me. Three of you will be given to my ur-Ghosts, my scientists. We will drain you of what you know, and then use you to explore ways of killing humans. Oh, you will be bred first; we are running short of laboratory animals. The fourth will be flayed, kept alive, and sent back where you came from. Perhaps *you*, the commander. A warning, you see; a statement of intent. Don't you think I know human psychology well?'

'Not well enough,' Borno said.

Hex snapped, 'Gunner—'

'For the Engineers!'

With a roar Borno straightened his legs and hurled himself out of his palette station, straight at the Ghost's bland black hide. In mid-flight his suit slit open and fell away, leaving him naked save for underwear, his head, hands and feet bare. His last breath frosted in the vacuum, his mouth gaping. But he held out his hands like claws.

Jul screamed, 'What's he doing? He's killing himself!'

Hex, stunned, could only watch.

Borno landed on the Ghost's night-dark hide and grabbed big handfuls, pulling and crumpling. The Black Ghost rolled, trying to shake off its assailant. Around it the other Ghosts bobbed, agitated, but they had no way to help; they couldn't fire on Borno for fear of hitting the Black Ghost itself.

Then Borno took a mouthful of hide, bit down hard, and arched his back. The Ghost's hide ripped, and a clear fluid laced with crimson boiled within the wound. Borno's eyes were bleeding now, his ears too, but he dug into the Black Ghost with his teeth and nails, the only weapons he had left.

'We have to help him,' Hella called. She breathed hard; Hex sensed her psyching herself up to follow Borno. 'Are you with me?'

'All right,' Hex said. 'On my mark—'

Before they could move one of the Ghosts broke ranks. A perfect silver sphere, it swept down purposefully on the Black Ghost and its clinging human assailant. A slit opened in its own belly, a weapon nozzle protruded – and a projectile fired neatly into the black hide through the wound Borno had opened. The Black Ghost emitted no sound, but it quivered and thrashed. Borno clung on, but he was limp now.

And every other Ghost among the million arrayed around them froze in place.

As the Black Ghost suffered its death throes, the assassin came drifting to Borno's vacated station.

Hex asked, 'Integumentary?'

Hella said, 'How do you keep *doing* this?'

'I suggest you get us out of here, pilot,' said the Ghost. 'Without leadership the troops are paralysed, but they will react soon. If you want to live—'

'Not without Borno,' Jul said.

'He's already dead,' said the Ghost.

'No!'

The Integumentary spun in its station and spat another bullet, this time neatly lancing through Borno's limp body. 'Now can we go?'

Hex grimly drew her hands towards her lap. The palette shot backwards out of the bastion, and into open space.

## VII

The palette hovered at the rim of the system. The misty, dying star of the Ghosts was still visible, as was its intensely blue companion.

'They won't find you here,' the Integumentary said, still nestling in Borno's vacated pod.

Commodore Teel's disembodied head appeared before Hex. 'So the Black Ghost is dead. Good. Now we will see how the war turns out. You did well, Hex.'

'Borno did well.'

'He will be remembered.'

The Integumentary seemed to feel its plan had worked out as it hoped. It had been able to penetrate the Black Ghost's bastion, even smuggle in a weapon so crude it wasn't picked up by the defensive systems. But it could never have penetrated the Black Ghost's hide if not for Borno's attack, which the Black Ghost clearly hadn't anticipated.

Teel said, 'So the most powerful Ghost in generations was defeated by human qualities: Borno's raw anger and courage, and the Black Ghost's own arrogance.'

The Integumentary murmured, 'And what could be more human than savagery and arrogance?'

Hex was still trying to understand what had happened. 'Ghost, when your sun died, there was a bloody battle for survival. You've spent a million years denying that about yourselves. But the Black Ghost saw it was precisely that streak of primitive brutality you had to rediscover to fight humanity. It might even have succeeded. But you couldn't bear the image of yourself it showed you, could you?'

The Integumentary said, 'The Black Ghost was an anomaly. This is not what we are, what we aspire to be.'

Teel looked at Hex. 'Pilot, it isn't just their past that the Ghosts want to expunge, but what they have glimpsed of their future – or anyhow that's what the analysts in the Commission for Historical Truth have made of this incident.'

It was a question of natural selection. For centuries, Ghosts had been losing battles to humanity. Only those capable of dealing with humans

– of anticipating human intentions, of *thinking* like a human – survived to breed. 'It's a selection pressure,' Teel said. 'Only those Ghosts who are most like us have been surviving. So maybe it's not surprising that there should emerge a Black Ghost, a Ghost so like a human it organises its own hierarchical society, fights a war like a human commander. What do you think about that, Ghost?'

The Integumentary rose up out of the palette cradle. 'I am relieved our business together is done. The Black Ghost is dead. The exploitation of interdimensional energy will be closed down, the research destroyed. It is a weapon too dangerous to be used.'

'Until we rediscover it,' Hella murmured.

Teel wasn't done yet. 'You can't stand this, can you, Ghost? You needed humanity to resolve this problem among yourselves. And to do it, *you had to think like a human yourself*, didn't you?'

The Integumentary said, 'It is true that we would rather go to extinction than to become like you. Is that something you take pride in? Pilot, the ancient star system will be restored to its proper time. You have only seconds before the energy pulse that will follow. I tell you this as a courtesy. We will not speak again.' And it disappeared, as if folding out of existence.

Jul said, 'Seconds?'

Hella said, 'How fast can this thing go, pilot?'

'Let's find out,' Hex said, and she flexed her gloved hands. 'Everybody locked in? Three, two, one—'

*The Black Ghost inspired its kind's last effective stand. After its fall, the Ghosts' political unity fragmented, and they fell back everywhere.*

*For the Ghosts, the consequence of defeat was dire.*

# THE GHOST PIT

AD 7524

As soon as the Spline dropped out of hyperspace our flitter burst from its belly.

After our long enclosure in the crimson interior of the huge living ship, it was like being reborn. Even though I had to share this adventure with L'Eesh, my spirits surged.

'Pretty system,' L'Eesh said. He was piloting the flitter with nonchalant ease. He was about sixty years old, some three times my age, a *lot* more experienced – and he didn't miss a chance to let me know.

Well, pretty it was. The Jovian and its satellites were held in a stable gravitational embrace at the corners of a neat equilateral triangle, the twin moons close enough to the parent to be tidally locked. And beyond it all I glimpsed a faint blue mesh thrown across the stars: an astonishing sight, a net large enough to enclose this giant planet, with struts half a million kilometres long.

I grinned. That netting, that monstrous grandiosity, was typical Ghost. It was proof that this Jovian system was indeed a Ghost pit – a new pit, an unopened pit.

Which was why its discovery had sent such a stir through the small, scattered community of Ghost hunters. And why L'Eesh and I were prepared to fire ourselves into it without even looking where we were going. We were determined to be the first.

Already we were sweeping down towards one of the moons. Beneath a dusty atmosphere the surface was brick red, a maze of charred pits.

'Very damaged landscape,' I said. 'Impact craters? Looks as if it's been bombed flat . . .'

'You know,' said L'Eesh laconically, 'there's a bridge between those moons.'

At first his words made no sense. Then I peered up. He was right: a fine arch leapt from the surface of one moon and crossed space to the other.

'Lethe,' I swore. I couldn't understand how I hadn't seen it immediately. But then, you don't *look* for such a thing.

L'Eesh grunted. 'I hope you have a strong stomach, Raida. Hily never did. Like mother like daughter—'

He had me off balance. 'What about my mother?'

'*Bogeys.*'

And suddenly they were on us, a dozen angular craft that looped around the flitter, coming from over our heads like falling fists.

L'Eesh yanked at the stick. We flipped backwards and sped away. But the bogeys were faster. I cowered, an ancient, useless reflex; I wasn't used to being in a dogfight that humans aren't dominating.

'Remarkable accelerations,' murmured L'Eesh. 'An automated defence?'

The bogeys surrounded us in a tidy cloud, and hosed us with a crimson haze.

'There is nothing we can do.' L'Eesh sat stoically at his controls; blood-red light glinted from the planes of his shaven scalp.

Abruptly the bogeys tipped sideways and squirted away. As the mist cleared I let out my breath.

At first it seemed the unexpected assault had done us no harm. We were still descending to the moon, which was flattening out from a closed-in crimson ball to a landscape beneath us.

Now my softscreen filled with the mournful face of Pohp, the agent who had brought us both here, calling from the Spline. But her image was broken up, her words indistinct: *classification of . . . Ghost . . . vacuum energy adjustment, which . . .*

A warning chimed.

'Raida, help me.' L'Eesh was battling his controls. 'We've lost telemetry from the portside drive.'

It was worse than that. Through the crystal hull I saw a drive pod tumbling away, surrounded by a cloud of frozen fluids and bits of hull material.

I tried my controls. With half our drive gone, they felt soggy.

I looked up to that impossible bridge, a line drawn across the sky, aloof from our petty struggles. There are times when you just can't believe what you are seeing. A survival mechanism, I guess.

More alarms.

'Another drive pod has cut out.' L'Eesh sat back, pressing his fists against his softscreen in genteel frustration.

We tipped down, suddenly buffeted by thickening air. A pink-white plasma glow gathered, hiding the stars, the bridge, and the land below.

There was a howling noise. My pressure suit stiffened suddenly. Peering down I saw a hole in the hull, a ragged gash reaching right through the hull's layers; I stared, fascinated, as fluffy clouds shot past my feet.

L'Eesh turned in his couch. 'Listen to me, child. We may yet survive this. The flitter is designed to keep us alive, come what may. It should be able to withstand a gliding descent from orbit on a world this size.'

'But we're breaking up.'

His grin was feral. 'Let's hope the hull ablates slowly enough.'

The blasted landscape flattened out further. The sky above had turned pink-brown. Rocks and craters shot beneath the prow. There was a last instant of calm, of comparative control. I clung to my couch.

The flitter bellied down.

Orange dust flew. The nose crumpled. The inertial suspension failed and I was flung forward. Foam erupted around me. I was trapped, blinded, feeling nothing.

Then the foam popped and burst, quickly evaporating, and I was dropped into rust-red dirt.

. . . *Down*, just like that, deposited in silence and stillness and orange-brown light, amid settling debris.

I brushed at the dirt with my gloved hand. There were bits of white embedded in the dust: shards and splinters that crackled, the sound carrying through my suit hood. *Bones?*

L'Eesh was lying on his back, surrounded by wreckage, peering up at the muddy sky. He barked laughter. 'What a ride. Lethe, what a ride!' He lifted his hands over his head, and bits of bone tumbled in the air around him, languidly falling in the low gravity.

When I was a kid, rogue Ghost cruisers still sailed through the less populated sectors of the Expansion. As parties of hunters scoured those great tangles of silvery rope, my mother would send me into Ghost nurseries armed with knives and harpoons. *Watch your back*, she would call, as I killed. *Use your head. There is always an option.* I was five years old, six.

That was how I started in this business.

L'Eesh was the most formidable Ghost hunter of his generation. And he was here because he was after what I believed to be rightfully my prey.

Once this system, in the crowded Sagittarius Arm, had been at the heart of the range of the Silver Ghosts. But the Third Expansion had rolled right through here, a wave of human colonisation heading for the centre of the Galaxy. Until a few decades back some Ghost nests survived within the Expansion itself; that fast-moving front left great unexplored voids behind it. My mother, a hunter herself, took part in such actions. She never came back from her last operation, the cleansing of a world called Snowball.

But those nests have long been cleaned out. The last wild Ghosts have retreated to their pits – like the one L'Eesh and I had gotten ourselves stuck in.

I had thought I would be first here. I had been dismayed to find L'Eesh had grabbed a place on the same Spline transport as me. Though I had warily gone along with his proposal that we should pool our resources and split the proceeds, I wasn't about to submit to him.

Not even in the mess we found ourselves in now.

We dug ourselves out of the dirt.

Our med systems weren't functioning, so we put each other through brisk checks – limbs, vision, coordination. Then we tested out the equipment. Our pressure suits were lightweight skinsuits, running off backpacks of gen-enged algae. The comms system worked on pale blue bioluminescent glyphs that crawled over each suit's surface.

I poked around in the dirt. Remnants of struts and hull plates crumbled. The little ship had broken up, sacrificing the last of its integrity to save us as it was designed to, and then it had broken up some more. There was nothing to salvage. We had the suits we wore, and nothing else.

L'Eesh was watching me. His augmented Eyes were like steel balls in his head; when he blinked you could hear the whirr of servomotors. 'It doesn't surprise you that your suit works, does it? Even here – it doesn't occur to you to ask the question.'

I glared back, not wishing to give him any satisfaction.

He dug a weapon out of the scattered wreckage of the flitter; it looked like a starbreaker hand-gun. 'This is a Ghost pit.' He crushed the gun like a dead leaf. 'Stuff like this happens. Pits are pockets of spacetime where nothing works right, where you can't rely on even the fundamental laws of physics and chemistry. But the Ghosts always arrange it so that living things are conserved – including us, and the little critters that live in our backpacks. You see? We know very little of how all this works. We don't even know how they could tell what is alive. And *all of this is engineered* – remember that.'

I knew all this, of course. 'You're full of shit, L'Eesh.'

He grinned. At some point in his life his teeth had been replaced by a porcelain sheet. 'You bet I am. Shit from battlefields a thousand years old.' He had an air of wealth, control, culture, arrogance; he was effortlessly superior to me. 'We're on our own down here. Pohp may be able to see us. But she can't speak to us, can't reach us.' He took a deep breath, as if he could smell the air. 'What now, Raida?'

There was one obvious place to go. 'The bridge between the moons.'

'It must be a hundred kilometres away,' he said. 'Our transportation options are limited.'

'Then we walk.'

He shrugged, dropped the remains of the gun. There was nothing to carry, nothing to be done with the remains of the flitter. Without preamble, he set off.

I followed. I'd sooner be watching L'Eesh's back than the other way around.

Soon our lower suits were stained bright orange by the dust.

This trapped moon was too small for tectonic cycling. The land was old, eroded to dust, mountains and crater rims worn flat. Iron oxides made the ground and the air glow crimson. On the horizon, dust devils spun silently. It was a museum of dust, that had nowhere to go.

Everywhere you looked – every time you dug a trench with your toe – you found more bits of bone. Perhaps there had been a vast flood, I thought, that had washed up this vast assemblage of remains. Or perhaps there had been a drought, and this was a place where animals had gathered around the drying water holes, fighting to suck at the mud, while the predators watched and waited.

Or maybe it was a battlefield.

Whatever the story of this place, it was long over. Nothing moved, save us and the dust. Not even the sun: the 'days' here lasted as long as an orbit of the moon around the Jovian, which was about ten standard days.

Over it all loomed the bridge. It rose lumpily from beyond the horizon. It looked crude – almost unfinished – but it became a thread that arrowed through the clouds, making the sky stretch into a third dimension.

And what a complex sky it was. The sister moon scowled down, scarred and bitter, and the Jovian primary loomed massively on the horizon, the corners of a great celestial triangle forever frozen in place.

The Spline ship rolled over the horizon, tracking its low orbit. It was like a moon itself, a mottled, meaty moon made grey by the dusty air. Even from here I could see the big green tetrahedron on its hull, the sigil of free humanity. The leathery hull-epidermis of the Spline was pocked with sensor arrays; we had spent a lot of money to ensure our capture of any wild Ghosts was recorded and certified, to preserve the value of the hides. Of course our problem was we had no way to get back up to the Spline, which we could see so clearly.

As we walked L'Eesh studied me, his inhuman Eyes glistening. 'It looks as if we are going to spend some time together.' I didn't reply.

'So. Tell me about yourself.'

'I'm not interested in playing head games with you, L'Eesh.'

'So defensive, little Raida! I did know your mother.'

'That doesn't give you the right to know me.' I saw a chance to get the upper hand. 'Listen to me, L'Eesh. I think I know what's going on here.'

*Know your prey*. This was my first pit, but I had prepared myself. The Ghosts seem to use only a small number of pit types – our flitter had been designed to cope with some of the common variants – and when Pohp sent us her cryptic message, I knew what she must have been talking about.

Vacuum energy: even in 'empty' space there has to be some energy, a ground energy level, because of quantum uncertainty. What was important for us was the effect this had – and the effect of the Ghosts' tinkering.

'Think of an atom,' I said. 'Like a little solar system with the electrons as planets, right? But what keeps a negative electron out of the positive nucleus?'

'Vacuum energy?'

'Right. The electron, and everything else, is surrounded by a sea of vacuum energy. And as fast as the electron loses energy and tries to spiral in, the vacuum sea supplies some more. So the electron stays in orbit.' I peered up at the complicated sky. 'Those weapons extracted some of the vacuum energy from the substance of our flitter. Or lowered the level of the background, so the vacuum energy drained away: something like that. All the electrons spiralled in, and molecular structures fell apart.'

L'Eesh listened, his face unreadable. Presumably he knew all this. His silence was more impressive than my babbling, even to me.

We walked on.

I felt naked without a weapon. I dug around among a thick patch of bones. I found a long, thin shaft that might have been a thigh-bone. I cracked it against a rock; it splintered, leaving a satisfactorily vicious point. As we walked I put myself through elementary drill routines.

A spear will take down a Ghost, but you have to be careful. The key resource you get from a Ghost is his hide – a perfectly reflective heat trap, with a thousand applications. Now that Ghosts are so rare, wild hides are a luxury item. People sell little squares and triangles of hide for use as charms, curios: this was, after all, a lucky species that survived the death of its sun, so the story goes.

Anyhow if you come at a Ghost with a jabbing weapon, you should try to get your spear into the carcase along the spin axis, where the hide is a little thinner, and you won't rip it unnecessarily. Then you just follow the trail of excrement and blood and heat until he dies, which might take a day or two. *Ghosts don't leave spoor*, my mother used to say. *So you have to cut him an asshole.*

L'Eesh was watching me analytically. 'You're, what, twenty, twenty-one? No children yet?'

'Not until I can afford to buy them out of the Coalition draft.'

He nodded. 'As Hily did you. I knew her ambition for you. It's good to see it realised so well. It must have been hard for you when she died. I imagine you got thrown into a cadre by the Commissaries – right?'

'I won't talk to you about my mother, L'Eesh.'

'As you wish. But you need to keep your mind clear, little Raida. And you might want to think about saving your energy. We have a long way to go.'

I worked with my bone spear and tried to ignore him.

\*

We had to sleep in our suits, of course. I dug a shallow trench in the dust. I couldn't shut out the crimson light. I slept in patches.

I woke up in my own stink. The recycled gloop from my hood nipples already tasted stale, my skinsuit was chafing in a dozen places, and I felt bruises from that landing that hadn't registered at the time.

If the sun had moved across the sky at all, I couldn't see it.

It's a strange thing, but it wasn't until that second 'morning' that I took seriously the possibility that I might die here. I guess I had been distracted by the hunt, my conflict with L'Eesh. Or maybe I just lack imagination. Anyhow my adrenaline rush was long gone; I was numb, flat, feeling beaten.

Through that endless day, we walked on.

We came to what might once have been a township. There was little left but a gridwork of foundations, a few pits like cellars, bits of low wall. I thought I could see a sequence, of older buildings constructed of massive marble-like blocks, later structures made of what looked like the local sandstone or else bits of broken-up marble ruins.

All of it trashed, burned out, knocked flat.

I squatted, chewing on a glucose tab.

L'Eesh, his suit scuffed and filthy, began poking around a large battleship-shaped mound of rubble. 'You know, there's something odd here. I thought this was a fort, or perhaps some equivalent of a cathedral. But it looks for all the world as if it *crashed* here.'

'You don't make aircraft from brick.'

'Whatever made such a vast, ungainly structure fly through the air is gone now. Nevertheless there was clearly once a pretty advanced civilisation here. On the way in I glimpsed extensive ruins. And some of those impact craters looked deliberately placed. This whole world is an arena of war. But it seems to have been a war that was fought with interplanetary weapons, and then flying brick fortresses, and at last fire and clubs.

'It's likely both moons were inhabited. Life could have been sparked on either moon, in some tidal puddle stirred by the Jovian parent. And then panspermia would work, spores wafting on meteorite winds, two worlds developing in parallel, cross-fertilising . . .'

On he talked. I wasn't interested. I was here for Ghosts, not archaeology.

I waited until he took the lead, and we walked on, leaving the ruined township behind.

*

Another 'night', another broken sleep in the dirt. Another 'day' on that endless plain. In places the surface had been blasted to glass; it prickled my feet as I staggered across it. We didn't seem to get any closer to that damn bridge.

We had nothing to do but talk.

A lot of it was L'Eesh's refined bragging. 'You know, the Commission was always very tolerant of us, we hunters. Under the Coalition, you aren't supposed to get old and rich. The species is the thing! Of course the Coalition found us useful, in the closing phases of its war with the Ghosts. It is not comfortable to feel one has been manipulated, even controlled. But it has been glorious nevertheless.'

It turned out L'Eesh had taken part in that great Ghost massacre on Snowball.

'Snowball was actually the first Ghost planet anybody found. Did you know that? The site of first contact two thousand years ago. When Ghost numbers collapsed the Commission slapped on conservation orders – some nonsense about preserving cultural diversity – but there wasn't a great deal of will behind the policing. On the day the orders were lifted we were already in orbit around Snowball. We made a huge circle around the major Ghost nest, with aerial patrols overhead, and we just worked our way in on foot, firing at will, until we met in the centre. The major challenge was counting up the carcases.

'So it went: while those big nests lasted it was a feeding frenzy. You were born too late, Raida. You know, a thousand years ago the Ghosts' pits of twisted spacetime struck dread into human hearts. They were deployed as fortresses, a great wall right across the disc of the Galaxy. Magnificent! . . . And now we hunt down the Ghosts like animals, for their hides. An intelligent species hunted as game. Remarkable! Appalling!'

'Who cares? Ghosts are predators.'

'They are colony creatures,' he said gently. 'Communities of symbiotes. You have been listening to too much Commission propaganda.'

'After all you've done, why go on? Why risk your neck in places like this, for the last few scraps of hide?'

'Because some day there will be a last Ghost of all. I must be there when he is brought down. It is the logic of my whole life.'

*

We walked on, across a land like a dusty table-top. L'Eesh kept up his dogged, unspectacular plod, hour after hour. He looked determined, sharp, as if he had plenty of reserve.

I was determined not to let my own gathering weakness show. I continued to carry that bone spear.

At the end of the third 'day' we reached the bridge.

Exhausted, filthy, uncomprehending, I peered up. About a hundred paces across, it was just a rough pile of mud bricks. And yet it towered above me, reaching up to infinity.

L'Eesh was breathing hard, sucking water. 'Magnificent,' he said. 'Mad. They built a brick tower to reach to heaven! . . .'

I went exploring.

I came to a crumbled gap in the base of the tower. I crawled into an unlit interior. My suit's low-output bioluminescent lamp glowed. I craned my neck. The bridge rose up vertically above me, a tunnel into the sky.

Metal gleamed amid the rubble on the floor.

I kicked aside half-bricks and uncovered a squat cuboid about half my height. It was featureless except for a fat red button. When I pressed the button the cube rose magically into the air, trailing a rose-coloured sparkle, like the bogeys' vacuum-energy weapon; I kept out of the way of the wake. When I released the button the cube dropped again.

It was pretty obviously a lifting palette.

There was another palette buried in the wall of the bridge – and further up another, and another beyond that.

'Now we know how they made their castles fly,' L'Eesh said. 'And how they raised this bridge.' He was standing beside me, his suit glowing green. I saw he had scraped a channel in mould-softened brick with his thumb. Beneath it, something gleamed, copper-brown. 'It's not metal,' he said. 'Not even like Xeelee construction material.'

'Maybe that's the original structure.'

'Yes. No suite of moons is stable enough to allow the building of a brick bridge between them; the slightest tidal deflection would be enough to bring it tumbling down. There must be something more advanced here – perhaps the moons' orbits are themselves regulated somehow . . . The bridge itself is just a clumsy shell. The inhabitants must have constructed it after the intervention.'

'What intervention?'

He sighed. 'Think, child. Try to understand what you see around you. Imagine millennia of war between the two moons.'

'What was there to fight over?'

'That scarcely ever matters. Perhaps it was just that these were sibling worlds. What rivalry is stronger? Finally the moons were ruined, serving only as a backdrop for the unending battles – until peacemakers sent down blood-red rays, vacuum energy beams that turned the weapons to dust.'

'Peacemakers? Silver Ghosts?'

'Well, it's possible,' he said. 'Though it's not characteristic of Ghost behaviour. It was a draconian solution: a quarantine of technology, the trashing of two spacefaring civilisations . . . How arrogant. Almost human.'

I felt uncomfortable discussing Ghosts with human-like motives. 'What about these lift palettes?'

'It makes a certain sense,' he said. 'From the point of view of a meddling Ghost anyhow. A simple technology to help the survivors rebuild their ruined worlds – something you surely couldn't turn into a weapon – but it didn't work out.' He smiled thinly. 'Instead the populations used the gifts to build this insane bridge.'

'How is this going to help us find the Ghosts?'

He seemed surprised by the question. 'There are no Ghosts here, child.'

Of course he was right. I saw it as soon as he said it. Ghosts spread out over every world they infest. We would have seen them by now, if they were here. The Ghosts had intervened here but they had not inhabited this world. I'd known this for a while, I guess, but I hadn't wanted to face the possibility that I'd thrown away my life for nothing.

I slumped to the littered floor. The strength seemed to drain out of me.

In retrospect I can see his tactics. It was as if he had designed the whole situation as a vast trap. He waited until I had reached the bottom – at the maximum point of my tiredness, as I was crushed with disappointment at the failure of the hunt, surrounded by alien madness.

*Then* he struck.

The length of bone came looming out of the dark, without warning, straight at my head.

\*

I ducked. The bone clattered against the wall. 'L'Eesh, you bastard—'

'It's just business, little Raida.'

My heart hammered. I backed away until my spine was pressed against the rough wall. 'You've found something you want. The vacuum-energy weapons. Is that it?'

'Not what we came for, but I'll turn a profit, if I can manage to get off this moon.'

'It's not as if you need to do this, to rob me,' I said bitterly.

He nodded. 'True. You actually have the stronger motive here. Which is why I have to destroy you.' He spoke patiently, as if instructing a child. He raised the bone, its bulging end thick, hefting it like a club, and he moved towards me, his movements oily, powerful.

I felt weak before his calm assurance. He was better than me, and always would be; the logic of the situation was that I should just submit.

In desperation I jumped onto the lift palette – it was like standing on a bobbing raft – and stamped on the button. I rose immediately, passing beyond the reach of his swinging club. I had been too fast, faster than his reactions. The advantage of youth.

But L'Eesh easily prised another palette out of the wall and followed me up into the darkness.

My palette accelerated, bumping against walls that were as rough as sandpaper. L'Eesh's green glow followed me, bioluminescent signals flickering.

Thus our ascension, two dead people racing into the sky.

On an interplanetary scale the tunnel arched, but from my petty human point of view it rose straight up. All I could see was a splash of bio light on the crude brickwork around me, sliding past, blurred by my speed.

L'Eesh tried to defeat me with words.

'Imagine, Raida,' he said softly. 'They must have come here from across the moon, carrying their mud bricks, a global pilgrimage that must have lasted generations. What a vision! They sacrificed everything – abandoned their farms, trashed their biosphere down to the slime on the rocks . . . And you know what? *The two populations must have worked together to build their bridge, so they could continue their war.* I mean, you couldn't build it just from one end or the other, could you? They cooperated so they could get at each other and carry on fighting. In the end, the war became the most important thing in their universe. More important than life, the continuation of the species.'

'Insane,' I whispered.

'Ah, but once *we* built vast structures, waged terrible wars, all in the names of gods we have long forgotten. And are we so different now? What of our magnificent Galaxy-spanning Expansion? Isn't that a grandiose folly built around an idea, a mad vision of cosmic destiny? Who do you think we more resemble – this moon's warmongers or its peacemakers?'

I was exhausted. I clung to my scrap of ancient technology as it careened up into the dark.

That sleek voice whispered in my ear, on and on. 'You can never live up to Hily's memory, little Raida. You do see that, don't you? You needn't feel you have failed. For you could never have succeeded . . . I saw your mother die.'

'Shut up, L'Eesh.'

'I was at her side—'

'Shut *up*.'

He fell silent, waiting.

I knew he was manipulating me, but I couldn't help but ask. 'Tell me.'

'She was shot in the back.'

'*Who?*'

'It doesn't matter. She was killed for her catch, her trophies. Her death wasn't dishonourable. She must even have expected it. We are a nation of thieves, you see, we hunters. You shouldn't feel bitter.'

'I don't feel anything.'

'Of course not.'

His brooding glow was edging closer.

I closed my eyes. What would Hily have said? *Use your head. There is always an option.*

I took my hand off the button. The palette rocked to a halt. 'Get it over,' I panted.

Now he had nothing to say; his words had fulfilled their purpose. He closed, that eerie green glow sliding over the crude brickwork.

And I jammed my hand back on the button. My palette lumbered into motion. I watched the exhaust gather into a thick crimson mist below me.

L'Eesh hurtled up into the mist, crouching on his palette – which abruptly cracked apart and crumbled. Stranded in the air, he arced a little higher, and then began to fall amid the fragments.

I sat there until my heart stopped rattling. Then I followed him down.

'My fall is slow,' he said, analytic, observing. 'Low gravity, high air resistance. You could probably retrieve me. But you won't.'

'Come on, L'Eesh. It's business, just as you said. You know what happened. These palettes extract their energy from the vacuum energy sea.'

'Leaving some kind of deficit in their wake, into which I flew. Yes? And so we both die here.' He forced a laugh. 'Ironic, don't you think? In the end we've cooperated to kill each other. Just like the inhabitants of these desolate moons.'

But I was thinking it over. 'Not necessarily.'

'What?'

'Suppose I head up to the midpoint of the bridge and burn my way through the wall. Pohp ought to see me and come in for me. I'd surely be far enough out of the vacuum field for the Spline to approach safely.'

'What about the quarantine ships?'

'They must primarily patrol the moons' low orbits. Perhaps I'd be far enough from the surface of either moon to leave them asleep.'

He considered. 'It would take days to get there. But it might work. You have something of your mother's pragmatism, little Raida. I guess you win.'

'Maybe we both win.'

There was silence. Then he said coldly, 'Must I beg?'

'Make me an offer.'

He sighed. 'There has been a sighting of a school of Spline. Wild Spline.'

I was startled. *'Wild?'*

'These Spline are still spacegoing. But certain of their behavioural traits have reverted to an ancestral state. They believe they swim in their primordial ocean—'

I breathed, 'Nobody has ever hunted a Spline.'

'It would be glorious. Like the old days. Hily would be proud.' It was as if I could hear his smile.

I was content with the deal. It was enough that I'd beaten him; I didn't need to destroy him.

Not yet. Not until I knew who killed my mother.

We argued percentages, all the way down towards the light.

*The human victory was probably always inevitable. We were better at waging war: after all, we had spent a hundred thousand years practising on each other.*

*But the war transformed humanity too. After seventeen hundred years of conflict the Coalition's grip on mankind, body and soul, was total.*

*We undying kept out of sight, tending our own long-term concerns. But we never went away.*

*The Expansion swept on across the face of the Galaxy, centralised, united, purposeful, ideological, purified by war.*

*It was not healthy to be in its way.*

# THREE

## ASSIMILATION

# LAKES OF LIGHT

## AD 10,102

The Navy ferry stood by. From the ship's position, several stellar diameters away, the cloaked star was a black disc, like a hole cut out of the sky.

Pala was to descend to the star alone in a flitter – alone save for her Virtual tutor, Commissary Dano.

The flitter, light and invisible as a bubble, swept inwards, silent save for the subtle ticking of its instruments. The star had about the mass of Earth's sun and, though it was dark, Pala imagined she could feel that immense mass tugging at her.

Her heart hammered. This really was a star, but it was somehow cloaked, made perfectly black save for pale, pixel-small specks, flaws in the dark mask, specks that were lakes of light. She'd seen the Navy scouts' reports, even studied the Virtuals, but until this moment she hadn't been able to believe in the extraordinary reality.

But she had a job to do, and had no time to be overawed. The Navy scouts said there were humans down there – humans living with, or somehow *on* the star itself. Relics of an ancient colonising push, they now had to be reabsorbed into the greater mass of mankind, their energies engaged in the project of the Expansion. But the Galaxy was wide, and Pala, just twenty-five years old, was the only Missionary who could be spared for this adventure.

Dano was a brooding presence beside her, peering out with metallic Eyes. His chest did not rise and fall, no breath whispered from his mouth. He was projected from an implant in her own head, so that she could never be free of him, and she had become resentful of him. But Pala had grown up on Earth, under a sky so drenched with artificial light you could barely see the stars, and right now, suspended in this

207

three-dimensional arena, she was so disoriented she was grateful for the company even of a Commissary's avatar.

And meanwhile that hole in the sky, the cloaked star, swelled until its edges passed out of her field of view.

The flitter dipped and swivelled, and swept along the line of the star's equator. Now she was flying low over a darkened plain, with a starry night sky above her. The star was so vast, its diameter more than a hundred times Earth's, that she could see no hint of curvature in its laser-straight horizon.

'Astonishing,' she said. 'It's like a geometrical exercise.'

Dano murmured, 'And yet, to the best of our knowledge, the photosphere of a star roils not a thousand kilometres beneath us, and if not for this – sphere, whatever it is – we would be destroyed in an instant, a snowflake in the mouth of a furnace. What's your first conclusion, Missionary?'

Pala hesitated before answering. It was so recently that she had completed her assessments in the Academies on Earth, so recently that the real Dano had, grudgingly, welcomed her to the great and ancient enterprise that was the Commission for Historical Truth, that she felt little confidence in her own abilities. And yet the Commission must have faith in her, or else they wouldn't have committed her to this mission.

'It is artificial,' she said. 'The sphere. It must be.'

'Yes. Surely no natural process could wrap up a star so neatly. And if it is artificial, who do you imagine might be responsible?'

'The Xeelee,' she said immediately. Involuntarily she glanced up at the crowded stars, bright and vivid here, five thousand light years from Earth. In the hidden heart of the Galaxy mankind's ultimate foe lurked; and surely it was only the Xeelee who could wield such power as this.

There was a change in the darkness ahead. She saw it first as a faint splash of light near the horizon, but as the flitter flew on that splash opened out into a rough disc that glowed pale blue-green. Though a speck against the face of the masked star, it was sizeable in itself – perhaps as much as a hundred kilometres across.

The flitter came to rest over the centre of the feature. It was like a shard of Earth, stranded in the night: she looked down at the deep blue of open water, the mistiness of air, the pale green of cultivated land and forest, even a greyish bubbling that must be a town. All of this was contained under a dome, shallow and flat and all but transparent. Outside the dome what looked like roads, ribbons of silver, stretched away into the dark. And at the very centre of this strange scrap of landscape was a shining sheet of light.

'People,' Dano said. 'Huddling around that flaw in the sphere, that lake of light.' He pointed. 'I think there's some kind of port at the edge of the dome. You'd better take the flitter down by hand.'

Pala touched the small control panel in front of her, and the flitter began its final descent.

They cycled through a kind of airlock, and emerged into fresh air, bright light.

It wasn't quite daylight. The light was diffuse, like a misty day on Earth, and it came not from the sky but from the ground, to be reflected back by mirrors on spindly poles. The atmosphere was too shallow for the 'sky' to be blue, and through the dome's distortion Pala saw smeared-out star fields. But the 'sky' contained pale, streaky clouds.

A dirt road led away from the airlock into the domed ecology. Looking along the road Pala glimpsed clusters of low buildings, the green of forest clumps and cultivated fields. She could even smell wood smoke.

Dano sniffed. 'Lethe. *Agriculture*. Typical Second Expansion.'

This pastoral scene wasn't a landscape Pala was familiar with. Under Coalition ideology Earth was dominated by sprawling Conurbations, and fields in which nanotechnologies efficiently delivered food for the world's billions. Even so this was a human scene, and she felt oddly at home here.

But she wasn't at home. The Navy scouts had determined that the stellar sphere was rotating as a solid, and that this equatorial site was moving at only a little less than orbital speed. This arrangement was why they experienced such an equable gravity; if not for the compensating effects of centrifugal force, they would have been crushed by nearly thirty times Earth standard. She could *feel* none of this, but nevertheless, standing here, gazing at grass and trees and clouds, she was really soaring through space, actually circling a star in less than a standard day.

'It takes a genuine effort of will,' she said, 'to remember where we are.'

'That it does. And here comes the welcoming party,' Dano said dryly.

Two people walked steadily up the road, a man and a woman. They were both rather squat, stocky, dark. They wore simple shifts and knee-length trousers, practical clothes, clean but heavily repaired. The man might have been sixty. His hair was white, his face a moon of wrinkles. The woman was younger, perhaps not much older than Pala. She wore her black hair long and tied into a queue that nestled over her spine, quite unlike the short and severe style of the Commission. Her shift had a sunburst pattern stitched into it, a welling up of light from below.

The man spoke. 'My name is Sool. This is Bicansa. We have been delegated to welcome you.' Sool's words, in his own archaic tongue, were seamlessly translated in Pala's ears. But underneath the tinny murmuring in her ear she could hear Sool's own gravelly voice. 'I represent this community, which we call Home . . .'

'Inevitably,' Dano said.

'Bicansa comes from a community to the north of here.' Pala supposed he meant another inhabited light lake. She wondered how far away that was; she had seen nothing from the flitter.

The woman Bicansa simply watched the newcomers. Her expression seemed closed, almost sullen. She could not have been called beautiful, Pala thought; her face was too round, her chin too weak. But there was a strength in her dark eyes that intrigued Pala.

Pala made her own formal introductions. 'Thank you for inviting us to your community.' Not that these locals had had any choice. 'We are emissaries of the Commission for Historical Truth, acting on behalf of the Interim Coalition of Governance, which in turn directs and secures the Third Expansion of mankind . . .'

The man Sool listened to this with a pale smile, oddly weary. Bicansa glared.

Dano murmured, 'Shake their hands. Just as well it isn't an assessment exercise, Missionary!'

Pala cursed herself for forgetting such an elementary part of contact protocol. She stepped forward, smiling, her right hand outstretched.

Sool actually recoiled. The custom of shaking hands was rare throughout the worlds of the Second Expansion; evidently it hadn't been prevalent on Earth when that great wave of colonisation had begun. But Sool quickly recovered. His grip was firm, his hands so huge they enclosed hers. Sool grinned. 'A farmer's hands,' he said. 'You'll get used to it.'

Bicansa offered her own hand readily enough. But Pala's hand passed through the woman's, making it break up into a cloud of blocky pixels.

It was this simple test that mandated the handshake protocol. Even so, Pala was startled. 'You're a Virtual.'

'As is your own companion,' said Bicansa levelly. 'I'm close by actually – just outside the dome. But don't worry. I'm a projection, not an avatar. You have my full attention.'

Pala felt unaccountably disappointed that Bicansa wasn't really here.

Sool indicated a small car, waiting some distance away, and he offered them the hospitality of his home. They walked to the car.

Dano murmured to Pala, 'I wonder why this Bicansa hasn't shown up in person. I think we need to watch that one.' He turned to her, his cold Eyes glinting. 'Ah, but you already are – aren't you, Missionary?'

Pala felt herself blush.

Sool's village was small, just a couple of dozen buildings huddled around a scrap of grass-covered common land. There were shops and manufactories, including a carpentry and pottery works, and an inn. At the centre of the common was a lake, its edges regular – a reservoir, Pala thought. The people's water must be recycled, filtered by hidden machinery, like their air. By the shore of the lake, children played and lovers walked.

All the raw material of this human settlement had come from cometary impacts, packets of dirty ice from this star's outer system that had splashed onto the sphere since its formation. It was remarkable that this peaceful scene could have originated in such violence.

This was a farming community. In the fields beyond the village, crops grew towards the reflected glare of spindly mirror towers, waving in breezes wafted by immense pumps mounted at the dome's periphery. And animals grazed, descendants of cattle and sheep brought by the first colonists. Pala, who had never seen an animal larger than a rat, stared, astonished.

The buildings were all made of wood, neat but low, conical. Sool told the visitors the buildings were modelled after the tents the first colonists here had used for shelter. 'A kind of memorial to the First,' he said. But Sool's home, with big windows cut into the sloping roof, was surprisingly roomy and well lit. There were traces of art. On one wall hung a kind of schematic portrait, a few lines to depict a human face, lit from below by a warm yellow light.

Sool had them sit on cushions of what turned out to be stuffed animal hide, to Pala's horror. In fact everything seemed to be made of wood or animal skin. But these people could generate Virtuals, Pala reminded herself; they weren't as low tech as they seemed.

Sool confirmed that. 'When the First found this masked star they created the machinery that still sustains us – the dome, the mirror towers, the hidden machines that filter our air and water. We must maintain the machines, and we go out to bring in more water ice or frozen air.' He eyed his visitors. 'You must not think we are fallen. We are surely as technologically capable as our ancestors. But every day we acknowledge our debt to the wisdom and heroic engineering of the First.' As he said this, he touched his palms together and nodded his head reverently, and Bicansa did the same.

Pala and Dano exchanged a glance. Ancestor worship?

A slim, pretty teenage girl brought them drinks of pulped fruit. The girl was Sool's 'daughter'; it turned out his 'wife' had died some years previously. Thanks to her training Pala was familiar with such terms. The drinks were served in pottery cups, elegantly shaped and painted deep blue, with more inverted-sunburst designs. Pala wondered what dye they used to create such a rich blue.

Dano watched the daughter as she politely set a cup before himself and Bicansa; these colonists knew Virtual etiquette. Dano said, 'You obviously live in nuclear families.'

'And you don't?' Bicansa asked curiously.

'Nuclear families are a classic feature of Second Expansion cultures. You are typical of your era.' Pala smiled brightly, trying to be reassuring, but Bicansa's face was cold.

Dano asked Sool, 'And you are the leader of this community?'

Sool shook his head. 'We are few, Missionary. I'm leader of nothing but my own family, and even that only by my daughter's grace! After your scouts' first visit the Assembly asked me to speak for them. I believe I'm held in high regard; I believe I'm trusted. But I'm a delegate, not a leader. Bicansa represents her own people in the same way. We have to work together to survive; I'm sure that's obvious. In a sense we're all a single extended family here . . .'

Pala murmured to Dano, 'Eusocial, you think? The lack of a hierarchy, an elite?' Eusociality – hive living – had been found to be a common if unwelcome social outcome in crowded, resource-starved colonies.

Dano shook his head. 'No. The population density's nowhere near high enough.'

Bicansa was watching them. 'You are talking about us. Assessing us.'

'That's our job,' Dano said levelly.

'Yes, I've learned about your job,' Bicansa snapped. 'Your mighty Third Expansion that sweeps across the stars. You're here to assimilate us, aren't you?'

'Not at all,' Pala said earnestly. It was true. The Assimilation was a separate programme, designed to process the alien species encountered by the Third Expansion wavefront. Pala worked for a parallel agency, the Office of Cultural Rehabilitation which, though controlled by the same wing of the Commission for Historical Truth as the Assimilation, was intended to handle relic *human* societies implanted by earlier colonisation waves, similarly encountered by the Expansion. 'My mission is to welcome you back to a unified mankind. To introduce you to the Druz Doctrines which shape all our actions.'

Bicansa wasn't impressed. Her anger flared, obviously pent up. 'Your arrogance is dismaying,' she said. 'You've only just landed here, only just come swooping down from the sky. You're confronted by a distinct culture five thousand years old. We have our own tradition, literature, art – even our own language, after all this time. And yet you think you can make a judgement on us immediately.'

'Our judgement on your culture, or your lack of it, doesn't matter,' said Dano. 'Our mission is specific.'

'Yes. You're here to enslave us.'

Sool said tiredly, 'Now, Bicansa—'

'You only have to glance at the propaganda they've been broadcasting since their ships started to orbit over us. They'll break up our farms and use our land to feed their Expansion. And we'll be taken to work in their factories, our children sent to worlds a thousand light years away.'

'We're all in this together,' Dano said. 'The Third Expansion is a shared enterprise of all humanity. You can't hide, madam, not even here.'

Pala said, 'Anyhow it may not be like that. We're Missionaries, not the draft. We're here to find out about you. And if your culture has something distinctive to offer the Third Expansion, why then—'

'You'll spare us?' Bicansa snapped.

'Perhaps,' said Dano. He reached for his cup, but his gloved fingers passed through its substance. 'Though it will take more than a few bits of pottery.'

Sool listened to this, a deep tiredness in his sunken eyes. Pala perceived that he saw the situation just as clearly as Bicansa did, but while she was grandstanding, Sool was absorbing the pain, seeking to find a way to save his way of life.

Pala, despite all her training, couldn't help but feel a deep empathy for him. 'We're here to save you,' she insisted, longing to be reassuring. It didn't seem to work.

They were all relieved when Sool stood. 'Come,' he said. 'You should see the heart of our community, the Lake of Light.'

The Lake was another car journey away. The vehicle was small and crowded, and Dano, uncomplaining, sat with one Virtual arm embedded in the substance of the wall.

They travelled perhaps thirty kilometres inwards from the port area to the centre of the lens-shaped colony. Pala peered out at villages and farms. Mirror-masts towered over the buildings. It was as if they were driving through a forest of skeletal trees, impossibly tall, crowned by light.

'You see we are comfortable,' Sool said anxiously. 'Stable. We are at peace here, growing what we need, raising our children. This is how humans are meant to live. And there is room here, room for billions more.' That was true; Pala knew that the sphere's surface would have accommodated ten thousand Earths, more. Sool smiled at them. 'Isn't that a reason for studying us, visiting us, understanding us – for letting us be?'

'But you are static,' Dano said coolly. 'You have achieved nothing. You've sat here in the dome built by your forefathers five thousand years ago. And so have your neighbours, in the other colonies strung out along this star's equator.'

'We haven't needed any more than this,' Sool said. 'Must one expand?' But his smile was weak.

Bicansa, sitting before Pala, said nothing throughout the journey. Her neck was narrow, elegant, her hair finely brushed. Pala wished she could talk to this woman alone, but that was of course impossible.

As they approached the Lake there was a brighter glow directly ahead, like a sun rising through trees. They broke through the last line of mirror towers.

The car stopped, and they walked. Under their feet, as they neared the Lake itself, the compacted comet dirt thinned and scattered. At last Pala found herself standing on a cool, steel-grey surface – the substance of the sphere itself, the shell that enclosed a sun. It was utterly lifeless, disturbingly blank.

Dano, more practical, kneeled down and thrust his Virtual hand through the surface. Images flickered before his face, sensor readings rapidly interpreted.

'Come,' Sool said to Pala, smiling. 'You haven't seen it yet.'

Pala walked forward to the Lake of Light itself.

The universal floor was a thin skin here, and a white glow poured out of the ground to drench the dusty air. Scattered clouds shone in the light from the ground, bright against a dark sky.

As far ahead as she could see the Lake stretched away, shining. It was an extraordinary, unsettling sight, a flood of light rising up from the ground, baffling for a human sensorium evolved for landscape and sun, as if the world had been inverted. But the light was being harvested, scattered from one great mirrored dish to another, so that its life-giving glow was spread across the colony.

Sool walked forward, onto the glowing surface. 'Don't worry,' he said to Pala. 'It's hot, but not so bad here at the edge; the real heat is towards the Lake's centre. But even that is only a fraction of the star's output, of course. The sphere keeps the rest.' He held out his arms and smiled. It was as if he was floating in the light, and he cast a shadow upwards into the misty air. 'Look down.'

She saw a vast roiling ocean, almost too bright to look at directly, where huge vacuoles surfaced and burst. It was the photosphere of a star, just a thousand kilometres below her.

'Stars give all humans life,' Sool said. 'We are their children. Perhaps this is the purest way to live, to huddle close to the star-mother, to use all her energy . . .'

'Quite a pitch,' Dano murmured in her ear. 'But he's targeting you. Don't let him take you in.'

Pala felt extraordinarily excited. 'But Dano – here are people living, breathing, even growing crops, a thousand kilometres above the surface of a sun! Is it possible this is the true purpose of the sphere – *to terraform a star?*'

Dano snorted his contempt. 'You always were a romantic, Missionary. What nonsense. Stick to your duties. For instance, have you noticed that the girl has gone?'

When she looked around, she realised that it was true; Bicansa had disappeared.

Dano said, 'I've run some tests. You know what this stuff is? *Xeelee construction material*. Your first intuition was right. This cute old man and his farm animals and grandchildren are living on a Xeelee artefact. And it's just ten centimetres thick.'

'I don't understand,' she admitted.

'All this is a smokescreen. We have to go after her,' Dano said. 'Bicansa. Go to her "community in the north", wherever it is. I have a feeling that's where we'll learn the truth of this place.'

While Dano murmured this sinister stuff in her ear, Sool was still trying to get her attention. His face was underlit by sunlight, she saw, reminding her of the portrait in his home. 'You see how wonderful this is? We live on a platform, suspended over an ocean of light, and all our art, our poetry is shaped by our experience of this bounteous light. How can you even think of removing this from the spectrum of human experience?'

Pala felt hopelessly confused. 'Your culture will be preserved,' she said hopefully, still wanting to reassure him. 'In a museum.'

Sool laughed tiredly, and he walked around in the welling light.

Pala accepted they should pursue the mysterious girl, Bicansa. But she impulsively decided she had had enough of being remote from the world she had come to assess.

'Bicansa is right. We can't just swoop down out of the sky. We don't know what we're throwing away if we don't take the time to look.'

'But there is no time,' Dano said wearily. 'The Expansion front is encountering thousands of new star systems every *day*. Why do you think you're here alone?'

'Alone save for you, my Virtual conscience.'

'Don't get cocky.'

'Well, whether you like it or not, I am here, on the ground, and I'm the one making the decisions.'

And so, she decided, she wasn't going to use her flitter. She would pursue Bicansa as the native girl had travelled herself – by car, over the vacuum road laid out over the star sphere.

'You're a fool,' snapped Dano. 'We don't even know how far north her community *is*.'

He was right, of course. Pala was shocked to find out how sparse the scouts' information on this star-world was. There were light lakes scattered across the sphere from pole to pole, but away from the equator the compensating effects of centrifugal force would diminish. In their haste the scouts had assumed that no human communities would have established themselves away from the standard-gravity equatorial belt, and hadn't mapped the sphere that far out.

She would be heading into the unknown, then. She felt a shiver of excitement at the prospect. But Dano admonished her for being distracted from her purpose.

He insisted that she shouldn't use one of the locals' cars, as she had planned, but a Coalition design shipped down from the Navy ferry. And, he said, she would have to wear a cumbersome hard-carapace skinsuit the whole way. She gave in to these conditions with bad grace. It took a couple of days for the preparations to be completed, days she spent alone in the flitter at Dano's order, lest she be seduced by the bucolic comfort of Home.

At last everything was ready, and Pala took her place in the car.

She set off. The road ahead was a track of comet-core metal, laid down by human engineering across the immense face of the star sphere. To either side were scattered hillocks of ice, purple-streaked in the starlight. They were the wrecks of comets that had splashed against the unflinching floor of the sphere.

The road surface was smooth, the traction easy. The blue-green splash of the domed colony receded behind her. The star sphere was so immense it was effectively an infinite plain, and she would not see the colony pass beyond the horizon. But it diminished to a line, a scrap of light, before becoming lost in the greater blackness.

When she gave the car its head it accelerated smoothly to astounding speeds, to more than a thousand kilometres an hour. The car, a squat bug with big, tough, all-purpose tyres, was state-of-the-art Coalition engineering, and could keep up this pace indefinitely. But there were no landmarks save the meaningless hillocks of ice, the arrow-straight road laid over blackness, and despite the immense speed, it was as if she wasn't moving at all.

And, somewhere in the vast encompassing darkness ahead, another car fled.

'Xeelee construction material,' Dano whispered. 'It's like no other material we've encountered. You can't cut it, bend it, break it. Even if we could build a sphere around a star and set it spinning in the first place, it would bulge at the equator and tear itself apart. But *this* shell is perfectly spherical, despite those huge stresses, to the limits of our measurements. Some believe the construction material doesn't even belong to this universe. But it can be shaped by the Xeelee's own technology, controlled by gadgets we call "flowers".'

'It doesn't just appear out of nowhere.'

'Of course not. Even the Xeelee have to obey the laws of physics. Construction material seems to be manufactured by the direct conversion of radiant energy into matter, one hundred per cent efficient. Stars burn by fusion fire; a star like this, like Earth's sun, probably converts some six hundred million tonnes of its substance to energy every second . . .'

'So if the sphere is ten centimetres thick, and if it was created entirely by the conversion of the star's radiation—' She called up a Virtual display before her face, ran some fast calculations.

'It's maybe ten thousand years old,' Dano said. 'Of course that's based on a lot of assumptions. And given the amount of comet debris the sphere has collected, that age seems too low – unless the comets have been *aimed* to infall here . . .'

She slept, ate, performed all her biological functions in the suit. The suit was designed for long-duration occupancy, but it was scarcely comfortable: no spacesuit yet designed allowed you to scratch an itch properly. However she endured.

After ten days, as the competition between the star's gravity and the sphere's spin was adjusted, she could feel the effective gravity building up. The local vertical tipped forward, so that it was as if the car was climbing an immense, unending slope. Dano insisted she take even more care moving around the cabin, and spend more time lying flat to avoid stress on her bones.

Dano himself, of course, a complacent Virtual, sat comfortably in an everyday chair.

'Why?' she asked. 'Why would the Xeelee create this great punctured sphere? What's the point?'

'It may have been nothing more than a simple industrial accident,' he said languidly. 'There's a story from before the Qax Extirpation, predating even the Second Expansion. It's said that a human traveller once saved himself from a nova flare by huddling behind a scrap of construction material. The material soaked up the light, you see, and expanded dramatically . . . The rogue scrap would have grown and grown, easily encompassing a star like this, if the traveller hadn't found the "Xeelee flower", the off-switch. It's probably just a romantic myth. Or this may alternatively be some kind of technology demonstrator.'

'I suppose we'll never know,' she said. 'And why the light lakes? Why not make the sphere perfectly efficient, closed, totally black?'

He shrugged. 'Well, perhaps it's a honey trap.' She had never seen a bee, or tasted honey, and she didn't understand the reference. 'Sool was right that this immense sphere-world could host billions of humans – trillions. Perhaps the Xeelee hope that we'll flock here, to this place with room to breed almost without limit, and die and grow old without achieving anything, just like Sool, and not bother them any more. But I think that's unlikely.'

'Why?'

'Because the effective gravity rises away from the equator. So the sphere isn't much of a honey trap, because we can't inhabit most of it. Humans here are clearly incidental to the sphere's true purpose.' His Virtual voice was without inflection, and she couldn't read his mood.

They passed the five-gravity latitude before they even glimpsed Bicansa's car. It was just a speck in the high-magnification sensor displays, not visible to the naked eye, thousands of kilometres ahead on this tabletop landscape. It was clear that they weren't going to catch Bicansa without going much deeper into the sphere's effective gravity well.

'Her technology is almost as good as ours,' Pala gasped. 'But not quite.'

'Try not to talk,' Dano murmured. 'You know, there are soldiers, Navy tars, who could stand multiple gravity for days on end. You aren't one of them.'

Pala was lying down, cushioned by her suit, kept horizontal by her couch despite the cabin's apparent tilt upwards. But even so the pressure on her chest was immense. 'I won't turn back,' she groaned.

'I'm not suggesting you do. But you will have to accept that the suit knows best.'

When they passed six gravities, the suit flooded with a dense, crimson fluid that forced its way into her ears and eyes and mouth. The fluid, by filling her up, would enable her to endure the immense, unending pressure of the gravity. It was like drowning.

Dano offered no sympathy. 'Still glad you didn't take the flitter? Still think this is a romantic adventure? Ah, but that was the point, wasn't it? *Romance.* I saw the way you looked at Bicansa. Did she remind you of gentle comforts, of thrilling under-the-blanket nights in the Academy dormitories?'

'Shut up,' she gasped.

'Didn't it occur to you that as she was only a Virtual image, that image might have been *edited*? You don't even know what she looks like.'

The fluid tasted of milk. Even when the feeling of drowning had passed, she never learned to ignore its presence in her belly and lungs and throat; she felt as if she was on the point of throwing up, all the time. She slept as much as she could, trying to shut out the pain, the pressure in her head, the mocking laugh of Dano.

But, trapped in her body, she had plenty of time to think over the central puzzle of this star-world – and what to do about it. And still the journey continued across the elemental landscape, and the astound-ing, desolating scale of this artificial world worked its way into her soul.

They drove steadily for no less than forty days, and traversed a great arc of the star sphere stretching from the equator towards the pole, across nearly a million kilometres. As gravity dominated the diminish-ing centrifugal forces, the local vertical tipped back up and the plain seemed to level out.

Eventually the effective gravity force reached more than twenty standard.

The car drew to a halt.

Pala insisted on seeing for herself. Despite Dano's objections she had the suit lift her up to the vertical, amid a protesting whine of exo-skeletal motors. As the monstrous gravity dragged at the fluid in which she was embedded, waves of pain plucked at her body.

Ahead of the car was another light lake, another pale glow, another splash of dimly lit green. But there were no trees or mirror towers, she saw; nothing climbed high above the sphere's surface here.

Bicansa appeared in the air.

She stood in the car's cabin, unsuited, as relaxed as Dano. Pala felt there was some sympathy in her Virtual eyes. But she knew now without doubt that this wasn't Bicansa' s true aspect.

'You came after me,' Bicansa said.

'I wanted to know,' Pala said. Propped up in her suit, her voice was a husk, muffled by the fluid in her throat. 'Why did you come to the equator – why meet us? You could have hidden here.'

'Yes,' Dano said grimly. 'The Navy's careless scouting missed you.'

'We had to know what kind of threat you are to us. I had to see you face to face, take a chance that I would expose' – she waved a hand – 'this.'

'You know we can't ignore you,' Dano said. 'This great sphere is a Xeelee artefact. We have to learn what it's for.'

'That's simple,' Pala said. She had worked it out, she believed, during her long cocooning. 'We were thinking too hard, Dano. *The sphere is a weapon.*'

'Ah,' Dano said grimly. 'Of course. And I always believed your thinking wasn't bleak enough for this job, Pala. I was wrong.'

Bicansa looked bewildered. 'What are you talking about? Since the First landed, we have thought of this sphere as a place that gives life, not death.'

Dano said, 'You wouldn't think it was so wonderful if you inhabited a planet of this star as the sphere slowly coalesced – if your ocean froze out, your air began to snow . . . Pala is right. The sphere is a machine that kills a star – or rather, its planets, while preserving the star itself for future use. I doubt if there's anything special about this system, this star.' He glanced at the sky, metal Eyes gleaming. 'It is probably just a trial run of a new technology, a weapon for a war of the future. One thing we know about the Xeelee is that they think long term.'

Bicansa said, 'What a monstrous thought. My whole culture has developed on the hull of a weapon! But even so, it is my culture. And you're going to destroy it, aren't you? Or will you put us in a museum, as you promised Sool?'

'Not necessarily,' Pala whispered.

They both turned to look at her. Dano murmured threateningly, 'What are you thinking, Missionary?'

She closed her eyes. Did she really want to take this step? It could be the end of her career if it went wrong, if Dano failed to back her. But she had sensed the gentleness of Sool's equatorial culture, and had now experienced for herself the vast spatial scale of the sphere – and here, still more strange, was this remote polar colony. This was an immense place, she thought, immense both in space and time – and yet humans had learned to survive here. It was almost as if humans and Xeelee were learning to live together. It would surely be

221

wrong to allow this unique world to be destroyed, for the sake of short-term gains.

And she thought she had a way to keep that from happening.

'If this is a weapon, it may one day be used against us. And if so we have to find a way to neutralise it.' The suit whirred as she turned to Bicansa, 'Your people can stay here. You can live your lives the way you want. I'll find ways to make the Commission accept that. But there's a payback.'

Bicansa nodded grimly. 'I understand. You want us to find the Xeelee flower.'

'Yes,' whispered Pala. 'Find the off-switch.'

Dano faced her, furious. 'You don't have the authority to make a decision like that. Granted this is an unusual situation. But these are still human colonists, and you are still a Missionary. Such a *deal* would be unprecedented.'

'But,' Pala whispered, 'Bicansa's people are no longer human. Are you, Bicansa?'

Bicansa averted her eyes. 'The First were powerful. Just as they made this star-world fit for us, so they made us fit for it.'

Dano, astonished, glared at them both. Then he laughed. 'Oh, I see. A loophole! If the colonists aren't fully human under the law you can pass the case to the Assimilation, who won't want to deal with it either . . . You're an ingenious one, Pala! Well, well. All right, I'll support your proposal at the Commission. No guarantees, though.'

'Thank you,' Bicansa said to Pala. She held out her Virtual hand, and it passed through Pala's suit, breaking into pixels.

Dano had been right, Pala thought, infuriatingly right, as usual. He had seen something in her, an attraction to this woman from another world she hadn't even recognised in herself. But Bicansa didn't even *exist* in the form Pala had perceived, not if she endured this gravity. Was she, Pala, really so lonely? Well, if so, when she got out of here she would do something about her personal life.

And she would have to think again about her career choice. Dano had always warned her about an excess of empathy. It seemed she wasn't cut out for the duties of a Missionary – and next time she might not be able to find a legal loophole to spare the victims of the Commission's heavy charity.

With a last regretful glance, Bicansa's Virtual sublimated into dusty light.

Dano said briskly, 'Enough's enough. I'll call down the flitter to get you out of here before you choke to death.' He turned away, and his pixels flickered as he worked.

Pala looked out through the car's window at the colony, the sprawling, high-gravity plants, the dusty, flattened lens of shining air. She wondered how many more colonies had spread over the varying gravity latitudes of the star shell, how many more adaptations from the standard human form had been tried – how many people actually lived on this immense artificial world. There was so much here to explore.

The door of Bicansa's car opened. A creature climbed out cautiously. In a bright orange pressure suit, its body was low-slung, supported by four limbs as thick as tree trunks. Even through the suit Pala could make out immense bones at hips and shoulders, and massive joints along the spine. It lifted its head and looked into the car. Through a thick visor Pala could make out a face – thick-jawed, flattened, but a human face nonetheless. The creature nodded once. Then it turned and, moving heavily, carefully, made its way towards the colony, and its lake of light.

*Pala was right that the Xeelee star-cloak was a weapon. One day this strange apparition would return, to haunt human history.*

*What a pity Bicansa's people never did find an off-switch.*

*This was an age when every resource in the Galaxy had to be harnessed to feed the Expansion. So the Missionaries and Assimilators drove on.*

*But, at the very edge of the human front, they were never very safe vocations.*

# BREEDING GROUND

## AD 10,537

The starbreaker pod exploded in her face.

Mari was hurled backwards, landing with a jarring impact against the weapons emplacement's rear bulkhead. Something gushed over her eyes – something sticky – blood? With sudden terror she scraped at her face.

The emplacement's calm order had been destroyed in an instant. Alarms howled, insistent. There was screaming all around her, people flailing. The transparent forward bulkhead had buckled inwards, and the row of starbreaker pods behind it, including her own, had been crushed and broken open. Charred shadows still clung to some of the stations, and there was a stink of smoke, of burned meat. She had been lucky to have been thrown back, she realised dully.

But beyond the forward bulkhead the battle was continuing. She saw black extragalactic space laced by cherry-red starbreaker beams, a calm enfilade caging in the bogey, the Snowflake, the misty alien artefact at the centre of this assault. The rest of the flotilla hovered like clouds around the action: Spline ships, fleshy scarred spheres, sisters of the living ship in which she rode, each wielding a huge shield of perfectly reflective Ghost hide.

Then the gravity failed. She drifted away from the wall, stomach lurching. In the misty dark, something collided with her, soft and wet; she flinched.

There was a face in front of her, a bloody mouth screaming through the clamour of the alarm. 'Gunner!'

That snapped her back into focus. 'Yes, sir.'

This was Jarn, a sub-lieutenant. She was bloodied, scorched, one arm dangling; she was struggling to pull herself into a pressure cloak.

'Get yourself a cloak, then help the others. We have to get out of here.'

Mari felt fear coil beneath her shock. She had spent the entire trip inside this emplacement, a station stuck to the outer flesh of a Spline ship; here she had bunked, messed, lived; here was her primary function, the operation of a starbreaker beam. *Get out?* Where to?

'. . . Academician Kapur first, then Officer Mace. Then anybody else who's still moving . . .'

'Sir, the action—'

'Is over.' For a heartbeat Jarn's shrill voice softened. 'Over for us, gunner. Now our duty is to keep ourselves alive. Ourselves, and the Academician, and the wetback. Is that clear?'

'Yes, sir.'

'Move it.' Jarn spun away, hauling pressure cloaks out of lockers.

Mari grabbed a cloak out of the smoke-filled air. Jarn was right; the first thing you had to do in a situation like this was to make sure you could keep functioning yourself. The semi-sentient material closed up around her, adjusting itself as best it could. There was a sharp tingle at her forehead as the cloak started to work on her wound. The cloak was too small; it hurt as it tried to enfold her stocky shoulders, her muscular legs. Too late to change it now.

Jarn had already opened a hatch at the back of the emplacement. She was pushing bodies through as fast as she could cram them in. Seeing Mari, she jabbed a finger, directing Mari towards Kapur.

The Academician – here because he was the nearest thing to an expert on the action's target – was drifting, limbs stiff, hands clutched in front of his face. Mari had to pull his hands away. His eye sockets were pits of ruin; the implanted Eyes there had burned out.

No time for that. She forced herself to close the cloak over his face. Then she pushed him by main force towards Jarn's open hatchway.

Next she came to Mace, the wetback, the Navy officer. He was bent forward over a sensor post. When she pulled him back she saw that both legs had been crudely severed, somewhere below the knee. Blood pumped out of broken vessels in sticky zero-G globules. His mouth gaped, strands of bloody drool floating around his face.

Her cloak had a medical kit. She ripped this open now and dug out a handful of gel. Shuddering at the touch of splintered bone and ragged flesh, she plastered the gel hastily over the raw wounds. The gel settled into place, turning pale blue as it sealed vessels, sterilised, dissolved its substance into a blood replacement, and started the process of promoting whatever healing was possible. Then she dragged a cloak around Mace and hurled him bodily towards Jarn and the hatch.

Under the alarm, she realised now, the noise had subsided. No more screaming. Nobody left in the emplacement was moving, nobody but her.

Beyond the forward bulkhead the Snowflake, the target, was beginning to glow internally, pink-white, and subtle structures crumbled. Fleshy Spline hulls drifted across the artefact's immense, complex expanse, purposeful, determined.

But the bulkhead was blistering, about to give way.

She dived through the hatch. Jarn slammed it closed. Mari felt a soundless explosion as the bulkhead failed. The alarm was cut off at last.

She was in a kind of cave, roughly spherical, criss-crossed by struts of some cartilaginous material. It was dark here, a crimson obscurity relieved only by the glow of the cloaks. She could see portals in the walls of the cave – not hatchways like decent human engineering, but *orifices*, like nostrils or throats, leading to a network of darker chambers beyond. There was some kind of air here, surely unbreathable. Little motes moved in it, like dust.

When she touched a wall, it was warm, soft, moist. She recoiled.

She was stuck inside the body of a Spline.

Mari had never forgotten her first view of a Spline ship.

Its kilometres-wide bulk had dwarfed her flitter. It was a rough sphere, adorned by the tetrahedral sigil of free humanity. The hull, actually a wrinkled, leathery hide, was punctured by vast navels within which sensors and weapons glittered. In one pit an *eye* had rolled, fixing Mari disconcertingly; Mari had found herself turning away from its huge stare.

The Spline – so went below-decks scuttlebutt – had once scoured the depths of some world-girdling ocean. Then, unknown years ago, they rebuilt themselves. They plated over their flesh, hardened their internal organs – and rose from their ocean like vast, studded balloons.

What it boiled down to was that Spline ships were alive: living starships.

On the whole, it was best not to think about it. Cocooned in the metal and ceramic of a gun or sensor emplacement, you mostly didn't have to. Now, however, Mari found herself immersed in deep red biological wetness, and her flesh crawled.

Jarn, strapping her own damaged arm tightly to her side, watched her with disgust. 'You're going to have to get used to it.'

'I never wanted to be a wetback. Sir.' The wetbacks were the officers and ratings who interfaced between the Spline vessel and its human cargo. Mace, the Navy officer who had been assigned to escort Academician Kapur during the action, was a wetback.

'We're all wetbacks now, gunner.' Jarn glanced around. 'I'm senior here,' she said loudly. 'I'm in charge. Gunner, help me with these people.'

Mari saw that Jarn was trying to organise the survivors into a rough line. She moved to help. But there was just a handful here, she saw – eight of them, including Mari and Jarn, just eight left out of the thirty who had been working in the emplacement at the time of the assault.

Here was Kapur, the spindly Academician with the ruined Eyes, sunk in sullen misery. Beside him Mace drifted in the air, his cloak almost comically truncated over those missing legs. Next to Mace were two squat forms, wrapped in misted cloaks, clutching at each other. Round faces peered up at Mari fearfully.

She reached for their names. 'Tsedi. Kueht. Right?'

They nodded. They were supply ratings, both male, plump, soft-skinned. They spoke together. 'Sir, what happened?' 'When will we get out of here?'

Academician Kapur turned his sightless face. 'We made a bonfire. A bonfire of wisdom almost as old as the universe. And we got our fingers burned.'

The ratings quailed, clutching tighter.

Useless, Mari thought analytically. Dead weight. Rumour had it they were cadre siblings, hatched in some vast inner-Expansion Con-urbation; further rumour had it they were also lovers.

She moved on down the line of cloaked bodies. Two more survivors, roughly wrapped in their cloaks. She recognised Vael, a gunner ranked below herself, and Retto, a sub-lieutenant who had been officer of the watch at the time of the attack. Good sailors both. Even the officer.

Except they weren't survivors at all. She could see that even through the layers of their imperfectly fitting cloaks, which had turned a subtle blue colour, the colour of death. Mari's heart sank; it would have been good to have these two at her side.

Jarn had extracted a kit of what looked like hypodermic needles from a pack at Mace's waist. 'Take their cloaks. Retto's and Vael's.'

Jarn was one rank below the CO and his First Officer, with nominal responsibilities for communications. Mari knew her as a prissy idiot who routinely dumped any responsibility downwards. And now, in this grim situation, she had issued a stupid order like that. 'Sir, they're *dead*.'

Kapur turned blindly. A thin, intense, withdrawn man, he wore his head shaven after the ancient fashion of the Commission for Historical Truth, and he had a clutch of bright red vials strapped to his waist: mnemonic fluid, every droplet a backup record of everything that had happened during the action. He said, 'I can read your tone of voice, gunner. I can tell what you're thinking. Why did such good comrades have to die, when such a rabble as this has survived?'

'Academician, shut up,' Jarn snapped. 'Sir. Just do it, gunner. There's nothing to be done for them now. And we're going to need those cloaks.' Fumbling one-handed, she began to jab needles into the fleshy wall of the little cavern, squirting in thick blue gunk.

Of course Kapur was right. Mari surveyed her surviving companions with disgust: Jarn the pompous ass-muncher of a junior officer, Mace the half-dead wetback, Kapur the dried-up domehead, the two soft-bodied store-stackers. But there was nothing to be done about it.

Keeping her face stony, Mari peeled the cloaks off the inert bodies of Vael and Retto. Vael's chest had been laid open, as if by an immense punch; blood and bits of burned meat floated out of the cavity.

Jarn abandoned her needle-jabbing. 'The Spline isn't responding.' She held up the emptied hypodermics. 'This is the way you communicate with a Spline – in an emergency, anyhow. Chemicals injected into its bloodstream. Lieutenant Mace could tell you better than I can, if he were conscious. I think this Spline must be too badly wounded. It has withdrawn from us, from human contact.'

Mari gaped. 'We can't control the ship?'

Kapur sighed. 'The Spline do not belong to us, to humanity. They are living ships, independent, sentient creatures, with whom we negotiate.'

The siblings huddled fearfully. The fatter one – Tsedi – stared with wide eyes at Jarn. 'They'll come to get us. Won't they, sir?'

Jarn's face flickered; Mari saw she was out of her depth herself, but she was working to keep control, to keep functioning. Maybe this screen-tapper was stronger than Mari had suspected. 'I'm a communications officer, remember.' That meant she had a Squeem implant, an alien fish swimming in her belly, her link to the rest of the crew. She closed her eyes, as if tapping into the Squeem's crude group mind. 'There is no *they*, rating.'

Tsedi's eyes were wide. 'They're dead? The crew? *All* of them?'

'We're on our own. Just focus on that.'

*Alone*. Kapur laughed softly. Mari tried to hide her own inner chill.

As if on cue, they all felt a subtle, gut-wrenching displacement.

'Hyperdrive,' Mari said.

The siblings clutched each other. 'Hyperdrive? The Spline is moving? Where is it taking us?'

Kapur said, 'Wherever it wants. We have no influence. Probably the Spline doesn't even know we are here. This is what you get when your warship has a mind of its own.'

Impatiently, Jarn snapped, 'Nothing we can do about that. All right, we have work to do. We should pool what we have. Med kit, supplies, weapons, tools, anything.'

There was precious little. They had the cloaks, plus the two spares scavenged from the bodies of Vael and Retto. The cloaks came with med-kits, half depleted already. There was some basic planet-fall survival gear, carried routinely by the crew: knives, water purification tablets.

Jarn rubbed her wounded arm, gazing at the kit. 'No food. No water.' She glared at Kapur. 'You. Academician. You know anything about Spline?'

'More than the rest of you, I suspect,' Kapur said dryly. 'For all you use them to fly around the Expansion from one battle to another. But little enough.'

'The cloaks will keep us alive for twenty-four hours. We might use the spares to stretch that a little longer. But we need to replenish them. How? Where do we go?'

I wouldn't have thought so far ahead, Mari considered. Again she was reluctantly impressed by Jarn.

Kapur pressed his fists to his burned-out Eyes. 'Inwards. The Spline has storage chambers in a layer beneath its hull. I think.'

Tsedi said, 'If only Lieutenant Mace was conscious. He's the expert. He would know—'

'But he isn't,' Jarn snapped, irritated. There's just us.'

They were silent.

'All right.' Jarn looked around, and selected an orifice directly opposite the one they had entered through. 'This way,' she said firmly. 'I'll lead. Academician, you follow me, then you two, Tsedi and Kueht. Gunner, bring up the rear. Here.' She thrust one of the knives into Mari's hand. 'Keep together.'

Kapur asked, 'What about Mace?'

Jarn said carefully, 'We can't take him. He's lost a massive amount of blood, and I think he may be in anaphylactic shock.'

'We take him.'

'Sir, you're our priority.' That was true, Mari knew. You were always supposed to preserve the Academicians and Commissaries first, for the sake of the knowledge they might bring forward to the next engagement. And if that couldn't be managed, then you retrieved the mnemonic vials the domeheads kept with themselves at all times. Everything else was expendable. Everything and everyone. Jarn said, 'We don't have energy to spare for—'

'We take him.' Kapur reached for Mace. Grunting, he pulled the Navy man to him and arranged him on his back, arms around his neck, head lolling, half-legs dangling.

Jarn exchanged a glance with Mari. She shrugged. 'All right. You others, get ready.'

'I don't like this situation, sir,' Mari said, as she gathered up her kit.

'Me neither,' Jarn muttered. 'The day the Expansion takes full control of these Lethe-spawned Spline the better. In the meantime, just do your job, sailor. Form up. Keep together. Let's go.'

One by one they filed through the orifice, into the crimson-black tunnel beyond. Mari, as ordered, took the rear of the little column, and she watched the dim yellow glow of the others' cloaks glistening from the organic walls.

She couldn't believe this was happening. But she breathed, she moved, she followed orders; and she seemed to feel no fear. You're in shock, she told herself. It will come.

In the meantime, do your job.

Without gravity there was no up, no down. Their only orientation came from the tunnel around them. Its clammy walls were close enough to touch in every direction, the space so cramped they had to proceed in single file.

The tunnel twisted this way and that, taking them sideways as much as inwards. But with every metre Mari was descending deeper into the carcase of this wounded Spline; she was very aware that she was crawling like some parasitic larva *under* the skin of a living creature.

What made it worse was the slow going.

Jarn and Mari moved OK, but Kapur blundered blindly, and Tsedi and Kueht seemed unaccustomed to the lack of gravity. The siblings stayed as close to each other as they could get in the confined space, touching and twittering like birds. Mari growled to herself, imagining what the master-at-arms would have said about *that*.

They couldn't have gone more than a few hundred metres before Mace's cloak turned blue. But Kapur, bathed in a cerulean glow he couldn't see, refused to leave Mace behind. He toiled doggedly on, his inert burden on his back.

Jarn snapped, 'I don't have time for this. Gunner, sort it out.'

'Sir. How?'

'With the tact and sensitivity you starbreaker grunts are famous for. Just do it. You two, move on.' She took the lead again, hustling Tsedi and Kueht behind her.

Mari took her place behind Kapur, at a loss. '. . . I guess you knew each other a long time, sir.'

Kapur turned. 'Mace and I? How old are you, gunner?'

'Eighteen standard, sir.'

'Eighteen.' He shook his head. 'I first met Mace before you were born, then. I was seconded here by the Commission, on the failed first contact with the Snowflake.'

'Seconded?'

'I was a Guardian, a policeman. As the Expansion grows, the rate of Assimilation itself accelerates, and specialists are rare . . . My own brand of forensic intelligence proved adequate for the role. My job was to understand the Snowflake. Mace's was to destroy it.'

Mari understood the tension. Resources were always short. The Assimilation, the processing of newly contacted alien species on an industrial scale, followed an accelerating Expansion that now spanned a quarter of the Galaxy's disc and had reached the great globular clusters beyond.

And, in one of those clusters, they had found the Snowflake. It surrounded a dwarf star, a tetrahedron fourteen million kilometres on a side: a stupendous artefact, a vast setting for an ancient, faded jewel of a star.

So far as anybody knew, the Snowflake had been constructed to observe: simply that, to gather data, as the universe slowly cooled. Since the building of the Snowflake, thirteen billion years had shivered across the swirling face of the Galaxy.

Assimilation was a matter of processing: contact, conquest, absorption – and, if necessary, destruction. If Kapur had been able to determine the goals of the Snowflake and its builders, then perhaps those objectives could be subverted to serve human purposes. If not, then the Snowflake had no value.

Mari guessed, 'Lieutenant Mace gave you a hard time.'

Kapur shook his head. 'Mace was a good officer. Hard, intelligent, ambitious, brutal. He knew his job and he carried it out as best he could. I was in his way; that was uncomfortable for me. But I always admired him for what he was. In the end the Snowflake resisted Mace's crude assaults.'

'How?'

'We were – brushed aside.'

He tried to explain what had happened. Their ship had been hit by a beam of lased gravity waves, that had come from outside the Galaxy. It seemed that the Snowmen, the builders of the 'Flake, had been able to manipulate something humans called Mach's principle. *Mach*, or *Mar-que*, it was a name all but lost in the Qax Extirpation.

Kapur said, 'You are embedded in a universe of matter. That matter tugs at you with gravity fields – but the fields surround you uniformly; they are equal in all directions, isotropic and timeless. The Snowmen had a way of making the field . . . unequal.'

'How?'

Kapur laughed uneasily. 'We still don't know. I guess you learn a lot in thirteen billion years.

'It has taken twenty-two years for the Academies to figure out how to deal with the Snowflake. For deal with it we must, of course. Its stubborn, defiant existence is not a direct threat to us, but it is a challenge to the logic of our ideology.' Now he smiled, remembering. 'After our failed mission we corresponded, Mace and I. I followed Mace's career with a certain pride. Do you think it's getting hot?'

'Sir—'

'When I was assigned to this second assault on the Snowflake, Mace was seconded to accompany me. He had risen to lieutenant. It galled him to have to become a wetback.'

'Sir. Lieutenant Mace is dead.'

Kapur drifted to a halt, and sighed. 'Ah. Then knowing me did him little good in the end. What a pity it ends like this.'

Gently Mari pulled the broken body from Kapur's back. Kapur didn't resist; he drifted to the wall, running his fingers over its moist surface. Mari pulled the cloak off Mace's inert body, but it had been used up by its efforts to keep Mace alive.

She was surprised to learn of a friendship between a straight-and-true Navy man and a domehead. And then Kapur had attempted to haul his friend along with him, even though it must have been obvious that Mace couldn't survive – even though Kapur, as their passenger Academician, would have been in his rights to demand that the rest of them carry *him* along.

People always surprised you. Especially those without military training and the proper orientation. But then, she had never gotten to know any domeheads before, not before this disaster, today.

She shoved the body back the way they had come, up into the darkness. When she was done she was sweating. Maybe it *was* getting hotter in here, as they penetrated deeper into the core of the Spline. 'It's done, sir. Now we have to—'

There was a flash of light from deeper inside the tunnel. And now came a high-pitched, animal scream.

Mari shoved Kapur out of the way and hurled herself down the tunnel.

It was Tsedi, the fat rating. He looked as if he had been shot in the stomach. The cloak over his fat belly was scorched and blackened, flaking away. Kueht bounced around the cramped tunnel, screaming, eyes bugging wide, flapping uselessly.

Jarn was struggling with one of the spare cloaks. 'Help me.' Together Jarn and Mari wrapped the cloak around Tsedi's shivering form.

And when she got closer Mari saw that whatever had burned through the rating's cloak had gone on, digging a hole right *into* Tsedi's body, exposing layers of flesh and fat. Inside the hole something glistened, wet and pulsing.

She retched.

'Hold it in,' Jarn said, her own voice tremulous. 'Your cloak would handle the mess, but you'd smell it for ever.'

Mari swallowed hard, and got herself under control. But her

hand went to the knife tucked into her belt. 'Did someone fire on us?'

Jarn said, 'Nothing like that. It was the Spline.'

'The Spline?'

Kapur was hovering above them, anchored to the wall by a fingertip touch. 'Haven't you noticed how hot it has become?'

Jarn said evenly, 'I remember hearing rumours about this. It's part of their – um, lifecycle. The Spline will dive into the surface layers of a star. Normally, of course, they drop off any human passengers first.'

Mari said, 'We're inside a *star*? Why?'

Jarn shrugged. 'To gather energy. To feed – to refuel. Whatever. How should I know?'

'And to cleanse,' Kapur murmured. 'They bathe in starstuff. Probably our Spline's damaged outer layers have already been sloughed away, taking what was left of our emplacements with it.'

'What about Tsedi?'

'There was a sunbeam,' Jarn said. 'Focused somehow.'

'An energy trap,' Kapur said. 'A way for the Spline to use the star's heat to rid itself of internal parasites. Like us,' he added with cold humour.

Jarn said, 'Whatever it was, it caught this poor kid in the gut. And – oh, Lethe.'

Tsedi convulsed, blood-flecked foam showing at his mouth, limbs flapping, belly pulsing wetly. Jarn and Mari tried to pin him down, but his flailing body was filled with unreasonable strength.

It finished as quickly as it had started. With a final spasm, he went limp.

Kueht began to scream, high-pitched.

Jarn sat back, breathing hard. 'All right. All right. Take the cloak off him, gunner.'

'We can't stay here,' Kapur said gently. 'Not while the Spline bathes in its star.'

'No,' Jarn said. 'Deeper, then. Come on.'

But Kueht clung to Tsedi's corpse. Jarn tried to be patient; in the gathering heat she drifted beside the rating, letting him jabber. 'We grew up together,' he was saying. 'We looked after each other in the Conurbation, in the cadres. I was stronger than he was and I'd help him in fights. But he was clever. He helped me study. He made me laugh. I remember once . . .'

Mari listened to this distantly.

Kapur murmured, 'You don't approve of family, gunner?'

'There is no such thing as family.'

'You grew up in a Conurbation?'

'Navy run,' she growled. 'Our cadres were broken up and reformed every few years, as per Commission rules. The way it should be. Not like *this*.'

Kapur nodded. 'But further from the centre, the rules don't always hold so well. It is a big Expansion, gunner, and its edges grow diffuse . . . Humanity will assert itself. What's the harm in family?'

'What good is "family" doing that rating now? It's only hurting him. Tsedi is *dead*.'

'You despise such weakness.'

'*They* lived while good human beings died.'

'Good human beings? Your comrades in arms. *Your* family.'

'No—'

'Do you miss them, gunner?'

'I miss my weapon.' Her starbreaker. It was true. It was what she was trained for, not this sticky paddling in the dark. Without her starbreaker she felt lost, bereft.

In the end Jarn physically dragged Kueht away from the stiffening corpse of his cadre sibling. At last, to Mari's intense relief, they moved on.

They seemed to travel through the twisting tunnel-tube for hours. As the semi-sentient cloaks sought to concentrate their dwindling energies on keeping their inhabitants alive, their glow began to dim, and the closing darkness made the tunnel seem even more confining.

At last they came to a place where the tunnel opened out. Beyond was a chamber whose mottled walls rose out of sight, into darkness beyond the reach of their cloaks' dim glow. Jarn connected a line to a hook which she dug into the Spline's fleshy wall, and she and Mari drifted into the open space.

Huge fleshy shapes ranged around them. Some of them pulsed. Fat veins, or perhaps nerve trunks, ran from one rounded form to another. Even the walls were veined: they were sheets of living tissue and muscle, nourished by the Spline's analogue of blood.

Mari found herself whispering. 'Is it the brain?'

Jarn snorted. 'Spline don't have brains as we do, tar. Even I know that much. Spline systems are – distributed. It makes them more robust, I guess.'

'Then what is this place?'

Jarn sighed. 'There's a lot about the Spline we don't understand.' She waved a hand. 'This may be a, a factory. An organic factory.'

'Making what?'

'Who knows?' Kapur murmured. He lingered by the wall, sightless gaze shifting. 'We are not the only clients of the Spline. They provide services for other species, perhaps from far beyond the Expansion, creatures of whom we may have no knowledge at all. But not everybody uses the Spline as warships. That much is clear.'

'It is hardly satisfactory,' Jarn said through clenched teeth, 'that we have so little control over a key element of the Expansion's strategy.'

'You're right, lieutenant,' Kapur said. 'The logic of the Third Expansion is based on the ultimate supremacy of mankind. How then can we *share* our key resources, like these Spline? But how could we control them – any more than we can control this rogue in whose chest cavity we ride helplessly?'

Mari said, 'Lieutenant.'

Jarn turned to her.

Mari glanced back at Kueht. The rating huddled alone at the mouth of the tunnel from which they had emerged. She made herself say it. 'We could make faster progress.'

Before Jarn could respond, Kapur nodded. 'If we dump the weak. But we are not strangers any more; we have already been through a great deal together. Mari, will *you* be the one to abandon Kueht? And where will you do it? Here? A little further along?'

Mari, confused, couldn't meet Kapur's sightless glare.

Jarn clutched her wounded arm. 'You're being unfair, Academician. She's trained to think this way. She's doing her job. Trying to save *your* life.'

'Oh, I understand that, lieutenant. She is the product of millennia of methodical warmaking, an art at which we humans have become rather good. She is polished precision machinery, an adjunct to the weapon she wielded so well. But in this situation, we are all stranded outside our normal parameters. Aren't we, gunner?'

'This isn't getting us anywhere,' Jarn snapped. She picked out a patch of deeper darkness on the far side of the chamber. 'That way. The way we were heading. There must be an exit. We'll have to work our way around the walls. Mari, you help Kapur. Kueht, you're with me . . .'

More long hours.

As its energy faded, Mari's cloak grew still more uncomfortable – tighter on her muscular body, chafing at armpits and groin and neck. It was tiring for her to struggle against its elasticity. And, though she had been able to resist throwing up, the cloak was eventually full of her own sour stink.

Meanwhile, her back ached where she had been rammed against the emplacement bulkhead. That gash on her head, half-treated by the cloak, was a permanent, nagging pain. Mysterious aches spread through her limbs and neck. Not only that, she was *hungry*, and as thirsty as she had ever been; she hadn't had so much as a mouthful of water since the assault itself. She tried not to think about how much Kueht was slowing them down, what had transpired in the 'factory'. But there wasn't much else to think about.

She knew the syndrome. She was being given too much time in her own head. And thinking was always a bad thing.

They came at last to another chamber.

As far as they could see in their cloaks' failing light, this was a hangar-like place of alcoves and nooks. The bays were separated by huge diaphanous sheets of some muscle-like material, marbled with fat. And within the alcoves were suspended great pregnant sacs of what looked like water: green, cloudy water.

Jarn made straight for one of the sacs, pulled out her knife and slit it open. The liquid pulsed out in a zero-G straight-line jet, bubbling slightly. Jarn thrust a finger into the flow, and read a sensor embedded in her cloaked wrist. She grinned. 'Sea water. Earth-like, salty sea water. And this green glop is blue-green algae, I think. We found what we came for.' She lengthened the slit. 'Each of you pick a sac. Just climb in and immerse yourself; the cloaks will take what they need.' She showed them how to work nipples in their cloaks that would provide them with desalinated water, even a mushy food based on the algae.

Mari helped Kapur, then clambered inside a sac of her own. She didn't lose much water when she slit the sac; surface tension kept it contained in big floating globules that she was able to gather up in her hands. She folded the sac like a blanket, holding it closed over her chest. The water was warm, and her cloak, drinking in nutrients, began to glow more brightly.

'Blue-green algae,' she murmured. 'From a human world.'

'Obviously,' Kapur said.

'Maybe this is one of the ways you pay a Spline,' Jarn said. 'I always wondered about that.' She moved around the chamber, handing out vials of an amber fluid that she passed through the sac walls. 'I think we deserve this. Pass it through your cloak.'

Kapur asked, 'What is it?'

Mari grinned. 'Poole's Blood.' For *Michael Poole*, the legendary pre-Extirpation explorer of Earth.

'Call it a stimulant,' Jarn said dryly. 'An old Navy tradition, Academician.'

Mari sucked down her tot. 'How long should we stay here?'

'As long as the cloaks need,' Jarn said. 'Try to sleep.'

That seemed impossible. But the rocking motion of the water and its swaddling warmth seemed to soothe the tension out of her sore muscles. She thought about her starbreaker station: the smooth feel of the machinery as she disassembled it for servicing, the sense of its clean power when she worked it.

Mari closed her eyes, just for a moment.

When she opened her eyes, three hours had passed. And Kueht had gone.

'He must have gone back,' Jarn said. 'Back to where we left his sibling.'

'That was hours ago,' Mari said. She looked from one to the other. 'We can't leave him.' Without waiting for Jarn's reaction she plunged back into the tunnel they had come from.

Jarn hurried after Mari, calling her back. But Mari wasn't about to listen. After a time, Jarn seemed to give up trying to stop her, and just followed.

Through the factory-like chamber they went, then back along the twisting length of muscle-walled tunnel.

*. . . Why am I doing this?*

Kueht was fat, useless and weak; before the disaster Mari wouldn't have made room for him in the corridor. All her training and drill, and the Expansion's Druz Doctrines that underpinned them, taught that people were *not* of equal worth. It was an individual's value to the species as a whole that counted: nothing more, nothing less. And it was the duty of the weak to lay down their lives for the strong, the worthless for the valuable.

But it wasn't working out like that. When it came down to it Mari just couldn't abandon even a helpless, useless creature like Kueht; she couldn't be the one to leave him behind, just as Kapur had said. *Humanity will assert itself.*

She was thinking too much again.

At last they reached the place where Mari had jammed Tsedi's burned body. Kueht was here, sprawled over his sibling. They pulled at Kueht's shoulders, turning him on his back. His cloak flapped open. His face was swollen, his tongue protruding and blackened.

Mari said, 'Kapur talked about opening our cloaks. Maybe that gave him the idea.'

'It must have been hard,' Jarn said. 'The cloak would have resisted being opened; it is smart enough to know that it would kill its occupant if it did. And asphyxiation is a bad way to die.' She shrugged. 'He told us he didn't want to go on without Tsedi. I guess we just didn't believe it.'

Mari shook her head, unfamiliar emotions churning inside her. Here were two comical little fat men, products of some flawed cadre somewhere, helpless and friendless save for each other. And yet Kueht had been prepared to die rather than live without the other. '*Why?*'

Jarn put her hand on Mari's arm; it was small over Mari's bunched bicep. 'Don't think about it.'

They paused to strip Kueht of his cloak. Even now, Mari realised, Jarn was thinking ahead, planning the onward journey.

They made good speed back the way they had come, to where Kapur was waiting. That was because they had after all lost the weak and slow, Mari reflected. It wasn't a thought that gave her any pleasure.

'We could just stay here,' Jarn said. 'There is food. We could last a long while.'

Jarn seemed to have withdrawn into herself since the loss of Kueht. Maybe exhaustion was weakening her resolve. She was, after all, just a screen-tapper.

'You've done well,' Mari said impulsively.

Jarn looked at her, startled.

Kapur said, 'There's no point staying here. We have to assume we will be rescued, plan for it. Anything else is futile, simply waiting to die.'

Jarn said, 'We're stuck inside a Spline warship, remember. Epidermis like armour.'

Kapur nodded. 'Then we must go to a place where the epidermis can be penetrated.'

'Where?'

'The eyes,' Kapur said. 'That's the only possibility I can think of.'

Jarn frowned. 'How will we find our way to an eye?'

'A nerve trunk,' said Mari. Jarn looked at her. Mari said defensively, 'Why not? Sir. Every eye must have an optic nerve connecting it to the rest of the nervous system. Or something like it.'

Jarn shook her head. 'You keep springing surprises on me, Mari.'

Kapur laughed out loud. 'That's human beings for you.'

They filled up the spare cloaks with sea water. Then, each of them trailing a massive, sluggish balloon by a length of rope, they formed up, Jarn leading, Kapur central, Mari bringing up the rear.

As they left the chamber, mouth-like nozzles puckered from the walls and began to spew sprays of colourless liquid. Mari's cloak flashed a warning. Stomach acid, she thought. She turned away.

Once they were in motion the inertia of her water bag gave Mari a little trouble, and when the tunnel curved she had some work to do hauling the bag around corners and giving it fresh momentum. But she worked with a will. Physical activity: better than thinking.

In some places the tunnels were scarred: once damaged, now healed. Mari remembered more scuttlebutt. Some of the great Spline vessels were very old, perhaps more than a million years, according to the domeheads. And they were veterans of ancient wars, fought, won and lost long before humans had even existed.

They had been moving barely half an hour when they came to another chamber.

This one was something like the organic 'factory'. A broad open chamber criss-crossed by struts of cartilage was dominated by a single pillar, maybe a metre wide, that spanned the room. It was made of something like translucent red-purple skin, and Mari made out fluid moving within it: blood, perhaps, or water. And there were sparks, sparks that flew like birds.

Kapur sniffed loudly. 'Can you smell that?' Their cloaks transmitted selective scents. 'Ozone. An electric smell.'

Jarn's water bag, clumsily sealed, was leaking; Mari had been running into droplets all the way up the tunnel. But now she saw that the droplets were *falling* – drifting away from Jarn, following slowly curving orbits, falling in towards the pillar that dominated the centre of the room.

Jarn, fascinated, followed the droplets towards the pillar.

Something passed through Mari's body, a kind of clench. She grunted and folded over.

'*Oh*,' said Kapur. 'That was a tide. Lethe—'

Without warning he hurled himself forward. He collided clumsily with Jarn, scrabbled to grab her, and spun her around. His momentum was carrying the two of them towards the pillar. But he tried to shove her away.

'No, you don't, sir,' Jarn grunted. With a simple one-armed throw she flipped him back towards Mari. But that left her drifting still faster towards the pillar.

Kapur scrabbled in the air. 'You don't understand.'

'Hold him, gunner.' Behind Jarn, Mari saw, those water droplets had entered tight, whirling orbits, miniature planets around a cylindrical sun. Jarn said, 'We haven't brought him all this way to—'

And then she folded.

As simple as that, as if crumpled by an invisible fist. Her limbs were thrust forward, her spine and neck bent over until they cracked. Blood and other fluids, deep purple, flooded her cloak, until that broke in turn, and a gout of blood and shit sprayed out.

Mari grabbed Kapur's bent form and threw her body across his, sheltering him from the flood of bodily fluids.

Kapur was weeping, inside his cloak. 'I heard it. I *heard* what happened to her.'

'What?'

'This is the hyperdrive chamber. Don't you see? Inside a Spline, even a star drive grows organically. Oh, you are seeing miracles today, gunner. Miracles of the possibilities of life.'

'We have to get you out of here.'

He straightened, seeming to get himself under control. 'No. The lieutenant—'

Mari shrieked into his face, 'She's dead!" He recoiled as if struck. She forced herself to speak calmly. 'She's dead, and we have to leave her, as we left the rest. I'm in charge now. Sir.'

'The Squeem,' he said evenly.

'What?'

'Jarn's implant. If we're to have any chance of rescue, we need it . . . Once the Squeem conquered the Earth itself. Did you know that? Now they survive only as unwilling symbiotes of mankind.'

Mari glanced back at Jarn's body, which was drifting away from the pillar. She seemed to have been compressed around a point somewhere above her stomach. Her centre of gravity, perhaps. 'I can't.'

'You have to. I'll help.' Kapur's voice was hard. 'Take your knife.'

They travelled on for perhaps a day.

Mari's cloak began to fail, growing cloudy, stiff, confining. Kapur moved increasingly slowly and feebly, and, though he didn't complain or even ask, he needed a lot of help. It seemed he had been wounded somehow, maybe internally, by the shock that had killed Jarn. But there wasn't anything Mari could do about that.

Once the tunnel they were using suddenly flooded with a thick gloopy liquid, crimson flecked with black. Blood maybe. Mari had to anchor them both to the wall; she wrapped her arms around Kapur and just held him there, immersed in a roaring, blood-dark river, until it passed. Then they kept on.

At last they found an eye.

It turned out to be just that: an *eye*, a fleshy sphere some metres across. It swivelled this way and that, rolling massively. At the back was a kind of curtain of narrow, overlapping sheets – perhaps components of a retina – from which narrower vine-like fibres led to the nerve bundle they had followed.

Mari parted the fibres easily. A clear fluid leaked out into the general murk.

She pulled Kapur into the interior of the eye. It was a neat spherical chamber. Unlike the tunnels and chambers they had passed through there were no shadows here, no lurking organic shapes; it was almost cosy.

She lodged Kapur against the wall. She found places to anchor their bundles of water, and the scrap of cloak within which swam the Squeem, the tiny alien not-fish which had inhabited Jarn's stomach.

She pushed at the forward wall. Her hand sank into a soft, giving, translucent surface. A lens, maybe. But beyond there was only veined flesh. 'If this is an eye, why can't I see out?'

'Perhaps the Spline has closed its eyelids.'

The floor under Mari seemed to shudder; the clear fluid pulsed, slow waves crossing the chamber, as the eye swivelled. 'But the eye is moving.'

Kapur grinned weakly. 'Surely Spline dream.'

Then the Spline eyelid opened, like a curtain raising. And, through a dense, distorting lens, Mari saw comet light.

They were deep within a solar system, she saw. She could tell because the comet had been made bright by sunlight. Its dark head was obscured by a glowing cloud, and two shining tails streaked across the black sky, tails of gas and dust.

To Mari it was a strange, beautiful sight. In most Expansion systems such a comet wouldn't be allowed to come sailing so close to a sun, because of the danger to the inhabitants of the system, and of the comet itself – all that outgassing would make the nucleus a dangerous place to live.

But she saw no signs of habitation. 'I don't get it,' she said. 'I don't see any lights. Where are the people? . . . Oh.'

Kapur turned when he heard her gasp.

Spline came sailing out of the glare of the comet's diffuse coma: great fleshy bodies, a dozen of them, more. She peered, seeking the green sigil of humanity, the telltale glitter of emplacements of weapons and sensors; but she saw nothing but walls of hardened flesh, the watery glint of eyes. This flotilla was moving like none she had seen before – coordinated, yes, but with an eerie, fluid grace, like a vast dance. Some of the Spline were smaller than the rest, darting little moons that orbited the great planets of the others.

And now they were gathering around the comet core.

'They are grazing,' she said. 'The Spline are grazing on the comet.'

Kapur smiled, but his face was grey. 'This is not a flotilla. It is a – what is the word? – it is a *school*.'

'They are wild Spline.'

'No. They are simply Spline.'

The school broke and came clustering around Mari's ship. Huge forms sailed across her vision like clouds. She saw that the smaller ones – infants? – were nudging almost playfully against her Spline's battered epidermis. It was a collision of giants – even the smallest of these immature creatures must have been a hundred metres across.

And now the Spline rolled. Mart's view was swivelled away from the comet, across a sky littered with stars, and towards a planet.

It was blue: the blue of ocean, of water, the colour of Earth. But this was not a human world. It was swathed in ocean, a sea broken only by a scattered litter of gleaming ice floes at the poles, and a few worn, rusty islands. She could see features on the shallow ocean floor: great craters, even one glowing pit, the marks of volcanism. An out-of-view sun cast glittering highlights from that ocean's silvery, wrinkled hide, and a set of vast waves, huge to be visible from this altitude, marched endlessly around the water-world.

And now she saw a fleet of grey-white forms that cut through the ocean's towering waves, leaving wakes like an armada of mighty ships, visible even from space.

'Of course,' Kapur said, his voice a dry rustle as she described this to him. 'It must be like this.'

'What?'

'The home world of the Spline. The breeding ground. We knew they came from an ocean. Now they swim through the lethal currents of space. But biology must not be denied; they must return here, to their original birthing place, to spawn, to continue the species. Like sea turtles who crawl back to the land to lay their eggs.' Kapur folded on himself, tucking his arms into his chest. 'If only I had my Eyes! . . . I often wondered *how* the Spline made that transition from ocean to vacuum. As giant ocean-going swimmers, they surely lacked limbs, tools; there would be no need for the sort of manipulative intelligence that would enable them to redesign themselves. There must have been others involved – don't you think? Hunters, or farmers. For their own reasons they rebuilt the Spline – and gave them the opportunity to rebel, to take control of their destiny.'

'Academician,' Mari said hesitantly. 'I don't recognise the stars. I don't see any sign of people. I never heard of a world like this. What part of the Expansion are we in?'

He sighed. 'Nobody has seen the home world of the Spline before. Therefore we can't be in the Expansion. I'm afraid I have no idea where we are.' He coughed, feebly, and she saw he was sweating.

It was getting hot.

She glanced out of the window-lens. That blue world had expanded so that it filled up her window, a wall of ocean. But the image was becoming misty, blurred by a pinkish glow. Plasma.

'I think we're entering the atmosphere.'

'The Spline is coming home.'

Now the glow became a glaring white, flooding the chamber. The temperature was rising savagely, and the chamber walls began to shudder. She found herself pulled to the floor and pressed deep into yielding tissue.

*I'm not going to live through this*, she thought. They were simply too far from home, too far from rescue, the situation too far out of control. It was the first time she had understood that, deep in her gut. And yet she felt no fear: only concern for Kapur. She cradled him in her arms, trying to shield him from the deceleration. His body felt stick-thin. He gasped, his face working from pain from which she couldn't save him. Nevertheless she tried to support his head. 'There, there,' she murmured.

'Do you have any more of that Poole blood?'

'No. I'm sorry.'

'Pity . . .' He whimpered, and tried to raise his hands to his ruined Eyes. He had never once complained of that injury, she realised now, even though the agony must have been continual and intense.

She had always thought of herself as strong, but there were different sorts of strength, she thought now. She felt as if her head was full of boulders: huge thoughts, vast impressions that rattled within her skull, refusing her peace. 'Lieutenant Jarn turned out to be a good officer. Didn't she, sir?'

'Yes, she did.'

'I never liked her, before. But she sacrificed her life for you.'

'That was her duty. You would have done the same.'

'Yes,' said Mari doggedly, 'but *you* tried to save *her*. Even though you didn't have to. Even though you would have been killed yourself in the process.'

He tried to turn his head. 'Gunner, I sense you believe you have failed, because you aren't dead yet. Listen to me now. You haven't failed. In the end, what brought us so far was not your specialist training but deeper human qualities of courage, initiative, endurance. Empathy. In the end it will be those qualities that will win this war, not a better class of weapon. You should be proud of yourself.'

She wasn't sure about that. 'If I ever did get out of this I'd have to submit myself for reorientation.'

'The Commission would have its work cut out, I think – Ah.' His face worked. 'Child.' She had to bend to hear him. He whispered, 'Even now my wretched mind won't stop throwing out unwelcome ideas. You still have a duty to perform. *Remember.*'

'Remember?'

'You saw the stars. Given that, one could reconstruct the position of this world, this Spline home. And how valuable that piece of information would be. It is the end of the free Spline,' he said. 'What a pity. But I am afraid we have a duty. *You must remember.* Tell the Commissaries what you saw.'

'Sir—'

He tried to grasp her arm, his ruined face swivelling. 'Tell them.' His back arched, and he gasped. '*Oh.*'

'No,' she said, shaking him. 'No!'

'I am sorry, gunner Mari. So sorry.' And he exhaled a great gurgling belch, and went limp.

She continued to cradle Academician Kapur, rocking him like a child, as the homecoming Spline plunged deeper into its world's thick atmosphere.

But as she held him she took the vials of mnemonic fluid from his waist, and drank them one by one. And she took the Squeem from its cloak bag – it wriggled in her fingers, cold and very alien – and, overcoming her disgust, swallowed it down.

In the last moments, the Spline's great eyelid closed.

Accompanied by Lieutenant-Commander Erdac, Commissary Drith stepped gingerly through the transfer tunnel and into the damaged Spline eye.

Drith's brow furrowed, sending a wave of delicate creases over her shaved scalp. It was bad enough to be immersed *inside* the body of a living creature like this, without being confronted by the gruesome sight the salvage teams had found here. Still, it had been a prize worth retrieving.

Erdac said, 'You can see how the Squeem fish consumed this young gunner, from inside out. It kept alive that way, long enough anyhow for it to serve as a beacon to alert us when this Spline returned to service in human space. And there was enough of the mnemonic fluid left in the gunner's body to—'

'A drop is sufficient,' Drith murmured. 'I do understand the principle, Commander.'

Erdac nodded stiffly, his face impassive.

'Quite a victory, Commander,' Drith said. 'If the breeding ground of the Spline can be blockaded, then the Spline can effectively be controlled.'

'These two fulfilled their duty in the end.'

'Yes, but we will profit personally from this discovery.' The Commander didn't respond to that; maybe he thought the remark was a personal test, a trap.

Drith looked down at the twisted bodies and poked at them with a polished toecap. 'Look how they're wrapped around each other. Strange. You wouldn't expect a dry-as-a-stick Academician and a boneheaded Navy grunt to get so close.'

'The human heart contains mysteries we have yet to fathom, Commander.'

'Yes. Even with the mnemonic, I guess we'll never really know what happened here.'

'But we know enough. What else matters?' Drith turned. 'Come, Commander. We both have reports to file, and then a mission to plan, far beyond the Expansion's current limits . . . quite an adventure!'

They left, talking, planning. The forensic teams moved in to remove the bodies. It wasn't easy. Even in death they were closely intertwined, as if one had been cradling the other.

*The Assimilated 'Snowflake' technology would turn out to be very valuable, much later, when I, Luru Parz, rediscovered it in decaying archives.*

*In the meantime Kapur's intuition was right. This was a turning point. With the Spline harnessed the Third Expansion accelerated. Mankind burned across the Galaxy.*

*The vanguard soldiers and Assimilators were reckless.*

*Destructive.*

*Magnificent.*

# THE DREAMING MOULD

## AD 12,478

Tomm found a new patch of dreaming mould. Snuggled into the shade of a damp tree root, it had settled down into a grey circle the size of a dinner plate. Where it had crossed the crimson soil it had left a slimy trail. You often found moulds in shady places like this. They didn't like the brightness of the growth lights. The muddled starlight cast diffuse colours over the mould, but it was always going to look ugly.

Tomm pressed his hands into the mould. It felt cold, slimy, not bad when you got used to it.

And the mould started to talk to him.

As always, it was like waking up. Suddenly he could smell the ozone tang of the growth lights, and hear the bleating of the goat at the Gavil place over the horizon, and he seemed to be able to see every one of the one hundred and twenty thousand stars in the crowded sky.

And then he spread out sideways, that was the way he thought of it, he *reached out*, left and right. The crowded stars froze over his head – or maybe they wheeled around and around, blurring into invisibility. He was with the mould now. And he could see its long, simple, featureless life all of a piece, from beginning to end, pulled out of time like a great grey slab of rock hauled out of the ground.

Even his heart stopped its relentless pumping.

But there was a flitter, a spark against the orange stars.

He dropped back into time. He stood and wiped his slimy hands on his trousers, watching the spaceship approach.

He was eight years old.

Kard's metallic Eyes gleamed in the complex starlight. 'Lethe, I love it all. Is there any sight more beautiful than starbreaker light shining through the rubble of a planet?'

This was a globular cluster, orbiting far out of the Galaxy's main disc. The sky was packed with stars, orange and yellow, layer upon layer of ancient lanterns that receded to infinity. But before those stars, paler lights moved purposefully. They were human-controlled ships. And Xera saw scattered pink sparks, silent detonations. Each of those remote explosions was the dismantling of a world.

The flitter's hull was transparent because Rear Admiral Kard liked it that way. Even the controls were no more than ghostly rectangles written on the air. It was as if Xera, with Kard and Stub, their young pilot, was falling defenceless through this crowded sky, and she tried to ignore the churning of her stomach.

Xera said carefully, 'I compliment you on the efficiency of your process.'

He waved that aside. 'Forget *efficiency*. Forget *process*. Commissary, this cluster contains a million stars, crowded into a ball a hundred light years across. It's only four decades since we first arrived here. And we will have processed them *all*, all those pretty lights in the sky, within another fifty to sixty years. What do you think of that?'

'Admiral—'

'*This* is the reality of Assimilation,' he snapped. 'Ten thousand ships, ten *million* human beings, in this fleet alone. And it's the same all over the Expansion, across a great spherical front forty thousand light years across. I doubt you even dream of sights like this, back in the centre. Commissary, watch and learn . . .'

Without warning, planets cannonballed out of the sky. She cowered.

Kard laughed at her shock. 'Oh. And here is our destination.'

Stub, the rodent-faced young pilot, turned to face them, grinning. 'Sir, wake me up when it gets interesting.'

Stub called Xera a domehead when he thought she wasn't listening. She tried not to despise them both for the way they bullied her.

There were three worlds in this sunless system, locked into a complex gravitational dance. Xera could see them all, sweeping in vertiginously, pale starlit discs against a crowded sky. Only one of them was inhabited: she saw the blue of water and the grey-green of living things splashed against its rust-red hide. It was called, inevitably, 'Home', in the language of the first human colonists to have reached this place, millennia before.

Xera was a xenoculturalist. She was here because the inhabitants of Home had reported an indigenous sentient species on their world. If this was true the planet might be spared from the wrecking crews, spared from demolition for the sake of its inner iron, its natives put to a more subtle use: mind was valuable. The fate of whole cultures, alien and human, the fate of a world, could depend on her assessment of the inhabitants' claim.

But her time was cruelly brief. Rear Admiral Kard's own impatient presence here – he hadn't wanted to spare any of his line officers to check out what he called 'earthworm grunting' – told her all she needed to know about the Navy's attitude to her mission.

Belatedly she remembered to deploy her data desk; she needed to record the triple worlds' orbital dynamics. Here in this crowded cluster, stellar close approaches were frequent, and worlds were commonly ripped free of the stars that had borne them. Most planets floated alone, but this world, Home, was unusual in having its two gravitationally locked companion worlds. The nature of their mutual orbit was apparently puzzling to the Academicians, and they had asked her to check it out. Orbital dynamics were hardly her priority, but nobody else was going to get a chance to study this unique jewel-box of worlds. She held up her desk, letting it record.

But already the flitter had begun its brisk closing descent, and the opportunity was over.

She flew through a spectacular orbital picket of Snowflakes, the giant tetrahedral artefacts the Navy employed as surveillance and communications stations. Then Home opened out into a landscape that fled beneath her, a land of lakes and forests and farms and scattered townships, of green growing things illuminated by floodlights mounted on unlikely stalks.

It was all so complex, so fascinating, but she had so little time. This was the reality of Assimilation: the processing of alien worlds and species on an industrial scale. Out here, you just did what you could before the starbreaker teams moved in. It was rescue work, really. The only consolation was that you would never know what you had missed—

She was plunged into blackness. Impact foam encased her.

Xera had no idea what had happened. But she felt a guilty stab of satisfaction that Kard and his magnificent Navy had screwed up after all.

*

To Tomm the flitter had been an all but invisible bubble, sweeping down through the air, with its three passengers suspended inside. But then it stopped dead, as if it had run into a wall, and its hull appeared out of nowhere. Opaqued, the flitter was an ugly, lumpy thing. It hung for a heartbeat. Then the flitter tipped up until it pointed at the ground, and fell without ceremony.

On impact the hull broke up into compartments that dropped into the dirt. Hatches popped open, and a gooey white liquid ran into the rust-red ground.

Two people tumbled out. They were wearing bright orange skin-tight suits, to which the sticky liquid clung. They staggered a few paces from the wreck and collapsed to their knees. They were a woman and a man, Tomm saw.

The man had silvery fake eyes. He didn't see Tomm, or if he did he didn't care. He immediately got up and stalked back into the wreckage of the flitter, ripping debris out of the way.

The woman was younger. Her head was shaved. She got to her feet more slowly. She looked around, as if she had never seen stars, dirt, growth lights before. She looked right at Tomm.

Then, coming to herself, she ran to the flitter's wrecked forward section. Tomm made out splashes of blood in there. The woman stepped back, a look of horror on her face. She glanced around, but there was nobody in sight, nobody but Tomm.

She walked back and spoke to him. He waited as she tapped at a panel on her chest, and a box floated up into the air by her shoulder. 'Can you understand me?' the box asked.

'Yes,' he said.

'I need help.'

Together they prised open the ripped hull. There wasn't much to see. Opaqued, the hull looked like scuffed metal, and all the pod's control surfaces were blank, dead. But there was a man – Tomm guessed he was the pilot – crumpled up into the nose of the pod, the way you'd wad a tissue into your pocket.

The woman bent over the pilot, feeling at his neck. 'He's still alive. Fluttery pulse . . . Lethe, I'm not trained for this. What's your name?'

'Tomm.'

'All right, Tomm. I'm Xera. I need you to pass me a med cloak. In the compartment behind you.'

The door was stiff, but Tomm was strong. The cloak was brilliant orange, so bright it seemed to dazzle. Xera just threw the cloak at the pilot. It immediately began to work its way around the body, then it filled up with more white goo.

When the cloak had set hard Xera took the pilot's shoulders, Tomm his legs. The pilot felt lighter than he looked. They got him out through the ripped hull, and set him on the ground. He lay there in the dirt, wrapped up like a bug in a cocoon, only his bruised face showing.

'He looks young,' Tomm said.

'He's only fifteen.' She glanced at him. 'How old are you?'

'Eight. How old are *you*?'

She forced a smile. 'Twenty-five standard. I think you're very brave.' She waved a trembling hand. 'To cope with all this. A crashing spaceship. An injured man.'

Tomm shrugged. He had grown up on a farm. He knew about life, injury, death.

He waited to see what happened next.

The air was warm, and smelled of rust. The land was like a tabletop, worn flat.

Kard had dumped heaps of equipment out of the flitter onto the ground, and was pawing through it.

Xera said, 'Admiral – what happened?'

'The Squeem,' Kard said bluntly. 'Dead, every last one of them. All the systems are down. We didn't even get a mayday out.' He glanced at the complex sky. 'The controllers don't know we are here. It's happened before. Nobody knows how the little bastards manage it.'

'You're saying the Squeem *killed* themselves to sabotage us?'

'Oh, you think it's a coincidence it happened just as we came into our final descent?'

The Squeem were group-mind aquatic creatures, a little like fish. Once, it was said, they had conquered Earth itself. Now, long Assimilated, they were used as communications links, as a piece of technology. Some humans had even taken Squeem implants. But it seemed that the Squeem were still capable of defiance. Maybe, she thought, the Assimilation wasn't as complete as it was presented by Commission propagandists.

Kard's hard gaze slid over the bundled pilot, as if reluctant to look at him too closely.

Xera said, 'Stub is hurt. The cloak will keep him alive for a while, but—'

'We need to get to the base camp. It's north of here, maybe half a day's walk.'

She looked about dubiously. There was no sun, no moon. Even Home's sibling worlds were invisible. There were only stars, a great uniform wash of them, the same wherever you looked. 'Which way's north?'

Kard glared, impatient. He seemed to see Tomm for the first time. 'You. Aboriginal. Which way?'

Tomm pointed, without hesitation. His feet were bare, Xera noticed now.

'Then that's the way we'll go. We'll need a stretcher. Xera, rig something.'

Tomm said, 'My home's closer.' He pointed again. 'It's just over that way. My parents could help you.'

Xera looked at Kard. 'Admiral, it would make sense.'

He glared at her. 'You do *not* take an injured Navy tar to an aboriginal camp.'

Xera tried to control her irritation. 'The people here are not animals. They are farmers. Stub might die before—'

'End of discussion. You. Earthworm. You want to come show us the way?'

Tomm shrugged.

Xera frowned. 'You don't need to tell your parents where you are?'

'You're the Navy,' Tomm said. 'We're all citizens of the Third Expansion. You have come here to protect us. That's what you told us. What harm can I come to with you?'

Kard laughed.

The ground was densely packed crimson dirt, hard under her feet. Soon she was puffing with exertion, her hips and knees dryly aching. After half a year in the murky gut of a Spline ship Xera wasn't used to physical exercise.

Kard, a bundle on his back, walked stiffly, with obvious distaste for the very dust under his feet.

At least the ground was level, more or less. And Stub, on his improvised stretcher, wasn't as heavy as he should have been. Evidently the smart med-care cloak contained some anti-gravitational trickery. Stub wasn't improving, though, despite the cloak's best efforts. Around his increasingly pale face, the cloak's hem glowed warning blue.

The boy, Tomm, just seemed interested in the whole adventure.

Away from the cultivated areas the ground looked nutrient-leached, and the only hills were eroded stumps, as dust-strewn as the rest. This was an old place, she thought. The population was evidently sparse, no more than this worn-out land could support.

And the sky was baffling.

Xera had grown up on a small planet of 70 Opiuchi, less than seventeen light years from Earth itself. There, in the Galaxy's main disc, three thousand stars had been visible in the night sky. In this globular cluster there were *forty times* as many. Shoals of stars swam continually above the horizon, casting a diffuse light laced with pale, complex, shifting shadows. There were too many of them to count, to identify, to track. This world had no sun and too many stars; it knew no day, no night, only this unchanging, muddy starlight. Here, time washed by unmarked, and in every direction the sky looked the same.

They had to cross a cultivated field. A floodlight bank loomed over the green growing things, presumably intended to supplement the starlight.

Kard hauled a semi-transparent suit out of the scavenged bundle he carried, and tied off the arms and legs. 'You,' he said to Tomm. 'Take this. We need supplies.'

Xera made to protest at this casual theft of somebody's crop. But Tomm was already running alongside Kard's long strides. They began pulling handfuls of green pods into the tied-off suit. Xera waited by Stub.

Kard snapped, 'Tell me what you eat here.'

'Peas,' said Tomm brightly. 'Beans. Rice. Wheat.'

'No replicators?'

Xera said, 'Admiral, Tomm's ancestors are here because they fled the Qax Occupation of Earth, seven thousand years ago. Nano replicators are Qax technology. To the colonists here, such things are hated.'

Kard glanced around. 'So how did they terraform this place?'

'The hard way. Apparently it took them centuries.'

'And now they grow wheat.'

'Yes.'

Kard laughed. 'Well, our suits will filter out the toxins.'

'We have goats too,' said the boy.

'Oh, imagine that.'

They came to an ancient, tangled tree, and Kard bent to inspect its roots. He pulled out a handful of what looked like fungus. 'What's this?'

'Dreaming mould,' said Tomm.

'Say what?'

Xera hurried over. 'That is why we're here. It's a relic of the native ecology, spared in the terraforming.'

Kard hefted the greyish stuff. '*This* is supposed to be sentient?'

'So the locals claim.'

'It can't even *move*.'

'It can,' insisted Tomm. 'It moves like slimy bugs.'

Xera held up her data desk, showing Kard images. 'On the move it absorbs nutrients from organic detritus, local analogues of leaves and grass. Then the protoplasm hardens into a definite shape as the mould prepares to fruit. In some species you get little parasols and rods.'

This organism was actually like the slime moulds of Earth: a very ancient form from a time when categories of life were blurred, when the higher plants had yet to split off from the fungi, and all animal life had streamed in protoplasmic shapelessness. What was more controversial was whether these moulds were sentient, or not. Already she was wondering how she could complete her assessment – how could she possibly *tell*?

Kard saw her doubts. He turned to the kid. 'How can this mould of yours be so smart if it can't use tools?'

'They used to,' said Tomm.

'What?'

'Once they built starships. They came from over there.' He pointed into the murky roof of stars – but the way he was pointing, Xera realised, was towards the Galaxy's main disc.

She asked, 'How do you know such things?'

'When you touch them.' The boy shrugged. 'You just know.'

'And why,' Kard asked, 'would they come to a shithole like this? It hasn't even got a sun.'

'They didn't want a sun. They wanted a sky like that,' pointing up again.

'Why?'

'Because you can't tell the time by it.'

Kard was glaring at Xera, hefting the mould. 'Is *this* all there is? What in Lethe are we doing here, Commissary?'

'Let's just try on the idea before we dismiss it,' Xera said quickly. 'Suppose there *was* an ancient race, done with' – she raised a hand at the sky, where worlds burned – 'with all this. Colonising, building—'

Kard snapped, 'So they came to this worn-out dump. They dismantled their starships, and dissolved into slime. Right? But it isn't even *safe*, here in this cluster. Have you any idea what it would be like to live through a Galaxy plane-crossing?' He shook his head. He threw the native life form into the hopper, along with the pea pods and runner beans.

'Admiral—'

'End of discussion.'

On they walked.


The stars were sombre. Most were orange or even red, floating silently in their watchful crowds. All this cluster's stars were about the same age, and all were old. Even the planets were so old the radioactivity trapped in their interiors had dwindled away. Which explained the exhausted landscape: no tectonics, no geology, no mountain-building.

This was what you got in a globular cluster. Like a diffuse planet, this whole cluster orbited the centre of the Galaxy. Every hundred million years it plunged through the Galaxy's disc, and in those catastrophic interludes all the dust was stripped out of the spaces between the stars. Thus there was no unburnt gas to make new stars out of, no rock dust to make new planets. That was why the fleet needed to demolish planets for their iron. Rock, metals were scarce between the worlds.

Of course Kard was right about the hazards of a main disc crossing. This planet would be bombarded with spiral-arm hydrogen and dust. A single dust grain would deliver the energy of a fission bomb. The place would be flooded with X-rays, if the atmosphere wasn't stripped off completely.

Maybe, maybe. But – Xera learned, checking her data desk, which she'd hung around her neck – the last plane crossing was only a couple of million years ago. There were nearly a hundred megayears yet before that calamity had to be faced again. Time enough for anybody.

This wasn't an academic debate. If she could prove the planet harboured intelligence, it might be spared demolition, its human colonists allowed to continue their way of life. If not . . .

Kard stopped again, breathing hard. 'Take a break.' He dumped the stretcher and squatted down, took a handful of pea pods from his improvised backpack, and crammed them into his mouth, pods and all.

The spare suit had extracted some water from the vegetable matter. Xera took one of its sleeves and dribbled water into the mouth of Stub. His breathing was irregular, his face pasty. She opened the cloak a little at his neck, trying to make him easier.

Kard recoiled from the stink that came out of the cloak, an earthy melange of blood and shit, the smell of a wounded human. 'Lethe, I hate this.' He turned away. 'You think the base is far?'

'I don't know. Not far, surely.'

He nodded, wordless, not looking at her.

Tomm sat quietly and watched them, bare feet tucked under his legs. He didn't ask for food or drink. Of the three of them he was by far the freshest.

Xera glanced again at her data desk. It had been working on the observations she'd been able to make before the landing. Now the desk showed that Home and its two siblings were locked into a figure-of-eight orbital motion. It was an exotic but stable solution to the ancient problem of how three bodies would swarm together under gravity. More common solutions resembled planets conventionally orbiting a sun, or three worlds at the corners of a rotating equilateral triangle.

She tried to discuss this with Kard. He knew a lot more about orbital dynamics than she did. But he was definitely not interested.

Xera pulled the dreaming mould out of the tied-up suit. A little dehydrated, it was cold to the touch but not unpleasant. She could tell nothing by just looking at it.

Uncertainly she handed it to Tomm.

The boy pressed his hands against the mould. He looked vaguely disappointed. 'This one's too dry.'

'Tomm, what happens when you touch the mould?'

'Like if you're sick.' Tomm shrugged. 'The mould helps you.'

'How?'

He said some things the floating translator unit couldn't handle. Then he said, 'Time stops.'

Kard sat up. *'Time stops?'*

'Like that. The mould doesn't see time—' Tomm made chopping motions. 'One bit after another. Step, step, step. It sees time all as a piece. All at once.'

257

Kard raised hairless eyebrows.

Xera felt like defying him. 'We need to keep open minds, Admiral. We're here to seek out the strange, the unfamiliar. That's the whole point. We know that time is quantised. Instants are like grains of sand. *We* experience them linearly, like a bug hopping from one grain to another. But other perceptions of time are possible. Perhaps—'

Kard looked disgusted. 'These dirt-diggers would call my ass sentient if it would hold back the starbreakers one more day.' He leaned towards the boy, who looked scared. 'Do you understand what we're doing here? Planets like yours are rare, in a globular cluster. That's why we need to blow up your world. So we can use what's inside it to make more ships and weapons.'

'So you can blow up *more* worlds.'

'Exactly. Slime mould and all.'

'Isn't that what the Qax did to humans?'

Xera choked a laugh.

Kard glared. 'Listen to me. You're just a snot-nosed earthworm kid and I'm a rear admiral. And any time I want to I could—'

Stub's med cloak abruptly turned bright blue.

Xera hurried to the dying pilot. Kard swore, stood up and walked away.

Tomm stared.

Xera felt for a pulse – it was desperately feathery – and bent her ear to Stub's mouth, trying to detect a breath. I'm here to stand in judgement on another race, perhaps much more ancient than my own, she thought. But I can't even save this wretched boy, lying in the dirt.

Kard stalked around. The crimson dust had stained his gleaming boots. 'We walked all this way for nothing.'

'It was your call,' she snapped. 'If we had gone to the farmers for help, maybe we could have saved him.'

Kard wasn't about to accept that. He turned on her. 'Listen to me, Commissary—'

Tomm was pressing bits of the dreaming mould into Stub's mouth.

Kard grabbed Tomm's arm. 'What are you doing?'

'The mould wants to help him. This is what we do.'

Xera asked quickly, 'When you hurt, when you die, you do this?'

'You take him out of time.'

Kard said, 'You'll choke him, you little grub.' He was still holding the boy's arm.

'Admiral, let the kid go.'

He said dangerously, 'This is a Navy man.'

'But we failed him, Kard. The cloak can't help. *He's dying*. Let the boy do what he wants. If it makes him feel better . . .'

Kard's face worked. But he broke away.

Bleakly, helplessly, Xera watched the boy patiently feed bits of the mould into the pilot's mouth.

*You take him out of time.*

Could it be true? How would it be to loosen the grasp of time – to have a mind filled with green thoughts, like a vegetable's perhaps – to be empty of everything but self? Kard had said the mould had no goals. But what higher goal could there be? Who needed starships and cities and wars and empires, when you could free yourself at last of the fear of death? And what greater empathy could there be than to share such a gift with others?

Or maybe the mould was just some hallucinogen, chewed by bored farmers.

Stub's breathing, though shallow, seemed a little easier.

She said, 'I think it's working.'

Kard wouldn't even look down. 'No.'

'Admiral—'

He turned on her. 'I know the sentience laws. What defines intelligence? You need to have goals, and pursue them. What goals has a slime mould got? Second, you need to have empathy: some kind of awareness of intelligence in others. And, most fundamentally, you need a sense of *time*. Life can only exist in a universe complex enough to be out of equilibrium – there could be no life in a mushy heat bath, with no flows of energy or mass. So tracking time is fundamental to intelligence, for a sense of time derives from the universal disequilibrium that drives life itself. *There*. If these creatures really don't have a time sense they *can't* be intelligent. How do you answer that? *There's nothing here*, Commissary. Nothing for you to save.'

She pressed her fingers to her temples. 'Admiral – the history of human understanding is about discarding prejudices, about ourselves, about others, about the nature of life, mind. We have come a long way, but we're still learning. Perhaps even an insistence on a time sense itself is just another barrier in our thinking . . .'

Kard, she could see, wasn't listening.

But, she thought, it isn't just about the sentience laws, is it, Admiral?

You can't accept that you made the wrong call today. Just as you can't accept that the humble creatures here, the farmers and this boy and even the mould, might know something you don't. You'd rather destroy it all than accept that.

Data scrolled across her desk. She glanced down. The desk had continued patiently to work on the orbital data. The figure-of-eight configuration was *rare*, the desk reported now, vanishingly unlikely. Surely too improbable to be natural. She felt wonder stir. Had they been vain, at the last? Before they dissolved down into this humble form, even gave up their shape, had they left a grandiose dynamic signature scrawled across the sky? . . .

But it's too late, too late. This place will be destroyed, and we'll never know what happened here.

Kard raised his engineered face, restless, trapped on the ground. 'Lethe, I hate this, the dust and the pain. The sooner I get back to the sky the better. You know what? None of this matters. Whether you're right or wrong about the mould, your petty moral dilemmas are irrelevant, Commissary. Because the Assimilation is nearly over. We've cleaned out this Galaxy. There's nothing left to oppose us now – nothing but one more opponent.'

'I have my assessment to finish—'

'Nothing happened here, Commissary. *Nothing.*'

Tomm sat back, smiling.

It seemed to Xera that the young pilot's face relaxed, that he breathed a little easier, before he was still.

*Personally I have more sympathy for Xera and her complex ethical dilemmas than with Kard.*

*But it was Kard's arrogant impatience that caught the flavour of the times.*

*Mayfly generations tick by terribly quickly. And almost all mayflies, embedded in history, believe that their epoch is eternal, that things will be this way until the end of time. Almost all. It takes a special mayfly to understand that he is living through a time of flux, a time when great forces are shifting – and even more special to be able to influence those forces.*

*Kard turned out to be one such.*

*Just as he had said, the Galaxy was cleaned out. Only one more opponent remained. Only one war remained to be completed.*

*But it had to be started first.*

# THE GREAT GAME

## AD 12,659

We were in our blister, waiting for the drop. My marines, fifty of them in their bright orange Yukawa suits, were sitting in untidy rows. They were trying to hide it, but I could see the tenseness in the way they clutched their static lines, and their unusual reluctance to rib the wetbacks.

Well, when I looked through the blister's transparent walls and out into the dangerous sky, I felt it myself.

We had been flung far out of the main disc, and the sparse orange-red stars of the halo were a foreground to the Galaxy itself, a pool of curdled light that stretched to right and left as far as you could see. But as our Spline ship threw itself gamely through its complicated evasive manoeuvres, that great sheet of light flapped around us like a bird's broken wing. I could see our destination's home sun – it was a dwarf, a pinprick glowing dim red – but even the target star jiggled around the sky as the Spline bucked and rolled.

And, leaving aside the vertigo, what twisted my own stress muscles was the glimpses I got of the craft that swarmed like moths around that dwarf star. Beautiful swooping ships with sycamore-seed wings – unmistakable, they were Xeelee nightfighters. The Xeelee were the Spline Captain's responsibility, not mine. But I couldn't stop my over-active mind speculating on what had lured such a dense concentration of them so far out of the Galactic Core, their usual stamping ground.

Given the tension, it was almost a relief when Lian threw up.

Those Yukawa suits are heavy and stiff, meant for protection rather than flexibility, but she managed to lean far enough forward that her bright yellow puke mostly hit the floor. Her buddies reacted as you'd imagine.

'Sorry, Lieutenant.' She was the youngest of the troop, at seventeen ten years younger than me.

I handed her a wipe. 'I've seen worse, marine. Anyhow you've left the wetbacks something to clean up. Keep them busy when we've gone.'

'Yes, sir.'

The mood was fragile, but I was managing it. What you definitely don't want at such moments is a visit from the brass. Which, of course, is what we got.

Admiral Kard came stalking through the drop blister, muttering to the loadmaster, nodding at marines. At Kard's side was a Commissary – you could tell that was her role at a glance – a woman, tall, ageless, in the classic costume of the Commission for Historical Truth, a floor-sweeping gown and shaved-bald head. She looked as cold and lifeless as every Commissary I ever met.

Admiral Kard picked me out. 'Lieutenant Neer, correct?'

I stood up, brushing vomit off my suit. 'Sir.'

'Welcome to Shade,' he said evenly.

I could see how the troops were tensing up. We didn't need this. But I couldn't have thrown out an admiral, not on his flagship.

'We're ready to drop, sir.'

'Good.'

Just then the destination planet, at last, swam into view. We grunts knew it only by a number. That eerie sun was too dim to cast much light, and despite low-orbiting sunsats much of the land and sea was dark velvet. But great orange rivers of fire coursed across the black ground. This was a suffering world; you could see that from space.

The Commissary peered out at the tilted landscape, hands folded behind her back. 'Remarkable. It's like a geology demonstrator. Look at the lines of volcanoes and ravines. Every one of this world's tectonic faults has given way, all at once.'

Admiral Kard eyed me. 'You must forgive Commissary Xera. She does think of the universe as a textbook, set out before us for our education.'

He was rewarded for that with a glare.

I kept silent, uncomfortable. Everybody knows about the strained relations between Navy, the fighting arm of mankind's Third Expansion, and Commission, implementer of political will. Maybe that structural rivalry was the reason for this impromptu walk-through, as the Commissary jostled for influence over events, and the Admiral tried to score points with a display of his fighting troops.

Except that right now they were *my* troops, not his.

To her credit, Xera seemed to perceive something of my resentment. 'Don't worry, Lieutenant. It's just that Kard and I have something of a history. Two centuries of it, in fact, since our first encounter on a world called Home, thousands of light years from here.'

I could see Lian look up at that. Two centuries? According to the book, *nobody* was supposed to live so long. I guess at seventeen you still think everybody follows the rules.

Kard nodded. 'And you've always had a way of drawing subordinates into our personal conflicts, Xera. Well, we may be making history today. Neer, look at the home sun, the frozen star.'

I frowned. 'What's a *frozen star?*'

The Commissary made to answer, but Kard cut across her. 'Skip the science. You know the setup here. The Expansion reached this region five hundred years ago. When our people down there called for help, the Navy responded. That's our job.' He had cold artificial Eyes, and I sensed he was testing me. 'And those Xeelee units are swarming like flies. We don't know *why* the Xeelee are here. But we do know what they are doing to this human world.'

'That's not proven,' Xera snapped.

Of course she was right. One of our objectives, in fact, was to pick up proof that the Xeelee were responsible for the calamities befalling the colonists on this battered world, Shade. But even so I could see my people stir at the Admiral's words. There had been tension between humanity and Xeelee for centuries, but none of us had ever heard of a direct attack by the Xeelee on human positions.

Lian said boldly, 'Admiral, sir.'

'Yes, rating?'

'Does that mean we are at war?'

Admiral Kard sniffed up a lungful of ozone-laden air. 'After today, perhaps we will be, at long last. How does that make you feel, rating?'

Lian, and the others, looked to me for guidance. I looked into my heart.

Across seven thousand years of the Third Expansion humans had spread out in a great swarm through the Galaxy, even reaching the halo beyond the main disc, overwhelming other life forms as we encountered them. We had faced no opponent capable of systematic resistance since the collapse of the Silver Ghosts – none but the Xeelee, the Galaxy's other great power, who sat in their great concentrations at the Core, silent, aloof.

This had been the situation for *five thousand years*. In my officer training I'd been taught the meaning of such numbers – for instance, that was an interval as long as that between the invention of writing and the launch of the first spaceships from Earth. It was a *long* time. But the Coalition was older yet, and its collective memory and clarity of purpose, all held together by the Druz Doctrines, even across such inhuman spans of time, was flawless. Marvellous when you thought about it.

And now – perhaps – here I was at the start of the final war, the war for the Galaxy. What I felt was awe. Also fear, maybe. But that wasn't what the moment required.

'I'll tell you what I feel, sir. Relief. *Bring it on!*'

That won me a predictable hollering, and a slap on the back from Kard. Xera studied me blankly, her face unreadable.

Then there was a flare of plasma around the blister, and the ride got a lot bumpier. The Spline was entering the planet's atmosphere. I sat before I was thrown down, and the loadmaster at last hustled away the brass.

'Going in hard,' called the loadmaster. 'Barf bags at the ready. Ten minutes.'

We were skimming under high, thin, icy clouds. The world had become a landscape of burning mountains and rivers of rock that fled beneath me. All this in an eerie silence, broken only by the shallow breaths of the marines.

The ship lurched up and to the right. To our left now was a mountain; we had come so low already that its peak was above us. According to the centuries-old survey maps the locals had called it Mount Perfect, and, yes, once it must have been a classic cone shape, I thought, a nice landmark for an earthworm's horizon. But now its profile was spoiled by bulges and gouges, ash had splashed around it, and deeper mud-filled channels had been cut into the landscape, splayed like the fingers of a hand.

Somewhere down there, amid the bleating locals, there was an Academician called Tilo, dropped by the Navy a couple of standard months earlier, part of a global network who had been gathering data on the causes of the volcanism. Tilo's job, bluntly, had been to prove that this was all the Xeelee's fault. The Academician had somehow got himself cut off from his uplink gear. Our mission, along with helping with the evacuation of the locals, was to find and retrieve Tilo and his data. No wonder Xera had been so hostile, I thought; the Commissaries, paranoid about their own power, were famously suspicious of the alliances between the Navy and the Academies.

Green lights marked out the hatch in the transparent wall. Show time.

The loadmaster came along the line. 'Stand up! Stand up!' The marines complied clumsily. 'Thirty seconds,' the loadmaster told me. He was a burly, scarred veteran, attached to a rail by an umbilical as thick as my arm. 'Winds look good.'

'Thank you.'

'All clear aft. Ten seconds. Five.'

The green lights began to blink. We pulled our flexible visors across our faces.

'Three, two—'

The hatch dilated, and the sudden roar of the wind made all this real. The loadmaster stood by the hatch, screaming, 'Go, go, go!'

As the marines passed I checked each static line one last time with a sharp tug, before they jumped into blackness. The kid, Lian, was the second last to go and I was the last of all.

So there I was, falling into the air of a new world.

My static line went taut and ripped free, turning on my suit's Yukawa-force gravity nullifier. That first shock of no-gravity can be a jolt to the stomach, but to me, after maybe fifty drops in anger, it came as a relief.

I looked up and to my right. I saw a neat line of marines falling starfished through the air. One was a lot closer to me than the rest – Lian, I guessed. Past them I made out our Spline vessel, its hull charred from its hurried entry into the atmosphere. Our open drop blister was a glistening scar on its flank. The Spline looked immense, its pocked hull like an inverted landscape above me. It was a magnificent sight, an awe-inspiring display of human power and capability.

But beyond it I saw the hulking majesty of that mountain, dwarfing even the Spline. A dense cloud of smoke and ash lingered near its truncated summit, underlit by a fiery glow.

I looked down, searching for the valley I was aiming for.

I was able to pick out the target. The Commission's maps, two centuries old, had shown a standard-issue Conurbation surrounded by broad, shining replicator fields, where the ground's organic matter was processed seamlessly into food. But the view from the air was different. I could see the characteristic bubble-cluster shape of the domed Conurbation, but it looked dark, poorly maintained, while suburbs of blockier buildings had sprouted around it, as if the colonists had moved out of the buildings provided for them. Well, you expected a little drift from orthodoxy, out here on the edge of everything.

Still, that Conurbation was our target for the evacuation. Amid the domes I could see the squat cone shape of a heavy-lift shuttle, dropped here on the Spline's last pass through the atmosphere, ready to lift the population.

But I had a problem, I saw now. My marines were heading straight for the nominal target, the Conurbation, just as they should. But there was another cluster of buildings and lights, much smaller, stranded halfway up the flank of the mountain. There was no sign of domed Conurbation architecture, but there seemed no doubt this was human. Another village? And then I saw a pale pink light blinking at me from the middle of that cluster of shacks.

I'm not sentimental, and I don't go for heroic gestures. In a given situation, with given resources, you do what you can, what's possible. Given a free hand I'd have concentrated my energies on evacuating the Conurbation which undoubtedly held the bulk of the population. I wouldn't have gone after that isolated handful of people, wouldn't have approached that village at all – if not for that pink light. It was Tilo's beacon. Kard had made it clear enough that unless I came home with the Academician, or at least with his data, next time I made a drop it would be without a Yukawa suit.

I slowed my fall and barked out orders. I knew my people would be able to supervise the evacuation of the main township without me; it was a simple mission. Then I redirected my own descent, down towards the smaller community. I'd go get Tilo out of there myself.

It was only after I had committed myself that I saw one of my troop had followed me: the kid, Lian.

No time to think about that now. A Yukawa suit is good for one drop, one way. You can't go back and change your mind. Anyhow I was already close. I glimpsed a few ramshackle buildings, upturned faces shining like coins.

Then the ground raced up to meet me. Feet together, knees bent, back straight, roll when you hit – and then a lung-emptying impact on hard rock.

I allowed myself three full breaths, lying there on the cold ground, as I checked I was still in one piece.

Then I stood and pulled off my visor. The air was breathable, but thick with the smell of burning, and of sulphur. But the ground quivered under my feet, over and over. I wasn't too troubled by that – until I reminded myself that I wasn't on a ship any more, that planets were supposed to be *stable*.

Lian was standing there, her suit glowing softly. 'Good landing, sir,' she said.

I nodded, glad she was safe, but irritated; if she'd followed orders she wouldn't have been here at all. I turned away from her, a deliberate snub that was enough admonishment for now.

I tried to get my bearings. The sky was deep. Beyond clouds of ash, sunsats swam. And past *them* I glimpsed the red pinprick of the true sun, and the wraith-like Galaxy disc.

I was just outside that mountainside village. Below me the valley skirted the base of Mount Perfect, neatly separating it from more broken ground beyond. The landscape was dark green, its contours coated by forest, and clear streams bubbled into a river that ran down the valley's centre. A single, elegant bridge spanned the valley, reaching towards the old Conurbation on the far side. Further upstream I saw what looked like a logging plant, giant pieces of yellow-coloured equipment standing idle amid huge piles of sawn trees. Idyllic, if you liked that kind of thing, which I didn't.

On this side of the valley, the village was just a huddle of huts – some of them made from *wood* – clustered on the lower slopes of the mountain. Bigger buildings might have been a school, a medical centre maybe, and there were a couple of battered ground transports. Beyond, I glimpsed the rectangular shapes of fields – apparently ploughed, not a glimmer of replicator technology in sight. It was like a living-history exhibit. But today it was all covered in ash.

People were standing, watching me, grey as the ground under their feet. Men, women, children, infants in arms, old folk, people in little clusters. There were maybe thirty of them.

Lian stood close to me. 'Sir, I don't understand. The way they are standing together—'

'These are *families*,' I murmured. 'You'll pick it up.'

'Dark matter.' The new voice was harsh, damaged by smoke.

A man was limping towards me. About my height and age but a lot leaner, he wore a tattered Navy coverall, and was he using an improvised crutch to hobble over the rocky ground, favouring what looked like a broken leg. His face and hair were grey with the ash.

I said, 'You're the Academician.'

'Yes, I'm Tilo.'

'We're here to get you out.'

He barked a laugh. 'Sure you are. Listen to me. *Dark matter*. That's why the Xeelee are here, meddling in this system. It may have nothing to do with *us* at all. Things are going to happen fast. If I don't get out of here . . . whatever happens, just remember that one thing – *dark matter*.'

A woman hurried towards me. One of the locals, she was wearing a simple shift of woven cloth, and leather sandals on her feet; she looked maybe forty, strong, tired. An antique translator box hovered at her shoulder. 'My name is Doel,' she said. 'We saw you fall.'

'Are you in charge here?'

'I—' She smiled wearily. 'Yes, if you like. Will you help us get out of here?'

She didn't look, or talk, or act, like any Expansion citizen I had ever met. Things truly had drifted here. 'You are in the wrong place.' I was annoyed how prissy I sounded. I pointed to the Conurbation, on the other side of the valley. '*That's* where you're supposed to be. The evacuation point.'

'I'm sorry,' she said, bemused. 'We've lived here in the village since my grandfather's time. We didn't like it, over in Blessed. We came here to live a different way. No replicators. Crops we grow ourselves. Clothes we make—'

'Mothers and fathers and grandfathers,' Tilo cackled. 'What do you think of that, Lieutenant?'

'Academician, why are you here, in this village?'

He shrugged. 'I came to study the mountain, as an exemplar of the planet's geology. I accepted the hospitality of these people. That's all. I got to like them, despite their – alien culture.'

'But you left your equipment behind,' I snapped. 'You don't have comms implants. You didn't even take your mnemonic fluid, did you?'

'I brought my pickup beacon,' he said smugly.

'Lethe, I don't have time for this.' I turned to Doel. 'Look, if you can get your people across the valley, to where that transport is, you'll be taken out with the rest.'

'But I don't think there will be time—'

I ignored her. 'Academician, can you walk?'

Tilo laughed. 'No. And *you* can't hear the mountain, can you?'

That was when Mount Perfect exploded.

Tilo told me later that, if I'd known where and how to look, I could have seen the north side of the mountain bulging out. The immense chthonic defect had been growing visibly, at a metre a day. Well, I didn't notice that. Thanks to some trick of acoustics I didn't even hear the eruption – though it was heard by other Navy teams working hundreds of kilometres away.

But the aftermath was clear enough. With Lian and Doel, and with Academician Tilo limping after us, I ran to the crest of a ridge to see down the length of the valley.

As we watched, a billion tonnes of rock slid into the valley in a monstrous landslide. Already a huge grey thunderhead of smoke and ash was rearing up to the murky sky. A sharp earthquake had caused the mountain's swollen flank to shear and fall away.

But that was only the start of the sequence of geological events, for the removal of all that weight was like opening a pressurised can. The mountain erupted – not upwards, but *sideways*, like the blast of an immense weapon, a volley of superheated gas and pulverised rock. The eruption quickly overtook the landslide, and I saw it demolish trees, imports from distant Earth, sentinels centuries old flattened like straws. I was stupefied by the *scale* of it all.

And there was more to come. From out of the ripped-open side of the mountain, a chthonic blood oozed, yellow-grey, viscous, steaming hot. It began to flow down the mountainside, spilling into rain-cut valleys.

'That's a lahar,' Tilo murmured. 'Mud. The heat is melting the permafrost – the mountain was snow-covered two weeks ago; did you know that? – making up a thick mixture of volcanic debris and meltwater. I've learned a lot of esoteric geology here, Lieutenant.'

'So it's just mud,' said Lian uncertainly.

'*Just* mud. You aren't an earthworm, are you, marine?'

'Look at the logging camp,' Doel said.

Already the mud had overwhelmed the heavy equipment, big yellow tractors and huge cables and chains used for hauling logs, crumpling it all like paper. Piles of sawn logs were spilled, immense wooden beams shoved downstream effortlessly. The mud, grey and yellow, was steaming, oddly like curdled milk.

*Just mud*. For the first time I began to consider the contingency that we might not get out of here.

In which case my primary mission was to preserve Tilo's data. I quickly used my suit to establish an uplink. We were able to access Tilo's records, stored in cranial implants, and fire them up to the Spline. But in case it didn't work—

'Tell me about dark matter,' I said. 'Quickly.'

Tilo pointed up at the sky. 'That star – the natural sun, the dwarf – shouldn't exist.'

'What?'

'It's too small. It has only around a twentieth of Earth's sun's mass. It should be a planet: a brown dwarf, like a big, fat Jovian. It shouldn't burn – *not yet*. You understand that stars form from the interstellar medium – gas and dust. Originally the medium was just Big-Bang hydrogen and helium. But stars bake heavy elements, like metals, in their interiors, and eject them back into the medium when the stars die. So as time goes on, the medium is increasingly polluted.'

Impatiently I snapped, 'And the point?'

'The point is that an increase in impurities in the interstellar medium lowers the critical mass needed for a star to be big enough to burn hydrogen. So as time goes by and the medium gets murkier, smaller stars start lighting up. Lieutenant, *that* star shouldn't be shining. Not in this era, not for trillions of years yet; the interstellar medium is too clean . . . You know, it's so small that its surface temperature isn't thousands of degrees, like Earth's sun, but the freezing point of water. It is a star with ice clouds in its atmosphere. There may even be liquid water on its surface.'

I looked up, wishing I could see the frozen star better. Despite the urgency of the moment I shivered, confronted by strangeness, a vision from trillions of years downstream.

Tilo said bookishly, 'What does all this mean? It means that out here in the halo, something, some agent, is making the interstellar medium dirtier than it ought to be. The only way to do that is by *making the stars grow old*.' He waved a hand at the cluttered sky. 'And if you look, you can see it all over this part of the halo; the stellar evolution diagrams are impossibly skewed.'

I shook my head; I was far out of my depth. What could make a star grow old too fast? . . . Oh. 'Dark matter?'

'The matter we're made of – baryonic matter, protons and neutrons and the rest – is only about a tenth of the universe's total. The rest is dark matter: subject only to gravity and the weak nuclear force, impervious to electromagnetism. Dark matter came out of the Big Bang, just like the baryonic stuff. As our Galaxy coalesced the dark matter was squeezed out of the main disc . . . But it lingered here. *This* is the domain of dark matter, Lieutenant. Out here in the halo.'

'And this stuff can affect the ageing of stars.'

'Yes. A dark matter concentration in the core of a star can change temperatures, and so affect fusion rates.

'You said an "agent" was ageing the stars. You make it sound intentional.'

He was cautious now, an Academician who didn't want to commit himself. 'The stellar disruption appears non-random.'

Through the jargon, I tried to figure out what this meant. 'Something is *using* the dark matter? . . . Or are there life forms *in* the dark matter? And what does that have to do with the Xeelee, and the problems here on Shade?'

His face twisted. 'I haven't figured out the links yet. There's a lot of history. I need my data desk,' he said plaintively.

I pulled my chin, thinking of the bigger picture. 'Academician, you're on an assignment for the Admiral. Do you think you're finding what he wants to hear?'

He eyed me carefully. 'The Admiral is part of a faction within the Navy that is keen to go to war with the Xeelee – if necessary, even to provoke conflict. Some call them extremists. Kard's actions have to be seen in this light.'

Actually I'd heard such rumours, but I stiffened. 'He's my commanding officer. That's all that matters.'

Tilo sighed. 'I understand. But—'

'Lethe,' Lian said suddenly. 'Sorry, sir. But that mud is moving *fast*.'

So it was, I saw.

The mud was filling up the valley, rising rapidly, even as it flowed towards us. It was piling up behind a front that was held back by its own viscosity. As it surged forward the mud ripped away the land's green coat to reveal bare rock, and was visibly eating away at the walls of the valley itself. Overlaying the crack of tree trunks and the clatter of rock there was a noise like the feet of a vast running crowd, and a sour, sulphurous smell hit me.

The gush out of the mountain's side showed no signs of abating. That front was already tens of metres high, and would soon reach the village.

'I can't believe how fast this stuff is rising,' I said to Tilo. 'The volume you'd need to fill up a valley like this—'

'You and I are used to spacecraft, Lieutenant,' Tilo said. 'The dimensions of human engineering. Planets are *big*. And when they turn against you—'

'We can still get you out of here. With our suits we can get you over that bridge and to the transport.'

'What about the villagers?'

I was aware of the woman, Doel, standing beside me silently, just waiting. Which, of course, made me feel worse than if she'd yelled and begged.

There was a scream. We looked down the ridge and saw that the mud had already reached the village's lower buildings. A young couple with a kid were standing on the roof of a low hut, about to get cut off.

Lian said, 'Sir? Your orders?'

I waited one more heartbeat, as the mud began to wash over that hut's porch.

'Lethe, Lethe.' I ran down the ridge until I hit the mud.

On the mud's surface were dead fish that must have jumped out of the river to escape the heat. There was a lot of debris in the flow, from dust to pebbles to small boulders: no wonder it was so abrasive.

Even with the suit's strength augmentation the mud was difficult stuff to wade through – lukewarm, and with a consistency like wet cement. The stench was bad enough for me to pull my visor over my mouth. By the time I reached the cottage I was already tiring badly.

I found the little 'family', parents and child, terrified, glad to see me. The woman was bigger, obviously stronger than the man. I had her hold her infant over her head, while I slung the man over my shoulder. With me leading, and the woman grabbing onto my belt, we waded back towards the higher ground.

All this time the mud rose relentlessly, filling up the valley as if it had been dammed, and every step sapped my energy.

Lian and Doel helped us out of the dirt. I threw myself to the ground, breathing hard. The young woman's legs had been scoured by rocks in the flow; she had lost one sandal, and her trouser legs had been stripped away.

'We're already cut off from the bridge,' Lian said softly.

I forced myself to my feet. I picked out a building – not the largest, not the highest, but a good compromise. It turned out to be the hospital. 'That one. We'll get them onto the roof. I'll call for another pickup.'

'Sir, but what if the mud keeps rising?'

'Then we'll think of something else,' I snapped. 'Let's get on with it.'

She ran to help as Doel improvised a ladder from a trellis fence.

My first priority was to get Tilo safely lodged on the roof. Then I began to shepherd the locals up there. But we couldn't reach all of them before the relentless rise of the mud left us all ankle-deep. People began to clamber up to whatever high ground they could find – verandas, piles of boxes, the ground transports, even rocks. Soon maybe a dozen were stranded, scattered on rooftop islands around a landscape turning grey and slick.

I waded in once more, heading towards two young women who crouched on the roof of a small building, like a storage hut. But before I got there the hut, undermined, suddenly collapsed, pitching the women into the flow. One of them bobbed up and was pushed against a stand of trees, where she got stuck, apparently unharmed. But the other tipped over and slipped out of sight. I reached the woman in the trees and pulled her out. The other was gone.

I hauled myself back onto the hospital roof for a break. All around us the mud flowed, a foul-smelling grey river, littered with bits of wood and rock.

My emotions were deep and unwelcome. I'd never met that woman, but her loss was visceral. It was as if, against my will, I had become part of this little community, as we huddled together on the roof of that crudely built hospital. Not to mention the fact that I now wouldn't be able to fulfil my orders completely.

I prepared to plunge back into the flow.

Tilo grabbed my arm. 'No. Not yet. You are exhausted. Anyhow you have a call to make, remember? If you can get me a data desk—'

Lian spoke up. 'Sir. Let me bring in the stranded locals.' She said awkwardly, 'I can manage that much.'

Redemption time for this young marine. 'Don't kill yourself,' I told her.

With a grin she slid off the roof.

Briskly, I used my suit's comms system to set up a fresh link to the Spline. I requested another pickup – was told it was impossible – and asked for Kard.

Tilo requested a Virtual data desk. He fell on it as soon as it appeared. His relief couldn't have been greater, as if the mud didn't exist.

When they grasped the situation I had gotten us all into, Admiral Kard and Commissary Xera both sent down Virtual avatars. The two of them hovered over our wooden roof, clean of the mud, gleaming like gods among people made of clay.

Kard glared at me. 'This is a mess, Lieutenant.'

'Yes, sir.'

'You should have gotten Tilo over that damn bridge while you could. We're heavily constrained by the Xeelee operations. You realise we probably won't be able to get you out of here alive.'

It struck me as somewhat ironic that in the middle of a Galaxy-spanning military crisis I was to be killed by mud. But I had made my choice. 'So I understand.'

'But, Kard,' Xera said, her thin face fringed by blocky pixels, 'he has completed his primary mission, which is to deliver Tilo's data back to us.'

Kard closed his Eyes, and his image flickered; I imagined Tilo's data and interpretations pouring into the processors which sustained this semi-autonomous Virtual image, tightly integrated with Kard's original sensorium. Kard said, 'Your report needs redrafting, Tilo. Sharpening up. There's too much about this *dark matter* crud, Academician.'

Xera said gently, 'You were here on assignment from your masters in the Navy, with a specific purpose. They wanted to know what the Xeelee are up to. But it's hard to close your eyes to the clamouring truth, isn't it, Academician?'

Tilo sighed, his face mud-covered.

'We must discuss this,' Kard snapped. 'All of us, right now. We have a decision to make, a recommendation to pass up the line – and we need to assess what Tilo has to tell us, in case we can't retrieve him.'

I understood immediately what he meant. We were about to put the Xeelee in the dock – *us*, right here on this beaten-up planet, while the mud rose up around us. And the recommendation we made today might reach all the way back to the great decision-making councils on Earth itself. I felt a deep thrill. Even the locals stirred, apparently aware that something historically momentous was about to happen, even in the midst of their own misfortunes, stuck as we were on that battered wooden roof.

So it began.

At first Tilo wasn't helpful.

'It simply isn't proven that this volcanism is the result of Xeelee action – and certainly not that it's deliberately directed against humans,' Despite Kard's glare, he persisted, 'I'm sorry, Admiral, but it isn't *clear*.

'Look at the context.' He pulled up historical material – images, text that scrolled briefly in the murky air. 'This is not a new story. There is evidence that human scientists were aware of dark-matter contamination in the stars *before* the beginning of the Third Expansion. They called the dark-matter life forms they found "photino birds". It seems an engineered human being was once sent into Sol itself to study them . . . An audacious project. But this learning was largely lost in the Qax Extirpation, and after that – well, we had a Galaxy to conquer. There was a later incident, a project run by the Silver Ghosts concerning a "soliton star", but—'

Kard snapped, 'What do the Xeelee care about dark matter?'

Tilo rubbed tired eyes with grubby fists. 'However exotic they are, the Xeelee are baryonic life forms, like us. It isn't in their interests for the suns to die young, any more than for us.' He shrugged. 'Perhaps they are trying to stop it. Perhaps *that's* why they have come here, to the halo. Nothing to do with us.'

Kard waved a Virtual hand at Mount Perfect's oozing wounds. 'Then why all this, just as the Xeelee show up? Coincidence?'

Xera protested, 'Admiral—'

'This isn't a Commission trial, Tilo,' Kard said. 'We don't need absolute proof. The imagery – human refugees, Xeelee nightfighters swooping overhead – will be all we need to implicate the Xeelee in this destruction.'

Xera said dryly, 'Yes. All we need to sell a war to the Coalition, the governing councils, and the people of the Expansion.' They seemed to forget the rest of us as they engaged in an argument they had clearly been pursuing before. 'This is wonderful for you, isn't it, Admiral? It's what the Navy has been waiting for, along with its Academy cronies. An excuse to attack.'

Kard's face was stony. 'The cold arrogance of you cosseted intellectuals is sometimes insufferable. It's true that the Navy is ready to fight, Commissary. That's our job. And we *are* ready. We have the plans in place—'

'But does the existence of the plans *require* their fulfilment? And let's remember how hugely the Navy itself will benefit. As the lead agency, a war would clearly support the Navy's long-term political goals.'

Kard glared. 'We all have something to gain. Xera, you Commissaries are responsible for maintaining the unity of mankind; the common principles, common purpose, the *belief* that has driven the Expansion so far. But isn't it obvious that you are failing? Look at this place.' He waved a Virtual hand through Doel's hair; the woman flinched, and the hand broke up into drifting pixels. 'This woman is a *mother*, apparently some kind of matriarch to her extended *family*.' He pronounced those words with loathing. 'They don't even live in their Coalition-provided Conurbation domes. It's as if Hama Druz never existed!

'And if the Druz Doctrines were to collapse, the Commission would have no purpose. Think of the good you do, for you know so much better than the mass of mankind how they should think, feel, live and die. Your project is actually humanitarian! It has to continue. But if it is to prevail mankind needs purification. An ideological cleansing. And *that's* what the bright fire of war will give us.'

I could see that his arguments, aimed at the Commissary's vanity and self-interest, were leaving a mark. I got a sense of the great agencies of the Coalition as shadowy independent empires, engaging in obscure and shifting alliances. And now each agency would contemplate the possibility of a war as an opportunity to gain political capital. It was queasy listening. But there's a lot I didn't want to know about how the Coalition is run. Still don't, in fact.

They had forgotten the Academician. But Tilo was still trying to speak. He showed me more bits of evidence he had assembled on his data desk – me, because I was the only one still listening. 'But I think I know now why the volcanism started here, Lieutenant. Forget the star: *this planet* has an unusually high dark-matter concentration in its core.

Under such densities the dark matter annihilates with ordinary matter and creates heat.'

I listened absently. 'Which creates the geological upheaval.'

He closed his eyes, thinking. 'Here's a scenario. The Xeelee have been driving dark-matter creatures out of the frozen star – and, fleeing, they have lodged here – and that's what set off the volcanism. It was all inadvertent. The Xeelee are trying to *save stars*, not harm planets. They probably don't even know humans are here . . . The damage to the planet is entirely coincidental.'

But nobody paid any attention to that. For, I realised, we had already reached a point where evidence didn't matter.

Kard ignored the Academician; he had what he wanted. He turned to the people of the village, muddy, exhausted, huddled together on their rooftop. 'What of you? *You* are the citizens of the Expansion. There are reformers who say you have had enough of colonisation and conflict, that there are enough people in the sky, we should seek stability and peace. Well, you have heard what we have had to say, and you have seen our mighty ships. Will you live out your lives on this drifting rock, helpless before a river of mud – or will you transcend your birth and die for an epic cause? War makes everything new. War is the wildest poetry. *Will you join me?*'

Those ragged-ass, dirt-scratching, orthodoxy-busting farmers hesitated for a heartbeat. You couldn't have found a less likely bunch of soldiers for the Expansion. But, would you believe, they started cheering the Admiral: every one of them, even the kids. Lethe, it brought a tear to my eye.

Even Xera seemed coldly excited.

Kard closed his Eyes; metals seams pushed his eyelids into ridges. 'We are just a handful of people in this desolate, remote place. And yet here a new epoch is born. They are listening to us, you know – listening in the halls of history. And *we* will be remembered for ever.'

Tilo's expression was complex. He clapped his hands, and the data desk disappeared in a cloud of pixels, leaving his work unfinished.

We mere fleshy types had to stay on that rooftop through the night. We could do nothing but cling to each other as the muddy tide rose slowly around us, and the kids cried from hunger.

When the sunsats returned to the sky, the valley was transformed. The channels had been gouged sharp and deep by the lahar, and the farms had been smothered by lifeless grey mud, from which only occasional trees and buildings protruded. But the lahar was flowing only sluggishly now.

Lian cautiously climbed to the edge of the roof and probed at the mud with her booted foot. 'It's very dense.'

Tilo said, 'Probably the water has drained out of it.'

Lian couldn't stand on the mud, but if she lay on it she didn't sink. She flapped her arms and kicked, and she skidded over the surface. Her face grey with the dirt, she laughed like a child. 'Sir, look at me! It's a lot easier than trying to swim or wade . . .'

So it was, when I tried it myself.

And that was how we got the villagers across the flooded valley, one by one, to the larger Conurbation – not that much was left of that by now – where the big transport waited to take us off. In the end we lost only one of the villagers, the young woman who had been over-whelmed by the surge. I tried to accept that I'd done my best to fulfil my contradictory mission objectives – and that, in the end, was the most important outcome for me.

As we lifted, Mount Perfect loosed another eruption.

Tilo, cocooned in a med cloak, stood beside me in an observation blister, watching the planet's mindless fury. He said, 'You know, you can't stop a lahar. It just goes the way it wants to go. Like this war, it seems.'

'I guess.'

'We humans understand so little. We *see* so little. But when you add us together we combine into huge historical forces that none of us can deflect, any more than you can dam or divert a mighty lahar . . .'

And so on. I made an excuse and left him there.

I went down to the sick bay, and watched Lian tending to the young from the village. I had relieved her of her regular duties, as she was one of the few faces on board that was familiar to the traumatised kids, so she was useful here. With the children now she was patient, competent, calm. I felt proud of that young marine; she had grown up a lot during our time on Shade.

And as I watched her simple humanity, I imagined a trillion such acts, linking past and future, history and destiny, a great tapestry of hard work and goodwill that united mankind into a mighty host that would some day rule a Galaxy.

To tell the truth I was bored with Tilo and his niggling. *War!* It was magnificent. It was inevitable. I didn't understand what had happened down on Shade, and I didn't care. What did it matter *how* the war had started, in truth or lies? We would soon forget about dark matter and the Xeelee's obscure, immense projects, just as we had before; we humans didn't think in such terms. All that mattered was that the war was here, at last.

The oddest thing was that none of it had anything to do with the Xeelee themselves. We needed a war. Any enemy would have served our purposes just as well.

I began to wonder what it would mean for me. I felt my heart beat faster, like a drumbeat.

We flew into a rising cloud of ash, and bits of rock clattered against our hull, frightening the children.

*Yes, war was inevitable. Too many wanted it too badly. But it did strike me as ironic that the triggering incident was a Xeelee action concerned with a different war entirely, a war in which we were always bystanders – a war which would one day overwhelm all of us.*

*With the final conflict begun at last, the Galaxy-spanning civilisation of mankind underwent a drastic reconfiguration. For millennia, under the Coalition, it had been a machine for expansion and conquest. Now it became a machine of war.*

*Humanity resplendent. We undying hid away, waiting for the storm to pass.*

*And human hearts, evolved for a long-forgotten savannah, had to adapt to the dilemmas of interstellar battlefields.*

# FOUR

## RESPLENDENT

# THE CHOP LINE

## AD 20,424

### I

W e'd had no warning of the wounded Spline ship's return to Base 592, in the heart of the Galaxy.

*Return:* if you could call it that. But this was before I understood that every faster-than-light spaceship is also a time machine. That kind of puzzling would come later. For now, I just had my duty to perform.

As it happened we were off the Base at the time, putting the *Admiral Kard* through its paces after a refit and bedding in a new crew. *Kard* is a corvette: a small, mobile yacht intended for close-in sublight operations. I was twenty years old, still an ensign, assigned for that jaunt as an assistant to Exec Officer Baras. My first time on a bridge, it was quite an experience, and I was glad of the company of Tarco, an old cadre sibling, even if he was a male and a lard bucket. In cold Galaxy-centre light we had just run through a tough sequence of speed runs, emergency turns, full backdown, instrument checks, fire and damage control.

It was thanks to our fortuitous station on the bridge that Tarco and I were among the first to see the injured ship as it downfolded out of hyperspace. It was a Navy ship – a Spline, of course, a living ship, like a great meaty eyeball. It just appeared out of nowhere. We were close enough to see the green tetrahedral sigil etched into its flesh. But you couldn't miss the smoking ruins of the weapons emplacements, and a great open rent in the hull, thick with coagulated blood. A swarm of lesser lights, huddling close, looked like escape pods.

The whole bridge crew fell silent.

'Lethe,' Tarco whispered. 'Where did *that* come from?' We didn't know of any action underway at the time.

But we had no time to debate it.

Captain Iana's voice sounded around the corvette. 'That ship is the *Assimilator's Torch*,' he announced. 'She's requesting help. You can all see her situation. Stand by your stations.' He began to snap out brisk orders to his heads of department.

Well, we scrambled immediately. But Tarco's big moon-shaped face was creased by a look I didn't recognise.

'What's wrong with you?'

'I heard that name before. *Assimilator's Torch*. She's due to arrive here at Base 592 next year.'

'Then it's a little early. So what?'

He stared at me. 'You don't get it, buttface. I saw the manifest. The *Torch* is a newborn Spline. It hasn't even left Earth.'

But the injured Spline looked decades old, at least. 'You made a mistake. Buttface yourself.'

He didn't rise to the bait. Still, that was the first indication I had that there was something very wrong here.

The *Kard* lifted away from its operational position, and I had a grand view of Base 592, the planet on which we were stationed. From space it is a beautiful sight, a slow-spinning sphere of black volcanic rock peppered with the silver-grey of shipyards, so huge they are like great gleaming impact craters. There are even artificial oceans, glimmering blue, for the benefit of Spline vessels, who swim there between missions.

592 has a crucial strategic position, for it floats on the fringe of the 3-Kiloparsec Spiral Arm that surrounds the Galaxy's Core, and the Xeelee concentrations there. Here, some ten thousand light years from Earth, was as deep as the Third Expansion of mankind had yet penetrated into the central regions of the main disc. 592 was a fun assignment. We were on the front line, and we knew it. It made for an atmosphere you might call frenetic. But now I could see ships lifting from all around the planet, rushing to the aid of the stricken vessel. It was a heart-warming, magnificent sight, humanity at its best.

As we approached the Spline, the *Kard* hummed like a well-tuned machine. Right now, all over the ship, I knew, the whole crew – officers and gunners, cooks and engineers and maintenance stiffs, experienced officers and half-trained rookies – everybody was getting ready to save human beings from the great void that had tried to kill them. It was what you did. I looked forward to playing my part.

Which was why I wasn't too happy to hear the soft voice of Commissary Varcin behind me. 'Ensign. Are you' – he checked a list – 'Dakk? I have a special assignment for you. Come with me.' Varcin, gaunt and tall, served as the corvette's political officer, as assigned to every ship of the line with a crew above a hundred. He had an expression I couldn't read, a cold calculation.

Everybody is scared of the Commissaries, but this was not the time to be sucked into a time-wasting chore. 'I take my orders from the exec. Sir.' I looked to the Executive Officer.

Baras's face was neutral. I knew about the ancient tension between Navy and Commission, but I also knew what Baras would say. 'Do it, ensign. You'd better go too, Tarco.'

I had no choice, crisis or not. So we went hurrying after the Commissary.

Away from the spacious calm of the bridge, the corridors of the *Kard* were a clamour of motion and noise, people running every which way lugging equipment and stores, yelling orders and demanding help.

As we jogged I whispered to Tarco, 'So where has this bucket come from? Where's the action right now? SS 433?'

'Not there,' Tarco said. 'Don't you remember? At SS 433 we suffered no casualties.'

That was true. SS 433, a few hundred light years from 592, is a normal star in orbit around a massive neutron star; gravitationally squeezed, it emits high-energy jets of heavy elements – very useful. A month before, the Xeelee had shown up in an effort to wreck the human processing plants there. But thanks to smart intelligence by the Commission for Historical Truth they had been met by an overwhelming response. It had been a famous victory, the excuse for a lot of celebration.

If a little eerie. Sometimes the Commission's knowledge of future events was so precise we used to wonder if they had spies among the Xeelee. Or a time machine, maybe. Scary, as I said. But there is a bigger picture here. After fifteen thousand years of the Third Expansion, and eight thousand years of all-out war with the Xeelee, humanity controls around a quarter of the disc of the Galaxy itself, a mighty empire centred on Sol, as well as some outlying territories in the halo clusters. But the Xeelee control the rest, including the Galaxy centre. And, gradually, the slow-burning war between man and Xeelee is intensifying.

So I was glad the Commissaries, with their apparent powers of prophecy, were on my side.

We descended a couple of decks and found ourselves in the corvette's main loading bay. The big main doors had been opened to reveal a wall of burned and broken flesh. The stink was just overwhelming, and great lakes of yellow-green pus were gathering on the gleaming floor.

The wall was the hull of the injured Spline. The *Kard* had docked with the *Assimilator's Torch* as best she could, and this was the result. The engineers were at work, cutting a usable opening in that wall. It was just a hole in the flesh, another wound. Beyond, a tunnel stretched, organic, less like a corridor than a throat.

I could see figures moving in the tunnel – *Torch* crew, presumably. Here came two of them labouring to support a third between them. *Kard* crew rushed forward to take the injured tar. I couldn't tell if it was a he or a she. That was how bad the burns were. Loops of flesh hung off limbs that were like twigs, and in places you could see down to bone, which itself had been blackened.

Tarco and I reacted somewhat badly to this sight. But already med cloaks were snuggling around the wounded tar, gentle as a lover's caress.

I looked up at the Commissary, who was standing patiently. 'Sir? Can you tell us why we are here?'

'We received ident signals from the *Torch* when it downfolded. There's somebody here who will want to meet you.'

'Sir, who—'

'It's better if you see for yourself.'

One of the *Torch* crew approached us. She was a woman, I saw, about my height. There was no hiding the bloodstains and scorches and rips, or the way she limped; there was a wound in her upper thigh that actually smoked. But she had captain's pips on her collar.

I felt I knew her face – that straight nose, the small chin – despite the dirt that covered her cheeks and neck, and the crust of blood that coated her forehead. She had her hair grown out long, with a ponytail at the back, quite unlike my regulation crew-cut. But – this was my first impression – her face seemed oddly reversed, as if she was a mirror image of what I was used to.

I immediately felt a deep, queasy unease.

I don't know many captains, but she immediately recognised me. 'Oh. It's *you*.'

Tarco had become very tense. It turned out he had thought the situation through a little further than I had. 'Commissary, what engagement has the *Torch* come from?'

'The Fog.'

My mouth dropped. Every tar on Base 592 knew that the Fog is an interstellar cloud – and a major Xeelee concentration – situated *inside* 3-Kilo, a good hundred light years deeper towards the centre of the Galaxy. I said, 'I didn't know we were hitting the enemy so deep.'

'We aren't. Not yet.'

'And,' Tarco said tightly, 'here we are greeting a battle-damaged ship that hasn't even left Earth yet.'

'Quite right,' Varcin said approvingly. 'Ensigns, you are privileged to witness this. This ship is a survivor of a battle *that won't happen for another twenty-four years.*'

Tarco kind of spluttered.

As for me, I couldn't take my eye off the *Torch*'s captain. Tense, she was running her thumb down the side of her cheek.

'I do that,' I said stupidly.

'Oh, Lethe,' she said, disgusted. 'Yes, tar, I'm your older self. Get over it. I've got work to do.' And with a glance at the Commissary she turned and stalked back towards her ship.

Varcin said gently, 'Go with her.'

'Sir—'

'Do it, ensign.'

Tarco followed me. 'So in twenty-four years you're still going to be a buttface.'

I realised miserably he was right.

The three of us pushed through the narrow passageway into the *Torch*. The gravity was lumpy, and I suspected that it was being fed in from the *Kard*'s inertial generators.

I had had no previous exposure to the organic 'technology' of a Spline. We truly were inside a vast body. Every time I touched a surface my hands came away sticky, and I could feel salty liquids oozing over my uniform. The passage's walls were raw flesh, much of it burned, twisted and broken, even far beneath the ship's epidermis.

But that was just background to my churning thoughts. *Captain Dakk*, for Lethe's sake.

The captain saw me staring again. 'Ensign, back off. We can't get away from each other, but over the next few days life is going to get complicated for the both of us. It always does in these situations. Just take it one step at a time.'

'Sir—'

She glared at me. 'Don't question me. What interest have *I* got in giving *you* bad advice? I don't like this situation any more than you do. Remember that.'

'Yes, sir.'

We found lines of wounded, wrapped in cloaks. Crew were labouring to bring them out to the *Kard*. But the passageway was too narrow. It was a traffic jam, a real mess. It might have been comical if not for the groans and cries, the stink of fear and desperation in the air.

Dakk found an officer. He wore the uniform of a damage control worker. 'Cady, what in Lethe is going on here?'

'It's the passageways, sir. They're too ripped up to get the wounded out with the grapplers. So we're having to do it by hand.' He looked desperate, miserable. 'Sir, I'm responsible.'

'You did right,' she said grimly. 'But let's see if we can't tidy this up a little. You two,' she snapped at Tarco and me. 'Take a place in line.'

And that was the last we saw of her for a while, as she went stomping into the interior of her ship. She quickly organised the crew, from *Torch* and *Kard* alike, into a human chain. Soon we were passing cloaked wounded from hand to hand, along the corridor and out into the *Kard*'s loading bay in an orderly fashion.

'I'm impressed,' Tarco said. 'Sometime in the next quarter-century you'll be grafted a brain.'

'Shove it.'

The line before us snarled up. Tarco and I found ourselves staring down at one of the wounded – conscious, looking around, waiting to be moved out. He was just a kid, sixteen or seventeen.

If this was all true, in my segment of time he hadn't even been *born* yet.

He spoke to us. 'You from the *Kard*?'

'Yeah.'

He started to thank us, but I brushed that aside. 'Tell me what happened to you.'

Tarco whispered to me, 'Hey. Don't ask him about the future. You never heard of time paradoxes? I bet the Commission has a few regulations about *that*.'

I shrugged. 'I already met myself. How much worse can it get?'

Either the wounded man didn't know we were from his past, or he didn't care. He told us in terse sentences how the *Torch* had been involved in a major engagement deep in the Fog. He had been a gunner, with a good view of the action from his starbreaker pod.

'We came at a Sugar Lump. You ever seen one of those? A big old Xeelee emplacement. But the nightfighters were everywhere. We were taking a beating. The order came to fall back. We could see that damn Sugar Lump, close enough to touch. Well, the captain disregarded the fallback order.'

Tarco said sceptically, 'She *disregarded an order?*'

'We crossed the chop line.' A chop line is actually a surface, a military planner's boundary between sectors in space – in this case, between the disputed territory inside the Fog and Xeelee-controlled space. 'The Xeelee had been suckered by the fallback, and the *Torch* broke through their lines. 'We only lasted minutes. But we fired off a Sunrise.'

Tarco said, 'A what?' I kicked him, and he shut up.

Unexpectedly, the kid grabbed my arm. 'We barely got home. But, Lethe, when that Sunrise hit, we nearly shook this old fish apart with our hollering, despite the pasting we were taking.'

Tarco asked maliciously, 'How do you feel about Captain Dakk?'

'She is a true leader. I'd follow her anywhere.'

All I felt was unease. *No heroes*: that's one lesson of the Druz Doctrines, the creed that has held mankind together across fifteen thousand years, and drilled into every one of us by the Commissaries at their orientation sessions every day. If my future self had forgotten about that, something had gone wrong.

But now the gunner was looking at me intently. I became aware I was rubbing my thumb down my cheek. I dropped my hand and turned my face away.

Captain Dakk was standing before me. 'Recognition. You'd better get used to that.'

'I don't want to,' I groused. I was starting to resent the whole situation.

'I don't think what you, or I, want has much to do with it, ensign.'

I muttered to Tarco, 'Lethe. Am I that pompous?'

'Oh, yes.'

Dakk said, 'I think we're organised here for now. I'll come back later when I can start thinking about damage control. In the meantime we've been ordered to your captain's wardroom. Both of us.'

Tarco said hesitantly, 'Sir – what's a *Sunrise*?'

She looked surprised. 'Right. You don't have them yet. A Sunrise is a human-driven torpedo. A suicide weapon.' She eyed me. 'So you heard what happened in the Fog.'

'A little of it.'

She cupped my cheek. It was the first time she had touched me. It was an oddly neutral sensation, like touching your own skin. 'You'll find out, in good time. It was *glorious*.'

Dakk led us back through *Kard*'s officer country. Commissary Varcin met us there.

Here, the partitions had hastily been taken down to open up a wide area of deck that was serving as a hospital and convalescent unit. There were crew in there in all stages of recovery. Some of them were lying on beds, weak and hollow-eyed. Many of them seemed to be pleading with the orderlies to be put back on the *Torch* despite their injuries – once you lose contact with your ship in a war zone it can be impossible to find it again. And many of them asked, touchingly, after the *Torch* itself. They really cared about their living ship, I saw; that battered old hulk was one of the crew.

An awful lot of them sported ponytails, men and women alike, apparently in imitation of their captain. Very non-Doctrinal.

When they saw Dakk they all shouted and cheered and whistled. The walking wounded crowded around Dakk and thumped her on the back. A couple just turned their heads on their pillows and cried softly. Dakk's eyes were brimming, I saw; though she had a grin as wide as the room, she was on the point of breaking down.

I glanced at Tarco. It wasn't supposed to be like this.

Among the medics I saw a figure with the shaven head and long robes of the Commission. She was moving from patient to patient, and using a needle on them. But she wasn't treating them. She was actually extracting blood, small samples that she stored away in a satchel at her side.

This wasn't the time or place to be collecting samples like that. I stepped forward to stop her. Well, it was a natural reaction. Luckily for me Tarco held me back.

Commissary Varcin said dryly, 'I can see you have your future self's impetuosity, ensign. The orderly is just doing her duty. It's no doubt as uncomfortable for her as it is for you. Commissaries are human beings too, you know.'

'Then what—'

'Before they went into battle every one of these crew will have been injected with mnemonic fluid. That's what we're trying to retrieve. The more viewpoints we get of this action, the better we can anticipate it. We're ransacking the ship's databases and logs too.'

Call me unimaginative. I still didn't know what unlikely chain of circumstances had delivered my older self into my life. But that was the first time it had occurred to me what a potent weapon had been placed in our hands. 'Lethe,' I said. 'This is how we'll win the war. If you know the course of future battles—'

'You have a lot to absorb, ensign,' Varcin said, not unkindly. 'Take it one step at a time.'

Which, of course, had been my own advice to myself.

At last, somewhat to my relief, we got Dakk away from her crew. Varcin led us down more corridors to Captain Iana's plush wardroom.

Tarco and I stood in the middle of the carpet, aware of how dinged-up we were, scared of spreading Spline snot all over Iana's furniture. But Varcin waved us to chairs anyhow, and we sat down stiffly.

I watched Dakk. She sprawled in a huge chair, shaking a little, letting her exhaustion show now she was away from her crew. She was *me*. My face – reversed from the mirror image I'd grown up with. I was very confused. I hated the idea of growing so old, arrogant, unorthodox. But I'd seen plenty to admire in Dakk: strength, an ability to command, to win loyalty. Part of me wanted to help her. Another part wanted to push her away.

But mostly I was just aware of the bond that connected us. It didn't matter whether I liked her or loathed her; whichever way, she was always going to be *there*, for the rest of my life. It wasn't a comfortable notion.

Varcin was watching me. I got the idea he knew what I was feeling. But he turned to business, steepling his fingers.

'Here's how it is. We're scrambling to download data, to put together some kind of coherent picture of what happened downstream.' *Downstream* – not the last bit of time-hopping jargon I was going to have to get used to. 'You have surprises ahead of you, Ensign Dakk.'

I laughed a bit shrilly, and waved a hand at the captain. 'Surprising after *this*? Bring it on.'

Dakk looked disgusted. Tarco placed a calming hand on my back.

Varcin said, 'First, you – rather, *Captain* Dakk – will be charged. There will be a court of inquiry.'

'Charged? What with?'

Varcin shrugged. 'Negligence, in recklessly endangering the ship.' He eyed Dakk. 'I imagine there will be other counts, relating to various violations of the Druz Doctrines.'

Dakk just smiled, a chilling expression. I wondered how I ever got so cynical.

Varcin went on, 'Ensign, you'll be involved.'

I nodded. 'Of course. It's my future.'

'You don't understand. *Directly* involved. We want you to serve as the prosecuting advocate.'

'*Me*? Sir.' I took a breath. 'You want me to prosecute *myself*. For a crime, an alleged crime anyhow, I won't commit for twenty-four years. Is there any part of that I misunderstood?'

'No. You have the appropriate training, don't you?'

Dakk laughed. 'This is their way, kid. After all who knows me better?'

I stood up. 'Commissary, I won't do it.'

'Sit down, ensign.'

'I'll go to Captain Iana.'

'*Sit. Down.*'

I'd never heard such a tone of command. I sat, frightened.

'Ensign, you are immature, and inexperienced, and impetuous. You will have much to learn to fulfil this assignment. But you are the necessary choice.

'And there's more.' Again, I glimpsed humanity in that frosted-over Commissary. 'In four months' time you will report to the birthing complex on Base 592. There you will request impregnation by Ensign Hama Tarco, here.'

Tarco quickly took his hand off my back.

'Permission will be granted,' said Varcin. 'I'll see to that.'

I didn't believe it. Then I got angry. I felt like I was in a trap. 'How do you know I'll *want* a kid by Tarco? No offence, butthead.'

'None taken,' said Tarco, sounding bemused.

Now the Commissary looked irritated. 'How do you *think* I know?

Haven't you noticed the situation we're in? Because it's in the *Torch*'s record. Because the child you will bear—'

'Will be on the *Torch*, with me,' said Dakk. 'His name was Hama.'

I swear Tarco blushed.

'*Was*? The kid *was* called Hama?' I felt a kind of panic. Perhaps it was the tug of a maternal bond that couldn't yet exist, fear for the well-being of a child I'd only just learned about. 'He's dead, isn't he? He died, out there in the Fog.'

Varcin murmured, 'One step at a time, remember, ensign.'

Dakk leaned forward. 'Yes, he died. *He rode the Sunrise*. He was the one who took a monopole bomb into the Xeelee Sugar Lump. You see? Your child, Dakk. *Our* child. He was a hero.'

One step at a time. I kept repeating that to myself. But it was as if the wardroom was spinning around.

## II

In Dakk's yacht, I sailed around the huge flank of the *Assimilator's Torch*. Medical tenders drifted alongside, hosing some kind of sealant into the living ship's mighty wounds.

The injured Spline had been allowed to join a flotilla of its kind, regular ships of the line. Living starships the size of cities are never going to be graceful, but I saw that their movements were coordinated, a vast dance. They even snuggled against each other, like great fish jostling.

Dakk murmured, 'Some of these battered beasts have been in human employ for a thousand years or more. We rip out their brains and their nervous systems – we amputate their minds – and yet something of the self still lingers, a need for others of their kind, for comfort. So we let the distressed swim together for a while.'

I listened absently.

The yacht docked, and the captain and I were piped aboard the *Torch*. I found myself in a kind of cave, buttressed by struts of some cartilaginous material. The lighting had been fixed, the on-board gravity restored.

We wandered through orifices and along round-walled passageways, pushing deeper into the body of the Spline. We saw none of Dakk's crew, only repair workers from the Base.

Dakk said to me, 'You haven't served on a Spline yet, have you? The ship is alive, remember. It's *hot*. At sleep periods you can walk around the ship, and you find the crew dozing all over the vessel, many of them naked, some sprawled on food sacks or weapons, or just on the warm surfaces, wherever they can. You can hear the pulsing of the Spline's blood flow – even sometimes the beating of its heart, like a distant gong. That and the scrambling of the rats.'

It sounded cosy, but not much like the Navy I knew. 'Rats?'

She laughed. 'Little bastards get everywhere.'

On we went. It wasn't as bad as that hour in the chaotic dark when the Spline first came limping in, and we had to haul a wounded crew out of a wounded ship. But even so it was like being in some vast womb. I couldn't see how I was ever going to get used to this environment, how I could serve on a ship like this. But Dakk seemed joyful to be back, so I was evidently wrong.

We came to a deep place Dakk called the 'belly'. This was a hangar-like chamber separated into bays by huge diaphanous sheets of some muscle-like material, marbled with fat. Within the alcoves were suspended sacs of what looked like water: green, cloudy water.

I prodded the surface of one of the sacs. It rippled sluggishly. I could see drifting plants, wriggling fish, snails, a few autonomous bots swimming among the crowd. 'It's like an aquarium,' I said.

'So it is. A miniature ocean. The green plants are hornweeds: rootless, almost entirely edible. And you have sea snails, swordtail fish and various microbes. There is a complete self-contained biosphere here. This is how we live; this little farm feeds us. These creatures are actually from Earth's oceans. Don't you think it's kind of romantic to fly into battle against Xeelee super-science with a droplet of primordial waters at our core?'

'How do you keep it from getting overgrown?'

'The weed itself kills back overgrowth. The snails live off dead fish. And the fish keep their numbers down by eating their own young.'

I guess I pulled a face at that.

'You're squeamish,' she said sharply. 'I don't remember *that*.'

We walked on through the Spline's visceral marvels. I didn't take in much.

The truth is I was struggling to function. I'm sure I was going through some kind of shock. Human beings aren't designed to be subject to temporal paradoxes about their future selves and unborn babies.

And my head was full of my work on the inquiry into Dakk's actions.

The inquiry procedure was a peculiar mix of ancient Navy traditions and forensic Commission processes. Commissary Varcin had been appointed president of the court, and as prosecutor advocate I was a mix of prosecutor, law officer and court clerk. The rest of the court – a panel of brass who were a kind of mix of judge and jury combined – were Commissaries and Navy officers, with a couple of civilians and even an Academician for balance. It was all a political compromise between the Commission and the Navy, it seemed to me.

But the court of inquiry was only the first stage. If the charges were established Dakk would go on to face a full court martial, and possibly a trial before members of the Coalition's Grand Conclave itself. So the stakes were high.

And the charges themselves – aimed at my own future self, after all – had been hurtful: *Through Negligence Suffering a Vessel of the Navy to be Hazarded; Culpable Inefficiency in the Performance of Duty; Through Disregard of Standing and Specific Orders Endangering the War Aims of the Navy; Through Self-Regard Encouraging a Navy Crew to Deviate from Doctrinal Thought* . . .

There was plenty of evidence. We had Virtual reconstructions based on the *Torch*'s logs and the mnemonic fluids extracted from the ship's crew. And we had a stream of witnesses, most of them walking wounded from the *Torch*. None of them was told how her testimony fitted into the broader picture, a point which many of them got frustrated about. But all of them expressed their loyalty and admiration towards Captain Dakk – even though, in the eyes of Commissaries, such idolising would only get their captain deeper into trouble.

All this could only help so far. What I felt I was missing was motive. I didn't understand *why* Dakk had done what she had done.

I felt I couldn't get her into focus. I oscillated between despising her and longing to defend her – and all the time I felt oppressed by the paradoxical bond that locked us together. I sensed she felt the same. Sometimes she was as impatient with me as with the greenest recruit, and other times she seemed to try to take me under her wing. It can't have been easy for her either, to be reminded that she had once been as insignificant as me. But if we were two slices of the same person, our situations weren't symmetrical. She had *been* me, long ago; I was doomed to *become* her; it was as if she had paid dues that still faced me.

Anyhow, that was why I had requested a break from the deliberations, so I could spend some time with Dakk on her home territory. I had to get to know her – even though I felt increasingly reluctant to be drawn into her murky future.

She brought me to a new chamber, deep within the Spline ship. Criss-crossed by struts of cartilage, this place was dominated by a pillar made of translucent red-purple rope. There was a crackling stench of ozone.

I knew where I was. 'This is the hyperdrive chamber.'

'Yes.' She reached up and stroked fibres. 'Magnificent, isn't it? I remember when I first saw a Spline hyperdrive muscle—'

'Of course you remember.'

'What?'

'Because it's *now*. This is *my* first time seeing this. And I'm *you*.' Some day, I thought gloomily, I would inevitably find myself standing on the other side of this room, looking back at my own face. 'Don't you remember this? Being me, twenty years old, meeting – you?'

Her answer confused me. 'It doesn't work like that.' She glared at me. 'You do understand how come I'm stuck back in the past, staring at your zit-ridden face?'

'No,' I admitted reluctantly.

'It was a Tolman manoeuvre.' She searched my face. 'Every faster-than-light starship is a time machine. Come on, ensign. That's just special relativity! Even "Tolman" is the name of some long-dead pre-Extirpation scientist. They teach this stuff to four-year-olds.'

I shrugged. 'You forget all that unless you want to become a navigator.'

'With an attitude like that you have an ambition to be a captain?'

'I don't,' I said slowly, 'have an ambition to be a captain.'

That gave her pause. But she said, 'The bottom line is that if you fight a war with FTL starships, time slips are always possible, and you have to anticipate them . . . Think of it this way. There is no universal *now*. Say it's midnight here. We're a light-minute from the Base. So what time is it in your fleapit barracks on 529? What if you could focus a telescope on a clock on the ground?'

I thought about it. It would take a minute for an image of the clock on the Base to reach me at lightspeed. So that would show a minute before midnight . . . 'OK, but if you adjust for the time lag needed for signals to travel at lightspeed, you can construct a standard *now* – can't you?'

'If everybody was stationary, maybe. But suppose this creaky old Spline was moving at half lightspeed. Even you must have heard of time dilation. *Our* clocks would be slowed as seen from the base, and *theirs* would be slowed as seen from here. Think it through further. There could be a whole flotilla of ships out here, moving at different velocities, their timescales all different. They could never agree.

'You get the point? Globally speaking there is no past and future. There are only events – like points on a huge graph, with axes marked *space* and *time*. That's the way to think of it. The events swim around, like fish; and the further away they are the more they swim, from your point of view. So there is *no* one event on the Base, or on Earth, or anywhere else which can be mapped uniquely to your *now*. In fact there is a whole range of such events at distant places, moving at different speeds.

'Because of that looseness, histories are ambiguous. A single location on Earth itself has a definite history, of course, and so does the Base. But Earth is maybe ten thousand light years from here. It's pointless to map dates of specific events on Earth against Base dates; they can vary across a span of millennia. You can even have a history on Earth that runs *backwards* as seen from a moving ship.

'Now do you see how faster-than-light screws things up? Causality is controlled by the speed of light. As long as light has time to travel from one event to another they can't get out of order, from wherever they are viewed, and causality is preserved. But in a ship moving faster than light, you can hop around the spacetime graph at will. I took a FTL jaunt to the Fog. When I was *there*, from my point of view the history of the Base *here* was ambiguous over a scale of decades . . . When I came home I simply hopped back to an event *before* my departure.'

I nodded. 'But it was just an accident. Right? This doesn't always happen.'

'It depends on the geometry. Fleeing the Xeelee, we happened to be travelling at a large fraction of lightspeed towards the Base when we initiated the hyperdrive. So, yes, it was an accident. But you can make Tolman manoeuvres deliberately. And during every operation we always drop Tolman probes: records, log copies, heading for the past.'

I did a double-take. 'You're telling me it's a *deliberate tactic* of this war to send information to the past?'

'Of course. If such a possibility's there you have to take the opportunity. What better intelligence can there be? The Navy has always cooperated with this fully. In war you seek every advantage.'

'But don't the Xeelee do the same?'

'Sure. But the trick is to try to stop them. The intermingling of past and future depends on relative velocities. We try to choreograph engagements so that we, not they, get the benefit. And of course they reciprocate.' Dakk grinned wolfishly. 'It's a contest in clairvoyance. But we punch our weight.'

I tried to focus on what was important. 'OK,' I said. 'Then give me a message from the future. Tell me how you crossed the chop line.'

She paced around the chamber, while the Spline's weird hyperdrive muscles pulsed. 'Before the fallback order came, we'd just taken a major hit. Do you know what that's like? Your first reaction is sheer surprise that it has happened to *you*. Surprise, and disbelief, and resentment. And anger. The ship is alive; it's part of your crew. And you live in it; it's as if your home has been violated. So there was shock. But most of the crew went to defence posture and began to fulfil their duties, as per their training. There was no panic. Pandemonium, yes, but no panic.'

'And in all this you decided to disobey the fallback order.'

She looked me in the eye. 'I had to make an immediate decision. We had an opportunity; we were close enough to strike, I believed, and we were in a situation where my orders weren't valid. So I believed. I decided to go ahead.

'We went straight through the chop line and headed for the centre of the Xeelee concentration, bleeding from a dozen hits, starbreakers blazing. That's how we fight the Xeelee, you see. They are smarter than us, and stronger. But we just come boiling out at them. They think we are vermin, so we fight like vermin.'

'You launched the Sunrise.'

'Hama was the pilot.' My unborn, unconceived child. 'He rode a monopole torpedo: the latest stuff. A Xeelee Sugar Lump is a fortress shaped like a cube, thousands of kilometres on a side, a world with edges and corners. We punched a hole in its wall like it was paper.

'But we were taking a beating. Hit after hit.

'We had to evacuate the outer decks. You should have seen the hull, human beings swarming like flies on a piece of garbage, scrambling this way and that, fleeing the detonations. They hung onto weapons mounts, stanchions, lifelines, anything. We fear the falling, you see. I think some of the crew feared that more than the Xeelee. The life pods got some of them. We lost hundreds . . . Her face worked, and she seemed to reach for happier memories. 'You know why the name "Sunrise"? Because it's a planet thing. The Xeelee are space dwellers. They don't know day and night. Every dawn is *ours*, not theirs – one thing they can't take away from us. Appropriate, don't you think? And you should see what it's like when a Sunrise pilot comes on board.'

'Like Hama.'

'As the yacht conies out of port, you get a flotilla riding along with it, civilian ships as well as Navy, just to see the pilot go. When the pilot comes aboard the whole crew lines the passageways, chanting his or her name.' She smiled. 'Your heart will burst when you see Hama.'

I struggled to focus. 'So the pilots are idolised. We aren't supposed to have heroes.'

'Lethe, I never knew I was such a prig! Kid, there is more to war than doctrinal observance. Anyhow what are the Sunrise pilots but the highest exemplars of the ideals of the Expansion? *A brief life burns brightly*, remember – Druz said it himself – and a Sunrise pilot puts that into practice in the brightest, bravest way possible.'

'And,' I said carefully, 'are you a hero to your crew?'

She scowled at me. Her face was a mask of lines, grooves carved by years into my own flesh. She had never looked less like me: 'I know what you're thinking. I'm too old, I should be ashamed even to be alive. Listen to me. Ten years after this meeting, you will take part in a battle around a neutron star called Kepler's. Look it up. *That's* why your crew will respect you, for what you will achieve that day – even though you won't be lucky enough to die. And as for the chop line, I don't have a single regret. We struck a blow, damn it. I'm talking about hope. That's what those fucking Commissaries never understand. Hope, and the needs of the human heart. *That's* what I was trying to deliver . . .' Something seemed to go out of her. 'But none of that matters now. I've come through another chop line, haven't I? Through a chop line in time, into the past, where I face judgement.'

'I'm not assigned to judge you.'

'No. You do that for fun, don't you?'

I didn't know what to say. I felt pinned. I loved her, and I hated her, all at the same time. She must have felt the same way about me. But we knew we couldn't get away from each other. Perhaps it is never possible for copies of the same person from two time slices ever to get along. After all it's not something we've evolved for.

In silence we made our way back to Dakk's wardroom. There, Tarco was waiting for us.

'Buttface,' he said formally.

'Lard bucket,' I replied.

On that ship from the future, in my own future wardroom, we stared at each other, each of us baffled, maybe frightened. We hadn't been alone together, not once, since the news that we were to have a child together. And even now Captain Dakk was sitting there like the embodiment of destiny.

Under the Druz Doctrines, love isn't forbidden. But it's not the *point*. But then, I was learning, out here on the frontier, where people died far from home, things were a little more complex than my training and conditioning had indicated.

I asked, 'What are you doing here?'

'You sent for me. Your future, smarter, better-looking self.'

Captain Dakk said dryly, 'Obviously you two have – issues – to discuss. But I'm afraid I can't give you the time. Events are pressing.'

Tarco turned to face her. 'Then let's get on with it, sir. Why did you ask for me?'

Dakk said, 'Navy intelligence have been analysing the records from the *Torch*. They have begun the process of contacting those who will serve on the ship – or their cadres, if they are infants or not yet born – to inform them of their future assignments. It's the policy.'

Tarco looked apprehensive. 'And that applies to me?'

Dakk didn't answer directly. 'There are protocols. When a ship returns from action, it's customary for the captain or senior surviving officer to send letters of condolence to cadres who have lost loved ones, or visit them.'

Tarco nodded. 'I once accompanied Captain Iana on a series of visits like that.'

I said carefully, 'But in this case the action hasn't happened yet. Those who will die haven't yet been assigned to the ship. Some haven't even been born.'

'Yes,' Dakk said gently. 'But I have to write my letters even so.'

That was incomprehensible to me. 'Why? Nobody's dead yet.'

'Because everybody wants to *know*, as much as we can tell them. Would it be better to lie to them, or keep secrets?'

'How do they react?'

'How do you think? Ensign Tarco, what happened when you did the rounds with Iana?'

Tarco shrugged. 'Some took it as closure, I think. Some wept. Some were angry, even threw us out. Others denied it was real . . . They all wanted more information. How it happened, what it was for. Everyone seemed to have a need to be told that those who had died had given their lives for something worthwhile.'

Dakk nodded. 'After a time hop you see all those reactions too. Some won't open the messages. They put them in time capsules, as if putting history back in order. Others take a look, find other ways to cope with the news. We don't tell people how to react. But we don't keep anything from them; that's the policy,' She studied me. 'This is a time-travellers' war, ensign. A war like none we've fought before. We are stretching our procedures, even our humanity, to cope with the consequences. But you get used to it.'

Tarco said apprehensively, 'Sir, please – *what about me?*'

Gravely, Dakk handed him a data desk.

'Hey, buttface,' he said, reading. 'You make me your exec. How about that. Maybe it was a bad year in the draft.'

I didn't feel like laughing. 'Read it all.'

'I know what it says.' His broad face was relaxed.

'You don't make it home. That's what it says, doesn't it? *You're going to die out there*, in the Fog.'

He actually smiled. 'I've been anticipating this since the *Torch* came into port. Haven't you?'

My mouth opened and closed, as if I was a swordtail fish in the belly of a Spline. 'Call me unimaginative,' I said. 'How can you accept this assignment, *knowing it's going to kill you*?'

He seemed puzzled. 'What else would I do?'

'Yes,' the captain said. 'It is your duty. Can't you see how noble this is, Dakk? Isn't it *right* that he should know – that he should live his life with full foreknowledge of the circumstances of his death, and do his duty even so, right up to the final foretold instant?'

Tarco grabbed my hand. 'Hey. It's years off. We'll see our baby grow.'

I said dismally, 'Some love story this is turning out to be.'

'Yes.'

Commissary Varcin's Virtual head coalesced in the air. Without preamble he said, 'Change of plan. Ensign, it's becoming clear that the evidence to hand will not be sufficient to establish the charges. Specifically it's impossible to say whether Dakk's actions hindered the overall war aims. To establish that we'll have to go to the Libraries, at the Commission's central headquarters.'

I did a double-take. 'Sir, that's on Earth.'

The disembodied head snapped, 'I'm aware of that.'

I had no idea how bookworm Commissaries on Earth, ten thousand light years away, could possibly have evidence to bear on this front-line incident. But the Commissary explained, and I learned there was more to this messages-from-the-future industry than I had yet imagined. On Earth, the Commission for Historical Truth had been mapping the future. For fifteen thousand years.

I said, 'Things weren't weird enough already.'

My future self murmured, 'You get used to it.'

Varcin's expression softened a little. 'Think of it as an opportunity. Every Expansion citizen should see the home world before she dies.'

'Come with me,' I said impulsively to Tarco. 'Come with me to Earth.'

'All right.'

Dakk put her hands on our shoulders. 'Lethe, but this is a magnificent enterprise.'

I hated her; I loved her; I wanted her out of my life.


III


It was all very well for Varcin to order us to Earth. The Navy wasn't about to release one of its own to the Commission for Historical Truth without a fight, and there was lengthy wrangling over the propriety and even the legality of transferring the court of inquiry to Earth. In the end a team of Navy lawyers was assigned to the case.

We were a strange crew, I guess: two star-crossed lovers, court members, Navy lawyers, serving officers, Commissaries and all. Not to mention another version of me. The atmosphere was tense all the way from Base 592.

But at journey's end all our differences and politics and emotional tangles were put aside, as we crowded to the hull to sightsee our destination.

Earth!

At first it seemed nondescript: just another rocky ball circling an unspectacular star, in a corner of a fragmented spiral arm. But Snowflake surveillance stations orbited in great shells around the planet, all the way out as far as the planet's single battered Moon, and schools of Spline gambolled hugely in the waves of a mighty ocean that covered half the planet's surface. It was an eerie thought that down there somewhere in that sea was another *Assimilator's Torch*, a junior version of the battered old ship we had seen come limping into port.

This little world had become the capital of the Third Expansion, an empire that stretched across all the stars I could see, and far beyond. And it was the true home of every human who would ever live. I was thrilled. As our flitter cut into the atmosphere and was wrapped in pink-white plasma, I felt Tarco's hand slip into mine.

At least during the journey in we had had time to spend together. We had talked. We had even made love, in a perfunctory way.

But it hadn't done us much good. Other people knew far too much about our future, and we didn't seem to have any choice about it anyhow. There could be no finer intelligence than a knowledge of the future – an ability to see the outcome of a battle not yet waged, or map the turning points of a war not yet declared – and yet what use was that intelligence if the future was fixed, if we were all forced to live out pre-programmed lives? I felt like a rat going through a maze. What room was there for joy?

I hoped I was going to learn this wasn't true in the Commission's future libraries. Of course I wasn't worrying about the war and the destiny of mankind. I just wanted to know if I really was doomed to become Captain Dakk, battered, bitter, arrogant, far from orthodox – or whether I was still *free*, free to be me.

The flitter swept over a continent. I glimpsed a crowded land, and many vast weapons emplacements, intended for the eventuality of a last-ditch defence of the home world. Then we began to descend towards a Conurbation. It was a broad, glistening sprawl of bubble-dwellings blown from the bedrock, and linked by canals. But the scars of the Qax Occupation, fifteen thousand years old, were still visible. Much of the land glistened silver-grey where starbreaker beams and nano-replicators had once worked, turning plains and mountains into a featureless silicate dust.

The Commissary said, 'This Conurbation itself was Qax-built. It is still known by its ancient Qax registration of 11729. It was more like a forced labour camp or breeding pen than a human city. It was here that Hama Druz himself developed the Doctrine that has shaped human destiny ever since. It is the headquarters of the Commission. A decision was made to leave the work of the Qax untouched. It shows what will become of us again, if we should falter or fail . . .'

And so on. His long face was solemn, his eyes gleaming with a righteous zeal. He was a little scary.

We were taken to a complex right at the heart of the old Conurbation. It was based on the crude Qax architecture, but internally the bubble dwellings had been knocked together and extended underground, making a vast complex whose boundaries I never glimpsed.

Varcin introduced it as the Library of Futures. Once the Libraries had been an independent agency, Varcin told us, but the Commission had taken them over three thousand years ago. Apparently there had been an epic war among the bureaucrats.

Tarco and I were each given our own quarters. My room seemed *huge*, itself extending over several levels, and very well equipped, with a galley and even a bar. I could tell from Captain Dakk's expression exactly what she thought of this opulence and expense. That bar made a neat Poole's Blood, though.

It was very strange to be in a place where a 'day' lasted a standard day, a 'year' a year. Across the Expansion the standards are set by Earth's calendar – of course; what else would you use? A 'day' on Base 592, for instance, lasted over two hundred standard days, which was actually longer than its 'year', which was around half a standard. But on Earth, everything fit together.

On the second day, the court of inquiry was to resume. But Varcin said that he wanted to run through the Commission's findings with us – me, Captain Dakk, Tarco – before it all unravelled in front of the court itself.

So, early on that crucial day, the three of us were summoned to a place Varcin called the Map Room.

It was like a vast hive, a place of alcoves and bays extending off a gigantic central atrium. On several levels, shaven-headed, long-robed figures walked earnestly, alone or in muttering groups, accompanied by gleaming clouds of Virtuals.

I think all three of us lowly Navy types, Tarco and I, even the older Dakk, felt scruffy and overwhelmed.

Varcin stood at the centre of the open atrium. In his element, he just smiled. And he waved his hand, a bit theatrically.

A series of Virtual dioramas swept over us like the pages of an immense book.

In those first few moments I saw huge fleets washing into battle, or limping home decimated; I saw worlds gleaming like jewels, beacons of human wealth and power – or left desolated and scarred, lifeless as Earth's Moon. And, most wistful of all, there were voices. I heard roars of triumph, cries for help.

I knew what I was seeing. I was thrilled. These were the catalogued destinies of mankind.

Varcin said, 'Half a million people work here. Much of the interpretation is automated – but nothing has yet replaced the human eye, human scrutiny, human judgement. You understand that the further away you are from a place, the more uncertainty there is over its timeline compared to yours. So we actually see furthest into the future concerning the most remote events . . .'

'And you see war,' said Tarco.

'Oh, yes. As far downstream as we can see, whichever direction we choose to look, we see war.'

I picked up on that. *Whichever direction* . . . 'Commissary, you don't just map the future here, do you? I mean a single future.'

'No. Of course not.'

'I knew it,' I said gleefully, and they all looked at me oddly. *'You can change the future.'* And I wasn't stuck with becoming Captain Dakk. 'So if you see a battle will be lost, you can choose not to commit the fleet. You can save thousands of lives with a simple decision.'

'Or you could see a Xeelee advance coming,' Tarco said excitedly. 'Like SS 433. So you got the ships in position – it was a perfect ambush.'

Dakk said, 'Remember the Xeelee have exactly the same power.'

I hadn't thought of that. 'So if *they* had foreseen SS 433, they could have chosen not to send their ships there in the first place.'

'Yes,' Varcin said. 'In fact if intelligence were perfect on both sides, there would never be *any* defeat, any victory. It is only because future intelligence is not perfect – the Xeelee *didn't* foresee the ambush at SS 433 – that any advances are possible.'

Tarco said, 'Sir, what happened the first time? What was the outcome of SS 433 *before* either side started to meddle with the future?'

'Well, we don't know, ensign. Perhaps there was no engagement at all, and one side or the other saw a strategic hole that could be filled. It isn't very useful to think that way. You have to think of the future as a rough draft, that we – and the Xeelee – are continually reworking, shaping and polishing. It's as if we are working out a story of the future we can both agree on.'

I was still trying to figure out the basics. 'Sir, what about time paradoxes?'

Dakk growled, 'Oh, Lethe, here we go. Somebody always has to ask about time paradoxes. And it has to be you, doesn't it, ensign?'

I persisted. 'I mean' – I waved a hand at the dioramas – 'suppose you pick up a beacon with data on a battle. But you decide to change the future; the battle never happens . . . What about the beacon? Does it pop out of existence? And *now you have a record of a battle that will never happen*. Where did the information come from?'

Tarco said eagerly, 'Maybe parallel universes are created. In one the battle goes ahead, in the other it doesn't. The beacon just leaks from one universe to another.'

Dakk looked bored.

Varcin was dismissive. 'We don't go in for metaphysics much around here. The cosmos, it turns out, has a certain common sense about these matters. If you cause a time paradox there is no magic. Just an anomalous piece of data that nobody created, a piece of technology with no origin. It's troubling, perhaps, but only subtly, at least compared to the existence of parallel universes, or objects popping in and out of existence. What concerns us more, day to day, are the consequences of this knowledge.'

'Consequences?'

'For example, the leakage of information from future into past is having an effect on the evolution of human society. Innovations are transmitted backward. We are becoming – static. Rigid, over very long timescales. Of course that helps control the conduct of a war on such immense reaches of space and time. And regarding the war, many engagements are stalemated by foresight on both sides. It's probable that we are actually *extending* the war.'

My blood was high. 'We're talking about a knowledge of the future. And all we're doing with it is set up stalemate after stalemate?'

For sure Varcin didn't welcome being questioned like that by an ignorant ensign. He snapped, 'Look, nobody has run a war this way before. We're making this up as we go along. But, believe me, we're doing our best.

'And remember this. Knowledge of the future does not change certain fundamentals about the war. The Xeelee are *older* than us. They are more powerful, more advanced in every which way we can measure. Logically, given their resources, they should defeat us, whatever we do. We cannot ensure victory by any action we make *here*, that much is clear. But we suspect that if we get it wrong we could make *defeat* certain.' His face closed in. 'If you work here you become – cautious. Conservative. The further downstream we look the more extensive our decisions' consequences become. With a wave of a hand in this room I can banish trillions of souls to the oblivion of non-existence – or rather, of never-to-exist.'

'So you don't wave your hand,' said Tarco pragmatically.

'Quite. All we can hope for is to preserve at least the possibility of victory, in some of the futures. And we believe that if not for the Mapping, *humanity would have lost this war by now.*'

I wasn't convinced. 'You can change history. But you will still send Tarco out, knowing he will die. Why?'

Varcin's face worked as he tried to control his irritation. 'You must understand the decision-making process here. We are trying to win a war, not just a battle. We have to try to see beyond individual events to the chains of consequences that follow. That is why we will sometimes commit ships to a battle we know will be lost – why we will send warriors to certain deaths, knowing their deaths will not gain the slightest immediate advantage – why *sometimes we will even allow a victory to turn to a defeat*, if the long-term consequences of victory are too costly. And *that* is at the heart of the charges against you, Captain.'

Dakk snapped, 'Get to the point, Commissary.'

Varcin gestured again.

Before the array of futures, a glimmering Virtual diagram appeared. It was a translucent sphere, with many layers, something like an onion. Its outer layers were green, shading to yellow further in, with a pin-point star of intense white at the centre. Misty shapes swam through its interior. It cast a green glow on all our faces.

'Pretty,' I said.

'It's a monopole,' said Dakk. 'A schematic representation.'

'The warhead of the Sunrise torpedo.'

'Yes.' Varcin walked into the diagram, and began pointing out features. 'The whole structure is about the size of an atomic nucleus. There are W and Z bosons in this outer shell here. Further in there is a region in which the weak nuclear and electromagnetic forces are unified, but strong nuclear interactions are distinct. In this central region' – he cupped the little star in his hand – 'grand unification is achieved.'

I spoke up. 'Sir, so how does this hurt the Xeelee?'

Dakk glared at me. 'Ensign, the monopole is the basis of a weapon which shares the Xeelee's own physical characteristics. You understand that the vacuum has a structure. That structure contains flaws. The Xeelee actually use two-dimensional flaws – sheets – to power their nightfighters. But in three-dimensional space you can also have one-dimensional flaws – strings – and zero-dimensional flaws.'

'Monopoles,' I guessed.

'You got it.'

'And since the Xeelee use spacetime defects to drive their ships—'

'The best way to hit them with is with another spacetime defect.' Dakk rammed her fist into her hand. 'And *that's* how we punched a hole in that Sugar Lump.'

'But at a terrible cost.' Varcin made the monopole go away. Now we were shown a kind of tactical display. We saw a plan view of the Galaxy's central regions – the compact swirl that was 3-Kilo, wrapped tightly around the Core. Prickles of blue light showed the position of human forward bases, like Base 592, surrounding the Xeelee concentration in the Core.

And we saw battles raging all around 3-Kilo, wave after wave of blue human lights pushing towards the core, but breaking against stolid red Xeelee defence perimeters.

'This is the next phase of the war,' Varcin said. 'In most futures these assaults begin a century from now. We get through the Xeelee perimeters in the end, through to the Core – or rather, we can see many futures in which that outcome is still possible. But the cost in most scenarios is enormous.'

Dakk said, 'All because of my one damn torpedo.'

'Because of the intelligence you will give away, yes. You made one of the first uses of the monopole weapon. So after your engagement the Xeelee knew we had it. The fallback order you disregarded was based on a decision at higher levels *not* to deploy the monopole weapon at the Fog engagement, to reserve it for later. By proceeding through the chop line you undermined the decision of your superiors.'

'I couldn't have known that such a decision had been made.'

'We argue that, reasonably, you should have been able to judge that. Your error will cause great suffering, unnecessary death. The Tolman data proves it. *Your judgement was wrong.*'

So there it was. The Galaxy diagram collapsed into pixels. Tarco stiffened beside me, and Dakk fell silent.

Varcin said to me, 'Ensign, I know this is hard for you. But perhaps you can see now why you were appointed prosecutor advocate.'

'I think so, sir.'

'And will you endorse my recommendations?'

I thought it through. What would *I* do in the heat of battle, in Dakk's position? Why, just the same – and that was what must be stopped, to avert this huge future disaster. Of course I would endorse the Commission's conclusion. What else could I do? It was my duty.

We still had to go through the formalities of the court of inquiry, and no doubt the court martial to follow. But the verdicts seemed inevitable.

You'd think I was beyond surprise by now, but what came next took me aback.

Varcin stood between us, my present and future selves. 'We will be pressing for heavy sanctions.'

'I'm sure Captain Dakk will accept whatever—'

'There will be sanctions against you too, ensign. Sorry.'

I would not be busted out of the Navy, I learned. But a Letter of Reprimand would go into my file, which would ensure that I would never rise to the rank of captain – in fact, I would likely not be given postings in space at all.

It was a lot to absorb, all at once. But even as Varcin outlined it, I started to see the logic. To change the future you can only act in the present. There was nothing to be done about Dakk's personal history; she would carry around what she had done for the rest of her life, a heavy burden. But, for the sake of the course of the war, my life would be trashed, so that I could never become *her*, and never do what she had done.

Not only that, any application I made to have a child with Tarco would not be granted after all. Hama would never be born. The Commissaries wanted to make doubly sure nobody ever climbed on board that Sunrise torpedo.

I looked at Tarco. His face was blank. We had never had a relationship, not really – never actually had that child – and yet it was all being taken away from us, becoming no more real than one of Varcin's catalogued futures.

'Some love story,' I said.

'Yeah. Shame, buttface.'

'Yes.' I think we both knew right there that we would drift apart. We'd probably never even talk about it properly.

Tarco turned to Varcin. 'Sir, I have to ask—'

'Nothing significant changes for you, ensign,' said Varcin softly. 'You still rise to exec on the *Torch* – you will be a capable officer—'

'I still don't come home from the Fog.'

'No. I'm sorry.'

'Don't be, sir.' He actually sounded relieved. I don't know if I admired that or not.

Dakk looked straight ahead. 'Sir. Don't do this. Don't erase the glory.'

'I have no choice.'

Dakk's mouth worked. Then she spoke shrilly. 'You fucking Commissaries sit in your gilded nests. Handing out destinies like petty gods. Do you ever even *doubt* what you are doing?'

'All the time, Captain,' Varcin said sadly. He put a hand on Dakk's shoulder. 'We will take care of you. You aren't alone. We have many other relics of lost futures. Some of them are from much further downstream than you. Many have stories which are – interesting.'

'But,' said Dakk stiffly, 'my career is finished.'

'Oh, yes, of course.'

There was a heartbeat of tension. Then something seemed to go out of Dakk. 'Well, I guess I crashed through another chop line. My whole life is never going to happen. And I don't even have the comfort of popping out of existence.'

I faced Dakk. 'Why did you do it?'

Her smile was twisted. 'Why would *you* do it? Because it was worth it, ensign. Because we struck at the Xeelee. Because Hama – *our son* – gave his life in the best possible way.'

At last I thought I understood her.

We were, after all, the same person. As I had grown up it had been drummed into me that there was no honour in growing old – and something in Dakk, even now, despite all she had gone through, still felt the same way. After surviving her earlier engagements she was not content to be a living hero. On some deep level she was ashamed to be alive. So she had let Hama, our lost child, live out her own dream – a dream of certain youthful death. Even though in the process she violated orders. Even though it damaged humanity's cause. And now she envied Hama his moment of glorious youthful suicide, even though it was an incident lost in a vanished future.

I think Dakk wanted to say more, but I turned away. I was aware I was out of my depth; counselling your elder self over the erasure of her whole career, not to mention her child, isn't exactly a situation you come across every day.

Anyhow I was feeling elated. Despite disgrace for a crime I'd never committed, despite my own screwed-up career, despite the loss of a baby I would never know, despite the wrecking of any relationship I might have had with Tarco, I was relieved. Frankly, I was glad I wouldn't turn into the beat-up egomaniac I saw before me. And I would never have to live through this scene again, standing on the other side of the room, looking back at my own face.

Is that cruel? I couldn't help it. *I was free.*

Tarco had a question to ask. 'Sir – *do we win?*'

Varcin kept his face expressionless. He clapped his hands, and the images over our heads changed.

It was as if the scale expanded.

I saw fleets with ships more numerous than the stars. I saw planets burn, stars flare and die. I saw the Galaxy reduced to a wraith of crimson stars that guttered like dying candles. I saw people – but people like none I'd ever heard of: people living on lonely outposts suspended in empty intergalactic spaces, people swimming through the interior of stars, people trapped in abstract environments I couldn't even recognise. I saw shining people who flew through space, naked as gods.

And I saw people dying, in great waves, unnumbered hordes of them.

Varcin said, 'We think there is a major crux in the next few millennia. A vital engagement at the centre of the Galaxy. Many of the history sheaves seem to converge at that point. Beyond that everything is uncertain. The farther downstream, the more misty are the visions, the more strange the protagonists, even the humans . . . There are paths to a glorious future, an awesome future of mankind victorious. And there are paths that lead to defeat – even extinction, all human possibilities extinguished. Your question isn't a simple one, ensign.'

Dakk, Tarco and I shared glances. Our intertwined destinies were complex. But I bet the three of us had only one thought in our minds at that moment: that we were glad we were mere Navy tars, that we did not have to deal with *this*.

That was almost the end of it. The formal court was due to convene; the meeting was over.

But there was still something that troubled me. 'Commissary?'

'Yes, ensign?'

'Do we have free will?'

Captain Dakk grimaced. 'Oh, no, ensign. Not us. We have duty.'

We walked out of the Map Room, where unrealised futures flickered like moth wings.

*As the two sides worked over their successive drafts of history, as timescales stretched to fit the vast spatial arena of a Galactic war, the Coalition laboured to keep mankind united. It succeeded, to an astonishing degree.*

*But there was always plenty of room, plenty of time, for things to drift.*

*One such dark corner was an Observation Post, flung far out of the Galaxy itself.*

# IN THE UN-BLACK

## AD 22,254

On the day La-ba met Ca-si she saved his life.

She hadn't meant to. It was un-Doctrine. It just happened. But it changed everything.

It had been a bad day for La-ba. She had been dancing. That wasn't un-Doctrine, not exactly, but the cadre leaders disapproved. She was the leader of the dance, and she got stuck with Cesspit detail for ten days. It was hard, dirty work, the worst.

And would-be deathers flourished there, in the pit. They would come swimming through the muck itself to get you.

That was what happened just two hours after she started work. Naked, she was standing knee-deep in a river of unidentifiable, odourless muck. Two strong hands grabbed her ankles and pulled her flat on her face. Suddenly her eyes and mouth and nose and ears were full of dense, sticky waste.

La-ba reached down to her toes. She found hands on her ankles, and further up a shaven skull, wide misshapen ears.

She recognised him from those ears. He was a We-ku, one of a batch of look-alikes who had come down from the Birthing Vat at the same time, and had clung together ever since. If they had ever had their own names, they had long abandoned them.

She wasn't about to be deathed by a We-ku. She pressed the heels of her hands into his eyes and shoved.

Her ankles started to slide out of his hands. The harder he gripped, the more his clutching fingers slipped. She pointed her toes and shoved harder.

Then she was free.

She pushed up to the surface and blew out a huge mouthful of dirt.

313

She prepared to take on the We-ku again, elbows and knees ready, fingers clawing for the knife strapped to her thigh.

But he didn't come for her, not for one heartbeat, two, three. She took the risk of wiping her eyes clear.

The We-ku had already found another victim. He was pressing a body into the dirt with his great fat hands. If he got his victim to the floor, his piston legs would crack the spine or splinter the skull in seconds.

The We-ku was a surging monster of blood and filth. His eyes were rimmed with blackness where she had bruised him.

Something in La-ba rose up.

At a time like this, a time of overcrowding, there was a lot of deathing.

You could *see* there were too many babies swarming out of the Birthing Vat, the great pink ball that hovered in the air at the very centre of the Observation Post. At rally hours you could look beyond the Vat to the other side of the Post, where the people marched around on the roof with their heads pointing down at you, and you could *see* that almost every Cadre Square was overfull.

Commissaries would come soon, bringing Memory. They would Cull if they had to. The less the Commissaries had to Cull, the happier they would be. It was the duty of every citizen of every cadre to bring down their numbers.

If you did well you would fly on a Shuttle out of here. You would fly to Earth, where life un-ended. That was worded by the cadre leaders. And if you hid and cowered, even if the amateur deathers didn't get to you, then the Old Man would. *That* was worded in the dorms. Earth as paradise, as life; the Old Man as a demon, as death. That was all that lay beyond the walls of the Post.

La-ba had no reason to un-believe this. She had seen hundreds deathed by others. She had deathed seventeen people herself.

La-ba was tall, her body lithe, supple: good at what she was trained for, deathing and sexing and hard physical work.

La-ba was five years old. Already half her life was gone.

She leapt out of the muck and onto the We-ku's back, her knife in her hand.

The We-ku didn't know whether to finish the death at his feet, or deal with the skinny menace on his back. And he was confused because what La-ba was doing was un-Doctrine. That confusion gave La-ba the seconds she needed.

Still, she almost had to saw his head clean off before he stopped struggling.

He sank at last into the dirt, which was now stained with whorls of deep crimson. The head, connected only by bits of gristle and skin, bobbed in the muck's sticky currents.

The We-ku's intended victim struggled to his feet. He was about La-ba's height and age, she guessed, with a taut, well-muscled body. He was naked, but crusted with dirt.

She was aroused. Deathing always aroused her. Glancing down at his crotch, at the stiff member that stuck out of the dirt there, she saw that this other felt the same.

'You crimed,' he breathed, and he stared at her with eyes that were bright white against the dirt.

He was right. She should have let the deathing go ahead, and then taken out the We-ku. Then there would have been two deaths, instead of one. She had been un-Doctrinc.

She glanced around. Nobody was close. Nobody had seen how the We-ku died.

Nobody but this man, this intended victim.

'Ca-si,' he said. 'Cadre Fourteen.' That was on the other side of the sky.

'La-ba. Cadre Six. Will you report?' If he did she could be summarily executed, deathed before the day was out.

Still he stared at her. The moment stretched.

He said, 'We should process the We-ku.'

'Yes.'

Breathing hard, they hauled the We-ku's bulky corpse towards a hopper. The work brought them close. She could feel the warmth of his body.

They dumped the We-ku into the hopper. It was already half-full, of tangled limbs, purple guts, bits of people. La-ba kept back one ugly We-ku ear as a trophy.

La-ba and Ca-si sexed, there and then, in the slippery dirt.

Later, at the end of the shift, they got clean, and sexed again.

Later still they joined in a dance, a vast abandoned whirl of a hundred citizens, more. Then they sexed again.

He never did report her crime. By failing to do so, of course, he was criming himself. Maybe that bonded them.

They kept sexing, whatever the reason.

*

Hama stood beside his mentor, Arles Thrun, as the citizens of the Observation Post filed before them. The marching drones stared at Hama's silvered skin, and they reached respectfully to stroke the gleaming egg-shaped Memory that Arles held in his hand: the treasure, brought from Earth itself, that the Commissaries were here to present to the drones of this Post.

One in three of the drones who passed was assigned, by Arles's ancient, wordless gesture, to the Cull. Perhaps half of those assigned would survive. Each drone so touched shrank away from Arles's gleaming finger.

When Hama looked to the up-curving horizon he saw that the line of patiently queuing drones stretched a quarter of the way around the Post's internal equator.

This Observation Post was a sphere, so small Hama could have walked around its interior in a day. The folded-over sky was crowded with Cadre Squares, dormitory blocks and training and indoctrination centres, and the great sprawls of the Post's more biological functions, the Cesspits and the Cyclers and the Gardens, green and brown and glistening blue. The great Birthing Vat itself hung directly over his head at the geometric centre of the sphere, pink and fecund, an obscene sun. Drones walked all over the inner surface of the sphere, stuck there by inertial generators, manipulated gravity. The air was thick with the stink of growing things, of dirt and sweat. To Hama, it was like being trapped within the belly of some vast living thing.

It didn't help his mood to reflect that just beyond the floor beneath his feet the host planet's atmosphere raged: a perpetual hydrogen storm, laced with high-frequency radiation and charged particles.

Absently he reached into his drab monastic robe and touched his chest. He stroked the cool, silvered Planck-zero epidermis, sensed the softly gurgling fluid within, where alien fish swam languidly. *Here* in this dismal swamp, immersed in the primeval, he could barely sense the mood even of Arles, who stood right next to him. He longed for the cool interstellar gulf, the endless open where the merged thoughts of Commissaries sounded across a trillion stars . . .

'Hama, pay attention,' Arles Thrun snapped.

Hama focused reluctantly on the soft round faces of the drones, and saw they betrayed agitation and confusion at his behaviour.

'Remember this is a great day for them,' Arles murmured dryly. 'The first Commission visit in a thousand years – and it is happening in the brief lifetime of *this* creature.' His silvered hand patted indulgently at the bare head of the drone before him. 'How lucky they are, even if we will have to order the deaths of so many of them. There is so little in their lives – little more than the wall images that never change, the meaningless battle for position in the cadre hierarchies . . .

And the dance, Hama thought reluctantly, their wild illegal dance. 'They disgust me,' he hissed, surprising himself. Yet it was true.

Arles glanced at him. 'You're fortunate they do not understand.'

'They disgust me because their language has devolved into jabber,' Hama said. 'They disgust me because they have bred themselves into over-population.'

Arles murmured, 'Hama, when you accepted the burden of longevity you chose a proud name. I sometimes wonder whether you have the nobility to match that name. *These* creatures' names were chosen for them by a random combination of syllablcs.'

'They spend their lives on make-work. They eat and screw and die, crawling around in their own filth. What need has a candle-flame of a name?'

Arles was frowning now, sapphire eyes flickering in the silver mask of his face. 'Have you forgotten the core tenet of the Doctrines? *A brief life burns brightly*, Hama. These creatures and their forebears have maintained their lonely vigil, here beyond the Galaxy – monitoring the progress of the war – for *five thousand years*. We have neglected them; isolated, they have – drifted. But these drones are the essence of humanity. And we Commissaries – doomed to knowledge, doomed to life – we are their servants.'

'Perhaps. But this "essence of humanity" is motivated by lies. Already we understand their jabber well enough to know that. These absurd legends of theirs—'

Arles raised a hand, silencing him quickly. 'Belief systems drift, just as languages do. The flame of the Doctrines still burns here, if not as brightly as we would wish. And, Doctrinal or not, this Post is useful. Always remember that, Hama: utility is a factor. This is a war, after all.'

Now two of the drones came before Hama, hand in hand, male and female, nude like the rest. This pair leaned close to each other, showing an easy physical familiarity.

They had made love, he saw immediately. Not oncc, but many timcs. Perhaps even recently. He felt an unwelcome pang of jealousy. But on a thong around her neck the female wore what looked hideously like a dried human ear. The fish in his chest squirmed.

He snapped: 'What are your names?'

They didn't understand his words, but comprehended the sense. They pointed to their chests. '*La-ba.*' '*Ca-si.*'

Arles smiled, amused, contemptuous. 'We have the perspective of gods. They have only their moment of light, and the warmth of each other's body . . . What is it, Hama? Feeling a little attraction, despite your disgust? A little *envy*?'

With an angry gesture, Hama sentenced both the drones to the Cull. The drones, obviously shocked, clung to each other.

Arles laughed. 'Don't worry, Hama. You are yet young. You will grow – distant.' Arles passed him the Memory.

Hama weighed the Memory; it was surprisingly heavy. It contained the story of the war since the Commission's last visit to this backwater Observation Post, a glorious story rendered in simple, heroic images. The contents of the Memory would be downloaded into the Post's fabric and transcribed on its walls, in images timeless enough to withstand further linguistic drift. Nothing else could be written or drawn on the surfaces of the Post – certainly nothing made by the inhabitants of this place. What had they to write or draw? What did they need to read, save the glorious progress of mankind?

'Carry on alone. Perhaps it will be a useful discipline for you. One in three for the Cull. And remember – as you condemn them, *love them.*' Arles walked away.

The drone couple had moved on. More ugly shaven heads moved past him, all alike, meaningless.

Later that night, when the Post's sourceless light dimmed, Hama watched the drones dance their wild untutored tangoes, sensual and beautiful. He clung to the thought of how he had doomed the lovers: their shocked expressions, the way they had grabbed each other's arms, their distress.

After another sleep, La-ba and Ca-si were thrust out of the Observation Post. Only one of them, La-ba or Ca-si, would come back – one, or neither, depending on the outcome of their combat. This was the Cull. A way of sifting out the strongest, while keeping down the population.

To La-ba, stiff in her hardsuit, it was a strange and unwelcome experience to pass through the shell of the Post, to feel gravity shift and change, to feel *up* become *down*. And then she had to make sense of a floor that curved away beneath her, to understand that the horizon now hid what lay beyond rather than revealed it.

The Post was adrift in a cloud, a crimson fog that glowed around La-ba. The endless air, above and below, was racked by huge storms. Far below she saw the smooth glint of this world's core, a hard plain of metallic hydrogen, unimaginably strange. Lightning crackled between immense black clouds. Rain slammed down around her, a hail of pebbles that glowed red-hot. They clattered against the smooth skin of the Post, and her hardsuit.

The clouds were a vapour of silicates. The rain was molten rock laced with pure iron.

The Post was a featureless ball that floated in this ferocious sky, a world drifting within a world. A great cable ran up from the floor before her, up into the crowded sky above her, up – it was said – to the cool emptiness of space beyond. La-ba had never seen space, though she believed it existed.

La-ba, used to enclosure, wanted to cringe, to fall against the floor, as, it was said, some infants hugged the smooth warm walls of the Birthing Vat. But she stood tall.

A fist slammed into the back of her head.

She fell forward, her hardsuited limbs clattering against the floor.

There was a weight on her back and legs, pressing her down. She felt a scrabbling at her neck. Fingers probed at the joint between her helmet and the rest of the suit. If the suit was breached she would death at once.

She did not resist.

She felt the fingers pull away from her neck.

With brisk roughness she was flipped on her back. Her assailant sat on her legs, heavy in his hardsuit. Rock rain pattered on his shoulders, red-gleaming pebbles that stuck for a second before dropping away, cooling to grey.

It was, of course, Ca-si.

'You un-hunted me,' he said, and his words crackled in her ears. 'And now you un-resist me.' She felt his hands on her shoulders, and she remembered how his skin had touched hers, but there was no feeling through the hardsuits. He said, 'You crime if you un-death me. You crime if you let me death you.'

'It is true.' So it was. According to the Doctrines that shaped their lives, it was the duty of the strong to destroy the weak.

Ca-si sat back. 'I will death you.' But he ran his gloved hands over her body, over her breasts, to her belly.

And he found the bulge there, exposed by the contoured hardsuit.

His eyes widened.

'Now you know,' she screamed at him.

His face twisted behind the thick plate. 'I must death you even if you have babied.'

'Yes! Death me! Get it over!'

'. . . No. There is another way.'

There was a hand on Ca-si's shoulder. He twisted, startled.

Another stood over them, occluding the raging rock clouds. This other was wearing an ancient, scuffed hardsuit. Through a scratched and starred faceplate, La-ba made out one eye, one dark socket, a mesh of wrinkles.

It was the Old Man: the monster of whom infants whispered to each other even before they had left the Birthing Vat.

Ca-si fell away. He was screaming and screaming, terrified. La-ba lay there, stunned, unable to speak.

The Old Man reached down and hauled La-ba to her feet. 'Come.' He pulled her towards the cable which connected the Post to space.

There was a door in the cable.

Hama kept Ca-si in custody.

The boy paced back and forth in the small cell Hama had created for him, his muscles sliding beneath his skin. He would mutter sometimes, agitated, clearly troubled by whatever had become of his lost love.

But when Ca-si inspected the Commissary's silvered epidermis and the fish that swam in his chest, a different look dawned on his fleshy, soft face. It was a look of awe, incomprehension, and – admit it, Hama! – *disgust*.

He knew Arles disapproved of his obsession with this boy. 'The result of your assignment of them to the Cull was satisfactory,' he had said. 'Two went out; one came back. What does it matter?'

But Hama pointed to evidences of flaws – the lack of trophies from the body being the most obvious. 'All these disgusting drones take trophies from their kills. There's something wrong here.'

'There is more than one way of manifesting weakness, Hama. If the other let herself die it is better she is deleted from the gene pool anyhow.'

'That is not according to the strict Doctrines.'

Arles had sighed, and passed a glimmering hand over the silver planes of his cheek. 'But even our longevity is a violation of the Doctrines – if a necessary one. Druz is seventeen thousand years dead, Hama. His Doctrines have become – mature. You will learn.'

But Hama had not been satisfied.

Hama faced the boy. He forced his silvered face into a smile. 'You have been isolated here a long time.'

'A hundred births,' the boy said sullenly.

That was about right: a thousand years since the last Commission visit, a hundred of these drones' brief generations. 'Yes. A hundred births. And, in enough time, languages change. Did you know that? After just a few thousand years of separation two identical languages will diverge so much that they would share no common features except basic grammatical constructs – like the way a language indicates possession, or uses more subtle features like ergativity, which . . .'

The boy was just staring at him, dull, not even resentful.

Hama felt foolish, and then angry to be made to feel that way. He said sternly, 'To rectify language drift is part of our duty. The Commission for Historical Truth, I mean. We will reteach you Standard. Just as we will leave you the Memory, with the story of mankind since you were last visited, and we will take away your story to tell it to others. We bind up mankind on all our scattered islands. Just as it is your duty—'

'To death.'

'To die. Yes. You are hidden inside a planet, a gas giant, out of sight of the enemy. The machines here watch for the enemy. They have watched for five thousand years, and they may watch for five thousand years more. If the enemy come you must do everything you can to destroy them, and if you cannot, you must destroy the machines, and the Post, and yourself.'

This boy was actually no more than a backup mechanism, Hama thought. A final self-destruct, in case this station's brooding automated defences failed. For this sole purpose, five hundred generations of humans had lived and loved and bred and died, here in the intergalactic waste.

Ca-si watched him dully, his powerful hands clenched into fists. As he gazed at the planes of the boy's stomach Hama felt an uncomfortable inner warmth, a restlessness.

On impulse he snapped, 'Who do we fight? Do you know?'

'We fight the Xeelee.'

'*Why* do we fight?'

The boy stared at him.

Hama ordered, 'Look at me.' He pulled open his robe. 'This silver skin comes from a creature called a Silver Ghost. Once the Ghosts owned worlds and built cities. Now we farm their skins. The fish in my belly are called Squeem. Once they conquered mankind, occupied Earth itself. Now they are mere symbiotes in my chest, enabling me to speak to my colleagues across the Galaxy. These are triumphs for mankind.'

The look on Ca-si's face made Hama think he didn't regard his condition as a triumph.

Angry, oddly confused, Hama snapped, 'I know you didn't kill the girl. Why did you spare her? Why did she spare you? *Where is she?*'

But the boy wouldn't reply.

It seemed there was nothing Hama could do to reach Ca-si, as he longed to.


La-ba ascended into strangeness.

The hollow cable had a floor that lifted you up, and windows so you could see out. Inside, she rode all the way out of the air, into a place of harsh flat light.

When she looked down she saw a floor of churning red gas. Auroras flapped in its textured layers, making it glow purple. When she looked up she saw only a single burning, glaring light.

The Old Man tried to make her understand. 'The light is the sun. The red is the world. The Post floats in the air of the world. We have risen up out of the air, into space.'

She couldn't stop staring at his face. It was a mass of wrinkles. He had one eye, one dark purple pit. His face was much stranger than the sun and the churning world.

The cable ended in another giant ball, like the Post. But this ball was dimpled by big black pits, like the bruises left by the heels of her hands in the face of the We-ku. And it floated in space, not the air. It was a moon, attached to the cable.

Inside the ball there was a cavity, but there were no people or Cadre Squares and no Birthing Vat: only vast mechanical limbs that glistened, sinister, sliding over each other.

'No people live here,' she said.

He smiled. 'One person does.'

He showed her his home inside the tethered moon. It was just a shack made of bits of shining plastic. There were blankets on the floor, and clothes, and empty food packets. It was dirty, and it smelled a little.

She looked around. 'There is no supply dispenser.'

'People give me food. And water and clothes. From their rations.'

She tried to understand. 'Why?'

He shrugged. 'Because life is short. People want—'

'What?'

'Something more than the war.'

She thought about that. 'There is the dance.'

He grinned, his empty eye socket crumpling. 'I never could dance. Come.'

He led her to a huge window. Machines screened out the glare of the sun above, and the glower of the overheated planet below.

Between sun and planet, there was only blackness.

'No,' the Old Man said gently. 'Not blackness. *Look*.'

They waited there for long heartbeats.

At last she saw a faint glow, laced against the black. It had structure, fine filaments and threads. It was beautiful, eerie, remote.

'It is un-black.'

He pointed at the sun. 'The sun is alone. If there were other suns near, we would see them, as points of light. The suns gather in pools, like that one.' He pointed down, but the Galaxy's disc was hidden by the bulk of the planet. 'The un-black is pools of suns, very far away.'

She understood that.

'Others lived here before me,' he said. 'They learned how to see with the machines. They left records of what they saw.' He dug into a pocket and pulled out a handful of bones: human bones, the small bones of a hand or foot. They were scored by fine marks.

'They speak to you with *bones*?'

He shrugged. 'If you smear blood or dirt on the walls it falls away. What else do we have to draw on, but our bones, and our hearts?' He fingered the bones carefully.

'What do the bones say?'

He gestured at the hulking machinery. 'These machines watch the sky for the trace of ships. But they also see the un-black: the light, the faintest light, all the light there is. Some of the light comes from the suns and pools of suns. Most of the light was made in the birthing

323

of the universe. It is old now and tired and hard to see. But it has patterns in it . . .'

This meant nothing to her. Bombarded by strangeness, she tried to remember the Doctrines. 'I crimed. I did not death, and I wanted to be deathed. Even the wanting was a crime. Then you crimed. You could have deathed me. And here—'

'Here, I crime.' He grinned. 'With every breath I crime. Every one of these bones is a crime, a record of ancient crimes. Like you, I was safed.'

'Safed?'

'Brought here.'

She asked the hardest question of all. 'When?'

He smiled, and the wrinkles on his face gathered up. 'Twenty years ago. Twice your life.'

She frowned, barely comprehending. She leaned against the window, cupping her hands and peering out.

He asked, 'What are you looking for now?'

'Shuttles to Earth.'

He said gently, 'There are no Shuttles.'

'The cadre leaders—'

'The cadre leaders say what is said to them. Think. Have you ever known anybody leave on a Shuttle? *There are no Shuttles.*'

'It is a lie?'

'It is a lie. If you live past age ten, the cadre leaders will death you. *They* believe they will win a place on the Shuttles. But they in turn are deathed by other cadre leaders, who believe they will steal their places on the Shuttles. And so it goes. Lies eating each other.'

*No Shuttles.* She sighed, and her breath fogged the smooth surface of the window. 'Then how will we leave?'

'We un-can leave. We are too remote. Only the Commissaries come and go. Only the Commissaries. Not us.'

She felt something stir in her heart.

'The Shuttles are un-real. Is Earth real? Is the war real?'

'Perhaps Earth is a lie. But the war is real. Oh, yes. The bones talk of how distant suns flare up. The war is real, and all around us, but it is very far away, and very old. But it shapes us.' He studied her. 'Soon the cadre leaders will pluck that baby from your belly and put it in the Birthing Vat. It will life and death for one purpose, for the war.'

She said nothing.

The Old Man said dreamily, 'Some of the Old Men before me have seen patterns in the un-black. They have tried to understand them, as the cadre leaders make us understand the Memory images of the war. Perhaps they are thoughts, those patterns. Frozen thoughts of the creatures who lived in the first blinding second of the universal birth.' He shook his head and gazed at the bones. 'I un-want death. I want more than the war. I want to learn *this*.'

She barely heard him. She asked, 'Who gives you food?'

He gave her names, of people she knew, and people she un-knew.

The number of them shocked her.

Hama and Arles Thrun drifted in space, side by side, two silver statues. Before them, this hot-Jupiter world continued its endless frenetic waltz around its too-close sun. The sun was a rogue star that had evaporated out of its parent galaxy long ago, and come to drift here, a meaningless beacon in the intergalactic dark.

Hama was comfortable here, in space, in the vacuum, away from the claustrophobic enclosure of the Post. Alien creatures swam through his chest cavity, subtly feeding on the distant calls of Commissaries all over the Galaxy. To Hama it was like being in a vast room where soft voices murmured in every shadowed corner, grave and wise.

'A paradox,' Arles Thrun murmured now.

'What is?'

'You are. You know, your rebuilding has extended beyond the superficial. You have been re-engineered, the layers of evolutionary haphazardness designed out of you. The inner chemical conflicts bequeathed by humanity's past do not trouble you. You do not hear voices in your head, you do not invent gods to drive out your internal torment. You are one of the most *integrated* human beings who ever lived.'

'If I am still human,' Hama said. 'We have no art. We are not scientists. We do not dance.'

'No,' said Arles earnestly. 'Our re-engineered hearts are too cold for that. Or to desire to make babies to fill up the empty spaces. Yet we are needed, we long-lived ones.

'It is impossible to begin to grasp the scale and complexity of an interstellar war in a human lifetime. And yet the brevity of human life is the key to the war: we fight like vermin, for to the Xeelee we are vermin – *that* is the central uncomfortable truth of the Doctrines. We, who do not die, are a paradoxical necessity, maintaining the attention span of the species.

'*But we know our flaws, Hama*. We know that those brutish creatures down there in the Post, busily fighting and fornicating and breeding and dying, *they* are the true heart of humanity. And so we must defer to them.' He eyed Hama, waiting for him to respond.

Hama said with difficulty, 'I am not – happy.'

'You were promised integration, not happiness.'

'I failed to find the girl. *La-ba.*'

Arles smiled in the vacuum. 'I traced her. She escaped to the sensor installation.'

'What installation?'

'In the tethered asteroid. Another renegade lives up there. To what purpose, I can't imagine.'

'This place is flawed,' Hama said bitterly.

'Oh, yes. Very flawed. There is a network of drones who provision the renegade. And there are more subtle problems: the multiple births occurring in the Vat; the taking of trophies from kills; the *dancing* . . . These drones seek satisfaction beyond the Doctrines. There has been ideological drift. It is a shame. You would think that in a place as isolated as this a certain purity could be sustained. But the human heart, it seems, is full of spontaneous imperfection.'

'They must be punished.'

Arles looked at him carefully. 'We do not punish, Hama. We only correct.'

'How? A programme of indoctrination, a rebuilding—'

Arles shook his head. 'It has gone too far for that. Even arguments of utility cannot outweigh the gross Doctrinal drift here. There are many other Observation Posts. We will allow these flawed drones to die.'

There was a wash of agreement from the Commissaries all over the Galaxy, all of them loosely bound to their thinking, all of them concurring in Arles's decision.

Hama found he was appalled. 'They have done their duty here for five thousand years, and now you would destroy them so casually, for the sake of a little deviance?'

Arles gripped Hama's arms and turned him so they faced each other. Hama glimpsed cold power in his eyes; Arles Thrun was already five centuries old. 'Look around, Hama. Look at the Galaxy, the vast stage, deep in space and time, on which we fight. Our foe is unimaginably ancient, with unimaginable powers. And what are we but half-evolved apes from the plains of some dusty, lost planet? Perhaps we are not *smart* enough to fight this war. And yet we fight even so.

'And to keep us united in our purpose, this vast host of us scattered over more galaxies than either of us could count, we have the Doctrines, our creed of mortality. Let me tell you something. The Doctrines are not perfect. *They may not even enable us to win the war*, no matter how long we fight. But they have brought us this far, and they are all we have.'

'And so we must destroy these drones, not for the sake of the war—'

'But for the sake of the Doctrines. Yes. Now, at last, you begin to understand.'

Arles released him, and they drifted apart.

La-ba stayed with the Old Man.

She woke. She lay in silence. It was strange not to wake under a sky crowded with people. She could feel her baby inside her, kicking as if it was eager to get to the Birthing Vat.

The floor shuddered.

The Old Man ran to her. He dragged her to her feet. 'It begins,' he said.

'What?'

'They are cutting the cable. You must go back.' He took her to the hatch that led to the hollow cable.

A We-ku was there, inside the cable, his fat face split by a grin, his stick-out ears wide.

She raised her foot and kicked the We-ku in the forehead. He clattered to the floor, howling.

The Old Man pulled her back. 'What did you do?'

'He is a We-ku.'

'Look.' The Old Man pointed.

The We-ku was clambering to his feet and rubbing his head. He had been carrying a bag full of ration packs. Now the packs were littered over the floor, some of them split.

The Old Man said, 'Never mind the food. Take her back.' And he pushed at La-ba again, urging her into the cable. Reluctantly, following the We-ku, she began to climb down.

She felt a great sideways wash. The whole of this immense cable was vibrating back and forth, as if it had been plucked by a vast finger.

She looked up at the circle of light that framed the Old Man's face. She was confused, frightened. 'I will bring you food.'

He laughed bitterly. 'Just remember me. Here.' And he thrust his hand down into hers. Then he slammed shut the hatch.

When she opened her hand, she saw it contained the scrimshawed bones.

The cable whiplashed, and the lights failed, and they fell into darkness, screaming.

Hama stood in the holding cell, facing Ca-si. The walls were creaking. He heard screaming, running footsteps.

With its anchoring cable severed, the Post was beginning to sink away from its design altitude, deeper into the roiling murk of the hot Jupiter's atmosphere. Long before it reached the glimmering, enigmatic, metallic-hydrogen core, it would implode.

Ca-si's mouth worked, as if he was gulping for air. He said to Hama, 'Take me to the Shuttles.'

'There are no Shuttles.'

Ca-si yelled, 'Why are you here? What do you *want*?'

Hama laid one silvered hand against the boy's face. 'I love you,' he said. 'Don't you see that? It's my job to love you.' But his silvered flesh could not detect the boy's warmth, and Ca-si flinched from his touch, the burned scent of vacuum exposure.

'. . . *I* know what you want.'

Ca-si gasped. Hama turned.

La-ba stood in the doorway. She was dirty, bloodied. She was carrying a lump of shattered partition wall. Fragmentary animated images, of glorious scenes from humanity's past, played over it fitfully.

Hama said, '*You*.'

She flicked a fingernail against the silver carapace of his arm. 'You hate being like this. You want to be like us. That's why you tried to death us.'

And she lifted the lump of partition rubble and slammed it into his chest. Briny water gushed down Hama's belly, spilling tiny silver fish that struggled and died.

Hama fell back, bending over himself. His systems screamed messages of alarm and pain at him – and, worse, he could feel that he had lost his link with the vaster pool of Commissaries beyond. 'What have you done? Oh, what have you done?'

'Now you are like us,' said La-ba simply.

The light flickered and darkened. Glancing out of the cell, Hama saw that the great Birthing Vat was drifting away from its position at the geometric centre of the Post. Soon it would impact the floor in a gruesome moist collision.

'I should have gone with Arles,' he moaned. 'I don't know why I delayed.'

La-ba stood over Hama and grabbed his arm. With a grunting effort, the two drones hauled him to his feet.

La-ba said, 'Why do you death us?'

'It is the war. Only the war.'

'Why do we fight the war?'

In desperation Hama said rapidly, 'We have fought the Xeelee for ten thousand years. We've forgotten why we started. We can see no end. We fight because we must. We don't know what else to do. We can't stop, any more than you can stop breathing. Do you see?'

'Take us,' said La-ba.

'*Take you?* Take you where? Can you even imagine another place?'

Perhaps she couldn't. But in La-ba's set face there was ruthless determination, a will to survive that burned away the fog of his own weak thinking.

The Doctrines are right, he thought. Mortality brings strength. *A brief life burns brightly.* He felt ashamed of himself. He tried to stand straight, ignoring the clamouring pain from his smashed stomach.

The girl said, 'It is un-Doctrine. But I have deathed your fish. Nobody will know.'

He forced a laugh. 'Is that why you killed the Squeem? . . . You are naïve.'

She clutched his arm harder, as if trying to bend his metallic flesh. 'Take us to Earth.'

'Do you know what Earth is like?'

Ca-si said, 'It is a place where you live on the outside, not the inside. It is a place where water falls from the sky, not rock.'

'How will you live?'

La-ba said, 'The We-ku helped the Old Man live. Others will help us live.'

Perhaps it was true, Hama thought. Perhaps if these two survived on some civilised world – a world where other citizens could see what was being done in the name of the war – they might form a focus for resistance. No, not resistance: *doubt.*

And doubt might destroy them all.

He must abandon these creatures to their deaths. That was his clear duty, his duty to the species.

There was a crack of shattering partition. The Post spun, making the three of them stagger, locked together.

Ca-si showed his fear. 'We will be deathed.'

'Take us to Earth,' La-ba insisted.

Hama said weakly, 'I would have to hide you from Arles. And you broke my link to the Commission. I may not be able to find my way. The link helps me – navigate. Do you see?'

'Try,' she whispered. She closed her eyes, and pressed her cheek against the cold of his silvered chest.

Hama's flitter floated in vacuum.

The sun glared, impossibly bright. The planet was a floor of roiling gas, semi-infinite. Above, Hama could see the Post's sensor installation. It was drifting off into space, dangling its tether like an impossibly long umbilical. It was startlingly bright in the raw sunlight, like a sculpture.

From beneath the planet's boiling clouds, a soundless concussion of light flickered and faded. Five thousand years of history had ended, a subplot in mankind's tangled evolution; the long watch was over. La-ba squirmed, distressed, her hands clasped over the bump at her belly.

Hama held the two lovers close.

The flitter turned and squirted into hyperspace, heading for Earth.

*Much later, the primordial cosmic thoughts detected by the 'drones' of that Observation Post would be recognised, and valued – and the monads, minds from the dawn of time, would play a crucial role in the human capture of the Galaxy Core. All that later.*

*It is amusing to see mayflies forget and rediscover, forget and rediscover, over and over. Commissaries like Arles and Hama with their alien symbiotes imagined that their longevity treatments were new, their long lives a novel strategy.*

*To us even they were mayflies.*

*The Galaxy blazed with war. Still time stretched, the past forgotten, the foreknown future static. The war became perpetual, a grinder of humanity.*

*Yet humanity prevailed.*

# RIDING THE ROCK

## AD 23,479

I

When Luca arrived in the Library conference room, the meeting between Commissary Dolo and Captain Teel was already underway. They sat in hard-backed armchairs, talking quietly, while trays of drinks hovered at their elbows.

Over their heads Virtual dioramas swept by like dreams, translucent, transient. These were the possible destinies of mankind, assembled from the debris of interstellar war by toiling bureaucrats here in Earth's Library of Futures, and displayed for the amusement of the Library's guests. But neither Dolo nor Teel were paying any attention to the spectacle.

Luca waited by the door. He was neither patient nor impatient. He was just a Novice, at twenty years old barely halfway through his formal novitiate into the Commission, and Novices expected to wait.

But he knew who this Captain Teel was. An officer in the Green Navy, she had come from her posting on the Front – the informal name for the great ring of human fortification that surrounded the Core of the Galaxy, where the Xeelee lurked, mankind's implacable foe. The Navy and the Commission for Historical Truth were also, of course, ancient and unrelenting enemies. There was no way Teel, therefore, would adopt the ascetic dress code of the Commission, even here in its headquarters. But her uniform was a subdued charcoal grey shot through with green flashes, and her hair, if not shaved, was cut short; this fighting officer had shown respect, then, for the hive of bureaucrats she had come to visit.

At last Dolo noticed Luca.

Luca said, 'You sent for me, Commissary.'

Captain Teel turned her head towards him. She looked tired, but

331

Luca saw how the complex, shifting light of multiple futures softened her expression.

Dolo was watching Luca, the corner of his mouth pulled slightly, as if by a private joke. Dolo had no eyebrows, and his skull was shaved, as was Luca's. 'Yes, Novice, I called you. I think I'm going to need an assistant on this project, and Lethe knows *you* need some field experience.'

'A project, Commissary?'

'Sit down, shut up, listen and learn.' Dolo waved a hand, and a third chair drifted in from a corner of the room.

Luca sat, and absently followed their continuing talk.

From scuttlebutt in the dormitories he already had an idea why Captain Teel had been called here to Earth. In a unit of troopers at some desolate corner of the Front, there had been an outbreak of anti-Doctrinal thinking which, it sounded to Luca's ill-informed ears, might even be *religious* in character. If so, of course, it was perilous to the greater efficiency of the Third Expansion. An important issue, then. But not very *interesting*.

Surreptitiously, as they talked, he studied Teel.

He supposed he had expected some battle-scarred veteran of raids on Xeelee emplacements. But this Navy officer was young, surely about the same age as he was himself, at twenty years. Her face was long, the nose narrow and well-carved, her nostrils flaring slightly; her mouth was relaxed but full. Her skin was unblemished – though it was pale, almost bloodless; he reminded himself that of all the countless worlds now inhabited by mankind, on only a handful could a human walk in the open air without a skinsuit. But that paleness gave her skin a translucent quality. But it was not Teel's features that drew him – she was scarcely conventionally beautiful – but something more subtle, a quality of stillness about her that seemed to pull him towards her like a gravitational field. She was *solid*, he thought, as if she was the only real person in this place of buzzing bureaucrats. Even before she spoke to him, he knew that Teel was like no one he had ever met before.

'Novice.' The Commissary's gaze neatly skewered Luca.

To his mortification, Luca felt his face flush like a child's in a new cadre. Captain Teel was looking a little past him, expressionless. 'I'm sorry,' he said.

Dolo brushed that aside. 'Tell me what you are thinking. The surface of your mind.'

Luca looked at Teel. 'That, with respect, the Captain is young.'

Dolo nodded, his voice forensic. 'How could one so young – actually *younger than you*, Novice – have achieved so much?'

Luca said, ' "A brief life burns brightly." '

Teel's lips parted, and Luca thought she sighed. The ancient slogan hung in the air, trite and embarrassing.

Dolo's smile was cruel. 'I have come to a decision. I will visit the site of this Doctrinal infringement. And you, Novice, will come with me.'

'Commissary – you want me to go to *the Core*?' It was all but unheard of for a novice to travel so far.

'I have no doubt it will help you fulfil your fitful promise, Luca. Make the arrangements.'

Suddenly he was dismissed. Luca stood, bowed to the Commissary and Captain, and turned to leave.

Emotions swirled in Luca: embarrassment, surprise, fear – and a strange, unexpected grain of hope. Of course this was all just some game to the Commissary; Dolo had spotted Luca's reaction to Teel and had impulsively decided to toy with him. Dolo was hugely arrogant. You could hardly expect to become one of the most powerful members of a bureaucracy that ruled the disc of a Galaxy without learning a little arrogance along the way. But for Luca it was a good opportunity, perhaps an invaluable building block for his future career.

And none of that mattered, he knew in his heart, for whatever the wider context Luca was now going to be in the company of this intriguing young Navy officer for weeks, even months to come, and who could say where *that* would lead?

At the door he glanced back. Teel and Dolo continued to talk of this uninteresting Doctrinal problem at the Galaxy's Core; still she didn't look at him.


They were to climb to orbit in a small flitter, and there join the Navy yacht that had brought Teel to Earth.

Luca had only been off Earth a couple of times during his general education, and then on mere hops out of the atmosphere. As the flitter lifted off the ground its hull was made transparent, so that it was as if the three of them were rising inside a drifting bubble. As the land fell away Luca tried to ignore the hot blood that prickled at his neck, and the deeply embarrassingly primeval clenching of his sphincter.

He tried to draw strength from Teel's stillness. Her eyes were blue,

Luca noticed now. He hadn't been able to make that out before, in the shifting light of the Library.

As they rose the Conurbation was revealed. It was a glistening sprawl of bubble-dwellings blown from the bedrock. The landscape beyond was flat, a plain of glistening silver-grey devoid of hills, and there were no rivers, only the rectilinear gashes of canals. The only living things to be seen, aside from humans, were birds. It was like this over much of the planet. The alien Qax had begun the transformation of the land during their Occupation of Earth, their starbreaker beams and nano-replicators turning the ground into a featureless silicate dust.

They spoke of this. Teel murmured, 'But the Qax were here only a few centuries.'

Dolo nodded. The silvery light reflected from the planes of his face; he was about fifty years old. 'Much of this is human work, Coalition work. The Qax tried to destroy our past, to cut us adrift from history. Their motivation was wrong – but their methods were valid. Remember, we have been in direct conflict with the Xeelee for *eleven thousand years*. We have done well. We have swept them out of the plane of the Galactic disc. But they remain huddled in their fortress in the Core, and beyond our little island of stars they swarm in uncounted numbers. We must put the past aside, for it is a distraction. If the Xeelee defeat us, *we will have no future* – and in that case, what will the past matter?'

'Your ideology is powerful.'

Dolo nodded. 'A single idea powerful enough to keep mankind united across a hundred thousand light years, and through tens of millennia.'

Teel said, 'But the mountains and rivers of Earth were far older than mankind. How strange that we have outlived them.'

Luca was startled by this anti-Doctrinal sentiment. Dolo merely looked interested, and said nothing.

The yacht soared upwards, out through the great ranks of Snowflake surveillance stations that stretched as far as Earth's Moon, and the planet itself turned into a glistening pebble that fell away into the dark.

It would take them a day to reach Saturn. Luca, on this first trip out of Earth's gravitational well, had expected to glimpse Earth's sister worlds – perhaps even mighty Jupiter itself, transformed millennia ago into a gleaming black hole in a futile gesture of rebellion. But he saw nothing but darkness beyond the hull, not so much as a grain of dust, and even as they plunged through the outer system the stars did not shift across the sky, dwarfing the journey he was making.

Saturn itself was a bloated ball of yellow-brown that came swimming out of the dark. It was visibly flattened at the poles, and rendered misty in the diminished light of the already remote sun. Rings like ceramic sheets surrounded it, gaudy. The world itself was an exotic place, for, it was said, mighty machines of war had been suspended in its clouds, there to defend Sol system should the unthinkable happen and the alien foe strike at the home of mankind. But if the machines existed there was no sign of them, and Luca was disappointed when the yacht stopped its approach when the planet was still no larger than he could cover with his hand.

But Saturn wasn't their destination.

Dolo murmured, '*Look*.'

Luca saw an artefact – a tetrahedron, glowing sky-blue – sailing past the planet's limb. Kilometres across, it was a framework of glowing rods, and brown-gold membranes of light stretched across the open faces. Those membranes held tantalising images of star fields, of suns that had never shone over Saturn, or Earth.

'A wormhole Interface,' Luca breathed. It was like a dream of a forbidden past.

Wormholes were flaws in space and time which connected points separated by light years – or by centuries – with passages of curved space. On the scale of the invisibly small, where the mysterious effects of quantum gravity operated, spacetime was foam-like, riddled with tiny wormholes. It had taken the genius of the legendary engineer Michael Poole, more than twenty thousand years ago, to pull such a wormhole out of the foam and manipulate it to the size and shape he wanted: that is, big enough to take a spacecraft.

'Once it must have been magnificent,' Teel said now. 'Poole and his followers built a wormhole network that spanned Sol system, from Earth to the outermost ice moon. At Earth itself wormhole gates of all sizes drifted across the face of the planet like sculptures.' This evocation was surprisingly poetic. But then Teel had been brought up within the Core itself – you couldn't get much further from Earth than that – and Luca wondered how much this trip to the home system meant to her.

But Dolo said sternly, 'That was before the Occupation, of course. The Qax broke it all up, destroyed the Poole wormholes. But now we are building a mighty new network, a great system of arteries that runs, not just across Sol system, but all the way to the Core of the Galaxy itself. There are a thousand wormhole termini orbiting in these rings. And if we have *that* in the present, we don't need dreams of the past, do we?'

Teel did not respond.

The yacht swept on, tracking the great ring system into the shadow of the planet.

Ships swarmed everywhere, pinpricks in the dark. Saturn, largest planet in the system now that Jupiter had been imploded, was used merely as a convenient gravitational mooring point for the mouths of the wormholes, tunnels through space and time. And its rings were being mined, ice and rock fragments hurled into the wormhole mouth to feed humans at remote destinations. Luca had heard mutterings in the seminaries at the steady destruction of this unique glory. In another couple of centuries, it was predicted, the ravenous wormholes would have gobbled up so much the rings would be barely visible, mere wraiths of their former selves. But, as Dolo would have remarked had Luca raised the point, if the victorious Xeelee caused the extinction of mankind, all the beauty in the universe would have no point, for there would be no human eyes to see it.

Now they were approaching a wormhole Interface. One great triangular face opened before Luca, wider and wider, until it was like a mouth that would swallow the yacht. A spark of light slid over the grey-gold translucent sheet that spanned the face, the reflected light of the yacht's own drive.

Suddenly Luca realised that he was only moments from being plunged into a wormhole mouth himself, and his heart hammered.

Blue-violet fire flared, and the yacht shuddered. Fragments of the Interface's exotic matter framework were already hitting the yacht's hull. That grey-gold sheet dissolved into fragments of light that fled from a vanishing point directly before him. This was radiation generated by the unravelling of stressed spacetime, deep in the throat of the flaw. For the first time since they had left Earth there was a genuine sensation of speed, of limitless, uncontrollable velocity, and the yacht seemed a fragile, vulnerable thing around him, a flower petal in a thunderstorm.

Luca gripped a rail. Aware of Teel at his side he tried not to cower, to hide his head from the stretched sky which poured down over him.

*

After a few days of hyperdrive hops and falls through branching wormholes, they reached the Orion Line. This was the innermost section of the Galactic spiral arm which contained Earth's sun. They emerged at a new clustering of wormhole Interfaces, a huge interchange that dwarfed the port at Saturn, carrying the commerce of mankind across thousands of light years.

Here they transferred to a Spline, a living thing transformed into a Navy warship. In the increasingly dangerous regions into which they would now venture, such protection was necessary.

Before they resumed their journey to the centre they took dinner, just the three of them, in a transparent blister set on the Spline's outer hull. At their small table they were served, not by automata but by humans, Navy ratings who hovered with cutlery, plates, dishes, even a kind of wine. It was a surreal experience for Luca, for all around the table, outside the blister's glimmering walls, the Spline's epidermis stretched away like the surface of a fleshy moon, and beyond its close horizon wormhole mouths glimmered like raindrops.

Commissary Dolo seemed slightly drunk. He was holding forth about the history of the Orion Line. 'Do you know the geography of the Galaxy, Novice? Look over there.' He pointed with his fork. 'That's the Sagittarius Arm, the next spiral arm in from ours. The Silver Ghosts strove for centuries to keep us out of those lanes of stars.' He talked on about the epochal defeat of the Ghosts and the thunderous Expansion since, and how the great agencies of the Coalition, the Navy, the Commission, the Guards, the Academies and the rest, had worked together to achieve those victories – and how officials like the Surveyor of Revenues and the Auditor-General laboured to maintain the mighty economic machine that fuelled the endless war – and, of course, how his own department within the Commission, the Office of Doctrinal Responsibility, oversaw the rest. He made it sound as if the conquest of the Galaxy was an exercise in paperwork.

As the Commissary talked, when he thought Dolo wasn't watching him, Luca studied Teel.

There was something animal in her deft actions with her cutlery, the powerful muscles that worked in her cheeks. It was as if she could not be sure when her next meal would come. Everything she did was so much more solid and vivid than anything else in his life – and far more fascinating than the great star clouds that illuminated the human empire. He was thrilled that they shared this transient bubble of isolation.

When Dolo fell silent, Luca took his chance. He leaned subtly closer to Teel. 'I suppose the food we eat is the same from one end of the Galaxy to the other.'

She didn't look directly at him, but she turned her head. 'Since this food comes from the belly of this Spline ship, and since the Spline are used all over the Galaxy – yes, I imagine you are right, Novice.'

'But not everything is the same,' he found himself babbling. 'We are about the same age, but our two lives could hardly have been more different. There is much about you that I envy.'

'You know very little about my life.'

'Yes, but even so—'

'What do you envy most?'

'Comradeship. I was born in a birthing centre and placed in a cadre. That's how it was for everybody. The cadres are broken up in cycles; you aren't allowed to get too close to your cadre siblings. Even at the seminaries I am in competition with the other novices. Intimacy is seen as inevitable, but is regarded as a weakness.'

'Intimacy?'

'I have had lovers,' he said, 'but I have no comrades.' He regretted the foolish words as soon as they were uttered. 'At the Front, everybody knows—'

'What *everybody knows* is always to be questioned, Novice,' said Dolo. Suddenly he no longer seemed drunk, and Luca wondered if he had fallen into some subtle trap. Dolo turned in his chair, waving his empty glass at the attendant ratings.

When Luca looked back, Teel had turned away. She was peering at the Sagittarius Arm's wash of light, as if with her deep eyes she could see it more clearly.


The Galaxy was a hundred thousand light years across, and over most of its span the stars were scattered more sparsely than grains of sand spread kilometres apart. On such a scale even the greatest human enterprise was dwarfed. And yet, as they neared the centre, the sense of activity, of industry, accelerated.

They moved within the 3-Kiloparsec Arm, the innermost of the spiral arms proper, wrapped tightly around the Core region. Here, no more than a few thousand light years from the Core itself, the Spline was replenished in orbit around a world that glistened, entirely covered in metal. This was a factory world, devoted to the production of armaments. Great clusters of wormhole mouths hovered over its gleaming surface, amid a cloud of Snowflake surveillance posts.

On a data desk, Dolo sketched concentric circles. 'The Core itself is surrounded by our fortresses, our warrior worlds and cities. As you'll see, Novice. Behind that, out here we are in the hinterland. Around a belt hundreds of light years thick, factory worlds churn out the material needed to wage the war. And behind *that* there is an immense and unending inward resource flow from across the Galaxy's disc, a flow through wormhole links and freighters of raw materials for the weapons factories, the lifeblood of a Galaxy all pouring into the centre to fuel the war.'

'It is magnificent,' Luca breathed. 'An organisation Galaxy-wide, built and directed by humans.'

'But,' Teel said dryly, 'do you think the Galaxy even notices we are here?'

Again Luca was disturbed by her flirting with non-Doctrine.

Dolo laughed softly. He said to Luca, 'Tell me what you have learned about our mission. Why are we here? Why was Captain Teel required to travel all the way out to Earth? What is there in this outbreak of faith so far from Earth that concerns us?'

What concerns me, Luca thought, is my relationship with Teel. But beyond that was his duty, of course: he aspired to become a Commissary, for the Commission for Historical Truth was the mind and conscience of the Third Expansion, and he did take his mission very seriously. 'It is only the Druz Doctrines that unite us, that enable the efficient working of the Expansion. If even our front-line troops are allowed to waste energy on foolish non-Doctrinal maundering—'

'Captain? What do you think?'

Teel pulled her lip, and Luca saw tiny hairs there, shining in the starlight. 'I think there is more at stake here than mere efficiency.'

'Of course there is. Perhaps I am training the wrong novice,' Dolo said ruefully. 'Luca, human history is not a simple narrative, a story told to children. It is more like a pile of sand.'

'Sand?'

'Heaped up,' Dolo said, miming just that. 'And as you add more grains – one at a time, random events added to the story – the heap organises itself. But the heap, the angle of the slope, is always at a state at which it is liable to collapse with the addition of just one more grain

– but you can never know *which* grain. This is called *"self-organised criticality"*. And so it is with history.'

Luca frowned. 'But the Coalition controls history.'

Dolo laughed. 'None of us is arrogant enough to believe that we *control* anything – and certainly not the historical arc of a society spanning a Galaxy, even one as unified as ours. Even the fore-knowledge of the future compiled by the Libraries is of no help. All we can do is watch the grains of sand as they fall.'

Luca found this terrifying, the notion that the great structure of the Expansion was so fragile. Equally terrifying was the realisation of how much knowledge he still had to acquire. 'And you think the religious outbreak at the Core is one such destabilising grain?'

'I'm hoping it won't be,' Dolo said. 'But the only way to know is to go there and see.'

'And stop the grain falling.'

'And make the right decision,' Dolo murmured, correcting him.

They left the factory world and passed ever inwards towards the Core, through more veils of stars.

At last they faced a vast wall of light. These were star-birthing clouds. Against the complex, turbulent background Luca could pick out globular clusters, tight knots of stars. Ships sailed silently everywhere, as deep as the eye could see. But from behind the curtain of stars and ships a cherry-red light burned, as if the centre of the Galaxy itself was ablaze.

Teel said, 'We are already within the Core itself, strictly speaking. Surrounding the Galaxy's centre is a great reservoir of gas some fifteen hundred light years across – enough to bake a hundred billion stars, crammed into a region smaller than that spanned by the few thousand stars visible to human eyes from Earth. That wall you see is part of the Molecular Ring, a huge belt of gas and dust clouds and star-forming regions and small clusters. The Ring surrounds the centre itself, and the Xeelee concentrations there.'

Dolo said evenly, 'The Ring is expanding. It is thought that it was thrown off by an explosion in the Core a million years ago. We have no idea what caused it.'

'How remarkable,' Luca said. 'In this dense place, *this* is the debris of an explosion: a great rolling wave of star birth. And what is that pink light that glows through the clouds?'

For the first time in the days since he had met her Teel looked directly at him. Her blue eyes seemed as wide as Earth's oceans, and he felt his breath catch. 'That,' she said simply, 'is the Front. By that light people are dying.'

Luca felt a complex frisson of fear and anticipation. All his life he had lived in a human space thousands of light years deep. He could look up into the sky and pick out any star he chose, and *know* that either humans were there, or they had been there and moved on, leaving the system lifeless and mined out. But now it was different. This slab of sky with its teeming clouds and young stars was *not human*. Up to now, he had been too concerned with his relationships with Teel and Dolo, and beyond that his duty, to have thought ahead. He realised he had no idea what he might find here at the Core, none at all.

He said reflexively, ' "A brief life burns brightly." '

'Here we have a different slogan,' murmured Teel. ' "Death is life." '

The Spline ship moved on, cautiously approaching the vast clouds of light.

## II

The asteroid had an official number, even an uplifting name, provided by a Commissary on distant Earth. But the troopers who rode it just called it the Rock.

'But then,' Teel quietly told Luca, 'they call every asteroid the Rock.'

And from this Rock's surface, everything was dwarfed by the magnificent sky. They were very close to the Galaxy's heart now, and the heavens were littered with bright hot beacons which, further out, merged into the clouds of light where they had been born. Beyond that was the curtain of shining molecular clouds that walled off the Galaxy's true centre – a curtain through which cherry-red light poured unceasingly, a battle glow that had already persisted for centuries.

The three of them, with a Navy guard, were walking on the Rock's surface in lightweight skinsuits. The asteroid was just a ball of stone some fifty kilometres across, one of a swarm that surrounded a hot blue-white star. The young sun's low light cast stark shadows from every crater, of which there were many, and from every dimple and dust grain at Luca's feet. He found himself fascinated by small details – the way the dust you kicked up rose and fell through neat parabolas, and clung to your legs so that it looked as if you had been dipped in black paint, and how some craters were flooded with a much finer blue-white powder that, somehow bound electrostatically, would flow almost like water around your glove.

But it was a difficult environment. His inertial-control boots glued his feet to the dusty rock, but in the asteroid's microgravity his body had no perceptible weight, and he felt as if he was floating in some invisible fluid, stuck by his feet to this rocky floor – or, if he wasn't careful about his sense of perspective, he might feel he was walking up a wall, or even hanging from a ceiling. He knew the others, especially Teel, had noticed his lack of orientation, and he was mortified with every clumsy glue-sticky step he took.

Meanwhile, all across the surface of this Rock, by the light of the endless war, soldiers toiled.

The troopers wore military-issue skinsuits, complex outfits replete with nipples and sockets and grimy with rubbed-in asteroid dirt. Some of the suits had been repaired; they had discoloured patches and crude seams welded into their surfaces. These patched-up figures moved through great kicked-up clouds of black dust, while machines clanked and hovered and crawled around them.

Most of the troopers' heads were crudely shaved, a practicality if you were doomed to wear your skinsuit without a break for days at a time. With grime etched deep into their pores it was impossible to tell how old they were. They looked tired, and yet kept on with their work even so, long past the normal limits of humanity. They were nothing like the steel-eyed warriors Luca had imagined. They looked like experts in nothing but endurance.

It seemed to Luca that what they were basically doing was *digging*. Many of them used simple shovels, or even their bare hands. They dug trenches and pits and holes, and excavated underground chambers, each trooper, empowered by microgravity, hauling out huge masses of crumpled rock. Luca imagined this scene repeated on a tremendous swarm of these drifting rocky worldlets, soldiers digging endlessly into the dirt, as if they were constructing a single vast trench that enclosed the Galaxy Core itself.

Dolo made a remark about the patched-up suits.

Teel shrugged. 'Suits are expensive here. Troopers themselves are cheaper.'

Luca said, 'I don't understand why they are digging holes in the ground.'

'To save their lives,' Teel said.

'It's called "riding the Rock", Novice,' Dolo said.

When it was prepared, Luca learned, this asteroid would be thrown out of its parent system, and in through the Molecular Ring towards the Xeelee concentrations. The first phase of the journey would be powered, but after that the Rock would fall freely. The troopers, cowering in their holes in the ground, would 'run silent', as they called it, operating only the feeblest power sources, making as little noise and vibration as possible. The point was to fool the Xeelee into thinking that this was a harmless piece of debris, and for cover many unoccupied rocks would be hurled in along similar trajectories. At closest approach to a Xeelee emplacement – a 'Sugar Lump' – the troopers would burst out of their hides and begin their assault.

'It sounds a crude tactic, but it works,' said Dolo.

'But the Xeelee hit back,' said Luca.

'Oh, yes,' Teel said, 'the Xeelee hit back. The rocks themselves generally survive. Each time a rock returns we have to dig out the rubble, and build the trenches and shelters again. And bury the dead.'

Luca frowned. 'But why dig by hand? Surely it would be much more efficient to leave it to the machines.'

Dolo said carefully, 'The soldiers seem to believe that a shelter constructed by a machine will never be as safe as one you have dug out yourself.'

'That doesn't make sense,' Luca said. 'All that matters is a shelter's depth, its structural qualities—'

'We aren't talking about *sense*,' Dolo said. 'We are touching here on the problem we have come to study. Come, Novice; recall your studies on compensatory belief systems.'

Luca had to dredge up the word from memory. 'Oh. *Superstition*. The troopers are superstitious.'

Dolo said, 'It's a common enough reaction. The troopers have little control of their lives, even of their deaths. So they seek to control what they can – like the ground they dig, the walls that shelter them – and they come to believe that such actions in turn might placate greater forces. All utterly non-Doctrinal, of course.'

Luca snorted. 'It is a sign of weakness.'

Teel said without emotion, 'Imagine this Rock cracking like an egg. Sometimes that happens, in combat. Imagine humans expelled, sent wriggling defenceless into space. Imagine huddling in the dark, waiting for that to happen at any moment. Now tell me how weak we are.'

'I'm sorry,' Luca said, flustered.

Dolo was irritated. 'You're sorry, you're sorry. Child, open your eyes and close your mouth. That way we'll all get along a lot better.'

They walked on.

The horizon was close and new land ahead hove constantly into view, revealing more pits, more toiling soldiers. Luca had the disconcerting sensation that he was indeed walking around the equator of a giant hall of rock, and his vertigo threatened to return.

It was because he was so busy trying to master his queasiness that he didn't notice the arch until they had almost walked under it. It was a neat parabola, perhaps twenty metres tall. A single trooper was standing beneath it, hands behind her back, stiffening to attention as Teel approached.

'Ah,' said Dolo, breathing a little heavily with the exertion of the suited walk. 'So *this* is what we have come so far to see.'

Luca stood under the arch. Its fine span narrowed above him, making a black stripe across the complex sky. The arch was so smoothly executed that he thought at first it must have been erected by machine, perhaps from blown rock. But when he bent closer he saw that the arch was constructed from small blocks, each no larger than his fist, stone that had been cut and polished. On each block writing was etched: names, he saw, two or three on each stone.

Teel stood at one side of the arch, picked up a pebble of conglomerate, and with care lobbed it upwards. It followed a smooth airless arc that almost matched the arch's span. 'Geometrically the arch is almost perfect,' she said.

Dolo bent to inspect the masonry. 'Remarkable,' he murmured. 'There is no mortar here, no pinning.'

'It was built by hand,' Teel said. 'The troopers started with the keystone and built it up side by side, lifting what was already completed over the new sections. Easy in microgravity.'

'And the stone?'

'Taken from deep within the asteroid – kilometres deep. The material further up has been gardened by impacts, shattered and conglomerated. They had to dig special mines to get to it.'

'And all done covertly, all kept from the eyes of their commanders.'

'Yes.'

Dolo turned to Luca. 'What do you make of it, boy?'

Luca would have had to dredge for the word if he hadn't been studying this specific area of deviancy. 'It is a *chapel*,' he said. A chapel of the dead, he thought, whose names are inscribed here. He glanced up at the arch's span. There was writing up to the limits of his vision. Hundreds of names, then.

'Yes, a chapel.' Dolo walked up to the single trooper standing under the arch. She held her place, but returned the Commissary's scrutiny apprehensively.

Teel said, 'This is Bayla.'

'The one on the charge.'

'She faces a specimen charge of anti-Doctrinal behaviour. Similar charges will be applied to others of the unit here depending on the outcome of the hearing – on your decision, gentlemen.'

Dolo looked the trooper up and down, as if he could read her mind by studying her suited body. 'Trooper. You understand the charge against you. Are you guilty?'

'Yes, sir.'

'Tell me about Michael Poole.'

Bayla was silent for a moment, visibly frightened; the visor of her skinsuit was misted. She glanced at Teel, who nodded.

And so Bayla stammered a tale of how the great engineer of ancient times, Michael Poole, had ridden one last wormhole to Timelike Infinity, the end of time itself. There he waited, watching all the events of the universe unfolding – and there he was ready to welcome those who remembered his name, and honour those who had fallen – and from there his great strength would reach out to save those who followed his example.

Dolo listened to this dispassionately. 'How many times have you ridden the Rock?'

'Twice, sir.'

'And what are you most afraid of, trooper?'

Again Bayla glanced at Teel. 'That you won't let me back.'

'Back where?'

'To ride the Rock again.'

'Why does that frighten you?'

Because she does not want to abandon her comrades, Luca thought, watching her. Because she is guilty to be alive where others have fallen around her. Because she fears they will die, leaving her to live on alone.

But Bayla said only, 'It is my duty, Commissary. A brief life burns brightly.'

Teel said, 'Simply say what you believe, trooper; it won't help you to mouth slogans.'

'Yes, sir.'

Luca walked back to the arch, for now Teel was standing under it, running her gloved hand over its surface. 'It's beautiful,' he essayed.

She shrugged. 'It's a tribute, not a work of art. But yes, it is beautiful.'

After his foolish remark about weakness he wanted to rebuild his connection with her. 'The names.' He glanced up at the arrayed letters over his head. He said boldly, 'To record the fallen may be non-Doctrinal, but here it seems – appropriate. If I had time I would climb this arch and count all the names.'

'It might take you longer than you think.'

'I don't understand.'

She pointed to a name, inscribed in the surface before his face. 'What do you see?'

' "Etta Maris",' he read. 'A name.'

'Now look at the first letter. Your suit visor has a magnification option; just tell it what you want to do.'

It took a couple of tries before he got it right. A Virtual flickered into existence before his face, the magnified letter. Even on this scale the carving was all but flawless – a labour of devotion, he saw, moved. But now he looked more closely, and he saw there were more names, inscribed *within* the carved-out grooves of the letter.

He stepped back, shocked. 'Why, there must be as many names here, in this single letter, as are inscribed on the whole of the arch.'

'I wouldn't know,' Teel said coolly. 'Pick a name and look again.'

Again he magnified a single letter from one inscribed name – and again he found more names, thousands of them, crowded in far beneath the level of human visibility.

'The names in the top layer were carved by hand,' Teel said. 'Then they used waldoes, and lasers, and ultimately replicator nanotech . . .'

He increased the magnification again and again, finding more layers of names nested one within the other. There were more layers than he could count, more names than could ever read if he stood here for the rest of his life. *Just on this one Rock.* And perhaps there were similar memorials on all the other bits of battered debris at every human emplacement, all the way around the core of the Galaxy, a great band of death stretching three thousand light years across space and two thousand years deep in time. He stepped back, shocked.

Teel studied his face. 'Are you all right?'

His eyes were wet, he found. He tried to blink away the moisture, but to his chagrin he felt a hot tear roll down his cheek. It was a dark epiphany, this shock of the names.

'I shouldn't have to teach you the Doctrines,' Teel said, comparatively gently. 'We each have one life. We each die. The question is how you spend that life.' She reached up with a gloved finger to touch his moist cheek – but her finger touched his visor, of course, and she dropped her hand and looked away, almost shyly.

He was astonished. In this brief moment of his own weakness, when he had been overwhelmed by something so much greater than he was, he had at last acquired some stature in her eyes; he had at last made the kind of contact with her that he had dreamed about since they had met.

After several hours on the surface they were escorted to what Teel called a *bio facility*, a pressurised dome where the soldiers could tend their bodies and their skinsuits, eat, drink, void their wastes, sleep, fornicate, play.

Around the perimeter of a central atrium there were small private cubicles, including dormitories, toilets and showers. Dolo and Luca were going to have to share one small, grimy compartment, at which Dolo scowled. Luca found a toilet and used it with relief. He had been unable to use the facilities in his skinsuit, in which you were just supposed to let go and allow the suit to soak it all up; it hadn't helped that the suits were semi-transparent.

He wandered uncertainly through the large central area. Under its fabric roof the facility was too hot. There was a stink of overheated food from the replicator banks, and the floor was grimy with sweat and ground-in asteroid dirt. The troopers, dressed in dirty coveralls, walked and laughed, argued and wrestled. While Luca had kept his inertial-control boots on, the soldiers mostly went barefoot; they jumped, crawled, even somersaulted, at ease in the low gravity environment. Many of them were sitting in solemn circles singing songs, sometimes accompanied by flutes and drums that had been improvised from bits of kit. They played sentimental melodies, but Luca could not make out the words; the troopers' vocabulary was strange and specialised, littered with acronyms.

There was graffiti on the walls. One crude sketch showed the unmistakable flared shape of a Xeelee nightfighter conflated with the ancient symbol of a fanged demon, and there were references by one sliver of a sub-unit to the incompetence and sexual inadequacy of the troopers in another, startlingly obscene. A couple of slogans caught his eye: 'Love unto the utmost generation is higher than love of one's neighbour. What should be loved of man is that he is in transition.' And: 'I am become Death, the Destroyer of Worlds.' Another hand had added: 'I am become Boredom, the Destroyer of Motivation.'

He joined Dolo on a small stage that had been set up before rows of seats. The daily briefing was soon to begin here. Luca reported on the graffiti he had seen. 'I don't recognise the sources.'

'Probably pre-Occupation. Oh, don't look so shocked. There is plenty of the stuff out there; we can't control everything. In fact I think I recognise the first. *Frederick Nietzsche.*' His pronunciation was strangulated.

'It sounded a good summary of the Druz Doctrines to me.'

'Perhaps. But I wonder how much harm those words have done, down across the millennia. Tell me what you think of our proto-religion here.'

'The elements are familiar enough,' Luca said. 'The old legend of Michael Poole has been conflated with the beliefs of the Friends of Wigner.' During the Qax Occupation the rebel group called the Friends had concocted a belief, based on ancient quantum-philosophical principles, that no event was made real until it was observed by a conscious intelligence – and hence that the universe itself would not be made real until all of its history was observed by an Ultimate Observer at Timelike Infinity, the very end of time. If such a being existed, then perhaps it could be appealed to – which was what the Friends had intended to achieve during their ultimately futile rebellion against the Qax. 'It's just that in this instance Poole himself has *become* that Observer.'

Dolo nodded. 'Oddly, Michael Poole *was* lost in time – in a sense – his last act, so it is said, was to fly his ship deliberately into an unending network of branching wormholes, in order to save mankind from an invasion from the future. Perhaps he is still out there somewhere, wherever *there* is. You can certainly see the resonance of his story for these rock jockeys. Poole sacrificed his life for the sake of his people – and yet, transcendent, he lives on. What a role model!' He actually winked at Luca. 'I sometimes think that even if we could achieve a state of total purity, of totally blank minds cocooned from the history of mankind, even then such beliefs would start sprouting spontaneously. But you have to admit that it's a good story.' He sounded surprisingly mellow.

Luca was shocked. 'But – sir – surely we must act to stop this drift from Doctrinal adherence. This new faith is insidious. You aren't supposed to pray for personal salvation; it is the species that counts. If this kind of thing is happening all over the Front, perhaps we should consider more drastic steps.'

Dolo's eyes narrowed. 'You're talking about excision.'

In the seminaries there had been chatter for millennia about the origin of the religious impulses which endlessly plagued the swarming masses under the Commission's care. Some argued that these impulses came from specific features of the human brain. Thus perhaps the characteristic sense of oneness with a greater entity came from a temporary disconnection within the parietal lobe, detaching the usual sense of one's self – controlled by the left side of this region – from the sense of space and time, controlled by the right. And perhaps a sense of awe and significance came from a malfunction of the limbic system, a deep and ancient system keyed to the emotions. And so on. If a mystical experience was simply a symptom of a malfunctioning brain – like, say, an epileptic fit – then that malfunction could be fixed, the symptoms abolished. And with a little judicious tinkering with the genome, such flaws could be banished from all subsequent generations.

'A future without gods,' said Luca. 'How marvellous that would be.'

Dolo nodded. 'But if *you* had had such an excision – and you had stood under the arch of names – could you have appreciated its significance? Could you have understood, have *felt* it as you did? Oh, yes, I watched you. Perhaps those aspects of our brains, our minds, have evolved *for a purpose*. Why would they exist otherwise?'

Luca had no answer. Again he was shocked.

'Anyhow,' said Dolo, reverting to orthodoxy, 'tampering with human evolution – or even passively allow it to happen – is itself against the Druz Doctrines. We win this war as humans or not at all – and we bend that rule at our peril. We have stayed united, across tens of thousands of light years and unthinkably huge populations, *because we are all the same*. Although that's not to say that evolution isn't itself taking mankind away from the norm that Hama Druz himself might have recognised.'

'Commissary?'

'Well, look around you. Most of these soldiers are the children of soldiers – obviously, how could it be otherwise? And the relentless selection of war is working to shape a new kind of human, better equipped for the fight. Combat survivors are the ones who get to breed, after all. Already their descendants are wiry, lithe, confident in the three-dimensional arena of low or zero gravity. Some studies even suggest that their eyes are adapting to the pressure of three-dimensional combat – that some of them can *see* velocity, for example, by perceiving subtle Doppler shifts in the colours of approaching or receding objects. Think what an advantage that would be in the battle-field! Another few thousand years of this and perhaps we will not recognise the soldiers who fight for the rest of us.'

'I think I'm losing my bearings,' said Luca truthfully.

Dolo patted his shoulder. 'No. You're just learning, is all.'

'And what have you learned about my troopers?' Teel had joined them on the small stage, and the troopers began to line up in rows before them.

Luca had learned to be honest with her. 'I find them – strange.'

'Strange?'

'They have all ridden the Rock, yes?'

'Most of them.'

'Then they have seen comrades fall. They know they will be sent out again to a place where they must face the same horror. And yet, here and now, they laugh.'

Teel thought about that and answered carefully. 'Away from the Front you don't talk about what happens out there. It's like – a secret. You've seen something beyond normal human experience. If you show your fear, or even admit it to yourself, then you're allowing a leak between *this*, normal human life, and what lies out there. You're letting it in. And if that happens there will be nowhere safe. Do you understand?'

He watched her face; there was sweat on her brow, traces of asteroid grime. 'Is that how you feel?'

'I try not to feel anything,' she said.

Luca looked around the dome. 'And this place is so *shabby*.' He felt a kind of self-righteous anger, and he encouraged it in himself, hoping to impress Teel. 'If these people are willing to die for the Expansion, they should have some comfort.'

Dolo shook his head. 'Again you don't understand, Novice. Think about the life of a soldier. It is a limited existence: moments of birth and growth, comradeship, determination, isolation – and finally, after the briefness of the light, an almost inevitable conclusion in pain and death. They have to know they are fighting for something better. And so they have to see that the present is imperfect. The soldiers *must* live in an eternal now of shabbiness and toil, so that they can be made to believe that we will progress from such places until a glorious victory is won, and everything will be made perfect – even if no such progress is ever actually *made*.'

'Then everything here is designed for a purpose,' Luca said, wondering. 'Even the shabbiness.'

'This is a machine built for war, Novice.'

A junior officer called the troops to order. On their crude seats, just blocks of asteroid rock, they fell silent.

Teel stood up. She said clearly, 'Eighteen thousand, three hundred and ninety-one years ago an alien force conquered humanity's home planet. We are here to ensure that never happens again.' She held up a data desk and read a single short obituary, a summary of one ordinary soldier's life and death. Here was another memorial, Luca supposed, for those who had fallen – and again, not strictly Doctrinal. Then Teel went on to a kind of situation report, summarising incidents from right around the Molecular Ring that circled the Galaxy's centre.

The troops listened carefully. Luca watched their faces. Their gazes were fixed on Teel as she spoke, their mouths open like rapt children's, some of them even quietly echoing the words she used. When she finished – 'Let's hurl the Xeelee starbreakers down their own Lethe-spawned throats!' – there was cheering, and even some tears.

Teel invited Dolo to get to his feet. As an emissary of the Coalition, he was to make a short address to these far-from-home troopers. He was greeted with whistles and foot-stamping. Luca thought he looked small and out of place in his pristine Commissary's robe.

Dolo talked in general terms about the war. He said that the 'Ring theatre' was a testing ground for future operations, including the eventual assault on the Xeelee concentrations in the Core itself – which, he hinted, might be closer than anybody expected. 'This a momentous time,' he said, 'and you have a momentous mission. You have been commissioned by history. This is total war. Our enemy is implacable and powerful. But if we let our vision of the universe and ourselves go forth, and we embrace it entirely, those who remember us will sing songs about us years from now . . .'

351

Luca let the words slide through his awareness. When the troops dispersed he found a way to get close to Teel.

She said, 'So do you think you have seen the comradeship you envied so much?'

'They love you.'

She shook her head. 'They think I'm a lucky commander. I've ridden this Rock four times already, and I'm still in one piece. They hope I'll give them some of my good fortune. And anyhow they have to love me; it's part of my job description. They won't let their brains be blown out for a stuffed shirt—'

'No, it's more than that. They will follow you anywhere.' His blood surging, longing to be part of her life, he said recklessly, 'As would I.'

That seemed to take her aback. 'You don't know what you're saying.'

He leaned closer. 'You've known there is something between us, a connection deeper than words, since the moment we met—'

But here was Dolo, and the moment was already over. The Commissary held up a small data desk, 'Novice, tomorrow we have a chance to advance your education. We will accompany a press gang.'

'Sir?'

'Be ready early.'

Teel had taken advantage of the interruption to slip away to join her troops. Luca saw how her face lit up when she spoke to those with whom she had fought. He was hopelessly jealous.

Dolo murmured, 'Don't lose yourself in her, Novice. After tomorrow, we will see if you still envy these troopers.'

III

The blue planet came swimming out of the dark.

Dolo said, 'You know that planets are rare here. This close to the Core, with so many stars crowding, stable planetary orbits are uncommon. All the unformed debris, which elsewhere might have been moulded into worlds, here makes up huge asteroid belts – which is why the rocks are used as they are; they are plentiful enough.

'This pretty world, though, was discovered by colonists of the Second Expansion – oh, more than twenty thousand years ago. Almost inevitably, they call it New Earth: names of colonised planets are rarely original. They brought with them a very strange belief system and primitive technology, but they made a good fist of terraforming this place. It lies a little close to its sun, though . . .'

Luca didn't feel able to reply. The world was like a watery Earth, he thought, with a world-ocean marked by tiny ice caps at the poles and a scatter of dark brown islands. He felt unexpectedly nostalgic.

Dolo was watching his face. 'Remember, though you are a Novice, you represent the Commission. We are the ultimate source of strength for these people. Keep your fear for the privacy of your quarters.'

'I understand my duty, sir.'

'Good.'

The yacht slid neatly into the world's thick air. Under a cloud-littered blue sky the ocean opened out into a blue-grey sheet that receded to a misty horizon.

The yacht hovered over the largest archipelago, a jumble of islands formed from ancient and overlapping volcanic caldera, and settled to the ground. It landed in a Navy compound, a large complex marked out in bright Navy green and surrounded by a tall fence. Beyond the fence, the rocky land rolled away, unmodified save for snaking roads and scattered farms and small villages.

Luca and Dolo joined a handful of troopers in an open-top skimmer. Hovering a couple of metres above the ground the skimmer shot across the Navy compound – Luca glimpsed bubble domes, unpressurised huts, neat piles of equipment – and then slid through a dilating entrance in the outer wall and hurtled over the countryside.

They had to wear face masks. Even after twenty thousand years of terraforming of this world, there was still not enough oxygen in the air; it had taken half that time just to exterminate most of the native life. But they could leave their skinsuits behind, and Luca welcomed the feeling of sunlight on his exposed skin.

Dolo said, over the wind noise, 'What you're going to see is where many of those troopers you envy come from.'

Luca said, 'I imagined birthing centres.' Like the one into which he had been born, on Earth.

'Yes. The children of soldiers are incubated in such places. But you've seen yourself that there is a – drift – in such populations, under the relentless selection pressure of combat. It's a good idea to freshen up the gene pool with infusions of wild stock.'

'Wild? Commissary, what is a "press gang"?'

'You'll see.'

The skimmer arrived at a village by the coast.

Luca stepped out of the hovering vehicle. The volcanic rock felt lumpy through the thin soles of his boots. A harbour, a rough crescent shape, had been blasted into the rock, and small boats bobbed languidly on oily water. Even through the filters in his mask Luca could smell the intense salt of the sea air, and the electric tang of ozone. But the volcanic rock was predominantly black, as were the pebbles and sand, and the water looked eerily dark.

He looked back along the coast. Dwellings built of volcanic rock were scattered along a road that led back to a denser knot of buildings. Here and there green flashed amidst the black – grass, trees, Earth life struggling to prosper in this alien soil. It was clear these people fed themselves through agriculture: crops grown on the transformed land, fish harvested from the seeded seas. The Second Expansion had occurred before the Qax had brought effective replicator technology to Earth, an unintended legacy which still fed the mass of the human population today. And so these people farmed, a behavioural relic.

From the doorway of the nearest house a child peered out at him, a girl aged about ten, finger thrust into one nostril, wide-eyed and curious. She wore no mask; the locals were implanted with respiratory equipment at birth.

He said, wondering, 'This is not a Coalition world.'

'No, it is not,' said Dolo. 'Ideally all human beings, across the Galaxy, would think exactly the same thought at every moment; that is what we must ultimately strive for. But out here on the fringe of the Expansion, where resources are limited, things are – looser. The three million inhabitants here have been left to their own devices – such as their own peculiar form of government, which lapsed into a kind of monarchy. The war against the Xeelee is a priority over cleansing the minds of a few fisher-folk on a dirt ball like this.'

'As long as they pay their taxes.'

Dolo grinned at him. 'An unexpectedly cynical remark from my idealistic young Novice! But yes, exactly so.'

They walked with the troopers towards the house. The little girl disappeared indoors. Luca could smell cooking, a baking smell like bread, and a sharper tang that might have been some kind of bleach. Simple domestic smells. Flowers adorned the top of the doorway, a colourful stripe, and two small bells dangled from the door itself, too small to be useful as a signal to the occupants, a cultural symbol Luca couldn't decode. The troopers in their bright green uniforms looked strikingly out of place, the shapes and colours all wrong, as if they had been cut out of some other reality and inserted into this sunlit scene.

There is a whole world here, Luca thought, a society which has followed its own path for twenty thousand years, with all the subtlety and individuality that that implies. I know nothing about it, had never even heard of it before coming here into the Core. And the Galaxy, which I as a Commissary will presume to govern, must be full of such places, such worlds, shards of humanity scattered over the stars.

A woman came to the door – the little girl's mother? – strong-faced, about forty, with hands grimy from work in a field, or garden. She looked resigned, Luca thought on first impression. Her gaze ran indifferently over the Commissaries, and she turned to the lead trooper.

She spoke a language he didn't recognise. The artificial voice of the trooper's translating desk was small and tinny.

Luca said, 'They must have brought their language with them. This woman speaks a relic of a pre-Extirpation tongue.' He felt excited, intellectually. 'Perhaps that aboriginal tongue could be reconstructed. Populations are scattered on this island world, isolated. Their languages must have diverged. By comparing the dialects of different groups—'

'Of course that would be possible,' said Dolo, sounded vaguely irritated. 'But why would you want to do such a thing?'

Now the woman pressed her hand against the trooper's data desk, a simple signature, and she called a name. The little girl came back to the door. She was a thin child with an open, pretty face; she looked bewildered, not scared, Luca thought. The mother reached down and gave the girl a small valise. She placed her hand on the girl's back, as if to push her to the troopers.

Luca understood what was happening a moment before the girl herself. 'We are here to take her away, aren't we?'

Dolo held up a finger, silencing him.

The girl looked at the tall armour-clad figures. Her face twisted with fear. She threw down the valise and turned to bury her face in her mother's belly, yelling and jabbering. The mother was weeping herself, but she tried to pull the child away from her legs.

'She's just a child,' Luca said. 'She doesn't want to leave her mother.'

Dolo shrugged. 'Child or not, she should know her duty.'

At first the troopers seemed tolerant. They stood in the sun, watching impassively as the mother gently cajoled the child. But after a couple of minutes the lead trooper stepped forward and put his gloved hand on the girl's shoulder. The girl squirmed away. The trooper seemed to have misjudged the mother's mood, for she jabbered angrily at him, pulled the child inside the house and slammed the door. The troopers glanced at each other, shrugged wearily, and fingered the weapons at their belts.

Dolo tugged Luca's sleeve. 'We don't need to see the resolution of this little unpleasantness. Come. Let me show you what will happen to that child.'

The lead trooper agreed that Dolo could take the skimmer if a replacement was sent out. So Luca climbed back into the skimmer alongside Dolo, leaving the harbour village behind them. It did not take long before they were back within the enclosing wall of the Navy compound, with the complex disorderly local world of sea and rock and light shut out. Luca felt a huge relief, as if he had come home.

Dolo directed the skimmer to a cluster of buildings huddled within the wall. These blocky huts had been set around a rectangle of cleared ground, and fenced off from the rest of the Navy base. Once inside this compound within a compound, Dolo and Luca got out of the skimmer and walked across obsessively swept dirt.

Everywhere Luca could see children. They were of varying ages from ten or so through to perhaps sixteen. One group marched in formation, another was lined up in rows, a third was undergoing some kind of physical training over a crude obstacle course, a fourth was standing in a rough square, watching something at the centre. Luca imagined this place must be big enough to hold a thousand children, perhaps more.

'What is this place?'

'Call it a school,' Dolo said. 'Keep your eyes open; listen and learn. And remember—'

'I know. I am the Commission. I mustn't show what I feel.'

'Better yet that you should feel nothing inappropriate in the first place. But not showing it is a start. First impressions?'

'Regularity,' Luca said. 'Straight lines everywhere. Everything planned, everything ordered. Nothing spontaneous.'

'And the children?'

Luca said nothing. There was silence save for barked commands; none of the children seemed to be saying anything.

Dolo said, 'You must understand that children brought in from the wild are more difficult to manage than those raised in birthing centres from soldier stock, for whom the war is a way of life; they know nothing else. These wild ones must be *taught* there is nothing else. So they will spend six or more years of their lives in places like this. Of course past the age of thirteen – or younger in some cases – they are used in combat.'

'Thirteen?'

'At that age their usefulness is limited. Those who survive are brought back for further training, and to shape the others. It helps them become accustomed to death, you see, if they are returned from the killing fields to a place like this, which keeps filling up with more people, people, people, so that mortality becomes trivial, a commonplace of statistics . . . Here now; this is where that pretty little girl from the coast will be brought, when the troopers extract her from her clinging mother.'

It was a nondescript building, before which children had been drawn up in rows. Male and female, no older than ten or eleven, they were dressed in simple orange coveralls, and were all barefoot. A woman stood before them. She had a short club in her hand. The children's posture was erect, their heads held still, but Luca could see how their eyes flickered towards the club.

One child was called forward. She was a slim girl, perhaps a little younger than the rest. The woman spoke to her almost gently, but Luca could hear she was describing, clinically, some small crime to do with not completing laundry promptly. The girl was wide-eyed and trembling, and Luca, astonished, saw urine trickle down her leg.

Then, without warning, the woman drew her club and slammed it against the side of the child's head. The child fell in the dust and lay still. Luca would have stepped forward, but Dolo had anticipated his reaction and grabbed his arm. Immediately the woman switched her attention to the others. She stepped over the prone form and walked up and down their rows, staring into their faces; she seemed to be smelling their fear.

Luca had to look away. He glanced up. The Galaxy's centre glowed beyond a milky blue sky.

Dolo murmured, 'Oh, don't worry. They know how to do such things properly here. The child is not badly hurt. Of course the other children don't know that. The girl's crime was trivial, her punishment meaningless – save as an example to the others. They are being exposed to violence; they have to get used to it, not to fear it. They must be trained not to question the authority over them. And— ah, yes.'

The woman had pulled a boy out of the ranks of silent children. Luca thought she could see tears glistening in his round eyes. Again the woman's club flashed; again the child fell to the ground.

Luca asked, aghast, 'And what was *his* crime?'

'He showed feelings for the other, the girl. That too must be programmed out. What use would such emotions be under a sky full of Xeelee nightfighters?' Dolo studied him. 'Luca, I know it is hard. But it is the way of the Doctrines. One day such training may save that boy's life.'

They walked on, as the children were made to pick up their fallen comrades.

They came to a more ragged group of children. Some of these were older, Luca saw, perhaps twelve or thirteen. It disturbed him to think that there might actually be combat veterans among this group of barefoot kids. At the centre of the group, two younger children – ten-year-olds – were fighting. The others watched silently, but their eyes were alive.

Dolo murmured, 'Here is a further stage. Now the children have to learn to use violence against others. The older ones have been put in charge of the younger. Beaten regularly themselves, now they enjoy meting out the same treatment to others. You see, they are forcing these two to fight, perhaps just for entertainment.'

At last one of the fighters battered her opponent to the ground. The fallen child was dragged away. The victor was a stocky girl; blood trickled from her mouth and knuckles. One of the older children walked into the crude ring, grinning, to face the stocky girl.

Dolo nodded with a connoisseur's approving glance. 'That fighter is strong,' he said. 'But now she will learn afresh that there are many stronger than she is.'

'These barefoot cadets must long to escape.'

'But their prison is not just a question of walls. In some places the regime is – harsher. When they are taken from their homes, the children are sometimes made to commit atrocities there.'

'Atrocities?'

Dolo waved a hand. 'It doesn't matter what. There are always criminals of one class or another who require corrective treatment. But after committing such an act the child is instantly transformed, in her own heart, and in the hearts of her family. The family may not even want the child back. So she knows that even if she escapes this place, she can never go back home.' He smiled. 'Ideally, of course, it would be a family member who is struck down; that would be the purest blow of all.'

'How efficient.'

'Even in the face of violence a child's social and moral concepts are surprisingly resilient; it takes a year or more before such things as family bonds are finally broken. After that the child crosses an inner threshold. Her sense of loyalty – why, her sense of *self* – becomes entwined not with her family but with the regime. And, of course, the first experience of combat itself is the final threshold. After that, with all she has seen and done, she cannot go home. She has been reborn. She doesn't even *want* to be anywhere else.'

They walked on to the edge of the compound. Beyond the rows of buildings there was a break in the fence. On the rocky plain beyond, a group of children, with adult overseers, were lying on their bellies in crude pits dug into the ground. They were working with weapons, loading, dismantling, cleaning them, and firing them at distant targets. The weapons seemed heavy, dirty and noisy; every firing gave off a crack that made Luca jump.

Dolo asked, 'Now. Do you see what is happening here?'

'More indoctrination. The children must be trained to handle weapons, to deploy destructive forces – and to kill?'

'There are native animals – flying, bird-like creatures – which they hunt. These days the animals are raised for that purpose, of course; it has ironically saved them from extinction. Yes, they must learn to kill.'

'And people?'

'The Xeelee are not like us – but they are sentient. Therefore it helps to be exposed to the moral conflict of killing a sentient creature, before it is necessary to do it to save one's life. So, yes, people too, when appropriate.'

'Commissary, must we commit such barbarism to wage our war?'

Dolo looked surprised. 'But there is no barbarism here. Novice, what did you *expect*? This regime, this crude empire of mud and clubs and blood, is actually a sophisticated processing system. It turns human beings, children, into machines.'

'Then why use human beings at all? Why not fight the war with machines?' It shocked him to find himself even mouthing such ideas.

Dolo seemed patient. 'This is a question everybody must ask at least once, Luca. We fight as we do because of the nature of our foe, and ourselves. The Xeelee are not like humans, not even like species such as the Silver Ghosts, our starfaring rivals in the early days of the Expansion. Read your history, Novice. With the Xeelee there has never been a possibility of negotiation, diplomacy, compromise. *None*. In fact there has been no contact at all – other than the brutal collision of conflict. The Xeelee ignore us until we do something that disturbs them – and then they stomp on us hard, striking with devastating force until we are subdued. To them we are vermin. Well, the vermin are fighting back.'

'And we are doing so,' Luca said, 'by consuming our children.'

'Yes, our children – our human flesh and blood. Because that is all we have.' Dolo held up his hands and flexed his fingers in Galaxy light. 'We weren't designed for waging a Galactic war – as the Xeelee seem to have been. We carry our past in our bodies, a past of cowering in trees, of huddling on plains, without weapons, without even fire to protect us, as the predators closed. But we fought our way out of that pit, just as we're fighting our way out of this one – not by denying our nature but by exploiting it, by breeding, breeding, breeding, filling up every empty space with great swarms of us. We are nothing but flesh and blood – but in overwhelming numbers even soft flesh can win the day. Our humanity is our only, our final weapon, and *that* is how we will win.' As he talked his broad face was alive with a kind of pleasure.

Around Luca the squads of children went through their routine of training, punishment, reward and abuse, their young minds shaped like bits of heated metal. He conjured up the face of Teel, her soft humanity above the stiff collar of the military uniform.

Dolo was watching him again. 'You're thinking of the lovely Captain. This is where she came from.' He waved a hand. 'An inductee into this dismal boot camp, here on New Earth, she was a tough fighter. Saw her first action at twelve, survived, went back for more. Why do you think I brought you here?'

Luca, bewildered, looked down at the dirt.

Dolo, at random, beckoned a small boy standing in a row of others. With a glance at his overseer the boy came running and stood at attention before them. His eyes were bright, lively. Dolo bent down and smiled. 'Do you know who we are?'

'No, *sir*,' snapped the boy.

'Then who are you?'

'Who I am does not matter. Sir,' he appended hastily.

'Good. Then what are you?'

'I am a little boy now, and I must study. But when I am big enough to operate a weapon I will join the unending war, and avenge those who have fallen, and fight for the future of mankind.'

Dolo straightened up. Luca would have sworn he could see a tear in his eye. 'Novice, it has taken us twenty thousand years – perhaps even longer – to get to this point. But, step by step, we are reaching our goal. I give you the child soldier: the logical future of mankind.'

When Dolo nodded dismissal the boy turned away and walked back to his section. Luca could see he was struggling to contain his youthful energy, trying not to skip or run.

When they got back to the Rock, an evacuation and hasty re-equipping was underway. Non-combatants were removed from the Rock, equipment, stores and people hurried underground, weapons, sensor and drive emplacements rapidly completed and tested. Meanwhile the troopers were checking their skinsuits and other kit, and injecting themselves with mnemonic fluid, a record which might help the military analysts reconstruct whatever happened to them.

It turned out that orders had been changed. The Rock was to be hurled on its new mission to the Front in just a few more days, weeks ahead of the old schedule. Perhaps, Luca thought with a shiver, the prognosticating librarians on distant Earth had discerned some shifting in their misty maps of the future, and the Rock was to be sent to secure some famous preordained victory – or to avert some predetermined disaster.

But for him the most important consequence of this chain of events was that he was to be taken off the Rock and flown out to another station, while Teel was to ride the Rock once more to the Front itself.

He hurried to her quarters.

Aside from a small bathroom area there were just two pieces of furniture, a simple bed and table. She was sitting on the bed studying a data desk. The top button of her uniform was undone; he found his eyes drawn to the tiny triangle of flesh that showed there.

She put down the desk. 'I knew you would come.'

'You did?'

'You have learned about the new orders. Your emotions are confused.'

Tentatively he sat beside her on the bed. 'I'm not confused. I don't want to be parted from you.'

'Do you think I should defy my duty? Or you yours?'

'No. I just don't want to lose you.'

Her blue eyes were wide, deep as oceans. 'It's not that. You've been to New Earth. Now you know where I come from – what I am. You want to *save* me, don't you?'

He was hot, miserable, perplexed. 'I can't tell if you are mocking me.'

She took his hand and enclosed it in hers. 'Go home.'

'Take me with you,' he said.

'What?'

It was as if he was framing the thoughts even as the words emerged from his mouth. 'To the Front. Give me a posting on the Rock.'

'That's absurd. You're a Commissary – a Novice at that. You don't have the training.'

He let his voice harden. 'I could surely be as useful as the twelve-year-old conscripts who will be riding with you.'

'Do you know what you will face?'

'I know you will be there.' He moved his face closer to hers, just a little, until he could feel her breath on his mouth. It was his last voluntary act.

Her passion was primal, like the way she ate, as if after this moment there would be no more to savour. And all through the love-making, and the hours later they spent asleep together, he could sense the strength in her – a strength she held back, as if afraid of damaging him.


## IV

Luca huddled at the bottom of the trench. It was just a gouge scraped roughly in the surface of the Rock.

He stared up at a great stripe of sky that was full of cherry-red light, a sky where immense rocks sailed like clouds. Sometimes they came so close to his own Rock he could actually see people moving on their inverted surfaces. It seemed impossible that such vast objects could be crowded so close. The slightest touch of one of these great jostling rocks against another could crush him and these shallow trenches and chambers, utterly erasing him and any trace to show he had ever existed, scraping clean his life from the universe. He was in a heavily armoured skinsuit, but he felt utterly defenceless. He was just a mote of soft blood and flesh, trapped in this nightmare machinery of churning rock and deadly light.

All of this in utter, inhuman silence, save for the shallow scratch of his own breathing, the constant incomprehensible chatter over his comms.

The Rock itself was a swarm of continual, baffling activity. Troopers crowded constantly past him, great files of them labouring from place to place carrying equipment and supplies. They were blank-faced, dogged, their suits carefully dusted with asteroid dirt in the probably vain hope that such camouflage would help them survive. Sometimes they stepped on Luca's feet or legs, and he cowered against the dirt in his trench, trying to make himself small and invisible.

Bayla, the trooper on the charge of religious sedition, was with him, though. She had been assigned by Teel to 'supervise' him. Luca hadn't seen anything of Teel herself since they had broken through the last cordon of Navy Spline ships and into the full battle light, and the final preparations had begun. Whatever fantasies he had had of working alongside Teel, of somehow participating in this effort, had long evaporated. The only human comfort he drew was from the warm pressure of Bayla's leg against his own.

Bayla kept checking a chronometer and consulting lists that scrolled over the surface of her skinsuit sleeve. But every few minutes she took the time to check on Luca. 'Are you all right?'

'Yes.' Again he had to push back to let a file of troopers past. 'I don't understand how they can do their jobs.'

'What else is there to do?'

'They must be afraid.'

He could see her frown. 'You learn to live with the fear. Like living with an illness.'

'A fear of death, or injury?'

'No, not that.' She spoke slowly. She seemed serene. 'It's more that it might not make sense. You feel you're in the wrong world, the wrong time. That it shouldn't be like this. If you let that in, that's the true fear.'

He didn't understand, of course.

A patch of Bayla's sleeve flashed orange. 'Excuse me.' Bayla barked a command.

A file of troopers came scurrying through the dirt and took their position. They were carrying tools, he saw. The troopers all seemed small, light. *Young*, he realised. Bayla held up her hand, checked the time again – then brought her arm down in a chop. The troopers swarmed up over the side of the trench, using rungs and cables or just footholds gouged into the harder rock.

In response, light stormed.

Some of the troops fell back immediately, limp, like dolls. The rest of the troopers flattened themselves on their bellies in the dirt, under the light, and began to crawl away, face down, out of Luca's sight. Other troopers came scurrying along the trench with med cloaks. They wrapped up the fallen and took them away, limp bundles that were awkward to handle in the low gravity.

There was a swirl of cubical pixels before Luca. It coalesced into the compact form of Dolo. He wasn't wearing a skinsuit, and his robe was clean. In this place of dirt and rock and fire he was like a vision of an unattainable paradise. He smiled. 'How are we bearing up, Novice?'

Luca found it difficult to speak. 'Those troopers who went out of the trench in the first wave. They were *children*.' Perhaps some of them had come from the induction camp on New Earth.

'Think of it in terms of efficiency. They are agile, easy to command. But they are poor soldiers. They suffer higher casualty rates than their adult counterparts, in part because their lack of maturity and experience leads them to take unnecessary risks. And their young bodies are more susceptible to complications if injured. But little has yet been invested in their training.'

'So they are expendable.'

'We are *all* expendable,' Dolo said. 'But some are more expendable than others. They will not suffer, Luca: if it comes, death here is usually rapid. And if they see their fellows fall they will not grieve; their childish empathy has been beaten out of them.' The Virtual floated closer to Luca, studying his face, close enough for Luca to see the graininess of the pixels. 'You are still thinking this is inhuman, aren't you? The evolution of your conscience is proving a fascinating study, Novice. Of course it is inhuman. All that matters are the numbers, the rates of mortality, the probabilities and cost of success. This is a statistical war – as wars have always been.'

There was a piercing whistle-like blast over the comms unit. Virtual Dolo popped out of existence, grinning.

A few of the child soldiers scrambled back over the trench's lip – a very few, and several of them were nursing injuries. More troops came scurrying like files of rats along the trench. Soon there was a double line of them, most carrying hand weapons or tools, peering up at the sky.

For a few heartbeats everybody was still, waiting.

Bayla was beside Luca, as intent as the rest. Luca whispered to her, 'What was the last thing you did before we left the bio facility?'

'I sent my daughter a Virtual.'

*A daughter*. Sons and daughters, like family life in general, were strictly anti-Doctrinal. 'Where is she?'

'On New Earth. I told her how as a baby she laughed when she looked at my face. How she slept in my arms, how we bathed together. I told her that when she grows up and wants to know about me she should ask her father or her aunt. Whatever becomes of me, she must never think of herself as a child without a mother. I will always be watching her.'

'From your place at Timelike Infinity,' he hazarded.

'I want her to be good, and to be the kind of person others would like. But I told her I was sorry that I had been a poor mother, an absent mother. When she was very small she had a doll, a soldier. I carry it with me as a good-luck charm.' She patted her dust-covered tunic. Luca saw a slight bulge there. 'This way she is always with me. The last time I saw her was during my last leave on New Earth. She was with the other children. They lined up to wave flags and sing for us. It's burned in my mind, her face that day. I told her that when she hears of my death she should be happy for me, for I will have achieved my ambition.'

'You embrace death, but you dream of your family.'

Bayla glanced at him. 'What else is there to do?'

Another piercing shriek in Luca's comms unit. No, it was a *word*, he realised, a word yelled so loud it overwhelmed the system itself. In response there was a muffled roar – more voices, thousands of voices, shouting together, maybe every trooper on the Rock.

Bayla raised her hand again, watching lights flash on her sleeve. 'Wait, wait.' The cherry-red light in the sky was growing brighter, shading to pink. It was like a silent, gathering sunrise, as if the Rock was turning to face some vast source of heat, and the noise rose in response.

Bayla brought her arm chopping down.

The first row of troopers swarmed forward, struggling to get out of the trench. Red light flared. Most of them fell back immediately, broken, limp, gases venting from ruined suits, and the yelling was broken now by screams of pain. Without hesitation the second line pushed after the first. They trampled on the fallen bodies of their comrades, even those who still moved, pushing their way over flesh and dirt to get to the lip of the trench. But they fell back in their turn, as if their bodies were exploding. Yet another line of troopers gathered and began to rush over the lip of the trench.

Suddenly Luca felt swept up, as if a great tide of blood was lifting these yelling troopers into battle. Without conscious thought he tore at the dirt with clumsy hands and hoisted his body out of the trench.

He was standing in a flood of light. Hardly anyone was standing with him, of the hundreds who had gone before him. There was a huddled heap of skinsuit every few paces, and bodies drifted helplessly above like moons of this asteroid, out of contact with the surface, to be pierced by relentless flickering beams of crimson light. When he looked back he saw that still another wave of troops was coming out of the trench. They were twitching like dolls as the darting light threaded through them. Soon the next wave were struggling to advance through a space that was clogged with corpses.

Space was sewn with cherry-red beams, a great flat sheet of them that flickered, vanished, came again. When he looked up he could see more of the beams, layer on layer, absolutely straight, that climbed up like a geometrical demonstration. The light crowded space until it seemed there wasn't room for it all, that the beams must start to cut and destroy each other.

And still people fell, all around him. He had never imagined such things were possible. It was as if he had been transported into some new and unwelcome reality, where the old physical laws didn't apply—

Somebody punched him in the back.

With agonising slowness, he fell to the dirt. Something landed on top of him. It wasn't heavy, but he could feel how massive it was; its inertia knocked the wind out of him. For an instant he was pressed face down, staring at the fine-grained asteroid soil and the reflection of his own hollow-eyed face. But still the cherry-red light dazzled him; even when he closed his eyes he could see it.

He twisted and thrashed, pushing the mass off his back. It was a trooper, he saw. She was struggling, convulsing. A crater had been torn in her chest. Blood was gushing out, immediately freezing into glittering crystals, as if she was just pouring herself out into space. Her eyes locked on Luca's; they were blue like Teel's, but this was not Teel. Luca, panicking and revolted, thrashed until he had pushed her away.

But without the trooper on his back he was uncovered. Some instinct made him try to dig himself into the dirt. Perhaps he could hide there. But deeper than a hand's breadth or so the dirt was compact, hardened by aeons, resistant to his scrabbling fingers.

A shadow moved across the light. Luca flinched and looked up. It was a ship, a vast graceful ship silhouetted against the light of battle.

The Xeelee nightfighter was a sycamore seed wrought in black a hundred metres across. The wings swept back from the central pod, flattening and thinning until at their trailing edges they were so fine Luca could see starbreaker fire through them. The Xeelee was swooping low over the asteroid's surface – impossibly low, impossibly graceful, utterly inhuman. Threads of starbreaker light connected it to the ground, pulses of death dealt at the speed of light. Luca couldn't tell if their source was the ship or the ground. Where the ship's shadow passed explosions erupted from the asteroid's surface, and bodies and bits of equipment were hurled up to go flying into space on neat straight-line trajectories.

Beneath the gaze of that dark bird, Luca felt utterly exposed.

There was a fresh crater not metres away, a scrap of shelter. He closed his eyes. 'One, two, three.' He pushed himself to hands and knees and tried a kind of low-gravity crawl, pulling at the surface with his hands and digging his toes into the dust, squirming over the ground like an insect.

He reached the crater and threw himself into it. But again the low gravity had fooled him, and he took an age to complete his fall.

The massive wing of the nightfighter passed over him. It was only metres above him; if he had jumped up he could have touched it. He felt a tugging, like a tide, passing along his body, and light flared all around him. He clamped his hands over his head and closed his eyes.

The cherry-red light faded, and that odd sensation of tugging passed. He risked looking up. The Xeelee had moved beyond him. It was tracking over the asteroid's close horizon, setting like a great dark sun, and it dragged a webbing of red light beneath it as it passed.

There was a brief lull. The light of more distant engagements bathed the ground in a paler, more diffuse glow.

Something moved on the ground. It was a trooper, crawling out of a hole a little deeper than Luca's. He, she, moved hunched over, looking only half human. One leg was dragging. Luca saw now that the trooper had lost a foot, cleanly scythed, and that the lower leg of the skinsuit was tied off by a crude tourniquet. More troopers came clambering out of holes and trenches, or even out of the cover of the bodies of their comrades. They crawled, walked, flopped back towards their trenches.

But the red light erupted again, raking flat across the curved landscape. The beams lanced through the bodies of the wounded as they tried to crawl, and they staggered and fell, cut open and sliced – or they simply exploded, the internal pressure of their bodies destroying them in silent, bloody bursts.

Still Luca was unharmed, as if this withering fire was programmed to avoid him. But, turned around and battered, he didn't know where his trench was, where he should go. And dust was thrown up around him by silent detonations, obscuring his vision. He saw a brighter light ahead, a cool whiteness, as if seen through a fog of dust and frozen blood. He pulled himself out of the crater and crawled that way.

Again the fire briefly faded. There was no air to suspend the dust, and as soon as the firing ceased it fell quickly back to the ground, or dispersed into space. As the dust cleared the white light was revealed.

It was no human shelter but the Sugar Lump itself, looming towards the Rock.

The Xeelee emplacement, a huge projection of power, was a cube, shining white, that spun slowly about shifting axes: it was an artefact the size of a small planet, a box that could have contained Earth's Moon. And it was beautiful, Luca thought, fascinated, like a toy, its faces glowing sheets of white, its edges and corners a geometrical ideal. But its faces were scarred and splashed with rock.

He saw this through a stream of rocks that soared through their complex orbits towards the Sugar Lump. They looked like gravel thrown against a glowing window. But these were asteroids, each like his own Rock, kilometres across or more.

Red light punched through his shoulder. He stared, uncomprehending, as blood founted in a pencil-thin spray, before his suit sealed itself over and the flow stopped. He was able to raise his arm, even flex his fingers, but he couldn't feel the limb, as if he had been sleeping on it.

He could sense the pain, though, working its way through his shocked nervous system.

An explosion erupted not metres away.

A wave of dirt and debris washed him onto his back. At last pain pulsed in his arm, needle-sharp. But the dust cleared quickly, the grains settling out on their millions of parabolas to the surface from which they had been hurled, and the open sky was revealed again.

A face of the Sugar Lump was over him, sliding by like a translucent lid across the world, the edges too remote to see. Asteroids slid past its surface, sparking with weapons' fire. The plane face itself rippled, holes dilating open like stretching mouths, and more Xeelee ships poured out, nightfighters like darting birds whose wings opened tentatively.

But a new fire opened up from the Rock, a blistering hail of blue-white sparks that hosed into the surface of the Sugar Lump itself. This was fire from a monopole cannon, Luca knew, and those blue-white sparks were point defects in spacetime. The Xeelee craft emerging from the Sugar Lump tried to open their wings. But the blue sparks ripped into them. One nightfighter went spinning out of control, to plummet back into the face of the Sugar Lump.

These few seconds of closest approach were the crux of the engagement, its whole purpose. Monopoles, point defects, would rip a hole in a nightfighter wing, or a Sugar Lump face. But you had to get close enough to deliver them. And you had to hit the Xeelee craft when they were vulnerable, which meant the few seconds or minutes after the nightfighters had emerged from the Sugar Lump emplacements, when they were slow, sluggish, like baby birds emerging from a nest. That was why you had to get in so close to the Sugar Lump, despite the ferocious fire, and you had to use the precious seconds of closest approach as best you could – and then try to get out before the Xeelee assembled their overwhelmingly superior weaponry. That was why Luca was here; that was why so many were screaming and dying around him.

Luca felt hate well up inside him, hate for the Xeelee and what they had done to mankind, the deaths and pain they had inflicted, the massive distortion of human destiny. And as the human weapons ripped holes in the Xeelee emplacement he roared a visceral cry of loathing and triumph.

But now somebody stood over him, shadowed against the Sugar Lump face.

'Bayla? Teel?'

A heavy hand reached down, grabbed a handful of his tunic, and hauled Luca up. He was carried across the surface, floppy-limbed, with remarkable speed and efficiency. The sky, still crowded with conflict, rocked above him.

He was hurled into a hole in the ground. He fell through low gravity and landed in darkness on a heap of bodies, a tangle of limbs. Med cloaks were wrapped around the injured, but many of the cloaks glowed bright blue, the colour of death, so that this chamber in the rock was filled with eerie electric-blue shadows.

More bodies poured in after Luca, tumbling on top of him. The mouth of the tunnel closed over, blocking out the light of battle. There was a second of stillness. Luca squirmed, trying to get out from under the heap of bodies.

Then the stomping began. It was exactly as if some immense boot was slamming down on the asteroid. The people in the chamber were thrown up, dropped back, shaken. Splinters of bright white light leaked into the tunnel through its layers of sealing dirt. Luca found himself rolling, kicked and punched. Ignoring the pain in his shoulder he fought with his fists and feet until he found himself huddled in a corner of wall and floor. He hugged his knees to his chest, making himself a small, hard boulder.

Still the slamming went on. He could feel it in his bones, his very flesh. He closed his eyes. He tried to think of the Conurbation where he had been born, and joined his first cadres. It had been an open place of parks and ruined Qax domes. In the mornings he would run and run, his cloak flapping around his legs, the dewy grass sharp under his bare feet. He had never been more alive – certainly more than now, sealed up in this suit in a hole in the shuddering ground.

He huddled over, dreaming of Earth. Perhaps if he dug deep down inside himself he would find a safe place to live, inside his memory, safe from this war. But still the great stamping went on and on, as he remembered the dew on the grass.

*Luca. Novice Luca.*

He had never understood.

Oh, logically he knew of the endless warfare at the heart of the Galaxy, the relentless deaths, the children thrown into the fire. But he had never *understood* it, on a deep, human level. So many human dead, he thought, buried in meaningless rocks like this or scattered across space, as if the disc of the Galaxy itself is rotten with our corpses. There they wait until the latest generation joins them, falling down like sparks into the dark.

*Luca.*

He tried to remember his ambitions, how he used to feel, when the war had been a fascinating exercise in logistics and ideology, a source of endless career opportunities for bright young Commissaries. How could he have been so dazzled by such fantasies?

It was as if a great crime was being committed, out of sight. Whether humans won this war or not, nothing would ever be the same – nothing ever could compensate for the relentless evil being committed here. We're like those wretched children on New Earth forced to commit atrocities against those they love, he thought. We can't go back. Not after what we have done here.

*Luca. Luca.* '. . . Luca. You are alive, like it or not. Look at me, Novice.'

Reluctantly, shedding the last of his cocoon of grass-green memory, he opened his eyes. He was still in the chamber of dirt. There was no light but the dimming glow of med cloaks. Nothing moved; everybody was still. But the stomping had stopped, he realised.

And here was Dolo's Virtual head, a fuzzy ball of pixels, floating before him, glowing in the dark.

'I'm in my grave,' Luca said.

'Less melodrama, please, Novice. The Navy knows you're here. They're on the way to dig you out.'

'Teel—'

'Is dead. So is Bayla, our anti-Doctrinal religionist.' Dolo reeled off more names, everybody Luca could think of in the units he had met. 'Everybody is dead, except you.'

*Teel was dead.* He tried to remember his feelings for Teel, that peculiar wistful love reciprocated by her on some level he had never understood. It had been everything in the world to him, he thought, just hours ago, and even after what he had seen of the child soldiers on New Earth and the rest, his head had been full of dreams of fighting alongside her – and, yes, of saving her from this place, just as she had understood. Now it all seemed remote, a memory of a memory, or the memory of a story told by somebody else.

As if they were back in the seminary, Dolo said, 'Tell me what you are thinking. The surface of your mind.'

'I have no sense of the true scale of this, the moral scale. I don't even know what my own life is worth. I'm too small. I've nothing to measure it against.'

'But it was that very scale that saved you. What defence do we have, we feeble humans, against the Xeelee?'

'None.'

'Wrong. Listen to me. We are fighting a war on an interstellar scale. The Xeelee push out of the Core; we push them back, endlessly. The Front is a vast belt of friction, right around the Galaxy's centre, friction between huge wheels spun by the Xeelee and ourselves, rubbing away lives and material as fast as we can pour them in. It's been this way, virtually static, for *two thousand years*.

'But if you are caught in the middle of it, your defence is *numbers*. Your defence is *statistical*. If there are enough of you, even if others are taken, you might survive. We have probably been using such strategies all the way back to the days without fire or tools, on some treeless plain on Earth. When the predators come, let them take *her* – the slowest, the youngest or oldest, the weakest, the unlucky – but *I* will survive. Death is life, remember; that was what Teel said: the death of others is *my* life.'

Luca looked into Dolo's eyes; the low-quality image had only empty, staring sockets. 'It is a vermin's strategy.'

'We *are* vermin.'

'Does the arch still stand?'

'It is sited on the far side of the asteroid, away from the main weapons sites. Yes, it stands.'

'Let it be,' Luca said. 'The religion. The worship of Poole at Timelike Infinity.'

Dolo's head pushed closer. 'Why?'

'Because it gives the troopers a meaning the dry Doctrines can't supply. A belief in a simple soldiers' heaven makes no difference.'

'But it does make a difference,' Dolo said quietly. 'Remember that we need to manage the historical stability of the Expansion. Far from being damaging, I now believe this proto-religion might actually be useful in *ensuring* that.' He laughed. 'We will probably support it, discreetly. Perhaps we will even write some scripture for it. We have before. In the end we don't care what they think they are fighting for, as long as they fight.'

'Why?'

'Why what?'

'Why do *you* do this? And—'

'And why do I so obviously enjoy it? Ha!' Dolo tipped back his Virtual face. 'Because it is a kind of exploration, Novice. There will always be another battlefield – another star, even, one day, another Galaxy – and each is much like the last. But here we are exploring the depths of humanity itself. How far can a human being be degraded and brutal-ised before something folds up inside? I can tell you, we haven't reached the bottom of that yet, and we're still digging.

'And then there is the war itself, the magnificence of the enterprise. Think about it: we are trying to build a perfect killing machine from soft human components, from swarming animals who evolved in a very different place, very far from here. It is a marvellous intellectual exercise – don't you think?'

Luca dropped his face. He said, 'How can we win this war?'

Dolo looked puzzled. 'But we have no interest in mere *winning*, but in the perfecting of humanity. And to achieve that we need eternity, an eternal war. Victory is trivial compared to that.'

'No,' Luca said.

'Novice—'

Dirt showered over him. Fragments rained through Dolo's Virtual, making it flicker. Luca looked up. A machine had broken through the roof of the cavern, revealing the light of the Galaxy Core.

Skinsuited troopers clustered around the hole. One leapt down and just picked up Luca under his shoulders. Luca cried out at the pain of his wound, but he was hoisted up towards the sky and released.

For a second, two, he floated up through the vacuum, as if dreaming.

Then more strong hands caught him. He was wrapped in a med cloak. It snuggled around him and he immediately felt its warmth.

Everywhere he looked he saw more teams digging, and bodies floating out of the dirt. It was as if the whole Rock were a cemetery fifty kilometres across, disgorging its dead. And over his comms system he could hear a great murmuring groan. It was the merging of thousands of voices, he realised, the thousands of wounded that still littered this battered Rock, who themselves were far outnumbered by the dead.

'No,' he muttered.

A visored face loomed over him. 'No what?'

'We have to find a way to win this war,' Luca whispered.

'Sure we do. Save your strength, buddy.' The med cloak probed at his shoulder. He felt a sharp pain.

And then sleep engulfed him, shutting out the light of the war.

*The seed inadvertently planted by Dolo and others, in allowing the soldiers' new religion to survive, took a long time to bear fruit.*

*In the meantime Luca was right. Humanity had to find a way to win its war before it lost through sheer exhaustion. It was through the slow sedition of Luca and others like him that the victory came about.*

*But it would take two more bloody millennia before the heroics of what became known as the 'Exultant generation' broke the logjam of the Front, and mankind's forces swept on into the Core itself.*

*I had a small part to play in that victory. We undying, hidden away, have sometimes seen fit to steer human history. With patience you can make a difference. But mayflies, blind to the long term, are impossible to herd. You never get everything you want.*

*Still, a victory.*

*Suddenly the Galaxy was human.*

*Victorious child soldiers peered around at what they had won, uncomprehending, and wondered what to do next.*

*Mankind sought new purposes.*

*For the first time in many millennia voyages of discovery, not conquest, were launched. Some even sailed beyond the Galaxy itself.*

*And even there they found relics of mankind's complicated history.*

*Some were almost as old as I am.*

# FIVE

# THE SHADOW OF EMPIRE

# MAYFLOWER II

## AD 5420–24,974

I

Twenty days before the end of his world, Rusel heard that he was to be saved.

'Rusel. Rusel . . .' The whispered voice was insistent. Rusel rolled over, trying to shake off the effects of his usual mild sedative. The room responded to his movement, and soft light coalesced around him. His pillow was soaked with sweat.

His brother's face was hovering in the air at the side of his bed. Diluc was grinning. The Virtual image made his face look even wider than usual, his nose more prominent.

'Lethe,' Rusel said hoarsely. 'You ugly bastard.'

'You're just jealous,' Diluc said. 'I'm sorry to wake you. But I just heard – you need to know – '

'Know what?'

'Blen showed up in the infirmary.' Blen was the nanochemist assigned to Ship Three. 'Get this: he has a heart murmur.' Diluc's grin returned.

Rusel frowned. 'For that you woke me up? Poor Blen.'

'It's not that serious. But, Rus – it's congenital.'

The sedative dulled Rusel's thinking, and it took him a moment to figure it out.

The five Ships were to evacuate the last, brightest hopes of Port Sol from the path of the incoming peril, the forces of the young Coalition. But they were slower-than-light transports, and would take many centuries to reach their destinations. Only the healthiest, in body and genome, could be allowed aboard a generation starship. And if Blen had a hereditary heart condition—

'He's off the Ship,' Rusel breathed.

'And that means you're aboard, brother. You're the second-best

377

nanochemist on this lump of ice. You won't be here when the Coalition arrives. You're going to live!'

Rusel lay back on his crushed pillow. He felt numb.

His brother kept talking. 'Did you know that families are *illegal* under the Coalition? Their citizens are born in tanks. Just the fact of our relationship would doom us, Rus! I'm trying to fix a transfer from Five to Three. If we're together, that's something, isn't it? I know it's going to be hard, Rus. But we can help each other. We can get through this . . .'

All Rusel could think about was Lora, whom he would have to leave behind.

The next morning Rusel arranged to meet Lora in the Forest of Ancestors. He took a bubble-wheel surface transport, and set out early.

Port Sol was a planetesimal, an unfinished remnant of the formation of Sol system. Inhabited for millennia, its surface was heavily worked, quarried and pitted, and littered by abandoned towns. The Qax had never come here; Port Sol was a museum, some said, of pre-Occupation days. But throughout Port Sol's long human usage some areas had been kept pristine, and as he drove Rusel kept to the marked track, to avoid crushing the delicate sculptures of frost that had coalesced here over four billion years.

And visible beyond the close horizon of the ice moon was a squat cylinder, a misty sketch in the faint sunlight. That was Ship Three, preparing for its leap into the greater dark.

This was the very edge of Sol system. The sky was a dome of stars, with the ragged glow of the Galaxy hurled casually across its equator. Set in that diffuse glow was the sun, the brightest star, bright enough to cast shadows, but so remote it was a mere pinpoint. Around the sun Rusel could make out a tiny puddle of light: the inner system, the disc of worlds, moons, asteroids, dust and other debris that had been the arena of all human history before the first interplanetary voyages some three thousand years earlier, and still the home of all but an invisible fraction of the human race. This was a time of turmoil, and today, invisible in that pale glow, humans were fighting and dying. And even now a punitive fleet was ploughing out of that warm centre, heading for Port Sol.

The whole situation was an unwelcome consequence of the liberation of Earth from the alien Qax, just thirteen years earlier. The Interim

Coalition of Governance, the new, ideologically pure and viciously determined central authority that had emerged from the chaos of a newly freed Earth, was already burning its way out through the worlds and moons of Sol system. When the Coalition ships came, the best you could hope for was that your community would be broken up, your equipment impounded, and that you would be hauled back to a prison camp on Earth or its Moon for 'reconditioning'.

But if a world was found to be harbouring anyone who had collaborated with the hated Qax, the penalties against it were much more extreme. The word Rusel had heard was 'resurfacing'.

Now the Coalition had turned its attention to Port Sol. This ice moon was governed by five 'pharaohs', as they were called locally, an elite group who had indeed collaborated with the Qax – though they described it as 'mediating the effects of the Occupation for the benefit of mankind' – and they had received anti-ageing treatments as a reward. So Port Sol was a 'nest of illegal immortals and collaborators', the Coalition said, and dispatched its troops to 'clean it out'. It seemed indifferent to the fact that, in addition to the pharaohs, some fifty thousand people called Port Sol home.

The pharaohs had a deep network of spies on Earth, and they had had some warning of the coming of the Coalition. As the colonists had only the lightest battery of antiquated weaponry – indeed the whole ice moon, a refuge from the Occupation, was somewhat low-tech – nobody expected to be able to resist. But there was a way out.

Five huge Ships were hastily thrown together. On each Ship, captained by a pharaoh, a couple of hundred people, selected for their health and skill sets, would be taken away: a total of a thousand, perhaps, out of a population of fifty thousand, saved from the incoming disaster. There was no faster-than-light technology on Port Sol; these would be generation starships. But perhaps that was as well. Between the stars there would be room to hide.

All these mighty historical forces had now focused down on Rusel's life, and they threatened to tear him away from his lover.

Lora was waiting for him at the Forest of Ancestors. They met on the surface, embracing stiffly through their skinsuits. Then they set up a dome-tent and crawled through its collapsible airlock.

In the Forest's long shadows, Rusel and Lora made love: at first urgently, and then again, more slowly, thoughtfully. In the habs, inertial generators kept the gravity at one-sixth standard, about the same as Earth's Moon. But there was no gravity control out here in the Forest, and as they clung to each other they drifted in the tent's cool air, light as dreams.

Rusel told Lora his news.

Rusel was an able nanochemist, he was the right age for Ship crew, and his health and pedigree were immaculate. But unlike his brother he hadn't been good enough to win the one-in-fifty lottery and make the cut to get a place on the Ships. He was twenty-eight years old: not a good age to die. But he had accepted his fate, so he believed – for Lora, his lover, had no hope of a berth. At twenty she was a student, a promising Virtual idealist but without the mature skills to have a chance of competing for a berth on the Ships. So at least he would be with her, when the sky fell in.

He was honest with himself, and unsentimental; he had never been sure if his noble serenity would have survived the appearance of the Coalition ships in Port Sol's dark sky. And now, it seemed, he was never going to find out.

Lora was slim, delicate. The population of this low-gravity moon tended to tallness and thin bones, but Lora seemed to him more elfin than most, and she had large, dark eyes that always seemed a little unfocused, as if her attention was somewhere else. It was that sense of other-world fragility that had first attracted Rusel to her.

With blankets bundled over her legs, she took his hand and smiled. 'Don't be afraid.'

'I'm the one who's going to live. Why should I be afraid?'

'You'd accepted dying. Now you've got to get used to the idea of living.' She sighed. 'It's just as hard.'

'And living without you.' He squeezed her hand. 'Maybe that's what scares me most. I'm frightened of losing you.'

'I'm not going anywhere.'

He gazed out at the silent, watchful shapes of the Ancestors. These 'trees', some three or four metres high, were stumps with 'roots' that dug into the icy ground. They were living things, the most advanced members of Port Sol's low-temperature aboriginal ecology. This was their sessile stage. In their youth, these creatures, called 'Toolmakers', were mobile, and were actually intelligent. They would haul themselves across Port Sol's broken ground, seeking a suitable crater slope or ridge face. There they would set down their roots and allow their nervous systems and their minds to dissolve, their purposes fulfilled.

Rusel wondered what liquid-helium dreams might be coursing slowly through the Ancestors' residual minds. They were beyond decisions now; in a way he envied them.

'Maybe the Coalition will spare the Ancestors.'

She snorted. 'I doubt it. The Coalition only care about humans – and their sort of humans at that.'

'My family has lived here a long time,' he said. 'There's a story that says we rode out with the first colonising wave.' It was a legendary time, when the engineer Michael Poole had come barnstorming all the way through the system to Port Sol to build his great starships.

She smiled. 'Most families have stories like that. After thousands of years, who can tell?'

'This is my home,' he blurted. 'This isn't just the destruction of us, but of our culture, our heritage. Everything we've worked for.'

'But that's why you're so important.' She sat up, letting the blanket fall away, and wrapped her arms around his neck. In Sol's dim light her eyes were pools of liquid darkness. 'You're the future. The pharaohs say that in the long run the Coalition will be the death of mankind, not just of *us*. Somebody has to save our knowledge, our values, for the future.'

'But you—' You will be alone, when the Coalition ships descend. Decision sparked. 'I'm not going anywhere.'

She pulled back. 'What?'

'I've decided. I'll tell Pharaoh Andres, and my brother. I can't leave here, not without you.'

'You must,' she said firmly. 'You're the best for the job, believe me; if not the pharaohs wouldn't have selected you. So you have to go. It's your duty.'

'What human being would run out on those he loved?'

Her face was set, and she sounded much older than her twenty years. 'It would be easier to die. But you must live, live on and on, live on like a machine, until the job is done, and the race is saved.'

Before her he felt weak, immature. He clung to her, burying his face in the soft warmth of her neck.

Nineteen days, he thought. We still have nineteen days. He determined to cherish every minute.

But as it turned out they had much less time than that.

Once again he was woken in the dark. But this time his room lights were snapped full on, dazzling him. And it was the face of Pharaoh

Andres that hovered in the air beside his bed. He sat up, baffled, his system heavy with sedative.

'—thirty minutes. You have thirty minutes to get to Ship Three. Wear your skinsuit. Bring nothing else. If you aren't there in thirty minutes, twenty-nine forty-five, we leave without you.'

At first he couldn't take in what she said. He found himself staring at her face. Her head was hairless, her scalp bald, her eyebrows and even her eyelashes gone. Her skin was oddly smooth, her features small; she didn't look young, but as if her face had sublimated with time, like Port Sol's ice landscapes, leaving this palimpsest. She was rumoured to be two hundred years old.

'Don't acknowledge this message, just move. We lift in twenty-nine minutes. If you are Ship Three crew, you have twenty-nine minutes to get to—'

She had made a mistake: that was his first thought. Had she forgotten that there were still sixteen days to go before the Coalition ships were due? But he could see from her face there was no mistake.

*Twenty-nine minutes.* He reached down to his bedside cabinet, pulled out a nano pill and gulped it down dry. Reality bleached, becoming cold and stark.

He dragged on his skinsuit and sealed it roughly. He glanced around his room, at his bed, his few pieces of furniture, the Virtual unit on the dresser with its images of Lora. Bring nothing. Andres wasn't a woman you disobeyed in the slightest particular.

Without looking back he left the room.

The corridor outside was bedlam. A thousand people shared this under-the-ice habitat, and all of them seemed to be out tonight. They ran this way and that, many in skinsuits, some hauling bundles of gear. He pushed his way through the throng. The sense of panic was tangible – and, carried on the recycled air, he thought he could smell burning.

His heart sank. It was obviously a scramble to escape – but the only way off the moon was the Ships, which could take no more than a thousand. Had the sudden curtailing of the time left triggered this panic? In this ultimate emergency had the citizens of Port Sol lost all their values, all their sense of community? What could they hope to achieve by hurling themselves at Ships that had no room for them, but to bring everybody down with them? But what would I do? He could afford the luxury of nobility; he was getting out of here.

Twenty minutes.

He reached the perimeter concourse. Here, surface transports nuzzled against a row of simple airlocks. Some of the locks were already open, and people were crowding in, pushing children, bundles of luggage. His own car was still here, he saw with relief. He pulled open his skinsuit glove and hastily pressed his palm to the wall. The door hissed open.

But before he could pass through, somebody grabbed his arm.

A man faced him, a stranger, short, burly, aged perhaps forty. Behind him a woman clutched a small child and an infant. The adults had blanket-wrapped bundles on their backs. The man wore an electric-blue skinsuit, but his family were in hab clothes.

The man said desperately, 'Friend, you have room in that thing?'

'No,' Rusel said.

The man's eyes hardened. 'Listen. The pharaohs' spies got it wrong. Suddenly the Coalition is only seven days out. Look, friend, you can see how I'm fixed. The Coalition breaks up families, doesn't it? All I'm asking is for a chance on the Ships.'

But there won't be room for you. Don't you understand? And even if there were— There were to be no children on the Ships at launch: that was the pharaohs' harsh rule. In the first years of the long voyage, everybody aboard had to be maximally productive. The time for breeding would come later.

The man's fist bunched. 'Listen, friend—'

Rusel shoved the man in the chest. He fell backwards, stumbling against his children. His blanket bundle broke open, and goods spilled on the floor: clothes, diapers, children's toys.

'Please.' The woman approached him, stepping over her husband. She held out a baby. 'Don't let the Coalition take him away. Please.'

The baby was warm, soft, smiling. Rusel automatically reached out. But he stopped himself cold, and turned away.

He pushed into his car, slammed shut the door, and stabbed a preset routine into the control panel. The woman with the baby continued to call after him. How could I do that? I'm no longer human, he thought.

The car ripped itself away from the airlock interface, ignoring all safety protocols, and began to haul itself on its bubble wheels up the ramp from the under-the-ice habitat to the surface. Shaking, Rusel opened his visor. He might be able to see the doomed family at the airlock port. He didn't look back.

It wasn't supposed to be like this.

Andres's Virtual head coalesced before him. 'Sixteen minutes to get to Ship Three. If you're not there we go without you. Fifteen forty-five. Fifteen forty . . .'

The surface was almost as chaotic as the corridors of the hab, as transports of all types and ages rolled, crawled or jumped. There was no sign of the Enforcers, the pharaohs' police force, and he was apprehensive about being held up in the crush.

He made it through the crowd and headed for the track that would lead through the Forest of Ancestors to Ship Three. Out here there was a lot of traffic, but it was more or less orderly, everyone heading out the way he was. He pushed the car up to its safety-regulated maximum speed. Even so, he was continually overtaken. Anxiety tore at his stomach.

The Forest, with the placid profiles of the Ancestors glimmering in Sol's low light, looked unchanged from when he had last seen it, only days ago, on his way to meet Lora. He felt an unreasonable resentment that he had suddenly lost so much time, that his careful plan for an extended farewell to Lora had been torn up. He wondered where she was now. Perhaps he could call her.

Thirteen minutes. No time, no time.

The traffic ahead was slowing. The vehicles at the back of the queue weaved, trying to find gaps, and bunched into a solid pack.

Rusel punched his control panel and brought up a Virtual overhead image. Ahead of the tangle of vehicles, a ditch had been cut roughly across the road. People swarmed, hundreds of them. Roadblock.

Eleven minutes. For a moment his brain seemed as frozen as Port Sol ice; frantic, bewildered, filled with guilt, he couldn't think.

Then a heavy-duty long-distance truck broke out of the pack behind him. Veering off the road to the left, it began to smash its way through the Forest. The elegant eightfold forms of the Ancestors were nothing but ice sculptures, and they shattered before the truck's momentum. It was ugly, and Rusel knew that each impact wiped out a life that might have lasted centuries more. But the truck was clearing a path.

Rusel hauled at his controls, and dragged his car off the road. Only a few vehicles were ahead of him in the truck's destructive wake. The truck was moving fast, and he was able to push his speed higher.

They were already approaching the roadblock, he saw. A few suit lights moved off the road and into the Forest, to stand in the path of the lead truck; the blockers must be enraged to see their targets evade them so easily. Rusel kept his speed high. Only a few more seconds and he would be past the worst.

But there was a figure standing directly in front of him, helmet lamp bright, dressed in an electric-blue skinsuit, arms raised. As the car's sensors picked up the figure, its safety routines cut in, and he felt it hesitate. He slammed his palm to the control panel, overriding the safeties. Nine minutes.

He closed his eyes as the car hit the protester.

He remembered the blue skinsuit. He had just mown down the man from the airlock, who had been so desperate to save his family. He had no right to criticise the courage or the morals or the loyalty of others, he saw.

We are all just animals, fighting to survive. My berth on Ship Three doesn't make me any better. He hadn't even had the guts to watch.

Eight minutes. He disabled the safety governors and let the car race down the empty road, its speed ever increasing.

He had to pass through another block before he reached Ship Three – but this one was manned by Enforcers. They were in an orderly line across the road, dressed in their bright yellow skinsuit uniforms. Evidently they had pulled back to tight perimeters around the five Ships. At least they were still loyal.

The queuing was agonising. With only five minutes before Andres's deadline, an Enforcer pressed a nozzle to the car's window, flashed laser light into Rusel's face, and waved him through.

Ship Three was directly ahead of him. It was a drum, a squat cylinder about a kilometre across and half as tall. It sat at the bottom of its own crater, for Port Sol ice had been gouged out and plastered roughly over the surface of its hull. It looked less like a ship than a building, he thought, a building coated by thick ice, as if long abandoned. But it was indeed a starship, a ship designed for a journey of not less than centuries, and fountains of crystals already sparkled around its base in neat parabolic arcs: steam from the Ship's rockets, freezing immediately to ice. People milled at its base, running clumsily in the low gravity, and scurried up ramps that tongued down from its hull to the ground.

Rusel abandoned the car, tumbled out onto the ice and ran towards the nearest ramp. There was another stomach-churning wait as an Enforcer in glowing yellow checked each identity. At last, after another dazzling flash of laser light in his eyes, he was through.

He hurried into an airlock. As it cycled it struck him that as he boarded this Ship, he was never going to leave it again: whatever became of him, this Ship was his whole world, for the rest of his life.

The lock opened. He ripped off his helmet. The light was emergency red, and klaxons sounded throughout the ship; the air was cold, and smelled of fear. Lethe, he was aboard! But there could only be a minute left.

He ran along a cold, ice-lined corridor towards a brighter interior.

He reached an amphitheatre, roughly circular, carpeted by acceleration couches. Andres's voice boomed from the air: 'Get into a couch. Any couch. It doesn't matter. Forty seconds. Strap yourself in. Nobody is going to do it for you. Your safety is your own responsibility. Twenty-five seconds.' People swarmed, looking for spare couches. The scene seemed absurd to Rusel, like a children's game.

'Rus! Rusel!' Through the throng, Rusel made out a waving hand. It was Diluc, his brother, wearing his characteristic orange skinsuit. 'Lethe, I'm glad to see you. I kept you a couch. Come on!'

Rusel pushed that way. Ten seconds. He threw himself down on the couch. The straps were awkward to pull around the bulk of his suit.

As he fumbled, he stared up at a Virtual display that hovered over his head. It was a view as seen from the Ship's blunt prow, looking down. Those tongue ramps were still in place, radiating down to the ice. But now a dark mass boiled around the base of the curving hull: people, on foot and in vehicles, a mob of them closing in. In amongst the mass were specks of bright yellow. Some of the Enforcers had turned on their commanders, then. But others stood firm, and in that last second Rusel saw the bright sparks of weapon fire, all around the base of the Ship.

A sheet of brilliant white gushed out from the Ship's base. It was Port Sol ice, superheated to steam at tens of thousands of degrees. The image shuddered, and Rusel felt a quivering, deep in his gut. The Ship was rising, right on time, its tremendous mass raised on a bank of rockets.

When that great splash of steam cleared, Rusel saw small dark forms lying motionless on the ice: the bodies of the loyal and disloyal alike, their lives ended in a fraction of a second. A massive shame descended on Rusel, a synthesis of all the emotions that had churned through him since that fateful call of Diluc's. He had abandoned his lover to die; he had probably killed others himself; and now he sat here in safety as others died on the ice below. What human being would behave that way? He felt the shame would never lift, never leave him.

Already the plain of ice was receding, and weight began to push at his chest.

II

Soon Port Sol fell away, and even the other Ships were lost against the stars, and it was as if Ship Three was alone in the universe.

In this opening phase of its millennial voyage Ship Three was nothing more than a water rocket, as its engines steadily sublimated its plating of ice and hurled steam out of immense nozzles. But those engines drew on energies that had once powered the expansion of the universe itself. Later the Ship would spin up for artificial gravity and switch to an exotic ramjet for its propulsion, and its true journey would begin.

The heaviest acceleration of the whole voyage had come in the first hours, as the ship hurled itself away from Port Sol. After that the acceleration was cut to about a third standard – twice lunar gravity, twice what the colonists of Port Sol had been used to. For the time being, the acceleration couches were left in place in that big base amphitheatre, and in the night watches everybody slept there, all two hundred of them massed together in a single vast dormitory, their muscles groaning against the ache of the twice-normal gravity.

The plan was that for twenty-one days the Ships would actually head *towards* the sun. They would penetrate Sol system as far as the orbit of Jupiter, where they would use the giant planet's gravity field to sling-shot them on to their final destinations. It seemed paradoxical to begin the exodus by hurling oneself deep into the inner system, the Coalition's home territory. But space was big, the Ships' courses had been plotted to avoid the likely trajectory of the incoming Coalition convoy, and the Ships were to run silently, not even communicating with each other. The chances of them being detected were negligible.

Despite the wearying gravity the first days after launch were busy for everybody. The Ship's interior had to be rebuilt from its launch configuration to withstand this high-acceleration cruise phase. And the daily routines of the long voyage had to be set up – the most important of them being cleaning.

The Ship was a closed environment and its interior had plenty of smooth surfaces where biofilms, slick detergent-proof cities of bugs, would quickly build up. Not only that, the fall-out of the Ship's human cargo – flakes of skin, hair, mucus – were seed beds for bacterial growth. All of this had to be eliminated; Captain Andres declared she wanted the Ship to be as clean as a hospital.

The most effective way to achieve that – and the most 'future-proof', in Andres's persistent jargon – was through the old-fashioned application of human muscle. Everybody had to pitch in, even the Captain herself. Rusel put in his statutory half-hour per day, scrubbing vigorously at the walls and floors and ceilings around the nanofood banks that were his primary responsibility. He welcomed the mindlessness of the work; he continued to seek ways in which to distract himself from the burden of thought.

He was briefly ill. In the first couple of weeks, everybody caught colds from everybody else. But the viruses quickly ran their course through the Ship's small population, and Rusel felt obscurely reassured that he would likely never catch another cold in his life.

A few days after launch Diluc came to find him. Rusel was up to his elbows in slurry, trying to find a fault in a nanofood bank's waste vent. Working non-stop, Rusel had seen little of his brother. He was surprised by how cheerful Diluc appeared, and how energetically he threw himself into his own work on the air cycling systems. He spoke brightly of his 'babies', fans and pumps, humidifiers and dehumidifiers, filters and scrubbers and oxygenators.

In their reaction to the sudden severance of the launch, the crew seemed to be dividing into two rough camps, Rusel thought. There were those like Diluc who were behaving as if the outside universe didn't exist; they were bright, brash, too loud, their laughter forced. The other camp, to which Rusel felt he belonged, retreated the other way, into an inner darkness, full of complicated shadows.

But today Diluc's mood seemed complex. 'Brother, have you been counting the days?'

'Since launch? No.' He hadn't wanted to think about it.

'It's day seven. There's a place to watch. One of the observation lounges. Captain Andres says it's not compulsory, but if . . .'

It took Rusel a moment to think that through. *Day seven*: the day the Coalition convoy was due to reach Port Sol. Rusel flinched from the thought. But one of his worst moments of that chaotic launch day was when he had run down that desperate father and driven on, without even having the courage to watch what he was doing. Perhaps this would atone. 'Let's do it,' he said.

Ship Three, like its four siblings, was a fat torus. To reach the observation lounge the brothers had to ride elevators up through several decks to a point in the Ship's flattened prow, close to the rim. The lounge, crammed with Virtual generation gear, was already configured for the spin-up phase to come, and most of its furniture was plastered to the walls, which would become the floor. It was big enough for maybe fifty people, and it was nearly full; Rusel and Diluc had to crowd in. Pharaoh Andres – now Captain Andres, Rusel reminded himself – was here, sitting in a deep, heavy-looking chair, front and centre before an immense, shining Virtual.

A ball of ice spun grandly before their eyes. It was Port Sol, of course; Rusel immediately recognised its icy geography of ancient craters, overlaid by a human patterning of quarries and mines, habitats and townships, landing ports. In the inhabited buildings lights shone, defiantly bright in outer-system gloom. It was a sculpture in white and silver, and it showed no sign of the chaotic panic that must be churning in its corridors.

The sight took Rusel's breath away. Somewhere down there was Lora; it was an almost unbearable thought, and he wished with all his heart he had stayed with her.

The Coalition convoy closed in.

Its ships materialised from the edge of the three-dimensional image, as if sliding in from another reality. The fleet was dominated by five, six, seven Spline warships. Confiscated from the expelled Qax, they were living ships each a kilometre or more wide, their hulls studded with weapons and sensors and crudely scrawled with the green tetrahedron that was the sigil of liberated humanity.

Rusel's stomach filled with dread. 'It's a heavy force,' he said.

'They've come for the pharaohs,' Diluc said grimly. 'The Coalition is showing its power. Images like this are no doubt being beamed throughout the system.'

Then it began. The first touch of the energy beams, cherry-red, was almost gentle, and Port Sol ice exploded into cascades of glittering shards that drifted back to the surface, or escaped into space. Then more beams ploughed up the ice, and structures began to implode, melting, or to fly apart. A spreading cloud of crystals began to swathe Port Sol in a temporary, pearly atmosphere. It was silent, almost beautiful, too large-scale to make out individual deaths, a choreography of energy and destruction.

'We'll get through this,' Diluc muttered. 'We'll get through this.'

Rusel felt numbed, no grief, only shame at his own emotional inadequacy. This was the destruction of his home, of a *world*, and it was beyond his imagination. Worse, Port Sol, which had survived the alien occupation of the solar system, was being devastated by humans. How could such things happen? He tried to focus on one person, on Lora, to imagine what she must be doing if she was still alive: perhaps fleeing through collapsing tunnels, or crowding into deep shelters. But, in the ticking calm of this lounge, with its fresh smell of new equipment, he couldn't even picture that.

As the assault continued, numbers flickered across the status display, an almost blasphemous tallying of the estimated dead.

Even after the trauma of Port Sol, work had to continue on booting up the vital systems that would keep them all alive.

Rusel's own job, as the senior nanochemist on the Ship, was to set up the nanofood banks that would play a crucial part in recycling waste into food and other consumables like clothing. The work was demanding from the start. The banks were based on an alien technology, nanodevices purloined from the occupying Qax; only partially understood, they were temperamental and difficult.

It didn't help that of the two assistants he had been promised a share of – most people were generalists in this small, skill-starved new community – only one had made it onto the Ship. It turned out that in the final scramble about ten per cent of the crew had been left behind; conversely, about ten per cent of those who actually were aboard shouldn't have been here at all. A few shame-faced 'passengers' were yellow-uniformed Enforcers who in the last moments had abandoned their posts and fled to the sanctuary of the Ship's interior.

The work had to get done anyhow. And it was urgent; until the nanofood was available the Ship's temporary rations were steadily depleting. The pressure on Rusel was intense. But Rusel was glad of the work, so hard mentally and physically in the high gravity he had no time to think, and when he hit his couch at night he slept easily.

On the fifteenth day Rusel achieved a small personal triumph as the first slab of edible food rolled out of his nanobanks. Captain Andres had a policy of celebrating small achievements, and she was here as Rusel ceremoniously swallowed the first mouthful of his food, and she took the second. There was much clapping and back-slapping. Diluc grinned in his usual huge way. But Rusel, numbed inside, didn't feel much like celebrating. People understood; half the crew, it was estimated, were still in some kind of shock. He got away from the crush as quickly as he could.

On the twenty-first day the Ship was to encounter Jupiter.

Captain Andres called the crew together in the acceleration-couch amphitheatre, all two hundred of them, and she set up a Virtual display in the air above them. Few of the crew had travelled away from Port Sol before; they craned to see. The sun was just a pinpoint, though much brighter than seen from Port Sol, and Jupiter was a flattened ball of cloud, racked with storm systems like bruises – the result, it was said, of an ancient battle.

The most intriguing sight of all was four sparks of light that slid across the background of stars. They were the other Ships, numbers One, Two, Four and Five; the little fleet would come together at Jupiter for the first time since leaving Port Sol, and the last.

Andres walked though the crowd on their couches, declaiming loudly enough for all to hear, her authority easy and unforced. 'We pharaohs have been discussing destinations,' she said. 'Obviously the targets had to be chosen before we reached Jupiter; we needed to plan for our angles of emergence from Jupiter's gravity well. The Coalition is vindictive and determined, and it has faster-than-light ships. It will soon overtake us – but space is big, and five silent-running generation starships will be hard to spot. Even so it's obviously best to separate, to give them five targets to chase, not just one.

'So we have five destinations. And ours,' she said, smiling, 'is the most unique of all.'

She listed the other Ships' targets, star systems scattered through the disc of the Galaxy – none closer than five hundred light years. 'All well within the Ships' design parameters,' she said, 'and perhaps far enough to be safe. But *we* are going further.'

She overlaid the image of the shining Ships with a ruddy, shapeless mass of mist. 'This is the Canis Major Dwarf Galaxy,' she said. 'Twenty-four thousand light years from Sol. It is the closest of the satellite galaxies – *but it is beyond the main Galaxy itself*, surely far outside the Coalition's grasp for the foreseeable future.'

Rusel heard gasps throughout the amphitheatre. To sail beyond the Galaxy? . . .

Andres held her hands up to quell the muttering. 'Of course such a journey is far in excess of what we planned. No generation starship has ever challenged such distances before, let alone achieved them.' She stared around at them, fists on hips. 'But if we can manage a thousand years of flight, we can manage ten, or fifty – why not? We are strong, we are just as determined as the Coalition and its drones – more so, for we know we are in the right.'

Rusel wasn't used to questioning the pharaohs' decisions, but he found himself wondering at the arrogance of the handful of pharaohs to make such decisions on behalf of their crew – not to mention the generations yet unborn.

There was no serious protest. Perhaps it was all simply beyond the imagination. Diluc muttered, 'Can't say it makes much difference. A thousand years or ten thousand, I'll be dead in a century, and *I* won't see the end . . .'

Andres restored the images of the Ships. Jupiter was expanding rapidly now, and the other Ships were swarming closer.

Andres said, 'We have discussed names for our vessels. On such an epic voyage numbers won't do. Every Ship must have a name! We have named our Ship-homes for great thinkers, and great vessels of the past.' She stabbed her finger around the Virtual image. '*Tsiolkovsky. Great Northern. Aldiss. Vanguard.*' She looked at her crew. 'And as for us, only one name is possible. Like an earlier band of pilgrims, we are fleeing intolerance and tyranny; we sail into the dark and the unknown, carrying the hopes of an age. We are *Mayflower.*'

You didn't study history on Port Sol. Nobody knew what she was talking about.

At the moment of closest approach Jupiter's golden-brown cloudscape bellied over the upturned faces of the watching crew, and the Ships poured through Jupiter's gravity well. Even now the rule of silence wasn't violated, and the five Ships parted without so much as a farewell message.

From now on, wherever this invisible road in the sky took her, the second *Mayflower* was alone.

## III

As the days stretched to weeks, and the weeks to months, Rusel continued to throw himself into work – and there was plenty of it for everybody.

The challenges of running a generation starship were familiar to the crew to some extent, as the colonists of Port Sol had long experience in ecosynthesis, in constructing and sustaining closed artificial environments. But on Port Sol they had had external resources to draw on, the ice, rock and organic chemistry of the ice moon itself. The Ship was now cut off from the outside universe.

So the cycles of air, water and solids would have to be maintained with something close to a hundred per cent efficiency. The sealing of the Ship against leakages was vital, and so nano-machines laboured to knit together the hull. The control of trace contaminants and pests would have to be ferociously tight: more swarms of nano-bots were sent scurrying in pursuit of flakes of hair and skin.

Not only that, the Ship's design had been hastily thrown together, and the vessel wasn't even completed on launch. The construction had been a hurried project anyhow, and the shaving-off of those final ten or twelve days of preparation time, as the Coalition fleet sneaked up in the dark, had made a significant difference. So the crew laboured to complete the ship's systems in flight.

The most significant difficulty, Rusel believed, was the sudden upping of the design targets. A thousand-year cruise, the nominal design envelope, was one thing. Now it was estimated that, cruising at about half lightspeed, it would take Ship Three *fifty times* as long to reach Canis Major. Even relativistic time dilation would only make a difference of a few per cent to the subjective duration. As a consequence the tolerances on the Ship's systems were tightened by orders of magnitude.

There was yet another goal in all this rebuilding. A key lesson of ecosynthesis was that the smaller the biosphere, the more conscious control it would require. The Ship was a much smaller environment than a Port Sol habitat, and that presented problems of stability; the ecological system was poorly buffered and would always be prone to collapse. It was clear that this small, tight biosphere would always have to be consciously managed if it were to survive.

That was manageable as long as the first crew, educated on Port Sol, were in command. But to ensure this in the long term the Ship's essential systems were to be simplified and automated as far as possible, to reduce the skill level required to maintain them. They couldn't foresee all that might befall the Ship, and so they were trying to 'future-proof' the project, in Andres's jargon: to reduce the crew to the status of non-productive payload.

As Diluc put it with grim humour, 'We can't allow civilisation to fall in here.'

Despite the horror of Port Sol, the hard work, and the daunting timescale Andres had set – which Rusel suspected nobody believed anyhow – the rhythms of human life continued.

Diluc found a new partner, a plump, cheerful woman of about thirty called Tila. Diluc and Tila had both left lovers behind on Port Sol, and Tila had been forced to give up a child. Now they seemed to be finding comfort with each other. Diluc was somewhat put out when they were both hauled into Andres's small private office to be quizzed about their relationship, but Andres, after much consulting of genetic maps, approved their continuing liaison.

Rusel was pleased for his brother, but he found Tila a puzzle. Most of the selected crew had been without offspring, back on Port Sol; few people with children, knowing they would have to leave them behind, had even offered themselves for selection. But *Tila had abandoned a child*. He saw no sign of this loss in her face, her manner; perhaps her new relationship with Diluc, and even the prospect of more children with him in the future, was enough to comfort her. He wondered what was going on inside her head, though.

As for Rusel, his social contacts were restricted to work. He found himself being subtly favoured by Captain Andres, along with a number of others of the Ship's senior technicians. There was no formal hierarchy on the Ship – no command structure below Andres herself. But this group of a dozen or so, a meritocracy selected purely by proven achievement, began to coalesce into a kind of governing council of the Ship.

That was about as much social life as Rusel wanted. Otherwise he just worked himself to the point of exhaustion, and slept. The complex mass of emotions lodged inside him – agony over the loss of Lora, the shock of seeing his home destroyed, the shame of living on – showed no signs of breaking up. None of this affected his contributions to the Ship, he believed. He was split in two, split between inside and out, and he doubted he would ever heal. In fact he didn't really want to heal. One day he would die, as so many others had, as Lora probably had; one day he would atone for his sin of survival in death.

Meanwhile there was always the Ship. He slowly widened the scope of his work, and began to develop a feel for the Ship as a whole. As the systems embedded, it was as if the Ship was slowly coming alive, and he learned to listen to the rhythm of its pumps, feel the sighing of its circulating air.

Though Andres continued to use the fanciful name she had given it, Rusel and everybody else thought of it as they always had: as Ship Three – or, increasingly, just the Ship.

Almost a year after Jupiter, Andres called her 'council' of twelve together in the amphitheatre at the base of the Ship. This big chamber had been stripped of its acceleration couches, and the dozen or so of them sat on temporary chairs in the middle of an empty grey-white floor.

Andres told them she wanted to discuss a little anthropology.

In her characteristic manner she marched around the room, looming over her crew. 'We've had a good year, for which I thank you. Our work on the Ship isn't completed – in a sense it never will be completed – but I'm now satisfied that *Mayflower* will survive the voyage. If we fail in our mission, it won't be the technology that betrays us, but the people. And that's what we've got to start thinking about now.'

*Mayflower* was a generation starship, she said. By now mankind had millennia of experience of launching such ships. 'And as far as we know, every last one of them has failed. And why? Because of the people.

'The most basic factor is population control. You'd think that would be simple enough! The Ship is an environment of a fixed size. As long as every parent sires one kid, on average, the population ought to stay stable. But by far the most common causes of mission loss are population crashes, in which the number of crew falls below the level of a viable gene pool and then shuffles off to extinction – or, more spectacularly, explosions in which too many people eat their way to the hull of their ship and then destroy each other in the resulting wars.'

Diluc said dryly, 'Maybe that proves it's just a dumb idea. The scale of the journey is just too big for us poor saps to manage.'

Andres gazed at him challengingly. 'A bit late to say that now, Diluc!'

'Of course it's not just numbers but our population's genetic health that we have to think about,' pointed out Ruul. This lanky, serious man was the Ship's senior geneticist. 'We've already started, of course. All of us went through genetic screening before we were selected. There are only two hundred of us, but we're as genetically diverse a sample of Port Sol's population as possible. We should avoid the *founder effect* – none of us has a genetically transmitted disease to be spread through the population – and, provided we exert some kind of control over breeding partnerships, we should be able to avoid genetic drift, where defective copies of a gene cluster.'

Diluc looked faintly disgusted. '"Control over breeding partnerships"? What kind of language is that?'

Andres snapped, 'The kind of language we're going to have to embrace if we're to survive. We must control reproductive strategies. Remember, on this Ship the purpose of having children is not for the joy of it or similar primate rewards, but to maintain the crew's population levels and genetic health, and thereby to see through our mission.' She eyed Diluc. 'Oh, I'm not against comfort. I was human once! But we are going to have to separate companionship needs from breeding requirements.' She glanced around. 'I'm sure you are all smart enough to have figured that out for yourselves. But even this isn't enough, if the mission objectives are to be ensured.'

Diluc said, 'It isn't?'

'Of course not. This is a desperately small universe. We will always rely on the Ship's systems, and mistakes or deviances will be punished by catastrophe – for as long as the mission lasts. Non-modified human lifespans average out at around a century; we just haven't evolved to think further. But a century is but a moment for our mission. *We must future-proof*; I've said it over and over. And to do that we will need a continuity of memory, purpose and control far beyond the century-long horizons of our transients.'

*Transients*: it was the first time Rusel had heard her use that word.

He thought he saw where all this was leading. He said carefully, 'Port Sol was not a normal human society. With respect. Because it had you pharaohs at its heart.'

'Yes,' she said approvingly, her small face expressionless. 'And *that* is the key.' She lifted her hand before her face and studied it. 'Two centuries ago the Qax Governor made me ageless. Well, I served the Qax – but my deeper purpose was always to serve mankind. I fled

Earth, with others, to escape the Qax. Port Sol was always a refuge for the undying. Now I have had to flee Sol system itself to escape my fellow human beings. But I continue to serve mankind. And it is the continuity I provide, a continuity that transcends human timescales, that will enable this mission to succeed, where even Michael Poole failed.'

Diluc pulled a face. 'What do you want from us – to worship you as a god?'

There were gasps; you didn't speak to a pharaoh like that. But Andres seemed unfazed. 'A god? No – though a little awe from you wouldn't come amiss, Diluc. And anyhow, it probably won't be *me*. Remember, it wasn't a human agency that gave me my anti-ageing treatments, but the Qax . . .'

The Qax's own body architecture had nothing in common with humanity's. They were technically advanced, but their medicinal manipulation of their human subjects was always crude.

'The success rate was only ever some forty per cent,' Andres said. She inspected her hand, pulling at slack skin. 'Oh, I would dearly love to live through this mission, all fifty millennia of it, and see it through to its conclusion. But I fear that's unlikely to happen.' She gazed around at them. 'I can't do this alone; that's the bottom line. I will need help.'

Diluc suddenly saw it, and his mouth dropped open. 'You aren't serious.'

'I'm afraid so. It is necessary for the good of the mission that *some of the people in this room do not die*.'

Ruul the geneticist unfolded his tall frame from his chair. 'We believe it's possible. We have the Qax technology.' Without drama, he held up a yellow pill.

There was a long silence.

Andres smiled coldly. 'This is no privilege. We can't afford to die. We must remember, while everybody else forgets.

'And we must manage. We must achieve *total* social control – control over every significant aspect of our crew's lives – and we must govern their children's lives just as tightly, as far as we can see ahead. Society has to be as rigid as the bulkheads which contain it. Oh, we can give the crew freedom within limits! But we need to enforce social arrangements in which conflict is reduced to negligible, appropriate skill levels kept up – and, most importantly, a duty of maintenance of the Ship is hammered home into every individual at birth. That is why a long-lived elite must ensure perfect continuity and complete control.'

Rusel said, 'Elite? And what about the rights of those you call the transients? We pharaohs would he taking away all meaningful choice from them – and their children, and their children's children.'

'Rights? Rights?' She loomed over him. 'Rusel, a transient's only purpose is to live, reproduce and die in an orderly fashion, thus preserving her genes to the far future. There is no room on this Ship for democracy, no space for love! A transient is just a conduit for her genes. She has no rights, any more than a bit of pipe that carries water from source to sink. Surely you thought this through. When we get to Canis Major, when we find a world to live on, when again we have an environment of surplus – then we can talk about rights. But in the meantime we will control.' Her expression was complex. 'But you must see that we will control through love.'

Diluc gaped. '*Love*?'

'The Qax technology was based on genetic manipulation. We pharaohs were promised that our gift would be passed on to our children. And we had those children! But we pharaohs rarely bred true. I once had a child myself. She did not survive.' She hesitated, just for a second. Then she went on, 'But by now there are genes for immortality, or at least longevity, scattered through the human population – even among *you*. Do you see now why we had to build these arks – why we couldn't flee and abandon you, or just take frozen zygotes or eggs?' She spread her hands wide. 'Because you are my children, and I love you.'

Nobody moved. Rusel thought he could see tears in her stony eyes. She is grotesque, he thought.

Diluc said carefully, 'Pharaoh, would I be able to bring Tila with me? And our children, if we have them?'

'I'm sorry,' she said gently. 'Tila doesn't qualify. Besides, the social structure simply wouldn't be sustainable if—'

'Then count me out.' Diluc stood up.

She nodded. 'I'm sure you won't be the only one. Believe me, this is no gift I'm offering you. Longevity is a heavy burden.'

Diluc turned to Rusel. 'Brother, are you coming with me?'

Rusel closed his eyes. The thought of his eventual death had actually been a comfort to him – a healing of his inner wounds, a lifting of the guilt he knew he would carry throughout his life. Now even the prospect of death was being taken away, to be replaced by nothing but an indefinite extension of duty. But he had to take it on, he saw. As

Lora herself had told him, he had to live on, like a machine, and fulfil his function. That was why he was here; only that way could he atone.

He looked up at Diluc. 'I'm sorry,' he said.

Complex emotions crossed his brother's face: anger, despair, perhaps a kind of thwarted love. He turned and left the room.

Andres behaved as if Diluc had never existed.

'We will always have to combat cultural drift,' she said. 'It is the blight of the generation starship. Already we have some pregnancies; soon we will have the first children, who will live and die knowing nothing but this Ship. And in a few generations – well, you can guess the rest. First you forget where you're going. Then you forget you're going anywhere. Then you forget you're on a damn ship, and start to think the vessel is the whole universe. And so forth! Soon nothing is left but a rotten apple full of worms, falling through the void. Even the great engineer Michael Poole suffered this; a fifteen-hundred-year generation starship he designed – the first *Great Northern* – barely limped home. Oh, every so often you might have a glorious moment as some cannibalistic savage climbs the decks and peers out in awe at the stars, but that's no consolation for the loss of the mission.

'Well, not this time. You engineers will know we're almost at the end of our GUTdrive cruise phase; the propellant ice is almost exhausted. And that means the Ship's hull is exposed.' She clapped her hands – and, to more gasps from the crew, the amphitheatre's floor suddenly turned transparent.

Rusel was seated over a floor of stars; something inside him cringed.

Andres smiled at their reaction. 'Soon we will leave the plane of the Galaxy, and what a sight *that* will be. In a transparent hull our crew will never be able to forget they are on a Ship. There will be no conceptual breakthroughs on *my* watch!'


IV


With the ice exhausted, the Ship's banks of engines were shut down. From now on a dark matter ramjet would provide a comparatively gentle but enduring thrust.

Dark matter constituted most of the universe's store of mass, with 'light matter' – the stuff of bodies and ships and stars – a mere trace. The key advantage of dark matter for the Ship's mission planners was that it was found in thick quantities far beyond the visible disc of the

Galaxy, and would be a plentiful fuel source throughout the voyage. But dark matter interacted with its light counterpart only through gravity. So now invisible wings of gravitational force unfolded ahead of the Ship. Spanning thousands of kilometres, these acted as a scoop to draw dark matter into the hollow centre of the torus-shaped Ship. There, concentrated, much of it was annihilated and induced to give up its mass-energy, which in turn drove a residuum out of the Ship as reaction mass.

Thus the Ship ploughed on into the dark.

Once again the Ship was rebuilt. The acceleration provided by the dark matter ramjet was much lower than the ice rockets, and so the Ship was spun about its axis, to provide artificial gravity through centrifugal force. It was an ancient solution and a crude one – but it worked, and ought to require little maintenance in the future.

The spin-up was itself a spectacular milestone, a great swivelling as floors became walls and walls became ceilings. The transparent floor of the acceleration-couch amphitheatre became a wall full of stars, whose cool emptiness Rusel grew to like.

Meanwhile the new 'Elders', the ten of them who had accepted Andres's challenge, began their course of treatment. The procedure was administered by geneticist Ruul and a woman called Selur, the Ship's senior doctor. The medics took the process slowly enough to catch any adverse reactions, or so they hoped. For Rusel it was painless enough, just injections and tablets, and he tried not to think about the alien nano-probes embedding themselves in his system, cleaning out ageing toxins, repairing cellular damage, rewiring his very genome.

His work continued to be absorbing, and when he had spare time he immersed himself in studies. All the crew were generalists to some degree, but the ten new Elders were expected to be a repository of memory and wisdom far beyond a human lifespan. So they all studied everything, and they learned from each other.

Rusel began with the disciplines he imagined would be most essential in the future. He studied medicine; anthropology, sociology and ethics; ecosynthesis and all aspects of the Ship's life-support machinery; the workings of the Ship's propulsion systems; techniques of colonisation; and the geography of the Galaxy and its satellites. He also buttonholed Andres herself and soaked up her knowledge of human history. Meanwhile, Qax-derived nano-systems were so prevalent throughout the Ship that Rusel's own expertise was much in demand.

His days passed in a dream, as if time itself flowed differently for him now. His major goal continued to be to use up as much of his conscious time as possible with work. The studying was infinitely expandable, and very satisfying to his naturally acquisitive mind. He found he was able to immerse himself in esoteric aspects of one discipline or another for days on end, as if he was an abstract intellect, almost forgetting who he was.

The Elders' placid lives were not without disturbance, however. The Qax biotechnology was far from perfect. In the first year of treatment one man suffered kidney failure; he survived, but had to be taken out of the programme.

And it was a great shock to all the Elders when geneticist Ruul himself succumbed to a ferocious cancer, as the technological rebuilding of his cells went awry.

The day after Ruul's death, as the Elders adjusted to the loss of his competence and dry humour, Rusel decided he needed a break. He walked out of the Elders' huddled quarters and through the body of the Ship, heading for the area where his brother had set up his own home with Tila.

On all the Ship's cylindrical decks, the interior geography had been filled by corridors and cabins, clustered in concentric circles around little open plazas – 'village squares'. Rusel knew the social theory: the Ship was supposed to be loosely partitioned into village-sized communities, but he quickly got lost in the detail; the layout of walls and floors and false ceilings was changed again and again as the crew sorted out their environment.

At last he came to the right doorway on the right corridor. He was about to knock when a boy, aged about five with a shock of thick black hair, rocketed out of the open door and ran between Rusel's legs. The kid wore a bland Ship's-issue coverall, long overdue for recycling judging by its grime.

This must be Tomi, Rusel thought, Diluc's eldest. Child and Elder silently appraised each other. Then the kid stuck out his tongue and ran back into the cabin.

In a moment Diluc came bustling out of the door, wiping his hands on a towel. 'Look, what in Lethe's going on— Rusel! It's you. Welcome, welcome!'

Rusel embraced his brother. Diluc smelt of baby sick, cooking and sweat, and Rusel was shocked to see a streak of grey in his brother's hair. Perhaps Rusel had been locked away in his studies longer than he had realised.

Diluc led Rusel into his home. It was a complex of five small interconnected cabins, including a kitchen and bathroom. Somebody had been weaving tapestries; gaudy, space-filling abstract patterns filled one wall.

Rusel sat on a sofa adapted from an acceleration couch, and accepted a slug of some kind of liquor. He said, 'I'm sorry I frightened Tomi. I suppose I've let myself become a stranger.'

Diluc raised an eyebrow. 'Two things about that. Not so much "stranger" as "strange".' He brushed his hand over his scalp.

Rusel involuntarily copied the gesture, and felt bare skin. He had long forgotten that the first side-effect of the pharaoh treatment had been the loss of his hair; his head was as bald as Andres's. Surrounded all day by the other Elders, Rusel had got used to it, he supposed. He said dryly, 'Next time I'll wear a wig. What's the second thing I got wrong?'

'That isn't Tomi. Tomi was our first. He's eight now. That was little Rus, as we call him. He's five.'

'*Five?*' But Rusel had attended the baby Rusel's naming ceremony. It seemed like yesterday.

'And now we're due for another naming. We've missed you, Rus.'

Rusel felt as if his life was slipping away. 'I'm sorry.'

Tila came bustling in, with an awestruck little Rus in tow, and an infant in her arms. She too seemed suddenly to have aged; she had put on weight, and her face was lined by fine wrinkles. She said that Tomi was preparing a meal – of course Uncle Rusel would stay to eat, wouldn't he? – and she sat down with the men and accepted a drink.

They talked of inconsequentials, and of their lives.

Diluc, having stormed out of Andres's informal council, had become something of a leader in his own new community. Andres had ordered that the two-hundred-strong crew should be dispersed to live in close-knit 'tribes' of twenty or so, each lodged in a 'village' of corridors and cabins. There were to be looser links between the tribes, for such purposes as finding marriage or breeding partners. Thus the Ship was united in a single 'clan'. Andres said this social structure was the most common form encountered among humans 'in the wild', as she put it, all the way back to pretechnological days on Earth, and was the most likely to be stable in the long run. Whether or not that was true, things had stayed stable so far.

Andres had also specified the kind of government each tribe should aspire to. In such a small world each individual should be cherished for her unique skills, and for the value of the education invested in her. People were interdependent, said Andres, and the way they governed themselves should reflect that. Even democracy wouldn't do, as in a society of valued individuals the subjection of a minority to the will of a majority must be a bad thing. So Diluc's tribe ran by consensus.

'We talk and talk,' Diluc said with a rueful grin, 'until we all agree. Takes hours, sometimes. Once, the whole of the night watch.'

Tila snorted. 'Don't tell me you don't like it that way. You always did like the sound of your own voice!'

The most important and difficult decisions the tribe had to make concerned reproduction, Most adults settled down into more-or-less monogamous marriages. But there had to be a separation between marriages for companionship and liaisons for reproduction; the gene pool was too small to allow matings for such trivial reasons as love.

Diluc showed Rusel a draft of a 'social contract' he was preparing to capture all this. 'First, on reaching adulthood you submit yourself to the needs of the group as a whole. For instance your choice of career depends on what we need as much as what you want to do. Second, you agree to have kids only as the need allows. If we're short of the optimum population level, you might have three or four or five, whether you want them or not, to bring up the numbers; if we're over the target, you might have none at all and die childless. Third, you agree to postpone parenthood for as long as possible, and to keep working as long as possible. That way you maximise the investment the tribe has made in educating you. Fourth, you can select your own breeding-spouse, who *may* be the same as your companionship-spouse—'

'We were lucky,' Tila said fervently.

'But she can't be closer than a second cousin. And you have to submit to having your choice approved by the Elders. That's you.' He grinned at Rusel. 'Your match will be screened for genetic desirability, and to maximise the freshness of the gene pool – all of that. And finally, if despite everything you're unlucky enough to have been born with some inheritable defect that might, if propagated, damage the Ship's chances of completing its mission, you agree not to breed at all. Your genetic line stops with you.'

Rusel frowned. 'That's eugenics.'

Diluc shrugged. 'What else can we do?'

Diluc hadn't studied Earth history, as Elder-educated Rusel now had, and without that perspective, Rusel realised, that word carried for him none of the horrific connotations it had once borne. As Diluc had implied, they had little choice anyhow given the situation they were in. Besides, eugenics through arranged couplings was lower-tech than genetic engineering: more future-proofing.

Rusel studied the draft contract. 'And what happens if somebody breaks the rules?'

Diluc was uncomfortable; suddenly Rusel was aware that he was an Elder, as well as this man's brother. 'We'll cross that bridge when we come to it,' Diluc said. 'Look, Rus, we don't have police here, and we don't have room for jails. Besides, everybody really is essential to the community as a whole. We can't coerce. We work by persuasion; we hope that such situations will be easily resolved.'

Diluc talked of personal things too: of the progress of his boys at school, how Tomi had always hated the hour's wall-cleaning he had to put in each day, while little Rus loved it for the friends he was making.

'They are good kids,' Rusel said.

'Yes. And you need to see more of them,' Diluc said pointedly. 'But, you know, Rus, they're not like us. They are the first Shipborn generation. They are *different*. To them, all our stories of Port Sol and Canis Major are so many legends of places they will never see. This Ship is *their* world, not ours: we, born elsewhere, are aliens here. You know, I keep thinking we've bitten off more than we can chew. For all Andres's planning, already things are drifting. No wonder generation starships always fail!'

Rusel tried to respond to their openness by giving them something of himself. But he found he had little to say. His mind was full of studying, but there was very little *human* incident in his life. It was if he hadn't been alive at all, he thought with dismay.

Diluc was appalled to hear of Ruul's death. 'That pompous geneticist – I suppose in a way it's fitting he should be the first to go. But don't let it take you, brother.' Impulsively he crossed to Rusel and rested his hand on his brother's shoulder. 'You know, all this is enough for me: Tila, the kids, the home we're building together. It's good to know that our lives serve a higher goal, but *this* is all I need to make me happy. Maybe I don't have much imagination, you think?'

Or maybe you're more human than I am, Rusel thought. 'We must all make our choices,' he said.

Diluc said carefully, 'But you can still make a different choice.'

'What do you mean?'

He leaned forward. 'Why don't you give it up, Rus? This crappy old Qax nano-medicine, this dreadful anti-ageing – you're still young; you could come out of there, flush the shit out of your system, grow your hair back, find some nice woman to make you happy again . . .'

Rusel tried to keep his face expressionless, but he failed.

Diluc backed off. 'Sorry. You still remember Lora.'

'I always will. I can't help it.'

'We've all been through an extraordinary experience,' Tila said. 'I suppose we all react differently.'

'Yes.' Tila, he remembered, had left behind a child.

Diluc looked into his eyes. 'You never will come out, will you? Because you'll never be able to cast off that big sack of guilt on your back.'

Rusel smiled. 'Is it that obvious?'

Tila was a gracious hostess. She perceived his discomfort, and they began to talk of old times, of the days on Port Sol. But Rusel was relieved when Toml came in to announce that the meal was ready, relieved to hurry through the food and get away, relieved to shut himself away once more in the bloodless monastic calm of his studying.

## V

He would remember that difficult visit again, much later, when a boy came to find him.

As time passed, the Elders withdrew further from the crew. They requisitioned their own sealed-off living area. It was close to the Ship's axis where the artificial gravity was a little lower than further out, a sop to muscles and bones expected to weaken with the centuries. Andres humorously called this refuge the 'Cloister'. And the Elders were spared the routine chores, even the cleaning, to which the rest of the crew were subject. Soon it was hard to avoid the feeling that the crew were only there to serve the Elders.

Of course it was all part of Andres's grand social design that there should eventually be an 'awe gap', as she put it, between Elders and transients. But Rusel wondered if a certain distancing was inevitable anyhow. The differential ageing of transients and Elders became apparent surprisingly quickly. When an Elder met a transient she saw a face that would soon crumble with age and vanish, while the transient saw a mysteriously unchanging figure who would see events that transpired long after the transient was dead. Rusel watched as friendships dissolved, even love affairs evaporated, under this stress.

However the increasingly isolated Elders, thrown on each other's company, were no chummy club. They were all bright, ambitious people; they wouldn't have been filtered out for Andres's inner circle otherwise, and there was always a certain tension and bickering. Doctor Selur remarked sourly that it was like being stuck with a bunch of jealous academics, *for ever*.

But the Elders were also cautious of each other, Rusel thought. Always at the back of his mind was the thought that he would have to live with these people for a *long* time. So he strove not to make any enemies – and conversely not to get too close to anyone. Eternity with a lover was one thing, but with an *ex*-lover it would be hellish. Better that things were insipid, but tolerable.

Life settled down. In the calm of the Cloister, time passed smoothly, painlessly.

One day a boy came knocking timorously, asking for Rusel. He was aged about sixteen.

Rusel thought he recognised him. He had spent a long time on his own, and his social skills were rusty, but he tried to focus and greet the boy warmly. 'Tomi! It's so long since I saw you.'

The boy's eyes were round. 'My name is Poro, sir.'

Rusel frowned. 'But that day I came to visit – you made us all a meal, me and Diluc and Tila, while little Rus played . . .' But that was long ago, he told himself, he wasn't sure *how* long, and he fell silent.

The boy seemed to have been prepared for this. 'My name is Poro,' he said firmly. 'Tomi was—'

'Your father.'

'My *grand*father.'

So this was Diluc's great-grandson. Lethe, how long have I spent inside this box?

The boy was looking around the Cloister. His eyes were unblinking, his mouth pulled back in a kind of nervous grin. None of the Elders was hot on empathy, especially with transients, but suddenly Rusel felt as if he saw this place through this child's eyes.

The Cloister was like a library, perhaps. Or a hospital room. The Elders sat in their chairs or walked slowly through the silence of the room, their every step calculated to reduce the risk of harm to their fragile, precious bodies. It had been this way since long before Poro had been born, these musty creatures pursuing their cold interests. And I, who once loved Lora when she wasn't much older than this child, am part of this dusty stillness.

'What do you want, Poro?'

'Diluc is ill. He is asking for you.'

'Diluc . . . ?'

'Your brother.'

It turned out that Diluc was more than ill; he was dying.

So Rusel went with the boy, stepping outside the confines of the Cloister for the first time in years.

He wasn't at home out here any more. The original crew had died off steadily, following a demographic curve not terribly different to that they would have endured had they remained on Port Sol. Rusel had grown used to seeing faces he had known since childhood crumple with age and disappear before him. Still, it had been a shock when that first generation reached old age – and, since many of them had been around the same age at launch, their deaths came in a flood.

He knew none of the faces of the younger transients. Everything about the new generations was *different*: the way they rebuilt the Ship's internal architecture, their manner with each other, the way they wore their hair – even their language, which was full of a guttural slang. The transients knew him, though, even the youngest. They stared at him with curiosity, or irreverence – or, worst of all, awe.

The basic infrastructure of the Ship itself, of course, remained unchanged. In a way he came to identify with that level of reality much more than with the flickering, fast-paced changes wrought by the transients. Though his senses were slowly dulling – the Qax treatment had slowed his ageing but not stopped it entirely – he felt he was becoming more attuned to the Ship's subtle vibrations and noises, its mechanical moods and joys. Transients came and went, fiddling with the partitions, and the other Elders were awkward old cusses, but the Ship itself was his constant friend, demanding only his care.

As they walked he saw that the boy had a bruise on his forehead. 'What happened to you?'

'Punishment.' Poro averted his eyes, ashamed. One of his teachers had whacked him with a ruler for 'impudence', which turned out to mean asking too-deep questions.

A paradox was emerging in the philosophy of education aboard the Ship. It had been quickly found that learning needed to be restrictive, and that curiosity couldn't be allowed to go unchecked. The students had to be bright and informed enough to be able to maintain the Ship's systems. But there was no room for expansion or innovation. There was unusually only one way to do things: you learned it that way.

It was necessary, Rusel knew. You couldn't have people tinkering. So you learned only what you needed to know, and were taught not to ask any more, not to explore. But he didn't like the idea of battering students into submission for the 'crime' of curiosity. Perhaps he would have a word with Andres about it, get a new policy formulated.

They reached Diluc's corridor-village.

Before he could see his brother he had to be met by a series of tribe worthies. Burly men and women in drab Ship's-issue clothing, they gathered with solemn expressions. Their greetings were lengthy and complicated. The transients seemed to be evolving elaborate rituals to be used on every social occasion: meeting, parting, taking meals. Rusel could see the value of such rituals, which used up time, and reduced social friction. But it was hard to keep up with the ever-changing rules. The only constant was that these politeness games always got more elaborate – and it was very easy to get something wrong and give offence.

The worthies looked concerned at the prospective loss of Diluc, as well they might.

Andres's imposition of 'rule-by-consensus' had been less than effective. In some of the Ship's dozen or so tribes, there was endless jaw-jaw that paralysed decision-making. Elsewhere strong individuals had begun to grasp power, more or less overtly. Andres wasn't too concerned as long as the job got done, the basic rules obeyed: whoever was in command among the transients had to get the approval of the Elders anyhow, and so Andres and her team were still able to exert a moderating influence.

The situation in Diluc's tribe had been more subtle, though. As the brother of an Elder Diluc had had a unique charisma, and he had used that power to push his peers to conclusions they might not otherwise have reached. He had been a leader, but of the best sort, Rusel thought, leading from the back, invisibly. Now he was about to be taken away, and his people knew they would miss him.

With the worthies out of the way, the Elder was presented to Diluc's children, grandchildren, great-grandchildren. All of them went through more elaborate transient-to-Elder rituals, even the smallest children, with an unsmiling intensity Rusel found disturbing.

At last, with reluctance, he entered Diluc's apartment. The rooms were much as he remembered them, though the tapestries on the wall had changed.

Tila was still alive, though she was bent, her hair white, and her face a crumpled mask. 'Thank you for coming,' she whispered, and she took Rusel's hands in her own. 'There are so few of us left, you know, so few not Shipborn. And he did keep asking for you.'

Rusel pressed her hand, reserved, awkward. He felt out of practice with people, with emotions; before this broken-hearted old woman he felt utterly inadequate.

Diluc himself lay on a bed, covered by a worn blanket. Rusel was shocked by how his brother had imploded with age. And he could see, even through the blanket, the swelling of the stomach tumour that was killing him.

He had thought Diluc was sleeping. But his brother opened one eye. 'Hello, Rusel,' he said, his voice a croak. 'You bastard.'

'I'm sorry—'

'You haven't been here in fifty years.'

'Not that long.'

'Fifty years! *Fifty years!* It's not as if—' He broke up in coughing. 'As if it's that big a Ship . . .'

They talked, as they had talked before. Diluc told rambling anecdotes about his grandchildren and great-grandchildren, all properly genetically selected, all wonderful kids.

Rusel had to tell him of a cull of the Elders.

It had had a variety of causes, according to Doctor Selur, but Andres had sniffed at that. 'I've seen it before. Call it a death wish,' she had said. 'You reach an age where your body knows it's time to die. You accept it. Maybe it's some kind of neural programming, a comfort as we face the inevitable.' She cackled; she was ageing too, and was now toothless. 'The Qax treatments don't do anything about it. And it

409

carries away more would-be immortals than you'd imagine. Strange, isn't it? That longevity should turn out to be a matter of the mind as much as the body.'

Rusel had spent some years in faint trepidation, wondering if and when his own dark-seeking mental programming might kick in. But it never did, and he wondered if he had some unsuspected strength – or, perhaps, a deficiency.

Now Diluc grimaced. 'So even immortals die.' He reached out his hand. Rusel took it; the bones were frail, the flesh almost vanished. 'Look after them,' Diluc said.

'Who?'

'Everybody. *You* know. And look after yourself.' He looked up at his brother, and Rusel saw pity in his brother's eyes – pity for *him*, from a withered, dying man.

He could bear to stay only a few minutes more. He would never see his brother again.

He tried to talk over his feelings about Diluc's death with the Captain. But Andres was dismissive. 'Diluc was a coward who shunned his duty,' she said. 'Anyhow, better when the first crew have all gone. *They* always saw us as peers, to some extent. So they resisted our ideas, our leadership; it was natural. We're totally alien to the new sort, and that will make them more malleable.

'And the new lot never suffered the trauma of seeing Port Sol trashed before their eyes. The psychological trauma ran deep, Rusel; you aren't the only one . . . This new batch are healthier, adjusted to the environment of the Ship, because they've known nothing else. When there's only them left, we'll be able to get things shaken down properly around here at last. You'll see.'

With relief Rusel returned to his studies, away from the complications of humanity. Once more time flowed smoothly past him, and that difficult day receded down the dimming corridors of his memory.

No more relatives came to see him, ever again.

## VI

'. . . Rusel. Rusel!' The voice was harsh – Andres's voice.

Sleep was deep these days, and it took him an age to emerge. And as he opened himself to the light he swam up through layers of dream and memory, until he became confused about what was real and what wasn't. He always knew *where* he was, of course, even in his deepest sleep. He was on the Ship, his drifting tomb. But he could never remember *when* he was.

He tried to sit up. The Couch responded to his feeble movements, and its back smoothly lifted him upright. He peered around in the dim, golden light of the Cloister. There were three Couches, great bulky mechanical devices half bed and half medical support system: only three, because only three of the Elders stayed alive.

Somebody was moving around him. It was a transient, of course, a young woman, a nurse. He didn't recognise her; she was new since he'd last been awake. She kept her eyes averted, and her hands fluttered through an elaborate greetings-with-apology ritual. He dismissed her with a curt gesture; you could eat up your entire day with such flim-flam.

Andres was watching him, her eyes sharp in her ruin of a face. She looked like a huge bug in her cocoon of blankets.

'Well?' he snapped.

'You are drooling,' she said mildly. 'Not in front of the transients, Rusel.'

Irritated, he wiped his chin with his sleeve.

'Oh,' she said, her tone unchanged, 'and Selur died.'

That news, so casually delivered, was like a punch in the throat. He turned clumsily, weighed down by blankets and life-sustaining equipment. The doctor's Couch was surrounded by transients who were removing her mummy-like body. Working in silence, cautiously, reverently, they were trembling, he saw dimly.

'I never did like her much,' Rusel said.

'You've said that before. Many times.'

'I'll miss her, though.'

'Yes. And then there were two. Rusel, we need to talk. We need a new strategy to deal with the transients. We're supposed to be figures of awe. Look at us. Look at poor Selur! We can't let them see us like this again.'

He glanced cautiously at the transient nurses.

'Don't worry,' Andres said. 'They can't understand. Linguistic drift. I don't think we should allow transients in here any more. The machines can sustain us. Lethe knows there are enough spare parts, now we have so many empty Couches! What I suggest is—'

'Stow it,' he said crossly. 'You're always the same, you old witch. You always want to jam a solution down my throat before I even know what the problem is. Let me gather my thoughts.'

'Stow it, stow it,' she parroted, grotesquely.

'Shut up.' He closed his eyes to exclude her, and laid back in his Couch. Through the implant in the back of his skull he allowed data from his body, the Ship, and the universe beyond filter into his sensorium.

His body first, of course, the slowly failing biomachinery that had become his prison. The good news was that, more than two centuries after his brother's death, his slow ageing had bottomed out. Since he had last checked – Lethe, all of a month ago, it seemed like yesterday, how long had he slept this time? – nothing had got significantly worse. But he was stuck in the body of a ninety-year-old man, and a frail old man at that. He slept almost all the time, his intervals of lucidity ever more widely separated, while the Couch fed him, removed his waste, gently turned him to and fro and manipulated his stick-thin limbs. Oh, and every few weeks he received a blood transfusion, an offering to the Elders from the grateful transients outside the Cloister. He may as well have been a coma victim, he thought grumpily.

His age was meaningless, his condition boring. Briskly he moved on.

His Virtual viewpoint roamed through the Ship. Despite the passage of centuries, the physical layout of the corridor-village that had been Diluc's was the same, save for detail, the same knots of corridors around the 'village square'. But the people had changed, as they always did, youth blossoming, old age crumbling.

The Autarch he remembered from his last inspection was still in place. He was a big bruiser who called himself Ruul, in subtle defiance of various inhibitions against taking the name of an Elder, even one long dead. He at least didn't look to have aged much since Rusel's last inspection. Flanked by two of his wives, Ruul received a queue of supplicants, all seeking the Autarch's 'wisdom' concerning some petty problem or other. Ruul's judgements were brisk and efficient, and as Rusel listened – though the time-drifted language was hard to decipher – he couldn't spot any immediate errors of doctrine in the Autarch's summary harshness.

He allowed his point of view to move on.

He watched the villagers go about their business. Four of them were scrubbing the walls clean of dirt, as they took turns to do every day.

Two plump-looking worthies were discussing a matter of etiquette, their mannerisms complex and time-consuming. There were some new bits of artwork on the walls, many of them fool-the-eye depth-perspective paintings, designed to make the Ship's corridors look bigger than they were. One woman was tending a 'garden' of bits of waste polymer, combing elaborate formations into it with a small metal rake. These transients, Shipborn for generations, had never heard of Zen gardens; they had rediscovered this small-world art form for themselves.

A little group of children was being taught to disassemble and maintain an air-duct fan; they chanted the names of its parts, learning by rote. They would be taught nothing more, Rusel knew. There was no element of *principle* here: nothing about how the fan as a machine worked, or how it fitted into the greater systems of the Ship itself. You only learned what you needed to know.

As he surveyed the village, statistics rolled past his enhanced vision in a shining column. Everything was nominal, if you took a wider perspective. Maintenance routines were being kept up satisfactorily. Reproduction rules, enforced by the Autarch and his peers in the other villages, were largely being adhered to, and there was a reasonable genetic mix.

The situation was stable. But in Diluc's village, only the Autarch was free.

Andres's uncharacteristically naïve dream of respectful communities governing themselves by consensus had barely outlasted the death of Diluc. In the villages strong characters had quickly taken control, and in most cases had installed themselves and their families as hereditary rulers. Andres had grumbled at that, but it was an obviously stable social system, and in the end the Elders, in subtle ways, lent the Autarchs their own mystical authority.

The Autarchs were slowly drifting away from their subject populations, though.

Some 'transients' had always proven to be rather longer-lived than others. It seemed that the Qax's tampering with the genomes of their pharaohs had indeed been passed on to subsequent generations, if imperfectly, and that gene complex, a tendency for longevity, was gradually expressing itself. Indeed the Autarchs actively sought out breeding partners for themselves who came from families that showed such tendencies.

So, with time, the Autarchs and their offspring were ageing more slowly than their transient subjects.

It was just natural selection, argued Andres. People had always acquired power so that their genes could be favoured. Traditionally you would propagate your genes by doing your best to outbreed your subjects. But if you were an Autarch, in the confines of the Ship, what were you to do? There was obviously no room here for a swarm of princes, bastards or otherwise. Besides, the Elders' genetic-health rules wouldn't allow any such thing. So the Autarchs were seeking to dominate their populations with their own long lives, not numbers of offspring.

Andres seemed to find all this merely intellectually interesting, a working-out of genetic games theory. Rusel wondered what would happen if this went on.

He continued his random wandering. Everybody was busy, intent on their affairs. Some even seemed happy. But it all looked drab to Rusel, the villagers dressed in colourless Ship's-issue clothing, their lives bounded by the polished-smooth bulkheads of the Ship. Even their language was dull, and becoming duller. The transients had no words for 'horizon' or 'sky' – but as if in compensation they had over forty words describing degrees of love.

He allowed his consciousness to return to his own body. When he surfaced, he found Andres watching him, as she so often did.

'We need a new way to interface with the transients,' she said again. 'Some of the Autarchs are tough customers, Rusel. If they start to believe we're weak – for instance, if we sleep for three days before delivering the answer to the simplest question—'

'I understand. We can't let the transients see us.' He sighed, irritated. 'But what else can we do? Delivering edicts through disembodied voices isn't going to wash. If they don't see us they will soon forget who we are.' 'Soon', in the language of the Elders, meaning in another generation or two.

'Right,' she snapped. 'So we have to repersonalise our authority. What do you think of this?' She gestured feebly, and a Virtual coalesced in the air over her head.

It showed Rusel. Here he was as a young man, up to his elbows in nanofood banks, labouring to make the Ship sound for its long journey. Here he was as a young-ish Elder, bald as ice, administering advice to grateful transients. There were even images of him from the vanishingly remote days before the launch, images of him with a smiling Lora.

'Where did you get this stuff?'

She sniffed. 'The Ship's log. Your own archive. Come on, Rusel, we hardly have any secrets from each other after all this time! Pretty girl, though.'

'What are you intending to do with this?'

'We'll show it to the transients. We'll show you at your best, Rusel, you at the peak of your powers, you walking the same corridors they walk now – you as a human being, yet *more* than human. That's what we want: engagement with their petty lives, empathy, yet awe. We'll put a face to your voice.'

He closed his eyes. It made sense, of course; Andres's logic was grim, but always valid. 'But why me? It would be better if both of us—'

'That wouldn't be wise,' she said. 'I wouldn't want them to see me die.'

It took him a while to work out that she meant that she, Andres, the first of the Elders, was failing at last. Rusel found this impossible to take in: her death would be to have a buttress of the universe knocked away. 'But you won't see the destination,' he said peevishly, as if she was making a bad choice.

'No,' she said hoarsely. 'But the *Mayflower* will get there! Look around, Rusel. The Ship is functioning flawlessly. Our designed society is stable and doing its job of preserving the bloodlines. And *you*, you were always the brightest of all. You will see it through. That's enough for me.'

It was true, Rusel supposed. Her design was fulfilled; the Ship and its crew were working now just as Andres had always dreamed they should. But only two hundred and fifty years had worn away, only *half of one per cent* of the awesome desert of time he must cross to reach Canis Major – and now, it seemed, he was going to have to make the rest of that journey alone.

'No, not alone,' said Andres. 'You'll always have the Ship . . .'

Yes, the Ship, his constant companion. Suddenly he longed to escape from the endless complications of humanity and immerse himself in its huge technological calm.

He lay back in his Couch and allowed his mind to roam once more. This time his awareness drifted away from the bright warm human bubble at the Ship's heart, out through the crowded torus of the hull to the realm of the pulsing ramjet engines, the wispy gravitational wings behind which the Ship sailed, and the vast spaces beyond. The Ship had covered only a fraction of its epic journey, but already it was climbing out of the galactic plane and the Core, the crowded heart of the Galaxy, rose like a sun from the dust-strewn lanes of the spiral arms. It was a stunning, comforting sight.

By the time he came back from his intergalactic dreaming, Andres was gone, her Couch disassembled for spare parts, her body removed to the cycling tanks.

## VII

Rusel was woken from his long slumber by the face of a boy, a face twisted with anger – an anger directed at *him*.

In retrospect Rusel should have seen the rebellion coming. All the indicators had been there: the drift of the transients' social structures, the gathering tensions. It was bound to happen.

But it was so hard for him to pay attention to the brief lives of these transients, their incomprehensible language and customs, their petty concerns and squabbling. After all, Hilin was a boy of the forty-fifth generation since launch: *forty-five generations*. Lethe, nearly a thousand years . . .

The exploits of Hilin, though, forced themselves on his attention.

Hilin was sixteen years old when it all began. He had been born in Diluc's corridor-village.

By now the Autarchs of the different villages had intermarried to form a seamless web of power. They lived on average twice as long as their subjects, and had established a monopoly on the Ship's water supply. A water empire ruled by gerontocrats: their control was total.

Hilin was not one of the local Autarch's brood; his family were poor and powerless, like all the Autarch's subjects. But they seemed to accept their lot. As he played in corridors whose polymer floors were rutted by generations of passing feet, Hilin emerged as a bright, happy child. He seemed compliant when he was young, cheerfully swabbing the bulkheads when it was his turn, and accepting the cuffs of his teachers when he asked impudent questions.

He had always been oddly fascinated by the figure of Rusel himself – or rather the semi-mythical presence portrayed to the villagers through the cycling Virtual storyboards. Hilin soaked up the story of the noble Elder who had been forced to choose between a life of unending duty and his beloved Lora, eventually becoming an undying model to those he ruled.

As he had grown, Hilin had flourished educationally. At fourteen he was inducted into an elite caste. As intellectual standards declined, literacy had largely been abandoned, and ancient manuals had anyhow crumbled to dust. So these monkish thinkers now committed to memory every significant commandment regarding the workings of the Ship and their own society. You would start on this vital project at fourteen, and wouldn't expect to be done until you were in your fifties, by which time a new generation of rememberers was ready to take over anyhow.

Rusel dryly called these patient thinkers Druids: he wasn't interested in the transients' own names for themselves, which would change in an eye-blink generation anyhow. He had certainly approved of this practice when it emerged. All this endless memorising was a marvellous way to use up pointless lives – and it established a power-base to rival the Autarchs.

Again Hilin had flourished, and he passed one Druidic assessment after another. Even a torrid romance with Sale, a girl from a neighbouring village, didn't distract him from his studies.

When the time came, the couple asked their families for leave to form a companionship-marriage, which was granted. They went to the Autarch for permission to have children. To their delight, it turned out their genetic make-ups, as mapped in the Druids' capacious memories, were compatible enough to allow this too.

But even so the Druids forbade the union.

Hilin, horrified, learned that this was because of the results of his latest Druidic assessment, a test of his general intelligence and potential. He had failed, not by posting too low a score, but too *high*.

Rusel, brooding, understood. The eugenic elimination of weaknesses had in general been applied wisely. But under the Autarch-Druid duopoly, attempts were made to weed out the overbright, the curious – anybody who might prove rebellious. So, if you were bright, you mustn't be allowed to breed. Rusel would have stamped out this practice, had he even noticed it. If this went on, the transient population would become passive, listless, easily manipulated by the Autarchs and the Druids, but useless for the mission's larger purposes.

It was too late for Hilin. He was banned from ever seeing his Sale again. And he was told by the Autarch's ministers that this was by order of the Elder himself, though Rusel, dreaming his life away, knew nothing about it.

After that Hilin spent long hours in the shrine-like enclosure where Rusel's Virtuals played out endlessly. He tried to understand. He told himself the Elder's wisdom surpassed his own; this severance from his lover must be for the best, no matter what pain it caused him. He even tried to draw comfort from what he saw as parallels between his own doomed romance and Rusel and his lost Lora. But understanding didn't come, and his bewilderment and pain soon blossomed to resentment – and anger.

In his despair, he tried to destroy the shrine of the Elder.

As punishment, the Autarch locked him in a cell for two days. Hilin emerged from his confinement outwardly subdued, inwardly ready to explode.

Rusel would later castigate himself for failing to see the dangers in the situation. But it was so hard to see anything at all now.

His central nervous system was slowly deteriorating, so the Couch informed him. He could still move his arms and legs – he could still walk, even, with a frame – but he felt no sensation in his feet, nothing but the faintest ache in his fingertips. As pain and pleasure alike receded, he felt he was coming loose from the world. When he surfaced into lucidity he was often shocked to find a year had passed like a day, as if his sense of time was becoming logarithmic.

And meanwhile, as he became progressively disconnected from the physical world, his mind was undergoing a reconstruction of its own. After a thousand years his memories, especially the deepest, most precious memories of all, were, like the floors of the Ship's corridors, worn with use; he was no longer sure if he *remembered*, or if he only had left memories of memories.

If he couldn't rely even on memory, if he came adrift from both present and past, what was he? Was he even human any more? Certainly the latest set of transients meant less than nothing to him: why, each of them was made up of the atoms and molecules of her ancestors, cycled through the Ship's systems forty times or more, shuffled and reshuffled in meaningless combinations. They could not touch his heart in any way.

At least he thought so, until Hilin brought him the girl.

The two of them stood before Rusel's Virtual shrine, where they believed the Elder's consciousness must reside. Trying to match the

Elder's own timescales they stayed there for long hours, all but motionless. Hilin's face was set, pinched with anger and determination. She, though, was composed. .

At last Rusel's lofty attention was snagged by familiarity. The girl was taller than most of the transients, pale, her bones delicate. And her eyes were large, dark, somehow unfocused even as she gazed into unseen imaging systems.

*Lora.*

It couldn't be, of course! How could it? Lora had had no family on the Ship. And yet Rusel, half-dreaming, immersed in memory, couldn't take his eyes off her image.

As Hilin had planned.

And as Rusel gazed helplessly at 'Lora's' face, the uprising broke out all over the Ship. In every village the Autarchs and their families were turned out of their palatial cabins. The Autarchs, having commanded their short-lived flocks for centuries, were quite unprepared, and few resisted; they had no conception such an uprising was even possible. The old rulers and their peculiar children were herded together in a richly robed mass in the Ship's largest chamber, the upturned amphitheatre where Rusel had long ago endured the launch from Port Sol.

The revolt had been centrally planned, carefully timed, meticulously executed. Despite generations of selective breeding to eliminate initiative and cunning, the transients no longer seemed so sheepish, and in Hilin they had discovered a general. And it was over before the Elder's attention had turned away from the girl, before he had even noticed.

Now Hilin, king of the corridors, stood before the Elder's shrine. And he pulled at the face of the girl, the Lora look-alike. It had been a mask, just a mask; Rusel realised shamefully that with such a simple device the boy had manipulated the emotions of a being more than a thousand years old.

A bloody club in his hand, Hilin screamed his defiance at his undying god. The Cloister's systems translated the boy's language, after a thousand years quite unlike Rusel's. 'You allowed this to happen,' Hilin yelled. 'You allowed the Autarchs to feed off us like [*untranslatable – body parasites?*]. We wash the decks for them with our blood, while they keep water from our children. And you, you [*untranslatable – an obscenity?*] allowed it to happen. And do you know why?' Hilin stepped closer to the shrine, and his face loomed in Rusel's vision. 'Because you don't exist. Nobody has seen you in centuries – if they ever did! You're a lie, cooked up by the Autarchs to keep us in our place, that's what I think. Well, we don't believe in you any more, not in any of that [*untranslatable – faeces?*]. And we've thrown out the Autarchs. We are free!'

'Free' they were. Hilin and his followers looted the Autarchs' apartments, and gorged themselves on the food and water the Autarchs had hoarded for themselves, and screwed each other senseless in blithe defiance of genetic-health prohibitions. And not a single deck panel was swabbed down.

After three days, as the chaos showed no signs of abating, Rusel knew that this was the most serious crisis in the Ship's long history. He had to act. It took him another three days to get ready for his performance, three days mostly taken up with fighting with the inhibiting protocols of his medical equipment.

Then he ordered the Cloister door to open, for the first time in centuries. It actually stuck, dry-welded in place. It finally gave way with a resounding crack, making his entrance even more spectacular than he had planned.

But there was nobody around to witness his incarnation but a small boy, no more than five years old. With his finger planted firmly in one nostril, and his eyes round with surprise, the kid looked heartbreakingly like Tomi, Diluc's boy, long since dead and fed to the recycling banks.

Rusel was standing, supported by servomechanisms, gamely clutching at a walking frame. He tried to smile at the boy, but he couldn't feel his own face, and didn't know if he succeeded. 'Bring me the chief Druids,' he said, and a translation whispered in the air around him.

The boy yelled and fled.

The Druids actually knelt before him, covering their faces. He walked very cautiously among them, allowing them even to touch his robe. He wanted to be certain they accepted his reality, to smell the dusty tang of centuries on him. Maybe in their hearts these monkish philosophers, like Hilin, had never really believed in the Elder's existence. Well, now their messiah had suddenly reincarnated among them.

But Rusel himself saw them as if through a flawed lens; he could hear little, feel less, smell or taste nothing. It was like walking around in a skinsuit, he thought.

He was an angry god, though. The rules of Shipboard life had been broken, he thundered. And he didn't just mean the recent mess. There must be no more water empires, and no knowledge empires either: the Druids would have to make sure that *every* child knew the basic rules, of Ship maintenance and genetic-health breeding.

He ordered that the Autarchs should not be returned to their seats of power. Instead, the governing would be done, for this generation, by a Druid – he picked out one terrified-looking woman at random. As long as she ruled wisely and well, she would have the Elder's backing. On her death the people would select a successor, who could not be more closely related to her predecessor than second cousin. No more dynasties.

The old Autarchs and their brood, meanwhile, were to be spared. They would be shut away permanently in their amphitheatre prison, where there were supplies to keep them alive. Rusel believed they and their strange slow-growing children would die off; within a generation, a tick of time, that problem would go away. He had done his share of killing, he thought.

Then he sighed. The worst of it had still to be faced. 'Bring me Hilin,' he ordered.

They dragged in the corridor king, tied up with strips of cloth. He had been assaulted, Rusel saw; his face was battered and one arm seemed broken. This erstwhile rebel was already being punished for his blasphemy, then, by those who sought the favour of the Elder. But Hilin faced Rusel defiantly, strength and intelligence showing in his face. Rusel's scarred heart ached a little more, for strength and intelligence were the last features you wanted in a transient.

Hilin had to die, of course. His flayed corpse would be displayed before the shrine of the Elder, as a warning to future generations. But Rusel didn't have the courage to watch it done. He remembered the man in the electric-blue skinsuit: he always had been a coward, he thought.

As he returned to his Cloister, he looked back once more. 'And clean up this damn mess,' he said.

He knew it would take a long time, even on his timescales, before he managed to forget the contemptuous defiance on Hilin's young face. But Hilin went into the dark like all his transient ancestors, and soon his siblings and nieces and nephews and everybody who looked remotely like him went too, gone, all gone into the sink of time, and soon only Rusel was left alive to remember the rebellion.

Rusel would never leave the Cloister again.

## VIII

Some time after that, there was a decimating plague.

It was brought about by a combination of factors: a slow unmonitored build-up of irritants and allergens in the Ship's environment, and then the sudden emergence of a latent virus in a population already weakened. It was a multiple accident, impossible for the pharaoh designers of the Ship to plan away, for all their ingenuity. But given enough time – more than five thousand years now – such low-probability events inevitably occurred.

The surviving population crashed to the threshold of viability. For a few decades Rusel was forced to intervene, through booming commands, to ensure that the Ship was maintained at a base level, and that genetic-health protocols were observed and breeding matches planned even more carefully than usually.

The low numbers brought benefits, though. The Ship's systems were now producing a large surplus of supplies, and there was no possibility of any more water empires. Rusel considered, in his glacial way, establishing a final population at a lower level than before.

It intrigued him that the occurrence of the low-probability plague mirrored the restructuring of his own mental processes. The day-to-day affairs of the Ship, and the clattering of the transient generations, barely distracted him now. Instead he became aware of slower pulses, deeper rhythms far beneath any transient's horizon of awareness.

His perception of risk changed. His endless analysis of the Ship's systems uncovered obscure failure modes: certain parameter combinations that could disrupt the governing software, interacting failures among the nano-machines that still laboured over the Ship's fabric inside and out. Such failures were highly unlikely; he estimated the Ship might suffer significant damage once every ten thousand years or so. On Earth, whole civilisations had risen and fallen with greater alacrity than that. But *he* had to plan for such things, to prepare the Ship's defences and recovery strategies. The plague, after all, was just such a low-risk event, but given enough time it had come about.

The transients' behaviour, meanwhile, adjusted on its own time-scales.

Once every decade or so the inhabitants of Diluc's corridor-village would approach the shrine of the Elder, where the flickering Virtual still showed. One of them would dress up in a long robe and march behind a walking frame with exaggerated slowness, while the rest cowered. And then they would fall on a manikin and tear it to pieces. Rusel had watched such displays several times before he had realised what was going on: it was, of course, a ritualised re-enactment of his own last manifestation, the hobbling leader himself, the manikin poor overbright Hilin. Sometimes the bit of theatre would culminate in the flaying of a living human, which they must imagine he demanded; when such savage generations arose, Rusel would avert his cold gaze.

Meanwhile, in the village in which Hilin's doomed lover Sale had been born, the local transients were trying another tactic to win his favour. Perhaps it was another outcome of Hilin's clever exploits, or perhaps it had been inherent in the situation all along.

*Girls*, elfin girls with dark elusive eyes: as the generations ticked by, he seemed to see more of them running in the corridors, making eyes at muscular wall-scrubbing boys, dandling children on their knees. They were like cartoon versions of Lora: tall Loras and short, thin Loras and fat, happy Loras and sad.

It was selective breeding, if presumably unconscious, people turning themselves into replicas of the images in the Virtual. They were appealing directly to his own cold heart: if the Elder loved this woman so much, then choose a wife that looks like her, if only a little, and hope to have daughters with her delicate looks, and so win favour.

Rusel was simultaneously touched, and appalled. But he did not interfere. They could do what they liked, he told himself, as long as they got their jobs done.

Meanwhile in the old amphitheatre, on the other side of the barricade he had erected, the Autarchs and their long-lived families had not died out as Rusel had expected – indeed hoped. They had lived on. And as they inbred ferociously, their lives were stretched out longer and longer.

Again this made sense in terms of their heredity, he thought. In their cordoned-off compartment there was simply no room to expand their population. So the genes' best bet of propagating themselves into the future, always their only objective, was to stretch out the lives of their carriers. Adults in there now lived for centuries, and for the vanishingly few children born, childhood lasted decades.

Rusel found these creatures, with their blank eyes and wizened-faced children, peculiarly disturbing. On the other hand, he still couldn't bring himself to kill them off. Perhaps in them he saw a distorted reflection of himself.

There was one constant throughout the Ship. On both sides of the barrier the transients were clearly getting dumber.

As generations passed – and by now, for fear of repeating Hilin's fate, potential mates were repelled by any signs of higher-than-average intelligence – it was obvious that the transients were breeding themselves into stupidity. If anything the Autarchs' environment was less stimulating than that of their cousins in the rest of the Ship, and despite their slower generational cycle they were shedding their unnecessary intelligence with even more enthusiasm, perhaps a response to sheer boredom.

The transients kept the Ship working, however, and in their increasingly brutish liaisons followed the genetic-health mandates scrupulously. This puzzled Rusel: surely by now they could have no real understanding of *why* they were doing these peculiar things.

But he observed that when it came time to attract a mate the most vigorous deck-swabbers and cousin-deniers stood out from the crowd. It made sense: after all, a propensity to please the undeniable reality of the Elder was a survival characteristic, and therefore worth displaying if you had it, and worth preserving in your children's heredity. He filed away such observations and insights.

By now, nothing that happened inside the Ship's hull interested him as much as what happened outside.

He was thoroughly wired into the Ship, its electromagnetic and other equipment taking the place of his own failed biological senses. He cruised with it through the intergalactic gulf, feeling the tingle of dark-matter particles as they were swept into the Ship's gut, sensing the subtle caress of magnetic fields. It fascinated him to follow the million-year turning of the Galaxy, whose brilliant face continued to open up behind the fleeing Ship. Even the space between the galaxies was much more interesting than he had ever imagined. It wasn't a void at all. There was structure here, he saw, a complex webbing of the dark stuff that spanned the universe, a webbing in which galaxies were trapped like glowing flies. He learned to follow the currents and reefs of the dark matter which the Ship's gravitational maw greedily devoured.

He was alone with the galaxies, then, and with his own austere mind.

Once, just once, as he drifted in the dark, he heard a strange signal. It was cold and clear, like the peal of a trumpet, far off in the echoing intergalactic night. It wasn't human at all.

He listened for a thousand years. He never heard it again.

## IX

Andres came to him. He could see her face clearly, that worn-smooth expressionless skin. The rest of her body was a blur, a suggestion.

'Leave me alone, you nagging old witch,' he grumbled.

'Believe me, that would be my choice,' said Andres fervently. 'But there's a problem, Rusel. And you need to come out of your damn shell and sort it out.'

He longed for her to leave him, but he knew that wasn't an option. In a corner of his frayed mind he knew that this Virtual projection of his last companion, a synthesis of his own reflection and the Ship's systems, was an alarm, activated only when absolutely necessary.

'What kind of problem?'

'With the transients. What else? You need to take a look.'

'I don't want to. It hurts.'

'I know it hurts. But it's your duty.'

Duty? Had she said that, or had he? Was he awake, or dreaming? With time, everything blurred, every category, every boundary.

He was far beyond biology now, of course. It was only technology that kept him alive. With time, the Ship had infiltrated its treatments and systems deeper into the shell of what had been his body. It was as if he had become just another of the Ship's systems, like the air scrubbers or the water purifiers, just as old and balky, and just as much in need of endless tender loving care.

The decay of his central nervous system had proceeded so far that he wasn't sure if it returned any signals to the hardening nugget of his brain; he wasn't sure if he perceived the outside universe unfiltered at all. And even the walls of his consciousness were wearing away. He thought of his mind as a dark hall filled with drifting forms, like zero-gravity sculptures. These were his memories – or perhaps memories of memories, recycled, reiterated, edited and processed.

And *he* was here, a pinpoint awareness that flitted and flew between the drifting reefs of memory. At times, as he sailed through the abstraction of emptiness, free of memory or anticipation, indeed free

425

of any conscious thought save only a primal sense of *self*, he felt oddly free – light, unburdened, even young again. But whenever that innocent point settled into the dark tangle of a memory reef, the guilt came back, a deep muddy shame whose origins he had half-forgotten, and whose resolution he could no longer imagine.

He wasn't alone, however, in this cavernous awareness. Sometimes voices called from the dark. Sometimes there were even faces, their features softened, their ages indeterminate. Here was Diluc, his brother, or Andres, or Ruul or Selur or one of the others. He knew they were all long dead save for him, who lived on and on. He had vague memories of setting up some of these Virtual personas as therapy for himself, or as ways for the Ship to attract his attention – Lethe, even as company. But by now he wasn't sure what was Virtual and what was a dream, a schizoid fantasy of his rickety mind.

Lora was never there, however.

And Andres, the cold pharaoh who had become his longest-enduring companion, was his most persistent visitant.

'Nobody ever said this would be easy, Rusel.'

'You said that before.'

'Yes. And I'll keep on saying it until we get to Canis Major.'

'Canis Major? . . .' The destination. He'd forgotten about it again, forgotten that an end to all this even as a theoretical possibility might exist. The trouble was, thinking about such things as a beginning and an end made him aware of time, and that was always a mistake.

How long? The answer came to him like a whisper. Round numbers? Twenty thousand years gone. Twenty thousand years. It was ridiculous, of course.

'Rusel,' Andres snapped. 'You need to focus.'

'You're not even Andres,' he grumbled.

Her mouth was round with mock horror. 'Really? Oh, no! What an existential disaster for me.' She glared. 'Just do it, Rus.'

So, reluctantly, he gathered his scattered concentration, and sent his viewpoint out into the body of the Ship. He was faintly aware of Andres riding alongside him, a ghost at his shoulder.

He found the place he still thought of as Diluc's village. The framework of corridors and cabins hadn't changed, of course; it was impossible that it should. But even the non-permanent partitions that had once been built up and torn down by each successive generation of transients had been left unmoved since the last time he was here. Building things wasn't what people did any more.

He wandered into the little suite of rooms that had once been Diluc's home. There was no furniture. Nests were crammed into each corner of the room, disorderly heaps of cloth and polymer scraps. He had seen the transients take standard-issue clothing from the Ship's recycler systems and immediately start tearing it up with hands or teeth to make their coarse bedding. There was a strong stink of piss and shit, of blood and milk, sweat and sex, the most basic human biology. But the crew remained scrupulously clean. Every few days all this stuff would be swept up and carted off to the recycler bins.

This was the way people lived now. They nested in starship cabins.

Outside, the walls and partitions were clean, gleaming and sterile, as was every surface he could see, the floor and ceiling. One partition had been rubbed until it was worn so thin the light shone through it: another couple of generations and it would wear away altogether, he thought. The crew still kept up their basic duties; that had remained, while so much else had vanished.

But these latter transients were not crewing the Ship as his own generation once had, for conscious purposes. They were doing it for deeper reasons.

The transients competed in how well they did their chores in order to attract mates, and these selection pressures had, given time, sculpted the population. By now the transients were maintaining a starship's systems as bees had once danced, stags had locked antlers, and peacocks had spread their useless tails: *they were doing it for sex*, and the chance to procreate. As mind receded, Rusel thought, biology had taken over.

As long as they were doing it in the first place, Rusel didn't care. Besides, it worked in maintaining the ship. Sexual drivers seemed very effective in locking in behaviour with the precision required to keep the Ship's systems functioning: you could fix a ceiling ventilation grille with a show-off flourish or not, but you had to do it *exactly* correctly to impress the opposite sex, even if you didn't understand what it was for. Even when mind was gone, you had to do it right.

He heard weeping, not far away.

He let his viewpoint drift along the corridor, following the sound. He turned a corner, and came on the villagers.

There were perhaps twenty-five of them, adults and children. They were all naked, of course; nobody had worn clothes for millennia. Some of them had infants in their arms or on their backs. Squatting in the corridor, they huddled around a central figure, the woman who was doing the weeping. She was cradling something, a bloody scrap. The others reached out and stroked her back and scalp; some of them were weeping too, Rusel saw.

He said, 'Their empathy is obvious.'

'Yes. They've lost so much else, but not that.'

Suddenly their heads turned, all of them save the weeping woman, faces swivelling like antennae. Something had disturbed them – perhaps the tiny hovering drone that was Rusel's physical manifestation. Their brows were low, but their faces were still human, with straight noses and delicate chins. It was like a flower bed of faces, Rusel thought, turned up to his light. But their mouths were pulled back in fear-grins.

And every one of them looked like Lora, more or less, with that delicate, elfin face, even something of her elusive eyes. Of course they did: the blind filter of natural selection, operating for generations on this hapless stock, had long determined that though mind was no longer necessary, to look *this* way might soften the heart of the wizened creature who ruled the world.

The strange tableau of upturned Lora-faces lasted only a moment. Then the transients took flight. They poured away down the corridor, running, knuckle-walking, bounding off the walls and ceiling.

Andres growled, 'I'll swear they get more like chimps with every generation.'

In a few seconds they had gone, all save the weeping woman.

Rusel allowed his viewpoint to swim towards the woman. He moved cautiously, not wishing to alarm her. She was young – twenty, twenty-one? It was increasingly hard to tell the age of these transients; they seemed to reach puberty later each generation. This girl had clearly passed her menarche – in fact she had given birth, and recently: her belly was slack, her breasts heavy with milk. But her chest was smeared with blood, shocking bright crimson in the drab, worn background of the corridor. And the thing she was cradling was no child.

'Lethe,' said Rusel. '*It's a hand*. A child's hand. I think I'm going to throw up.'

'You no longer have the equipment to throw up. Take a closer look.'

A white stump of bone stuck out of a bloody mass of flesh. The hand had been severed at the wrist. And two tiny fingers had been almost stripped of flesh, ligament and muscle, leaving only tiny bones.

'That wrist,' Andres said pitilessly, 'has been bitten through. By *teeth*, Rusel. And teeth have been at work on those fingers as well. Think about it. With a bit of practice, you could take one of those little morsels between your incisors and just strip off the flesh and muscle—'

'Shut up! Lethe, Andres, I can see for myself. We always avoided cannibalism. I thought we beat that into their shrinking skulls hard enough.'

'So we did. But I don't think this is cannibalism – or rather, whatever did this wasn't *her* kind.'

Rusel elevated the viewpoint and cast around. He saw a trail of blood leading away from the woman, smeared along the walls and floor, quite unmistakable, as if something had been dragged away.

Andres said, 'I think our transients suddenly have a predator.'

'Not so suddenly,' Rusel said. A part of his scattered consciousness was checking over the Ship's logs, long ignored. This kind of incident had been going on for a couple of centuries. 'It's been rare before, once or twice a generation. Mostly it was the old who were taken, or the very young – vulnerable, dispensable, or replaceable. But now they seem to be upping the rate.'

'And making a dent in the transients' numbers.'

'Yes. You were right to bring me here.' This had to be resolved. But to do it, he thought with a deepening dread, he was going to have to confront a horror he had shut out of his awareness for millennia.

'I'm here with you,' Andres said gently.

'No, you're not,' he snapped. 'But I have to deal with this anyhow.'

'Yes, you do.'

His viewpoint followed the bloody trail as it wound through the corridor-villages of the transients. Broken in places, the trail slinked through shadows or through holes worn in the walls. It was the furtive trail of a hunter, he thought.

At last Rusel came to the bulkhead that cut the Ship in two, marking the limit of his transients' domain. He had long put out of his mind what lay beyond this wall: in fact, if he could have cut away the Ship's aft compartment and let the whole mess float off into space he would long ago have done so.

But there was a hole in the bulkhead, just wide enough to admit a slim body.

The bulkhead was a composite of metal and polymer, extremely tough, and a metre thick; the hole was a neat tunnel, not regular but smooth-walled, drilled right through. 'I can't believe they have tools,' he said. 'So how did they get through?'

'Teeth,' Andres said. 'Teeth and nails – and time, of which they have plenty. Remember what you're dealing with. Even if the bulkhead was made of diamond they'd have got through eventually.'

'I hoped they were dead.'

'Hope! Wishful thinking! That always was your weakness, Rusel. I always said you should have killed them off in the first place. They're just a drain on the Ship's resources.'

'I'm no killer.'

'Yes, you are—'

'And they are human, no less than the transients.'

'No, they're *not*. And now, it seems, they are *eating* our transients.'

His viewpoint drifted before the hole in the wall. Andres seemed to sense his dread; she didn't say anything.

He passed through the barrier.

He emerged in the upended chamber he still thought of as the amphitheatre, right at the base of the Ship. This was a big, bare volume, a cylinder set on its side. After the spin-up it had been used to pursue larger-scale reconstruction projects necessary to prepare the Ship for its long intergalactic voyage, and mounted on its floor and walls were the relics of heavy engineering, long abandoned: gantries, platforms of metal, immense low-gravity cranes like vast skeletons. Globe lights hovered everywhere, casting a yellow-white light complex with shadows. It was an oddly magnificent sight, Rusel thought, and it stirred memories of brighter, more purposeful days. On the wall of the chamber, which had been its floor, he could even make out the brackets which had held the acceleration couches on launch day.

Now, every exposed surface was corroded. Nothing moved. And that upturned floor, which Andres had turned transparent a mere year after the launch, was caked by what looked like rock. It was a hardened pack of faeces and cloth scraps and dirt, a wall of shit to block out the Galaxy.

At first, in this jungle of engineering, he couldn't make out anything living. Then, as he allowed the worn-out ambience of the place to wash over him, he learned to see.

They were like shadows, he thought, slim, upright shadows that flitted through the gantries, furtive, cautious. At times they looked human – clearly upright, bipedal, purposeful – though their limbs were spindly, their bellies distended. But then they would collapse to all fours and lope away with a bent gait, and that impression of humanity vanished. They didn't seem to be wearing clothes, any more than the transients did. But unlike the transients their bodies were coated with a kind of thick hair, dark brown, a fur.

Here and there hovering drones trailed the shambling creatures, carrying food and water. The creatures ignored these emissaries of the Ship that kept them alive.

Andres said grimly, 'I know you haven't wanted to think about these relics, Rusel. But the Ship has watched over them. They are provided with food, of course. Clothing, blankets and the like – they rip all that up to serve as nesting material, like the transients. They won't go to the supply hoppers as the transients will; drones have to bring them the stuff they need, and take out their waste. But they're really quite passive. They don't mind the drones, even when the drones clean them, or tend to wounds or sicknesses. They are used to being cared for by machines.'

'But what do they *do* all day?'

Andres laughed. 'Why, nothing. Nothing but eat the food we give them. Climb around the gantries a little, perhaps.'

'They must have some spark of curiosity, of awareness. The transients do! They're *people*.'

'Their ancestors used to be. Now they're quite mindless . . . There. Look. They are gathering at one of their feeding places. Perhaps we'll be able to see what they do.'

The feeding site was a shallow depression, worn into a floor of steel. Its base was smeared green and brown. A drone had delivered a cache of food to the centre of the pit, a pile of spheres and cylinders and discs, all sized for human hands, all brightly coloured.

From around the amphitheatre the animals came walking, loping, moving with the slow clumsiness of low gravity – and yet with an exaggerated care, Rusel thought, as if they were very fragile, very old. They gathered around the food pile. But they did not reach for the food; they just slumped down on the ground, as if exhausted.

Now smaller creatures emerged from the forest of gantries. They moved nervously, but just as cautiously as the larger forms. They must be children, Rusel thought, but they moved with no spontaneity or energy. They were like little old people themselves. There were far fewer children than adults, just a handful among perhaps fifty individuals.

It was the children who went to the food pile, broke off pieces of the brightly coloured fodder, and carried it to the adults. The adults greeted this service with indifference, or at best a snarl, a light blow on the head or shoulder. Each child servant went doggedly back to the pile for more.

'They're not particularly hygienic,' Rusel observed.

'No. But they don't have to be. Compared to the transients they have much tougher immune systems. And the Ship's systems keep the place roughly in order.'

Rusel said, 'Why don't the adults get the food themselves? It would be quicker.'

Andres shrugged. 'This is their way. And it is their way to eat another sort of food, too.'

At the very centre of the depression was a broad scar stained a deep crimson brown, littered with lumpy white shapes.

'That's blood,' Rusel said, wondering. 'Dried blood. And those white things—'

'Bones,' said Andres evenly. Rusel thought she seemed oddly excited, stirred by the degraded spectacle before her. 'But there's too much debris here to be accounted for by their occasional raids into transient country.'

Rusel shuddered. 'So they eat each other too.'

'No. Not quite. *The old eat the young*; mothers eat their children. It is their way.'

'Oh, Lethe . . .' Andres was right; Rusel couldn't throw up. But he was aware of his body, cradled by the concerned Ship, thrashing feebly in distress.

Andres said dispassionately, 'I don't understand your reaction.'

'I didn't know—'

'You should have thought it through – thought through the consequences of your decision to let these creatures live.'

'You are a monster, Andres.'

She laughed without humour.

Of course he knew what these animals were. They were the Autarchs – or the distant descendants of the long-lived, inbred clan who had once ruled over the transients. Over nearly twenty thousand years selection pressure had worked relentlessly, and the gene complex that had given them their advantage over the transients in the first place – genes for longevity, a propensity injected into the human genome by the Qax – had found full expression. And meanwhile, in the sterile nurture of this place, they had had even less reason to waste precious energy on large brains.

As time had passed they had lived longer and longer, but thought less and less. Now these Autarchs were all but immortal, and all but mindless.

'They're actually rather fascinating,' Andres said cheerfully. 'I've been trying to understand their ecology, if you will '

'Ecology? Then maybe you can explain how it can benefit a creature to treat its children so. Those young seem to be *farmed*. Life is about the preservation of genes: even in this artificial little world of ours, that remains true. So how does eating your kids help achieve that? . . . Ah.' He gazed at the hairy creatures before him. '*But these Autarchs are not mortal.*'

'Exactly. They lost their minds, but they stayed immortal. And when mind had gone, natural selection worked with what it found.'

Even for these strange creatures, the interests of the genes were paramount. But now a new strategy had to be worked out. It had been foreshadowed in the lives of the first Autarchs. There was no room to spread the genes by expanding the population – but if individuals could become effectively immortal, the genes could survive through them.

Andres said, 'But simple longevity wasn't enough. Even the longest-lived will die through some accident eventually. The genes themselves can be damaged, through radiation exposure for instance. Copying is safer! For their own preservation the genes need to see *some* children produced, and for some, the smartest and strongest, to survive.

'But, you see, living space is restricted here. The parents must compete for space against their own children. They don't *care* about the children. They use them as workers – or even, when there's an excess, as a cannibalistic resource . . . But there are always one or two children who fight their way through to adulthood, enough to keep the stock numbers up. In a way the pressure from the adults is a mechanism to ensure that only the smartest and strongest of the kids survive. It's a mixed strategy.'

'From the genes' point of view it's a redundancy mechanism,' Rusel said. 'That's the way an engineer would put it. The children are just a fail-safe.'

'Precisely,' Andres said.

It was biology, evolution: the destiny of the *Mayflower* had come down to this.

Rusel had brooded on the fate of his charges, and had studied how time had always shaped human history. And he had decided it was all a question of timescales.

The conscious purpose of the Ship had sustained its crew's focus for a century or so, until the first couple of generations, and the direct memory of Port Sol, had vanished into the past.

Millennia, though, were the timescale of historical epochs on Earth, over which empires rose and fell. His studies suggested that to sustain a purpose over such periods required the engagement of a deeper level of the human psyche: the idea of Rome, say, or a devotion to Christ. If the first century of the voyage had been an arena for the conscious, over longer periods the unconscious took over. Rusel had seen it himself, as the transients had become devoted to the idea of the Ship and its mission, as embodied by his own Virtual. Even Hilin's rebellion had been an expression of that cult of ideas. Call it mysticism: whatever, it worked over epochs of thousands of years.

That far, he believed, Andres and the other pharaohs had been able to foresee and plan for. But beyond that even they hadn't been able to imagine; Rusel had sailed uncharted waters.

And as time heaped up into *tens* of millennia, he had crossed a span of time comparable to the rise and fall, not just of empires, but of whole species. A continuity of the kind that kept the transients cleaning the walls over such periods could only come about, not through even the deepest layers of mind, but through much more basic biological drivers, like sexual selection: the transients cleaned for sex, not for any reason to do with the Ship's goals, for they could no longer comprehend such abstractions. And meanwhile natural selection had shaped his cradled populations, of transients and Autarchs alike.

Sometimes he felt queasy, perhaps even guilty, at the distorted fate to which generation upon generation had been subjected, all for the sake of a long-dead pharaoh and her selfish, hubristic dream. But individual transients were soon gone, their tiny motes of joy or pain soon vanishing into the dark. Their very brevity was comforting.

Of course, if biology was replacing even the deepest layers of mind as the shaping element in the mission's destiny, Rusel's own role became still more important, as the only surviving element of continuity, indeed of consciousness.

Whatever, there was no going back, for any of them.

Andres was still watching the Autarchs. 'You know, immortality, the defeat of death, is one of mankind's oldest dreams, But immortality doesn't make you a god. *You* have immortality, Rusel, but, save for your crutch the Ship, you have no power. And these – animals – have immortality, but nothing else.'

'It's monstrous.'

'Of course! Isn't life always? But the genes don't care. And in the Autarchs' mindless capering, you can see the ultimate logic of immortality: for an immortal, to survive, must in the end eat her own children.'

But everybody on this Ship was a child of this monstrous mother, Rusel thought, whose twisted longings had impelled this mission in the first place. 'Is that some kind of confession, pharaoh?'

Andres didn't reply. Perhaps she couldn't. After all this wasn't Andres but a Virtual, a software-generated comfort for Rusel's fading consciousness, at the limit of its programming. And any guilt he saw in her could only be a reflection of himself.

With an effort of will he dismissed her.

One of the adults, a male, sat up, scratched his chest, and loped to the centre of the feeding pit. The young fled at his approach. The male scattered the last bits of primary-colour food, and picked up something small and white. It was a skull, Rusel saw, the skull of a child. The adult crushed it, dropped the fragments, and wandered off, aimless, immortal, mindless.

Rusel withdrew, and sealed up the gnawed-through bulkhead. After that he set up a new barrier spanning the Ship parallel to the bulkhead, and opened up the thin slice of the vessel between the walls to intergalactic vacuum, so that nothing could come through that barrier. And he never again gave any thought to what lay on the other side.

## X

Twenty-five thousand years after the end of his world, Rusel heard that he was to be saved.

'Rusel. Rusel . . .'

Rusel wanted the voices to go away. He didn't need voices now – not Diluc's, not even Andres's.

He had no body, no belly, no heart; he had no need of people at all. His memories were scattered in emptiness, like the faint smudges that were the remote galaxies all around the Ship. And like the Ship he forged on into the future, steadily, pointlessly, his life empty of meaning. The last thing he wanted was *voices*.

But they wouldn't go away. With deep reluctance, he forced his scattered attention to gather.

The voices were coming from Diluc's corridor-village. Vaguely, he saw people there, near a door – the door where he had once been barrelled into by little Tomi, he remembered, in a shard of bright warm memory blown from the past – two people, by that same door.

People standing upright. People wearing clothes.

*They were not transients*. And they were calling his name into the air. With a mighty effort he pulled himself to full awareness.

They stood side by side, a man and a woman – both young, in their twenties, perhaps. They wore smart orange uniforms and boots. The man was clean-shaven, and the woman bore a baby in her arms.

Transients had clustered around them. Naked, pale, eyes wide with curiosity, they squatted on their haunches and reached up with their long arms to the smiling newcomers. Some of them were scrubbing frantically at the floor and walls, teeth bared in rictus grins. They were trying to impress the newcomers with their prowess at cleaning, the only way they knew how. The woman allowed the transients to stroke her child. But she watched them with hard eyes and a fixed smile. And the man's hand was never far away from the weapon at his belt.

It took Rusel a great deal of effort to find the circuits that would allow him to speak. He said, '*Rusel*. I am Rusel.'

As the disembodied voice boomed out of the air the man and woman looked up, startled, and the transients cowered. The newcomers looked at each other with delight. 'It's true,' said the man. 'It really is the *Mayflower*!' A translation whispered to Rusel.

The woman scoffed. 'Of course it's the *Mayflower*. What else could it be?'

Rusel said, 'Who are you?'

The man's name was Pirius, the woman's Torec.

'Are we at Canis Major?'

'No,' Pirius said gently.

These two had come from the home Galaxy – from Sol system itself, they said. They had come in a faster-than-light ship; it had overtaken the *Mayflower*'s painful crawl in a few weeks. 'You have come thirteen thousand light years from Port Sol,' Pirius said. 'And it took you more than twenty-five thousand years. It is a record for a generation starship! An astonishing feat.'

Thirteen thousand light years? Even now, the Ship had come only halfway to its intended destination.

Torec cupped the face of a transient girl in her hand – Lora's face. 'And,' Torec said, 'we came to find you.'

'Yes,' said Pirius, smiling. 'And your floating museum!'

Rusel thought that over. 'Then mankind lives on?'

Oh, yes, Pirius told him. The mighty Expansion from which the *Mayflower*'s crew had fled had burned its way right across the Galaxy. It had been an age of war; trillions had gone into the dark. But mankind had endured.

'And we won!' Pirius said brightly. Pirius and Torec themselves had been involved in some kind of exotic combat to win the centre of the Galaxy. 'It's a human Galaxy now, Rusel.'

'Human? But how are *you* still human?'

They seemed to understand the question. 'We were at war,' Pirius said. 'We couldn't afford to evolve.'

'The Coalition—'

'Fallen. Vanished. Gone. They can't harm you now.'

'And my crew?'

'We will take them home. There are places where they can be cared for. But, ah—'

Torec said, 'But the Ship itself is too big to turn around. Too much mass-energy. I'm not sure we can bring *you* back.'

Once he had seen himself, a stiff ageless man, through the eyes of Diluc's great-grandson Poro, through the eyes of a child. Now, just for an instant, he saw himself through the eyes of Pirius and Torec. A wizened, charred thing suspended in a webbing of wires and tubes.

That didn't matter, of course. 'Have I fulfilled my mission?'

'Yes,' Pirius said gently. 'You fulfilled it very well.'

He wasn't aware of Pirius and Torec shepherding the transients and Autarchs out of the Ship and into their own absurdly small craft. He wasn't aware of Pirius's farewell call as they shot away, back towards the bright lights of the human Galaxy, leaving him alone. He was only aware of the Ship now, the patient, stolid Ship.

The Ship – and one face, revealed to him at last: an elfin face, with distracted eyes, He didn't know if she was a gift of Pirius or even Andres, if she was outside his own head or inside. None of that seemed to matter when at last she smiled for him, and he felt the easing of a tension twenty-five millennia old, the dissolving of a clot of ancient guilt.

The Ship forged on into the endless dark, its corridors as clean and bright and empty as his thoughts.

*I knew Andres. I knew about the five Ships that sailed from Port Sol. I always wondered what happened to her.*

*Some of the Ships sailed on to even more exotic fates than her* Mayflower's. *But that's another story.*

*The conquest of the Galaxy was perhaps humanity's finest hour. The ministers, generals and Commissaries at the heart of the Coalition looked back on the immense achievement of their ideological government with, perhaps, justifiable pride.*

*But it was an irony that as soon as the victory was won, the Coalition lost its purpose, and its control.*

*And it was an irony, I thought, that a crude faith of child soldiers, outlawed by the Coalition, should not only outlive the Coalition itself but even shape the history that followed its demise.*

# BETWEEN WORLDS

## AD 27,152

I

'She wants to go home,' said the starship Captain.

'But she can't go home,' said the acolyte. Futurity's Dream was baffled by the very request, as if the woman who had locked herself inside a starship cabin, with a bomb, was making a philosophical mistake, a category error.

Captain Tahget said, 'She says she needs to speak to her daughter.'

'She hasn't got a daughter!'

'No, not according to the records. A conundrum, isn't it?'

Captain Tahget sat very still, his glare focused unblinking on the young acolyte. He was a bulky man of about forty, with scar tissue crusting over half his scalp. He obviously had military experience, but his unadorned body armour, like the bare walls of his private office, gave away nothing of his character; in these fluid, uncertain times, when sibling fought sibling, it was impossible to tell who he might have served.

Before this monolithic officer Futurity, just twenty years old, felt nervous, ineffectual – not just weak, but like a shadow, with no control over events.

Futurity lifted his data desk and checked the *Ask Politely*'s manifest again. The passenger's name stood out, highlighted in red: MARA. No mention of a daughter. 'She's a refugee. Home for her is Chandra. The black hole at the centre of the Galaxy.'

'I know what Chandra is.'

'Or rather,' Futurity said nervously, 'home is, or was, Greyworld, a worldlet in orbit around a satellite black hole, which in turn orbits Chandra—'

'I know all this too,' said the Captain stonily. 'Get on with it, acolyte.'

Tahget had been hired by Futurity's boss, the Hierocrat, to come to this processing station in orbit around Base 478. Here he was to pick up Mara, and other refugees displaced by the Kardish Imperium from their homes in the Galaxy's Core, and then carry them on to Earth, where the ruling Ideocracy had pledged to welcome its citizens. But Mara had refused to travel on. Because of her, the ship had been held in orbit around the Base, and the other refugees had been evacuated and sent back to holding centres on the surface.

And now it was up to Futurity to sort this mess out. He had no idea where to start.

Futurity licked his lips and looked again at the glowing cube on the Captain's desk. It was a fish-tank monitor, a Virtual realisation of the interior of the woman's cabin. Mara sat on her bunk, as still, in her way, as Tahget. She was slim, her head shaved; aged thirty-six, she looked modest, sensible, undemanding. Her small suitcase sat unopened on top of the low dresser that was the cabin's only other significant piece of furniture. The locked door was blocked by an upturned chair, a trivial barricade.

And before her on the floor was the reason she had been able to impose her will on a starship Captain, hundreds of refugees and at least three interstellar political entities. It was a blocky tangle of metal and polymer, an ugly sculpture quite out of place in the mundane shabbiness of the cabin. You could clearly see where it had been cut out of the weapons pod of some wrecked ship. It was a bomb, a monopole bomb. Dating from the time of the Coalition and their galactic war, it was at least two thousand years old. But the Coalition had built well, and there was no doubt that the bomb could destroy this ship and do a great deal of damage to Base 478 itself.

Futurity didn't know where the bomb had come from, though after millennia of war 478 was famously riddled with weapons caches. And he had no idea how the bomb had been smuggled on board the *Ask Politely*, this starship. But the Hierocrat had made it clear that Futurity didn't need to know any of that; all Futurity had to do was to resolve this messy situation.

'But she can't go home,' he said again feebly. 'Her home doesn't exist any more, legally speaking. And soon enough it won't exist physically either. She's a refugee.' Futurity didn't understand anything about this situation. 'We're trying to help her here. Doesn't she see that?'

'Evidently not,' Tahget said dryly. Tahget didn't move a muscle, but

Futurity could sense his growing impatience. 'Acolyte, none of the politics of the Galaxy, or the geography of the black hole, matter a jot to me.' He stabbed a finger at the fish-tank. 'All I care about is getting that woman away from that bomb. We can't disarm the thing. We can't force our way into the cabin without—'

'Without killing the woman?'

'Oh, I don't care about that. No, we can't get in without setting the thing off. Do you need to know the technical details, of Virtual trip-wires, of dead man's switches? Suffice it to say that force is not an option. And so I turn to you, acolyte. 478 is your church's world, after all.'

Futurity spread his hands, 'What can I do?'

Tahget laughed, uncaring. 'What you priests do best. Talk.'

The dread weight of responsibility, which had oppressed Futurity since he had been 'volunteered' for this assignment by the Hierocrat and projected into orbit, now pressed down on him hard. But, he found, his greatest fear was not for his own safety, nor even for the fate of this poor woman, but simply that he was making a fool of himself in front of this dour captain. *Shame on you, Futurity's Dream!*

He forced himself to focus. 'How do I speak to her?'

The Captain waved a hand. A Virtual of Mara's head coalesced in the air, and Futurity saw a miniature of himself pop into existence in the little diorama of her cabin. So he had been put in contact with this bomber.

He tried to read her face. She looked younger than her thirty-six years. Her face was a neat oval, her features rather bland – her nose long, her mouth small. She would never be called beautiful, though something about the shape of her skull, exposed by the close shaving of her hair in the Ideocratic style, was delicately attractive. As she studied him, evidently without curiosity, her expression was clear, her brow smooth. She looked *loving*, he thought, loving and contented in herself, her life. But tension showed around her eyes, in hollow stress shadows. This was a gentle woman projected into an horrific situation. She must be desperate.

A smile touched her lips, faint, quickly evaporating. She said to him, 'Aren't you going to say anything?'

The Captain rolled his eyes. 'Our terrorist is laughing at you! Good start, acolyte.'

'I'm sorry,' Futurity blurted. 'I didn't mean to stare. It's just that I'm trying to get used to all this.'

'It's not a situation I wanted,' Mara said.

'I'm sure we can find a way to resolve it.'

'There is a way,' she said without hesitation. 'Just take me home. It's all I've asked for from the beginning.'

*But that's impossible.* Futurity had never negotiated with an armed fugitive before, but he had heard many confessions, and he knew the value of patience, of indirection. 'We'll come to that,' he said. 'My name is Futurity's Dream. I live on the planet below, which is Base 478. Our government is called the Ecclesia.'

'You're a priest.'

He said reflexively, 'Just an acolyte, my child.'

She laughed at him openly now. 'Don't call me a child! I'm a mother myself.'

'I'm sorry,' he mumbled. But in his peripheral vision he checked over the manifest details again. She was travelling alone; there was definitely no mention of a child either on the ship or back at Chandra. Don't contradict, he told himself. Don't cross-examine. Just talk. 'You'll have to help me through this, Mara. Are you of the faith yourself?'

'Yes,' she sniffed. 'Not of your sort, though.'

Since the fall of the Coalition, the religion Futurity served, known as the 'Friends of Wigner', had suffered many schisms. He forced a smile. 'But I will have to do,' he said. 'The Captain turned to my Hierocrat for help. Mara, you must see that to sort out this situation you will have to talk to me.'

'No.'

'No?'

'I have to talk. That's obvious. But not to an acolyte. Or a priest, or a bishop, or a, a—'

'A Hierocrat.' He frowned. 'Then who?'

'Michael Poole.'

That ancient, sacred name shocked Futurity to brief silence. He glanced at Captain Tahget, who raised his eyebrows. *You see what I've been dealing with?* Perhaps this woman was deluded after all.

Futurity said, 'Mara, Michael Poole is our messiah. In the age of the First Friends he gave his life for the benefit of humanity by—'

'I know who he was,' she snapped. 'Why do you think I asked for him?'

'Then,' he said carefully, 'you must know that Poole has been dead – or at least lost to us – for more than twenty-three thousand years.'

'Of course I know that. But he's here.'

'Poole is always with us in spirit,' said Futurity piously. 'And he waits for us at Timelike Infinity, where the world lines of reality will be cleansed.'

'Not like that. *He's here*, on Base—'

'478.'

'478. You people keep him locked up.'

'We do?'

'I want Michael Poole,' Mara insisted. 'Only him. Because he will understand.' She turned away from Futurity. The imaging system followed her, but she covered her face with her hands, so he couldn't read her expression.

Captain Tahget said dryly, 'I think you need to talk to your Hierocrat.'

## II

The Hierocrat refused to discuss such issues on a comms link, so Futurity would have to return to the surface. Within the hour Futurity's flitter receded from the starship.

From space the *Ask Politely* was an astonishing sight. Perhaps a kilometre in length it was a rough cylinder, but it lacked symmetry on any axis, and its basic form was almost hidden by the structures which plumed from its surface: fins, sails, spines, nozzles, scoops, webbing. Hardened for interstellar space the ship shone, metallic and polymeric. But it had the look of something organic rather than mechanical, a form that had *grown*, like a spiny fish from Base 478's deep seas perhaps, rather than anything designed by intelligence.

There was something deeply disturbing about the ship's lack of symmetry. But, Futurity supposed, symmetry was imposed on humans by the steady straight-up-and-down gravity fields of planets. If you swam between the stars you didn't need symmetry.

And besides, so the seminary gossip went, despite the controlling presence of Tahget and his command crew, this wasn't really a *human* vessel at all. It certainly didn't look it, close to.

Futurity was relieved when his flitter pulled out of the ship's forest of spines and nets and began to swing back down towards Base 478.

478 was a world of ruins: from the high atmosphere the land looked as if it had been melted, covered over by a bubbling concrete-grey slag. Once every resource of this world had been dedicated to the

prosecution of a galactic war. Base 478 had been a training centre, and here millions of human citizens had been moulded into soldiers, to be hurled into the grisly friction of the war at the Galaxy's heart, from whence few had returned. Even now the world retained the number by which it had been registered in vanished catalogues on Earth.

But times had changed. The war was over, the Coalition fallen. Many of those tremendous wartime buildings remained – they were too robust to be demolished – but Futurity made out splashes of green amid the grey, places where the ancient buildings had been cleared and the ground exposed. Those island-farms laboured to feed 478's diminished population. Futurity himself had grown up on such a farm, long before he had donned the cassock.

He had never travelled away from his home world – indeed, he had only flown in orbit once before, during his seminary training; his tutor had insisted that you could not pretend to be a priest of a pan-Galactic religion without at least seeing your own world hanging unsupported in the Galaxy's glow. But Futurity had studied widely, and he had come to see that though there were far more exciting and exotic places to live in this human Galaxy – not least Earth itself – there were few places quite so orderly and *civilised* as his own little world, with its proud traditions of soldiery and engineering, and its deeply devout government. So he had grown to love it. He even liked the layers of monumental ruins that plated over every continent, for in the way they had been reoccupied and reused he took a lesson about the durability of the human spirit.

But a world so old hid many secrets. After his flitter had landed – and as the Hierocrat led him to a chamber buried deep beneath the Ecclesia's oldest College – Futurity felt his soul shrink from the suffocating burden of history.

And when Michael Poole opened his eyes and faced him, Futurity wondered which of them was the most lost.

The room was bare, its walls a pale, glowing blue. Its architecture was tetrahedral, a geometry designed respectfully to evoke an icon of Michael Poole's own past, the four-sided mouths of the wormholes the great engineer had once built to open up Sol system. But those slanting walls made the room enclosing: not a chapel, but a cell.

The room's sole occupant looked up as Futurity entered. He sat on the one piece of furniture, a low bed. Futurity was immediately reminded of Mara, in another plainly furnished room, similarly trapped by her own mysterious past. The man was bulky, small – smaller than Futurity had imagined. His hair was black, his eyes dark brown. He looked about forty, but this man came from an age of the routine use of AntiSenescence treatments, so he could be any age. The muscles of his shoulders were bunched, and his hands were locked together, big, powerful engineer's hands. He looked tense, angry, haunted.

As Futurity hesitated, the man fixed him with an aggressive gaze. 'Who in Lethe are you?' The language was archaic, and a translation whispered softly in Futurity's ear.

'My name is Futurity's Dream.'

'Futurity—?' He laughed out loud. 'Another infinity-botherer.'

It shocked Futurity to have *this* man speak so casually heretically. But he had had enough of being cowed today, and he pulled himself together. 'You are on a world of infinity-botherers, sir.'

The man eyed him with a grudging respect. 'I suppose I can't argue with that. I didn't ask to be here, though. Just you remember that. So I know who you are. Who am I?'

Futurity took a deep breath. 'You are Michael Poole.'

Poole raised his hand, and turned it back and forth, studying it. Then he stood up and without warning aimed a slap at Futurity's cheek. Poole's fingers broke up into a cloud of pixels, and Futurity felt nothing.

'No,' Poole murmured. 'I guess you're wrong. Michael Poole was a human being. Whatever I am it isn't that.'

For a second Futurity couldn't speak. He tried to hold himself together against this barrage of shocks.

To Futurity's surprise, Poole said, 'Sorry. Perhaps you didn't deserve that.'

Futurity shook his head. 'My needs don't matter.'

'Oh, yes, they do. Everything goes belly-up if you forget that.' He cast about the tetrahedral cell. 'What's a man got to do to get a malt whisky around here? . . . Oh. I forgot.' He looked up into the tetrahedron's squat spire, and held out his hand, cupping it. In a moment a glass appeared, containing a puddle of amber fluid. Poole sipped it with satisfaction. Then he dipped his fingers in the drink, and flicked droplets at Futurity. When they hit the acolyte's cassock, the droplets burst apart in little fragments of light. 'Consistency protocols,' Poole murmured. 'How about that? Why am I here, Futurity's Dream? Why am I talking to you – why am I conscious again?'

Futurity said bluntly, 'I need your help.'

Poole sat down, sipped his drink, and grunted. 'More of your decadent dumb-ass theology?'

'Not theology,' Futurity said evenly. 'A human life.'

That seemed to snag Poole's attention. But he said, 'How long this time?'

Futurity, briefed by the Hierocrat, knew exactly what he meant. 'A little more than a thousand years.'

Poole closed his eyes and massaged his temples. 'You bastards,' he said. 'I'm your Virtual Jesus. A simulacrum messiah. And I wasn't good enough. So you put me in memory store, a box where I couldn't even dream, and left me there for a *thousand years*. And now you've dug me up again. Why? To crucify me on a wormhole mouth, like the first Poole?'

Futurity was growing irritated. 'I know nothing of Jesus, or crucifying. But I always thought I understood Michael Poole.'

'How could you? He's been dead twenty millennia.'

Futurity said relentlessly, 'Then perhaps I misjudged his character. We didn't bring you back to harm you. We didn't bring you back for *you* at all. You're here because somebody in trouble is asking for your help. Maybe you should think about somebody other than yourself, as Michael Poole surely would have done.'

Poole shook his head. 'I don't believe it. Are you trying to manipulate me?'

'I wouldn't dream of it, sir.'

Poole sipped his unreal whisky. Then he sighed. 'So what's the problem?'

### III

Poole had no physical location as such; he 'was' where he was projected. It would have been possible for him to be manifested aboard the *Ask Politely* by projection from the Ecclesia's underground caches. But Poole himself pressed for the data that defined him to be downloaded into the ship's own store, as otherwise lightspeed delays would introduce a barrier between himself and this fragile woman who was asking for his help.

What Poole wanted, it seemed, Poole got.

It took a day for the Ecclesiast authorities to agree transfer protocols with Captain Tahget and his crew. Futurity, no specialist in such matters, found this delay difficult to understand, but it turned out that Poole's definition was stored at the quantum level. 'And you can transfer quantum information,' Poole said, 'but you can't copy it. So your monks can't make a backup of me, Futurity, any more than they can of you. Kind of reassuring, isn't it? And that's why the monks are twitchy.' But Poole was furious that the Ecclesiasts ensured that Tahget understood they owned the copyright in him and would protect their 'intellectual property' against 'piracy'. 'Copyright! In *me*! What do they think I am, a worm genome?'

Meanwhile, Captain Tahget was insulted by the very suggestion of piracy, and he complained about the delays for which nobody was compensating him, not to mention the risk of allowing the unstable situation of a woman with a bomb aboard his ship to continue for so long.

These transactions seemed extraordinary to Futurity, and terribly difficult to cope with. After all, when he had first gone up to the orbiting starship, Futurity hadn't even known this simulacrum of Michael Poole existed.

Virtual Poole was the deepest secret of the Ecclesia, his Hierocrat had said. Indeed, an acolyte as junior as Futurity shouldn't be hearing any of this at all, and the Hierocrat made it clear he blamed Futurity for not resolving the starship situation without resorting to this: in the Hierocrat's eyes, Futurity had failed already.

It had begun fifteen hundred years ago. It had been an experiment in theology, epistemology and Virtual technology, an experiment with roots that reached back to the establishment of the Ecclesia itself.

Poole himself knew the background. 'I – or rather, *he*, Michael Poole, the real one – has become a messiah figure to you, hasn't he? You infinity-botherers and this strange quantum-mechanical faith of yours. You had theological questions you thought Poole could answer. Your priests couldn't dig him up. And so you *made* him. Or rather, you made me.'

Technicians of the ancient Guild of Virtual Idealism had deployed the most advanced available technology to construct the Virtual Poole. Everything known about Poole and his life and times had been down-loaded, and where there were gaps in the knowledge – and there were many – teams of experts, technical, historical and theoretical, had laboured to extrapolate and interpolate. It had been a remarkable project, and somewhat expensive: the Hierocrat wouldn't say how much it cost, but it seemed the Ecclesia was still paying by instalments.

At last all was ready, and that blue tetrahedral chapel had been built. The Supreme Ecclesiarch had waved her hand – and Michael Poole, or at least *a* Michael Poole, had opened his eyes for the first time in more than twenty thousand years.

The whole business seemed vaguely heretical to Futurity. But when Poole popped into existence in the *Politely*'s observation lounge, surrounded by the gaping crew and nervous Ecclesiast technicians, Futurity felt a shiver of wonder.

Poole seemed to take a second to come to himself, as if coming into focus. Then he looked down at his body and flexed his fingers. In the brightness of the deck he seemed oddly out of place, Futurity thought – not flimsily unreal like most Virtuals, but *more* opaque, more dense, like an intrusion from another reality. Poole scanned the crowd of staring strangers. When he found Futurity's face he smiled, and Futurity's heart warmed helplessly.

But Poole's face was dark, intent, determined. For the first time it occurred to Futurity to wonder what Poole himself might want out of this situation. He was a Virtual, but he was just as sentient as Futurity was, and no doubt he had goals of his own. Perhaps he saw some advantage in this transfer off-world, some angle to be worked.

Poole turned and walked briskly to the big blister-window set in the hull. His head scanned back and forth systematically as he took in the crowded view. 'So this is the centre of the Galaxy. You damn priests never even let me see the sky before.'

'Not quite the centre. We're inside the Core here, the Galaxy's central bulge.' Futurity pointed to a wall of light that fenced off half the sky. 'That's the Mass – the Central Star Mass, the knot of density surrounding Chandra, the supermassive black hole at the very centre.'

'Lethe, I don't know if I imagined people would ever come so far. And for millennia this has been a war zone?'

'The war is over.' Futurity forced a grin. 'We won!'

'And now humans are killing humans again, right? Same old story.' Poole inspected the surface of the planet below. 'A city-world,' he said dismissively. 'Seen better days.' He squinted around the sky. 'So where's the sun?'

Futurity was puzzled by the question.

Captain Tahget said, 'Base 478 has no sun. It's a rogue planet, a wanderer. Stars are crowded here in the Core, Michael Poole. Not like out on the rim, where you come from. Close approaches happen all the time.'

'So planets get detached from their suns.' Poole peered down at the farms that splashed green amid the concrete. 'No sunlight for photosynthesis. But if the sky is on fire with Galaxy light, you don't need the sun. Different spectrum from Sol's light, of course, but I guess they are different plants too . . .'

Futurity was entranced by these rapid chains of speculation and deduction.

Poole pointed to a shallow crater, a dish of rubble kilometres across, gouged into the built-over surface. 'What happened there?'

Futurity shrugged. 'Probably a floating building fell, when the power failed.'

Poole laughed uncomfortably. 'Layers of history! I don't suppose I'll ever know the half of it.' Now he took in the *Ask Politely*'s bubbling organic form. 'And what kind of starship is *this*?' At random he pointed at hull features, at spines and spires and shields. 'What is *that* for? An antenna, a sensor mast? And *that*? It could be a ramjet scoop, I guess. And that netting could be an ion drive.'

There was a stirring of discomfort. Futurity said, 'We don't ask such questions. It's the business of the Captain and his crew.'

Poole raised his eyebrows, but he got only a blank stare from Captain Tahget. 'Demarcation of knowledge? I never did like that. Gets in the way of the scientific method. But it's your millennium.' He clapped his hands. 'OK, so I'm here. Maybe we should get to work before your fruitcake in steerage blows us all up.'

The Ecclesia technicians muttered among themselves, and prepared Poole's relocation.

Futurity watched the scene in Tahget's fish-tank Virtual viewer. Mara's cabin looked just as it had before: the woman sitting patiently on the bed, the dresser, and the bomb sitting on the floor, grotesquely out of place. All that was different was a tray on top of the dresser with the remains of a meal.

Poole appeared out of nowhere, a little manikin figure in the fish-tank. Mara sat as if frozen.

Poole leaned down, resting his hands on his knees, and looked into her face. 'You're exhausted. Your eyes are piss-holes in the snow.'

Nobody in Tahget's office had ever seen snow; the translation routines had to interpret.

Poole snapped his fingers to conjure up a Virtual chair and sat down. Mara bowed down before him. 'Take it easy,' he said. 'You don't have to dry my feet with your hair.' Another archaic reference Futurity didn't understand. 'I know I'm tangled up in your myths. But I'm just a man. Actually, not even that.'

'I'm sorry,' Mara said thickly, straightening up.

'For what? You're the real person here, with the real problem.' He glanced at the sullen mass of the bomb.

Mara said, 'I made them bring you here. Now I don't know what to say to you.'

'Just talk. I don't think anybody understands what you want, Mara. Not even that bright kid Futurity.'

'Who? Oh, the acolyte. I told them, but they didn't listen.'

'Then tell me.' He laughed. 'I'm the sleeping beauty. Lethe knows *I've* got no preconceptions.'

'I want to go home. I didn't want to leave in the first place. They evacuated us by force.'

He leaned forward. 'Who did?'

'The troops of the new Kard.'

'Who . . . ? Never mind; I'll figure that out. OK. But home for you is a planetoid orbiting a black hole. Yes? A satellite black hole, born in the accretion disc of the monster at the heart of the Galaxy.' He rubbed his chin. 'Quite a place to visit. But who would want to *live* there?'

Mara sat up straighter. 'I would. I was born there.'

It had been a project of the first years after mankind's victory in the centre of the Galaxy, Mara told him. With the war won, the ancient Coalition, the government of a united mankind, abruptly crumbled, and successor states emerged across the Galaxy. A rump remnant of the Coalition that called itself the Ideocracy had clung on to Earth and other scattered territories. And at the Core, the scene of mankind's greatest victory, a new project was begun. Ideocrat engineers had gathered asteroids and ice moons which they had set spinning in orbit around the satellite black holes which studded Chandra's accretion disc. One such was the rock Mara called Greyworld.

'You say you were born there?'

'Yes,' Mara said. 'And my parents, and their parents before them.'

Poole stared at her. Then, in Futurity's view, Poole's little figure walked to the edge of the fish-tank viewer, and stared up challengingly. 'Hey, acolyte. Help me out here. I'm having a little trouble with timescales.'

Futurity checked his data desk. Under the Ideocracy, these accretion-disc colonies had been in place for two thousand years, almost since the final victory at the Galaxy's Core.

Poole, a man of the fourth millennium, seemed stunned. *'Two thousand years?'*

Captain Tahget leaned forward and peered into the fish-tank. 'Virtual, we once fought a war that spanned tens of thousands of light years. We learned to plan on a comparable scale in time. During the war there were single battles which lasted millennia.'

Poole shook his head. 'And I imagined I thought big. I really have fallen far into the future, haven't I?'

'You really have, sir,' Futurity said.

Poole sat down again and faced Mara. 'I can see why you didn't want to leave. Your roots were deep, on your Greyworld.'

'Time was running out,' she said. 'We knew that. Our black hole was slowly spiralling deeper into Chandra's accretion disc. Soon the turbulence, the energy density, the tides – it would have been impossible for us to hang on.'

'Although,' said Poole, 'the black hole itself will sail on regardless until it reaches Chandra's event horizon.'

'Yes.'

Poole said, 'I still don't understand. If you knew your world was doomed, you must have accepted you had to evacuate.'

'Of course.'

'Then what—'

'I just didn't like the way it was done.' Her face worked, deep emotions swirling under a veneer of control. 'I didn't get a chance to say goodbye.'

'Who to?'

'Sharn. My daughter.'

Poole studied her for a moment. Then he said gently, 'You see, you're losing me again, Mara. I'm sorry. According to the ship's manifest you don't have a daughter.'

'I did have one. She was taken away from me.'

'Who by?'

'The Ideocrats.'

'But you see, Mara, there's my problem. I saw the records. Once the evacuation was done, there was *nobody* left on Greyworld. So your daughter—'

'She wasn't on Greyworld.'

'Then where?'

'She lives in the satellite black hole,' Mara said simply. 'Where the Ideocrats sent her.'

'*In* the black hole?'

'She lives in it, as you, Michael Poole, live in light.'

'As some kind of Virtual representation?'

Mara shook her head. 'I'm sorry. I can't explain it better. We aren't scientists on Greyworld, like you.'

He thought that over. 'Then what are you?'

'We are farmers.' She shrugged. 'Some of us are technicians. We supervise the machines that tend other machines, that keep the air clean and the water flowing.'

Poole asked, 'But why are you there in the first place, Mara? What did the Ideocracy intend? What is your duty?'

She smiled. 'To give our children to the black hole. And that way, to serve the goals of mankind.'

Futurity said quickly, 'She's probably doesn't know any more, Michael Poole. This was the Ideocracy, remember, heir to the Coalition. And under the Coalition you weren't encouraged to know more than you needed to. You were thought to be more effective that way.'

'Sounds like every totalitarian regime back to Gilgamesh.' Poole studied Mara for a long moment. Then he stood. 'All right, Mara. I think that's enough for now. You've given me a lot to think about. Is there anything you need? More food?'

'I'm tired,' she said quietly. 'But I know if I lie down that Captain or the acolyte will sneak in here and disarm the bomb, or hurt me, and—'

Poole said, 'Look at me, Mara. Things will get flaky very quickly if you don't sleep. Nobody will hurt you, or change anything in here. *You can trust me.*'

She stared at his Virtual face. Then, after a moment, she lay down on her bunk, her knees tucked into her chest like a child.

Poole's fish-tank representation popped out of existence.

Poole, Tahget and Futurity faced each other across the table in Tahget's office.

Tahget said, 'We need to resolve this situation.'

Poole had another glass of Virtual whisky in his hand. 'That woman is determined. Believe me, you don't separate a mother from her child. She'll blow us all up rather than give in.'

Tahget said coldly, 'Then what do you suggest we do?'

'Comply with her wishes. Take her back to Chandra, back to the centre of the Galaxy, and to her black hole Garden of Eden. And help her find her kid.'

Futurity said, 'There is no child. She said the child lives *in* the black hole. That's just impossible. No human being—'

'Who said anything about it being human?' Poole snapped. 'I'm my mother's son, and I'm not human. Not any more. And black holes are complicated beasts, Futurity. You're a scholar; you should know that. Who's to say what's possible or not?'

'Actually I don't know anything about black holes,' Futurity said.

'You know, you've got a really closed mind,' Poole said. 'You Ecclesiasts have origins in an engineering guild, don't you? But now you want to be a priest, and the whole point of being a priest is to keep your knowledge to yourself. Well, maybe you're going to have to learn to think a bit more like an engineer and less like an acolyte to get through this.'

Tahget was glaring at Poole. 'If you insist on this absurd chase to the centre of the Galaxy, Michael Poole, you will have your way. You are accorded respect here. Too much, in my opinion.'

Poole grinned. 'Ain't that the truth?'

'At least it will buy us time,' Futurity said, trying to reassure Tahget. 'But you must hope to resolve this situation before you reach Chandra, where you will find there is no magical child in the singularity, and the woman's condition will veer from denial to desperation.'

'Or it all works out some other way,' Poole said evenly. 'Don't prejudge, acolyte; it's a nasty habit. One condition. I'm coming along too.'

They both looked at him sharply.

Futurity said hesitantly, 'I don't think the Hierocrat would—'

'Into Lethe with your bishops and their "copyright"! I didn't ask them to bring me back from the dead. I only want to see a little of the universe before I get switched off again. Besides, right now I'm the only sentient creature poor Mara trusts. I think you need me aboard, don't you, Captain?'

Futurity opened his mouth, and closed it. 'As the Captain said, if you ask for that I imagine it will be granted, though the Hierocrat's teeth will curl with anxiety.'

Tahget growled, 'Your Hierocrat will have more to think about than that.' He grabbed Futurity's wrist in one massive hand. 'If Michael Poole is joining this cruise of ours, so are *you*, acolyte. When this Virtual fool starts to cause trouble, I want somebody I can take it out on.'

Futurity felt panicked; for a boy who had never been further than low orbit before, this was becoming a daunting adventure, out of control.

Poole laughed and rubbed his hands together. 'Great! Just leave a piece of him for the Hierocrat to gnaw on.'

Tahget released Futurity. 'But I have a condition of my own.' He waved his hand over the table, and its surface turned into a schematic of the Galaxy. 'Here is our original route, planned but now abandoned.' It was a simple dotted line arcing from Base 478 in the Core out to the sparse Galactic rim, where Earth lay waiting. There were a few stops on the way, mostly at nominal political borders. One stop was at a flag marked '3-Kilo', outside the Core, and Tahget tapped it with his finger-nail. 'This is the Galaxy's innermost spiral arm, the 3-Kiloparsec Arm. Whatever our final destination, we go here first.'

Futurity didn't understand. 'But that's the wrong way. 3-Kilo is *outside the Core*.' Leaving the Base was bad enough. His dread deepened at the thought of being taken out of the brightly lit Core and into the sparse unknown beyond. 'If we're aiming for the centre of the Galaxy, we'll have to double back. And the bomb – the additional time this will take—'

'I know the urgency of the situation,' Tahget snapped.

Poole said, 'So why do you want to go to 3-Kilo?'

'I don't,' Tahget said. 'The *Ask Politely* does. On a ship like this, you go where *it* wants to go.' Tahget blanked the table display and stood. 'There is much you will never understand about this modern age, Michael Poole. Even about this ship. This meeting is over.' He walked out.

Futurity and Poole stared at each other. Poole said, 'So it isn't just a cutesy name. On this ship, you really do have to ask politely.'

Futurity peered into the fish-tank display of Mara's cabin, where the woman hadn't moved since she lay down in Poole's presence.

## IV

The *Ask Politely* spent another day in orbit around 478. Then the ship slid silently away into deep space.

Futurity stood alone in the observation lounge, watching his home planet fold over itself until it became a dull grey pebble, lost against the glare of the Galaxy Core. He really was heading out into the cold and the dark. He shivered and turned away from the blister-window. It would be three days' travel to 3-Kilo, said Tahget, with much delay at border posts as they cut across the territories of various squabbling statelets.

Futurity spent most of the first day alone. The bare corridors echoed; a ship meant to carry a hundred passengers seemed empty with just the three of them, counting Poole.

He quickly found his range of movement was limited. He had access to corridors and rooms only over two decks, confined to a lozenge-shaped volume near one end of the ship's rough cylinder. The corridors were bleak, panelled with bare blue-grey polymer, with not a bit of artwork or personalisation in sight. Even within the lozenge many rooms were closed to him, such as the bridge, or just plain uninteresting, such as the refectory, the nano-food banks and the air cycling gear.

The lozenge of access spanned no more than fifty metres, on a craft a kilometre long. In fact this whole pod of habitation was like an after-thought, he started to see, an add-on bolted onto *Ask Politely*, as if these corridors and the people in them were not the point of the ship at all.

And nobody would speak to him. Tahget and his crew were busy, and as a mere earthworm, as they called him, they just ignored Futurity anyhow. The woman Mara slept throughout the day. Michael Poole stayed in the Captain's office. He appeared to sit still for hours on end, immersed in his own deep Virtual reflections. Futurity didn't dare disturb him.

Futurity thought of himself as disciplined. He wasn't without inner resource. He had been assigned a cabin, and he had brought a data desk and other materials. So he sat down, faced his data desk, and tried to pursue his seminary studies – as it happened, into the divine nature of Michael Poole.

The Wignerian faith was based on the comforting notion that all history was partial, a mere rough draft. It was all based on quantum physics, of course, the old notion that reality is a thing of probabilities and might-bes, that collapses into the real only when a conscious mind makes an observation. But that conscious mind, with all its ob- servations, in turn wasn't realised until a *second* mind observed *it* – but that second in turn needed a *third* observer to become real, who needed a *fourth* . . .

This paradoxical muddle would be resolved at the end of time, said the Wignerians, when the Ultimate Observer, the final Mind, would make the last Observation of all, terminating chains of possibilities that reached back to the birth of the universe. In that mighty instant the sad history of the present, with its pain and war, suffering and brief lives and death, would be wiped away, and everybody who ever lived would find themselves embedded in a shining, optimal history.

This was the kernel of a faith that had offered profound hope during the last days of the Coalition, when the whole Galaxy had been infested with human soldiers, many of them not much more than children. The faith had always been illegal, but it was blind-eye tolerated by author- ities and commanders who saw the comfort it brought to their warriors.

And when the Coalition fell, the faith was liberated.

The Ecclesia of Base 478 had its origins in the Guild of Engineers, an ancient agency that had itself participated in the founding of the Coalition. The Guild had survived many political discontinuities in the past. Now it survived the fall of the Coalition and proved its adapt- ability again. The Guild took over an abandoned Coalition training base, 478, and set up an independent government. Like many others, it fully accepted the newly liberated Wignerian faith, seeing in the religion a short cut to power and legitimacy. Soon its Master of Guild- Masters proclaimed herself Supreme Ecclesiarch, announcing that she alone owned the truth about the faith – again, like many others.

The Guild-Masters, following their old intellectual inclinations, de- veloped an interest in the theological underpinnings of their new faith. Their Colleges on Base 478 quickly developed a reputation even among rival orthodoxies as hosting the best Wignerian thinkers in the Galaxy.

But in those heady early days of theological freedom, there had been constant schisms and splits, heresy and counter-heresy, as the scholars debated one of the religion's most fascinating and difficult elements: the strange career of Michael Poole. This entrepreneur, engineer and adventurer of humanity's remote history had, it was said, projected himself into the far future through a collapsing chain of wormholes. He had done this in order to save mankind. Poole, a redeemer who had confronted Timelike Infinity, came to embody and humanise the chilly quantum abstractions of the faith. He was a Son of that aloof Mother that was the Ultimate Observer.

There seemed no doubt that Poole really had existed as an historical figure. The question was: what was his relationship to the Ultimate Observer? Was Poole just another supplicant, if an extraordinary one, his life just one more thread in the tapestry contemplated by the Wignerian godhead? Or, some argued further, perhaps Poole and the Observer ought to be identified: perhaps Michael Poole *was* the Observer. The trouble with that argument was that Poole was undoubtedly human, whatever else he was, though his achievements had been anything but ordinary. So could a god be made incarnate?

It was an issue that had always fascinated Futurity. Indeed, it had so intrigued some of his predecessors that they had commissioned the Virtual Poole from the Idealists so they could ask him about it: it was a rough-and-ready engineer's approach to a deep theological question.

But oddly, with the real thing – or at least a disturbing simulacrum – just down the corridor of this ship, Futurity's dry scholarship seemed pointless. He found it hard to believe Poole himself would have any time for this dusty stuff.

After a couple of hours Futurity gave up. He left his cabin and went exploring again.

As he roamed the corridors he watched the crew at work. They all seemed to be command staff, aside from a few orderlies who performed such chores as serving the Captain his meals and shifting furniture around to set up passengers' cabins. It was puzzling. Futurity had no experience of life aboard starships, but he could not see how the crew's complicated discussions and endless meetings related to the ship's actual operations. And he never spotted an engineer, a person who might be in charge of the systems that actually made the ship *go*.

He was probably reading the situation all wrong. But Michael Poole, who had once built starships himself, also concluded that there was something very odd about this ship.

On the second day he talked it over with Futurity. Tahget had given Poole some limited access over where he could 'pop up', as he put it, and he had been able to roam a bit wider than Futurity had. But not much further. His own internal-consistency protocols, designed to give him some anchoring in humanity, made it impossible for him to roam into areas that would have been hazardous for humans. And when the

Captain had spotted that Poole was hacking into access-denied areas, such privileges had quickly been locked out.

'I saw a few sights before they shut me down, though,' Poole said, and he winked. *'We're not alone on this ship*. It's a big place, and we're confined to this little box. But in the longer corridors on the fringe of our cage, I saw things: shadows, furtive movements. Like ghosts. And if you look too closely what you see disappears into the shade.'

Futurity frowned. 'You're not saying the ship is haunted?'

'No. But I think there is, um, a *second* crew, a crew beneath the crew, who are actually flying the damn ship. And it's presumably to serve *their* needs that we're all jaunting out to 3-Kilo, because for sure it isn't for us. What I haven't yet figured out is who those people are, why they're hiding from us, and what their relationship is to Tahget and his bunch of pirates. But I'll get there,' he said cheerfully. 'I'll tell you something even odder. I'm not convinced that the squat little folk I glimpsed were even *wearing clothes*!'

Futurity never ceased to marvel at Poole. He was a tourist in this twenty-eighth millennium, a revenant from the deepest past. And yet he was finding his way around what must be a very strange future with far more confidence than Futurity felt he could muster in a hundred lifetimes.

By the morning of the third day the *Ask Politely* had swum out of the Core, and Futurity was growing disturbed by the sky.

They were still only a few thousand light years from the centre of the Galaxy, and behind the ship the Core was a mass of light, too bright to be viewed by a naked human eye. But Futurity could already tell he was in the plane of a galactic disc: there were stars all around, but they were more crowded in some directions than others. If he looked straight ahead the more distant stars merged into a band of light that streaked across the sky, a stellar horizon, but if he looked up or down, the stars scattered to thinness, and he could see through the veil of light to a sky that was noticeably empty – and *black*.

Futurity had never seen a black sky before. He felt as if his own mind was crumbling, as if the bright surface of reality was breaking down, to reveal an abyssal darkness beneath. He longed to be back on 478, where the whole sky was always drenched with light.

But Poole was animated. 'What a tremendous sky! You know, from Sol system you can make out only a few thousand stars, and the Galaxy is just a ragged band of mushy light. The Core ought to be visible from Earth – it should be as bright as the Moon – but the spiral-arm dust clouds get in the way, and it's invisible. Futurity, it was only a few decades before the first human spaceflight that people figured out they lived in a Galaxy at all! It was as if we lived in a shack buried in the woods, while all around us the bright lights of the city were hidden by the trees.'

Poole had a kindly streak, and was empathetic. He sensed Futurity's discomfort, and to distract him he brought the acolyte to the Captain's office, and encouraged him to talk about himself. Futurity was flattered by his interest – this was *Michael Poole*! – and he responded with a torrent of words.

Futurity had always been cursed with a lively, inquisitive mind. As a young boy on the family farm, surrounded by the lowering ruins of war, he had laboured to tease healthy plants from soil illuminated by pale Galaxy-centre light. It had been fulfilling in its way, and Futurity saw with retrospect that to spend his time on the processes of life itself had satisfied some of his own inner spiritual yearnings. But the unchanging rhythms of the farm weren't sufficient to sustain his intellect.

The only libraries on Base 478 were deep underground, where Ecclesiast scholars and scribes toiled over obscure aspects of Wignerian theology, and the only academic career available to Futurity was in a seminary. In fact, on a priest-run world, to become an Ecclesiast of some rank or other was the only way to build any kind of career. 'On 478 even the tax collectors are priests,' as Futurity's father had said ruefully.

So the boy said goodbye to the farm, and donned the cassock of a novice. He gave up his childhood name for a visionary Wignerian slogan: *Futurity's Dream*.

The study was hard, the rule of the Hierocrats and tutors imperious and arbitrary, but life wasn't so bad. His intellect had been fully satisfied by his immersion in the Ecclesia's endless and increasingly baroque studies of the historical, philosophical and theological roots of its faith. He recoiled with humility from the pastoral side of his work, though. It mortified him to hear the confession of citizens older and wiser than he was. But that very humility, one discerning Hierocrat had once told him, might mark him out as having the potential to be a fine priest.

Anyhow now, seven years later, his seemingly inevitable career choices had led him to this extraordinary situation.

'And who are these "Kards"?' Poole asked.

'The Kardish Imperium is a new power that has risen in the Core,' Futurity told Poole. 'Named after a famous admiral of the Core wars. Expansive, aggressive, intolerant, ambitious—'

'I know the type.'

The Kards were on the march. There was only one state, in a Galaxy quilted with petty statelets, capable of resisting the Kards – and that was the Ideocracy, the rump of the collapsed Coalition.

So far the Ideocracy had been as aloof concerning the Kardish as it was about all the successor states, which it regarded as illegal and temporary secessions from its own authority. But the Kards' challenge was profound. Earth, base of the Ideocracy, was the home of mankind. But the Galaxy Core had been the centre of the war, and more humans had died there, by an order of magnitude, than all those who had lived and died on Earth before the age of spaceflight. The Core was the moral and spiritual capital of *Homo galacticus*, said the new Kard. The question was, who was the true heir to the Coalition's mantle, Imperium or Ideocracy? The reputation of the Coalition still towered, and its name burned brightly in human imaginations; whoever won that argument might inherit a Galaxy.

This was the terrible friction that had rubbed away the life of Mara, and countless other refugees.

'And now,' Futurity said, 'they are cleaning out the last Ideocracy enclaves in the Core.'

'Ah. Like Mara's world.'

'Yes. There isn't much the Ideocracy can do, short of all-out war. As for us,' Futurity went on, 'the Ecclesia is just trying to keep the peace.' Through their faith the Ecclesia's acolytes and academics had links that crossed the new, shifting political boundaries. 'Michael Poole, the Wignerian faith was never legal under the Coalition, but it spanned the Galaxy, and in its way unified mankind. It survived the Coalition's fall. Now, despite our fractured politics, and even though the faith itself has schismed and schismed again, it still unites us – or at least gives us something to talk to each other about. And it provides a moral, civilising centre to our affairs. If not for the faith's moderating influence, the fall of the Coalition would have been *much* worse for most of humanity.'

460

Mara's fate was an example. Wignerian diplomatic links had been used to set up a reasonably safe passage for Ideocracy refugees from the Core. Thus at places like Base 478 refugees like Mara were passed off from one authority to another, following a chain of sanctuaries out of the Core to their new homes in the remote gloom of the rim.

Poole seemed cynical about this. 'A service for which you charge a handsome fee, no doubt.'

Futurity was stung. 'We're not a rich world, Michael Poole. We rely mostly on donations from pilgrims to keep us going. We have to charge the refugees or their governments for transit and passage; we'd fall into poverty ourselves otherwise.'

But Poole didn't seem convinced. 'Pilgrims? And what is it those pilgrims come to see on Base 478? Is it the shrine of the great messiah? Is it *me*? Have you dug up my bones? Do you have some gibbering manikin of me capering on a monument, begging for cash?'

Futurity tried to deny this: *not literally*. But there was truth in Poole's charge, he thought uncomfortably. Of course Poole's body had been lost when he fell into the wormhole to Timelike Infinity, and so he had been saved from the indignity of becoming a relic. But as the Wignerian religion had developed the Ecclesia had mounted several expeditions to Earth, and had returned with such treasures as the bones of Poole's father Harry . . .

Poole seemed to know all this. He laughed at Futurity's discomfiture.

The Captain called them. They had arrived at 3-Kilo, and Tahget, in his blunt, testing way, said his passengers might enjoy the view.


Poole was charmed by the clustering stars of 3-Kilo. To Futurity these spiral-arm stars, scattered and old, were a thin veil that barely distracted him from the horror of the underlying darkness beyond.

But it wasn't stars they were here to see.

Poole pointed. 'What in Lethe is *that*?'

An object shifted rapidly against the stars of 3-Kilo. Silhouetted, it was dark, its form complex and irregular.

Poole was fascinated. 'An asteroid, maybe – no, too spiky for that. A comet nucleus, then? I spent some time in the Kuiper Belt, the ice moon belt at the fringe of Sol system. I was building starships out there. Big job, long story, and all vanished now, I imagine. But a lot of those Kuiper objects were like that: billions of years of sculptures of frost and ice, all piled up in the dark. Pointlessly beautiful. So is this a

Kuiper object detached from some system or other? But it looks too small for that.'

Futurity was struck again by the liveliness of Poole's mind, the openness of his curiosity – and *this* was only an incomplete Virtual. He wondered wistfully how it might have been to have met the real Michael Poole.

Then Poole saw it. 'It's a ship,' he said. 'A ship covered with spires and spines and buttresses and carvings, just like our own *Ask Politely*. A ship like a bit of a baroque cathedral. I think it's approaching us! Or we're approaching it.'

He was right, Futurity saw immediately. He felt obscurely excited. 'And – oh! There's another.' He pointed. 'And another.'

Suddenly there were ships all over the sky, cautiously converging. Every one of them was unique. Though it was hard to judge distances and sizes, Futurity could see that some were larger than the *Ask Politely*, some smaller; some were roughly cylindrical like the *Politely*, others were spheres, cubes, tetrahedrons, even toroids, and some had no discernible regularity at all. And all of them sported gaudy features every bit as spectacular as *Politely*'s. There were immense scoop mouths and gigantic flaring exhaust nozzles, spindly spines and fat booms, and articulating arms that worked delicately back and forth like insect legs. Some of the ships even sported streamlined wings and fins and smooth noses, though none of them looked as if they could survive an entry into an atmosphere. These glimmering sculptures drifted all around the sky.

Poole said, 'Quite a carnival. Look at all that crap, the spines and spikes and nets and fins. It looks like it's been stuck on by some giant kid making toy spaceships. I can't believe there's any utility in most of those features.'

Futurity said, 'It's also *ugly*. What a mess!'

'Yes,' said Poole. 'But I have the feeling we're not the ones this stuff is supposed to impress.' He pointed. 'And that one looks as if it wants to get a bit more intimate than the rest.'

A huge ship loomed from the crowd and approached the *Ask Politely*. It was a rough sphere, but its geometry was almost obscured by a fantastic hull-forest of metal, ceramics and polymers. Moving with an immense slow grace, it bore down on the *Ask Politely*, which waited passively.

At last the big sphere's complex bulk shadowed most of the

observation lounge's blister. A jungle of nozzles and booms slid across the window. Futurity wondered vaguely how close it would come before it stopped.

And then he realised it wasn't going to stop at all.

Captain Tahget murmured, 'Brace for impact.' Futurity grabbed a rail.

The collision of the two vast ships was slow, almost gentle. Futurity, cupped in the *Ask Politely*'s inertial-control field, barely felt it, but he could hear a groan of stressed metal, transmitted through the ship's hull. Two tangles of superstructure scraped past each other; dishes were crashed and spines broken, before the ships came to rest, locked together.

Translucent access tubes sprouted from the hulls of both ships, and snaked across space like questing pseudopodia, looking for purchase. Futurity thought he saw someone, or something, scuttling through the tubes, but it was too far away to see clearly.

Poole gazed out with his mouth open. 'Look – here's another ship coming to join the party.'

So it was, Futurity saw. It was a relative dwarf compared to the monster that had first reached *Ask Politely*. But with more metallic grinding it snuggled close against the hulls of the two locked ships.

Poole laughed. 'Boy, space travel has sure changed a lot since my day!'

Captain Tahget said, 'Show's over. We'll be here two days, maybe three, before the swarming is done.'

Poole glanced at Futurity questioningly. *The swarming?*

Tahget said, 'Until then we maintain our systems and wait. Let me remind you it's the night watch; you passengers might want to get some sleep.' He glanced at Poole. 'Or whatever.'

Futurity returned to his cabin, and tried to sleep. But there were more encounters in the night, more subtle shudderings, more groans of stressed materials so deep they were almost subsonic.

This experience seemed to him to have nothing to do with space-flight. I am in the belly of a fish, he thought, a huge fish of space that has come to this place of scattered stars to seek others of its kind. And it doesn't even know I am here, embedded within it.

V

During the 3-Kilo lay-off Captain Tahget had his crew scour through the ship's habitable areas, cleaning, refurbishing and repairing. It was make-work to keep the crew and passengers busy, but after a few hours Futurity conceded he welcomed the replacement of the ship's accumulated pale stink of sweat, urine and adrenaline with antisepsis.

But the continuing refusal of Mara, reluctant terrorist, to come out of her cabin caused a crisis.

'She has to leave her cabin, at least for a while,' Tahget thundered. 'That's the company's rules, not mine.'

'Why?' Poole asked evenly. 'You recycle her air, provide her with water and food. Give her clean sheets and she'll change her own bed, I'm sure.'

'This is a starship, Michael Poole, an artificial environment. In a closed, small space like that cabin there can be build-ups of toxins, pathogens. And I remind you she is sharing her cabin with a monopole bomb, a nasty bit of crud at least two thousand years old, and Lethe knows what's leaking out of that. We need to clean out her nest.'

Poole's eyes narrowed. 'What else?'

'That woman needs exercise. You've seen the logs. She only gets off her bed to use the bathroom, and even that's only a couple of times a day. What good will it do anybody if she keels over from a thrombosis even before we get to the Chandra? Especially if she's got a dead man's switch, as she claims.'

'Those are all reasons for separating Mara from her bomb, despite your promises to the contrary. I don't trust you as far as I can throw you, Captain. And if I don't, how can Mara?'

Captain Tahget glared; he was a bulky, angry, determined man, and his scar was livid. 'Michael Poole, my only concern is the safety of the ship, and everybody aboard – yes, including Mara. I am an honourable man, and if you have half the intuition for which your original was famous you will understand that. I give you my word that if she is willing to leave her room, briefly, for these essential purposes, Mara's situation will not be changed. When she is returned, everything will be as it was. I hope that we can progress this in a civilised and mutually trusting fashion.'

Poole studied him for long seconds. Then he glanced at Futurity, and shrugged. 'After all,' Poole said, 'she'll still be able to detonate her bomb whether she's in the cabin with it or not.'

So Mara emerged from her room, for the first time since before Futurity's first visit to the ship.

A strange procession moved around the ship, with Tahget himself in the van, and a handful of crew, mostly female, surrounding the central core of Poole, Futurity and Mara. Mara insisted that Poole and Futurity stay with her at all times, one on either side, and she brought a pillow from her cabin which she held clutched to her chest, like a shield. Futurity couldn't think of a thing to say to this woman who was holding them all hostage, but Poole kept up a comforting murmur of mellifluous small-talk.

Futurity saw that the crew checked over Mara surreptitiously. Maybe they were searching for the devices that linked her to her bomb. But there was nothing to be seen under her shapeless grey smock. Surely any such device would be an implant, he decided.

The peculiar tour finished in the observation lounge, where the view was still half obscured by the hull of an over-friendly ship that had sidled up to the *Ask Politely*. Further out, nuzzling ships drifted around the sky, like bunches of misshapen balloons.

Mara showed a flicker of curiosity for the first time since leaving her cabin. 'The ships are so strange,' she said.

'That they are,' Poole said.

'What are they doing?'

'I don't know. And the Captain won't tell me.'

She pointed. 'Look. Those two are fighting.'

Futurity and the others crowded to the window to see. It was true. Two ships had come together in an obviously unfriendly way. Both lumbering kilometre-long beasts, they weren't about to do anything quickly, but they barged against each other, withdrew, and then went through another slow-motion collision. As they spun and ground, bits of hull ornamentation were bent and snapped off, and the ships were surrounded by a pale cloud of fragments, detached spires and shields, nozzles and antennae and scoops.

'It's a peculiar sort of battle,' Futurity said. 'They aren't using any weapons. All they are doing is smashing up each other's superstructure.'

'But maybe that's the point,' Poole said.

'So strange,' Mara said again.

Captain Tahget blocked her way. 'But,' he said, 'not so strange as the fact that you, madam, were able to smuggle a monopole bomb onto my ship.'

The mood immediately changed. Mara, obviously frightened, shrank back against Poole, coming so close she brushed against him, making his flank sparkle with disrupted pixels.

Poole said warningly, 'Captain, you promised you wouldn't interfere with her.'

Tahget held up his big hands. 'And I will keep my word. Nobody will touch the bomb, or Mara here, and we'll go through with our flight to Chandra as we agreed.'

'But,' Poole said heavily, 'you had an ulterior motive in getting her out here, despite your promises.'

'All right,' Captain Tahget snapped. 'I need some answers. I must know how she got us all into this situation.'

Futurity asked, 'Why?'

Tahget barely glanced at him. 'To stop it happening again.' He glared at Mara. '*Who helped you*? Somebody must have. You're nothing but a refugee from Chandra; you came to 478 with nothing. Who helped you smuggle a bomb on board? Who equipped you with the means to use it? And *why*? I know what *you* want – I don't understand, but I've heard what you said. What I don't know is what your benefactors want. And I need to know.'

She returned his stare defiantly. 'I want to go back to my cabin.'

But Tahget wouldn't back down. The stand-off was tense, and Futurity, his heart pumping, couldn't see a way out.

Poole intervened. 'Mara, it may be best to tell him what he wants to know.'

'But—'

'Telling him who helped you will make no difference to you. You aren't going to come this way again, are you? And I can see the other point of view. Captain Tahget is responsible for his ship.' Mara hesitated, but Poole continued to reassure her. 'I believe he'll keep his word. Just tell him.'

She took a deep breath. 'Her name is Ideator First Class Leen.'

Tahget growled, 'Who?'

But Futurity was shocked. He knew the name: the person who had helped Mara set all this up was a priest belonging to the Guild of Virtual Idealism.

Poole's jaw dropped when he heard this. 'My own makers! How delicious.'

Mara began to explain how the Ideator had helped her smuggle the bomb and other equipment aboard, but Tahget waved her silent. 'If that bunch of illusionists was involved, anything could have been done to us and we wouldn't know it.' His suspicious frown deepened. 'And then, once you were aboard, you asked for Poole himself. So was that part of the scheme?'

'No,' she insisted. 'The Ideator did tell me Michael Poole had been reincarnated on 478. But it was my idea to ask for him, not hers.'

Poole shook his head. 'I'm not part of this, captain, believe me. I'm a mere creature of the Idealists – rather like Mara here, I suppose.'

Now the Captain's ferocious stare was turned on Futurity. 'And you,' Tahget snarled, his scar livid. 'What do you have to do with it? The truth, now.'

Futurity, flustered, protested, 'Why, nothing, Captain. You know why I was brought in – to negotiate with Mara. *You* asked for the Ecclesia's help! And I don't understand why you're even asking me such a question. I'm an Engineer, not an Idealist.'

Tahget snorted. 'But you're all alike, you Guilds. All of you clinging to your petty worldlets, with your stolen fragments of the soldier's faith, your saintly relics and your shrines!'

Futurity was shocked. 'Captain – believe me, Engineers and Idealists would never cooperate on a scheme like this. It's unthinkable.' He hunted for the right word. 'We may seem alike to you. But we are *rivals.*'

'Maybe that's the point,' Poole said smoothly. 'Acolyte, I imagine the Idealists have their own flow-through of pilgrims, along with their money.'

'Yes, that's true.'

'What, then, if Mara's bomb goes off? What will be the impact on the Ecclesia's trading?'

'We don't think of it as trading but a duty to helpless—'

'Just answer the question,' Tahget growled.

Futurity thought it through. 'It would be a disaster for us,' he conceded. 'A refugee makes her journey only once in her lifetime. She brings her children. If she can choose, nobody would come to a place so unsafe as to allow something like this to happen.'

'No more refugees with their meagre savings for you to cream,' Poole said, watching Futurity's reaction with a cold amusement. 'No more pilgrims and their offerings. Your rivals would have struck a mighty economic blow, would they not?'

Tahget said, 'My company certainly wouldn't touch your poxy little globe with a gloved hand, acolyte. Perhaps we won't anyhow.' A vein throbbed in his forehead. 'So we are all puppets of those illusionists. And there's not one of them within light years, whose head I can crack open!'

Mara had listened to all this. Now she said, 'None of this matters. What does matter is me, and my daughter.'

'And your bomb,' said Poole softly.

'Take me back to my cabin,' she said. 'And don't ask me to leave it again before we get to Chandra.'

With a curt nod, Tahget dismissed her.

Futurity went back to his own room. He was relieved the little crisis was over, but his cheeks burned with shame and anger that this whole incident had been set up to get at his own Ecclesia – that another Guild should be responsible – and it had taken Poole to see it, Poole, a Virtual designed by the Idealists themselves!

But as he thought it over, he did see how alike the two Guilds were. And, he couldn't help wondering, if the Idealists were capable of such deception, could it be that *his own Ecclesia* would not be above such dirty tricks? It was all politics, as Poole would probably say, politics and money, and a competition for the grubby trade of refugees and pilgrims. Perhaps even now the Ecclesiasts were plotting manoeuvres just as underhand and unscrupulous against their rivals.

An unwelcome seed of doubt and suspicion lodged in his mind. To burn it out he took his data desk and began furiously to write out a long report on the whole incident for his Hierocrat.

But before he had completed the work he was disturbed again. This time it wasn't Mara who was causing trouble for the crew, but Poole – who had gone missing.

Tahget met Futurity in the observation lounge.

Futurity said, 'I don't see how you can *lose* a Virtual.'

Tahget grunted. 'We know he's being projected somewhere. We can tell that from the energy drain. What we don't know is where. He isn't on the monitors. We've checked out all the permitted zones by eye. What's he up to, acolyte?'

Once again Futurity found himself flinching from Tahget's glare. 'You know, Captain, the way you use your physical presence to intimidate me—'

'Answer the question!'

'I can't! I'm on this voyage because of Poole – believe me, I wish I wasn't here at all – but I'm not his keeper.'

'Acolyte, if you're hiding something . . .'

Futurity was aware of a shadow passing over him. He turned.

There was Poole.

He was *outside* the hull, standing horizontally with his feet on the window's surface, casting a diffuse shadow into the lounge. He was dressed in a skinsuit, and he looked down at Futurity with a broad grin, easily visible through his visor. The Virtual rendition was good enough for Futurity to see the pattern on the soles of Poole's boots. Behind him, entangled ships drifted like clouds.

Futurity gaped. 'Michael Poole! Why – how—?'

'I can tell you how,' Tahget said. He walked up to the window, huge fists clenched. 'You hacked into your own software, didn't you? You overrode the inhibiting protocols.'

'It was an interesting experience,' Poole said. His voice sounded muffled to Futurity, as if he was in another room. 'Not so much like rewriting software as giving myself a nervous breakdown.' He held up a gloved hand. 'And you can see I didn't do away with all the inhibitions. I wasn't sure how far I could go, what was safe. Futurity, I think it's possible that if I cracked this visor, the vacuum would kill me just as quickly as it would kill you.'

Futurity felt an urge to laugh at Poole's antics. But at the same time anger swirled within him. 'Poole, what are you doing out there? You're the only one Mara trusts. All you're doing is destabilising a dangerous situation, can't you see that?'

Poole looked mildly exasperated. 'Destabilising? I didn't create this mess, acolyte. And I certainly didn't ask to be here, in this muddled century of yours. But given that I am here – what do *I* want out of it? To find out, that's what. That's all I ever wanted, I sometimes think.'

Tahget said, 'And what did you go spacewalking to find out, Poole?'

Poole grinned impishly. 'Why, Captain, I wanted to know about your Hairy Folk.'

Futurity frowned. 'What Hairy Folk?'

Tahget just glared.

Poole said, 'Shall I show him?' He waved a hand. A new Virtual materialised beside him, hanging in the vacuum. Its fragmentary images showed shadowy figures scurrying through the ship's corridors, and along those translucent access tubes that snaked between the intertwined ships.

At first they looked like children to Futurity. They seemed to run on all fours, and to be wearing some kind of dark clothing. But as he looked closer he saw they didn't so much crawl as scamper, climbing along the tube using big hands and very flexible-looking feet to clutch at handholds. There was something odd about the proportions of their bodies too: they had big chests, narrow hips, and their arms were long, their legs short, so that all four limbs were about the same length.

'And,' Futurity said with a shudder, 'that dark stuff isn't clothing, is it?'

For answer, Poole froze the image. Captured at the centre of the frame, clearly visible through an access tube's translucent wall, a figure gazed out at Futurity. Though this one's limbs looked as well-muscled as the others, it was a female, he saw; small breasts pushed out of a tangle of fur. Her face, turned to Futurity, was very human, with a pointed chin, a small nose, and piercing blue eyes. But her brow was a low ridge of bone, above which her skull was flat.

'A post-human,' Futurity breathed.

'Oh, certainly,' said Poole. 'Evidently adapted to microgravity. That even-proportioned frame is built for climbing, not for walking. Interesting; they seem to have reverted to a body plan from way back in our own hominid line, when our ancestors lived in the trees of Earth. The forests have vanished now, as have those ancestors or anything that looked like them. But a sort of echo has returned, here at the centre of the Galaxy. How strange! Of course these creatures would have been illegal under the Coalition, as I understand it. Evolutionary divergence wasn't the done thing in those days. But the Galaxy is a big place, and evidently it happened anyhow. *She* doesn't look so interested in the finer points of the law, does she?'

Futurity said, 'Captain, why do you allow these creatures to run around your ship?'

Poole laughed. 'Captain, I'm afraid he doesn't understand.'

Tahget growled, 'Acolyte, we call these creatures "shipbuilders". And I do not allow them to do anything – it's rather the other way around.'

Poole said cheerfully, 'Hence the ship's name – *Ask Politely!*'

'But you're the Captain,' Futurity said, bewildered.

Poole said, 'Tahget is Captain of the small pod which sustains you, acolyte, which I can see very clearly stuck in the tangle of the hull superstructure. But he's not in command of the ship. All he does is a bit of negotiating. You are all less than passengers, really. You are like lice in a child's hair.'

Tahget shrugged. 'You insult me, Poole, but I don't mind the truth.'

Futurity still didn't get it. 'The ships belong to these Builders? And they let you hitch a ride?'

'For a fee. They still need material from the ground – food, air, water – no recycling system is a hundred per cent efficient. And that's what we use to buy passage.'

Poole grinned. 'I pay you in credits. You pay them in bananas!'

The Captain ignored him. 'We have ways of letting the Builders know where we want them to take us.'

'How?' Poole asked, interested.

Tahget shuddered. 'The Shipbuilders are nearly mindless. I leave that to specialists.'

Futurity stared at Poole's images of swarming apes, his dread growing. 'Nearly mindless. But who maintains the *Ask Politely*? Who runs the engines? Captain, *who's steering this ship?*'

'The Hairy Folk,' Poole said.

It was all a question of time, said Michael Poole.

'In this strange future of yours, it's more than twenty thousand years since humans first left Sol system. *Twenty thousand years!* Maybe you're used to thinking about periods like that, but I'm a sort of involuntary time traveller, and it appals me – because that monstrous interval is a good fraction of the age of the human species itself.

'And it's more than enough time for natural selection to have shaped us, if we had given it the chance. The frozen imagination of the Coalition kept most of humanity in a bubble of stasis. But out in the dark, sliding between those islands of rock, it was a different matter: nobody could have controlled what was happening out there. And with time, we diverged.

'After the first humans had left Earth, most of them plunged straight into another gravity well, like amphibious creatures hopping between ponds. But there were some, just a fraction, who found it preferable to stay out in the smoother spaces between the worlds. They lived in bubble-colonies dug out of ice moons or comets, or blown from asteroid rock. Others travelled on generation starships, unsurprisingly finding that their ship-home became much more congenial than any destination planned for them by well-meaning but long-dead ancestors. Some of them just stayed on their ships, making their living from trading.'

'My own people did that,' Futurity said. 'So it's believed. The first Engineers were stranded on a clutch of ships, out in space, when Earth was occupied. They couldn't go home. They survived on trade for centuries, until Earth was freed.'

'A fascinating snippet of family history,' Tahget said contemptuously.

Poole said, 'Just think about it, acolyte. These Hairy Folk have been suspended between worlds for millennia. And that has shaped them. They have lost much of what they don't need – your built-for-a-gravity-well body, your excessively large brain.'

Futurity said, 'Given the situation, I don't see how becoming less intelligent would be an advantage.'

'Think, boy! You're running a starship, not a home workshop. You're out there *for ever*. Everything is fixed, and the smallest mistake could kill you. You can only maintain, not innovate. Tinkering is one of your strongest taboos! You need absolute cultural stasis, even over evolutionary time. And to get that you have to tap into even more basic drivers. There's only one force that could fix hominids' behaviour in such a way and for so long – and that's sex.'

'Sex?'

'Sex! Let me tell you a story. Once there was a kind of hominid – a pre-human – called *Homo erectus*. They lived on old Earth, of course. They had bodies like humans', brains like apes'. I've always imagined they were beautiful creatures. And they had a simple technology. The cornerstone of it was a hand-axe: a teardrop-shape with a fine edge, hacked out of stone or flint. You could use it to shave your hair, butcher an animal, kill your rival; it was a good tool.

'And the same design was used, with no significant modification, for *a million years*. Think about it, acolyte! What an astonishing stasis that is – why, the tool survived even across species boundaries, even when one type of *erectus* replaced another. But do you know what it was that imposed that stasis, over such an astounding span of time?'

'Sex?'

'Exactly! *Erectus* used the technology, not just as a tool, but as a way of impressing potential mates. Think about it: to find the raw materials you have to show a knowledge of the environment; to make a hand-axe you need to show hand-eye coordination and an ability for abstract thought; to use it you need motor skills. If you can make a hand-axe you're showing you are a walking, talking expression of a healthy set of genes.

'But there's a downside. Once you have picked on the axe as your way of impressing the opposite sex, the design has to *freeze*. This isn't a path to innovation! You can make your axes better than the next guy – or bigger, or smaller even – but never different, because you would run the risk of confusing the target of your charms. And *that* is why the hand-axes didn't change for a megayear – and that's why, I'll wager, the technology of these spiky starships hasn't changed either for millennia.'

Futurity started to see his point. 'You're saying that the Shipbuilders maintain their starships, as – as—'

'As *erectus* once made his hand-axes. They do it, not for the utility of the thing itself, but as a display of sexual status. It's no wonder I couldn't figure out the function of that superstructure of spines and scoops and nozzles. It has no utility! It has no purpose but showing off for potential mates – but that sexual role has served its purpose and frozen its design.'

Futurity recalled hearing of another case like this – a generation starship called the *Mayflower*, lost beyond the Galaxy, where the selection pressures of a closed environment had overwhelmed the crew. Evidently it hadn't been an isolated instance.

As usual Poole seemed delighted to have figured out something new. 'The *Ask Politely* is a starship, but it is also a peacock's tail. How strange it all is.' He laughed. 'And it would appal a lot of my old buddies that their dreams of interstellar domination would result in *this*.'

'You're very perceptive, Michael Poole,' the Captain said with a faint sneer.

'I always was,' said Poole. 'And a fat lot of good it's done me.'

Futurity turned to the Captain. 'Is this true?'

Tahget shrugged. 'I wouldn't have put it quite so coarsely as Poole. We crew just get on with our jobs. Every so often you have to let the Builders come to a gathering like this. They show off their ships, their latest enhancements. Sometimes they fight. And they throw those tubes between the ships, swarm across and screw their heads off for a few days. When they've worn themselves out, you can pass on your way.'

Futurity asked, 'But *why* use these creatures and their peculiar ships? Look at the detour we have had to make, even though we have a bomb on board! Why not just run ships under human control, as we always have?'

Tahget sighed. 'Because we have no choice. When the Coalition collapsed, the Navy and the state trading fleets collapsed with it. Acolyte, unless you are *extremely* powerful or wealthy, in this corner of the Galaxy a ship like this is the only way to get around. We just have to work with the Builders.'

Futurity felt angry. 'Then why not *tell* people? Isn't it a lie to pretend that the ship is under your control?'

Tahget blinked. 'And if you had known the truth? Would you have climbed aboard a ship if you had known it was under the control of low-browed animals like *those*?'

Futurity stared out as the Shipbuilders swarmed excitedly along their access tubes, seeking food or mates.

## VI

With the encounter at 3-Kilo apparently complete, the *Ask Politely* sailed back towards the centre of the Galaxy. To Futurity it was a comfort when the ship slid once more into the crowded sky of the Core, and the starlight folded over him like a blanket, shutting out the darkness.

But ships of the Kardish Imperium closed around the *Ask Politely*. Everybody crowded to the windows to see.

They were called greenships, an archaic design like a three-pronged claw. Part of the huge military legacy of the Galaxy-centre war, they had once been painted as green as their names – green, the imagined colour of distant Earth – and they had sported the tetrahedral sigil that had once been recognised across the Galaxy as the common symbol of a free and strong mankind. But all that was the symbology of the hated Coalition, and so now these ships were a bloody red, and they bore on their hulls not tetrahedrons but the clenched-fist emblem of the latest Kard.

Ancient and recycled they might be, but still the greenships whirled and swooped around the *Ask Politely*, dancing against the light of the Galaxy. It was a display of menace, pointless and spectacular and beautiful. The *Politely* crew gaped, their mouths open.

'The crew are envious,' Futurity murmured to Poole.

'Of course they are,' Poole said. 'Out there, in those greenships – that's how a human is supposed to fly. This spiky, lumbering beast could never dance like that! And this "crew" has no more control over their destiny than fleas on a rat. But I suppose you wouldn't sign up even for a ship like this unless you had something of the dream of flying. How they must envy those Kardish flyboys!'

Futurity understood that while the *Politely* had fled across the Galaxy there had been extensive three-way negotiations between the Ideocracy, the Imperium and the Ecclesia about the situation on *Politely*. All parties had tentatively agreed that this was a unique humanitarian crisis, and everyone should work together to resolve it, in the interests of common decency. But Earth was twenty-eight thousand light years away, and the blunt power of the Kard, here and now, was not to be denied.

So, with its barnstorming escort in place, the ship slid deeper into the crowded sky. The whole formation made bold faster-than-light jumps, roughly synchronised. Soon they penetrated the Central Star Mass.

Futurity found Poole in the observation lounge, staring out at the crowded sky. The nearest stars hung like globe lamps, their discs clearly visible, with a deep three-dimensional array of more stars hanging behind them – stars beyond stars beyond stars, all of them hot and young, until they merged into a mist of light that utterly shut out any disturbing darkness.

Against this background, Poole was a short, sullen form, and even the Mass's encompassing brilliance didn't seem to alleviate his heavy darkness. His expression was complex, as always.

'I can never tell what you're thinking, Michael Poole.'

Poole glanced at him. 'That's probably a good thing . . . Lethe, *this is the centre of the Galaxy*, and the stars are crowded together like grains of sand in a sack. It's terrifying! The whole place is bathed in light – why, if not for this ship's shielding we'd all be fried in an instant. But to you, acolyte, this is normal, isn't it?'

Futurity shrugged. 'It's what I grew up with.'

He tried to summarise for Poole the geography of the centre of the Galaxy. The structure was concentric – 'Like an onion,' Poole commented – with layers of density and complexity centred on Chandra, the brooding supermassive black hole at the centre of everything. The Core itself was the Galaxy's central bulge, a fat ellipsoid of stars and shining nebulae set at the centre of the disc of spiral arms. Embedded within the Core was the still denser knot of the Central Star Mass. As well as millions of stars crammed into a few light years, the Mass contained relics of immense astrophysical violence, expanding blisters left over from supernovas, and tremendous fronts of roiling gas and dust thrown off from greater detonations at the Galaxy's heart. Stranger yet was the Baby Spiral, a fat comma shape embedded deep in the Mass, like a miniature galaxy with its own arms of young stars and hot gases.

And at the centre of it all was Chandra itself, the black hole, a single object with the mass of millions of stars. The Galaxy centre was a place of immense violence, where stars were born and torn apart in great bursts. But Chandra itself was massive and immovable, the pivot of vast astrophysical machineries, pinned fast to spacetime.

Poole was intrigued by Futurity's rough-and-ready knowledge of the Core's geography, even though the acolyte had never before travelled away from 478. 'You know it the way I knew the shapes of Earth's continents from school maps,' he said. But he was dismayed by the brusque labels Futurity and the crew had for the features of the centre. *The Core, the Mass, the Baby*: they were soldiers' names, irreverent and familiar. In the immense glare of the Core there was no trace of mankind's three-thousand-year war to be seen, but those names, Poole said, marked out this place as a battlefield – just as much as the traces of complex organic molecules that had once been human beings, hordes of them slaughtered and vaporised, sometimes still detectable as pollutants in those shining clouds.

Something about the location's complexity made Poole open up, tentatively, about his own experience: the Virtual's, not the original.

'When I was made fully conscious the first time, it felt like waking up. But I had none of the usual baggage in my head you carry through sleep: no clear memory of where I had been when I fell asleep, what I had done the day before – even how old I was. The priests quizzed me, and I slowly figured out where I was, and even *what* I was. I was shocked to find out *when* I was. Let me tell you,' said Poole grimly, 'that was tougher to take than being told I was worshipped as a god.'

'You can remember your past life? I mean, Poole's.'

'Oh, yes. I remember it as if I lived it myself. I'm told they didn't so much programme me,' said Poole wistfully, 'as *grow* me. They put together as much as they could about my life, and then fast-forwarded me through it all.'

'So you lived out a computer-memory life.'

Poole said, 'My memory is sharp up to a point. I remember my father Harry, who, long after he was dead, came back to haunt me as a Virtual. I remember Miriam – somebody I loved,' he said gruffly. 'I lost her in time long before I lost myself. But it's all a fake. I *remember* having free will and making choices. But I was a rat in a maze; the truth was I never had such freedom.

'And the trouble is the records go fuzzy just at the point where my, or rather *his*, biography gets interesting to you theologians. What happened after I lost Miriam isn't like a memory, it's like a dream – a guess, a fiction somebody wrote out for me. Even to think about it blurs my sense of self. Anyhow I don't believe any of it!

'So I was a big disappointment, I think. Oh, the priests kept on developing me. They would download upgrades; I would wake up refreshed, rebooted. Of course I always wondered if I was still the same *me* as when I went to sleep. But I was never able to answer the theologians' questions about the Ultimate Observer, or my jaunt through the wormholes, or about what I saw or didn't see at Timelike Infinity. I wish I could! I'd like to know myself.

'In the end they shut me down one last time. They promised me I'd wake up soon, as I always had. But I was left in my Virtual casket for a thousand years. The bastards. The next thing I saw was the ugly face of your Hierocrat, leaning over me.'

'Perhaps they did crucify you, in the end.'

Poole looked at him sharply. 'You've got depths, despite your silly name, kid. Perhaps they did. What I really don't understand is why they didn't just wipe me off the data banks. Just sentimental, maybe.'

Futurity said, 'Oh, not that.' The Hierocrat in his hurried briefing had made this clear. 'They'd worked too hard on you, Michael Poole. They put in too much. Your Virtual representation is now more information-rich than *I* am, and information density defines reality. You may not be a god. You may not even be Michael Poole. But whatever you are, you are more *real* than we are, now.'

Poole stared at him. 'You don't say.' Then he laughed, and turned away.

Still the *Ask Politely* burrowed deeper into the kernel of the Galaxy.

## VII

At last the *Ask Politely*, with its Kardish escort, broke through veils of stars into a place the crew called the Hole. Under the same strict guarantees as before, Poole brought Mara to the observation deck.

The ship came to a halt, suspended in a rough sphere walled by crowded stars. This was a bubble in the tremendous foam of stars that crowded the Galaxy's centre, a bubble swept clean by a black hole's gravity. Captain Tahget pointed out some brighter pinpoints; they were the handful of stars, of all the hundreds of billions in the Galaxy, whose orbits took them closest to Chandra. No stars could come closer, for they would be torn apart by Chandra's tides.

When Futurity looked ahead he could see a puddle of light, suspended at the very centre of the Hole. It was small, dwarfed by the scale of the Hole itself. It looked elliptical from his perspective, but he knew it was a rough disc, and it marked the very heart of the Galaxy.

'It looks like a toy,' Mara said, wondering.

Poole asked, 'You know what it is?'

'Of course. It's the accretion disc surrounding Chandra.'

'Home,' Poole said dryly.

'Yes,' Mara said. 'But I never saw it like this before. The Kardish shipped us out in their big transports. Just cargo scows. You don't get much of a view.'

'And somewhere in there—'

'Is my daughter.' She turned to him, and the washed-out light smoothed the lines of her careworn face, making her look younger. 'Thank you, Michael Poole. You have brought me home.'

'Not yet I haven't,' Poole said grimly.

The *Ask Politely* with its escort swooped down towards the centre of the Hole. That remote puddle loomed, and opened out into a broad sea of roiling gas, above which the ships raced.

Infalling matter bled into this central whirlpool, the accretion disc, where it spent hours or weeks or years helplessly orbiting, kneaded by tides and heated by compression until any remnants of structure had been destroyed, leaving only a thin, glowing plasma. It was this mush that finally fell into the black hole. Thus Chandra was slowly consuming the Galaxy of which it was the heart.

Eventually Futurity made out Chandra itself, a fist of fierce light set at the geometric centre of the accretion disc, so bright that clumps of turbulence cast shadows light days long over the disc's surface. It wasn't the event horizon itself he was seeing, of course, but the despairing glow of matter crushed beyond endurance, in the last instants before it was sucked out of the universe altogether. The event horizon was a surface from which nothing, not even light, could escape, but it was forever hidden by the glow of the doomed matter which fell into it.

Poole was glued to the window. 'Astounding,' he said. 'The black hole is a flaw in the cosmos, into which a Galaxy is draining. And this accretion disc is a sink as wide as Sol system!'

It was Mara who noticed the moistness on Poole's cheeks. 'You're weeping.'

He turned his head away, annoyed. 'Virtuals don't weep,' he said gruffly.

'You're not sad. You're happy,' Mara said.

'And Virtuals don't get happy,' Poole said. 'It's just – to be here, to see this!' He turned on Futurity, who saw anger beneath his exhilaration, even a kind of despair, powerful emotions mixed up together. 'But you know what's driving me crazy? I'm not *him*. I'm not Poole. It's as if you woke me up to torture me with existential doubt! *He* never saw this – and whatever *I* am, he is long gone, and I can't share it with him. So it's meaningless, isn't it?'

Futurity pondered that. 'Then appreciate it for yourself. This is your moment, not his. Relish how this enhances your own identity – yours, uniquely, not *his*.'

Poole snorted. 'A typical priest's answer!' But he fell silent, and seemed a little calmer. Futurity thought he might, for once, have given Poole a little comfort.

Tahget said grimly, 'Before you get too dewy-eyed, remember this was a war zone.' He told Poole how Chandra had once been surrounded by technology, a net-like coating put in place by beings who had corralled a supermassive black hole and put it to work. 'The whole set-up took a lot of destroying,' Tahget said evenly. 'When we'd finished that job, we'd won the Galaxy.'

Poole stared at him. 'You new generations are a formidable bunch.'

There were stars in the accretion disc. Tahget pointed them out.

The disc was a turbulent place, where eddies and knots with the mass of many suns could form – and, here and there, collapse, compress and spark into fusion fire. These stars shone like jewels in the murky debris at the rim of the disc. But doomed they were, as haplessly drawn towards Chandra as the rest of the disc debris from which they were born. Eventually the most massive star would be torn apart, its own gravity no match for the tides of Chandra. Sometimes you would see a smear of light brushed across the face of the disc: the remains of a star, flensed and gutted, its material still glowing with fusion light.

Some stars didn't last even that long. Massive, bloated, these monsters would burst as supernovas almost as soon as they formed, leaving behind remnants: neutron stars – or even black holes, stellar-mass objects. Even Chandra couldn't break open a black hole, but it would gobble up these babies with relish. When a black hole hit Chandra, so it was said, that immense event horizon would ring like a bell.

It was towards one of these satellite black holes that the *Ask Politely* now descended.

Dropping into the accretion disc was like falling into a shining cloud; billows and bubbles, filaments and sheets of glowing gas drifted upwards past the ship. Even though those billows were larger than planets – for the accretion disc, as Poole had noted, was as wide as a solar system itself – Futurity could see the billows churning as he watched, as if the ship was falling into a nightmare of vast, slow-moving sculptures.

The approach was tentative, cautious. Captain Tahget said the Shipbuilders were having to be bribed with additional goodies; the swarming creatures were very unhappy at having to take their ship into this dangerous place. This struck Futurity as a very rational point of view.

In the middle of all this they came upon a black hole.

They needed the observation lounge's magnification features to see it. With twice the mass of Earth's sun, it was a blister of sullen light, sailing through the accretion clouds. Like Chandra's, the dark mask of its event horizon – in fact only a few kilometres across – was hidden by the electromagnetic scream of the matter it sucked out of the universe. It even had its own accretion disc, Futurity saw, a small puddle of light around that central spark.

And this city-sized sun had its own planet. 'Greyworld,' Mara breathed. 'I never thought I'd see it again.'

This asteroid, having survived its fall into Chandra's accretion disc, had been plucked out of the garbage by the Ideocrats and moved to a safe orbit around the satellite black hole. The worldlet orbited its primary at about the same distance as Earth orbited its sun. And Greyworld lived up to its name, Futurity saw, for its surface was a seamless silver-grey, smooth and unblemished.

To Mara, it seemed, this was home. 'We live under the roof,' Mara said. 'It is held up from the surface by stilts.'

'We used to call this paraterraforming,' Poole said. 'Turning your world into one immense building. Low gravity lets you get away with a lot, doesn't it?'

'The roof is perfectly reflective,' Mara said. 'We tap the free energy of the Galaxy centre to survive, but none of it reaches our homes untamed.'

'I should think not,' Poole said warmly.

'It is a beautiful place,' Mara said, smiling. 'We build our houses tall; some of them float, or hang from the world roof. And you feel safe, safe from the violence of the galactic storms outside. You should see it sometime, Michael Poole.'

Poole raised his eyebrows. 'But, Mara, your "safe" haven is about as unsafe as it could get, despite the magical roof.'

'He's right,' said Tahget. 'This black hole and its orbital retinue are well on their way into Chandra. After another decade or so the tides will pull the planetoid free of the hole, and after that they will rip off that fancy roof. Then the whole mess will fall into Chandra's event horizon, and that will be that.'

'Which is why Greyworld had to be evacuated,' Futurity said.

'The latest Kard is known for her humanitarian impulses,' Tahget said dryly.

Poole said, 'All right, Mara, here we are. What now? Do you want to be taken down to Greyworld?'

'Oh, no,' she said. 'What would be the point of that?' She seemed faintly irritated. 'I told you, Michael Poole. My Sharn isn't on Greyworld. She's *there*.' And she pointed to the glimmering black hole.

Tahget and his crew exchanged significant glances.

Futurity felt a flickering premonition, the return of fear. This journey into the heart of the Galaxy had been so wondrous that he had managed, for a while, to forget the danger they were in. But it had all been a diversion. This woman, after all, controlled a bomb, and now they approached the moment of crisis.

Poole drew him aside. 'You look worried, acolyte,' he murmured.

'I *am* worried. Mara is still asking for the impossible. What do we do now?'

481

Poole seemed much calmer than Futurity felt. 'I always had a philo-sophy. If you don't know what to do, gather more data. How do you *know* that what she wants is impossible?' He turned to Tahget. 'Captain, how close can you take us to the satellite black hole?'

Tahget shook his head. 'It's a waste of time.'

'But you don't have any better suggestion, do you? Let's go take a look. What else can we do?'

Tahget grumbled, but complied.

So the ship lifted away from Greyworld, and its retinue of Kardish greenships formed up once more. Mara smiled, as if she was coming home at last. But Futurity shivered, for there was nothing remotely human about the place they were heading to now.

Slowly the spiteful light of the satellite black hole drew closer.

'Acolyte,' Poole murmured. 'You have a data desk?'

'Yes.'

'Then start making observations. Study that black hole, Futurity. Figure out what's going on here. This is your chance to do some real science, for once.'

'But I'm not a scientist.'

'No, you're not, are you? You're too compromised for that. But you told me you were curious, once. That was what drove you out of the farm and into the arms of the Ecclesia in the first place.' He sighed. 'You know, in my day a kid like you would have had better opportunities.'

Futurity felt moved to defend his vocation. 'I don't think you understand the richness of theological—'

'Just get the damn desk!'

Futurity hurried to his cabin and returned with his data desk. It was the Ecclesia's most up-to-date model. He pressed the desk to the observation lounge blister, and checked it over as data poured in.

'I feel excited,' he said.

'You should,' Poole said. 'You might make some original discovery here. And, more important, you might figure out how to save all our skins, my Virtual hide included.'

'I'm excited but worried,' Futurity admitted.

'*That* sounds like you.'

'Michael Poole, how can a human child survive in a black hole?'

Poole glanced at him approvingly. 'Good; that's the right question to ask. You need to cultivate an open mind, acolyte. Let's assume Mara's serious, that she knows what she's talking about.'

'That she's not crazy.'

'Open mind! Mara has implied – I think – that we're not talking about the child in her physical form but some kind of download, like a Virtual.'

Futurity asked, 'But what information can be stored in a black hole? A hole is defined only by its mass, charge and spin. You need rather more than three numbers to define a Virtual. But no human science knows a way to store more data than that in a black hole – though it is believed others may have done so in the past.'

Poole eyed him. '*Others*? . . .' He slapped his own cheek. 'Never mind. Concentrate, Poole. Then let's look away from the hole itself, the relativistic object. We're looking for structure, somewhere you can write information. Every black hole is embedded in the wider universe, and every one of them comes with baggage. This satellite hole has its own accretion disc. Maybe there . . .'

But Futurity's scans of the disc revealed nothing. 'Michael Poole, it's basically a turbulence spectrum. Oh, there is some correlation of structure around a circumference, and over time tied into the orbital period around the black hole.'

'But that's just gravity, the inverse square law, defined by one number: the black hole's mass. All right, what else have we got?' Inexpertly Poole tapped at a Virtual clone of Futurity's desk. He magnified an image of the hole itself. It was a flaring pinprick, even under heavy magnification. But Poole played with filters until he had reduced the central glare, and had brought up details of the background sky.

A textured glow appeared. A rough sphere of pearly gas surrounded the black hole and much of its accretion disc, and within the sphere a flattened ellipsoid of brighter mist coalesced closer to the hole.

'Well, well,' said Poole.

Futurity, entranced, leaned closer to see. 'I never knew black holes had atmospheres! Look, Michael Poole, it is almost like an eye staring at us – see, with the white, and then this iris within, and the black hole itself the pupil.'

Tahget listened to this contemptuously. 'Evidently neither of you has been around black holes much.' He pointed to the image of the accretion disc. 'The hole's magnetic field pulls material out of the disc, and hurls it into these wider shells. We call the outer layers the corona.'

Futurity said, 'A star's outer atmosphere is also a corona.'

'Well done,' said Tahget dryly. 'The gas shells around black holes and stars are created by similar processes. Same physics, same name.'

Poole said, 'And the magnetic field pumps energy into these layers. Futurity, look at this temperature profile!'

'Yes,' said Tahget. 'In the accretion disc you might get temperatures in the millions of degrees. In the inner corona' – the eye's 'iris' – 'the temperatures will be ten times hotter than that, and in the outer layers ten times hotter again.'

'But the magnetic field of a spinning black hole and its accretion disc isn't simple,' Poole said. 'It won't be just energy that the field pumps in, but complexity.' He was becoming more expert with the data desk now. He picked out a section of the inner corona, and zoomed in. 'What do you make of that, Futurity?'

The acolyte saw wisps of light, ropes of denser material in the turbulent gases, intertwined, slowly writhing. They were like ghosts, driven by the complex magnetic fields, and yet, Futurity immediately thought, they had a certain autonomy. Ghosts, dancing in the atmosphere of a black hole! He laughed with helpless delight.

Poole grinned. 'I think we just found our structure.'

Mara was smiling. 'I told you,' she said. 'And that's where my daughter is.'

## VIII

It took a detailed examination of the structures in the black hole air, a cross-examination of Mara, input from the experienced Captain Tahget, and some assiduous searching of the ship's data stores – together with some extremely creative interpolation by Michael Poole – before they had a tentative hypothesis to fit the facts about what had happened here.

Like so much else about this modern age, it had come out of the death of the Interim Coalition of Governance.

Poole said, 'Breed, fight hard, die young, and stay human: you could sum up the Coalition's philosophy in those few words. In its social engineering the Coalition set up a positive feedback process; it unleashed a swarm of fast-breeding humans across the Galaxy, until every star system had been filled.' Poole grinned. 'Not a noble way to do it, but it worked. And we did stay human, for twenty thousand years. Evolution postponed!'

'It wasn't as simple as that,' Futurity cautioned. 'Perhaps it couldn't have been. The Shipbuilders slid through the cracks. There were even rumours of divergences among the soldiers of the front lines, as they adapted to the pressures of millennia of war.'

'Sure.' Poole waved a hand. 'But these are exceptions. You can't deny the basic fact that the Coalition *froze human evolution*, for the vast bulk of mankind, on epic scales of space and time. And by doing so, they won their war. Which was when the trouble really started.'

The heirs of the Coalition were if anything even more fanatical about their ideology and purpose than their predecessors had ever been. They had called themselves the Ideocracy, precisely to emphasise the supremacy of the ideas which had won a Galaxy, but of which everybody else had temporarily lost sight.

In their conclaves the Ideocrats sought a new strategy. Now that the old threat had been vanquished, nobody needed the Coalition any more. Perhaps, therefore, the Ideocrats dreamed cynically, a conjuring-up of *future* threats might be enough to frighten a scattered humanity back into the fold, where they would be brought once more under a single command – that is, under the Ideocrats' command – just as in the good old days. Whether those potential threats ever came to pass or not was academic. The cause was the thing, noble in itself.

The Ideocrats' attention focused on Chandra, centre of the Galaxy and ultimate symbol of the war. The great black hole had once been used as a military resource by the foe of mankind. What if now a *human* force could somehow occupy Chandra? It would be a hedge against any future return by the Xeelee – and would be a constant reminder to all mankind of the threat against which the Ideocracy's predecessor had fought so long, and on which even now the Ideocracy was focused. A greater rallying cry could hardly be imagined; Ideocracy strategists imagined an applauding mankind returning gratefully to its jurisdiction once more.

But how do you send people into a black hole? Eventually a way was found. 'But,' Poole said, 'they had to break their own rules . . .'

Far from resisting human evolution, the Ideocrats now ordered that *deliberate* modifications of mankind be made: that specifically designed post-humans be engineered to be injected into new environments. 'In this case,' Poole said, 'the tenuous atmosphere of a black hole.'

'It's impossible,' said Captain Tahget, bluntly disbelieving. 'There's no way a human could live off wisps of superheated plasma, however you modified her.'

'Not a human, but a *post*-human,' Michael Poole said testily. 'Have you never heard of pantropy, Captain? This is your age, not mine! Evolution is in your hands now; it has been for millennia. You don't have to think small: a few tweaks to the bone structure here, a bigger forebrain there. You can go much further than that. I myself am an example.

'A standard human's data definition is realised in flesh and blood, in structures of carbon-water biochemistry. *I* am realised in patterns in computer cores, and in shapings of light. You could project an equivalent human definition into any medium that will store the data – any technological medium, alternate chemistries of silicon or sulphur, anything you like from the frothing of quarks in a proton to the gravitational ripples of the universe itself. And then your post-humans, established in the new medium, can get on and breed.' He saw their faces, and he laughed. 'I'm shocking you! How delicious. Two thousand years after the Coalition imploded, its taboos still have a hold on the human imagination.'

'Get to the point, Virtual,' Tahget snapped.

'The point is,' Mara put in, 'there are people in the black hole air. Out there. Those ghostly shapes you see are *people*. They really are.'

'It's certainly possible,' Poole said. 'There's more than enough structure in those wisps of magnetism and plasma to store the necessary data.'

Futurity said, 'But what would be the point? What would be the function of these post-humans?'

'Weapons,' Poole said simply.

Even when Greyworld was ripped away and destroyed by Chandra's tides, the satellite black hole would sail on, laden with its accretion disc and its atmosphere – and carrying the plasma ghosts that lived in that atmosphere, surviving where no normal human could. Perhaps the ghosts could ride the satellite hole all the way into Chandra itself, and perhaps, as the small hole was gobbled up by the voracious central monster, they would be able to transfer to Chandra's own much more extensive atmosphere.

'Once aliens infested Chandra,' Poole said. 'It took us three thousand years to get them out. So the Ideocrats decided they were going to seed

Chandra with humans – or at least post-humans. Then Chandra will be ours for ever.'

Captain Tahget shook his head, grumbling about ranting theorists and rewritings of history.

Futurity thought all this was a wonderful story, whether or not it was true. But he couldn't forget there was still a bomb on board the ship. Cautiously, he said to Mara, 'And one of these – uh, post-humans – is your daughter?'

'Yes,' Mara said.

Tahget was increasingly impatient with all this. 'But, woman! Can't you see that even supposing this antiquated Virtual is right about pantropy and post-humans, whatever *might* have been projected into the black hole atmosphere can no more be your daughter than Poole here can be your son? You are carbon and water, *it* is a filmy wisp of plasma. Whatever sentimental ties you have, the light show in that cloud has nothing to do with you.'

'Not sentimental,' she said clearly. 'The ties are real, Captain. *The person they sent into that black hole is my daughter*. It's all to do with loyalty, you see.'

The Ideocrats, comparative masters when it came to dominating their fellow humans, had no experience in dealing with post-humans. They had no idea how to enforce discipline and loyalty over creatures to whom 'real' humans might seem as alien as a fly to a fish. So they took precautions. Each candidate pantropic was born as a fully biological human, from a mother's womb, and each spent her first fifteen years living a normal a life – *normal*, given she had been born on a tent-world in orbit around a black hole.

'Then, on her sixteenth birthday, Sharn was taken,' Mara said. 'And she was copied.'

'Like making a Virtual,' Poole mused. 'The copying must have been a quantum process. And the data was injected into the plasma structures in the black hole atmosphere.' He grinned. 'You can't fault the Ideocrats for not thinking big! And that's why there are people here in the first place – I mean, a colony with families – so that these wretched exiles would have a grounding in humanity, and stay loyal. Ingenious.'

'It sounds horribly manipulative,' said Futurity.

'Yes. *Obey us or your family gets it* . . .'

Mara said, 'We knew we were going to lose her, from the day Sharn was born. We knew it would be hard. But we knew our duty. Anyhow we weren't *really* losing her. We would always have her, up there in the sky.'

'I don't understand,' groused the Captain. 'After your daughter was "copied", why didn't she just walk out of the copying booth?'

'Because quantum information can't be cloned, Captain,' Poole said gently. 'If you make a copy you have to destroy the original. Which is why young Futurity's superiors were so agitated when I was transferred into this ship's data store: there is only ever one copy of *me*. Sharn could never have walked out of that booth. She had been destroyed in the process.'

Futurity gazed out at the wispy black hole air. 'Then – if this is all true – somewhere in those wisps is your daughter. The *only* copy of your daughter.'

Poole said, 'In a deep philosophical sense, that's true. It really is her daughter, rendered in light.'

Futurity said, 'Can she speak to you?'

'It was never allowed,' Mara said wistfully. 'Only the commanders had access, on secure channels. I must say I found that hard. I don't even know how she *feels*. Is she in pain? What does it feel like to be her now?'

'How sad,' Poole said. 'You have your duty – to colonise a new world, the strange air of the black hole. But *you* can't go there; instead you have to lose your children to it. You are transitional, belonging neither to your ancestors' world or your children's. You are stranded between worlds.'

That seemed to be too much for Mara. She sniffed, and pulled herself upright. 'It was a military operation, you know. We all accepted it. I told you, we had our duty. But then the Kard's ships came along,' she said bitterly. 'They just swept us up and took us away, and we didn't even get to say goodbye.'

Tahget glared. 'Which is why you hijacked my ship and dragged us all to the centre of the Galaxy!'

She smiled weakly. 'I'm sorry about that.'

Futurity held his hands up. 'I think what we need now is to find an exit strategy.'

Poole grinned. 'At last you're talking like an engineer, not a priest.'

Futurity said, 'Mara, we've brought you here as we promised. You can *see* your daughter, I guess. What now? If we take you to the planetoid, would you be able to talk to her?'

'Not likely,' Mara said. 'The Kardish troops were stealing the old Ideocracy gear even before we lifted off. I think they thought the whole project was somehow unhealthy.'

'Yes,' said Poole. 'I can imagine they will use this as a propaganda tool in their battle with the Ideocracy.'

'Pah,' spat Tahget. 'Never mind politics! What the acolyte is asking, madam, is whether you will now relinquish your bomb, so we can all get on with our lives.'

Mara looked up at the black hole, hesitating. 'I don't want to be any trouble.'

Tahget laughed bitterly.

'I just wish I could speak to Sharn.'

'If we can't manage that, maybe we can send a message,' said Michael Poole. He grinned, snapped his fingers, and disappeared.

And reappeared in his skinsuit, out in space, on the other side of the blister.

Captain Tahget raged, 'How do you *do* that? After your last stunt I ordered your core processors to be locked down!'

'Don't blame your crew, Captain,' came Poole's muffled voice. 'I hacked my way back in. After all, nobody knows *me* as well as I do. And I was once an engineer.'

Tahget clenched his fists uselessly. 'Damn you, Poole, I ought to shut you down for good.'

'Too late for that,' Poole said cheerfully.

Futurity said, 'Michael Poole, what are you going to do?'

Mara was the first to see it. 'He's going to follow Sharn. He's going to download himself into the black hole air.'

Futurity stared at Poole. 'Is she right?'

'I'm going to try. Of course I'm making this up as I'm going along. My procedure is untested; it's all or nothing.'

Tahget snorted. 'You're probably an even bigger fool than you were alive, Poole.'

'Oh?'

'All this is surmise. Even if it was the Ideocracy's intention to seed the black hole with post-humans, we have no proof it worked. There may be nothing alive in those thin gases. And even if there is, it may no longer be human! Have you thought of that?'

'Yes,' Poole said. 'Of course I have. But I always did like long odds. Quite an adventure, eh?'

Futurity couldn't help but smile at his reckless optimism. But he stepped up to the window. 'Michael Poole, please—'

'What's wrong, acolyte? Are you concerned about what your Hierocrat is going to do to you when you go home without his intellectual property?'

'Well, yes. But I'm also concerned for you, Michael Poole.'

Poole did a double-take. 'You are, aren't you? I'm touched, Futurity's Dream. I like you too, and I think you have a great future ahead of you – *if* you can clear the theological fog out of your head. You could change the world! But on the other hand, I have the feeling you'll be a fine priest too. I'd like to stick around to see what happens. But, no offence, it ain't worth going back into cold storage for.'

Mara said, her voice breaking, 'If you find Sharn, tell her I love her.'

'I will. And who knows? Perhaps we will find a way to get back in touch with you, some day. Don't give up hope. I never do.'

'I won't.'

'Just to be absolutely clear,' said Captain Tahget heavily. 'Mara, will this be enough for you to get rid of that damn bomb?'

'Oh, yes,' said Mara. 'I always did trust Michael Poole.'

'And she won't face any charges,' Poole said. 'Will she, Captain?'

Tahget looked at the ceiling. 'As long as I get that bomb off my ship – and as long as somebody *pays* me for this jaunt – she can walk free.'

'Then my work here is done,' said Poole, mock-seriously. He turned and faced the black hole.

'You're hesitating,' Futurity said.

'Wouldn't you? I wonder what the life expectancy of a sentient structure in there is . . . Well, I've got a century before the black hole hits Chandra, and maybe there'll be a way to survive that.

'I hope I live! It would be fun seeing what comes next, in this human Galaxy. For sure it won't be like what went before. You know, it's a dangerous precedent, this deliberate speciation: after an age of unity, will we now live through an era of bifurcation, as mankind purposefully splits and splits again?' He turned back to Futurity and grinned. 'And this is my own adventure, isn't it, acolyte? Something the original Poole never shared. He'd probably be appalled, knowing him. I'm the black sheep! What was that about *more real*?'

Mara said, 'I will be with you at Timelike Infinity, Michael Poole, when this burden will pass.'

That was a standard Wignerian prayer. Poole said gently, 'Yes. Perhaps I'll see you there, Mara. Who knows?' He nodded to Futurity. 'Goodbye, engineer. Remember – open mind.'

'Open mind,' Futurity said softly.

Poole turned, leapt away from the ship, and vanished in a shimmering of pixels.

After that, Futurity spent long hours studying the evanescent patterns in the air of the black hole. He tried to convince himself he could see more structure: new textures, a deeper richness. Perhaps Michael Poole really was in there, with Sharn. Or perhaps Michael Poole had already gone on to his next destination, or the next after that. It was impossible to tell.

He gave up, turned to his data desk, and began to work out how he was going to explain all this to the Hierocrat.

With the Shipbuilders swarming through their corridors and access tubes, the ship lifted out of the accretion disc of Chandra, and sailed for Base 478, and then for Earth.

*In the end the Ideocracy and the Kardish Imperium inevitably fell on each other.*

*Such wars of succession consumed millennia and countless lives. It was not a noble age, though it threw up plenty of heroes.*

*But time exerted its power. The wars burned themselves out. Soon the Coalition with all its works and its legacies was forgotten.*

*As for the Wignerian religion, it developed into the mightiest and deepest of all mankind's religions, and brought consolation to trillions. But in another moment it too was quite forgotten.*

*And humans, flung upon a million alien shores, morphed and adapted.*

*This was the Bifurcation of Mankind. How it would have horrified that dry old stick Hama Druz! There were still wars, of course. But now different human species confronted each other, and a fundamental xenophobia fuelled genocides.*

*As poor Rusel on the* Mayflower II *had understood, human destiny works itself out on overlapping timescales. An empire typically lasts a thousand years – the Coalition was a pathology. A religion may linger five or ten thousand years. Even a human subspecies will alter unrecognisably after fifty or a hundred thousand years. So on the longest of timescales human history is a complex dissonance, with notes sounding at a multitude of frequencies from the purposeful to the evolutionary, and only the broadest patterns are discernible in its fractal churning.*

*You learn this if you live long enough, like Rusel, like me.*

*The age of Bifurcation ended abruptly.*

*Sixty-five thousand years after the conquest of the Galaxy, genetic randomness threw up a new conqueror. Charismatic, monstrous, carelessly spending human life on a vast scale, the self-styled Unifier used one human type as a weapon against another, before one of his many enemies took his life, and his empire disintegrated, evanescent as all those before.*

*And yet the Unifier planted the seeds of a deeper unity. Not since the collapse of the Coalition had the successors of mankind recalled that their ancestors had shared the same warm pond. After ten thousand more years that unity found a common cause.*

*Mankind's hard-won Galaxy was a mere tidal pool of muddy light, while all around alien cultures commanded a wider ocean. Now those immense spaces became an arena for a new war. As in the time of the Unifier, disparate human types were thrown into the conflict; new sub-species were even bred specifically to serve as weapons.*

*This war continued in various forms for a hundred thousand years. In the end, like the Unifier, mankind was defeated by the sheer scale of the arena – and by time, which erodes all human purposes.*

*But mankind didn't return to complete fragmentation, not quite. For now a new force began to emerge in human politics.*

*The undying. Us. Me.*

*Since the time of Michael Poole, there had been undying among the ranks of mankind. Some of us were engineered to be so, and others were the children of the engineered. We emerged and died in our own slow generations, a subset of mankind.*

*The hostility of mortals was relentless. It pushed us together – even if, often, in mutual loathing. But we were always dependent on the mass of mankind. Undying or not, we were still human; we needed our short-lived cousins. We spent most of our long lives hiding, though.*

*We undying had rather enjoyed the long noon of the Coalition, for all that authority's persecution of us. Stability and central control was what we sought above all else. To us the Coalition's collapse, and the churning ages that followed, were a catastrophe.*

*When, two hundred thousand years after the time of Hama Druz, the storm of extragalactic war at last blew itself out, we decided enough was enough. We had always worked covertly, tweaking history here and there – as I had meddled in the destiny of the Exultants. Now it was different. In this moment of human fragmentation and weakness, we emerged from the shadows, and began to act.*

*We established a new centralising government called the Commonwealth. Slowly – so slowly most mayflies lived and died without ever seeing what we were doing – we strove to challenge time, to dam the flow of history. To gain control, at last.*

*And we attempted a deeper unity, a linking of minds called the Transcendence. This superhuman entity would envelop all of mankind in its joyous unity, reaching even deep into the past to redeem the benighted lives that had gone before. But the gulf between man and god proved too wide to bridge.*

*Half a million years after mankind first left Earth, the Transcendence proved the high water mark of humanity's dreams.*

*When it fell our ultimate enemies closed in.*

*At first there was a period of stasis – the Long Calm, the historians called it. It lasted two hundred thousand years. The stasis was only comparative; human history resumed, with all its usual multiple-wavelength turbulence.*

*Then the stars began to go out.*

*It was the return of the Xeelee: mankind's ultimate foe, superior, unforgiving, driven out of the home Galaxy but never defeated.*

*It had been thought the Xeelee were distracted by a war against a greater foe, creatures of dark matter called 'photino birds' who were meddling with the evolution of the stars for their own purposes – a conflict exploited by Admiral Kard long ago to trigger the human-Xeelee war. The Xeelee were not distracted.*

*It had been thought the Xeelee had forgotten us. They had not forgotten.*

*We called the Xeelee's vengeance the Scourge. It was a simple strategy: the stars that warmed human worlds were cloaked in an impenetrable shell of the Xeelee's fabled 'construction material'. It was even economical, for these cloaks were built out of the energy of the stars themselves. It was a technology that had actually been stumbled on long before by human migrants of the Second Expansion, then rediscovered by the Coalition's Missionaries – discovered, even colonised, but never understood.*

*One by one, the worlds of man fell dark. Cruellest of all, when humanity had been driven out, the Xeelee unveiled the cleansed stars.*

*People had forgotten how to fight. They fled to the home Galaxy, and then fell back further to the spiral arms. But even there the scattered stars faded one by one.*

*It took the Xeelee three hundred thousand years, but at last, a million years after the first starships, the streams of refugees became visible in the skies of Earth.*

*But the photino birds had been busy too, progressing their own cosmic project, the ageing of the stars.*

*When Sol itself began to die, its core bloated with a dark-matter canker, suddenly mankind had nowhere to go.*

# SIX

## THE FALL OF MANKIND

# THE SIEGE OF EARTH

c. AD 1,000,000

I

The canal cut a perfect line across the flat Martian landscape, arrowing straight for the crimson rim of sun at the horizon.

Walking along the canal's bank, Symat was struck by the sheer scale on which people had reshaped the landscape for a purpose – in this case, to carry water from Mars's perpetually warm side to the cold. Of course the whole world was engineered, but terraforming a world was beyond Symat's imagination, whereas a canal was not.

His mother had always said he had the instincts of an engineer. But it wasn't likely he would ever get to be an engineer, for this wasn't an age when people built things. A million years after the first human footsteps had been planted in its ancient soil, Mars was growing silent once more.

Symat was fourteen years old, however, and that was exactly how old the world was to him. And he was unhappy for much more immediate reasons than man's cosmic destiny. He stumbled on, alone.

It was hours since he had stormed out of his parents' home, though the changeless day made it hard to track the time. Nobody knew where he was. He had instructed the Mist, the ubiquitous artificial mind of Mars, not to follow him. But the journey had been harder than he had expected, and he was already growing hungry and thirsty.

It might have been easier if his journey had a destination, a fixed end. But he wasn't heading anywhere as much as escaping. He wanted to show his parents he was serious, that his refusal to join the great exodus from reality through the transfer booths wasn't just some fit of pique. Well, he'd done that. But his flight had a beginning but no end.

Trying to take his mind off his tiredness, he stared into the sliver of sun on the horizon. Sol was so big and red it didn't hurt his eyes, even when he gazed right into it. The sun never moved, of course, save for its slow rise as you walked towards it.

The sky of Mars had changed, across a million years. Symat knew that Mars's sky had once had three morning stars, the inner planets. But Venus and Mercury had long been eaten up by the sun's swelling, Earth wafted away, and Mars was the closest of the sun's remaining children.

And that sun never shifted in the sky. These days Mars kept one face turned constantly towards the sun, and one face away from it: one Dayside, one Nightside, and a band of twilight between where the last people lived.

Something briefly eclipsed the sun. He stopped, blinking; his eyes were dry and sore. He saw that he had passed through the shadow of a spire.

He walked on.

Soon he entered a city. The buildings were tall and full of sunlight, and bridges fine as spider web spanned the canal water. But there were no people walking over those bridges, no flitters skimming around the spires, and red dust lay scattered over the streets. It was like walking through a museum, solemn and silent.

One building bulged above his head, a ball of smooth, fossil-free Martian sandstone skewered on a spire of diamond. Clinging to the bank of the canal Symat gave it a wide berth: even after all this time human instincts remained shaped by the heavier gravity of Earth, where such an imbalanced structure would have been impossible.

Time had made its mark. Right in the heart of the city one slender bridge had collapsed. He could see its fallen stones in the water, a line of white under the surface.

Before he reached the ruined abutment on the canal bank he came to a scattering of loose stones. He gathered together a dozen or so cobbles and peered up resentfully at one of the more substantial buildings. Its flat windows, like dead eyes, seemed to mock him. He hefted a cobble, took aim, and hurled it. His first shot clattered uselessly against polished stone. But his second shot took out a window that smashed with a sparkling noise. The sound excited him, and he hurled more stones. But the noise stopped every time he quit throwing, reminding him firmly he was alone.

Dispirited, he dumped the last of his cobbles and turned back to the canal. On its bank, he sat with his feet dangling over blue running water, water that ran endlessly from the world's cold side to the warm.

Symat was very thirsty.

The canal bank was a wall of stone that sloped smoothly down to the water. It would be easy to slide down there, all the way into the water. He could drink his fill, and wash off the dust of Mars. But how would he get out? Glancing down the river he saw the ruins of that bridge. The bank beneath the abutment was broken up; surely he could find handholds.

Without water he was going to have to turn back. It was a defining moment in his odyssey.

Without letting himself think about it he pulled off his boots, pants and jacket, and slid down the smooth sloping wall. The water was so cold it shocked him, and it was deep; he couldn't feel the bottom. When he came bobbing back up he was faintly alarmed that he had already been washed some way towards the stump of the bridge. The current must be stronger than it looked.

With a couple of strokes he reached the canal wall. It was smooth, but by pushing his hands against it he was able to resist the current. Feeling safer, he ducked his head and scrubbed his hair clean of dust, and took long deep draughts of the water. It was chill, for it was meltwater from Nightside, and slightly sparkling; Mars's water was rich in carbon dioxide.

Refreshed, he felt his energy return. There were more cities strung out along the canal like pearls on a necklace. He could hide out for days, and how *that* would make his parents worry.

But he was starting to feel cold, deep inside. Time to get out. He pushed off from the wall and let himself drift downstream. When he reached the ruined abutment he grabbed at projecting stones. But they were all slick with some green slime, and slid maliciously out of his hands. Scared now, he shoved himself at the protruding stones. He managed to halt his slide down the river, but only by clinging on with all his limbs, like a spider, and the water still plucked at his legs and torso.

He was getting very cold, and tiring quickly, his muscles aching. He had walked along the canal for hours and had seen nothing but smooth walls. If he lost his grip here, he would be washed away until he drowned – or, even worse, the Mist would alert his parents, who would come sweeping down in the family flitter to rescue him. The first real decision he had made had been a stupid one, and all his defiant dreams of showing his parents he was worthy of their respect were imploding.

He was starting to shiver. He had no choice. He prepared to call for the Mist's help.

'Up here.'

The voice came from above. Looking up, he saw three heads silhouetted against the sky, three small curious faces peering down. 'Who are you?'

'Try there!' The middle figure leaned over and pointed. It was a girl, a bit younger than he was. She was pointing at a shelf on the canal wall, all but invisible from his position down here. With an effort he lifted up his hand and grabbed at the shelf. It was dry and he grasped it easily, and already felt safer.

'All right,' the girl called down. 'Now see if you can reach that foothold. To your left, just behind that broken stone . . .'

In this way, with the girl spotting one hand- or foothold after another, he managed to haul himself up out of the water.

Exhausted, he flopped on his belly on the bank.

He got his first good look at the children who had helped him. They were a girl and two boys. The girl looked about twelve, and the boys, wide-eyed, were no more than eight or nine. They wore simple shifts of bright blue cloth that looked oddly clean. They weren't alike, not like siblings, a family.

One of the boys approached him, and Symat reached out a hand. But there was a soft chime, and his fingers passed through the boy's palm. The boy yelped and drew back, as if it had hurt.

Symat looked at the girl. 'You're Virtuals.'

She shrugged. 'We all are. Sorry we can't help you up.'

'I can manage.' Not wanting to shame himself before this girl, he rolled on his back and sat up, panting hard.

The Virtuals stared at him. 'My name is Mela,' the girl said. 'This is Tod, this is Chem.'

'I got stuck,' Symat said, hotly embarrassed.

Mela nodded, but he saw the corners of her mouth twitch. 'You ought to put your clothes back on before you get too cold.'

One of the boys, Tod, said in a piping voice, 'We can't get them for you.'

'Sorry,' said the other, Chem. 'Would you like some food?'

'Yes.'

'We'll show you.'

Symat towelled himself on his jacket and dressed. His clothes dried quickly, and, sensing his low body temperature, warmed him. The three Virtual children watched him silently.

They led him into the city, away from the canal. They walked with a sound of rustling clothes, even of boots crunching on the scattered sand. But of the four of them only Symat left footprints.

'We saw you breaking the windows,' Tod said. 'Why did you do that?'

'Why not?'

Tod considered. 'It's wrong to break things.'

'But nobody's coming back here. People are leaving the planet altogether. What difference does it make?'

'*My* parents are coming back,' Chem said.

Mela said softly, 'Chem—'

'I wouldn't throw stones,' the boy said. 'My parents wouldn't like it.'

'What parents? . . . You couldn't throw stones anyway,' Symat said. 'You're a Virtual.'

That seemed to hurt the boy, and he glanced away.

Mela was slim, thoughtful, grave. She didn't react to this exchange one way or another. But somehow she made Symat feel ashamed of upsetting the Virtual boy.

They came to a building, an unprepossessing block in a neighbourhood of crystalline spires. It was as unlit as the others. 'There's food in here,' Tod insisted. 'Through that door.' They stood waiting for him to open the door.

'Why don't you go in? You're Virtuals. You could just walk through the wall.'

Mela said, 'Protocol violations. We aren't supposed to.'

'It hurts,' Chem said.

Symat said, 'I haven't been around Virtuals much.' He stepped forward, pushed at the door's polished surface, and it slid open.

The building was an apartment block. They wandered through suites of rooms. Heavy furniture remained, chairs and tables and beds, but smaller items had been taken away.

'I've seen people take stuff,' Symat said. 'Clothes and ornaments and toys, even sets of plates to eat dinner. They carry them in suitcases and boxes when they go through.'

Mela asked, 'Through where?'

'Through the transfer booths. Imagine carrying plates and forks and knives into another universe!'

'What are they supposed to take?' Mela asked reasonably.

They came to a kind of kitchen, where a nanofood replicator was still functioning. Symat asked it to prepare him something warm, and soon rich smells filled the air.

'It probably needs restocking,' Mela said. 'You can scrape up some algae from the canal, I guess.'

Chem said sharply, 'If you can keep from getting stuck!' He and Tod laughed.

Mela reproved the boys. Symat sat at a table and ate in dogged silence. The Virtuals stood around the table, watching him.

Chem said, 'Of course you won't have to put more glop in the nanofood box if your parents come for you.'

'They won't come,' Symat said, chewing. Mela watched him with that quiet gravity, and he felt impelled to add, 'They don't know I'm here.'

'Are you hiding?' Chem asked. 'Did you run away?'

'Did you do something wrong?' Tod asked, wide-eyed.

'They want me to go into a transfer booth with them. I don't want to go.'

Chem said, 'Why not?'

'Because it would feel like dying. I haven't done with *this* world.'

Chem said brightly, 'I'd go with *my* parents. I always do whatever they want.'

Tod said maliciously, 'They would go without *you*. They probably have already.'

'No, they haven't.' Chem's lips were working. 'They'll come back to me when—'

'When, when, when,' Tod sang. 'When is *never*. They're never coming back!'

'And nor are yours!'

'But I don't care any more,' Tod said. 'You do. Ha ha!'

Chem, in a tearful fury, flew at Tod. The wrestling boys fell to the floor and crashed through table legs. Pixels flew and protocol-violation warnings pinged, but the table didn't so much as quiver.

Symat watched curiously. He lived in a world saturated by sentience, where everything was aware, everything potentially had feelings. He understood Virtual children could be hurt, but he didn't necessarily know what might hurt them.

'Enough.' Mela waded into the mêlée and pulled the boys apart. Chem, crying copiously, ran from the room. Mela said to Tod, 'You know how it upsets him when you say such things.'

'It's true. Our parents are never coming back. *His* aren't. We all know that.'

Mela put her hand on her heart. 'He doesn't know it. Not in here.'

'Then he's stupid,' Tod said.

'Maybe he is, maybe not. But we have to look out for him. All we have is each other now. Go after him.'

'Aww—' Tod pulled a face, but he went out obediently.

Mela looked at Symat. 'Kids,' she said, smiling faintly.

Symat, his head full of his own issues, chewed his food.

When he had done eating, the apartment was a little more like a home, a little less like a strange place. And, his muscles still aching from his time in the water, he realised he felt tired. He found a bathroom, and a bedroom stripped of light furnishings. He sat on a pallet.

The three Virtuals clustered in the doorway, looking at him.

'I'm going to sleep,' he said.

'All right.' They receded into the shadows.

Symat lay down on the pallet, and his clothes, sensing his intentions, fluffed themselves up into a warm cocoon around his body. Experimentally he ordered the room to dim its lights; the command worked. He turned over and closed his eyes.

He thought he slept.

But he heard murmuring. He saw the two boys in the dim light, standing at the foot of his pallet – no, hovering, their feet just above the ground. And they were talking, softly, and too rapidly for him to hear, like speeded-up speech. He heard a name: '*The Guardians.*' Then one of them whispered, 'He's awake!' And they fled, sliding through the solid wall like spectres, accompanied by a soft pinging.

So much for protocol violations, Symat said to himself. Those Virtuals were creepy. He didn't understand where they had come from, what they wanted. But he reminded himself they were artificial; and like all artefacts they were here to serve humanity – him. He huddled down in his clothes and went back to sleep.

\*

When he rose and walked out of the apartment into the unchanging sunlight, the three Virtuals were waiting for him. They were sitting on a low stone wall, or at least they looked like they were doing so, Mela in the centre with the two boys to either side.

'Um, thank you for bringing me to this place. The food.'

'You're human. That's our job,' Mela said.

'I suppose it is. Thanks anyhow.' He walked off down the street towards the canal.

When he looked back they were following. Perhaps they were waiting for him to give them more commands. He wouldn't have admitted it, but he was glad to have some company.

Walking along the line of the canal they soon left the city behind. The canal continued to head towards the immobile sun, but now the water looked turbid, muddy.

While Mela walked with Symat, the two boys ran by themselves. They played elaborate games of hide and seek, which could involve hiding inside the fabric of a wall, which evidently didn't hurt that much; the air was full of warning pings, and the laughter of the boys. It reminded Symat uneasily of their odd behaviour in the bedroom last night. Maybe they had been inhibited about violating their protocols around him. If so, the inhibition was wearing off.

They came to a small township, as empty as the city. The boys ran off to explore. Mela and Symat sat on a low wall.

He asked her, 'How come I didn't see you yesterday, before you found me in the canal?'

'We didn't want you to see us.'

He wondered what a Virtual had to hide from. 'Why does Chem talk about "parents"? Virtuals don't have parents.'

'We did.'

It had been a craze, a few generations back. It began after humans had been pushed back to Sol system.

'People still wanted kids,' Mela said. 'But you don't want to bring kids into a defeated world. So they had us instead.'

A Virtual child could be a very convincing simulacrum of the real thing. You could raise it from infanthood, teach it, learn from it. It would have been trivial to realise a child physically, downloading complex sensoria into a flesh-and-blood shell, but such 'dolls' were unpopular, apparently violating some even deeper set of instincts. It was more comfortable to be with Virtuals, even if you couldn't cuddle them.

And Virtual kids actually had advantages. You could back them up, rerun favourite moments. You could even wipe them clean if you really made a hash of raising them, though sentience laws discouraged this.

One feature, popular but hotly debated ethically, was the ability to stop the growth of your child at a certain age. You could stretch out a childhood for as long as you wanted, enough to match your own long lifespan. Some people kept their Virtual children as perpetual infants; generally, however, eight to ten years old was the chosen plateau range.

'I'm twelve,' Mela said. 'Few ever got as old as me. For a long time I've been surrounded by kids younger than me.'

'A long time? How long?'

Mela considered. 'Oh, two hundred years, nearly.'

Symat, shocked, didn't know what to say.

Times changed, Mela said. Now, in increasing numbers, people were leaving the world behind altogether, passing through the transfer booths to an unknown destination beyond. And the Virtual children couldn't follow: you could take your pots and pans, but you couldn't take your Virtual child.

More than that, Mela told him mildly, Virtual children had simply gone out of fashion, as had so many technological toys before them. It became embarrassing to admit you needed such an emotional crutch.

For all these reasons, the children were shut down – or more commonly just abandoned, perhaps after centuries of companionship every bit as intense as the bond between a parent and a real child.

'Every last mother said she would come back. I always knew the truth. I was twelve years old. But Chem is only eight. He'll be eight for ever. And he still believes. Every day he is disappointed.'

Every day for centuries, Symat thought, Chem wakes up full of pointless hope, trapped in childhood. 'Tod seems to understand.'

'He's actually younger than Chem, but he's tougher minded.'

'How come?'

She shrugged. 'His parents had him designed that way. You could choose what you liked. Chem's parents must have wanted a child more dependent, more vulnerable.'

'But they abandoned him anyway.'

'Oh, yes.'

Symat said, 'But I still don't see—'

He heard a piercing scream. Mela broke off and ran into the township. Symat hurried after her.

*

They came to an open plaza. A number of children had gathered, perhaps a dozen, none older than eight or nine. No, not children – they were more Virtuals, as Symat could tell from the sparkling pixels and tiny pings that marked petty protocol violations. They all wore bland shifts and coveralls like Mela and the boys.

And these kids stood in a loose ring around Chem and Tod. The boys crouched on the floor, clinging to each other.

Mela ran forward. 'Get away from them!'

Symat hurried after her. 'What kind of game is this?'

'No game,' she called back. 'They are bloodsuckers. They are trying to kill the boys.'

'Kill them? How do you kill a Virtual?'

Mela didn't answer. She waded into the attacking children, grabbing them and pulling them aside. But there were too many of them; they gathered around her and pushed her back, jeering.

Symat ran forward, fists clenched. 'Back off.'

One of the girls faced him. She was shorter than he was, with a hard, cold face and her skin was waxy, almost translucent. She had drifted a long way from her core programming, he realised. 'Whose child are you?'

'I'm no child. I'm human.'

The girl jeered and pointed at Chem. '*He* thinks he's human.'

Symat swung a hand at her face. His fingers passed through her pale flesh, scattering pixels. She flinched, shocked; that had hurt.

'Do what I say,' Symat said. 'Leave my friends alone.'

The girl quickly recovered. 'You can't order us around. And you can't hurt us.'

'But we can hurt you,' said a sly-faced boy.

'Projections can't hurt a human.'

'Oh, yes, we can,' said the boy. 'We can come to you in the night. We can hide in walls, in your clothes, even in your body, *human*. You'll never sleep again.'

The girl said, 'You don't have to be real to inflict pain. We've learned that in the years we've been out here. We will haunt you.'

Chem was crying. 'Please, Symat, don't let them hurt us.'

Symat stood, hesitant. The out-of-control Virtuals' threats filled him with dread. And this wasn't his fight; after all he hadn't met Mela and the boys before yesterday. But Mela's eyes were on him. His fists clenched again, he stepped forward. 'Leave them alone or—'

The girl ran at him, burst through his chest, and pushed her hands *through* his skull so the insides of his eyeballs exploded with light. 'Or what? What will you do, human?'

But the others didn't follow her lead.

'Kiri,' the sly boy said. '*Look* at him.'

The girl turned, looked at Symat – and then stepped back, her mouth dropping.

Symat found himself surrounded by a circle of staring children. Even Mela and the boys were gazing at him wide-eyed. He saw that their protocol respect was weakening; some of them drifted up from the floor, and others tilted sideways, reaching impossible angles. They were like floating spectres, not children. They began to whisper, the strange, rapid speech he had heard from the boys in the night; he heard them mutter that strange name again – 'the Guardians'.

And somehow Symat sensed the circle of scrutiny expanding beyond the limited circle of these children. After all, he reminded himself, these Virtuals were merely manifestations of the Mist, the cloud of artificial sentience in which all of Mars was immersed – and suddenly he was the centre of attention.

He had no idea what was happening, but he ought to make use of it He raised his arms. 'Get away!'

The strange children turned and fled, leaving the two boys weeping on the ground.

Mela and Symat ran to them. Mela hugged them. Chem looked up at Symat, tears streaking down his face. 'Don't leave me again, Symat. Keep me safe until my parents come back for me. Oh, keep me safe!'

'I promise,' Symat said helplessly.


They left the town and walked on, following the canal, ever westward. The sun inched higher, showing more of its bloated red belly, and the air grew steadily warmer. The water in the canal was thick and sluggish now, and deep red-brown with sediment.

Symat was walking out of the twilight band and into the hemisphere of permanent daylight.

The Virtuals followed. The boys, subdued, stayed closer to Symat and Mela. They didn't complain, though Symat could see they were getting as hot and tired as he was. Their bodies apparently responded appropriately to the weather, one bit of protocol they couldn't violate.

'So,' he said to Mela. 'Bloodsuckers?'

'It's what we call them. A lot of the kids are too young to understand the truth.'

'Which is? . . .'

The bloodsuckers had learned to steal something far more precious to any Virtual than blood: processor time.

'The Mist's capacity is huge, but it's finite,' Mela said. 'There are rules that unnecessary programmes are eventually shut down.'

'Unnecessary like abandoned Virtual children?'

'Yes. But the bloodsuckers have learned a way to, um, integrate you into their own programming. That way they co-opt your ration of processor capacity.'

'And live longer.'

'That's the idea.'

Symat was stunned. Living in a city still occupied by humans, Virtuals had always been peripheral to him. He had no idea that this kind of cannibalistic savagery was going on among them, out of sight of mankind. 'So that's why you hid from me.'

Mela shrugged. 'We didn't know if you were a Virtual or not.'

'Not until you got stuck in the water,' Tod said, and Chem laughed.

What else didn't he know? 'Mela – when I was trying to sleep, I heard the boys muttering. Something about *Guardians*. And in the middle of the fight back there, you all looked at me strangely. I heard that name again. *Guardians*.' He looked at her uncertainly. 'What's going on?'

Mela flexed her hand, and held it up to the sun, as if trying to look through it. 'You understand that we Virtuals are individuals. But we are all projections, from the Mist, and of wider artificial minds beyond even that. So we aren't like you, Symat. We're – blurred. It's hard to explain . . .'

Mela was a projection of a mass artificial mind that, loosely integrated, spanned Mars, and what was left of Sol system – indeed, once it had spanned much of the Galaxy. Mars's Mist was just part of it. This interplanetary colloquium of minds, meshed together in an endless conversation, called itself the 'Conclave', Mela told him. And sometimes she and the other Virtuals could sense the deeper thoughts of that mind, the vast undercurrents of its consciousness.

How strange she was, Symat realised as she spoke, strange in layers. She looked like a rather serious twelve-year-old girl; most of the time she acted that way. But she was old – far older than him, centuries old.

She had been twelve all that time, looking after these other ageless children. And behind her, looking at him through her eyes, were misty ranks of ancient artificial minds.

'And the Conclave,' she said, 'is very aware of *you*, Symat.'

'Me? I'm not important. I'm just a kid.'

'Apparently you're more than that.'

The water had almost run dry. Reefs of baking mud clogged the basin of the canal.

They slowed to a halt, and stood in a glum group.

'We're past the point where the recycling pumps take back the water,' Mela said. 'Nobody tries to grow things further west than this any more. It's too hot and dry. And every year this point is pulled further back.' She looked up at Symat. 'So we can't go on.'

'Look.' Tod pointed at the bare ground, a hundred paces from the canal. 'There's a flitter.'

Symat shielded his eyes from the sun to see.

Mela said, 'It's your parents, isn't it? They've waited for you here, where you could walk no further.'

'I have to face them,' Symat said grimly. 'Maybe now they'll take me seriously.'

Another Virtual coalesced out of the dusty air. It was Symat's mother, grave, soberly dressed. Symat was astonished to see the streaks of tears under her eyes. 'Come home, son,' she said. 'We're here. In the flesh, in our flitter. We've come for you. Please come back.' She didn't even seem to see the Virtual children with him.

Impulsively Symat opened his arms. 'I've made friends. Let me take them back with me.'

'That's impossible.'

'One, then. Let me take one.'

His mother glanced sideways; Symat imagined her looking at his father back in the family flitter, listening to that gravelly voice. *Give him a victory. What does it matter?*

'Very well,' his mother said. 'Which one?'

Symat turned to Mela. 'Come with me.'

She hesitated. 'What about the boys?'

'I think I need your help.'

She looked at him, and again he had an odd sense that she knew more about him than he knew himself, that other minds watched him through her eyes. 'Maybe you do.'

'No!' Chem grabbed Mela. 'Don't leave us!'

Symat could see she was torn. 'I'll come back,' she said. 'This could be important. Just stay out of the way of the bloodsuckers and you'll be fine.'

Symat's mother put her own Virtual arm around Mela. 'Come, dear.' They started walking across the sand towards the flitter.

Chem, desperate, called after Symat, 'You promised you'd stay, you promised you'd keep us alive.'

'I'll come back.'

'They always say that. You won't. You won't! . . .'

Symat followed Mela and his mother, his heart breaking.

II

The flitter arrowed with perfect accuracy towards Kahra, capital city of Mars, where Symat had grown up. The ease of the journey was galling, after Symat's slog on foot through the echoing deserts.

And as the flitter dipped low over the rooftops of Kahra, he saw lines of people snaking towards the transfer booths. The human population of Mars was passively draining into another universe. Symat glanced at his father, wondering if this part of the flight had been set up deliberately to show him the booths and the patient lines, to make a point. Hektor returned his gaze, impassive.

Symat's parents' villa, on the outskirts of Kahra, was spacious, airy. Mela and Symat wandered through it. The glass walls shone like fire in the light of the sun. Even after a million years on Mars some deep instinct made you aware that this tall, open design would have been impossible on heavy Earth, and the place felt all the more remarkable.

'It's beautiful,' Mela said.

After his abortive adventure Symat wanted to puncture her awe. 'It isn't so special. There are much grander buildings than this, all over Kahra, in fact all around the twilight belt. All empty,' he said harshly. 'You can just walk in and take whatever you want.'

'But this is home, to you. That's the most important thing about it.'

'I don't like being here.'

'But you don't have anywhere else to go. You're all stuck here together, you and your family.'

He studied her. 'You're very smart about this stuff. Perceptive.'

'You think I'm too smart.' Just briefly her projected image seemed to waver.

Symal felt angry. Why did he have to make friends with a weird, superhuman two-hundred-year-old Virtual? Couldn't he just have found somebody normal? 'You're not even here, are you? Not really. You're just a projection of some vast cobwebby thing.'

'I'm here.' She tapped her head. 'It's just that I hear things. I can't help it. I'll go away, if you like.'

'No.' It had been a long time since anybody else of Symat's age had come here. There had been few children around to begin with, and all his childhood companions had long since followed their parents into the booths. He couldn't bear the thought of being left alone again. 'You'll have to do,' he said.

She seemed to understand; she nodded.

They completed a circuit of the villa and found Symat's parents. Hektor and Pelle sat in the grandest of the villa's living rooms, while a small, silent bot, glass-hulled in sympathy with the architecture, laid out food and drink on a table.

Hektor stayed seated, but Pelle, Symat's mother, stood up, a hopeful smile on her lips. 'You two. Come and sit down. Are you still hungry?' She waved her hand over the table; some of the dishes shimmered and broke up. 'We have something for you too, Mela.'

Mela smiled. 'Thank you.' She selected a seat and, cautiously, sat down. The smart environment gave her a surface that matched the real-world seat flawlessly. She reached forward, picked a piece of fruit, and began to eat.

Symat sat too. Back home, he felt as if he had been reduced to a child once more. But it was obvious his mother, at least, was making an effort to reach him; she was even being considerate to Mela. And somehow with Mela here it wouldn't have been right to show his resentment. So he accepted a drink.

As he had grown, Symat had often felt uncomfortable around his parents. They were so different from him, both tall and slender, matching the architecture of their Martian villa, while Symat was dumpy, squat, thick-set. Today Pelle was casually dressed, but Hektor wore the orange robe of a scholar, and his head was shaven. Both Symat's parents had dedicated their long lives to archiving the human past on Mars, participating in a community act of remembrance to be completed before the final transfer through the booths. But in this domestic environment the robe made Hektor look formal, severe, the contrast with his son only more accentuated.

When he spoke, however, Hektor's tone was mild. 'So where do we go from here?'

'We just want to know what you're feeling,' Pelle said to Symat. 'What made you—' She faltered.

'Run away?'

'You don't have to say sorry, son. We just want to understand.'

His father leaned forward. 'What I want to know is, where did you think you were going? You know your geography. There's nowhere *to* go.'

Pelle snapped, '*Hektor*. He's fourteen years old. What kind of plans do you expect him to make?'

Hektor said, 'This is all about the booths, isn't it? Everybody else goes through happily enough. All your little friends have gone.' He ticked off names on his fingers. 'Jann. C'peel. Moro—'

'I don't want to go into a booth,' Symat said testily.

As always his father seemed genuinely mystified. 'Why not?'

Symat waved a hand at the shining glass walls. 'Because this is my home. My world. My universe! I hardly know anything about it. Why would I want to walk into nothing?'

'Not *nothing*,' Hektor said. 'A pocket universe, connected to our own by an umbilical of—'

'Symat,' his mother cut in, 'I wouldn't change a hair on your head. Don't ever think that, not ever. But I want what's best for you. And this— it's as if you are refusing medical treatment, say. We can't just ignore it. Believe me, going into a booth would be the best choice – *the Xeelee are coming* – in the long run it's the *only* choice.'

'I think that's the trouble,' Mela put in brightly. 'The trouble is he *doesn't* believe you.'

Hektor snarled, 'Who asked you, Virtual?'

Mela flinched.

Pelle held up her hand. 'No. She's right. Symat, we've always tried to educate you. But on some level we've failed.' She seemed to be coming to a rehearsed suggestion. 'So let us show you. Give us one day, that's all. Just listen, watch, for one day. Try to see things from our point of view. And then you can see how you feel about the booths.'

Symat hesitated. 'What if I still don't want to do it?'

'Then we won't force you,' his mother said.

'In fact we can't,' Hektor said stiffly. 'That's the law. But you need to understand that *we're* going through the booths, with or without you. After that you can do what you want. Stay here. Move away. There are others who choose not to come. Other oddballs and deadbeats—'

'Just give us one day,' Pelle said firmly.

Symat glanced at Mela. She nodded. 'All right,' he said.

Hektor stood up. 'Then let's not waste any more time.' He spoke to the air. 'Ready the flitter. We leave in five minutes.' He clapped his hands, and the bot began to clear away the barely touched food.

Pelle patted Symat's arm. 'Don't worry,' she said. 'We can always eat on the ship—'

The flitter rose from Mars like a stone thrown from a crimson bowl. The little craft tumbled slowly as it climbed, sparkling. Mela peered out of the flitter's transparent hull, wide-eyed; evidently she had never seen the world like this.

From here you could clearly see how Mars was divided into two hemispheres, barren landscapes of hot and cold, separated by a narrow belt of endless twilight. The canals, shining blue-black, laced across this precious strip. Kahra, a capital city almost as old as man's occupation of Mars itself, was a green jewel that glimmered on the desert skin of the planet.

Looking down now, it struck Symat for the first time that Kahra was set slap in the middle of the twilight band, exactly poised between dark and light. But he knew that when Kahra had been founded Mars had still spun on its axis. He wondered if that positioning was a happy accident – or if the slowing rotation of Mars had somehow been managed so that Kahra ended up exactly where it needed to be. He had no idea how you might control the spin of a whole world, but then, it was said, the people of the past had had powers beyond the imagination of anybody now alive.

As the flitter swept through its rapid suborbital hop, the sun rose. Bloated, surrounded by a churning corona, the sun's scarlet face was pocked by immense spots. Symat's father had told him that the whole of the sun was a battleground between forces beyond human control, and from here it looked like it.

The flitter swooped down towards Dayside, the sunlit face of Mars.

513

On blasted crimson rock cities still glittered. But there was no sign of life, no movement in the cities, and the canals were bone dry.

Hektor said, 'Look down there. Nothing left but bugs in the deep rocks. Everything that can burn in those cities has gone already. Son, if you transplanted our villa down there it would turn into a shining puddle of melted glass. And it's getting worse.'

'Because the sun is still heating up.'

'So it is. There is nothing we can do to reverse this. Soon the twilight belt will close, squeezed between hot and cold, and Mars will be uninhabitable, just as it was before humans came and terraformed it. And the last of us will have to leave, or die.'

This desolate prospect filled Symat with gloom, which it was in his nature to resist. 'It might not come to that. What if the sun cools again?'

Pelle touched Symat's arm. 'It won't. Those who are destroying the sun won't allow it.'

To swell into a giant would have been the sun's eventual fate, but not for billions of years yet. This premature destabilisation of the sun was deliberate. Creatures, malevolent and relentless, swarmed in its core, puddling the fusion processes there, and so compressing aeons of a stellar lifetime into mere megayears. And Sol was not the only star being smothered in its own heat. You only had to look around the sky, littered with red stars, to see that. 'But it's not personal,' a teacher had told Symat once, with black humour. 'The photino birds in the heart of the sun probably don't even know we humans exist . . .'

'The sun is dying,' Hektor said with bleak finality, 'and Mars is dying with it, and there isn't a thing we can do about it. And then there's the Scourge.'

This was the trap of history, closing in Symat's lifetime. For even as one agency was murdering the sun, another, the Xeelee, was driving mankind back from the stars.

'We were left with nowhere to go,' Hektor said. 'Until we discovered the booths.'

Symat said suspiciously, '*Discovered?*'

'Yes, discovered. You didn't imagine they are a human invention?'

Symat supposed he had, but he had never thought hard about it. Besides, it just wasn't something you talked about.

A few generations back, the booths had simply appeared at scattered locations, studded around the cities and parks of mankind's remaining worlds. Their operation was simple, the execution awe-inspiring. If you walked through a booth, you would be transported, not just to another place as if this was some fancy teleport system, but to another *universe*: a pocket universe, as the cosmologists called it, a fold in the fabric of spacetime stitched to the parent by a wormhole-like umbilical. You could walk between universes with your luggage on your back and your child in your arms. And once you were through you would be safe, preserved from Xeelee and photino bird interventions alike.

Nobody was clear exactly *how* this common knowledge about the booths had reached the human population. Certainly not from the booths themselves, which were one way: nobody came back to tell the tale of what was on the other side. The folk wisdom just seemed to be there, suddenly, in the databases, in the air. But it was believed widely enough for a steadily increasing fraction of humanity to trust their own futures and their children's to this strange exit.

Hektor said, 'Obviously there has been speculation. The booths could be an ancient human design, I suppose; who can say what was once possible? Or they could come from some alien culture, though our habit of enslaving, assimilating or eliminating most aliens we came across might seem to argue against that.' He said conspiratorially, '*Perhaps it was the Xeelee themselves*. What do you think about that? Our greatest foe, eradicating us from the universe – and yet giving us a bolt-hole in the process.'

'And this is what you want me to walk into,' Symat said.

Hektor said stiffly, 'We can't tell you anything we haven't told you a dozen, fifty times before. Somehow it never stuck with you, the way it did with other children.'

'But I thought that if we *showed* you,' Pelle said, 'showed you the world, the sky, the state of things, then it might make things clearer.'

'*Clearer?* But walking into a booth is like dying. You can't come back. And you don't know what's on the other side, because nobody ever came back to tell us. Just like dying.'

'Here we go again,' Hektor growled. 'Pelle, I told you this was a waste of time. We've had conversations like this since he was five years old, and every time it finishes up the same. Us being reasonable, him getting angry and stubborn.'

Symat and Pelle spoke at once. 'And you think that's my fault?'
'Hektor, please—'

Unexpectedly Mela stepped forward. She said gravely, 'No wonder

515

you argue. You're starting out from different premises. Different positions. You're different kinds of people.'

Hektor's eyes narrowed.

'What do you mean, different?' Pelle said. 'He's my son. How different can he be?'

'The Scourge has been continuing now for *three hundred thousand years*. To the Xeelee the Scourge is a conscious project. To humans it has become our environment.' Mela's voice was neutral, her words not quite her own, Symat thought. 'A steady force applied to a population for long enough becomes a selection pressure. In such an environment those able psychologically to accept the reality of inevitable defeat will prosper. And that is why you are prepared to walk trustingly into the booths, even without knowing what lies beyond. Your ancestors have learned to accept similar bolt-holes without question, far back into your history. You've been preadapted to accept the booths for ten thousand generations! Perhaps even that was part of the grand design of the Scourge.'

Hektor said, 'You've got a wide perspective for a twelve-year-old.'

Symat, troubled, thought he glimpsed the Conclave, the vast composite mind for which Mela was sometimes, it seemed, a mouthpiece. 'She's right, though, isn't she? But why can't *I* just walk into the booths with the rest?'

'Because you're different,' Mela said, sounding almost amused. 'Can't you see that? You don't even *look* the same.'

Symat glanced around at his family, his tall, elegant, long-boned Martian parents towering over his own squat, thick-boned form.

Mela said, almost mischievously, 'The differences go all the way down to the genes. You could almost be called a throwback, Symat. But you know what? You're just as you're meant to be.'

Pelle snapped, 'What are you talking about?

Symat demanded, '*Who* meant me to be this way?'

Hektor turned on the girl. 'You're getting on my nerves. *Why are you here?*'

Mela seemed upset by the family's brief unity in hostility to her, but she quickly recovered. Symat thought it was as if new data were continually being downloaded into her head. 'Symat, you don't want to follow your parents into the booths. The trouble is you can't imagine an alternative. But there is another way out.'

'There is?'

'It depends on you. The Conclave wanted to reach you, Symat. *That's* why I'm here. If you hadn't found me, it would have been somebody else. Another Virtual. There is somebody who would like to meet you. Very much indeed.'

She no longer sounded like a twelve-year-old girl at all. Looking into her eyes, Symat began to feel frightened. In the corner of his eye he saw his mother, distressed, cling to Hektor's arm.

'Where will I have to go?'

'Far from Mars . . .' Mela smiled, suddenly herself again. 'Isn't it exciting?'

## III

Pelle insisted they loan her son the family flitter for his jaunt: 'At least it will keep him safe.' With very bad grace, Hektor agreed.

So Symat and Mela climbed aboard the ship once more, just the two of them. The flitter rose until the world shrank to a scrap of floor. Symat felt as if he had climbed to the top of a pole a million kilometres tall, and vertigo crowded his mind.

A Virtual of his mother's face appeared before him, concerned. 'We have to hand the ship over to the Mist,' she said.

Up to this point the ship had been under the override of his parents, down on Mars. But now the lofty agencies who had summoned Symat through Mela would take control of the flitter and guide him into the darkness, out of his parents' protection.

'You don't have to go, you know,' Virtual Pelle said in a rush. She glanced at Mela with a trace of malevolence. 'You don't have to do what *she* says. And you won't – oh, you won't *lose face* if you turn around and come back to us.'

'Mother, I'm caught up in some kind of mystery. I need to understand. I'm making an adult choice. I think.'

She nodded, her lips tight. 'Then I won't stop you. But I'll be tracking you every step of the way.' The Virtual shut itself down, dispersing in a cloud of pixels.

The ship flipped over, and Mars squirted away.

Mela was watching him. 'Are you OK?'

Symat felt a pang of regret. But he had made his choice, and now he had to follow it through. 'I'm fine. What about you?'

'I don't matter.'

'Yes, you do.'

'I'm all right.'

He tried to focus on the journey. Mars was gone, and the sun's huge hull was receding. 'We're going away from the sun. Where to? Saturn?' His knowledge of Sol system's geography was vague, but he knew Saturn was a giant world out in the dark, far out beyond the orbit of Mars.

'Not as far as that. Not at first.' Her small face was creased with concentration. It was as if she was listening to a faint voice only she could hear.

'So where? Jupiter?'

'No. Jupiter's on the far side of the sun right now.'

Symat was faintly disappointed. He'd have liked to see the black hole remnant and its shattered moons. 'Then what? An asteroid? There is a belt of asteroids between Mars and Jupiter.'

'There was. But the belt was mined out long ago. And then when the sun started heating up many of the remaining icy bodies were destroyed. Sol system was a lot more interesting, once.' She sounded wistful.

'So where are we going?'

She smiled. 'You'll see.'

He studied her, curious. 'What's it like?'

'What?'

'When you get stuff downloaded into your head.'

She frowned, trying to find words. 'It's as if I lost my memory, then recovered it.'

'It doesn't sound very comfortable. Not if it feels like you're sick.'

She sighed. 'It's not comfortable. And I don't have any control over it. The stuff just pours into my head when it's needed – when *you* need it. Sometimes even when I'm asleep, it comes.'

'I didn't know your kind slept,' he said. She looked hurt, and he added hastily, 'Sorry. And I'm sorry you're having to put up with this, for my sake.'

'It's not *your* fault. And anyhow if I hadn't been around when the Conclave decided it needed to speak to you, if they'd picked some other Virtual, I'd never have got to see all this.' She waved a hand at the utter darkness beyond the enclosing walls of the flitter, and they both burst out laughing.

Symat clapped his hands to opaque the hull, and suddenly the flitter felt like a cosy room. 'So shall we play a game?'

Mela smiled. 'OK.'

No longer children but not yet adults, the two of them ran and laughed through the confines of the tiny ship, as it sailed on into the mined-out emptiness of Sol system.

After a day of silent transit, their destination came swimming out of the dark.

It was just a lump of ice at first glance, maybe a couple of hundred kilometres across. Tinted an odd red-purple colour, it was only vaguely spherical. It was impossible to tell if the scars on its surface were natural or man-made, for the ice had obviously been heavily melted, and the ridges and crater walls were softened and slumped. But this island of ice was occupied. Symat saw lights, defiant green and white, gleaming in crater shadows.

And as the flitter skimmed low a spindly tower, kilometres tall, loomed above the crumpled horizon. It was absurdly out of proportion on this little world. When he looked carefully Symat saw a ghostly purple bloom at the top of the tower: rocket exhaust.

Even given the tower, this worldlet was hardly spectacular. But he had to admit he was impressed when Mela finally told him the name of this place. It was Port Sol.

'That's impossible,' Symat said immediately. 'Port Sol is a Kuiper object.' An ice moon, one of a vast flock drifting far beyond the orbit of the farthest planets. 'We're inside the orbit of Saturn. What's it doing *here*?'

A Virtual popped into existence in the middle of the cabin. 'I think I can answer that.' It was a man, perhaps as old as Symat's father, though it was hard to tell physical ages. But unlike Hektor he was short, squat, his limbs short and his belly large.

Symat resented this sudden intrusion. He snapped, 'Who are you?'

'Actually I don't have a name. You can call me by my role, which is the Curator.' Despite his persistent grin he looked like a curator. He was bald, and he wore an antique-looking robe, black, sweeping to the floor, its breast adorned with a green tetrahedral sigil.

Mela asked, 'Curator of what?'

'Why, of Port Sol, of course. One of mankind's most precious bastions – and still a working place today.'

Symat said, 'But Port Sol isn't in the Kuiper Belt any more.'

'No indeed. Now it swoops around a long elliptical path that reaches from Saturn all the way in to Earth's orbit. It has been brought in from the dark, along with a whole flock of other outer-system objects. All for a purpose.'

'Why are you so fat?' Mela asked bluntly.

The Curator patted his belly, apparently not offended. 'Do say what's on your mind, child! In the cold, the rounder your shape is the better off you are. Ask a Silver Ghost! And out where Port Sol came from, believe me, it's cold, even now. You're Mela, aren't you? There has been a lot of gossip in the Conclave about you. Metaphorically speaking, of course. You're doing a good job. A lot of us are jealous.' He reached out and ruffled Mela's short-cut hair. She flinched back, glaring.

Symat said heavily, 'Can't you tell she doesn't like that?'

'Actually, no. I'm a little light on sentience programming. In the empathy area, in fact. Though I hope that what I lack in personality I make up for in charm. Of course I could be wrong about that. But how would I ever know?' He laughed lightly.

Mela stared at him. 'How can you *be* like that? Don't you want more, to be whole?'

'Not really. Believe me, when you see the job I have to do, you'll understand why.' Even now he kept smiling. 'Welcome to Port Sol!'

Under the Curator's effortless control, the flitter dipped and swooped over Port Sol's eroded landmarks.

Every child in the system knew about Port Sol. It was itself ancient, a fragment of unprocessed rubble left over from the formation of Sol system. And its human history stretched far back too, almost as far back as man's first tentative steps off the home planet.

'Once they built starships here,' the Curator said. 'Before hyperdrive, even. They used the worldlet's own water ice for reaction mass, digging out great pits like that one.' The quarry he pointed out was a slumped hole in the ground, indistinguishable from a thousand others. 'When hyperdrive came this place was bypassed for a while. But then, because it was so hidden away and forgotten, the first of the Ascendents came here.'

'Ascendents?' Symat asked.

'Undying,' Mela said immediately.

The Curator raised a thin eyebrow. 'They've been called many names in their long history – jasofts, pharaohs – few of them complimentary. *Ascendents* isn't so bad, I think: we are all their descendants after all . . .

520

Whatever they're called, I care for them. That's my vocation! You'll see, anyhow. You'll meet them. They want to meet *you*, Symat.'

Symat tried to absorb that, and tried not to react to Mela's obvious fear.

The flitter circled this little world rapidly, and soon they once more approached the mast, with the flare of blue light at its tip. Buildings clustered at the base of the tower, while machines like giant beetles dug a pit in the ice that sliced through the pale marks of older workings.

Symat said, 'This is a rocket, isn't it? And it's pushing this moon.'

The Curator nodded. 'Very perceptive. We're actually at one spin pole of the moon – a good place to push.' He pointed. 'The engines are GUTdrives – one of mankind's oldest technologies, immensely reliable. The exhaust is plasma, charged matter, the outflow shaped by magnetic fields. And, just like in those ancient starship engines, the stuff of Port Sol itself is being consumed as reaction mass. You can see how the engineering here has churned up the old surface. Aside from Earth itself, Port Sol is probably the system's key historic site. But Ascendents care little for archaeology.' He sighed. 'I suppose you wouldn't if you could remember it all!'

Mela said, 'So this is an Ascendent project.'

'Well, of course. The mass of Port Sol is huge, and by comparison the rocket delivers only a small push. You have to keep shoving for a *very* long time before you can kick it out of its orbit. But that's just the sort of long-term, dogged programme the Ascendents excel at.'

The rocket tower dropped behind the horizon, and the flitter swept down towards a plain of ice, heavily melted by the heat of multiple landings. Nearby was a cluster of domes, evidently their destination.

As the ground fled beneath the descending flitter, Symat spotted a slim black pillar, obviously artificial, standing in the middle of what looked oddly like a forest, 'trees' sculpted from ice. 'Look, Mela. A transfer booth! Even here they are escaping.'

The Curator looked surprised. 'Oh, that's not for *people*. Did you imagine booths are just for humans?' He told them that when Port Sol had first been discovered it had an indigenous fauna, slow-moving inhabitants of the deep cold with liquid helium for blood. 'Once we farmed them; we transplanted them to other cold worlds. Somehow they survived a million years of cohabitation with mankind – even the dreadful summer we have brought to Port Sol by pushing it into the heart of the system. And now a booth has appeared, right in the middle of their Forest of Ancestors, and, with our help, the Toolmakers, the ones in their motile phase, are passing through to their own destiny. A slow process, I can tell you . . .' He seemed surprised at their incomprehension. 'There are many life forms in Sol system – or were, before we came along – but even now many of them survive. And as far as we can tell, every one of them with the remotest level of advancement has been supplied with booths so they can escape the destruction of the sun. Touching, isn't it? And not only that, there are suggestions in the records that other species, driven to extinction long ago, have been provided with similar escape routes. The Silver Ghosts, for example . . . The booths are evidently part of a long-term rescue strategy, by whoever is responsible. It could be the Xeelee,' he mused. 'Some say it is. The Xeelee relish the diversity of life, and seek to protect it, even when it snaps at them, as we have . . .'

The silvered domes at the base of the rocket tower turned out to be the upper levels of much more extensive structures, buried deep under the ice.

The Curator took them down through a hatch in the bottom of the flitter, through a kind of airlock, and then into the interior of the base. They never walked in the vacuum, out on the ice. Symat, who had never walked anywhere you would need a pressure suit, was faintly disappointed to lose out on a little bit of adventure.

The Curator led them along cold, echoing corridors, past closed-off rooms. Just as on Mars there were few people here, it seemed. Symat was getting a sense of Sol system as a series of empty planets and moons, like dusty rooms in a deserted house.

The Curator asked if they wanted to rest or eat, but they were both too excited, or apprehensive. The Curator gave in with a cheerful shrug. 'Then I'll take you to the Ascendents.'

He led them along more corridors until they came to a brightly lit area, a complex of corridors that stank strongly of antisepsis, like a hospital. The Curator paused at a door. 'Now before you go in,' he told Symat, 'try not to be afraid.'

Symat said testily, 'Let's get on with it.' He wasn't about to hesitate in front of Mela. He stepped forward boldly. The door slid aside.

He entered a low, wide room, white-walled, flooded with pale light. There were beds here – no, they were more like medical stations; each had boxes of equipment hovering in the air beside it. Bots cleaned the walls and ferried supplies. He saw no human attendants, but there were many Virtuals who nodded at the Curator. Rotund individuals like him, they all seemed to have broad faces and wide smiles.

Symat inspected a station more closely. A bot hovered suspiciously, but he wasn't impeded. The station was a pallet covered by a translucent bubble. It was marked with a number: 247, in bold digits. Inside the bubble, lying on the pallet, was a man. His limbs like sticks, his belly imploded, and with tiny bots crawling over his body, he looked more dead than alive. But as Symat cast a shadow over his face, that skull-like head turned. Symat shuddered and stepped back.

They walked on, between the rows of stations. The floor was soft and Symat's footsteps made no sound.

The Curator said, 'They are unimaginably old, some of them – and several of them, with no real memory of their own deepest past, don't even know how old they are themselves. The best way to date them is actually through the anti-ageing technology embedded in their bodies. But even that is unreliable.'

As they passed, the naked Ascendents stirred and whispered, dry skin rustling.

'We're disturbing them,' Mela said softly.

'Don't worry about it. They are creatures of routine as are we all, but in them it is taken to an extreme. And anything that disturbs that routine disturbs *them*. That's why only bots and Virtuals are used as attendants. You don't want to frighten them with a new face every century or so!'

Symat wondered how old the Curator himself was.

One old woman, to Symat's astonishment, was out of bed. She was naked, her skin so flaccid she looked as if she had melted, and tubes snaked out of all her orifices. But she managed to walk to a cabinet a few paces from her bed, where, with a trembling hand, she picked out fragments of food that she pushed into a toothless mouth.

'She likes to feed herself,' the Curator said. 'Or at least to believe she does. It's good for her to have some independence. But look here.'

The floor was cut through by a deep rut, hard metal and ceramic worn away by this old woman's soft feet. And where she had lain in her bed she had left the shape of her body compressed into the mattress.

The Curator said dryly, 'Perhaps you can see why many of us working in this place prefer to forgo personality. It's better not to think about it. Better still not to be *able* to think . . .'

The stations were set out in orderly rows, a neat rectangular grid.

Symat counted no more than twenty or twenty-five rows in each direction: there were only a few hundred Ascendents here.

The Curator seemed to know what he was thinking. 'Four hundred and thirty-seven. If you'd come here a decade ago there were four hundred and thirty-eight.'

Mela asked, 'This is all?'

'As a group they have been ineradicable. They have time on their side: that's what you always have to remember about Ascendents. If you try to get rid of them, no matter how strong you are, all they have to do is wait for you to grow old and die, and for your children and grandchildren to die too, wait until you're nothing but a sliver of data in a history text, and then they just walk back in.'

'They are dying out, though.'

The Curator shrugged. 'Nobody is making immortals any more. And entropy catches up with us all in the end. But despite their strangeness, they are mankind's treasures.'

Mela asked, 'Why do you say that?'

'For all they have seen,' the Curator said. 'For the wisdom they have accrued, when you can dig it out of them. And for all they have done for us – and continue to do. It was the undying who founded the Transcendence, who tried to bring us to a new plane of being altogether. They ultimately failed, but what a magnificent ambition!'

'And you say they still work for us?' Mela asked.

'By moving Port Sol,' Symat saw immediately.

'Yes,' the Curator said, 'But what they have done is rather more spectacular than pushing around a mere ice moon! You see, long ago, the undying resolved to move the Earth itself . . .'

It was the sun, of course.

As the downpour of solar radiation grew too intense, Earth's natural processes couldn't be sustained. And when the swelling sun's photosphere washed over it like a misty tide, would Earth be sterilised, scorched, melted, even vaporised? It would take a long time, hundreds of thousands of years, before Earth was destroyed entirely. But Ascendents fretted on long timescales. You could say that was the point of their existence.

How do you save a world from an overheating sun? Mankind had never had the power to tinker with the processes of stars themselves. Could you shield the world with mirrors and parasols lofted into space?

But any such shield would eventually be overwhelmed as the sun expanded. There was only one option: to move the Earth itself. But how?

You could push it. You could mount a giant rocket on a spin pole, as had been done on Port Sol, or even a series of rockets around the equator. But you would consume an immense amount of Earth's own matter in the process, and any instability could cause the planet's crust to shake itself to pieces. You might end up doing more harm than good.

Alternatively you could use gravity. If the Earth still had its Moon, you could have used that as a tug: push away the Moon as violently as you liked, and let lunar gravity gradually haul the Earth on a slow spiral away from the sun. But the Moon had been detached from the Earth in the course of a long-forgotten war.

Or you could do it piecemeal.

The Ascendents mounted venerable GUTdrive engines on a whole fleet of Kuiper Belt ice moons, including their own base, Port Sol. It took a long time for the slow push of the plasma rockets to make a difference, but at last the moons came swooping out of the dark into the inner system, entering complicated orbits that shuttled between Earth and the greatest planets, Jupiter and Saturn.

And with each moon's passage Earth's orbit was deflected, just slightly.

With a long series of slingshots Earth was gradually nudged outward from the sun, while the giants were subtly moved closer. It was as if the Ascendents had linked Earth to its giant cousins with immensely long chains, that drew them slowly together. It was going to take a *million* encounters with moons the size of Port Sol to move the Earth out to its destination, a new orbit around Saturn. At the rate of two or three encounters a year that would require thousands of centuries. But the undying always had time in abundance, time and patience. And Earth was on its way.

It was a typical undying project, on immense timescales, but low-tech. But you had to keep a sense of perspective, Symat thought. Where the Xeelee had blocked the light of suns across a supercluster of galaxies, all humans could manage was to nudge one little world across Sol system.

And in the end even this monumental exercise in persistence hadn't been enough. The immortals had saved Earth from the expansion of its sun. Now the Xeelee had come to Sol system, and a new danger loomed.

But again, it seemed, the undying had been preparing.

The three of them continued to walk among the ranks of immortals, each in her station, each with her number.

As they passed the dimly stirring figures, the Curator kept smiling.

Symat asked curiously, 'Why do you grin like that?'

'None of them can see well. But many of them respond to simple shapes.'

'A smiling human face,' said Mela, wondering. 'Like a baby. A baby can recognise a smiling face almost as soon as it's born.'

'Yes. Remarkable, isn't it? As if life is a great circle. *That's* why we smile all the time.' He tapped the green tetrahedron on his breast. 'A lot of them seem comforted to see this too. We're not sure why. It must be a very ancient symbol, of something.'

Symat asked the Curator about the medical-station numbers.

'They are for our purposes. We number them in order of age, as best we can. When one dies you have to renumber those younger – though *young* scarcely seems appropriate for creatures such as these! – but there are so few it isn't a great burden.'

As they walked the age numbers fell away, below twenty, fifteen, and at last to single figures. Symat felt his heart unaccountably thump. And then the Curator brought them to a bed, where a short, slim form lay, obscured by her translucent tent. The bed was adorned by a single digit: 1.

'The oldest,' Mela breathed.

'She has been called many names,' the Curator said. '*Leropa, Luru Parz*, other variants; perhaps one of these is her original given name. If she knows she won't tell us. She claims to know the date of her birth, but it's so long ago we can't reconcile her dates with current chronologies more precisely than within five thousand years . . . Take a good look, Symat. She is certainly the oldest human being any of us will ever see. She is probably a million years old. Think of that!'

Suddenly the woman's eyes flickered open. Mela gasped.

Symat stepped forward, his pulse hammering in his ears. And as he came by the bed a hand like a claw shot out to grab his wrist. He forced himself not to flinch, for fear he might snap bones like dry twigs.

Her black eyes were on him. She opened a ruined mouth and whispered, 'There are questions you need to ask.'

To a fourteen-year-old she was a figure from a nightmare. But her leathery palm was warm on his skin. She was old, she was very strange, but she was human, he could feel that. 'I don't know how it must be,' he said.

'What?'

'To be like you.'

She closed her eyes briefly; he could actually hear the dry skin rustle on her eyeballs. 'If you knew how many times I have been asked that . . . I have thought the same thoughts so often they don't need me to think them any more. Perhaps I am a robot, then. Certainly I am no longer human, if I ever was, since the moment I took that pill given me by Gemo Cana, that murderous witch . . .'

'Who?'

'But that is why I am valuable, you see. I and my kind. For, long after love and hate are gone, even after meaning is lost, we keep on and on and on. And, given enough time, we achieve greatness.'

'You moved the Earth.'

'Yes. A human Galaxy was just a dream. Earth is the home of man, and as long as Earth exists, man will endure.'

'But it isn't enough,' Symat said.

'No. Because the Xeelee are here.'

'People are fleeing. The booths—'

Her face, a mask of imploded skin, crumpled a little, showing disgust. 'The booths. A solution for cattle bred for defeat, beaten before they are even born. Have you ever heard of Original Sin?'

'No.'

'Child, *you* know there is a better way. And that is why you must go to Saturn.'

His mind was reeling. 'I don't know anything about Saturn. What must I do there?'

'You will know,' she said. She fell back on her pillow, her eyes closing, but she kept hold of his arm. 'It is why I made you, after all . . .'

Symat, electrified, astonished, could only stare at her.


IV


Port Sol fell away into the dark. Symat and Mela were travelling ahead of the ice moon on its endless cycling trajectory between the spheres of Earth and Saturn, but where Port Sol took years to complete a single orbit, the flitter would take only days.

527

And now the flitter had a third passenger. The Curator wore his antique robe with its tetrahedral sigil, and his broad face was fixed with his habitual smile. But as Port Sol dwindled to a point of crimson light Symat thought he saw fear in his Virtual eyes.

It had been Mela's idea to bring him. 'You might be able to help us,' she had told him. 'You know this Luru. You might be able to figure things out.'

'I'm a Curator,' he had protested. 'I keep these human museum pieces alive. I'm not designed to interpret their mad ramblings.' But Mela had kept on, pressing him to come.

Symat was reluctantly fascinated by this exchange. He reminded himself that they were both expressions of a much vaster interlinked awareness. As the Curator and Mela argued it was as if he was listening to the internal debate of a single mind.

They certainly weren't human, not even Mela; Symat was the only human here. And as the darkness closed in on the ship he felt increasingly alone, and far from home.

The flitter had internal partitions you could turn opaque, and he shut himself up inside a little boxy room. He didn't want to deal with the Curator and his resentful wittering, and he didn't much even want to be with Mela.

After a day of this Mela asked to see him. He wouldn't let her in, so she just walked through the walls, protocol warnings sounding. She shook her arms and flexed her fingers until all her rogue pixels had settled back into place. 'That hurt.'

Symat was lying on a pallet. 'Then don't do it.'

She sat down uncertainly. 'What are you doing?'

'Nothing.' He had been reading, watching silly kids' Virtuals, stuff he had liked years ago. Now he felt oddly self-conscious and shut it all down.

She asked, 'You want to play a game?'

'No, I don't want to play a stupid game.'

'What's the matter with you? You're not much fun.'

'I don't feel like *fun*. I feel—'

'What?'

'I'm sick of being pushed around. My parents wanted me to follow them into the booths. So I ran away. But then the Conclave got hold of me, through you. Now I find this stupid old woman, Luru, who says she planned me for some purpose long before I was even *born*. And I've ended up coming all the way out here, into the dark.'

'Welcome to my world,' Mela snapped. 'That's how I feel all the time. The Curator too, probably.'

'You aren't human.'

'But we're sentient,' she hit back. 'Is that how you think of me, just a part of some kind of trap?'

He flinched. 'I'm sorry. I didn't mean that.'

She softened a little. 'Anyway, Virtual or human, what difference does it make? Look around, Symat. Everything is *old*. Everything in the universe has been shaped by humans, or their enemies. Every important decision was made long ago. So we have very little choice about things. My mother used to feel the same way,' she said, a little wistfully.

It was the first time she'd mentioned any detail of her parents. 'She did?'

'She said she'd always felt like a child herself, a child who had grown up in the halls of some vast and dusty museum, where everything was frozen and on display, out of her reach . . . Look, Symat, if you do have some purpose, it must be important.'

'But if I've got no choice about any of this, what is there for *me*?'

She thought about that. 'Dignity?' She stood up. 'Come on. Let's go and wind up the Curator. I want to know what kind of underwear he has on under that stupid robe.'

Laughing, they left the cabin.


Saturn loomed out of the dark.

This wasn't like approaching Port Sol. They had come swooping down on that much-engineered little worldlet in a flash. The largest surviving planet in Sol system, Saturn was majestic and stately, a misty disc painted red by the sun. Its size was obvious, oppressive.

The ship hurled itself through Saturn's tremendous shadow. Symat saw lightning crackle purple and white across the clouds, as storms that could have engulfed the whole of Mars played themselves out. This was the power of nature, he thought, even now dwarfing humanity and its dreams. As he watched, Symat's heart pumped in a kind of retrospective panic. To think that he might have lived and died on Mars, or even followed his parents into a booth, without seeing such wonders as this!

The flitter swooped away from Saturn, climbing up and out of its deep gravity well, the energy of its incoming trajectory dumped. And the Curator showed Symat how to look for the moons.

Spacegoing mankind had swept like a storm through Sol system, shattering in a few millennia the patient geological assemblings of aeons. Saturn's ice moons, if not taken apart altogether, had been extensively mined. One moon was more interesting, though. The Curator called it 'Titan'. Once this small world had had decks of clouds beneath which complex chemical processes had played out; humans had sent scoop-ships and trawlers to mine the air and the hydrocarbon seas. But Titan, starved of heat, had never spawned life. Now, as the sun brightened, Titan was at last stirring from its chill slumber. It was a marvellous prospect, the birth of a new world right in the middle of Sol system: even in these desolate latter days you could still find new life. But no human scientists were studying the miracles unfolding in Titan's clouds. This was not an age for science.

They left Titan behind. And as the flitter continued to swoop around Saturn's gravity well, the true human purpose of this system was gradually revealed.

'Can you see?' The Curator ducked and pointed, picking out lights scattered among the moons. 'And that one? They are drones. Sensor stations, weapons platforms. All sentient.'

The sky was full of them, machines that flocked like metallic birds in the ever-changing gravity field of Saturn and its moons. Some of them gathered into rings that girdled Saturn's equator, which the Curator wistfully said were an echo of an even stranger wonder of the past, natural rings of ice and dust that had long been disrupted by war. And once you could have seen even more spectacular artefacts, the ruins of wormhole mouths, the remnant of a transit system that had once spanned a Galaxy but had collapsed with the demise of its builders, the Coalition.

But Symat understood that the beauty of the weapons clouds wasn't their point. Their purpose was lethality. The whole of the Saturn system was a fortress. And it was all because of the Ascendents.

When the vast retreat of man had begun, even when only the most remote of colonies had yet been evacuated, the undying with their eerie far-flung prescience had planned the end game. Before the siege of Earth itself began, it would be necessary to make a stand.

Saturn had always been a military stronghold. As long ago as the

Exultants' heroic effort to win the Galactic Core, huge war machines had been buried in the planet's deepest clouds, ready to leap to the defence of Earth if any foe dared attack the capital planet. These brooding machines, self-maintaining, self-enhancing, became known as the Guardians.

Now, as a far more formidable foe gathered, the Ascendents turned to Saturn once more. Earth itself was to be corralled with gravitation and brought out here, to circle on the rim of Saturn's mighty gravity well, where it could be protected. And the war machines under those clouds, already powerful, were enhanced with the accumulated learning of a million years of interstellar war.

The purpose of the undying had been unswerving. But this project was not quite as under their obsessive control as they would have preferred. There was risk.

'I don't understand,' Mela said. 'What risk?'

The Curator waved a hand, and the air was filled with a high-speed chatter of automated signals. Symat thought he picked out questions and responses, handshaking, a kind of dialogue. The Curator said, 'The Guardians are *very* old. They have long since got used to making their own decisions. When a ship like this comes sliding into their space, they get *very* suspicious. Can't you tell, from the way the drones are swarming around us? All that's keeping us from being destroyed right now is our flitter's responses to the Guardians' continual interrogation.'

'And when the Ascendents decided to move Earth here – Lethe, a whole planet sliding across Sol system – one false word and the home of mankind might have been blown to bits by machines meant to protect it.'

Symat said, 'We've been at war with the Xeelee for a million years. What can these Guardians have that's so powerful it could make a difference now? And why hasn't it been thrown into the war before?'

'I think I can answer that.' Mela's eyes clouded, and there was a sheen about her face, a waxy unreality. She screwed up her forehead as she tried to integrate the information pouring into her head.

Long ago, as mankind advanced across a Galaxy, under a purposeful programme called the Assimilation, whole alien cultures were eradicated or subsumed, their technology and learning purloined. Most such treasures, as Symat had guessed, had been thrown into the vast war effort. But some had been secreted away by the patient undying. Insurance for the future, they thought of it.

One such was the technology called the Snowflake. It had been found in orbit around an ancient star in a globular cluster out in the Galaxy's halo. It was a stunning artefact, a regular tetrahedron measuring over fourteen million kilometres along its edges. Humans gave it this name because like a snowflake the structure had a fractal architecture, with the tetrahedron motif repeated on all scales. And the Snowflake, it was discovered, was full of information: it was an iron-wisp web of data, a cacophony of bits endlessly dancing against the depredations of entropy.

The Snowmen, the human label for the vanished builders of this lacy monster, had an utterly alien motivation. The Snowmen decided that to record events – and only to record – was the highest calling of life. They took apart their world and rebuilt it as a monstrous data storage system. After that they watched time unravel – and waited for the universe to cool, so they could capture even more data.

Thus the Snowflake had hung in space for thirteen billion years. Then, during the Assimilation, a human ship came.

The Navy crew, intent on plunder, had been unsubtle – but their ship had been devastated by an unexpected blow, broken apart by a beam of directed gravity waves.

It had taken some time to work out what had happened, how the Snowflake had struck back.

Mela lacked the vocabulary to express the concepts downloading into her mind, and she looked at the Curator. Reluctantly, he closed his eyes, and began to speak deliberately. 'There is a profound principle at work. Once it was known as the Mach principle. Mach, Marque, something like that. Every particle in the universe is linked to every other. That is why inertia exists; when you push something, the universe itself drags it back.'

Symat frowned. 'What connections? Gravity?'

The Curator frowned. 'That, and quantum wave functions, and, and – I can see it, I can't say it! The ancients understood. If you use complex arithmetic to extend most theories of cosmology—'

Symat held up his hand. 'Just tell me what happened.'

'The Snowmen had a defensive system. They found a way of manipulating these cosmic linkages. A way to use them as a weapon.'

Symat barely understood enough to be amazed. 'How?'

'Does it matter? I guess you learn a lot in thirteen billion years.'

Thanks to its Mach-principle weapon the Snowflake was saved from the Assimilators, that first time. But the humans returned, of course, evaded the weapon, and took what they wanted. They used the technology of the Snowflake itself in their own information-storage systems across the Galaxy.

And they took away the strange global-manipulation weapons system, but that turned out to be much harder to understand. When it didn't yield early results it was reduced in priority, shuffled from one research centre to another, until it became so obscure, despite its potency, that a clique of undying were able to spirit it away and develop it for their own purposes.

The Curator peered at Saturn uneasily. 'And *that*, it seems, is what is held under those clouds. A weapon of last resort.'

'But,' said Symat, 'what has this got to do with me?'

Suddenly Mela's face worked, and the tone of her voice hoarsened. 'We need you because the Guardians won't listen to *us*. Is that clear enough for you?'

Symat was shocked. This time the intervention was crude, as if she had been possessed by a different personality altogether.

The Curator stepped forward and grabbed her arm, one Virtual handling another. 'Ascendent. Show yourself. Leave this child alone.'

Mela spasmed, and her eyes rolled up in their sockets, showing white. She blurred briefly and broke up into a rough sculpture of blocky pixels. Then Mela stumbled backwards, reforming as she emerged from the cloud of pixels.

And from that mist of light a new figure coalesced. Suddenly there were four of them, and the flitter's tiny cabin seemed very crowded.

The newcomer was a woman, dressed in a brown robe as drab as the Curator's. Small, dark, her face was smooth – but Symat immediately saw that the smoothness was a sign of great age.

Black eyes fixed on Symat.

'Ascendent One,' the Curator breathed.

'You can't be Luru,' Symat said immediately. 'I saw her. She's a dried-out skeleton. She could barely move.'

'I'm a projection,' the new Virtual said, unfazed. 'I am as *she* was long ago. And my sentience overlaps with hers, though time-shifted.'

The Curator sounded uneasy. 'Most of the Ascendents are conscious only briefly each day. It will take Luru, the real one, a long time to live through this Virtual's experiences. But she has time, of course.'

'Her will is mine,' said the Virtual. 'When I speak, *she* speaks. Remember that.'

Symat felt deeply disturbed. To see Mela split into two and give birth to this monstrous form was an unwelcome reminder of how strange all these Virtual creatures were, how inhuman – and how interconnected, their identities somehow flowing one into another. He gathered his defiance into a knot. 'You told me the Guardians won't listen to you.'

Luru eyed him. 'They'll listen to you, though.'

Symat felt the universe pivot around him, as if the Guardians' strange cosmic weapons had been turned on him. 'Me? *I* could command the Guardians?'

'Of course,' she said. 'That's why we bred you.' She stepped closer to him and he thought he could smell her, a dry scent like a musty library. 'I'll show you,' she said. 'Come to Earth.'


V


So Symat's strange odyssey ended on Earth, the planet of his most remote ancestors.

There was an Earth in Symat's head, mistily imagined, a world of water and life, of blue and green. It had been taken out of Mars's sky long ago, many generations before he had been born, and sent on its way to Saturn. It wasn't something you talked about, the loss of the home world.

But the Earth that came looming out of the outer-system cold was not like that story-book vision. The mountains were worn down, and the sea floors were rimmed by banks of salt, drained save for dark remnant puddles. The air seemed thin, supporting only wispy traces of cloud. And though a few cities still glittered, the ground of Earth shone brick red, the red of Mars, of rust and lifelessness.

'Earth has grown old,' he said.

Luru was watching him, apparently interested in his reaction. 'Old like its children.'

'It is well guarded,' Mela murmured.

'There is nothing more precious,' Luru said.

On its final approach to the planet the flitter cautiously descended through shells of automated sentinels, and artificial suns that swooped on low orbits, casting splashes of yellow light. Luru said that not all those satellites carried weapons. Earth's magnetic field had failed. The sun was far away now, but the electromagnetic environment around a gas giant was ferociously energetic. Where nature failed, humans had to step in; and so devices orbited the Earth to protect it with new shields of magnetism.

The flitter ducked deep into the air, and the sky turned a muddy red-brown. Everybody stayed silent as the ground of Earth fled under the ship's prow.

The cities were sparsely scattered, and Symat could see no logic to their positioning. Perhaps they had been placed along the banks of long-dried rivers, or at the shores of vanished oceans; the cities endured where geography had eroded away. Many of the buildings were airy confections of glass and light that wouldn't have looked out of place on Mars. But these modern cities were fragile flowers that grew out of mighty ruins, covered by drifts of red dust.

Mela picked out patterns. 'Look. Lots of those old ruins have got circles in them. See, Symat?'

She was right. Sometimes the circles were obvious, rings of foundations or low walls that could be kilometres across. In other places you could only spot the circles by the way other ruins fitted around them, filling up their interior spaces or crowding around their circumferences.

Luru's eyes, black as night, gleamed bright as she peered out at this ancient architecture. Perhaps in these traces she saw some trace of her own long life, Symat mused.

In every city they passed over Symat spotted transfer booths. Even Earth, which Luru and her Ascendents had laboured so long to save, was draining of its people.

Wild things lived on the lands between the last cities. The flitter passed over what looked like plains of grass, even forests of stunted trees, and occasionally its passage scattered herds of animals. But there were swathes of vegetation that wasn't even green.

The flitter at last swept over a southern continent that seemed even more worn-down than the rest, and came to rest at the outskirts of yet another city.

Symat deliberately jumped down from the hatch, falling a half-metre or so to the dusty ground. He fell slowly, though once his feet were planted in the dirt of Earth, invisible inertial systems ensured his weight felt normal to him. Gravity was indeed low here, he thought, somehow lower than Mars's. But Earth, the mother world, had always defined the standard of gravity: how, then, could its gravity be reduced?

He looked around. The city was unprepossessing. You could clearly see the usual circular tracings, but the structures they had supported were razed to the ground. Amid these ancient foundation arcs stood only a small, shabby cluster of more recent glass buildings.

There was nobody about. The Ascendent was quiet as she wandered around the circular profile of one vanished wall.

Symat asked, 'Luru, why have you brought us here?'

'I think this place means something to her,' Mela said. She guessed, 'Did you grow up here, Luru? Were you *born* here?'

Luru's face remained impassive, but she nodded. 'Yes, I was born here, or rather in the ruins of a still older city on this site – born in a tank, actually, for that was the way in those days.'

Symat found it hard to imagine Luru Parz ever having been young, ever being *born*.

'The whole of the Earth was in the grip of alien conquerors. They built this city, erasing the ruins. They called it Conurbation 5204. These circles you see were the bases of domes of blown rock. The place was beautiful, in its way. There were plenty of places to play, for me and my cadre siblings.'

'It was home,' Mela said.

'Oh, yes. Even a prison becomes a home.'

The Curator looked at her almost with compassion. 'You never told me any of this.'

'You were told what you needed to know,' Luru said harshly. 'I worked here, for an agency called the Extirpation Directorate. My job was to erase the human past. We humans were useful to our conquerors, but troublesome. To detach us from our history, to strip away our identity, was their strategy to control us.'

Symat felt disgusted. 'And you did this work for them?'

'I had no choice,' she murmured. 'And the work was challenging, intellectually. To eradicate is as satisfying as to build, if you don't think beyond the act itself. Of course we failed. Look around you!' She laughed and spread her arms; it was a grotesque sight. 'Since the great levelling of those days, more cities have been built on the foundations of the old, only to fall into ruin, over and over. History just keeps on piling up, whatever you do.'

Mela asked curiously, 'Did you have children, Luru Parz?'

'Not that I knew of. If I had I wouldn't have lived so long. There is a logic in immortality.'

'Lovers, then,' Mela said. 'You must have had lovers.'

Luru smiled. 'Yes, child. One lover. But we fell out. He was a ragamuffin. He escaped the conquerors' cities, preferring to live wild. We were on opposite sides of the argument on how to deal with the Occupation, you see. He died well, though. He died for what he believed in.' She said this neutrally, her face blank.

Mela asked softly, 'What was his name?'

Luru took a rattling breath. 'Suvan. Symat Suvan.'

Symat's mouth dropped open.

The Curator stared at him. 'So now we know why you have been conjured into existence, boy.' He laughed out loud.

The clustering artificial suns swarmed out of the sky, and night fell. There were still creatures on Earth that needed a cycling of day and night, it seemed. But the dark revealed a sky crowded with stars and weapons, with misty Saturn and swollen Sol.

Symat and his party returned to the flitter. Mela shared a cabin with Symat; she went to bed and seemed to fall asleep immediately. Symat could not settle. Too much strangeness was swirling around in his head – and nothing as disturbing as the fact that he had been named after the lover of an Ascendent, a man dead a million years.

When light began to seep into the sky, he slid out of the cabin without disturbing Mela. Outside the flitter the air was cool, but so dry there was no dew. The light was still an empty grey, and the dawn was complex, cast by multiple suns that swarmed restlessly over the horizon.

Luru Parz was standing in the shadow of the flitter's wing, a silent pillar watching him.

'I couldn't sleep,' he said.

She shrugged. 'You're young. You'll survive . . . Look.'

Peering into the half-light, Symat saw movement. The dark shapes were animals, a herd shifting slowly across the plain beyond the city. One animal, younger, broke away from the rest, and he saw its silhouette more clearly. He counted two, four, six legs.

Luru said, 'Interesting, isn't it? This planet was the capital of a Galactic empire. Now most of it is abandoned and gone wild.'

'I never saw an animal with six legs.'

'I believe they are called "spindlings". They are not native to Earth. And look at this.' She walked a few paces away from the flitter to a patch of grass.

Symat bent down and ruffled the grass with his fingers. It was dry as a bone, but it was alive, adapted to the aridity. And as the light lifted a little more he saw that among the green blades was some kind of fibrous growth, deep black.

'The green grass is probably native: there are lots of ways to exploit sunlight for energy, but using green chlorophyll is quite rare. Something to do with the spectrum of our sun, no doubt, before its modification by the photino birds. But that black mat is not a native, any more than a spindling. And – there!' Luru pointed, almost eagerly. 'See that?'

Symat saw a small shape moving through the miniature jungle of the grass. It had a silvered carapace, and he thought it might be a beetle. But then light speckled between its jaws.

'Laser light?'

'It's descended from tiny machines designed to crop the grass. Now it follows its own evolutionary agenda. If you turn them out into the wild, even machines evolve, Symat.'

Symat thought of the bit of wild technology he had seen for himself on Mars: abandoned Virtual children, turned cannibal. And he remembered the slow liquid-helium native fauna of Port Sol, scattered by mankind to other cold worlds across the Galaxy.

Luru said, 'Wherever they are deposited, living things, transported between the stars, even machines, find ways to combine, to form rich new ecologies. After a million years of spaceflight, every human world is like this. And even if mind disappeared from the Earth tomorrow, as long as the planet survives, you would be able to look at this interstellar mixing-up and say, yes, once people from this place reached the stars.'

'But this isn't the only trace of the past.' It was Mela; small, composed, she walked out from the shadow of the flitter. The Curator followed her.

'Oh, good,' Luru said dryly. 'Everybody's up.'

Symat said, 'What do you mean, Mela?'

'The collapsed magnetic field. The thin air, the drained oceans.' She jumped up and drifted back down to the ground, slow as a snowflake. Symat knew it was a Virtual illusion, but she made her point effectively: even Earth's gravity had been reduced.

Luru sighed. 'Earth got used up.'

Earth, home of mankind, had been the capital of an empire which had won a Galaxy, and beyond. And for all that time Earth itself had supported a surprisingly heavy burden of the resource load.

'Earth was only rarely attacked, and never fell into enemy hands, after the lifting of the Qax Occupation,' Luru said. 'But its air, its precious water were scattered in ships across the Galaxy. Its metals were sucked from its deep interior. Its inner heat was tapped for energy.'

That was why the magnetic field had collapsed: as the planet's heat had been drained its liquid core crystallised, and Earth's magnetism failed. The internal cooling had also weakened the great mantle currents. So there were no more volcanoes or earthquakes, and the mountains currently eroding away were the last the old world would ever see.

Luru whispered, 'In the final madness of their wars the engineers tapped into the planet's ultimate energy store, its gravity well. They sucked out mass-energy – they reduced the effective mass of the planet. That is why you feel so light on your feet, Symat; that is why we are able to put up buildings so delicate they would seem more suited to a dwarf world like Mars. Earth is the little world that fought a Galactic war! But in the end it could give us no more.'

'Which is why,' the Curator prompted, 'you believe we must save it now.'

'Yes. And I haven't spent half a million years striving to save the Earth from the swelling sun to see it put to the Xeelee flame now. I have a plan,' Luru said. 'Come. The dawn is rising. Walk with me into the light, and we'll talk.'

It all depended on the Guardians, and their Snowflake cosmic-linkage technology. Luru said, 'With such a technology you can do almost anything you can conceive of. Why, you can bend spacetime itself . . .'

And that was what Luru intended to do.

If you descended into a gravity well, you found your clocks turning more slowly than those of your colleagues on an orbiting ship, far above. All this was commonplace. Even in a gravity well as shallow as Earth's, time passed more slowly for Symat than for an observer up there in free space. In a black hole, the deepest gravity well possible, the time-stretching effect ultimately became dominant, until at the event horizon itself time would cease to flow for you altogether.

The Curator shook his head. 'Ascendent, I'm no physicist. Are you planning to turn the Earth into a black hole?'

'No. But I want to reshape its spacetime.'

Luru planned to make the Earth a pit of slow time. Just as if looking into a black hole, from the outside time on its surface would seem stretched out. Conversely if you stood on its surface, you would see blueshifted stars wheel across the sky, flaring and dying. It was possible to do all this, she claimed, by manipulating spacetime subtly; you didn't need the immense and concentrated mass of a black hole to do it.

Mela was looking oddly absent; Symat imagined massed intelligences looking through her eyes and listening through her ears, and crowding her mind with their speculations. She said, 'It would have to be quite a gradient. There would be a perceptible difference in the passage of time over the height of a human – a difference between your head and your toes!'

Symat scratched his head. 'That would be a strange place to live.'

'People adapt. And with their lives stretched out to megayears,' Luru said, 'the inhabitants of Earth would be safe from the depredations of the Xeelee, or anybody else. They wouldn't even need energy from outside, for Earth's inner heat, reduced to a trickle, would fuel their slow-moving biosphere. Of course there are a few details to work out. This must be a long-term solution. The saved Earth – or "Old Earth" as I think of it – will need a stocked ecology, a self-renewing biosphere, some equivalent of tectonic processing. It will need a day and a night. I haven't worked out how yet.'

The Curator laughed. 'A typical Ascendent solution – to save the world with a gift of time!'

'But,' Symat asked anxiously, 'will it work?'

'Oh, yes,' Luru said calmly. 'The Guardians can do this. I've been able to consult them about it. They can turn their weapons on the Earth itself, and use the resources of a universe to reshape it as they please.'

The Curator shook his head. 'If this Snowflake weapon is capable of such a remarkable feat, why not turn it on the Xeelee? We could scatter their fleets of nightfighters like swatting flies.'

'*We?*' Luru mocked him. 'For a shell of a programme with no personality, you have stored up a lot of aggression, Curator.'

He scowled at her taunting, and Symat could see centuries of bitterness in his expression. 'Why not just answer the question?'

'We are done with fighting. After all this time, perhaps we humans have learned a little wisdom – and humility.' She squinted up at the sky. 'We humans took on the Xeelee. Remarkable when you think about it: savannah apes against a supergalactic power. We did them some damage, we drove them out of the Galaxy. But the Xeelee are far more than we ever were; we could never defeat them. And we barely noticed the true enemy, a foe of both ourselves and the Xeelee and everything made of baryonic matter, matter like ourselves—'

'Dark matter,' said Mela. 'The photino birds in the sun.'

'In *every* sun – yes, child. You mayflies encountered them in the deep past, even found them in the core of Earth's sun, and you forgot about them. You found them again later, out in the halo of the Galaxy, where dark matter dominates – the Xeelee were already fighting them there, long before our war for the Galaxy – and again, in a generation or two, you forgot what you saw. You are so infuriatingly transient!

'Well, we can't fight the photino birds. We never could. Perhaps even the Xeelee can't, but they are trying. There is evidence that the Xeelee are engaged in supergalactic projects, stupendous in scale – some long-forgotten explorers told tantalising tales.

'But it doesn't matter. We humans are trapped, here in Sol system itself, between two immense forces, the destruction of the sun, and the extinguishing of the stars. Yes, Curator, we could wield our last sword and cut off a few more limbs. But we can't win. So I think it's better we simply vacate the stage, don't you?

'I believe my solution is the right one. The Guardians can do this, if they have the will – and if they are ordered to. But I can't give that order.'

Symat whispered, 'Which is where I come in, is it?'

'Listen, child. The sole purpose of the Guardians is to serve humanity. But *what is humanity*? Since the Guardians were first installed we humans have bifurcated, innovated, rebuilt and re-engineered ourselves. Even the stock who remained on Earth and Mars, like your own family, has adapted in its own quiet way. Each of these subtypes is "human", in that they can all trace their ancestry back to the common root. But none of them is *identical* to the root stock. And a biologist's definition of humanity isn't necessarily good enough for a weapons system.'

'Ah.' The Curator nodded. 'The Guardians are so old they no longer recognise the much-evolved descendants of their makers as human at all. Not even you, old one! What an irony.' He shook his head and laughed.

Luru ignored him. She said to Symat, 'I have found a solution for Earth – and I need the Guardians' help to implement it. But they won't listen to me. I needed a true human, Symat, at least "true" in the discriminating eyes of the Guardians. And, as I was unable to find one, I had to breed one . . .'

Genetic engineering had been considered. Even if nobody like the ur-stock of humanity still existed, there were records of their bio-molecules. But the Guardians would easily have been able to spot any such engineering; they would have rejected the wretched result as a fake.

So Luru had had to resort to more natural methods. She had surveyed the human population of Sol system. She had identified stretches of raw DNA in fragments, scattered over the worlds. And she had begun a programme of patient cross-breeding, seeking to gather together the strains she needed.

It took a thousand years. But a millennium was a moment for an undying.

'And it all culminated in me,' Symat said.

'I told you you're different, Symat!' Mela said. 'No wonder you don't look like your parents. And no wonder the Conclave was watching you.'

'You probably don't look much like an ur-human either,' Luru said dryly, 'but I think you'll fool the Guardians. And that's all that counts.'

The Curator said, 'And did these generations of toiling breeders *know* how you were using them, Ascendent?'

'It was safer for the project that they didn't. A little social engineering sufficed.'

'And this is your master plan? After a galactic war and a million years of history, the future of man comes down to the decision of a fourteen-year-old child? . . . Lethe, Ascendent, what gives you the right to make a choice that will fix the whole future of mankind – even through this boy?'

'Only I have the vision for such a solution,' she murmured. 'Only I have the longevity to see it through. That's what gives me the right.'

Symat said, 'What would I have to do?'

'The Guardians are watching you, Symat, through the Conclave, through all our Virtual eyes. All you have to do is formulate your decision, and it will be made so. You won't need to throw a switch.'

'It will happen straight away?'

'Why wait?'

Mela's eyes narrowed. 'And *what will become of Symat?*'

Luru frowned. 'For a brief moment he will be the epicentre of cosmic forces. Humans are frail creatures.'

'I wouldn't live through it,' Symat said slowly. 'I am going to die.' But somehow even that didn't perturb his eerie calm.

'Symat, you don't have to do this,' Mela said.

Luru reached out as if to touch him, but she could not, of course, 'Every true saviour must lay down his life,' she said.

'Just like your own Symat,' Mela said. 'He died for his beliefs, you said.'

'Yes,' the Curator snapped. 'And now you've cooked up another Symat to go the same way. What's going on in that head of yours, Ascendent? Is this really about saving Earth, or just working out your own million-year-old guilt? Is this all about *you?*'

'You disgust me, Curator, you and your inane grinning,' Luru said coldly. 'You disguise your fear of me within your hollowness. But I know you.'

The Curator was obviously shocked, and again Symat saw fierce resentment burn. But he persisted. 'And what will you do if he refuses? After all your planning and preparations, to be thwarted now by the whim of a boy—'

'I will start again,' she said smoothly. 'An Ascendent always has time. You should know that, Curator.'

'Enough,' Symat said.

They all fell silent.

He still felt calm, calmer than any of these Virtuals, it seemed. 'You're saying this is the only choice,' he said to Luru. 'The only way forward for humanity. It's this or the booths.'

'This or the booths,' she said.

He looked at a sky full of dying stars. He reminded himself he was a boy, just a boy with a judgement so poor he had almost got himself drowned in a canal. Who was he to make such a decision? But mankind couldn't stay here, in this imploding system. And he could never have walked into a booth himself. Perhaps others felt that way. So there was only one choice. Yes, he was a child, but he knew that no matter how long he lived the parameters of his life wouldn't change – and nor would his choice.

He said as clearly as he could, 'I have made my decision.'

And even as he spoke he thought he felt a stirring, emanating from deep under the clouds of Saturn, as if a great storm were brewing there.

Luru's black eyes shone. 'You've made a good choice. You've given humanity a chance.'

The Curator muttered, 'You have courage, boy. I just hope you've wisdom too.'

A wind rose, whipping up red dust that clouded the sky.

The Curator cried, 'Look!'

There was a new light in the sky. The clouds of Saturn were churning, and a harsh, pitiless light broke out. It was like a monstrous egg cracking, Symat thought.

Luru Parz laughed.

Mela cried, 'So quickly?'

Luru smiled. 'The Guardians have waited a million years to act. They are ready.'

But Symat wondered if *he* was ready. He knew he was too young to have come to terms with the idea of personal death. Now, suddenly, he was going to have to face it.

Mela ran to Symat and tried to grab him. The wind noise was too loud for him to hear the inevitable protocol chimes. Her eyes were wide, her face torn, as she yelled at him.

'What did you say?'

She screamed louder. 'It may not have to be this way . . .'

The egg cracked wider. Glass smashed somewhere in the city behind them, and every grain of dust on Earth took to the air. A tremendous light flooded the sky, dazzling him. And then—

## VI

'Can you hear me? Symat, can you hear?' It was Mela's voice, but she was far away.

It was like waking up. But he had no sense of his body, of a bed, of blankets and sheets. He was surrounded by light.

He *was* light, he thought, but the idea didn't disturb him. He was light, coming into focus.

And suddenly he could see. Mela's face hovered before him, creased with concern. Beside her were other children. He recognised Chem, Tod.

He was standing. For a moment he was disconcerted, as if finding his balance, and he staggered slightly.

He stood on dusty ground, beside the crystal waters of a canal. A malevolent sliver of red sun poked above the horizon, but the air was still and pleasantly cool.

'So I lived through it.'

'Sort of,' said Chem.

'Earth has gone,' Mela said. 'Sent off into the future. But Mars is still here.'

'My parents—'

'They are coming.' She looked more serious. 'It will be difficult for them. For you.'

He looked at his hand. 'I'm a Virtual.'

'Yes. You're a Virtual.'

'My mother won't be able to touch me. My parents will feel as if they have lost me.'

'And you have lost them. But you have found us.' Impulsively she reached for his hands – and held them. Her palms were warm and soft.

He smiled. 'I told you I'd come back,' he said to Chem.

Chem grinned.

'You took your time,' Tod said.

'Listen,' Mela said. 'Can you hear them?'

Symat glanced around. 'Hear what?'

'Not outside. Inside.' She tapped her chest.

When he listened inwardly, he could hear a distant murmuring, voices merging like a sea. It was the Conclave, the community of minds that spanned Sol system and now embraced him, a community of which he would be a part for ever. 'Yes,' he said. 'Yes, I hear them.'

'So what do you want to do now?'

'I don't know—' A child's shoe hit him in the chest.

Tod had thrown it. 'You can save the world, but you can't catch me!'

'Oh, yes? . . .'

The four of them ran, and their laughter echoed from the banks of the drying Martian canal.

*So Earth died but did not die. So Symat died, but did not die.*

*I did not die, of course.*

*How could I die? I had completed this project, but I have completed projects before, and history just keeps on piling up, whatever I do. So here I am, in the dark, alone.*

*Waiting for what comes next.*

*I remember so much, yet so little. I have seen mankind rise and fall – quite a story! But what stays with me are the faces, the endless torrent of faces, from Symat the ragamuffin whom I loved, to Symat the idealistic messiah-boy whom I bred to die. Each face blossoms like a flower and fades to dust, leaving me alone once more. Each face is a betrayal. Yet they are all I have.*

*Sometimes it feels as if it has all been a dream, from the instant I put Gemo Cana's pill into my mouth. Perhaps in a moment I will wake to find myself under the shining domes of Conurbation 5204. And then, with my cadre siblings, I will run, laughing, in Sol's yellow light.*

# TIMELINE

*Note*: this timeline refers to events in this book, and in the earlier books of the 'Destiny's Children' series (*Coalescent*, first published 2003, *Exultant*, 2004, and *Transcendent*, 2005); and also to earlier books of my 'Xeelee Sequence' (*Raft*, 1991, *Timelike Infinity*, 1992, *Flux*, 1993, *Ring*, 1994, and *Vacuum Diagrams*, 1997). See also the timeline in *Vacuum Diagrams*.

|  | Singularity: Big Bang |
| --- | --- |
| *ERA*: **Earth** | |
| AD 476–2005: | Events of *Coalescent*. Emergence of first human 'hive' in Rome. |
| AD 2047: | Events of *Transcendent*. |
| | |
| *ERA*: **Expansion** | |
| AD 3000+: | Opening up of Sol system. First Expansion of humanity to the stars begins. |
| AD 3700+: | Events of *Timelike Infinity*. |
| | |
| *ERA*: **Resurgence** | |
| AD 5088: | Conquest of human planets by Qax. |
| AD 5301: | 'Cadre Siblings'. |
| AD 5407: | 'Conurbation 2473'. Overthrow of Qax. |
| AD 5408: | 'Reality Dust'. Third Expansion begins under Coalition government. |
| AD 5420: | 'Mayflower II'. Launch of generation starship *Mayflower II*. (See also AD 24,974.) |
| AD 5478: | 'All in a Blaze'. |
| | |
| *ERA*: **The War with the Ghosts** | |
| AD 5499: | 'Silver Ghost'. Third Expansion: first contact with the Silver Ghosts. |

| AD 5802: | 'The Cold Sink'. The Ghost wars break out. |
| AD 6454: | 'On the Orion Line'. |
| AD 7004: | 'Ghost Wars'. End of effective resistance by the Ghosts. |
| AD 7524: | 'The Ghost Pit'. |

ERA: **Assimilation**

| AD 10,000+: | Humans dominant sub-Xeelee species. Rapid expansion and absorption of species and technologies. |
| AD 10,102: | 'Lakes of Light'. |
| AD 10,537: | 'Breeding Ground'. |
| AD 12,478: | 'The Dreaming Mould'. |
| AD 12,659: | 'The Great Game'. Initiation of hostilities with the Xeelee. |

ERA: **The War for the Galaxy**

| AD 20,424: | 'The Chop Line'. |
| AD 22,254: | 'In the Un-Black'. |
| AD 23,479: | 'Riding the Rock'. |
| AD 24,973: | Events of *Exultant*. The human conquest of the centre of the Galaxy. |

ERA: **The Shadow of Empire**

| AD 24,974: | 'Mayflower II'. Retrieval of generation starship *Mayflower II*. |
| AD 25,000+: | Collapse of central Coalition government. Conflict among successor states. |
| AD 27,152: | 'Between Worlds'. |
| AD 40,000+: | The Bifurcation of Mankind. |

ERA: **The War to End Wars**

| AD 90,000+: | Reunification. |
| AD 100,000+: | Human assaults on Xeelee concentrations across the supercluster. |
| AD 104,000+: | Events of *Raft*. |
| AD 190,000+: | Events of *Flux*. |
| AD 200,000+: | Establishment of Commonwealth by 'undying'. |
| c. AD 500,000: | Events of *Transcendent*. The high-water mark of human destiny. |

*ERA*: ***The Fall of Mankind***

AD 500,000+:     The retreat of mankind begins. The Long Calm.

AD 700,000+:     The Xeelee Scourge. Intervention of photino birds in stellar evolution becomes significant.

AD 1,000,000:     'The Siege of Earth'. Final siege of Sol system by Xeelee. Defeat and imprisonment of mankind.

AD 5,000,000+:     Events of *Ring*. Last humans return to Sol.

AD 10,000,000+: Virtual extinction of baryonic life.

Singularity: Timelike Infinity